THE TALES OF HAVERA

THE TALES OF HAVERA

ORB OF EMANCIPATION

DEREK SPICER

edited by Crayle Vanest
cover design by Kaila Lianne

Derek Spicer

Contents

To my Mom and Dad for their never-ending and unwavering support

First Printing, 2022

Prologue

The Icewalker was accelerating through negative space. The old, rusty tin can of Captain Veskor creaked and groaned with each passing light year. These sounds were all too familiar to Nat. He had been Captain Veskor's navigator for more than fifteen years. He was intimately familiar with every noise, every clang, every thud the ship made during a voyage like this. Nothing out of the ordinary with the sounds the old girl was making, regardless of the protests of their engineer. Yet, after all these years, the ship stank to him, even through his mechsuit's air filters.

"Are you ever going to upgrade this piece of junk?" Nat hissed through his mechsuit's re-breather.

The Rinvari captain laughed. "That's your Zokyon blood talking, Nat. No appreciation for vintage or the classics your kind has. If it's a year old, you waste all your precious Links replacing it with something only marginally better at almost double the cost. It's a small wonder y'all are in constant economic ruin. Broken glass everywhere."

Nat rolled his eyes. He was used to this sort of inter-species jabbing from the captain. It was all in good fun.

"How far away are we from the signal's triangulation?" the captain asked.

Nat checked his instruments and ran a quick calculation over the galactic map. "We'll arrive within the hour. Kewea's curse, who travels this close to the Point of Always Return?"

"We do, apparently," the captain replied.

Nat snorted. The Icewalker was the closest ship when they received the distress call. They were at the refueling station near the Cauduun-Rinvari border on the Beta spiral. After finishing their refueling, the

Icewalker diverted towards the western end of the Alpha spiral, far away from any civilization.

At the Icewalker's top speed, it would've taken them about three days to arrive. Unfortunately, to avoid an asteroid storm, the Icewalker had to exit negative space and manually divert around the flood of gargantuan rocks, which added an extra day to their journey.

"Whoever it was, they're probably dead by now," a familiar voice called out from behind him. Smoke, their Human engineer, was wiping his hands on a dirty rag, having just returned from inspecting the positive-mass engines as they prepared to exit negative space.

"More than likely," the captain replied. "But, we have to inspect and report, regardless."

Smoke spat. "I don't like being this close to the Borderlands, Captain. Too many strange stories about this part of the galaxy for my comfort; the Point of Always Return, unexplained space storms, ferocious glistening monsters, not to mention the Xizor. I don't want to end up as some anonymous star on the guild walls. We should turn around and make for the nearest port."

The captain spun in his chair to face him. Veskor was a large primate covered in thick creamy white fur that had begun to gray along the fringes. The quadruped walked on his huge, over-sized arms and knuckles, thumping the ground with each step. If he was in a hurry or if he was particularly angry, the captain was more than capable of charging on his hind legs. He had a billowy mane around his droopy, dark face. A colorful shade of light green. Like his body-hair, it was also starting to gray around the tips. His one good black horn curved at a slight angle towards his back; the other horn was broken off around the point where it would also curve back.

"Damn Naddine warbeast tore it off me during the war," the captain once told him, referring to the Century of Strife. The fifth war between the Zokyon Technocracy and the Naddine Confederacy was the longest and the most brutal conflict in known history, even more so than the Great Galactic War almost a thousand years ago. By the war's end, every race became involved. The number of war deaths totaled more than a billion souls. Although the Rinvari were never subjugated by either the Zokyo or the Naddine, many had fought as mercenaries while the war depleted the manpower of each respective side. Reinforcements from outside their territories had to be hired.

Nat had fought in that war when he was younger. 'Fought' wasn't really the correct term. He had never piloted a great mecha, going toe-to-toe with the savage warbeasts of the Naddine. In truth, he was a grease monkey. A simple mechanic. He loved ships; he loved fixing ships; he loved building ships; he loved flying in ships. He had come of age during the tail end of the fighting, thankfully never having to witness the horrors of battle. That was some twenty-five years ago now.

Nat had met Veskor when the Rinvari was piloting a squad of atmospheric planes on behalf of a smaller mercenary company hired by the Technocracy. His squad had returned to Zokyon space for repair. By Mordelar's luck, Nat, or Knt'u'Frm to use his formal name, was assigned to repair Veskor's ship. This chance encounter paid off almost a decade later when he was applying for a position with the Rangers. Veskor was already a prominent pilot in the guild, and he put in a good word for him with the guildmasters. They accepted his application only a day later. He had been with Captain Veskor ever since.

The look the captain gave Smoke he was all too familiar with. Nat had been on the receiving end of that look in his early Ranger days. It was not a comforting look.

"Even if the Rangers wouldn't expel us for dereliction of duty, Conclave law dictates all ships, regardless of species, must answer a distress call of any nonmilitary vessel. If you don't like it, there's the airlock, Engineer Smoke."

The Human was a short, stout man with a bald head and a long, unkempt black beard. He wore plain, ratty clothes in the typical Ranger fashion. The only remarkable feature about him was a tattoo of two disks, unequal in size, next to his left eye. The larger disk was a faded deep blue while the smaller disk, located up and to the right of the larger disk, was gray. He was the only Human Nat had ever met. They were hardly ever seen outside of Bokori space; the unfortunate side effect of being the last officially subjugated race in the galaxy. Smoke had joined the Rangers only a few years ago, having fled Bokori space from charges of spreading blasphemy. When Nat asked him about it, Smoke only grunted. Fortunately for Smoke, the Rangers were outside of Bokori jurisdiction, so he was safe from the long slender fingers of the grayskins so long as he remained in the guild.

"No need to get hostile, Captain. I'm only speaking my mind. I've heard the tales about the Borderlands and the Point of Always Return. I'm not eager to find out if they're true is all."

The captain lifted himself from his chair and slowly marched to Smoke, hitting the metal below his knuckled hands with extra emphasis on each step. Smoke took a step back, a flicker of fear in his eyes.

"I have gazed into the maws of Naddine warbeasts, zapped out of the sky by a Rorae Magi, and nearly suffocated by a Moan Metamorph pretending to be one of us. A few sailors' stories whispered in the ears of whelps and whores won't deter me. Now, report on the status of the positive-mass engine."

The Rinvari towered over the smaller Human. Smoke gulped. "It's old, decrepit, falling apart, and functioning as normal, Captain."

The captain smiled then burst into laughter that rattled the steel all around them. Veskor patted Smoke on the shoulder so hard it almost knocked the Human off his feet. "Kewea's curse, you frighten too easily, Smoke. Let's hope you find your nerves when we arrive. You'll be conducting the spacewalk."

Smoke gulped again. "Of...of course Captain Veskor, of course. I'll go get suited up."

Smoke turned and hustled away towards the bowels of the ship. Nat snickered. The Captain was giving Smoke a hard time. Veskor knew Nat's mechsuit was tailor made for spacewalks. It was a three-person crew, and someone had to be the humiliation lightning rod.

Zokyon mechsuits were primarily built for that purpose. It was impossible for them to survive in space otherwise. Their frail bodies and carbon dioxide & methane-based lungs made life difficult for them compared to the mostly oxygen-based lungs of the other major galactic species, save for the plantlike Rorae. They hardly ever took their mechsuits off, even on their homeworld, these days. Nat's mechsuit hugged his body tightly. It was not a combat model. It was simply for survival. Zokyon bodies were lanky; incredibly thin and smooth with long, oval appendages that gave them a noodle-like appearance. Even their heads were narrow and elongated with tiny mouths and beads for eyes close together on either side of their head. Their orb-like chests and hips provided the pivots for two sets of long, lean arms with a gaunt torso connecting the chest and the hips.

"I was watching his vitals on my HUD, Captain," Nat piped in when Smoke was out of sight. "I do right think you've scared away his wits."

The captain laughed. "The Humans will never regain their independence if they are all like Smoke. What a pity. They rose and fell so quickly those Humans. I hope they send those Bokori straight into the clutches of Kewea."

"Hear, hear," agreed Nat. The captain turned around and sat back down on his perch staring out the thin window as the Icewalker barreled through negative space, passing what must've been hundreds if not thousands of stars and planets along their way.

Silence settled in for a long moment. Nat decided to break it. "Smoke may be superstitious, Captain, but he ain't wrong."

The captain slowly whirled his chair to face him. "Is my translator glitching or did you just agree with Smoke? You really think we're going to run into Xizor out here? No one's seen them for over five-hundred years if they ever truly existed."

"Your translator is functioning properly, Captain," Nat said. "I don't know anything about Xizor or glistening monsters, but I do worry about pirates. I've heard rumblings about Excommunicated activity in this area. The Xizor may be just a story, but the knives of the Excommunicated are not. Something caused a ship to send out a distress signal. I'm afraid of what we'll find."

Veskor waved his hand at him dismissively. "Probably just another asteroid storm or perhaps they got too close to the remnants of a supernova. They are more common in this part of the galaxy. In any case, if we do run into hostility, the Icewalker is fast enough to get us out of trouble in no time. We have nothing to fear, Nat, trust me."

The captain turned his chair back to face his data screen, signaling the end of that discussion. Nat wasn't so sure. He had checked the buoy data feeds for that part of the galaxy when they left. No indication of an asteroid storm or any sort of space storm in that area.

Although this part of space was unoccupied, over the past several centuries, the Rangers had charted these interstellar paths along the spiral arms of the galaxy. Their forerunners had dropped satellite buoys all throughout the sector as navigational data for any ships in the future that wished to explore this part of the galaxy for colonization or monetization. Without the buoys, traveling to the distant parts of the galaxy would be treacherous. Ships could accidentally collide with stars, planets, asteroids, black holes, or other such dangers the galaxy held. The process of charting, documenting, and laying down buoys was a perilous job, but that's why the Rangers existed. The job may have gotten slightly easier in the recent few centuries, but the pay and benefits were still very lucrative.

The Icewalker was making small jobs in the local area, trying to find systems with black holes. The Coalition of Independent Nations (CIN), or Sinners as they were commonly known, had hired dozens of Rangers to find black holes, so they could mine and stockpile dark matter, the fuel needed to enter negative space for long distance interstellar travel. Black holes were the energy currency of the galaxy. The more black hole systems under a specie's control, the greater their wealth and reach. While the Sinners were a young coalition, forming at the end of the Century of Strife, they were seeking to make their mark on the galaxy. Captain Veskor, whose own Rinvari were members of the CIN, was making a killing off their rapid expansion, as was Nat by extension.

Nat couldn't complain about the long days and the months at a time they spent on the fringes of galactic society. Truth be told, Nat preferred the quiet solitude of space. The fact he was paid and paid well to do a job he loved was just a bonus.

An alert flashed across his screen along with a reaffirming series of beeps. "We're here, Captain."

Veskor pressed the intercom. "Smoke, I hope you're ready, because we're about to exit negative space."

A moment passed when they heard Smoke's voice reply. "Suited up and ready to go, Captain."

"Aye, brace yourselves."

The captain pulled a few levers on his control board. With a lurch, the Icewalker popped out of negative space. The inertia jolted Nat for but a moment. It was a relatively smooth transition, one Veskor had made thousands of times. He pressed a few more buttons on his board and the positive-mass engine kicked into gear. The ship groaned at the sudden change in speed and power. Nothing alarming to the trained ear.

"Status report," the captain demanded firmly.

"Engine's a bit creaky, but she's otherwise fine, Captain, full power ahead," Smoke declared over the com.

"Good. Navigator Nat, what do the scans read?"

Nat examined the data flashing past his screen. "No sign of supernovae, storms, or any other astrological disturbance, Captain. Only one contact bearing 210 degrees off the port side 20 degrees down angle. Huh, this is unexpected."

"What is it, Nat?"

"It's a Union ship, sir."

Veskor spun his chair around to face him. "That's not possible, Navigator. The Yunes don't send out distress calls on our frequencies. Why would they? They're damned bots!" the captain bellowed with a mixture of disbelief and frustration.

Nat double-checked the data. "It's confirmed, Captain. It's small, probably a scout ship. Cross-shaped design and signatures bear all the marks of a Union vessel. See for yourself," Nat said as he transferred the data from the ship's computer to his own HUD, then passed it along to Veskor's HUD. By the flick of his finger, Nat could tell the captain was scrolling through the data on his HUD, which Nat couldn't see.

"This makes no sense," Veskor declared after siphoning through the data.

Smoke's voice piped through the com. "Is there a problem, Captain? Are we going to search for survivors?"

"I don't see how? Do Yunes have survivors? I guess they are technically alive, but there's no organic matter to find. Standby, Smoke," Veskor said through the com.

"Did you say Yunes, Captain? As in The Union? We came all this way for a derelict ship of malfunctioning bots!" Smoke yelled. Veskor didn't respond.

Nat's sense of unease spiked. Something was wrong. "I'm beginning to agree with Smoke, Captain. This isn't right. We're a couple hundred light years off the beaten path and more than thirty thousand light years from Union space. There's no reason for them to be here on the opposite side of the galaxy. Yunes rarely leave Neutral Space or their own territory, and we haven't heard of a peep of their presence on the Alpha spiral in the half-monthly briefs. We should get out of here."

Nat's words hung in the air. Veskor's face was a wash of concern and excitement. Nat knew what he was going to say before the words left the captain's mouth.

"We have no choice, Navigator Nat. Protocols dictate we fully investigate the ship. The guildmasters will ask us why we didn't examine the vessel when we return to Concordia. I don't want to be brought up on charges. Besides, this might be a chance for the other races to get an edge on those damn Yunes. Any nugget of information on how to disable a Yune ship is worth a fortune. We go in," Veskor declared.

Nat didn't have a chance to protest. The captain activated engine thrusters, and the Icewalker slowly encroached on the vessel.

"Conduct a scan for lifeforms, Navigator," Veskor ordered. They closed the distance to only a few hundred miles. Nat activated the scanners as the Icewalker encircled the derelict ship from a safe distance. The panel beeped and spat out more data.

"No sign of lifeforms, Captain," Nat said.

The captain breathed a sigh of relief. "I suppose in this case that's a good thing. I shudder to think what would be living on a Union ship. How about heat signatures?"

"Negative, Captain," Nat replied. "The ship's temperature matches the local temperature, and there's no residual heat coming off the engines. Their defense turrets seem to be offline as well." The captain grumbled. "Makes sense. They've been out here for days. I'm going to bring us closer for a visual inspection."

"Captain..." Nat tried to protest. Veskor raised a fist to silence him.

"Just open the damn viewports, Navigator!" the captain barked.

"Aye, Captain," Nat responded, not daring to challenge Veskor when he was in command mode. Nat rose from his seat and flipped a switch on the nearby wall. The metal screen guards in front of the captain's viewport retracted, slowly bringing the outside into view. There was very little light. They were in a part of space between solar systems, and the closest star was five light years away. Nat could see the rough outline of the ship in the darkness. The cross-shaped outline of the Union ship indicated it was no larger than the Icewalker.

"Hit the lights," Veskor ordered. Nat flipped a second nearby switch. The floodlights attached to the Icewalker activated instantly. Nat's beady eyes adjusted to the sudden flash of lights. As the Icewalker orbited the Union ship along all three axes, Nat's anxiety flared again.

"There's nothing, Captain. No sign of structural damage, no heat blasts, no scorch marks. The Union ship is completely intact. It's just drifting through space."

The captain rubbed his chin. "Do you see anything on your end, Smoke?" he asked into the com.

"Negative, Captain. We've done our job. We should abandon the ship and go," Smoke said with a hint of nervousness in his voice.

"Stand by," the captain said, ignoring him. "Maybe that's how Union ships travel through deep space? They don't need a living crew to operate a ship. It's easy for them to go into hibernation for long voyages. Maybe that's what this is."

"Then, who sent the distress signal, Captain? There's no other contact in range on my scopes. Plus, without the constant monitoring of the stellar data, they could easily wander off course and crash into a star. If that is how they travel long distance, how can they get this far out without so much as a scratch?"

"Good question, Nat. Perhaps it was an automated response when they shut down. I guess Smoke is going to find out. Prepare for boarding," Veskor said with a smirk.

Union ships didn't have glass windows, so there was no way to physically see the inside of the ship. The only way was to attach themselves to a docking bay door and pry it open from the outside. The Icewalker sidled up next to the derelict ship and attached her umbilical cord to it.

"Smoke, initiate boarding procedures. If you don't find any signs of life, I want you to get the black box," Veskor said into the com.

"Absolutely not, Captain. This is insane!" Smoke yelled.

"Do as I command, Smoke, or I'll have you spaced," Veskor yelled back.

"I'm not going into that ship without a weapon at least, Captain," Smoke insisted.

Veskor sighed. "Fine! Take the plasma rifle. They're the most effective against Yunes. Don't fire unless fired upon! Just get the black box and get out if you're that much of a frightened child." Nat heard Smoke swear through the com. "Aye, Captain," Smoke responded. "Opening the umbilical door now."

Nat protested. "Captain, we cannot enter the vessel of a sovereign specie, especially a Proprietor race. Our obligation is to find the ship and search for survivors. Without a crew to grant us access, we'd need Conclave permission to enter."

"Kewea seize the Conclave," Veskor swore. "It's not a big deal. If there are functional Yunes on the ship, we'll say it was an honest mistake and be on our way. If there aren't, we'll grab the black box and go. We'll know exactly where this ship has been, how long it has been traveling, and what it has encountered. That black box will be worth enough for the three of us to retire on. The scans show no signs of activity. This will be easier than seducing a jade at a fueling station."

That did not alleviate Nat's concerns. They were treading on shaky legal ground, in addition to the general nerves Nat felt around this situation. Nonetheless, he followed Veskor's orders. The captain may be bold at times, but he had never led him astray in fifteen years.

Nat took a deep breath. "Smoke, turn on your suit cam," Nat said into the com. A few moments later, a video feed popped up on his screen. Smoke was moving deliberately down the corridor of the umbilical cord. When he reached the ship's exterior, he knocked hard on the door. A minute passed. No response from the inside. Smoke took that as his cue to put down his defense rifle and whip out his plasma torch. He ignited it and started burning a hole in the locking mechanisms. Nat was monitoring Smoke's vitals on his HUD. Smoke's heart was beating very fast, and Nat could hear him breathing heavily.

"Any issues so far, Smoke?" Nat asked.

"None. Still don't like this," Smoke replied.

"I don't either, but you have to relax. Don't go dying of a heart attack before you get inside, you hear?"

"Yeah, yeah," Smoke said, taking a deep breath. "I'm almost through."

A few more minutes passed when Smoke broke the seal on the outer door. He tugged at the door. It must've been heavier than he expected. He struggled to force the door open. When he did, he was nearly sucked into the ship as the umbilical cord's atmosphere equalized with that of the derelict ship. Smoke barely stayed on his feet as the force of the air almost caused him to be thrown into the ship's interior. His magboots were the only thing that prevented him from being tossed into a bulkhead.

"Kewea's curse!" Smoke swore. "There's no airlock."

"That's because there's no air," the captain replied with a chuckle. "Synthetic organisms don't need to breathe. Remember that when you try to open any more doors."

The captain was laughing. He glanced at Nat, expecting him to be laughing, too. Only Nat wasn't. He was too busy examining the feed from Smoke's suit cam.

Smoke was in what Nat presumed to be the long corridor of the

Union ship. Nat had never seen the interior of their ships. Save for what appeared to be control panels at various stages along the interior, the ship was completely empty. Nat supposed that made sense. Yunes wouldn't have much need for the same bells and whistles of a regular ship. No need for sleeping quarters, dining area, or even a bathroom. Still, the lack of a single bot, active or inactive, spooked Nat.

"Turn right, Smoke, the black box will be in the cockpit near the front," Nat said. Smoke didn't reply. Instead, he raised his rifle and proceeded to head towards the cockpit. His magboots kept him stabilized with the lack of artificial gravity. Smoke reached the door. It was locked. Smoke put his rifle down and pulled out his plasma torch again. Halfway through burning into the door, Smoke was jostled and let out a scream.

"What's happening?!" Nat asked fearfully. Smoke dropped his plasma torch and picked up his defense rifle. He was frantically searching all around him for the source of the jostling. Smoke's heart rate was through the roof.

"You need to calm down, Smoke," Veskor said coolly.

"Why don't you come over here and tell me to be goddess damn calm!" Smoke shouted. Smoke was frantically searching all around him finding nothing. Nat noticed something move on his cam.

"Smoke, look up," Nat said.

Sheepishly, Smoke raised his rifle upwards. He nearly screamed again. It was a Yune bot. Judging by its small size and vaguely rounded-shape, Nat supposed it was an engineering bot. It was floating in the air seemingly deactivated. Smoke yanked it to the floor and examined it more closely.

"It's disabled," Smoke said. "No sign of any damage, though. The power core is still intact just with no juice. Should I bring it with me?" Smoke asked.

"No, leave it. Once we get into range of a hub world, it might come back online. I don't want to have to explain to the entire Union what we were doing with one of their bots. Keep at the door," Veskor said.

Smoke managed to burn the lock on the cockpit door quickly. This time when he opened the door, he braced himself. Except, when the door opened, air didn't rush in to fill the vacuum like last time. Something flashed on Smoke's cam. Suddenly, the feed went dead. Only static filled the screen.

"Smoke, is everything okay," Nat asked nervously. No response. He tried again. "Smoke, come in. Your camera went offline." Still no reply. "Coms are down, Captain. I'm not getting anything."

"I can see that," Veskor said, unconcerned. "Check his vital signs."

Nat's heart skipped a beat. His words almost got caught in his throat. "His vital signs aren't there, Captain."

"What do you mean? He's dead?" Veskor asked.

"No, I mean they aren't there. Smoke has completely disappeared off my party HUD. It's as if he isn't there anymore."

"Nonsense," the captain insisted. He must've pulled up the team's vitals on his own HUD. "I don't understand, it's only reading you and me. Smoke doesn't register at all."

"Enough is enough, Captain, we need to leave now!" Nat insisted.

"And leave Smoke? Do you forget the Ranger bylaws, Navigator? No one shall be left behind. I'm sure it's just a malfunction. Go down there and find him," Veskor ordered.

There was a loud crashing sound below deck. The sound of metal on metal screeching and tearing.

"Kewea's curse. What was that? Smoke better not be wrecking my ship," the captain bellowed.

Nat jumped to his feet and dashed to the source of the noise as fast as his mechsuit would allow. He exited the cockpit and reached the railing overlooking the interior cargo bay. What Nat saw chilled him to the bone.

Standing in the middle of the cargo area among the ruins of the torn away umbilical door was a tall, slender sentient figure the likes of which Nat had never seen. It must've been seven or eight feet tall with cracked, rustic red skin. Its face was skeletal with a bony nose, and it was wearing what resembled goggles over where its eyes should be. Its pointy ears rose up from its skull and curved back towards its jet-black hair. Nat noticed the creature was wearing armor around most of its body save for the face. Even the creature's short, stunted tail had armor. Except, the armor was moving. Nat saw it slither around its body, growing and contracting. The organic armor had a metallic sheen that reflected the light of the Icewalker's interior. Nat's eyes wandered over to the large, bladed weapon in its hand. The blade swirled with an eerie black energy, giving the sword an almost amorphous appearance.

Nat froze. He held his breath, trying not to make a sound. His mind screamed at him to move, but his scrawny legs wouldn't budge. The creature turned its head slowly to stare at him. For a moment, Nat thought that the creature was smiling at him. Nat's instincts finally kicked in. He turned to flee. He couldn't move. He was pushing his muscles, but he felt like he was tightly bound by ropes.

No, this is the worst time for my armor to lock down!

He quickly scanned his HUD for his mechsuit's status. It was fully functional, and yet, Nat was completely immobile. Out of the corner of his eye, he saw the creature had his non-sword arm outstretched towards him. The creature opened its mandible mouth wide with a hiss. It was making this unsettling clicking sound at him. To Nat's horror, he finally noticed the creature was hovering off the ground and was now gliding in his direction. Nat had heard the stories about them, but never thought they were real. Until this moment.

Xizor!

Nat's body was slowly turning against his will. Nat tried to fight, but he was powerless to stop it. He was now face-to-face with this creature only a few feet away. The creature was still clicking at him with its mouth. Nat was pulled in closer and closer.

BANG BANG BANG.

Multiple shots rang out, striking the creature. The unexpected gunshots must've startled the intruder, for Nat was unceremoniously dropped to the ground. Nat turned to see Veskor with his sidearm in hand. "Get up, boy!" he yelled. Nat scrambled to his feet. He ran back to hide behind the burly captain. He expected his muscles to seize up again at any moment. They didn't. He reached the captain and turned to face the creature. It was gone.

Veskor inched closer to the railing to see where the creature had fallen. Nat followed close, not wanting to put any distance between him and the captain. Nat peered over the side and saw only the wreckage of the umbilical door.

"It's gone!"

Nat's heart was pounding. He whipped his head around as fast as his mechsuit would allow searching for the creature. It was nowhere to be seen. "Did you get him?" Nat asked.

Veskor was also searching for the creature. "Maybe. No body. Stick close to me. I'm not picking up anything on my HUD. We're going for the armory. We'll pick up better weapons and armor, then we'll seal the umbilical door with the emergency stasis field. I'm fairly confident protocol allows us to leave."

Nat wasn't sure if Veskor was trying to be funny or not. They creeped along the edge of the upper railing. The armory was on the opposite side of the ship from them and down one level. Veskor was pointing his outstretched gun at anything vaguely suspicious. Still no sign of the creature.

Nat noticed a glint in his peripheral vision. A little metallic ball was slowly ascending near them. The ball flashed with a burst of light so bright it almost blinded Nat. As his vision returned, Nat saw that all the lights in the vicinity had gone out. He heard Veskor grunting. A few seconds later, Veskor grunted again, this time making strange noises he had never heard the captain utter. He felt a tugging on his shoulder. Veskor was trying to say something to him, but all Nat heard was grunting and roaring. Nat had a sudden realization.

He is speaking to me, except his words aren't translating.

Nat noticed that all the information on his HUD was gone. He saw nothing but what his physical eyes were showing him. His UI System was completely shut down. Nat couldn't access his inventory, his data files, his vital statistics, nothing. In a panic, Nat thought that his mechsuit's breathing apparatus might've shut down, too. It hadn't. Nat breathed a sigh of relief. His mechsuit's functions were mostly mechanical in nature. Whatever that metal ball was, it had rendered anything electronic or digital useless.

Nat tried desperately to mime as much of that information as he could to Veskor. He wasn't sure if Veskor completely understood. He did seem to grasp their communications were down. He gestured to Nat to keep following. Nat's mind was racing. He couldn't keep his thoughts straight; the fear had penetrated his body to the core. Nat was fully aware his mechsuit made a thud with each step in the steel walkway beneath him. The creature knew exactly where they were at all times. Nat heard a clang from the other side of the walkway. Instinctively, Veskor fired in that direction striking nothing but the wall.

It's toying with us.

As if the creature read his thoughts, Nat felt Veskor suddenly lift right off the ground and slam right back down into the walkway below them. The old metal gave way like crumpled paper. The two of them were thrown into in the open cargo area, and the beams crashed around them. Nat's mechsuit absorbed most of the impact, but he had the wind knocked out of him. He pulled himself to his feet, then heard an ear-piercing scream. Nat whipped his head around to see the creature slashing its blade at Veskor. The blade carved a bloody path across the captain's chest. Veskor roared in pain. For a moment, it seemed as if Veskor's blood was sucked into the creature's blade. Nat turned to flee only to run into another person.

"Smoke!"

Nat's relief turned to terror as he beheld his former shipmate. The whites of Smoke's eyes were black, the color in his eyes bright red. The veins in his neck were huge and blackened. He made no sound.

Smoke lunged at Nat, succeeding in tackling him to the ground. Smoke was clawing at his face. The glass on the front of Nat's mechsuit was reinforced with clear, fused quartz. No way Smoke's bare hands could break it. Hoping the strength augments he had acquired in his youth would be enough, Nat grabbed Smoke and hurled the Human over his head. By stroke of luck, Nat managed to throw Smoke right into the creature, who had finished off Veskor by then.

The impact dazed his foe long enough for Nat to spring to his feet and dash in the direction of the escape pod. He reached the doorway that led to the connecting corridor when his body stalled again. The creature was holding him in place. Nat tried desperately to move, but he could only barely move his arms. Even the augments were no match for whatever power the creature had over his body. He could hear the creature walking towards him making that bone-chilling clicking noise. Nat knew he only had one chance. He forced his arm as close to his mechsuit as he could. With every last bit of strength he could muster, Nat took a deep breath and hit the emergency release button on his mechsuit. The mechsuit went flying off him in the direction of the creature with a loud crash. Without a second's hesitation, Nat took off as fast as his bony, mech-less legs could carry him. His plan must have worked. Like an attacker grabbing onto a piece of clothing, Nat had let his mechsuit be taken rather than him.

Nat's lungs were screaming at him. He held his breath, charging down the corridor. Zokyo could not last long in this environment. He had to reach the escape pod immediately. The creature would not be far behind. Nat had turned a corner just as a huge piece of metal crashed above him. Nat didn't stop to see what had happened. He kept racing towards the end of the corridor.

Fifty feet.

Forty feet.

Thirty feet.

Another hunk of metal was hurled in his direction, crashing near him. He had almost let out his breath in surprise.

Twenty feet.

Ten feet.

Nat had to dive to reach the pod. With his last bit of strength, he leaped forward into the escape pod. Nat hit the ground inside the pod with a thud, the last bit of air leaving his lungs. He was suffocating. Nat quickly hit the button to close the door on the escape pod and frantically searched the pod. Not a moment too soon, he found a portable rebreather. The Zokyo collapsed to the ground and took several deep breaths.

Not a moment later, Nat was forcefully pulled through the air. His body crunched against the window of the escape pod. Nat felt several bones break. Nat screamed in pain. His eyes welled up with tears. Nat watched the creature try to pull him through the sealed glass of the escape pod door with its outstretched hand. Nat felt like his insides were ripping apart. A sealed door wasn't enough to keep him safe. The Zokyo lifted his hand to the nearby lever, and, with a great tug, yanked it down. The pod was jettisoned from the Icewalker with a flash. The shockwave of the pod's departure caused the creature to lose his mental grip on him. Nat hit the ground with another bone crunching thud. The Zokyo yelped another cry of pain.

The pod's autopilot was putting a few miles between Nat and the Icewalker; between him and the creature. His body was wracked with internal trauma. He could hardly move. Yet, Nat never felt a stronger sense of relief. He was laughing. The pod contained all he needed to survive for at least a month, including a backup mechsuit. Although it lacked the capacity for negative space, he could fly it far away from that red-skinned demon. Eventually, someone would answer his pod's distress call.

Oh, the story I'll have when I get back.

He decided he'd visit a den of Anamea when he returned to Concordia. Find comfort in the arms of a vivacious Incubae. He laid there in pain for minutes. Maybe hours? He lost all sense of time. The soreness of his body was messing with his internal clock. There was beeping on the nearby monitor.

I haven't sent out the distress signal, yet. How could anyone be close by?

When Nat turned on the monitor, his eyes widened. Outside, closing fast, was an enormous ship in the shape of a three-sided pyramid, the peak pointed in his direction. The hull of the ship was contracting and expanding, slithering along its exterior with an eerie slight luminescent glow. Nat had served aboard a Titan-class warship during the Century of Strife. He estimated the pyramid-shaped ship was at least fifty percent larger. Nat felt the escape pod jerk in the direction of the ship. The ship was pulling the pod to it. Nat heard tapping on the window. He glanced out the window, and his heart sank. With no spacesuit, the cracked, rustic-skinned creature was hanging onto the side of the pod. It stared at him. This time it was unmistakable, the creature was smiling at him.

I

What the F?

I hope they don't put me in a box.

The thought washed over Adam as he watched the rows of mourners dressed all in white flank the coffin. His eyes fluttered upward to see an entire fleet of Bokori saucers dotting the sky over head. Pendulum blades prepared to strike. The looming husk of Bokor engulfed the entire sky, staring down at them. The steady drizzle of rain tapped their flesh and the ground around them, pricking them with a constant reminder of their perilous situation. The thick, soupy air of the humid jungle moon filled their lungs with dread and despair. A rotten stench of feces and odor permeated the local atmosphere, drifting up from the densely populated town below. This was humanity's reality; this was humanity's home.

A peculiar buzz of excitement filled the air. They had all gathered around the coffin of the dead man. As it strange as it was, this was an act of defiance. A moment of grief and sadness mixed with a feeling of hope and uncertainty. Media representing different species from all over the galaxy were huddled together just out of earshot. They had a perfect line of sight on Adam. Putting a body in the ground may have seemed like an ordinary affair to some observers, but to the Humans of Windless Tornado, it was anything but ordinary.

A few hundred thousand pairs of Human eyes were glued to screens, watching the events unfold from inside the illegal settlement of Arabella below. In his head, Adam tried to count the number of laws, regulations, and social norms violated by committing this act of humanity. Refusing to recycle the parts of a body was a great crime to the Bokori. Those that would enforce the Covenant, Human or Bokori, would scream and holler their protestations into the ether. Adam did not care. Above the pomp and circumstance of the moment, his gaze shifted between his weeping mother and consoling brother. A great weight on Adam's shoulders. Those that would expect something extraordinary from him would have to wait. This was about his father.

He tapped the air in front of him. His HUD displayed the notes he had taken when preparing for this moment. He did not want to misstep here. He did not want this to have the appearance of a political speech, so he eschewed the handheld emulator. Instead, he relied on the limited memory space of his UI System. Shown in front of his vision on his HUD, he had jotted down brief talking points. To all those observing, he was speaking from his heart. His words would be dissected by scores of sentients from Rema to Mthr, from Concordia to Terras-Ku, from the territories of the Sinners to wherever the Yunes call home. A balance needed to be struck, all while remembering he was still Human. He had to show the proper sorrow and bereavement expected from losing someone close to them. Adam had not been particularly close to his father. He loved him, as any son should, but he had spent so many years apart from his father, mother, and brother. Between growing up on the streets of the Sistine Slums, serving several years in the Bokori military, and the monstrosities inflicted upon him in rehab, Adam was numb. Whatever grief visible on the faces of his mother and brother, he did not feel it himself. Yet, through the confluence of circumstance and tragedy, Adam was the one requested to deliver the eulogy.

Adam cleared his throat. All eyes were on him. His back muscles tightened. "Those here that know me understand when I say I am a man of few words, so I will be brief. My father, Cloud Mortis, is a man history will not forget. I will go to my own grave to be certain of that.

From the simple act of *liberating* a statue to establishing the massive *community outpost* behind and below me, my father's legacy will be one of hope and disobedience. Our eyes always looking to the future, to the improvement of the Human condition. My brother told me our father's last moments were spent in laughter playing Conclave Conquest, a game my father and brother enjoyed playing together for many years. That is how I will choose to remember my father. As a happy, family man always wanting to do what is right for his children and those under his charge. We will not wait for permission to take charge of our future. With the eyes of the galaxy upon us, I can only say, 'What is lost, will be found.'"

The Humans around the casket all repeated the phrase. From the top of the high ridge, where the ceremony was performed, "What is lost, will be found," could be heard repeated by thousands of voices from Arabella. The phrase was repeated as a low, hushed chant for several seconds after Adam finished his brief eulogy. A few of the camera crews rushed to the side of the cliff to take video of the moment occurring beneath them.

Clad all in white, Adam approached the coffin. His father's name was engraved into the side of the dull gray wooden box. Underneath his name, the letter "F" from the Default language was prominently carved. Remembering the instructions taught to him by Havera, Adam pressed his left hand softly onto the letter "F." Adam felt incredibly silly standing there in the rain, holding his hand on the box. His eyes locked onto the tattoo on the back of his hand, hoping perhaps the inked symbol held some hidden wisdom for him to unlock. None came. After a few seconds, he let go.

Havera!

Adam surveyed the small crowd of white-clad mourners. Except for the few reporters off to the side, they were all Human. His eyes connected with Trissefer's. She smiled weakly at him. She bowed her head immediately to prevent others from seeing her understanding smile. The Cauduun was nowhere in sight.

Adam finished with his part in the ceremony and moved to join the others. He stood next to his best friend John Dark and his sister Samus. John subtly nodded his approval to Adam. Samus grabbed his hand and squeezed it with reassuring affection. Adam smiled weakly, which caused Samus to blush. Adam appreciated the gesture.

"I don't see Havera here, do you?" Adam whispered to his friend.

John shrugged. "Who is the Consul of Cloudboard? Probably for the best. It isn't appropriate for an alien to be so intimately involved in a Human affair."

"That's not fair," Adam replied. "This ceremony wouldn't have happened without her. She should be here."

Adam's brother Aaron shushed them. John glared at Aaron while Adam bowed his head in contrition. Samus squeezed her brother's hand. More so than his own flesh and blood, the raven-haired siblings were like family to him. He owed John a debt he could never repay. They grew up together in the Sistine Slums, they enlisted together, and it was John who liberated him from rehab. John and Samus' parents were sent to rehab for crimes of morality when they were young. The Bokori assigned John and Samus a Community to live with, common for Humans and Bokori these days. John and Adam were of an age while Samus was five years younger than them. After their parents finished their stint in rehab, they had emerged as Modders stripped of all dignity and self-respect. Despite his age, John had rejected the culture the Bokori attempted to impose upon them. He and his sister were little rebels, and they had roped Adam into their small acts of defiance. A few vandalisms here, a few destructions of propaganda there. By the time Adam's parents had rescued them from the slums, Adam and John decided that learning skills from the Bokori military were needed if they were to become effective revolutionaries.

The Bokori military was unusual by galactic standards in that most of the enlisted ranks were made up of Humans, including a large percentage of the officer corps. Modern Bokori shunned violence and any who sought out the "barbaric" profession. The only reason the Bokori kept an active military was to combat the pirates ravaging their eastern holdings, and, from what Adam understood, they were required to do so by Conclave law as a Proprietor race. In an ironic twist of fate, the Bokori military had become a major breeding ground for Human resistance. The Bokori political and morality officers embedded in the units and the fleets did little to quell the Human spirit. By the time of Adam's arrest, the Bokori were beginning to phase in bots to replace the Human soldiers.

John was comfortable leaving Samus in the care of the Mortis family and the budding settlement of Arabella. It was the hardest decision of John's life. The two were closer than anyone Adam had met. When John brought Adam back to Arabella, the two were inseparable.

Seven Humans stepped forward with old rifles. A voice called out for them to aim and fire. At once, all seven fired one shot into the air. They repeated this volley twice more. Adam thought this was a waste of projectiles. Arabella had so few bullets and even fewer weapons to go around. Their printers didn't have the resources to keep with the demand. Adam had pushed back when the independence faction argued for the twenty-one-gun salute. Havera explained to them about this ancient Human ritual gleaned from Stepicro.

Twenty-one-waste-of-projectiles salute, Adam had thought was more appropriate. Getting this funeral ceremony right was important to his mother, so it was important to him. They compromised by using makeshift projectiles with older weapons, whose usage was inconsequential to the defense of Arabella due to their age and the rust that had overtaken them. It was Trissefer who ultimately convinced him in the way she often did. She used him, and, in the short-term, Adam did not mind. He never had the mind or the stomach for such political intrigue. At least, not since he escaped rehab.

It was all the more reason he dreaded what was to come the next day. By acclamation, Adam was to be appointed to his father's seat on the Commission. The six-member Commission was responsible for the governance of Arabella. Each Commissioner in charge of certain sector of the settlement's welfare. Adam's father, Cloud, had been the Commissioner in charge of defense and security. Soon, it would be Adam's purview.

It should be Aaron's; Adam had thought when he was told of the appointment. His hot-headed younger brother had more of an appetite for this sort of work. Although he lacked the military experience Adam had, Aaron had spent most of his life in Arabella since their father helped establish the town. He knew the ins and outs of the settlement far better than Adam and had better working relationships with most of Arabella's people. Adam, by contrast, was a relative stranger to the settlement. He had only been there a couple years since his escape.

"It's a matter of symbolism," Trissefer had told him the other night. "Whether you like it or not, your presence gives Arabella focus and a cause to strive for." Adam wasn't sure why. He only did what he thought was right. Adam didn't need another constant reminder of what had happened as his back itched. Since word spread about the decision to replace their father with him, Aaron had treated him coolly, at best, and with outright hostility, at worst. He didn't blame him. Although they were brothers by blood, they hardly knew each other. The Bokori's communitarian policies had separated them when they were born. Their parents had rescued Aaron when he was still a baby. Adam wasn't as lucky. After he was eventually tracked down and reunited with his parents, Adam had enlisted in the military right away. It was only after John had liberated him did the four of them start to form a familial relationship. That was nearly three years ago.

They lowered his father's casket into the ground. One-by-one, mourners grabbed a nearby patch of dirt and tossed it into the hole as they walked by. Adam was the last. He scooped up a chunk of dirt and held his hand aloft over the hole.

"All those years those grayskins took from us, Dad, I will take them back in blood," he whispered. He let go of the dirt and with a soft thump he said goodbye to his father.

One last piece of the ceremony remained. Adam, Aaron, and their mother, Morrigan, stood near the edge of the cliff as the white-clad mourners lined up to give their condolences to each member of the family. There weren't many, but to Adam the line seemed endless. The space at the top of the cliff was small. Only those deemed most important were invited. To Adam's chagrin, they were the people he liked the least: the other Commissioners, leaders of commerce, and other so-called movers and shakers of Arabella. Besides the Dark siblings and Trissefer, the only one he remotely got along with was the Chief of Internal Security, Duke Drake, a tough dark-skinned Human Adam had known briefly in the navy. The scarred, bald man shook his hand and whispered, "I'm at your service, Commissioner." The man was at least twenty years his senior, yet, as the soon-to-be Commissioner for Defense and Security, Duke would report to him. The other Commissioners whispered their words of solace and good fortune. Trissefer was one of the last to approach. Her shoulder-length strawberry blonde hair had new streaks of pink Adam noticed. Her hair fluttered in the gentle breeze. She leaned in and kissed him on the cheek.

"Come see me tonight. Please?" she whispered. Adam nodded. Aaron shot him a sideways disapproving glance. Adam gazed into her pale green eyes. They were puffy. His father's death had been hard on her. Adam realized she probably had been closer to his father than he had. She walked away burying her face in her hands choking back tears.

"I don't like what's going on with you two," Aaron muttered when she was out of earshot.

"Dad approved. Why can't you?" Adam asked, not wanting to look his brother in the eye.

"Of course, he did. He thought you two would be the perfect match. He always had a blind spot when it came to her...and you. If only he knew how fleeting y'all's relationship truly was."

"And how would you know?" Adam asked, turning to face his brother. A sudden anger flared up inside him.

"Trissefer Quinn is only the latest passing fancy for you, and you're nothing but a political relationship to her. A way for her to boost her prestige," Aaron scoffed. "Not that I can see what's so prestigious about tussling in your bedroom."

"Enough! The two of you please stop bickering today of all days!" Morrigan said as loud as she could while maintaining a respectful tone.

"Sorry, Mom," the brothers said together.

The brothers stood there in rebuked silence. "Come with us, Morrigan. We'll take you home," John said, taking her by the hand. John led his mother to the awaiting ride back down the hill. Samus gave both Adam and Aaron one final hug as she went to join her brother. Adam and Aaron stood near the edge of the cliff alone but for a few reporters waiting to ask them questions. They looked down to see Arabella returning to its typical hustle and bustle. The muggy wet weather didn't stop the Humans from resuming their daily lives. If only that were the case for Adam and Aaron.

"Dad taught you well," Aaron said breaking the silence. "No one will be happy with that little speech. The Bokori will demand more supplication, and the hardcore Separatists will say you rhetorically compromised our cause by calling Arabella a "community outpost," treating this place like an extension of Bokori authority. It's the kind of speech Dad would've given."

"Would you prefer I acted more like Mom?" Adam asked.

"If Mom had given the speech, she would've had us grab our weapons, fly straight to Inclucity, and burn down the whole place down just to prove a point," Aaron replied.

The brothers shared a laugh, the tension between them slowly dissolving. Aaron glanced upward at the small fleet floating above their heads. The half-dozen or so saucers continued their rotational patrols in the sky between Windless Tornado and Bokor. Adam mimicked his brother. His eyes locked onto one of the smaller saucers, a black circular cloud closer than all the others. It was the only one not patrolling, instead hovering only a few thousand feet in the sky. "I half expected a storm of Hisbas to descend upon us as the box was lowered into the ground," Adam said, keeping his eyes on the black saucer.

"The Hisbaween's bark is loud, but the Bokori won't unleash them. Windless Tornado is sacred ground, and the Bokori are too weak-willed to so brazenly initiate violence. They prefer to keep their violent actions under wraps. Even the High Hisba wouldn't violate Bokori law just to stop us," said Aaron.

"I'm not so sure," Adam said, his heart skipping at the mention of the High Hisba. "He's Human. No telling what he'd be willing to do to stop the further 'degradation' of their moon. The Bokori might've surrendered themselves to cultural hysteria, but we know what Humans are capable of when pushed to the brink."

Aaron scoffed. "I'm surprised you of all people would call that creature Human. Modders strip themselves of all humanity when they go under the knife. Anything to honor the Covenant and the slave masters who hold us all hostage. Is Noah real, too?"

"We're the last species in the galaxy operating under a Covenant of Subjugation. You'd think the rest of the galaxy would give a damn," said Adam.

"Kewea seize the rest of the galaxy. The Proprietor races, the Conclave, the Sinners, the Xizor; The whole lot of them. Humanity is nothing but a joke to them. We're a relic of a bygone age when Human technology was the envy of the galaxy. It's all gone. Earth is gone. The Apocalypse took her along with any hope of a future. We're on our own and have been for over five-hundred years," said Aaron with increasing bitterness.

"What is lost will be found, Aaron."

Aaron sighed. "What is lost will be found. You're right. We must keep faith in the Long Con. If I'm honest, I don't know if I believe in it anymore. It's a fantastical a story, no different than Noah. Gone are the days when the Bokori were a major galactic power it's true, Proprietor status or no. I just don't know if we have the strength to win. Dad's Debbie won't be enough. I think maybe Mom has the right notion. We should march on Inclucity and put our fate in the goddesses' hands. Give the galaxy something to remember us by. We have the numbers to do it. We only need the guns. The Xizor will return. We must be ready."

Halfheartedly listening to his brother, Adam lowered his gaze back to the freshly buried pit. The raindrops continued pelting his face, disguising the tears gathering at the edge of his eyes. Adam tried turning his focus onto the environment around him. The dull gray trees with their muted leaves dominated the muddy landscape. He was trapped by an aura of mediocre desolation. He felt the jungle closing in all around him. Dizziness took him.

No, not now!

The panic set in. His heart fluttered at an alarming rate. His stomach churned. He wanted to puke. His breathing shallowed. He bent over bracing himself on his knees. Aaron realized what was happening. He braced his brother's back with his hand. The reporters must've noticed too, for they were rushing to swarm the pair of them.

"Aaron, deal with them. Please. I'm done." Adam took a few steps forward, then turned heel on the spot. Aaron let out a yell of protest. Adam ignored him. It was too much. He needed to get away. He needed to be free. With reckless disregard, he ran to the edge of the cliff...and jumped.

2

The Longtail

The wind rushed past Adam's face. His hair was ripped back towards the sky. The air pressed his cheeks into his skull. Adam closed his eyes and counted in his head. He knew exactly how long until his body would crunch into the ground. He held his pointer finger in place prepared to press a virtual button in the air. He had made this jump dozens of times. The rush of adrenaline surging through his body felt like an old creature comfort. Falling from huge heights was nothing new to Adam. He had made thousands of jumps during his Shocktrooper days. It was liberating plunging hundreds of feet from on high. The cold chill of the rushing air alleviated the heat and stickiness that permeated Windless Tornado's climate. He felt free. At the end of a stressful day, he would drag his ragged body up to the top of that hilltop, often taking hours battling the mud-soaked ground and constant steady downpour. The first time he jumped, he intended it to be his last. In his melancholier moods, he would often fantasize about letting the ground rush up to kiss him. A final intimate painless goodbye. Like falling asleep only quicker. There were days he would let his finger linger for just a moment too long. Maybe it would be easier to let go. End it once and for all. Today was not that day.

Less than a hundred feet from the ground, Adam tapped in the air and his HUD lit up. His eyes were still closed, but he could feel the clothes on his body instantly change. Gone was the white outfit, replaced with something more to Adam's liking. He tucked his body in and spun until his feet were facing downward. He clicked his newly materialized boots, igniting the orange flame boosters in the heels. Slowing his descent to a gentle fall, the boosters stabilized his body. He touched down with a gentle thud. He smiled after hitting the muddy ground.

His charcoal boots along with his faded green jumpsuit were relics from his time in the military. The boosters were a bonus he received as a member of the Shocktroopers, an elite branch of marines deployed at a moment's notice anywhere in Bokori space. Dropships would enter the atmosphere until they reached a low enough altitude that elite Shocktroopers would jump. Gliding in the air until they reached their destination, they would wait until the last possible moment until activating their boosters. Adam chose to put his in his boots. Some had special backpacks or helmets, but Adam found those either uncomfortable or overly cumbersome. The boosters in the boots weren't as powerful. They couldn't act as jump jets. Adam didn't care. He preferred the freedom and flexibility in the boots. He always found them strangely comfortable for military attire. He was grateful John was able to grab them from storage during his stadium escape.

Beyond the boots and the jumpsuit, Adam had one more article of clothing: a deep purple hooded duster coat washed out in the gray filter of Windless Tornado. It wasn't the most appropriate attire in this climate. Often times, Adam found himself sweating through his clothes with the coat on. Again, Adam didn't care. He wore it everywhere he could. His father had given it to him the day John brought him back from rehab. It was the only gift his father ever gave him. Adam treasured the coat. His father told him there was a special story about the coat, but Adam never bothered to ask. One of many regrets he was feeling.

He walked over to a nearby parked hoverbike. His hoverbike. He had parked it there earlier in the day, knowing full well he would take the scenic route down. That day, the funeral party was given lifts to the top of the cliff in various vehicles owned by fellow mourners or lent to them for just that occasion. Adam rode with his family to the funeral site he had suggested at the top of the cliff. It was a scenic overlook and provided the perfect escape for the awkward questions he would've been forced to answer had he stayed. Adam wiped the sweat off his brow and boarded his vehicle.

It was an old carbon fiber hoverbike. The Cauduun voluntourist who sold it to him explained it was a decades-old luxury drift bike. It was designed to take leisurely excursions over the water. As such, it moved quite slow. Not ideal for getting somewhere fast. Adam bought it because he liked the color scheme: silver with purple stripes. The seats had cracked white leather and the handles were a bit rusted, yet it operated quite smoothly for such an old bike. Anything to avoid walking on the muddy streets of Arabella. Adam bought it for only three hundred Links. He had more than covered the cost of the bike since. The hoverbike was a two-seater. He made some extra Links giving people rides around the compact village. He was never short on customers.

Every Human on Arabella wanted a chance to talk to him. In the first couple years, Adam hated that. He wanted to avoid other people at all costs. Not something easy to do on Arabella, where you couldn't swing your arm without hitting a bunch of people. The anxiety and nerves he felt around large, densely-packed crowds made him uneasy. It was John who encouraged him to put himself out there. John thought seeing and interacting with people who admired him would be therapeutic. John was right. Those first few rides were awkward. Overly eager passengers trying to suss every little bit of information about his experiences or amorous men and women dropping not so subtle hints they wanted to spend more time with him. Over time, Adam became more relaxed with those rides. He talked more about his life. He never spoke about his rehabilitation to anyone, but he would tell some of the younger kids about what he saw in the military. He sometimes talked to activists about the conditions of the Sistine Slums and the underground Human resistance hotbed within those slums. Not often, though, for he found them to be incredibly exhausting and boring more often than not.

Adam had made some modifications to the drift bike. He attached rigging to the sides of the bike to allow for a tarp to be thrown over the top with a small flap for him peek through. This gave Adam and whoever he was driving some modicum of privacy. It had the added benefit of keeping out the elements. It was a bit warmer with the tarp down, but it was a small price for Adam to pay to avoid curious eyes. It was how he met Trissefer, giving her a ride from one of the few operational restaurants in the town back to her home. She was running away from a bad first date. At first, Adam thought she was another optimistic Human political activist, rambling about the desire for Human independence and the creation of a new Earth. She must've sensed Adam's lack of interest for she quickly changed topics. What caught Adam's attention wasn't her physical beauty, although she had plenty of that to spare, rather she never asked him about rehab. She never once asked him about his imprisonment or what caused him to be arrested in the first place. She never asked him what it was like inside that stadium. Those were often the first questions people asked. Adam refused to indulge them. He'd remain silent until they asked something else. She was the first person outside of John, Sam, and his family to ask him how he was feeling, what he wanted to do in life here on Arabella. She wanted to know him, to understand how he thought and felt. The line of questioning shocked Adam to the point where he nearly crashed his slow-moving drift bike into the side of a repair shop. Adam opened up little by little to her. She didn't invite him inside the first time. That took several more rides and conversations. Adam refused her the first time she asked. He never did so again.

Adam pressed the ignition button on the bike, and the blades came to life. Straddling the bike, he felt the vehicle lift off the ground. He pulled the acceleration, and the bike jerked forward until it moved a slow, deliberate pace, hovering just above the ground. Arabella had no streets per se. More like wide open muddy lanes for people to traverse.

There weren't many hovercars in Arabella and certainly no aircars. Every so often a transport vessel smuggling in goods and resources would land in the nearby jungle. Most of the buildings were all stacked on top of each other. Salvaged old ships, re-purposed vehicles, stolen Bokori storage units and containers, and even donated alien structures comprised the "architecture" of the town. Buildings and hover vehicles were augmented with printed parts. Acquiring the right plans and resources to insert into the printers were a challenge. The jungles of Windless Tornado had an ample supply of wood and game but little else. Raw materials needed to print key pieces of infrastructure were harder to come by than fully functioning generators. Not to mention many, Adam included, wanted to use the printers to boost their weapons and ammo supply. They were a supplemental stopgap, nothing more.

Arabella was originally founded by a couple thousand Human settlers until it ballooned into the bustling small city it is today. A settlement of five-hundred thousand and rising. The site was chosen for its location. A clearing beneath a towering cliff that provided some protection from the weather and the creatures of Windless Tornado. It also created a defensible position against any potential Bokori hostile action. Windless Tornado was an environmentally protected no-go zone for any sentient species. Their mere presence on this jungle rock was a crime, and the list of offenses increased as the town grew. To appease the Bokori, the Humans tried not to build further out beyond the clearing; however, it created more problems for the living conditions. Sanitation and disease were massive headaches. The limited number of doctors, healers, and supplies constituted a crisis. Adam learned certain groups managed to appeal to the races of the Conclave. Despite Bokori objections, certain sentientarian supplies were dropped on the settlement and continued to this day. Creating and maintaining a basic economy was a whole other nightmare. He didn't envy Lara Shepard, the Commissioner in charge of the economy and infrastructure. As far as Adam understood, it involved a lot of begging, stealing, and smuggling. He supposed he would find out in greater detail tomorrow.

The crowd always parted for Adam's drift bike. It was about ten feet long, not easy to maneuver, so Adam was grateful for that. He had the tarp down today and his sign reading "NO RIDES" posted on either side of the cover. He didn't feel like talking to any one today. There would be plenty of time for talking tomorrow. Adam drove around listlessly, no particular destination in mind. He wanted to curl up in his bed and sleep.

He ended up in the town square, or what passed for a town square in Arabella. It was quite cramped. In the center of town was a rusted bronze statue of a woman. Adam knew this statue all too well. He drove closer to it and stopped.

He saw the visage of the woman holding a rifle in a running motion. She was charging into battle with no regard to her own safety. Only the safety of her fellow Humans. This was Arabella. The real Arabella, the person from whom the town derived its name. For good reason, this statue was the instigator of it all. Following the formation of the Covenant, the Bokori built statues and monuments honoring various Humans, who had fought in the Xizorian Invasion. It was the Bokori's way of appeasing Humans to keep them happy about their new life under the Covenant, the legal foundation for humanity's subjugation.

As the centuries wore on and Bokori attitudes about culture and freedoms changed, so too did their attitudes towards the monuments and what they represented. To the Bokori, they were a reminder of humanity's violent, backward past. They instigated a program to remove them post haste. Hundreds of monuments, large and small, were destroyed in this purge of Human history. Many Humans protested with some bolder people stealing the monuments and hide them in the Sistine Slums to protect them. The Bokori police, led by units of the Hisbaween, entered the slums to seize and destroy the stolen statues. All were lost, except for one: Arabella. Adam's parents along with a dedicated band of followers and believers decided the safest place to take the statue was to Windless Tornado. So forbidden were Bokori from setting foot on the jungle moon that shared an atmosphere with its mother planet, they dared not follow the rebellious Humans to the surface. Arrest warrants were issued by the hundreds for Adam's parents and all the Humans that joined them. Seeing no other choice, they decided to establish a settlement of their own. A new Earth, some called it. To all of them, it was now home. Thus, the Separatist movement was firmly established. No longer could their concerns be ignored.

Adam thought it was an odd turn of events to raise such a fuss on either side for a few pounds of bronze. However, he supposed symbolism mattered more than he cared to admit. Arabella herself was a source of mystery. As the story goes, during one of the last battles of the Xizorian Invasion, she flew her ship carrying the legendary Dewbie, a weapon of mass destruction constructed out of dark energy, straight into the heart of the Xizorian fleet. In a flash, half of the Xizorian ships were destroyed. Arabella herself was believed dead. Beyond that, no one really knows anything about her, least of all what she looked like. All those records were lost during the Apocalypse, the term Humans used for the disappearance of Earth. The statue was a basic likeness of a fit Human female with the features on the face notably plain. The rains and winds of Windless Tornado had worn at her remaining features over the past decade.

I wonder if Havera knows about Arabella...Havera!

Adam's thoughts quickly shifted to the Cauduun woman. She wasn't at the funeral and Adam wanted to ask her why. He turned his bike towards the western edge of the town and drove quickly to the outskirts and beyond. It took him quite a while.

Several hundred yards away from the outer edge of Arabella rested a spaceship parked on its own makeshift clearing. It was the largest personal vessel Adam had ever seen. He was used to ships of the fleet, so he had seen bigger spaceships. However, personal vessels were usually no larger than a hundred feet long. The Cicera, by Adam's estimate, was at least four or five-hundred feet long. It was oval-shaped, the façade resembling the visage of a tortoise. Four diamond-shaped protrusions on the four corners of the ship, its arms and legs, with a rounded cockpit up front creating a head. The ship's most interesting feature was a long, thick tail that protruded from the back, curling up to rest on top of the ship. Adam was vaguely familiar with Cauduun ship design. He had seen several while in the navy. The tail attached to a ship was their signature motif. Adam wasn't quite sure what the tail did, but it gave the Cicera a distinguished silhouette. The ship was covered in a thin layer of crimson-painted platinum all along its exterior with the occasional black pattern to break up the sea of red. Across the top of the ship under the curled tail was a prominent purple stripe painted from end to end. Havera told him once the platinum was merely decoration common in Cauduun constructs. The ship itself was built with a mixture of titanium and palerasteel, a powerful steel forged exclusively in the Paleria region of Rema, the Cauduun homeworld. The Cicera could take a full blast from a capital ship, although Havera said that claim had never been tested.

Adam pulled up to the ship. He saw a familiar figure working on dehumidifiers underneath the ship next to the boarding ramp. "How's it going, Dee?" Adam called out to him. Dee dropped a tool he was holding.

"Kewea's curse, Master Adam! You frightened me. You know it's rude to sneak up on someone. I figured a fleshsack like you would understand and practice proper etiquette and protocol," Dee said.

"I didn't realize a bot could be surprised, Dee. I learn something new every day," Adam said with a sarcastic smile. Adam hopped off his parked bike. Dee was a mechanical assistance robot, or bot, what most sentient beings called artificially intelligent constructs. He was metallic and covered in a thin layer of rusted hunter-green platinum with dimly-lit bronze eyes. His body was cauduunoid, mirroring a Human's physiology in many ways, but with six digits on each hand. Dee's "skull" was his most distinguishing feature. The headpiece was elongated at a forty-five-degree angle stretched by about a foot.

"You may find this surprising, Master Adam, but bots are capable of much you don't understand, which, judging by your lack of formal education and choice of wardrobe, I would say is quite a bit," Dee said.

"I'm being insulted by a bot," Adam said shaking his head.

"Yes, you are. It was quite easy. Not to be rude, but what in Cradite's name are you doing here? Do you wish to see the mistress?" Dee asked.

"Nothing gets by you, Dee. Is she here?" asked Adam.

Adam wasn't sure bots could scowl, but he was fairly confident Dee was scowling at him. "She's in the research room studying the latest update from Stepicro. Mind your manners," Dee said.

"Thanks, Dee. Good luck with those dehumidifiers. Windless Tornado has enough humidity to sink several capital ships," Adam said.

"Oh, trust me. I know," Dee said returning to his work. He heard the bot mutter "fleshsack" under his breath.

Adam left Dee to his own devices and traveled up the ramp. He had been inside the Cicera several times, yet he was always impressed by each visit. The ramp led into a spacious cargo area. The entire interior of the ship had padded brown and beige carpeting that felt wonderful under Adam's feet. He was accustomed to military and cargo vessels with lots of sterile steel grating. The Cicera, by contrast, felt more homely. He made sure to wipe his boots off when he entered. He could see the double door elevator leading to the engine room towards the back. Two stairwells in the middle on either side of the cargo bay led up to the main hold. Adam chose the right stairwell near the port side docking room.

He walked up the stairs into an intersection of corridors between several rooms. A circular conference room marked the center of the ship. Inside there was a round, wooden table in the middle of the room with several padded leather seats for people to sit and relax. Nearby was the port side observation room that doubled as Havera's library. She had shown him a sample of her collection. Rows and rows of old-fashioned covered books and discs adorned the walls. The ship also contained a medical room, bathroom and shower area, a training room, and a bar. Most of these rooms he had never visited.

Adam turned on his heel towards the research room in one of the diamond wings on the port side. As he approached, he could see the door to Havera's quarters next to the research room was shut. Beyond her quarters was a small walkway that separated the bridge and cockpit from the rest of the ship. Adam walked into the research room, and he spotted her.

Havera.

Her vibrant crimson skin had a radiance and emissivity Adam could not explain, even compared to the other fantastically-colored Cauduun Adam had met. As if the universe always wanted everyone to know where she was. She wore her Praetorian Order robes, a conservative snowy white overtunic with long sleeves overlaying a matching undertunic with hempen rope wrapped around her torso beneath her chest. She was barefoot, her caligulae three-toed sandals sat next to the doorway.

Her long tail, black as night, distinguished her as a member of the Cauduun race. It was wagging passively from side to side while she worked, poking through the slit of her robes in the back. Thick at the base, her tail was as long as she was tall, thinning out down the length. At its thinnest part, it was still about as thick as Adam's forearm. The tail rounded out into a bulbous tip.

Her mixed-colored hair was up in her usual prim fashion, a long, sleek ponytail that went halfway down the length of her back flanked by two smaller shoulder-length ponytails. "Three tails for the three moons of Rema," Havera had told him when he complimented her style.

She was wearing VR headgear and transcribing something onto physical paper. The headgear she was wearing covered her curved pointy ears, so Adam walked up to Havera and tapped on her shoulder to get her attention.

WHACK!

Adam was sent flying and crashed over a table into the opposite wall. Piles of notes and books fell on top of him with a hard thud. Adam was seeing spots dance in his vision. A sharp pain hit his chest as he tried to breathe. All the air had been knocked from his lungs.

"Oh, goddesses, Adam! Mea culpa! Mea culpa! Stay right there, don't move!" he heard Havera yell. He tried to move but was met with more sharp pain. His breathing was labored. He rubbed his chest. It was tender and sore. He groaned in pain when he tried to press it.

A few seconds later, Havera returned. She knelt down beside him, clearing away some of the debris pile around him. She tilted his head and fed him liquid from a vial. "It's a potion. Should stem any internal bleeding you might have. Let me look at it," Havera said.

He drank the concoction without protest. It was sweet on the way down but had an immediate, bitter aftertaste. Adam had to resist spitting it up. Havera removed Adam's duster coat and laid his head down on top of it. She unzipped the front of his jumpsuit to pull it down. A giant black and blue welt bigger than Adam's fist was present around his sternum. Adam blushed as she stared at his exposed chest.

She pulled out a small container of white, gooey sludge called sanagel and applied it to his bruise. It stung badly at first, causing Adam to let out a yell. The sanagel eventually cooled to the point that Adam felt relief. His breathing eased. He felt a tingle go down his spine. Whether this was from the potion or the sludge Adam couldn't tell. The pain subsided slightly. Adam felt comfortable sitting up.

"Are you okay? You shouldn't surprise me like that!" Havera said with a mixture of concern and anger. Her husky, feminine voice was authoritative as if she were used to doling out orders. Between that and her toned physique, Havera exuded steely confidence. Apart from her eyes, the only element of her sculpted body not red or black. Enchanting amethysts of the deepest purple, their glimmers revealed a kindness in the alien's soul. A kindness and a burning desire for something Adam could only guess. Despite their other physiological differences, Human and Cauduun faces were identical. He wasn't sure why, but Adam found that comforting.

"I hate Naddine potions. Was that your tail?" Adam asked as Havera helped pull him to his feet. The platinum bracers on her forearm tightened in his grip.

"Now you know it's not just for show," Havera said with a smirk.

Adam rubbed his chest. It was still tender but hurt less and less by the second. "Understood. Dee warned me to mind my manners. I will announce my presence next time. I would've done that anyway, but I wasn't sure if you could hear me. What were you working on?"

Havera laughed. "You should always listen to Dee. I was studying a newly decoded part of Stepicro. They concern your Spartans. Spartahns? Spart-ins?"

Adam shrugged. "Who is the Consul of Cloudboard? It's our history, you're the expert." Havera blushed. She stood there, staring down at her feet awkwardly. Adam felt bad. "Oh, no it's fine, Havera. It was a joke. It's true but still a joke," he said with a weak smile.

Havera ran her three-fingered hand through her hair nervously, highlighting another difference between Cauduun and Humans. It was not uncommon for Humans to dye their hair different and exotic colors. Adam himself had one streak of dyed silver among his muddy brown locks. Cauduun, on the other hand, had different flashy colors in their hair naturally. The sides of Havera's hair were raven-hued like her tail. The center of her hair, wrapped back into a long ponytail, was a bright scarlet distinguishable from the deep crimson of her emissive skin.

"I know, I know. I also know how you and the other Humans feel about the issue. If I could show you firsthand I would, but I would be asked to return to Rema and stripped of my Praetorian rank if I did. I'm still only a Quaestor."

The Stepicro Cache was the most important historical find in the last century. Rangers had stumbled upon a destroyed Human colony long abandoned, whose location had been lost to time since the days of the Apocalypse. Among the wreckage, they found an old terminal and downloaded terabytes of information. Most of the files were corrupted and unreadable. Galactic governments salivated over the potential windfall of what they discovered. The races of the galaxy desperately wanted the secrets of dark energy they believed humanity once knew at the height of the Xizorian Invasion. All that knowledge was lost during the Apocalypse.

The Cauduun called the find the Stepicro Cache, named after the first reconstructed file name "Stepicro," its meaning unknown. What the cache contained mystified historians and the wider public alike. The few bits of information available in text and picture files indicated it was a collection of ancient Human stories. Realizing it was the only true source of undiluted Human culture and history, many Humans wanted access to the cache. The Humans of Arabella demanded the entirety of Stepicro be turned over to them. The Bokori naturally protested. For years, it was a sore issue within the Human nation. As a compromise, the Praetorians took possession of the find.

They were an order of monks and historians originating from Rema. Initially a Cauduun organization, the Praetorians had long since opened their doors to other galactic species. The Conclave would allow Humans access to information in the cache after the Praetorians evaluated it for important and dangerous knowledge. In other words, if the secrets of dark energy were in the cache, they wanted it first. They sent one of their acolytes, an "expert" in pre-Conclave history, to share the knowledge decoded from Stepicro under her supervision. That's how Havera came to live on Windless Tornado.

The first morsel of knowledge she brought was a lengthy list of names gleaned from various files in the cache. Thousands of them. Since that day, Humans have adopted these names and variations of them. Adam had not always been Adam. Havera helped him pick out his name. His Bokori name he had pushed out of his mind. His mother picked out the name Mortis for the family. For the past two years, he was Adam Mortis of Arabella. His friends chose the names John and Samus with the family name Dark. John said it matched their hair.

"You would be surprised how I feel, Havera. Who or what are the Spartans, and what have you learned about them?" Adam asked Havera.

Havera fixed her ruffled tunic and picked up her dropped headgear. She placed it gingerly on the table. Adam helped her pick up her notes and books. "It's interesting. Their name pops up again and again in completely different epochs of history. I'm not sure what to make of it. The data indicates they were either a bronze age warrior people or they were a select group of space age super soldiers. Your friend John's name appears in the latter. There's even a hint that their name was used in sporting events. Like Orbital teams and their nicknames. I'm not completely sure. All we have on that are text files. No images. No readable sound files. Not yet anyway. The Praetorians are decrypting and defragmenting more information every day. It's a mystery, but that's what I'm here for," Havera said with a sigh.

"On that note," Adam said. "Why weren't you at the funeral?"

Havera blushed again and nervously ran her fingers through her hair. "I figured y'all would want your first Human burial in hundreds of years to be a Human-only occasion," she said, avoiding his eye contact.

"Havera, you're the reason we were able to have a successful ceremony in first place. I know my mother wanted to thank you for your efforts. Besides, every other species was there. No idea how or why the Bokori gave them approval to land. Media hounds wanting to document the historical defiance of the Bokori-Human Covenant. The Yunes even sent a cam bot to record the whole damn thing," Adam said.

Havera shuffled her feet, slowly raising her gaze. "I...I just wanted to be respectful is all. It was a team effort. The engineers on Rema were able to fast track decoding relevant data. It wasn't much, but it was the best I...we could do on such short notice. Mea culpa if it wasn't what you were expecting."

"I admit I did feel quite silly at times. I'm sure our ancestors had good reason and purpose conducting funerals the way they did. Other than the sticky weather and the Bokori saucers looming overhead, I think the ceremony went quite well. Thank you, Havera," Adam said, patting the Cauduun on the shoulder. Havera's tail wagged, coming to a rest on her shoulder. She overcame her embarrassment to look Adam in the eye, a soft smile across her glossy black lips. "I don't suppose you found anything in your notes about Noah?" Adam asked jokingly.

She raised an eyebrow at him. "I'm a historian, Adam. I don't chase after myths, no matter how exciting or lucrative they might be. Why are you asking me about Noah?"

"Aaron mentioned it in passing after the funeral. It's not important. Wishful, whimsical thinking between a pair of skeptics. Maybe I was seeking a place to run away from tomorrow is all," Adam said.

"Are they admitting you to the Commission?" Havera asked. Adam raised his eyebrow. "Trissefer told me," Havera responded. "During one of our Stepicro debriefs. That woman likes to talk...a lot. Especially about you. I think she likes you," Havera said with mischievous grin.

"Oh, ha ha. You and my brother both are giving me a hard time about her. She does like to talk though, you are right about that," Adam said.

"Do you like her?" asked Havera.

"Havera..." Adam sighed.

"What? Mea culpa I was only curious. She seems quite passionate and is very pretty. A little too grimdark and serious for my tastes. Why not settle down and pop out a few little Humans with her? I think you two have quite a bit in common," Havera said teasingly.

"My father suggested the very same idea," Adam shrugged. "I don't know if I can settle down. Between the situation with the Covenant and the responsibilities I'm taking on with the Commission, I feel too uneasy to relax," Adam said. He paused, wondering if he should say what he wanted to say. "I'm having nightmares again."

Havera scrounged up a pair of chairs and gestured Adam to sit down. "About the stadium?"

Adam nodded sitting down. "More than that. I'm experiencing imagery I've never encountered. Pounding hearts, infinite darkness, the most excruciating pain I've ever felt. I don't know why this is happening to me now."

"When did it start this time?" Havera asked.

"The night my brother told me our father was dead."

Silence hung in the air between them. In the distance, Dee's maintenance work was a barely audible humming in the background. Adam was staring at the ground, through the ground to the core of the moon and beyond.

"I've never told you about my dreams, have I?" Havera said. Adam snapped back to the present. He stared at the Cauduun. She was deep in thought. He shook his head. "For as long as I can remember, I've had these vivid dreams. Not dreams, visions. I see horrible things happen to me, to my friends, to my family. I see them dying. I see them falling.

Possibilities and scenarios playing out in my head. I've always felt these visions guiding me. I asked my mater if she had these visions, too, and she shot me the most frightening look. She demanded I forget about what I was seeing. I couldn't, I can't. The truly scary part is lately I've been experiencing these visions while I'm awake. I'll slip into a trance and see something horrible right before it happens. Only it doesn't happen, not exactly. I can't explain what is happening. I throw myself into my work in the hopes it can distract me."

"Does it help?" Adam asked.

Havera nodded. "A little bit." She reached over and squeezed his hand. "I understand what you're feeling and what you're going through. What I saw in that footage horrified me. It horrified an entire galaxy. If you need to talk, you know where to find me, Adam," Havera said.

"Someone close to you die, too?" Adam asked.

Havera withdrew her hand and stood up suddenly. "I should really get back to my work. I'll stop by your home tomorrow and call on your mater."

Adam stood up. "You should talk to the people in town more, Havera. They want to get to know you, too, and thank you as well. You can't keep isolating yourself out here. Trust me."

Havera nodded. "I talk to quite a few people, Adam. You'd be surprised. You're right, though. I'm heading to Inclucity tomorrow. Maybe people in town need something I can get for them."

"Cradite bless you. Arabella has many needs, but I know you have plenty of room in that cargo bay of yours," Adam said with chuckle.

"You're right, I do," she said, matching his chuckle. "What about you? Any plans?"

"Other than the Commission meeting tomorrow, not particularly. I know there's a delegation heading to Bokor in the afternoon. Luckily, that doesn't involve me. Oh, and I'm seeing Trissefer tonight," Adam said.

"Perhaps we could meet up in Arabella tomorrow when I get back? It'll be nice to get out and stretch our legs. Vale, Adam" Havera said. Adam picked up his coat off the ground. "Adam?" Havera called out.

Adam turned to see Havera pointing down the hall. "If you're going to see Trissefer, you should shower first."

3

You'll See Me Again

Adam was falling. It wasn't the gleeful exhilaration from earlier. He was terrified. Falling into a pit of never-ending darkness, Adam flailed about, unable to stop his descent. Nothing to grasp. A void more infinite than the chasm of space. Suddenly, solid surface rushed up to meet him. He hit a grassy field hard. He was no longer in darkness. He was inside the stadium, glaring hot lights illuminated the arena. Hundreds of thousands of screaming voices hollered down at him. He was bound and naked, forcibly pulled up to his knees.

"Do you repent?" a familiar haunting voice asked him.

Adam didn't respond. He gritted his teeth for what was about to happen.

SLASH!

Adam resisted the urge to cry out. "Do you repent?" the voice asked again. Adam said nothing again. He would not give them the satisfaction. The whip struck his back. He winced again. He bit his tongue so hard he felt his mouth fill with blood. The voices in the stadium cheered with each flick of the whip. He could feel more blood dripping down his back. "Do you repent, blasphemer?" the voice asked. Adam spit the blood out of his mouth, refusing to answer. The whip struck him eleven more times. Each time he kept up his defiance. The grayskins would not break him. The Modders would not break him. They would have to see with their very eyes what their ideology wrought. Adam collapsed to the ground. The cheers and jeers of the stadium attendees silenced. His ear to the ground, he could hear his heartbeat.

THUMP THUMP; THUMP THUMP; THUMP THUMP.

He felt the grass underneath him tremble. It wasn't his heart he was hearing. He lifted his head to see he was no longer bound inside the stadium. He was on a smooth rocky surface floating in space. He'd seen this place previously, yet he'd never been there. Adam felt the vast emptiness of the rock all around him.

THUMP THUMP; THUMP THUMP; THUMP THUMP.

Adam was ejected from the rock at great speed. Thrust out into expanding darkness, he could see the rock more clearly. It was a decahedron, a ten-sided elegant planetoid drifting through space and time. He could see the beating heart of the structure contract and expand. He reached for it, trying feverishly to return to the planetoid. Whatever was inside that structure held answers. The planetoid turned black and withered away into dust. Adam let out a scream.

The dust particles reformed into that of a familiar figure: a lithe, beautiful silvery-skinned woman. It was *her*. Adam flailed his arms even faster, attempting to swim in space towards her. He wouldn't lose her again. His muscles became ragged and tired, yet he wasn't getting to her any faster. She was slowly fading away. Adam screamed again. The cosmos ignored his pleas. The figure vanished into the vast emptiness of the void.

In her place emerged a swirling orb surrounded by a colorful mass. It was an awesome and terrifying sight to behold. Rings of light danced all around the singularity. Adam was pulled towards the orb. He tried thrashing the other direction, but his muscles were too tired to resist the pull. He was whipped around the singularity at increasingly fast speeds. Every molecule in his body was ripping apart, stretching further and further until he was nothing. His sight was pulled at great speed across the galaxy. Stars, asteroids, planets, moons, comets, all manner of celestial bodies rushed by his head. He decelerated rapidly, drifting lazily through space and time. The ages passed him by.

He glimpsed a pyramid of opaque, black glass buried deep beneath the soil. An entire abandoned underwater city of icy, white crystal. A dazzling kaleidoscopic tree so large it swallowed the landscape around it whole. Unspeakable horrors deep in a jungle where the sun never rose. Without warning, he crashed into something corporeal.

He realized he was back on the planetoid. It was burning. The ground was twisted and scarred with the sounds of screams echoing even with the lack of atmosphere. Adam saw what he bumped into. A tall skeletal figure with cracked sulfur skin and slithering armor stared down at him. It was wearing goggles, so Adam couldn't see its eyes. It was holding a blade of swirling black energy. The creature was emitting clicking noises from its mouth. Somehow, Adam could understand it.

"We will help you find what you seek."

Adam was sure the creature spoke with Adam's own voice. The creature raised his blade, preparing to strike. Adam raised his arms instinctively to block the strike. As the blade arced downward, a huge surge of bright light hit the creature, scattering it into dust. Adam turned towards the source of the light. All he saw was the decahedron, only this time it was made of icy, white crystal. He was no longer resting on it, but rather standing at the top of an impossibly tall, snow-covered mountain. A loud buzzing rattled his ears. The crystal rock grew smaller in his view until he realized it wasn't just a rock. It was an eye. A colossal face emerged from the darkness. Adam heard a different voice in his head this time. The voice was powerful, yet strangely beautiful and serene.

Awaken, protector of life.

Adam shot up in bed, letting out a gasp. He was sweating profusely, and his heart was pounding. His back throbbed and itched worse than ever. He tried scratching it by rubbing his back on his sheets. It didn't help. He wiped the sweat from his brow. The rest of his muscles ached like tiny daggers piercing his skin all over his body. He threw his legs over the side of his bed, burying his face in his hands. Next to him, Trissefer stirred.

"Adam," she said with a sleepy voice. "How come you're up?"

"It's fine, Triss. Go back to sleep," Adam said. He felt her run her fingertips down his back. He flinched unintentionally. Even her sensitive touch felt like a white-hot poker. He sensed her sit up in bed.

"Adam, you're tense and sweating. What's wrong? Was it another nightmare?" she asked.

He kept his face buried in his hands, not wanting to look her in the eye.

"Yes."

There was a pause. The pain was subsiding, but the itching remained. Trissefer ran her fingers up and down Adam's scars. Initially, Adam tensed again. His body felt conflicted. He loved it when she touched him like that, but his skin was so sensitive it screamed every time she brushed him with her fingertips. He could feel himself becoming excited; however, the sensitivity and pain increased with his excitement.

"Was it about *her*?" she asked.

Adam turned to face Triss. Her hair was down and ruffled. The streaks of pink mixed with the blonde. He pushed the hair out her face to see her eyes. He could barely make out the dusky green around her pupils in the reflected light of Bokor through her window. A comforting breeze circulated through the room. An earthy scent percolated his nostrils from Trissefer's nearby window garden. Something pleasantly sweet. A few beads of sweat were running down her neck to her bare breasts, glistening in the planetary glow.

"You've never asked me about *her*?"

"You've never had nightmares night after night since we've been together. I'm worried," she said.

"Together? I thought you wanted to keep this simple. Are we together now?" he asked.

"I did. I do. That doesn't mean I don't care," she said as she wrapped her arms around him, resting her head on his shoulder. "I've always respected you don't want to talk about what happened to you. I never want you to feel boxed in. I want you to feel safe with me. But tomorrow is going to be a big day. The stresses of governing will only add more pressure. I don't want to see you collapse under the weight of responsibility. Arabella needs you; I need you to be strong for all of us. The dead don't need for anything."

She kissed him on the cheek. He tilted his head to look her in the eyes. Her face was determined, not betraying any emotion she was feeling under the surface. It was one of Trissefer's gifts. Her honeyed words could convey whatever emotional support the recipient needed to hear without any actual empathy on her part. He could hear his brother's words gnawing at the back of his brain. *You're nothing but a political relationship to her.* He tilted his head further to kiss her, pushing his brother's poisonous thoughts out and filling his mind with the sweetness of her kisses. She ran her fingers through his messy hair and kissed him passionately. She pulled him down on top of her, beckoning him to her body. She wrapped her legs tightly around his torso, moaning into his mouth.

"It's going to be okay." Her words hit like daggers as he slid inside her. The words hung in the air like the final note of a song. He shut his eyes and tried to focus on Trissefer in the moment. His heart raced, and his breathing shallowed. A moment of panic overcame him as he thought of *her*. Not Trissefer, but the woman in his dream.

Don't worry about me. Everything is going to be okay. You'll see me again. I promise. He heard the woman's words in his head. The panic-induced mania threw off Adam's focus, causing his body to become unduly excited. He finished after only a minute. His breathing labored. The pain returned to his muscles. He rolled off Trissefer onto his back.

"I'm sorry. I guess I'm distracted is all," Adam said.

He heard her sigh softly. "It's alright. Why don't you try to get some sleep," she said, rolling onto to her side to face away from him. She pulled the covers over her body. Adam did the same trying to collect his thoughts. His mind raced with the imagery of the dream flashing in the forefront of his thoughts. He could hear Trissefer moaning softly next to him as she finished herself without him. He felt awful leaving her unsatisfied. Maybe his brother was right. He could never satisfy Trissefer Quinn. Not in the ways she wanted. He closed his eyes. Trissefer's moans stopped after a few minutes. The soreness of his body kept him up the rest of the night while she slept like the dead.

***

"Congratulations, Commissioner Mortis."

Adam exchanged an awkward handshake with Lara Shepard, the olive-skinned, brunette Commissioner, who administered his oath. The words meant little to Adam. A promise to defend the freedoms and the welfare of all Humankind. Not even Stepicro held any knowledge about Human oaths of office. Only that they had them. They did mention Humans used to greet each other by gripping each other's hand for a firm shake. The greeting had slowly spread throughout Arabella to the point where most people used it. Adam thought it was weird. He much preferred the Cauduun's hand over the heart salute. It felt more sincere. It helped that the gesture was a military salute. Nonetheless, Adam was now the Commissioner for Defense & Security. The office his father held.

Adam sat down in the uncomfortable metal chair while Shepard returned to the seat at the head of the hexagonal table. It was her turn in the rotation to chair the meeting. Adam studied the other Commissioners. They were the only ones in the room for these meetings by custom. A way to maintain secrecy for sensitive business.

To Adam's immediate left sat Hideo Auditore, a man a little more than ten years Adam's senior, with hooded, narrow, brown eyes. A professional man. He was hurriedly combing his compact dark hair. He was the Commissioner for Health & Education. He was one of the few Humans to leave Bokori space and come back, having trained as a doctor on Concordia. He straightened his white tunic, waiting for the meeting to start.

To his left, sat the oldest Commissioner, B.J. Doom. A weathered, leathery, pale-skinned man to whom Adam rarely spoke, Doom's purview was trade and diplomacy. He spent most of his time away from Arabella, pleading the Human cause to other civilizations. He was the most cautious of the group, and the one most opposed to unilateral Human independence. "Probably all the time spent with politicians whispering in his ear urging restraint," John told him when he asked about the other Commissioners. It was the only thing John said about Doom that was fit for polite company.

To his left sat Shepard. Adam could see the crow's feet prominent in her face. She brushed her graying hair out of her eyes. She was only a woman of fifty-five years, yet the stresses of managing Arabella had taken their toll. She played the role of internal diplomat on the Commission, so Adam was told. The Commission was split on how to achieve Human independence, and she was the neutral arbiter. She was one of the original founding members of the Commission along with Adam's father and Doom.

To her left was Handsome Snake. A little younger than Shepard, a little older than Auditore, Snake was an ex-cop with a shock of chaotic white hair. He joined the Commission around the time Adam was liberated from rehab. In fact, Snake's intel, along with that of a few other police defectors, aided the team's escape. He was eternally grateful to Snake for that. However, Snake also opposed unilateral Human independence. Not because he didn't believe in it, but because he was afraid the Bokori would send the military to crush them if they tried. His twenty-plus years' experience in law enforcement, seeing the inner workings of Bokori government and bureaucracy, led him to worry about antagonizing the Bokori too much. He was rubbing his prominent forehead, staring down at the table lost in his thoughts. Snake was an introspective man, preferring to let his heavily tattooed body speak for him. He rarely spoke, but when he did it was with the force of a man who lived a thousand lifetimes. Adam was going to work closely with Snake. He was the Commissioner for Law & Justice.

Finally, to Snake's left and Adam's right sat someone with whom he was intimately familiar. Her strawberry blonde hair with pink streaks was pulled back into a tight bun. She wore a simple faded blue jumpsuit. Her blue and gray discs tattoo, identical to Adam's, was featured prominently on the back of her neck. Trissefer Quinn, the

Commissioner for History & Culture. She tapped him playfully under the table when he sat down. Of all the Commissioners, Trissefer was the most adamant about Human independence. Adam often wondered if that's why she was so drawn to his father's influence or if was his father's influence rubbing off on her that molded her into a diehard. Either way, she was always crystal clear about where she stood. She had been on the Commission less than a few months. Adam's father pushed for the appointment not long after Adam and Trissefer started seeing each other.

Shepard spoke. "Let it be recorded, today, the 29th day of Anamead in the year 1600 of the Galactic Standard Calendar, Adam Mortis, the son of the late-Commissioner Cloud Mortis, has taken the oath of office as Commissioner for Defense & Security. Having accepted his oath and credentials, this Commission welcomes him with all its rights and privileges. May Cradite bless him with her wisdom. I, Commissioner Lara Shepard for Economy & Infrastructure, am presiding. Commissioner for Law & Justice, Handsome Snake, is tasked with the duty of secretary for this meeting. This Commission is now in session."

"I would like it to be known I still object to usage of Cauduun iconography and religion in blessing our meetings, and the continued usage of the G.S.C. for recording dates and times" said Trissefer right away.

"Noted, Commissioner," Snake said.

Doom responded with a cough. "You work with the Cauduun Praetorian on a regular basis. Has she informed us of any new information about Human goddesses or blessings since our last meeting?"

"She has not," conceded Trissefer.

"Then, do not waste your breath and our time until you have something concrete, *Commissioner for History & Culture*," Doom said mockingly emphasizing Trissefer's title.

"The Cauduun's reach is longer than their tails, Commissioners," said Shepard, defusing the tension. "We all know this. It is simply easier for us to work and operate within the customs of the galaxy-at-large.

None of the other Proprietor races object to the Cauduun-influenced G.S.C. I see no reason why we shouldn't either. Besides, it's the month of Anamead. Everyone loves love. I'm sure Commissioner Mortis would agree with me on that, do you not?"

Adam resisted the urge the smile. Anamea was the Cauduun goddess of love, passion, pleasure, and sex. The month that bears her name signified the beginning of spring on Rema, the Cauduun homeworld. Anamead was a time for love and romance, not to mention the occasional dalliance or tryst. It was Shepard's not-so-subtle way of jabbing at him and Trissefer. Their relationship was widely whispered, but no one said anything to their faces. It was a source of contention for Adam's membership on the Commission. A couple of the members, Doom in particular, thought it was a conflict of interest. Shepard overruled him, but she was subtly reminding Adam to tread carefully.

"I do, Commissioner. Although, I'm more of a Dasenor man myself. Holdover from my military days. So, when it comes time for y'all to put me in the ground, it better be with sword and shield, not chocolate and flowers. Be that as it may, I wouldn't object to anyone painting a nude Cauduun woman on said shield." The other Commissioners laughed. Trissefer smiled at him. Adam tried not to stare at her too hard.

"Well said, Commissioner. If all that nonsense is out of the way, let's move onto business. We'll keep it short since Commissioner Mortis needs time to get up to speed on everything within his purview. The Bokori summit this afternoon is scheduled for just past midday. Commissioner Doom and I are meeting with representatives of the People's House to discuss the state of Arabella and our overall cooperation within the confines of the Covenant," said Shepard, reading notes from her handheld emulator.

"What issues are on the table?" asked Auditore.

"Everything," said Doom. "We only got them to agree to this meeting by promising no issue would be untouched if either party so chose."

"We're meeting them unconditionally?" asked Adam astonished.

"Yes, our position on Arabella is weakening every moment we wait.

We simply don't have the leverage to hold out for conditions any longer. We need to get the Bokori to agree to allow the Conclave to approve an aid package," said Shepard.

"Our numbers are swelling! More and more Humans join our cause by the day. Now is not the time to concede, it is the time for bold action!" insisted Trissefer.

"Our numbers are indeed swelling, and that's part of the problem," said Shepard. "We don't have the resources to feed them, jobs to employ them, or simply the room to house them. The unofficial aid drops from the Sinners aren't enough. Neither are the voluntourists who use us to win popularity points on the Nexus. They take up more of our resources than they're worth."

"This settlement stands at over five-hundred thousand strong and growing by the day. We need the Bokori to lift their embargo and allow galactic trade to flow, officially. Smuggling can only get us so far," said Doom.

"This wouldn't be a problem if humanity were an independent race. We could form our own trade pacts. We wouldn't have to rely on the charity of others," insisted Trissefer.

"If we so much as whisper the word 'independence,' we'd have Shocktroopers dropping out of the sky. Commissioner Mortis will be able to speak more to that once he is fully acclimated. I'm sure he will tell you we don't have the strength to resist a Bokori onslaught. The Bokori can claim pacifism and peaceful solutions all they want; we all know better. The Bubble only has a few days' power. We wouldn't last half a month," Shepard said.

"We are not ready, Commissioner Quinn." It was Snake this time. "We must maintain the appearance of respecting the Covenant. To do otherwise, would bring death to us all."

Snake's words silenced Trissefer. She was only a couple years older than Adam, but she seemed a teenage girl in that moment. She looked to Adam for support. He held his tongue. He was waiting to get a better sense of the room. Trissefer was not pleased by his reaction.

"I don't expect this meeting to amount to much. The Bokori are likely to drag their heels as they're oft to do. In either event, keeping an open dialogue is critical," Doom said.

"How are the Bokori guaranteeing your safety? Technically, we're all wanted criminals. Some of us more so than others. What's stopping them from arresting you the moment you land?" Adam inquired.

"The Bokori have issued us temporary diplomatic status for the day. Officially, we are acting as representatives of a local Community," explained Shepard.

"You mean they're treating us like we're another Sistine Slum," said Trissefer bitterly.

"More or less, yes," said Shepard.

"If that's the case, Lara, I insist you bring Adam along with you," said Trissefer.

The room was stunned. "What?" asked Shepard, Doom, and Adam, simultaneously.

Adam leaned over to whisper. "Triss...Commissioner Quinn, what are you doing?"

She ignored him. "Commissioner Mortis has spent more time in the Sistine Slums than the rest of us combined. He can speak from experience about the abysmal conditions both in the slums and here in Arabella. He is someone even the Bokori can't impugn. They wouldn't dare object to what he has to say, especially if we leak it to one of the dozen or so reporters outside the Bokori are meeting with a man they tortured," said Trissefer.

"Triss!" Adam said more forcefully than he meant to. His pulse was pounding. The room was silent for a few seconds. Adam shifted uncomfortably in his seat. Shepard awkwardly coughed.

"Very well. Commissioner Mortis will accompany myself and Commissioner Doom to Bokor. We've arranged a shuttle to take us planetside. I'll brief you on the flight. If there is no other business, this Commission is dismissed," said Shepard.

The other Commissioners stood up and walked out. Trissefer was rising out of her chair when Adam grabbed her by the arm. "Don't move. I need to talk to you in private," he whispered. For a moment, he thought she would resist. She sat back down, an annoyed expression across her face. Shepard patted him on the shoulder and told him where to find the shuttle. Adam whispered his thanks. Once they were alone, Adam let his emotions get away from him. "What in Kewea were you trying to pull back there?" Adam asked angrily.

Trissefer sighed, tilting her head to peer over at him. "It's the right thing to do. We need someone in that meeting who won't give away everything. There needs to be a strong voice for Human independence in that room. They'd never let me go, and they'd never refuse you. It seemed like the perfect match," she explained.

Adam stood up in exasperation. He ran his fingers through his muddy brown hair, wiping away the burgeoning sweat from his brow. His five-day old scruff itched a bit. "I don't fault your logic, Triss. Give me a heads-up next time before you go off half-cocked. Going back to that planet is no simple task for me. The last time I was there wasn't exactly the happiest time of my life. I need more time than that to mentally prepare. My heart feels like it's going to explode just thinking about the prospect of going back," said Adam.

"Go to the medics and take of patch of Celeste. You'll calm down," she said.

"NO!" he screamed.

Trissefer flinched at Adam's sudden outburst. He didn't mean to do that. The mere mention of Celeste forced more haunting images back in his head. For a split second, he was back in cell. "*Confess your sins,*" said a voice in his head. "*Equality through sacrifice. Repeat these words. Embody them. You shall be rewarded.*" He instinctively reached for his left triceps, expecting to feel a patch. He bit his tongue so as not to blurt out those words. Thankfully, no patch was there. Only a distant memory. He buried his face in his shaking hands and took several deep breaths. His pulse slowed to a steady beat. He reoriented himself. He was inside the Commission meeting room with Trissefer, whose expression bordered on panic. She was afraid.

"I'm sorry," Adam said finally calm. "My past is mine. It is for me to deal with and process. It is not to be used by you to score political points. We're not close enough for that." He stormed out of the room without another word, leaving Trissefer stupefied.

4

Too Many Rotundas

Adam's hands were still shaking leaving the room. He braced his back up against a nearby wall and counted to ten. Twenty. Thirty. Forty. The shaking in his limbs ceased by the time he reached fifty. His brow was damp from the cold sweat. The churning in his stomach forced him to bend over in pain. As he reached sixty, he thought he had his anxiety attack under control until he vomited his breakfast all over the cavern wall.

"Commissioner? Commissioner, are you okay?" It was the voice of his Chief of Internal Security Duke Drake. Adam spat out the rest of the vomit, wiping off the remaining residue from his lips. Ironically, puking was probably the best thing that could've happened to Adam. His nerves settled down. He stood up straight composing himself.

"Do me a favor, Chief? Never ask if I'm okay. Ever," Adam said, trying to find his authoritative voice.

"As you wish, Commissioner. All the same, maybe you should go see a medic," Drake said. Between his tall stature, muscular build, scars, and tattoos, Adam felt Drake's suggestion was more of a command. It wasn't. Drake, despite his serious facade and his inexplicable ability to kill a man with his ring finger, was a jovial man. More importantly, he was a dependable man. He joined the Separatist cause at the beginning. He left the military to brave the jungles of Windless Tornado with the other Separatists. Under his leadership, Arabella was the safest place in the entirety of Bokori space. Petty crimes were at their lowest and not a single murder since he was appointed Chief of Internal Security. He was Cloud Mortis' right-hand man.

"My men and I are ready to get you up to speed on the status of the militia and Arabella's defenses at your leisure, Commissioner," Drake said.

"Walk with me, Chief," Adam said. They exited the secure cavern at the base of the cliff. Drake and two of his militiamen followed Adam. The rain had stopped. The ground was slick with mud, and Arabella's usual stench hit Adam especially hard. He suppressed the urge to vomit again. "Change of plans unfortunately, Chief. I've been volunteered to join Shepard and Doom on their little expedition to Bokor this afternoon. That briefing will have to wait."

"You're going to Bokor, sir?" asked Drake.

"It's Adam, Duke, you've known me for years," Adam said.

"Yes, sir," said Drake, brooking no argument.

Adam sighed. "Triss...I mean Commissioner Quinn thought it was a good idea. She says we need a strong voice for independence in that room," Adam said.

"If I may speak freely, sir?" inquired Drake. Adam nodded. "Commissioner Quinn is right. You should be in that room. The Bokori need to know what kind of people they're dealing with."

That's what I'm afraid of.

"Do you know where I can find John, Chief?" asked Adam changing topics.

"Commander Dark was one of those scheduled to brief you, Commissioner. He's waiting for us back at the security station," Drake said.

"Oh, good. Can you send him a message telling him I'm coming, but the others are dismissed for now? Better yet, have them double check our stockpile of munitions. I want to be able to have an accurate idea just how badly we'd lose in a full-scale assault. Same thing goes for the generators. The Bubble must have enough reserve power, goddesses-forbid, should we ever need to use it," Adam ordered.

"Yes, sir, right away," Drake said. Drake tapped the air to send those messages. He heard him mutter the orders through his HUD's communication network. Twenty minutes later, they arrived at the security station. A fairly large, stand-alone building, the security station was protected by several militiamen at all times. It was one of the first buildings erected in Arabella. It looked it too, with its cobbled together wall panels and rusted defensive barriers. Adam had gotten the full tour only a couple days ago. The building operated as both a de facto police headquarters and the central hub for Arabella's electricity. Half the building was dedicated to the power stations and generators needed to keep the city running. If Arabella were ever attacked, this was the primary hard target the Bokori would try to take. They kept Arabella's stockpiles of weapons and ammo in the basement. Most everybody in Arabella possessed a firearm in their personal inventory just in case. The stockpile was their insurance.

John was waiting for him inside. Wearing his own faded green jumpsuit and charcoal boots, he was sitting on a bench at the long table. He had a patch on his right triceps bearing the same symbol on the back of Adam's hand. Most of the militiamen had similar patches. The two embraced, followed by John giving him a mocking heart salute.

"Oh, knock it off, *Commander*. I'll have you tried for insubordination if you do that again," Adam said.

John laughed. "Careful! You know I'm not above staging a coup."

"Please, please, oh, please do so. That way you can go to this Cradite-forsaken meeting in my stead," pleaded Adam sarcastically.

"Ah, so the little minx actually went for it," John said.

"Wait! You knew?" Adam asked.

"Trissefer ran the idea by me. I was torn. Politically, I thought it prudent, but I was worried how'd you react. I was worried about the other thing, too," John said a hint of guilt in his voice.

"I chewed her out a little too hard," said Adam feeling regretful.

"You were right to be worried. I had an attack seconds after leaving the room. Drake saw me vomiting all over the cavern walls," Adam said.

John peered over Adam's shoulder at Drake. "At least you know you were in...capable hands," John said. His famished eyes lingered on the older, muscular security chief.

Adam snapped his fingers in John's face to get his attention. "Focus, John, focus."

"Right," John said, shaking his head. He turned his attention back to Adam. "How are you feeling?"

Adam sat down on the bench. John joined him on the opposite side of the long table. "I'm fine right now. In ten minutes, an hour, a day, a month? Who's to say?"

"Sam is worried about you, Adam. So is your mother. I am, too. I know the Commission is what your father wanted, and Arabella is far better off with you having a strong presence in its leadership. I just wonder if it's best for you."

"I'll be fine," Adam said unsure of himself. "The stadium was three years ago."

"No, it wasn't Adam. We may have liberated your body from that place three years ago, but you still aren't back to your old self," John said.

"I don't think that will ever be possible. I'm afraid I'll carry the scars from that place the rest of my life. It haunts me. The nightmares are getting worse. Trissefer's presence doesn't provide the comfort it once did," Adam said.

"Trissefer will continue to do what's best for Trissefer. I like her, Adam. Her mind is in the right place, but her heart only has room for one person: Trissefer Quinn," John said.

Aaron and John rarely ever agree on anything. Is this a sign? Are they both right?

"Havera thinks I should settle down with her and have a couple of kids," Adam said with a chuckle. "I went to see her after the funeral to thank her. I told her about my nightmares, too."

John leaned back and sighed. "I worry you confide too much in the longtail."

"Don't call her that, John. She's here to help," Adam said insistently.

"You don't know why she's here. You think the Conclave sends a warrior monk to piecemeal us versions of our own history out of the goodness of their hearts?" John said skeptically.

"Warrior monk?" Adam was confused.

John leaned in close. "I heard from somebody who heard from somebody that the Praetorians train their students to fight. That they're not a bunch of history and anthropology nerds. They're spies under the guise of spreading knowledge. It's the Conclave's way of keeping tabs on us. Make sure we don't get out of line. The Conclave may as well be doing the Bokori's bidding."

"I'm not so sure. Havera doesn't seem like the fighting type," Adam said. Then he remembered the blow he took from the business end of her tail. He rubbed the spot on his chest where she hit him. It had mostly healed with only a minor bruise visible under his jumpsuit.

It was only a reflex. It was a powerful reflex. She's quite strong...

"Either way," John said. "Be careful what you say to her. I don't trust her."

"It's not for the obvious reason, is it?" Adam asked, resting his chin on his fist.

John raised an eyebrow. "What reason would that be?"

Adam matched his expression, tilting his head in a you-know-what-I-mean sort of way.

John crossed his arms. "So, what if it is? You know as well as I do the only good people in this galaxy are Humans." Adam didn't share John's galactic view on this subject. He understood the mentality perfectly but didn't subscribe to it. Adam's mind flickered to *her* for an instant.

"Where is Sam by the way?" Adam said, pivoting away from the sudden awkwardness.

"She's on Bokor in fact," John said, agreeing with the change of subject. "She's up to her usual tricks, you know gathering intel, monitoring smuggling operations. She's meeting a contact in a few hours. I'm going to meet her afterwards."

"You're going there, too?" Adam asked surprised. "You can't stand that place."

"You're not the only one making sacrifices for the good of humanity, Adam," John said patting Adam on the shoulder in jest. "You're going to be fine. The Bokori will spend the entire time lecturing you and making idle threats about this-and-that. You'll be back here before you know it."

***

The shuttle ride between Bokor and Windless Tornado was pleasant, other than the looming threat that at any moment the Bokori could decide they've had enough and blast them out of the sky. The saucers of the Bokori fleet were monitoring their progress to the planet closely. Usually, these shuttles were used for smuggling. Their parts were easy to salvage or print. They had minimal positive core drives and certainly no negative space capability. Barely a step above aircars. The close proximity between the two celestial bodies enabled the functionality of such transports.

The rays from Bokor's twin white suns brushed Adam's face. It had been a long time since he laid his eyes on them. Windless Tornado's soupy atmosphere kept them hidden beneath a blanket of rain clouds. He was staring out the window while Commissioners Shepard and Doom conversed about protocol. Adam was ignoring most of it. He didn't plan on speaking much, if at all, during this meeting. The three of them agreed early on his presence was for show. That suited Adam perfectly. He'd leave the politicking to Shepard and Doom. Trissefer wouldn't be thrilled, but she was miles away now.

Other than Windless Tornado's incessantly overcast and humid weather, Bokor and Windless Tornado were nearly identical in temperament. The dull, dreary gray filter permeated both worlds. Windless Tornado was called a moon, but they were closer to twin planets. A relatively small world, Bokor had vast environmental diversity. Deserts, mountains, canyons, swamps, forests, et cetera. They had one thing in common: each were as stale as the rest. The entire landscape was a desaturated painting, dotted with various tones of gray. Watching the suns rise and set each day was enough to put even the most energetic child to sleep.

Bokor only had one notable feature: the massive mega urban center called Inclucity. Virtually every living person on Bokor lived inside Inclucity. They had no choice. It was the law. Few exceptions were made other than for military outposts and certain professions that required resources from the aforementioned regional environments around the planet. That order extended to all the colonies, too. Only the planet First Expedition, hundreds of light years away, maintained a sizable Bokori and Human civilian population to support the military bases there. Inclucity emerged as the Bokori capital in the centuries leading to the Bokori-Cauduun meeting on Concordia and the formation of the Conclave.

It was only in the last half-century that Inclucity was designated the sole living city of Bokor. Energy wars, environmental concerns, ideological rigidity, and sheer costs all contributed to the decision by the central planners of the People's House to uproot every town, village, hamlet, suburb, borough, and minor city on Bokor and relocate them to Inclucity. It was not a smooth transition. Those they couldn't bribe or cajole to migrate, they uprooted by force. Officially, the death toll was minimal and justified to the galaxy as necessary for the survival of Bokor's health and safety. This was bunk, of course. Rapid advancements in energy production and significant progress in terraforming technologies eliminated such concerns for the other Proprietor races. Only the Bokori's intractable desire for utopia drove them this far. Many of the ruins of Bokor's old cities could be seen dotting the landscape near Inclucity and around the planet. Samus told him those ruins often held valuable resources and provided perfect places to hide from the watchful eyes of the Bokori.

The shuttle descended into the lower atmosphere. Inclucity's urban sprawl stretched for miles. It was impossible to see the entirety of the city even thousands of feet in the air. From space, Inclucity resembled a series of spiraling stamps branded into the planet. A giant morass of dark gray on top of light gray, far less visually appealing than the galaxy above. Up close, Inclucity was bland, too. Modern Bokori architects were obsessed with rounded objects. Each building on Bokor, no matter the size, shared that uninspired visage. Far in the distance, Adam saw the domed shape outline break the city skyline and immediately turned away.

"The Bokori have agreed to use our political ranks, and, more importantly, our Human names. We tried to eliminate most of the nonsense trifles that could needlessly derail the meeting," Shepard said. Adam focused on her words to distract him from the city skyline and what may be lurking on the horizon.

"So, no mentioning their pastes taste like crap. Got it," Adam said sardonically.

"Don't joke. Little issues thwarted the first several attempts at this meeting. We don't want to give the Bokori an excuse to kick us out. Zokyon diplomats almost ended the Saptia Conference because they couldn't agree on a seating arrangement," Doom said referring to the peace conference that ended the Century of Strife. "Your dad and I saw firsthand how easily these sorts of talks could fall apart."

"Perhaps that will work to our advantage. The Bokori seem unreasonable with their requirements. We come out appearing stronger, more level-headed," Adam suggested.

"Believe me, we discussed it. If I thought it would help, I'd do it in a heartbeat. We simply don't have the leverage," Shepard said.

"I never noticed this until yesterday, but you sure say 'simply' more than anyone I've ever met. Nothing is simply simple, Lara," Adam said.

"Be that as it may, we simp...hmm. We need this meeting whether we like it or not. Perhaps we'll get lucky, and the galactic community will respond positively. It's the only reason reporters were given permission to land on the moon. The Bokori calculated we'd appear silly, not worthy of attention by the Conclave," Shepard said.

"A foolish miscalculation on their part. It'll be hard for the galaxy to ignore what they've seen, given how poor living conditions are in Arabella," Doom said.

"It's arrogance. The grayskins are so convinced of their own self-righteousness, they look down their nose-less faces at us. With limited Nexus access, we'll never know," Adam said, returning his gaze out the window.

Doom slid down his seat to join Adam by the window. "I weirdly possess a soft spot for Bokori architecture. It's boringly elegant," Doom said, matching Adam's distant gaze.

"Too many rotundas. I get dizzy," Shepard said, sliding over to join them.

"Better than the brutalist architecture on much of Concordia's station, let me tell you. The Conclave could match the Bokori rectangle for circle. All the same, nothing compares to the breathtaking forest retreats on Saptia. The Gilded Prairies, in particular, are a wondrous, natural marvel all should once in their, lifetime. The Palace at Saptia is a splendor of old Cauduun engineering. I could only imagine the splendor of the Platinum Palace on Rema herself," Doom said.

"You've been to Saptia?" Adam asked curiously.

"Oh, yes. I was at the signing of the Saptia Accords along with your father, among others. Part of the invited group of Human delegates to attend the Saptia Conference. Heck of a party, I'll tell you. That Orbital match was unforgettable. Awe-inspiring! Shame we got next to nothing out of it. Though, your father did acquire the coat you're wearing," said Doom.

Adam was surprised. "I didn't know that."

"Style of dress they wear in the outer Cauduun colonial worlds. Keeps the dust out. Vital when you live near the mines of Sorma or the shipyards of Docia. Your father and mother were inspired by the similarities between the Confederate cause and our own."

"Dad never did like to talk about what happened on Saptia."

Doom nodded mournfully. "Your father considered it his second greatest failure. The first being his inability to locate you until you were nearly fully grown." The Bokori's relocation policies split all Human children from their parents. Those not born on Arabella or lucky enough to be hidden away in the slums were sent away to be raised by Bokori or worse Modders in their communities. The Reclamation Service in Arabella did what it could to reunite Human children with their Human parents, though their reach was limited. Trissefer had worked for the Reclamation Service for years before she became a Commissioner.

"'Lucky.' Yeah, right. I escaped my assigned Community barely old enough to run. I hopped from shelter to shelter, slum to slum, scraping by. If not for John and Samus, I would've died or been forcibly relocated back to those jadespawn infested Bokori communities. That's twice I owe him now," Adam said, closing his eyes trying to suppress his memories.

"John is a capable man and a dedicated Human activist, but..." Doom said hesitating.

"Everything spoken until that 'but' was pointless. Say what you want to say, B.J." Adam demanded with a raised eyebrow.

"I understand why you care so deeply about him, Adam, but you're blinded by loyalty. John is a poisonous influence on you, on this entire movement. His...ideas...create much discomfort amongst the rest of us. He's too bloodthirsty. I don't want him whispering kooky notions in your ear. I'm uncomfortable with his position so high up within the militia," Doom said.

Adam's anger flashed. "Poisonous? You sound like a Bokori, Commissioner. I don't deny John is little rough around the edges. Nevertheless, we need people like John. Those willing to get their hands dirty for the good of humanity. I fear you've spent too much time bending over for the Bokori, Commissioner. I can see why Trissefer was so insistent I come. You'd sacrifice us all for a few popularity points with the Conclave. If anyone is poisonous, it is you, Commissioner Doom."

Doom's eye twitched. The old man's sensitivities were easy to spot. Doom was about to verbally retaliate when Shepard cut him off.

"Commissioners, there is no need for infighting. Not at this juncture. We must present a united front. Keep your squabbles to yourselves until we get home. Shape up. We're landing."

5

Not About Today

The People's House, the center of Bokori politics, was the cleanest building Adam had ever been in. On the outside, the building was unimpressive. Dull and rounded like any other building Inclucity had to offer. Inside, the floors were spotless. An army of janitors kept every nook and cranny pristine. Adorning the walls were a gallery of paintings and artwork dedicated to Bokori ideas and culture. Simple shapes and blobs all symmetrical and organized in various shades of gray. In other words, bland and utilitarian. Adam did recognize a few pieces of art with more style and pizzazz tucked away from the entrance by the restrooms. The few instances of real color hidden away for fear they might be inspiring. He noted all the dates of said pieces predated the current century. The building's rotunda had Inclucity's only functioning fountain.

Of course, bureaucrats would treat themselves.

Water was scarce in the city. Adam had no idea why. Enough rain fell on Windless Tornado to sink a thousand capital ships. Its sister world was not lacking for weather either. Bokor's population, while declining in recent centuries, stood at around 10.6 billion. Each sector of Inclucity was divided into Communities. These were communal living arrangements designed to eliminate heretical and treasonous attitudes and beliefs of the past. Bokori society wasn't always this way. In fact, much of this change occurred during the latter half of the Century of Strife. At first, only Bokori were obligated to join these Communities. Eventually, Humans were brought into the fold. Neither event was a smooth transition. Official licensed historians and sociologists erased much of what Bokori history was like prior to this new arrangement, so exact figures and details weren't available. Much like the transition to Inclucity, many Bokori died to realize this forlorn dream.

This nightmare. The Long Con isn't without its drawbacks.

Humans comprised less than 1% of Inclucity's overall population. Much of the Human population was contained in the relatively new Human-led Communities. A pet project of a well-intentioned but naïve Bokori social engineer named Benevolent Sistine. The Covenant had not been kind to the welfare of humanity. The life expectancy of a Human, though still a couple decades older than the average Bokori, had fallen to record lows. *Recorded not by Bokori, of course. Wouldn't want evidence of their failures dash their deluded dreams.* Humans were often the victims of hate crimes. Social welfare programs and anti-crime laws did little in the way of stopping this downward trend. If fact, they often spurred greater resentment.

As a revitalization effort, Benevolent Sistine proposed unused sections of Inclucity be set aside for Humans to run their own Communities. Initially, the practice was received with much enthusiasm by the Humans, including those with Separatist sympathies. However, reality quickly set in when it became abundantly clear these "Communities" were a way to identify those Humans with the strongest anti-Covenant sentiments and herd them all together. After uprooting their lives to relocate to these Communities, Humans in these settlements were largely abandoned by the People's House. Crime was rampant, infrastructure fell apart. That was humanity's lowest point since the Apocalypse. Humans began calling these settlements Sistine Slums. Benevolent Sistine went to its deathbed believing it had done good for humanity. In a way, it had. The Separatist movement had grown stronger due to its actions.

We ought to build it a statue right next to Arabella.

Not that the Bokori were much better off. The planet had been in the midst of an economic depression since the end of what is now known as the "Bokori Phase" of the Century of Strife almost a hundred years ago. It was a foolhardy attempt to use the conflict to seize black hole and mineral-rich systems near Neutral Space. The Bokori also took the opportunity to pursue a Covenant of Subjugation against the Rinvari, for the second time, and the Sezerene. They failed against both races. The Bokori were handed their worst defeat since the Great Galactic War more than one-thousand years ago. Naddine sorcery was blamed for that defeat, too. The People's House imposed rations on every good or service imaginable after their involvement in the war ended, rations which continued to this day. The military had to be called in to quash riot after riot. It's all the military had to do besides fight pirates and outlaw groups on the fringes of Bokori space.

The military is the key.

All that was in the back of Adam's mind as they were escorted to the meeting with the bureaucrats of the People's House. The journey was in total silence. It was eerie to Adam how quiet the building was. Hundreds of Bokori were wandering from room to room, going about their daily business. Not one word was spoken out in the open. The few Bokori that walked past them avoided eye contact, preferring to bury their faces under their hooded robes or behind their kyqads. The kyqad was a facial covering, usually a thin cloth, wrapped around the lower half of the face, leaving only the eyes uncovered. Few Humans wore kyqads and those that did were usually Modders.

On some level, Adam sympathized with their desire to not talk to them. The slightest misunderstanding could result in the Hisbaween knocking on the innocent Bokori's door that night. On the other hand, Adam couldn't shake the feeling he was in an evolving nightmare from which no one could awaken. Other than a simple greeting and a "follow me," their escort was dead silent. Their footsteps echoed throughout the ringed slate marble halls.

The group reached their destination, and Adam stopped dead in his tracks. His heart got stuck in his throat. Flanking the doorway to the meeting room were two guards dressed in black. He shut his eyes before he could get a good look at them. He didn't need to.

Hisbaween! I can't do this. I must leave.

Sensing his apprehension, Shepard slipped her arm under Adam's. "Just follow my lead. I'll handle this."

With a tug, she guided him towards the doorway. Adam refused to open his eyes, holding his breath the entire length of the hallway. His head was pounding. His stomach revolted on him. Shepard's firm grip kept him aloft. The scars on his back itched unbearably. They eventually crossed the threshold. It might've been Adam's imagination, but he thought he could feel the heat from their searstaffs.

Upon entering, Adam exhaled and opened his eyes. To his relief, there were no Hisbaween in the room. It was a barren, lifeless conference room with a circular table. The Bokori brought with them nine representatives, all sitting next to each other. They wore identical oversized gray hooded robes that disguised any hint about age or sex. All but one had their hoods up. All but one had their kyqad wrapped around their faces.

A murder of gray ghosts spooked by their own past, determined to haunt our future.

The central Bokori was standing, his kyqad lowered beneath its chin. It opened up its arms in a gesture of welcome. "On behalf of the representatives of the People's House, the true voice of the Bokori *and Human* peoples alike, welcome!" Adam bristled at the 'and Humans' part. As if Bokori could ever represent them.

Shepard matched the Bokori's gesture. "On behalf of the Commission representing the Community of Arabella, we thank you for your invitation," she said in her most diplomatic tone. The Bokori bowed their heads, and the Humans mimicked them.

"Before we begin, I just wanted to say, Commissioner Mortis, we all mourn the loss of your biological progenitor. Although the circumstances after his death could've been handled more delicately, by us all, all of Bokor mourns your loss. We grieve with you," the Bokori said.

Adam's heart was still pounding. His anxiety upon seeing the

Hisbaween had not settled. He coughed clearing his throat. "I thank you for your condolences on the loss of my *father.* I will be sure to pass them along to my *mother* and *brother,*" Adam said, emphasizing his familial relationships the Bokori had worked so hard to deny.

"Just so," the Bokori said.

"In that spirit, I was wondering if you could do me a favor?" Adam asked. Shepard and Doom shot him sideways glances.

"Of course. You need only ask," the Bokori said.

"The Hisbas guarding the door. If it is all the same to you, could you please ask them to leave," Adam requested.

The Bokori smiled. Adam felt a chill down his spine. "It is not a problem. The Committee for the Advancement of Love and Virtue are here to keep us safe. However, in the spirit of cooperation, I will ask them to move to the end of the hall away from the meeting. Do you find that satisfactory?"

Adam nodded. The Bokori nodded back. It walked around the round table to the door's exit. Adam could hear them talking through the door.

Shepard leaned over to whisper. "You shouldn't have done that. Now, they will expect a favor from you in return. Their goal is to appear reasonable with their demands, and you just dealt them a strong opening hand," Shepard said.

A flicker of panic sparkled in Adam's chest. The anxiety he was feeling almost physically pained him. His back screamed in protest.

I'm out of my depth here.

The Bokori returned. To calm himself, Adam focused on the Bokori's physical features. Focusing on the immediate environment around him was a technique Samus had taught him to ground himself. At times it helped. Adam prayed this was one of those times.

This Bokori appeared much like any other Bokori. On average, the grayskins were about a foot shorter than Humans and about forty-percent head. Shaped like an over inflated balloon, Bokori possessed giant craniums. The rest of their body seemed almost disproportionate to their heads. Like Humans, they had two arms and legs. Notably, only four digits on each extremity, with long, slender fingers mimicking their scrawny arms. They were completely hairless: no eyelashes, no eyebrows, no body hair, no head hair, and skin that felt like rough leather.

Not hers. Hers was soft.

Their faces were almost comically small compared to their heads. Thin lips and slits for a nose, their eyes stood out most of all. Unlike a Human's, which were horizontal rounded off at the top and bottom, Bokori eyes were vertical rounding off at the sides. Their pupil-less, chalk white eyes dominated the rest of their faces. Gratefully, Bokori blinked as much as Humans, otherwise Adam wasn't sure he could stomach staring at those faces for the next several hours.

I could stare at hers for hours. Hers were a stunning shade of ivory. Her lips a smooth pewter.

Thinking about her calmed Adam down. Regretfully, it was all she could do for him. He wished she could be there with him. Just the mere thought of her presence soothed him.

The Bokori returned to its side of the table. The other eight Bokori stood up. One-by-one, they were introduced. None of the other Bokori representatives were making eye contact with the Humans. "From the far side, that is Person Becoming Garden, Person Dragging Cotton, Person Folding Skies, Person Hopping Chains, Person Transforming Parlor, Person Broadening Horizons, Person Corresponding Solemnity, and Person Negotiating Business. I am Person Enduring Temptation," the Bokori said, pointing to each representative down the line. Modern Bokori shunned the usage of titles. They supposedly encouraged separation and elitism. In rare circumstances, Bokori could use their job as a title in order to clear up possible confusion. The moniker "Person" was used instead, which covered both Bokori and Humans. Fortunately, Shepard had said the Bokori would recognize their positions as Commissioners.

The term person is dehumanizing. What an ironic thing to think. Always about context.

"This is Commissioner B.J. Doom, Commissioner Adam Mortis, with whom you spoke, and I am Commissioner Lara Shepard," Shepard said.

Enduring Temptation gestured they sit, and they did so. Adam shifted back-and-forth in his seat. The Bokori valued function over fashion and comfort. These seats were clearly not designed with Humans in mind.

Enduring Temptation spoke first. "I believe it is best to get the...unpleasantness out of the way to start. If we can feel comfortable putting both our issues on the tables, I believe we could find a way to work towards a more amicable solution with the goal of reintegrating the Humans illegally occupying our sacred moon into civilized society. To that end, we wish to formally protest the unethical burial of a Human body. We do not wish to drudge up painful memories, but we humbly request the body be exhumed and returned to the People's House for recycling. To waste such valuable organs is appalling and to deny the right for medical students to study the deceased is unconscionable."

"Not allowing us to grieve in our own way is unconscionable, Person Enduring Temptation. My father is at rest. No one will disturb his grave site while I breathe," Adam said. He couldn't hold his tongue for five seconds. He could sense Shepard's disapproval.

"With all due respect, Commissioner, your progenitor's body belongs to the People's House, as do all deceased, Human and Bokori. Their value to the Community trumps your personal feelings," Enduring Temptation said.

"Y'all already pretense to own the living. You shall not do the same with our dead. It's non-negotiable. What's your next objection?" Adam said curtly.

"If this is how you are going to handle each of our reasonable requests, this may be a short meeting after all," Enduring Temptation said smugly.

"I think you can appreciate, Person Enduring Temptation, Commissioner Mortis' sensitivity on this particular issue. I agree, it is an issue worth discussing, but let's not get bogged down right out of the gate. Please, what other concerns do you have?" asked Shepard, ever the diplomat.

"Very well," Enduring Temptation said. It gestured to Negotiating Business to its right. The hooded Bokori slid it a binder so thick it was practically a lethal weapon. Enduring Temptation cracked open the binder, scanning its top pages quickly.

"It has come to our attention the Humans illegally occupying our sacred moon are using Links as a currency. All intraplanetary exchanges are legally required to use Striking Stamps, the only officially recognized currency of Bokor. The usage of Links undermines our whole economy and gives into the economic terrorism committed by the other races attempting to pressure us into compromising our shared ethical and moral values. Furthermore, we've learned some of the generators used for electricity are powered using combustible fuel in violation of the..."

It was nonstop. Every single page in that thick binder contained at least a dozen problems, large and small, the Bokori had with Arabella, the Separatist movement, and Humans in general. Adam sat there, rocking back-and-forth in his chair, listening to the Bokori ramble on-and-on about every issue conceivable. Issues Adam had no idea were an issue. Weirdly, Adam found the Bokori's never ending list of complaints comforting. Borderline comical.

The Long Con must truly be working if we're having this great an impact.

Adam peered over to his companions. *Bless her;* Adam thought about Shepard. She was completely composed. If one didn't know any better, she was hanging on every word, every complaint the Bokori were leveling at them. The sad part was she probably could recite everything the grayskins had said to the detail. She was steadfast. Doom, on the other hand, was half asleep. He struggled to keep his head up, his eyelids getting heavier by the minute. His old age and demeanor were not suited for this sort of gathering. Nevertheless, he plugged on, not wanting to show he wasn't the perfect diplomat.

At one point, around hour three, Enduring Temptation said this. "In addition, we find the seizure, caging, and grooming of nonconsenting animals from the protected ecosystem of the sacred moon to be reprehensible and request its immediate cessation. We also demand the freeing all living creatures into the custody of the People's House for reintegration into the wild."

Adam shot a sideways glance at Shepard, clearly confused. She leaned over to whisper in his ear. "It means we keep domesticated animals. You know, pets," Shepard said with half a snort. Adam physically had to restrain his jaw from dropping. His baffled expression begged further clarification from Shepard. "You know how seriously the Bokori take animal rights," she said.

Adam had no words. He was well aware of the Bokori attitude towards such issues. Never in a million years, though, did he expect for them to go that far. The Bokori outlawed hunting and ranching of animals for food. The Humans of Arabella had no such qualms. He glimpsed the raw, gray nutrient paste on the tray in front of him. It was the meal the Bokori had provided for the meeting. Adam hadn't touched it. He hated the stuff in the military, although he had grown accustomed to it. Since his arrival on Arabella, he found a new liking for bouncing bits, a giant hare found exclusively on Windless Tornado. It was the most abundant source of meat for the Humans of Arabella. Adam sniffed the paste in front of him and almost vomited.

"Keep it together," Shepard whispered, noticing his visual displeasure with their meal. "We only have a few more hours of this."

"Will we ever get a word in?" he asked whispering.

Shepard shrugged. "Who is the Consul of Cloudboard? I'm surprised we've been able to say anything at all. Bokori tend to be...self-important with their views. You just roll with it."

At the very least, Adam's anxiety disappeared. Listening to complaints was easy to Adam. He heard them all the time back home, mostly from his brother. Aaron and their mother would often get into heated discussions. Not arguments but discussions about the state of Arabella, Human emancipation, or whatever the issue of the day was. Aaron and his mother were very much alike in temperament. Adam was more like his late father. They sat back, quietly watching the two of them for hours tucker each other out with all the yelling. He and his dad often played Conclave Conquest, a game at which Adam sucked, or Adam would read a book, tuning them out while his dad would soak in the discussion. The Bokori were a breeze by comparison.

"...and finally, we must talk about the loss of tax revenue and economic activity from declining tourism. Twenty years ago, foreign tourism to Bokor accounted for around 250 trillion Striking Stamps. That number dropped dramatically to under 100 trillion Striking Stamps last year. With the economy...less than robust, the People's House needs all the revenue it can generate to keep the people of Bokor afloat until the economy fully rebounds. The Striking Stamp is 100-to-1 against the Link. This should bring in a flood of tourists hoping to capitalize on the trade exchange advantage. The fact they're not coming tells us it is something beyond the state of economic and trade affairs causing the decline in tourism. The only logical explanation is this ongoing dispute with the Humans illegally occupying our sacred moon. We need to end this dispute, so foreign tourists feel comfortable visiting us once again. It is science," said Enduring Temptation as it closed the binder.

"It is science," echoed the other eight Bokori.

Four hours of complaints, and they finish with taxation and trade disputes.

"With all due respect, the economy of Bokor has been sluggish since the early days of the Strife. All the People's House's attempts to boost the economy have been a miserable failure, and Humans are suffering the brunt of it," said Shepard, her voice cracking after hours of non-use.

"We dispute those assertions. The fundamentals of the Bokori economy are strong. It is science," said Enduring Temptation.

"It is science," echoed the other eight Bokori.

"Regardless," said Doom. "Humans would greatly benefit from having more direct say over our own affairs. There are needs exclusive to the Human community that cannot be addressed by an interstellar vote."

"Humans have an equal say to Bokori in all matters pertaining to quality of life. The People's House executes the will of the voters. Nothing more, nothing less. The people as a whole decide what is best for the whole people. Humans are no exception. What is good for Bokori is good for Humans. It is science," said Enduring Temptation.

"It is science," echoed the other eight Bokori.

I have a science lesson for them. Friction and fluid dynamics.

"Ask the people living on Windless Tornado, Person Enduring

Temptation. They don't feel as if their needs are being met," insisted Shepard.

"That's because Separatists have spread lies, deceptions, and blasphemous propaganda about life within the Democracy. The issue of Human independence and autonomy has been on every biannual ballot for the past five years. The People's House easily could've struck the issue from the ballot, but we decided to compromise. We allow a vote on the issue every single time. Overwhelmingly, the voters of Bokor have rejected each proposition. Do you know what percentage of the vote favoring Human independence received in the last ballot, Commissioner Shepard?" asked the Bokori

Shepard sighed. "Nine percent."

"Correct. Only nine percent of the fair and just people of Bokor voted for Humans to break away, including just thirty-two percent of Humans. You can't even muster a majority of your own race to see your twisted and heretical viewpoint. We are stronger together. Your kind would pull us apart," Enduring Temptation said with a not-so-subtle shot in Adam's direction.

"Thirty-two percent of Humans is the highest it's ever been, and the share of the vote is only increasing," said Doom.

"Just so, which we again blame on blasphemous propaganda and misinformation proliferated by the Separatists and your misguided supporters in the galaxy," said Enduring Temptation.

Adam interjected. "I'm not sure what you mean by 'misguided supporters in the galaxy,' Person. Humans and Humans alone push for our independence. No one comes to our aid. If they did, I'd welcome them with open arms."

"Do you take us for fools, Commissioner Mortis? We know seedy elements within the Conclave and the other Proprietor races are pushing this mischievous notion of independence within the Human community. Ever since Saptia, rogue actors have covertly supported your misguided, toxic ideas. We know criminal elements have aided your cause. The People's House and the Hisbaween have worked tirelessly to halt the spread of misinformation. It is not perfect, but we are making strides. If all Humans understood and acknowledged the truth, we would be in a century of prosperity. It is science," said Enduring Temptation.

"It is science," echoed the other eight Bokori. It was the only thing those eight ever said. Enduring Temptation had done all the talking. They still refused to look the Humans in the eye.

"Their support must be incredibly covert since we know nothing about it," Adam said. Shepard shot him a side-eyed glance.

She thinks I'm talking too much. Perhaps I am.

"You can issue as many denials as you wish, Commissioner. I want to state this on the record. Any attempt by galactic powers, criminal enterprises, or the rebellious Humans occupying our sacred moon to compromise the integrity of our elections will be met with severe consequences," Enduring Temptation said sternly.

"Your elections are already compromised!" Adam said, throwing caution to the wind.

"Commissioner!" Doom yelled startled. Shepard grabbed him by the knee with a threatening expression on her face.

Adam continued unabated. "Your economy is such trash that Bokori and Humans sell their votes each election to make ends meet. Everyone's vote is published for all to see. It's quite simple to confirm vote selling. We all know the Hisbaween and the People's House grease the landing gears to push an agenda, and those they can't bribe they threaten to haul off to rehabilitation in order to scare them into voting against their conscience. You can issue as many denials as you wish, Person. We know the truth."

"Are you accusing us of corruption and vote tampering without any evidence, Commissioner? Careful. You've already been sent to rehab once for your blasphemous tongue," Enduring Temptation said threateningly.

"I'm not accusing at all. I'm declaring it to be true. You Bokori and your Modder-enabling traitors to humanity. Keep applying the pressure. Like a volcano, it will eventually blow up in your collective faces," Adam said fully aware of his word choice.

If Bokori eyes could widen, they might've conveyed shock. It was hard to tell with grayskins. Enduring Temptation stood. The other eight Bokori quickly followed suit.

"This meeting is over. Your toxic language will not be tolerated by us. You're lucky you enjoy immunity for this day otherwise I'd have the Committee for the Advancement of Love and Virtue throw you back into a cell," declared Enduring Temptation.

Shepard and Doom stood for the Bokori preparing to exit the room. Adam remained seated. "Would you prefer I use more acceptable terms such as Humans who modify? Modified Humans? Humans with modifications? Would that sate your incoherent logic?" asked Adam mockingly. His rage kept his bubbling anxiety at bay.

The Bokori strode past exiting the room. Enduring Temptation lingered behind for a moment. "I'd watch your tongue, Flowing Courage." It used Adam's Bokori name. "You keep tossing around declarations like that, it'll be the end of your insignificant movement." The Bokori left the room.

I thought I'd never hear that name again. I hate it. I am not one of them. I am a free Human!

"Good work, jadespawn!" Doom cursed at him. "You've set us back years with that little stunt of yours."

Adam slowly rose to his feet. "Are you so naïve? Do you think we'd get any concessions out of that lot? We spent more than four hours at a lecture, not a negotiation." Adam strode over to Doom getting right in his face. "If you ever refer to my mother as a 'jade' again, I'll modify you myself, permanently." Doom took a step back nearly tripping over his chair. Shepard forced herself between them.

"Cool it. Both of you. Doom, go wait for us at the shuttle. Now, please," Shepard said. It was not a request. Doom nodded and left the room. Adam and Shepard stood staring at each other for a moment.

"Are you going to lecture me, too, Lara?" Adam asked.

Shepard shook her head. "Look. I understand how you feel. I understand how your mother, your father, Trissefer, John, Samus, and the thousands of other hardworking independents on Arabella feel about the situation. No, I'm not naïve. We weren't going to get a concession *today*. It's not about today, Adam. It's about tomorrow and the next day and the next after that. The Link wasn't built in a day. Neither will our freedom. We put up with those smug jadespawn now, and we might be able to win over hearts and minds later. Yes, times seem bleak. However, if we play our cards right, the Bokori themselves could vote us our independence. We build towards a watershed moment. The movement towards emancipation will be unstoppable. The galaxy will be behind with us! You just have to trust me. Progress, true progress, takes time."

Adam breathed deeply. He respected her words. Lara Shepard was one of the wisest women Adam had ever met. He was glad for her counsel. On some level, Adam saw the truth and wisdom in her words. Yet, something was nagging him at the back of his mind.

"What did the Bokori mean when he mentioned 'misguided galactic supporters?' Surely, it couldn't be referring to the pitiful sentientarian aid?" Shepard said nothing. She scratched her cheek while adjusting her jumpsuit. "Lara, is there something we need to talk about?"

Shepard leaned in close. "Not here. We'll talk more about this when we get back. We must restrategize."

There is no way in Kewea the other galactic powers care that much about the Human Separatist cause to risk provoking a Proprietor race. Is there? What isn't she telling me?

"You and Doom can head back. I'm sticking around here for a bit. Going to explore the city. I'll find my way back with Havera. She's in the city running errands," Adam said, walking to the door.

Shepard called out to him. "Be careful! The immunity only lasts a day and only for this meeting. It won't cover any offenses you might commit out there, so please, for the love of Cradite, hold your tongue. What do you plan on doing in Inclucity?"

Adam titled his head to peek over his shoulder. "I'm going to reacquaint myself with our enemy."

6

We're Everywhere

Leaving the building, Adam received the ping notification on his HUD. It was a voice message from John on their private channel. He opened it. John's voice was hushed and frantic.

"Adam, something's happened to Samus. We're in a huge bind. I won't say more even on a private channel while we're inside the city. The building on the corner across from where we acquired our first vehicle. Third floor. End of the hall. Usual signal. Come alone. Come quickly."

Adam hurried down the entrance stairs. A line of cab drivers were idling on the near side of the street. They were a mixture of Human and Bokori drivers. A couple of the Humans were visibly modded. They were standing around bored, waiting for someone to ask for a ride. Few ever did. Most people used the semi-legal private pickup services accessed through their HUDs. More than likely, many of these drivers also drove for them, but they maintained the appearance of legitimate state-approved cab services for legal and tax purposes. Adam didn't want to risk using his HUD to flag down a private pickup in case he was monitored. Instead, he knew of another way.

"Pardon me!" Adam called out to the row of drivers. They were shaken from their boredom at the prospect of a rare fare. "I'm searching for the best place to get my hair done in a traditional Human style. Do any of y'all know how to get to Sleeping Slashes?"

Adam hoped one of them would understand. He studied the faces of the drivers. They were all thoroughly confused. "I do! I can take you there," called out a Human male at the end of the row.

Adam breathed a sigh of relief. He approached the Human, a short older man with balding white hair and matching white goatee. "You can take me to Sleeping Slashes?" Adam asked.

"Absolutely. That place is tough to get to this time of day. Can you hook me up?" replied the driver?

"Not a problem. Would you mind waiting while I get my hair done?" asked Adam.

"I can't wait around all day waiting for someone to get their hair done. Not at this hour," the driver said.

"We'll forge a greater bond if you do," Adam said.

The driver sighed. "Alright. Hop in."

They were speaking in code. Travel to and from a Sistine Slum was highly regulated and expensive at that. Asking for a benign service in traditional Human style was the setup phrase. A few of the more friendly Human drivers were willing to take people to one of the slums, but only if paid in Links. They were worth far more on the open market than Striking Stamps, the official currency of Bokor. Haggling on price was also illegal, but Adam offered to pay him double to wait around in case they needed a quick getaway. Sleeping Slashes was the underground name for a slum near the northern end of the city. The slums weren't the safest place to be at any time of day. He could understand the driver's apprehension.

John's instructions brought Adam back to the Sistine Slum where they grew up. It was on the other side of the city from their current location. The aircar lifted off in that direction. The air traffic wasn't too bad, and Adam knew it would thin out when they reached the city aerial limits. "John, I'm on route. Be there in ten minutes. Hang on," Adam whispered into a message for John. He instructed the driver on the quickest pathway to avoid most of the remaining traffic. The driver grunted an affirmative to his request and steered accordingly.

The car whooshed through the air. Adam spotted a building he had hoped he'd never see again. Adam's breath got caught in his throat. A giant domed structure loomed over the neighborhood. Huge black banners hung over the front of the building as the aircar passed right by it. Adam could see the gray, open-palmed hand symbol on the front of the banners along with the words drilled forever into his brain.

"Equality through sacrifice!" Adam blurted out loudly. He bit his lip immediately while his whole body shook uncontrollable. Images of bright lights flashed in his mind. The scars on his back ached. He tasted iron in his mouth as blood leaked from where he bit his lip. He wrapped his arms around himself to stop the shaking.

"Person, are you okay?" the driver asked concerned about the sudden outburst and shaking.

"I'll be fine," Adam managed to huff out. "Keep driving."

Adam got the shaking under control. He wiped the blood off his mouth and spit the remaining blood into his sleeve. His back scars continued to ache and itch. He rubbed his back hard against the seat cushion to try and find relief. He received very little.

Get it together, you weakling! You're free of that horrible place. They cannot hurt you ever again. But they keep hurting me every day. They're hurting me right now. You've worked on this for years. The High Hisba is miles away. It'll always occupy a part of your mind.

Adam's mind was racing. All the self-doubt was rushing back to him. All the trauma he experienced in that building. All the thoughts and feelings he worked hard to suppress.

You can do it. For John. For Samus. For...her.

He focused on his hand tattoo. Its image centered his thoughts. What seemed like hours passed for Adam. He was so lost in his thoughts he didn't realize they had arrived at the exterior of the slum.

"Here we are," the driver said, lowering the car onto the street.

"We need to go further inward," Adam said.

"No. Too dangerous. I will wait for you here," the driver insisted.

"Head into the Cradite forsaken slum, or I'll tell the authorities you called me a Modder!" Adam declared.

The driver gaped at Adam with a mixture of rage and fear. Adam knew the accusation of blasphemy was louder than the truth. He felt guilty about threatening an innocent driver, but he had to reach John and Samus. The driver relented. He lifted the car back into the air and drove through the streets.

The slum was exactly as Adam remembered. Young Human boys and girls playing in the streets, Celeste dealers on every corner, cheap jades performing their services in the back alleys, the smell of death and failure all around them. Some of the buildings were so run-down Adam was surprised they hadn't collapsed. Adam could see the eyes scanning them. Aircars were not common in the slums. Hopefully, they could be in and out before anyone caused any trouble.

Adam directed the driver to the correct building. On the corner of a pothole-covered street was a three-story building only moderately nicer than the rest of the neighborhood. Adam recognized it as a local hostel used by transients and the few braver Bokori tourists that wished to get the full "Human experience." The building had a pair of muscular bodyguards outside the entrance. Whether that brought more or less comfort to the driver, Adam couldn't tell as the driver parked the car out front.

"Wait right here. No one will bother you with them here," Adam said, reinforcing the presence of the guards.

"Half the Links now or I leave!" the driver demanded. Adam didn't argue. He transferred half the agreed upon Links from his HUD to the driver's.

"I'll be back shortly," Adam said. The driver only grunted.

Adam exited the aircar. The bodyguards eyed his approach. Adam walked right by them exchanging a friendly nod. The lobby was surprisingly clean and polished. Adam hurried over to the concierge, a tiny older Human woman who was reading an old-fashioned paperback book. "Excuse me, which way to the elevators?"

"Elevators don't work," the woman said without regard to his presence. She pointed towards the back of the lobby. "You'll have to take the stairs."

"Thank you," Adam said. The woman ignored him. He located the doors to the stairwell. He hustled up the stairs passing by a young couple making out on the stairs. "Excuse me," Adam said rushing by them. The couple blushed and ran into the second-floor hallway. Adam reached the third floor and pushed open the door. The air was rank. A Human man was sleeping in the hallway covered in rags, a bottle of booze by his side. Adam tiptoed past him so as not to wake him. He reached the room at the end of the long circular hallway. He knocked on the door once, paused, knocked again, paused, then knocked two more times. The door opened. John stood in the doorway seeing if Adam was alone. Adam noticed the door had been kicked in previously.

"Where we *acquired* our first car? Cute euphemism for stole, John," Adam said with a slight chuckle.

"About time you showed up! No time for jokes. Come in," John said. He grabbed Adam by the scruff of his jumpsuit and dragged him in.

"Kewea's curse, John. You said something happened to Samus. Where is she?" Adam asked.

"She's in the bathroom cleaning up. I need to show you something first," John said.

He dragged Adam deeper into the room. Adam only just realized the front of John's jumpsuit was covered in blood. Gray blood. It was a tiny room. A messy double bed along with a small table and chair. John brought Adam around to the other side of the bed. Adam's eyes widened. Lying face up in a pool of gray blood was a dead Bokori. The Bokori was nude. A male. Adam guessed the Bokori was about twenty to twenty-five years old. The Bokori had a pair of gunshot wounds to the chest.

"Kewea take us! What happened here, John?" Adam asked.

John cleared his throat. "I was meeting Samus here. I had finished my business early, so I thought I'd come here and wait for her. I reached the door. I heard noises through the door. It was Samus' voice. She sounded in distress. I kicked in the door, and that's when I saw this Kewea-infected monster," John said pointing to the dead Bokori. "It was on top of her, its hands around her throat. It was assaulting her! I heard Samus scream, 'NO,' and my mind went blank. I remember struggling with the grayskin. Next thing I knew I heard two gunshots, and the grayskin was dead. I don't remember shooting."

Adam put his hand to his mouth. "Is Samus alright?"

John shook his head. "She hasn't said a word. She's in shock. We need to leave. We must get her back to Arabella."

"We're just going to leave without reporting this?" Adam asked.

"Are you crazy? Even if we could convince the grayskins it was self-defense, I'd get charged with possession of an illegal weapon. They'd probably tack on a charge of vigilantism since I took action without calling the authorities first. We're already on a dozen watch lists. They'll send us all to prison or worse to rehab!"

Adam winced. "I have a car downstairs waiting for us. I'll get Samus. Go downstairs and make sure the coast is clear."

John hesitated glimpsing in the direction of the bathroom door.

"No time to argue, John. Someone probably heard the shots, and the authorities might be here any minute. Your sister will be safe with me. I promise. Go," Adam said.

John nodded. He tucked his gun under his shirt and left the room. Adam reached the bathroom and knocked on the door. "Sam. Sam, it's Adam. Can I come in?"

No response. Adam could hear muffled weeping through the door. "Sam, please we can't stay here."

Adam heard hurried footsteps reach the door. The door wrenched open and Samus threw herself into Adam's arms. "I'm sorry. I'm so sorry. I don't know what happened," Samus said. She was sobbing into his chest, squeezing him tightly. Adam wrapped his arms around her tenderly.

"It's not your fault. We'll get you someplace safe," Adam said. She let go of him and took a step back. The whites of her eyes were bloodshot and her cheeks puffy. A pain and anguish swelled behind her bright brown eyes Adam could tell. Visible tears were streaming down her face. Adam noticed the bruises on her neck. They appeared to be finger marks. She had a minor abrasion on her left cheek and one of her sleeves was partially torn. Adam felt a rising anger to run over and kick the dead Bokori where it lay. Adam saw she was eyeing the body. Adam placed himself between her and the Bokori. "Come on, Sam. We shouldn't linger here any longer."

She nodded. Adam took off his duster jacket and wrapped it around her. She accepted it gratefully. He raised the hood to help keep her face hidden. Adam helped usher her out of the room. For an instant, Sam peeked over her shoulder back towards the dead Bokori. Adam closed the door behind him. The hallway was deserted. The passed-out drunk was gone. Thoughts flooded Adam's brain.

The drunk. The lovey-dovey couple. The concierge. The bodyguards. Soon, the driver. Who knows how many other potential witnesses there are?

Adam and Samus reached the lobby. John was waiting for them by the door. "All clear," John said when they met. "We're in luck. Your driver is still there."

Adam breathed a sigh of relief. He thought for sure the driver would've taken off by then. A few Links go a long way. The trio hustled out the doorway. Adam caught sight of the old woman concierge watching them leave. They walked swiftly past the guards and into the backseat of the car.

"Where to this time, friend?" the driver asked.

"Outskirts on the north side. Quickly," John said. The driver grunted and the aircar lifted off. The car flew out of the slum with a high rate of speed. Adam figured the driver had spent enough time in that place to not dawdle.

"We'll reach a smuggling area and get out that way. It's the quietest path back to Arabella," John said. Adam nodded. Due to the close proximity between Bokor and her moon, the Humans of Arabella operated dozens of smuggling routes all around the planet to transport goods and people to and from Bokor. The closest one was on the northern side of Inclucity. Adam had never used them, but John and Samus were well versed in that regard.

Only a couple minutes passed when everyone's HUD dinged an alert. Adam pulled up the notice. "Kewea's curse!" Adam swore under his breath. It was a city-wide wanted notification. Anyone with an active HUD within Inclucity received those alerts. Adam saw all three of their faces in the alert with the tagline 'wanted for questioning in a matter of seditious activity, heresy, and murder.'

That seems awfully fast.

John picked up on the notification, too. "What do we do now?" John asked nervously.

Adam thought for a second. He had an idea. "Change of plans," Adam said to the driver. "Take us the spaceport." The driver sighed. Adam prayed he hadn't checked his notifications, yet. The aircar banked left away from the direction of the outskirts towards the northwestern part of Inclucity.

"Spaceport?! We can't go that way. There'll be security everywhere!" John said in a raised whisper.

"They'll be watching any traffic at the outskirts. They'll search every aircar at the city limits, and they'll be monitoring the smuggling routes more closely. We need to leave by more legitimate means.

"How?" John asked incredulous.

"Havera is in Inclucity. Her ship will be at the spaceport. We can hide there. She'll take us back to Arabella no issue."

"You can't seriously trust her not to turn us in? I won't put my sister's safety and freedom in the hands of that longtail," John insisted.

"I trust her." It was Samus. She hadn't spoken the entire trip, only quietly sobbing under the hood of Adam's jacket. "Havera has always been kind to me. She'll help us I'm sure of it."

Adam looked to John and could see he wanted to protest. Seeing the resolve in his sister's eyes, he relented. "Alright, fine, but I won't be taken alive," John said. Adam could see his hand move towards where his gun was hidden. "No matter what happens, Adam, you get my sister out."

Adam nodded. The aircar was descending as if to land, but they were still a couple miles from the spaceport. Adam saw the driver was leering back at the three of them. A small bead of sweat dripped down the old man's forehead.

"We're compromised," Adam whispered to John.

John whipped out his gun and pointed it at the driver's head. "Keep driving, *friend*," John said, pressing the muzzle of the gun into the driver's temple. The driver panicked. He opened his door and leapt out the side while the car was still a dozen feet in the air. His sudden reaction shocked John. He tried to grab the steering wheel. The car crashed into the ground with a loud crunch. Adam instinctively wrapped his arms around Samus to shield her from the impact. The trio was thrown forward. Adam and Samus hit the padding of the backseat. John wasn't as lucky. He was hurtled through the glass of the windshield and hit the ground hard. He rolled along the ground before coming to a violent stop.

"No!" Adam yelled. He checked to see if Samus alright. "Sam, are you hurt?" She shook her head. Sam saw the hole in the windshield and gasped. "Come on," Adam said, kicking out the broken side door. He helped Samus exit the wreck. She rushed to her brother's side. Adam followed suit. He could hear his friend moaning as they got close.

"Owwwww," John moaned. "That reminded me too much of Shock-trooper training. Ow. Ow. Ow." He tried to get up, but his arms buckled under his weight. Adam and Samus helped lift him to his feet. "Ow! Gently. Gently! That pavement is really solid," he joked.

"Check your HUD vitals. Anything broken or any organ damage?" Adam asked concerned.

John shook his head. "We've both fallen from much higher heights than that. I'll live. I'll be sore for the next month though. Are you okay, Samus?" John asked his sister. She nodded. Several bystanders were observing them.

"We have to keep moving," Adam said. He braced John against his shoulder. The trio fled into the alleyways. The authorities had to be close by. Adam tapped his HUD until he found his contacts. He pressed Havera's signal to call her. It was a necessary risk. He needed to ensure she was still there.

Come on, Havera, pick up.

To his relief, the Cauduun answered. "Adam? I was wondering if I'd hear from you. There's a city-wide alert out on you! Are you okay?"

"Yes, we're mostly okay. Havera, we need a huge favor from you. Can you transport us back to Arabella? Samus is in danger, and we were in a car wreck. John isn't in great shape. I promise this is all a huge misunderstanding, but the Bokori won't give us a fair shake. Please."

Havera didn't hesitate. "Of course. I'll head back to my ship right away. I'll tell Dee to let you aboard. Are y'all far?"

"About a mile or so on foot. We're near the..." Adam's voice was caught in his throat. He only just realized they were right next to the stadium. The headquarters of the Hisbaween. The site where all rehabilitations occurred. He saw the propaganda posters plastered all around the side. 'Your children belong to us,' 'Report family, friends, and neighbors for blasphemous or heretical activity to the Committee for the Advancement of Love and Virtue,' 'For the good of the many.' The most prominent poster of all, in big bold letters, 'Equality Through Sacrifice.'

Adam tried to bite his lips, but the words slipped through them. "Adam, what was that? Did something happen?" Havera asked.

Adam felt a slap on his face. John had hit him. "Adam, focus. I understand what you're feeling, but my sister needs your help. Be strong for her," he said.

Adam regarded Samus. Her bright brown eyes had dried. Her face was awash with concern. Adam took a deep breath. "I'm fine, Havera. We're near the stadium. We should be there within the hour."

"Okay," Havera said. "Hurry. I can see the police aircars flying around. They're searching for y'all. My ship is in hangar bay ninety-four. Y'all should be able to just walk up to it. Dee will let y'all in. Stay safe."

"Thank you, Havera. I owe you," he said.

"We'll worry about that later. Just get there in one piece," she said.

Havera ended the call. "We're good to go," Adam said.

"I pray you're right about the longtail, Adam," John said.

Adam was certain Havera would come through for them. However, an uneasy thought dug into the back of Adam's mind. He could hear John's doubts creeping through his skull. Depending on the kindness of others was a surefire way to get killed in the slums. One always had to know exactly what the other party was getting out of the arrangement if one was to survive the harsh streets of Inclucity. Adam pushed those thoughts out of his head. They had no choice but to trust the Cauduun woman.

The trio hobbled their way through the streets, continuing northwest towards the spaceport away from the stadium. Adam was vaguely familiar with the layout of the streets in this part of the city. He had typically avoided the hustle of the spaceport. The high presence of police cars overhead pushed many of the residents to hide in their homes and businesses, allowing them to dart from alleyway to alleyway mostly unnoticed. The few Bokori that spotted them either paid no mind or actively turned away as if merely sighting them was a criminal offense.

John was weakening. His breathing was labored while he clutched at the side of his ribs. At one point, he coughed up a little blood, which he tried to hide by wiping it away. His internal injuries must have been worse than he led Adam to believe. Havera would have emergency medical supplies on her ship. They had to get there first.

Only a few blocks away from the spaceport, Adam peered around a corner. A parked patrol car was close by. An officer was interviewing people on the street. Adam wasn't certain but the officer appeared more Human than Bokori. It was risky to press this direction. The quickest way was to cut through an alley about halfway between them and the officer. To be safe, Adam thought it might be best to go loop back around. He gave John a once-over. His face was nearly chalk white, and he wheezed every breath. Samus and Adam exchanged glances. They had no choice.

We must chance it.

Adam peered around the corner again. The officer was in mid-conversation with a pair of Bokori children. He seemed adequately distracted. The alley exit was only a hundred or so feet down the block. "Now," Adam whispered. Samus and Adam lifted John slightly off his feet and carried him. They hurried swiftly trying not to make too much noise. Adam kept one eye on the officer. He hadn't noticed them, yet. John let out a huge cough, sprinkling blood on Adam's boots. Not wasting a moment, they rushed around the corner and out of sight.

Adam's heart sank. He had misremembered where this alley led. "Dead end," Adam said, swearing under his breath. He could hear footsteps coming from around the corner. "Hide behind the stairs," Adam hissed in a hushed whisper. These old buildings had solid stone circular staircases that led to the upper levels, which were meant to be fire escapes but often made for more convenient entryways to avoid filthy residential apartment lobbies. They hid around the nearest spiral staircase and pressed their backs up against the wall. The officer turned into the alley. Even in the middle of the day, the alleyway was dark. The officer pulled out a flashlight and his service weapon glancing down the alley. John's wheezing threatened to give away their position. Adam regretfully placed his hand over John's mouth. Samus shot him a frightened, angry expression. She tried mouthing something to him, but the translators wouldn't pick it up. He couldn't read her lips. John and Samus spoke Standard while Adam spoke Default. It didn't matter. Her face spoke volumes. The officer was about to leave when he spotted something on the ground. Adam realized what he saw.

John's blood!

The officer rubbed the blood on his fingers. He raised his weapon and flashlight cautiously moving into the alley. Adam's mind was frantic. He wasn't sure what to do. Samus was equally panicking. He could hear her emit the occasional worried cry. Not loud enough for the officer to hear, but persistent enough to keep Adam's heart racing.

Adam thought about reaching for John's gun. John coughed again into Adam's hand causing another trickle of blood to escape through his hand. The officer spotted them.

Everyone froze. No one dared make a move or utter a sound. The officer was indeed Human. He was a tall, slender, dark-skinned Human about Adam's age if he had to guess. The officer's expression was stony. He didn't react to the sight of the three of them. Adam was slowly moving his hand behind his coat to reach for John's gun. The officer noticed the movement. "Don't move," he said. It was more of a request than an order. The officer lifted his finger to his temple to talk into his HUD's radio. "Dispatch, this is Patrol Officer 141, I have completed my sweep of sector 27. No sign of the fugitives." He paused. "Copy that. Resuming search pattern."

Adam wasn't sure what to make of what the officer had said. As if to answer his confused expression, the officer lowered his gun. He shined the light on himself. He pulled down the front of his white uniform to reveal a tattoo: two circular disks, one large and blue and the other smaller and gray, up and to the right of the blue disk. The officer smiled at them.

"Where are y'all headed?" the officer asked.

Adam acted on instinct. "To the spaceport. We have a ride off the planet." The officer nodded. He gave John a once-over. The officer retrieved a small vial from his pocket and handed it to Adam. "Naddine potion. It should stymie the internal bleeding until he can receive proper medical attention." Adam uncorked the vial and lifted it to John's mouth. He swallowed the potion without protest. The liquid traveled down John's throat, causing him to cough more. The officer put his gun away. "Wait here for one minute, and then head to the spaceport with haste. The Hisbaween are searching for y'all. I'll lead them away." Adam nodded. The officer again lifted his finger to his temple. "Dispatch, this is Patrol Officer 141. I found a lead on the fugitives. They were spotted on the southeastern side of the stadium. Found blood. One of them is wounded. They couldn't have gotten far. Send all available units this way."

The officer lowered his finger and headed back towards his car.

"Thank you!" Samus blurted out.

The officer turned and nodded. "What is lost will be found," he said.

"What is lost will be found," Adam and Samus returned. The officer hopped back into his vehicle and lifted off. They waited one minute as requested. Adam noticed a few more patrol cars flying overhead away from their intended destination.

"We're everywhere," John said through a wheeze. "I told you. We can do this. We can achieve our freedom and independence once more. We just need the courage to seize it."

"We'll worry about that tomorrow," Adam said. "First, let's get you and Samus home."

With a renewed sense of confidence, the trio hurried through the streets. It was only a matter of time until the authorities figured out they weren't there. Adam hoped the officer would be alright. He couldn't dwell on those thoughts. Not yet. They were within sight of the spaceport. Adam and John waited around a corner while Samus, wearing Adam's hooded jacket, rushed up incognito to a sign that would tell them the location of hanger bay ninety-four. Samus returned promptly.

"It's close. This way."

Samus guided the two of them towards the hanger bay. The potion was taking effect. Adam could feel John walking under some of his own power once again. They reached the exterior of one of the nicer hangar bays. It was polished steel with the number "94" emblazoned at the top. Adam pressed the button on the intercom.

"Dee, you there? It's Adam. Let us in!" No response. "Dee, hurry! We can't linger out here."

"Excuse me!" a voice called out behind them. Adam glanced over his shoulder to see a Bokori security guard. The guard's eyes widened. It realized who they were. It lifted its finger to its temple and spoke frantically into its HUD com. The door into the hanger bay opened with a creak. Dee was waiting for them on the other side. "STOP!" the guard yelled out at them.

"I think y'all better get inside," Dee said dryly. They pushed their way through the door. Dee shut the door after them. The ramp to the interior of Havera's ship was down. "Hurry! Wait inside," Dee said.

"Is Havera at the helm?" Adam asked.

"Mistress Havera is on her way back. She was at the marketplace when she received your call. She should be here within a few minutes," Dee said.

"We don't have that kind of time, Dee! Security, the police, and the Hisbaween will be on us momentarily. We need to get out of here!" Adam yelled.

"It is not a problem, Master Adam. Wait inside Mistress Havera's ship. I will handle any trouble," Dee insisted.

Adam didn't argue. He wasn't sure what Dee could do. He wasn't a combat bot. As far as Adam knew, Dee was merely an assistant bot. What could he do to stop an entire planet's law enforcement bureaus?

They rushed John inside and placed him on a table in the medical room. He was still coughing blood. Adam searched the medical room and found another vial of Naddine health potion. He handed it to Samus and grabbed John's gun. "Whatever you do, do not open the door for anyone other than myself, Havera, or Dee. Understand? If I have to hijack this ship to get out of here, I will."

Samus nodded. Adam exited the medical room and sealed the door behind him. He climbed down the stairs and reached the open ramp in the cargo bay. He hid near some unopened crates marked "Ingredients." At any moment, Adam expected to see armed guards storm the ship. Adam intended to wait for Havera, but, if she didn't make it back on time, he would hold off the police and steal the ship. Havera might forgive him.

If I don't crash the ship. I've never flown a spaceworthy vessel.

Except, the armed guards never came. Adam could hear Dee's robotic voice pierce through the tense air, but he couldn't make out what Dee was saying. Adam inched closer to get a better vantage point. Adam could see the black clad uniforms of the Hisbaween from where he hid. He shut his eyes and took several deep breaths to calm himself. He opened his eyes to gaze at the instruments of his suffering. The jet-black uniforms covered them from head to toe. From their military boots to the long triangular shoulder pads, which gave them the appearance of wings, there wasn't an inch of skin showing. Their dark great helms, with a horizontal white sliver across the front of their opaque visors, were a terrifying visage to behold. Each one was armed with a rifle and a four-foot-long black searstaff, capable of burning any foe into submission. Topped off with a flowing black cloak, they were the dark angels from the deepest depths of Kewea. Whispers in the night to frighten adults and children alike into complying with the strict Bokori morality code. Their authority rested on murky legal grounds, but no one dared oppose them. Such was their reputation. They were the only people in Bokori society allowed to have a title. They were charged with upholding the dignity and order of "civilized society."

"Step aside, bot! There are three dangerous fugitives aboard that ship. We have full authority to go in there and get them!" a loud Bokori voice yelled out.

Dee did not flinch in the face of their demands. "I am afraid you are mistaken, Hisba. The Cicera is the property of a sovereign nation. You must receive authorization from the office of Queen Alexandra in order to enter the sovereign vessel of the Cauduun Monarchical Alliance. Violation of Cauduun sovereignty will lead to severe penalty against the Bokori from both the Alliance and the Conclave. You are already treading on dangerous waters by entering our hangar bay without express permission and threatening to keep the Cicera on lock down. The Duchess, when she returns, is well within her legal rights to leave if she wishes, no matter who or what is on board. If you wish to file a complaint, please speak to a representative of the Alliance at the embassy or at the Conclave. If you will pardon my language, get your Cradite-forsaken, fleshsack, jadespawn asses out of our hangar bay. Good day."

Duchess? Does Dee mean Havera?

The Hisba that Dee was arguing with had removed its helm. It was Bokori and, judging by the echoed inflection in its voice, Adam guessed it was a parthenogen, the rare third sex of the Bokori. Parthenogens were Bokori birthed without genitals, yet many had the ability to reproduce asexually. Ancient Bokori societies once viewed parthenogens as gods or heralds of gods, so Adam had learned. These days, their sexless, egalitarian features were a source of pride and esteem for those lucky enough to be born first among equals. Their lack of interest in physical relations allowed them to avoid the morally hazardous...complications commonplace among Bokori and Humans. Morally hazardous to the Hisbaween, at least. The Hisbas spent considerable effort policing relationships, stamping out behaviors and tendencies they considered problematic. Adam figured this Hisba must be Unbroken Tide, second-in-command to the High Hisba. Adam had never met Unbroken Tide, but he was well aware of its reputation. If the rumors were true, Unbroken Tide was more of a zealot than even the High Hisba. It was responsible for running and maintaining the rehab facilities within the stadium, making it directly responsible for Adam's torment. The scars on Adam's back itched and burned just seeing its muted gray face. Adam had to restrain himself from putting a bullet between its vertical, white eyes.

Beyond the Hisbaween stood a dozen other armed assailants. They were a mixture of the white clad police and the gray clad spaceport security. They were taking their cue from the Hisbaween with most of the security forces giving them a wide berth. Even other law enforcement officials were terrified of the Hisbaween.

Adam heard a door slide open just out of sight. Dee and the guards turned to see who entered. "Your Grace," Dee said with a bow. "These fleshsacks have broken into your hangar, demanding we give them access to your ship. I told them they are in violation of the law and diplomatic protocol; however, it seems these fleshsacks have the intelligence of a Kewean consort and the wits of her excrement. They are refusing to leave."

Havera strode into Adam's view. Her radiant crimson skin illuminated the area around her in Adam's eyes. "It is alright, Dee. I will handle this. Go inside and get ready for takeoff."

"Yes, Mistress," Dee said with a bow. Adam swore he heard Dee mutter "fleshsack" again under his breath. Dee walked up the ramp and spotted Adam. "Master Adam, why don't you wait for the mistress in the cockpit. She will be along shortly."

"Don't you mean the Duchess?" Adam asked pointedly.

"Did I stutter? I am sure the mistress will have much to talk about with you when she finishes putting those fleshsacks in their place. In the meantime, I will take the initiative to see what I can do to help Master John. I noticed he was leaking blood. Good day, Master Adam," Dee said as he walked away towards the medical room.

Adam did as he was told. He waited for Havera in the cockpit. Through the window of the Cicera's cockpit, Adam could see most of the guards dispersing out of the hangar. A faint violet glow was emanating just out of sight. The Hisbaween were leaving as well, except for Unbroken Tide. It was staring into the cockpit. Adam and it locked eyes. He could feel the Hisba's gaze burn through his soul. The hatred exuding off those eyes was palpable. Adam was amused at the irony. The Hisba spent so much effort eliminating what they deemed hate, yet Adam could not think of a more hateful, spiteful bunch than the Hisbaween. Through the pain and itching in his back, Adam simply smiled.

7

Bubbles and Beacons

"Should I call you ma'am? Your Highness? Your Duchesship?" Adam asked Havera half-jokingly, half-serious after the Cicera had lifted off.

"Call me Havera. *Only* Havera if you please," replied Havera a tinge of bitterness in her voice. "Did Dee tell you?"

"I'm surprised you didn't, *Only* Havera. I wish I knew I was in the company of royalty all this time," Adam said. "Dee invoked your title to stop the Hisbas from boarding the ship."

"I see. Regrettable," Havera said softly.

"I don't know understand why you seem so upset about it. Duchess sounds like a cool title. Are you in the line of succession? I don't know how your monarchy works," Adam said.

"No. It doesn't work like that. We're a Cognatic Monarchy. It's a mixture of a hereditary and electoral process. We don't choose the queen; we choose who will succeed her, the archduchess. After the coronation of a new queen, the duchesses from every part of the Alliance come together to pick a female successor from the line of Shele. When the queen dies or abdicates, the archduchess becomes queen. Only members of the Shelean Royal Family can become the archduchess and therefore sit the throne," Havera explained.

"All the duchesses? That means you get a vote, right? You must be really important back home," Adam said excitedly.

"Hardly," Havera said dismissively. "There are over six-hundred duchesses in the Platinum Court. Their numbers have increased many folds with many diverse political factions due to the growth of our colonies. My vote is completely inconsequential," Havera said.

"Are you part of the Shelean Royal Family? Could you become the next queen or archduchess, I guess? Who's the current archduchess? I know Queen Alexandra III has been on the throne for a couple decades. How do you feel about her?" Adam's curiosity increased with each question.

"If it's all the same to you, I'd rather we not keep discussing this. It's not a topic I like to talk about if you couldn't tell. I've only been a duchess for two years. It makes little difference to me," Havera said with a definitive end-of-conversation tone. She spent the rest of the short flight in silence without so much of a glance in his direction. He had never seen her act this way. In the two years he'd known her, she'd always treated him warmly and courteously.

A duchess for two years? That's how long she's been helping us. It can't be a coincidence. I wonder why it bothers her so much. Is she hiding from something or someone?

The more Adam thought about it, the more questions he had. Havera hadn't spent every day on Windless Tornado. She would often travel to pick up more data from Stepicro and come back. What else did she do on those excursions? Adam realized how little he knew about the Cauduun. All he knew was that she's a historian and a Praetorian, an organization which Adam was mostly ignorant. Beyond that and her sometimes awkward social mannerisms, Havera was a mystery. Adam wondered if that was intentional.

Is she keeping me and the other Humans at an arm's length for a reason?

John's words crept back into his head. "*They're spies under the guise of spreading knowledge. It's the Conclave's way of keeping tabs on us.*"

His curiosity would have to be sated later. The Cicera was descending to her usual landing zone near the outskirts of Arabella. Adam thought it best to leave the Cauduun to her thoughts. He exited the cockpit to check on John. He was unconscious. Dee and Samus had strapped him to a floating mobile stretcher.

"He's stable," Samus said. "Dee gave him a sedative. I've already contacted Commissioner Auditore. Apparently, we've stirred up a Bubil's nest. They're meeting us when we land."

Samus wasn't joking. The entirety of the Commission met them at the bottom of Cicera's ramp. Auditore examined John quickly and ordered his team of medics to take him to the makeshift hospital. Samus made to join them when Snake put out a hand to stop her.

"What in Kewea happened, Adam?!" asked Commissioner Doom hysterically. "The Hisbaween have issued an arrest warrant for Samus and John, and they want to detain you for questioning, too. Do you have any idea the damage that's been done? We have many questions for the two of you."

Why are the Hisbaween involved? Shouldn't this be a simple law enforcement issue?

Adam stepped between Samus and Snake. "Let her be with her brother. We'll talk about this away from prying ears. I'll answer any and all questions when we get to a secure room. In the meantime, send for Chief Drake. I need to put his men on alert. Activate the Bubble, immediately."

The other Commissioners grumbled a mixture of shock and anger. "The Bubble? It's that serious? What have you done, you idiot?!" barked Doom.

"Enough!" yelled Shepard. "Adam, are you certain about this? The Bubble only has so much power. We've never fully activated it outside of periodic testing. It's meant to be activated in case of dire emergencies."

Adam turned to face Shepard. "The Bubble is completely within my jurisdiction, yes?" Shepard nodded. "Then, do it, and do it quickly. I'm taking no chances with those demons."

***

Minutes later, an all-encompassing, translucent barrier surrounded the entirety of Arabella. The Bubble, so named for its appearance, was

Adam's father's pet project. A small-scale version of a planetary shield designed to prevent aerial bombardment from space. This type of technology had long fallen out of style in modern military engagements during the Strife. Military strategy had evolved, shifting the interest towards holding and repurposing enemy infrastructure and away from outright destroying it. Not to mention the amount of raw power such defensive shields consumed made them economically infeasible. Rumors abounded that the Cauduun's energy weapons' research could eventually render such defenses obsolete. That said, taking down such defenses required intense firepower, which could leave the attacker vulnerable to counterattacks from the surface. Projectile, laser, and plasma weaponry were still the most common for the average foot soldier and starship. The mere presence of a shield was often deterrent enough against fleets more suited to attacking soft targets. Without the necessary firepower, a ground assault was needed to take down a target protected by shields.

It was Cloud's most controversial decision to push for the creation of the Bubble. Scarce resources were devoted to building the infrastructure necessary to sustain such a defense. Dozens of relay stations properly positioned around Arabella had to be built or, more often than not, stolen. Thousands of man hours went into scrounging enough generators to power the shield for longer than a few seconds, which was another struggle altogether. A problem they hadn't quite solved. The most readily available generators were solar-powered, some stolen, some bought, some donated. Unfortunately, Arabella was notoriously overcast all the damn time. The twin white suns hardly shone through the moon's thick, billowing clouds. Energy storage was not economically or practically possible for Arabella. Recharging the generators required smugglers to travel to remote, sunny parts of Bokor. These smugglers were sometimes caught, their generators confiscated. The Bubble required so much raw power. Other vital services within Arabella needed power to function, too. Diverting resources to the Bubble meant fewer resources to homes, the hospital, the school, et cetera. All for a questionable deterrent.

Needless to say, the Bubble's activation caused much consternation. Concerned voices resounded throughout the dense settlement. No one knew what was happening. The militiamen under Drake's command did their best to try and instill calm. The group of commissioners pushed their way through a gathering crowd, all shouting and demanding answers. Those shouts grew louder as people stared up into the sky. The Bokori fleet constantly patrolling the skies above grew to well over thirty ships, including a handful of the black Hisbaween saucers.

The commissioners arrived at their meeting room inside the cavern. Drake and a handful of militia guarded the door from a growing crowd of petitioners. They waited a few minutes for Auditore to return.

"John is going to live," Auditore said when Adam asked about John's condition. "He has several cracked ribs, a collapsed lung, and his spleen was partially ruptured. The surgeons are repairing him now. They'll give him more Naddine draughts for the internal bleeding and pain along with a Zokyon torso brace to keep his ribs from fracturing further. He'll need to take it easy for a half a month, but I expect him to make a full recovery." The entire room breathed a sigh of relief.

"Alright, that's out of the way. Commissioner Mortis, tell us what happened after you left the meeting," Shepard said. The other Commissioners sat in their usual seats with bated breath. Adam relayed them the events from what he saw in the hotel to their escape from the city. He didn't mention anything about Havera's title. Only that as a Praetorian, she was entitled to diplomatic immunity.

"You caught a lucky break with the Cauduun," Trissefer said a hint of sarcasm in her voice. She was shooting him a suspicious look almost like she knew he was holding information back. Being the Commissioner for History & Culture, Trissefer spent many hours with Havera going over Stepicro data. Maybe she knew more about Havera than she led on.

"Yes, it would seem so," Shepard said. "We'll have to extend her our further thanks for returning y'all safely and relatively unharmed."

"Enough about the Praetorian. How we can be so certain what John told you was the truth?" asked Doom skeptically.

"I've known John almost my entire life. We grew up together. He is the reason I have my freedom. He's never given me cause to disbelieve him. I saw Samus not long after the attack. She was traumatized. I saw enough signs of assault to confirm the story," Adam said.

"You aren't exactly an impartial party by your own admission," insisted Doom.

"What are you implying?" Adam asked resentfully. "That I helped John murder an innocent Bokori and helped him cover it up?"

"We need to ask, Adam," Shepard interjected. "The Bokori sent us a communique. They're claiming the victim was shot twice in the chest execution-style. That there was no sign of a struggle. To make matters worse, they're saying the victim was an undercover Hisbaween."

"Kewea's curse!" Adam swore.

No wonder the Hisbas were pursuing us so vigilantly. Sam was meeting with a Hisba. Did she know? Why did it attack her? Execution-style. Not possible. It was self-defense. The Hisbaween must be lying.

Adam was stunned into silence. More questions flashed into his mind. He kept replaying the scene over and over again in his head. The dead Bokori was laying there in a pool of its own blood. He tried to focus harder on the room. Samus' terrified face kept clouding his mind. He could only hear John's words. "*It was assaulting her!*"

Shepard's words cut through his thoughts. "You didn't happen to examine Samus while you were evaluating John did you, Hideo?" Shepard asked Auditore.

He shook his head. "I noticed a minor abrasion on her forehead, so I offered. She vehemently refused. Visually, I inspected her up and down. She had obvious bruise marks around her neck that could easily be from manual strangulation. It's impossible to conclude one way or another if she was attacked without a full physical examination. However, her reaction to my offer was more telling. She flinched when I took a step towards her. She struck one of the medical bots in a reflex when it bumped into her. If I had to give a medical opinion, I would say she experienced some sort of trauma. Again, without a more thorough physical and mental evaluation, I cannot say definitively."

"Thank you, Commissioner. This whole situation is a mess. The Hisbaween have demanded we turn the three of you over to them," Shepard said meaning him, John, and Samus.

"We can't do that," Trissefer insisted. "We'd never hear from them again. Not in a million years would they give them a fair trial. It's unconscionable. John is half dead, Samus is more than likely a victim, and Adam..." She couldn't get the words out.

Adam finished for her. "...is a mentally broken-down man more suited to therapy than leadership. It's alright. Y'all think it, I'm just saying it. The only reason I'm on this Commission is because of who my father was and the unfortunate circumstances I helped create for myself. I won't make the situation worse than it already is. I'll turn myself in if it'll help spare Arabella any hardship she'll face from the fallout of this incident."

Adam stood up to leave. "Where do you think you're going?" Adam expected it to be Trissefer, but it was Snake who spoke. "Do you think we went to all that trouble breaking you out the first time to let you walk right back into that viper's nest? You walk out that door and you unwittingly endorse every horrible ordeal they put you through. That they put us all through. After everything's that happened, we're not letting you give up now. Arabella - no, Humans everywhere need your voice. Like it or not, you are a beacon of hope. A living representation of resistance to the cultural regime the Bokori imposed upon us. You have done nothing wrong. We won't let the Bokori tell us otherwise."

"Here, here!" Trissefer affirmed. Auditore and Shepard nodded their heads. Even Doom affirmed his approval. Adam was moved. He struggled to find his words.

"I honestly don't know what to say. Thank you. All of you. We still have to deal with the problem at hand. What are we going to do about those ships hanging above our heads?"

"I have an idea on how we can handle the situation," Shepard said. "It's going to take time and careful diplomacy, but I think we can..."

The lights in the room shut off cutting off Shepard's words. "Nothing to worry about. Outages are to be expected while the Bubble is up."

Adam heard shouts coming from the other side of the door. The shouts turned to screams. He heard other noises, too.

Gunshots!

Adam didn't have time to react. The door to the meeting room blew open with a thunderous explosion, forcing Adam to brace himself against the wall. Instinctively, Adam shut his eyes and covered his ears. As he expected, a bright, ear-shattering explosion engulfed the room, blinding and deafening everyone within the interior. The sounds of laser blasts penetrated the ringing of the flashbang's explosion. Through the dimming light of the grenade, Adam saw them. The dark-winged shoulder pads, the black helms with white eye slivers, and the billowing cloaks like shadows in the night. The Hisbaween had come for him.

8

Combat Mode

Someone flipped the hexagonal table over to provide cover for the Commissioners. Adam couldn't reach the cover without exposing himself. A Hisba was firing into the room from just outside the door. He heard screams and cries of pain from behind the table, but he couldn't distinguish voices. His adrenaline was pumping too hard.

A Hisba attempted to enter the room, firing while it crossed the threshold. A fatal mistake. The bulky, ridiculous shoulder pads the Hisbas wore only allowed for one to enter at a time. They had to turn their bodies at an angle to enter the narrow, blown out doorway. The Hisba had its back towards Adam. Adam grabbed the edge of the winged shoulder pad and whipped the Hisba around, slamming the zealot into the wall with a crack! He seized the Hisba by helm and repeatedly smashed it against the wall until the Hisba stopped moving. Adam picked up the fallen Hisba's searstaff and jammed it into the side of another Hisba trying to enter the room. The Hisba screamed. Its uniform singed from the tip of the searstaff pressed into its torso. The Hisba's size and scream denoted it as a Bokori. Shots from a projectile weapon reverberated around the room as slugs struck the burning Hisba. It collapsed onto the ground dead.

Adam turned to see Shepard, Trissefer, and Snake with handguns drawn. Snake was clutching his leg and collapsed to the ground. Another Hisba breached the door, striking Trissefer in the shoulder with a laser blast. Enraged, Adam smacked the laser rifle out of the Hisba's hands and repeatedly struck the Hisba with the searstaff. The Hisba tried reaching for its own staff but was pinned in between the wall and Adam's onslaught. It couldn't reach the staff. Adam slammed the staff into the Hisba until it collapsed onto the floor. Adam could hear its whimpers. This one was Human. He reached down to raise the Hisba's visor. Adam saw the scars from modification on the Hisba's face. Its eyes altered to be vertically long.

"Modder scum!" Adam roared. He raised the burning tip of the staff. The Hisba tried to raise its hands, pleading. Adam drove the staff through the opening in the visor with all his strength. The Hisba's arms fell limp. He left the staff buried in the Hisba's face, only the sound of flesh sizzling emanated from its dead body.

Adam heard groaning from the other side of the table barricade. "Triss!" he called out. Adam wheeled around the table to see Auditore pressing a rag into Trissefer's shoulder. Shepard was tightening a makeshift tourniquet around Snake's thigh.

"It's nothing. I'm fine," insisted Trissefer.

"Quit moving or you'll tear open your shoulder further," Auditore said, pressing the rag harder into Triss' wound. Trissefer let out a little yelp of pain. Adam bent over to examine her.

"How is she?" Adam asked Auditore.

"Her shoulder is dinged up. She'll need stitches and ointment for the laser burns. Otherwise, she'll be fine. As long as she doesn't do anything stupid like trying to fight treatment!" Auditore emphasized that last part.

"It's only a flesh wound. I'll live," insisted Trissefer as she tried to stand. Adam pressed her lightly to remain still.

"Stay! Let the doctor treat you first. Lara, how's Snake?" Adam asked turning his attention to the other two.

"Through-and-through. No major arteries. Doom...wasn't as lucky."

Adam saw the old man prone on the ground, a smoking laser blast between his eyes. "Are you hurt?" Shepard asked. Adam shook his head.

"The Bokori didn't give us a chance to respond. They're already unleashing their monsters on us!" Trissefer yelled.

"They probably wanted to get the jump on us before we had the chance to prepare any defenses. The Bubble's activation forced their hand," said Auditore.

"Are you saying this is my fault?" asked Adam angrily.

"I'm saying they knew if they waited any longer, we'd be too far entrenched for them to take you and the Dark siblings by force," said Auditore.

"They weren't here to capture anything," said Snake, struggling to his feet. Shepard helped brace him against the wall. "Those weapons weren't on stun. This was a kill squad."

"Kewea's curse! Do you mean they have cancellation orders out on Adam?" asked Shepard.

"Not just Adam," Snake said, grimly gesturing to Doom's lifeless body. "They want to wipe out our entire political leadership. I fear each one of us has a cancellation order out on them."

"Kewea take them!" yelled Auditore. "How could they be this reckless? There are more than five-hundred thousand lives on this moon. Do they expect to kill us all?"

"Even the Bokori wouldn't go that far. Too many people watching. No, they want the biggest troublemakers gone with the hopes the rest of us will fall back into line," Shepard said.

An idea popped into Adam's head.

"We don't know that. They have just made the worst mistake imaginable. The Bokori have launched an unprovoked, unrestrained attack upon a peaceful Human settlement acting in self-defense. Who's to say genocide is not exactly what they're trying to do. We can use this. Please, please tell me one of the galactic news crews is still here."

"I think a reporter from Neutral Space Features Monthly is at the school, working on a piece about the living conditions here. They wanted to shoot some B-roll footage, I told them it was fine," Auditore said.

"So, they have a working camera and Nexus access?" asked Adam.

"I would assume so," Auditore said.

"Good." Adam picked up a pair of the dropped Hisba laser rifles and tossed one each to Shepard and Auditore. "Why don't you track them down and have them point the camera where we want. Feed them what we want them to hear. Maybe we can get the rest of the galaxy to give a damn. Lara, you stay here keep the others safe. I'll send some militia your way as backup."

"Where are you going?" asked Trissefer.

Adam picked up the final dropped laser rifle and confirmed the rifle was set to kill. "I'm going to get John and Sam."

***

He marched out into the cave, checking the corners. He saw several bodies on the ground, most were Human militia. Adam spotted one familiar Human body. His heart sunk. With his dagger sunk into the visor of a dead Hisba, Duke Drake lay motionless. Adam flipped his body over. His eyes stared straight up, lifeless. At least twenty smoking holes dotted his face and torso. It required that many shots to bring down the seasoned veteran. Adam slid Drake's eyelids down gently. He retrieved Drake's bloodied dagger and placed it on his chest, folding the chief's hands around the blade. "It's your turn to join our fallen brothers and sisters charging into the hells of Kewea. May Dasenor welcome your sword with open arms," Adam prayed. It was a warrior's prayer.

Two Hisba were standing sentry outside the cavern. They were waiting for their squadmates to emerge after they completed their cancellation orders. Instead, they received two laser blasts to the face courtesy of Adam. He charged into the panicked crowds. Auditore followed him out of the cavern and darted off in the opposite direction.

The situation was total chaos. A torrential downpour pounded the ground with high winds whipping the rain violently into Adam's face. It was hard to see exactly what was happening. He could see people running in all directions. Distant sounds of gunfire were barely audible over the wind. The Bubble prevented an aerial assault. It didn't prevent ground forces from entering nor did it stop the weather. There could be hundreds of Hisbas in the city.

He reached up to tap onto his HUD. He needed to get a communique out. He decided to compose a citywide notice under Commission authority. The Hisbaween would pick up on the notification, but he suspected it wouldn't matter. They were probably already at their intended targets. "Arabella is under attack by forces of the Hisbaween. Barricade your homes. All militia and any volunteers with arms report to the security station or the hospital. Assume anyone with a black helm and cloak has hostile intent. Cancellation orders have been issued on any Human the Hisbas encounter. What is lost will be found."

Adam came to a fork in the road. One way led to the security station, the other to the hospital. Adam didn't hesitate. Most militia would rush to defend the security station. John, still recovering from his wounds, was exposed. Sam would more than likely be with him. The hospital wasn't designed against an incursion.

On this day, Adam chose family over duty.

Two more Hisbas emerged from a side street, shooting at a few Humans who returned fire from around the corner. Adam dispatched the Hisbas with ease. "GO!" he yelled. The muddied, rain-soaked Humans rushed past him in the security station's direction. None of them were official militia. Today, every Human on Arabella was a militiaman. The streets were unusually empty. Most people were heeding Adam's warning and barricading their homes. He passed several frighten faces hunkering down, hugging each other for comfort too scared to move. He couldn't stop to help them; he couldn't stop to lead them. He needed to get to John and Sam.

He reached the block with the hospital building. Bodies of Humans and Hisba were scattered around the entrance to the three-story building. He rushed inside. He could hear a smattering of screams and gunfire deep within the building. The hospital was cobbled together from wings and parts from old alien hospitals and medical bays of decommissioned ships. It was one of Arabella's biggest buildings. The

Darks could be anywhere. Grimly, he followed the sounds of battle. If there was still fighting, he must be still alive.

I hope Sam isn't hurt. She'll go down fighting if anyone tries to harm her brother.

Adam tapped on his HUD and switched the display to combat mode. It had been a while since he'd done this. Several years in fact. Combat mode cleared up the UI in his HUD and displayed only critically necessary information. His vitals were displayed in the top-left, a mini-map of the immediate surrounding area in the bottom-left, and ammo readout for his current weapon in the bottom-right. The top-right he reserved for distance to waypoint, which currently was blank since he had no definitive location on John or Sam.

It was fortunate he switched to combat mode. He realized his scavenged current weapon was near its overheating point. The standard-issue Hisbaween laser rifle, Cultural Justice, like all laser weapons, had no physical ammo. They relied on an internal power core that converted volatile gases into laser beams fired in rapid succession. Deadly against flesh. Behind projectile firearms, laser weapons were the galaxy's most common. The drawback was laser weapons were prone to overheating, especially guns forged from cheap steel like the Cultural Justice. If a laser weapon overheated, it needed time to cool, otherwise the gun was prone to melting or even exploding. They also had a difficult time penetrating armor or shields. Unfortunately for Adam, he possessed neither. The Hisbaween wore armor too thin to be effective against laser weapons. They valued intimidation, speed, and swiftness over a sturdy defense. It was however resistant to projectile weapons, the bulk of Arabella's weapons stockpile. He was worried for the security station. The electricity was still on, so the Hisbas couldn't have taken it. Adam hoped their sheer numbers would be enough to repulse the invaders with no idea the number of attacking Hisbas.

He reached a station desk. Hiding behind it were a pair of clerks and a nurse. The nurse was attending to a badly wounded security guard. They yelped when they saw Adam until they recognized him.

"Commissioner, what's going on?! Why are the Hisbas attacking us?!" asked one of the frightened clerks. She was a Human around Sam's age.

"I'm here for John Dark. Where is he?" He didn't have time to comfort them.

"Re...recovery Room F, other side of the first floor," the clerk stuttered.

"Do any of y'all have a weapon?" Adam asked. His everyday sidearm only had sixteen rounds. Not enough if got into a protracted fight.

"Wally did," she said gesturing to the wounded guard. "They shot him without warning. Are we going to be okay?"

Adam took a deep breath. "Wait right here, don't move. Reinforcements should be coming any minute. Take this," Adam said as he handed her the rifle. "It's close to overheating. You probably only have one good burst until it's depleted. Give me Wally's gun and transfer me your local map data while you're at it. I need the exact layout of the hospital." The clerk squeaked. She scooped up Wally's gun and handed it to Adam. She frantically tapped the air in front of her. Adam heard a beep and checked his mini-map. He had a complete layout of the hospital with rooms labeled. He found Recovery Room F and set his waypoint. It was only a few hundred feet away. "Thank you. Be safe. What is lost will be found," Adam said.

"What is lost will be found," the others repeated.

Adam cycled to his inventory on his HUD. He selected his personal sidearm, an old pre-Strife era Bokori semi-automatic pistol. Its grip was a bit small for his larger Human hands, but Adam liked its simple, economical design. Probably the only piece of Bokori tech he liked. He selected the gun from his inventory. In an instant, the gun materialized in his right hand. The guard's gun in his left hand was a long-barreled concussion pistol, most likely Moan in design, converted to use projectiles. It was in rough shape. He glanced at the weapon's information on his HUD.

MP-190 Bayonet model. Condition is poor. Only 7 rounds?!

Adam sighed. It was better than nothing. He checked his vitals. His heart rate was elevated but steady. It was never combat that induced his anxiety. He had a knack for keeping calm during a firefight. It was the stresses of civilian life that gave Adam grief. Up until this point, his only combat experience was fighting pirates on the eastern reaches of Bokori space. Despite whom he was facing, he did not flinch. Perhaps with a weapon in hand, he felt better about confronting the disciples of the High Hisba. Both weapons raised, he rushed deeper into the hospital. His HUD generated a flashing blue line on the ground to guide him to his waypoint. The map information he obtained aided the waypoint's pathing. Without precise coordinates, waypoints could only give a general direction.

He reached a corner and peeked around it. No one in sight. Recovery Room F was at the end of this hall and around another corner to the right. His mini-map indicated a handful of life signs in the various side rooms on either side of the hall. Without proper attunement data, it was impossible to tell friend from foe. He listened for sounds of battle. He didn't hear any gunshots, rather distant shouts. No time to search all the rooms thoroughly for Hisbaween, he chanced it.

They have to be closing in on John and Samus.

He rushed forward swiftly towards the end of the corridor. Thankfully, if any Hisbaween were in any of the side rooms, they didn't notice him. Pressing himself against the wall, he poked his head around the next corner. The shouts turned into grunts and screams. Adam rounded the corner. As soon as he did, a body crashed through thin plastered wall and landed at Adam's feet. It was a Hisba. Its chest was completely caved in.

What in Kewea?

Adam peered through the hole in the wall. It led into Recovery Room F. Adam stood there, mouth agape at what he was witnessing. Positioning herself between three Hisbas and Samus was Havera. The platinum bracers Havera wore were glowing with a faint violet light. She held up her arms in a defensive posture. Her fists glowed in the same manner as her bracers. The three Hisbas twirled their double-bladed searstaffs, taunting the Cauduun. Two of them were unhelmed. Both were Bokori. Another Hisba was dead at their feet. The room was cramped. Not much space for maneuverability. Samus was guarding what Adam presumed to be John's bed. No one noticed his arrival.

Adam whistled at them. Two of the Hisbas turned to the source of the whistle. Havera used the distraction to seize the nearest Hisba by its searstaff, pulling it close to her. She caved in her adversary's helm with one backhanded punch, crumpling the combatant to the ground. The violet glow of her bracer flashed brighter on impact. Adam shot at the closest Hisba, who lunged at him with his searstaff. The bullet impacted, causing the Hisba to stumble. Adam tried to fire the Bayonet handgun, but it jammed. Adam tossed it angrily aside as his foe closed the distance. The Hisba struck Adam in his right hand, disarming him. Its searstaff glowed orange from the heat. Swinging the staff wildly, Adam dodged each slash. Adam seized the staff's center grip. Using his momentum to fall backwards, Adam launched the Hisba over his head into the wall behind him. Adam stood up and slashed the tip of the staff at his foe's helm, knocking it out cold.

He turned around to see what was happening with Havera. The remaining Hisba was trying to pierce Havera's defenses with stab after stab, slash after slash. Havera used her glowing bracers to parry each thrust seemingly with ease. Her expression was focused. She was in full control. She slammed down on her opponent's staff, snapping it half. The Hisba stumbled backwards. Havera strode towards it. It put his hands up in a fruitless effort to defend itself. With one swing of her tail, she knocked off the Hisba's helm, sending it crashing into the nearby wall. It was Human. With a second swing of her tail, she wrapped it around the helpless, unprotected Hisba's neck. She squeezed tightly as the Hisba desperately tried to pull the tail off its throat. Havera lifted it a couple feet off the ground, and with a slight twitch of her tail, she broke the Hisba's neck with a loud CRACK! She loosened her tail's grip, dropping its lifeless body to the ground. The glow on her bracers dimmed.

Adam dropped the searstaff he was holding in disbelief. *Warrior monk indeed;* Adam thought, remembering what John had said. Havera wiped the sweat from her brow, breathing heavily.

"I've never met a history nerd who could do that," Adam said.

Havera ran her fingers through her hair and smirked at him. "How many history nerds do you know besides me?"

Adam walked up to her. "You and I are going to have a conversation later," Adam said a determined look in his eye.

Havera nodded. "I imagine you have a ton of questions, but we have to get your friends out of here."

"Adam!" Sam pushed past Havera and wrapped Adam in a tight hug. "Havera saved us. She wanted to check up on me and John when those demons attacked. She took them out like they were nothing."

"I noticed. How are you? What's John's condition?" Adam asked.

"He's stable. They just brought him to recovery when we were attacked. I can't believe what's happening. I mean we only scarcely returned home and they...LOOK OUT!"

Adam turned to see the Hisba he thought he had knocked out sitting up against the wall. Its tightly clutched laser rifle was pointed at them. Adam twisted his body to shield Sam. He felt a sudden rush of air followed by the sound of a laser blast. He expected to feel pain; none came. He turned back around to see Havera holding up her bracer, glowing brightly again, between him and the Hisba. He saw beyond her that the Hisba was dead. A smoking laser blast in its forehead. He put two-and-two together.

"You deflected it! Right back at it! What else can those things do?" Adam asked, pointing to Havera's platinum bracers dimming once more.

"I'll explain later. First, let's get y'all out of here," Havera said.

"Right. Let's go," Adam said.

They heard loud running footsteps approaching their room. Adam and Sam picked up searstaffs and Havera reignited her bracers, waiting for whomever was around the corner. To their relief, they recognized them.

"Shepard! What are you doing here?" Adam asked. She wasn't alone. Limping near her were Trissefer and Snake, both bleeding through their bandages. Behind them were at least two dozen militia and armed volunteers, wet and muddy.

"Did you really think we were going to wait in that cave?" Trissefer asked sarcastically. She glanced past Adam and Samus to see Havera, her bracers dimmed once more. "Havera, is that you? What are you doing here?"

Adam answered. "She's here to help." He gestured to the bodies of the dead Hisbaween all around them. Havera suppressed a smile, embarrassed. She lowered her gaze to the floor, running her fingers through her hair. The group of Humans all seemed impressed.

"Your message worked," Shepard said stepping forward. "The Hisbaween attacked the security station in force. They almost broke through until hundreds of armed reinforcements showed up. They scattered once they realized they were outgunned. Unfortunately, many good people died defending the station. Some of the generators were damaged, too. The Bubble is intact, but I don't know how long we can keep them operating."

Adam bowed his head. *If I had gone to the security station like I should've, I would've been able to save more. Havera was here. She didn't need me.* Shepard patted him on the shoulder. "We did the best we could. No one could've seen this coming," she said, reassuring him almost like she could read his thoughts. Shepard spotted something next to him. "Wait a moment, I recognize that Hisba!" Shepard bent over to examine the dead Human Hisba. "Yes, his name is Logan. He's a sanitation engineer. He was helping us with our plumbing issues. What's he doing in a Hisba uniform?"

"Trying to kill me," a hoarse voice called out. John Dark was struggling to his feet. Adam and Sam rushed over to brace him. They helped lift him out of bed. "We have infiltrators," John said wincing through his post-op pain. Worried murmurs erupted from the crowd, each person giving the nearest person a suspicious glance over. Adam and Sam eased John into a nearby wheelchair. "Drake was going to brief you, Adam.

We've long suspected the Bokori and/or the Hisbaween planted spies and infiltrators in our midst to try and gather intelligence on our weak spots. Hit us when and where we're most vulnerable." Adam couldn't help but notice he shot a sideways glance at Havera. If Havera noticed, she didn't acknowledge it.

"John, Drake is dead," Adam said solemnly. John hung his head. He knew the news would devastate him. It was best to get it out of the way sooner rather than later.

John took a deep breath. "If that's the case, the chain of command dictates I am next in line for Chief of Internal Security," he said without missing a beat. Adam looked to Shepard, who nodded her approval.

"Seems you were right, Commissioner. They tried to cut off the head of the snake and the body for good measure. We've no other reports of Hisbaween movement beyond the Commission chambers, the security station, and here. We're safe now," Shepard said.

"We're far from safe, Commissioner," John said with authority. "Logan here cannot be the only infiltrator, and we have not confirmed all the Hisbas are dead or have fled. We must capture one if we can. We need to check every home."

Samus gasped. "Adam, if they were going for you, there's one other place they might be. Your home!" she said.

Adam grasped her words. Panic set in.

"Mom!"

9

Consider This a Declaration

All Adam heard was ringing. The blood pounded through his veins.

How could I be so stupid?!

It never occurred to Adam to check in at home. He was so focused on John and Sam. They had already attacked him at the cavern. The threat to his person was over. Why would they attack his home? How would they know where he lived?

"We have infiltrators." Kewea take the Hisbaween!

Adam shoved his way through the crowd in the hospital, sprinting at full speed. He ignored all call outs. He ran faster than he ever had in his life, faster than the day he escaped rehab. He had to reach home. The wind had stopped howling. Only a steady downpour remained.

He tapped on his HUD and filtered through his contacts. He tried calling his brother. "Aaron, pick up! Aaron. Aaron!" No answer. He tried his mother next. "Mom! Mom, please answer. Mom!" Again, no answer. He howled in frustration. "GAH! No, no, no, no. I will kill every last one of them, I swear it!" His yells startled a few people, who had poked their heads up to see what was going on. He slipped rounding a corner, falling flat on his face. A couple militia tried helping him to his feet, but he shoved them aside. He was covered in sweat, mud, and fear. He scrambled up and dashed towards his home's block. He wanted desperately to puke. He forced the bile back down his throat. His breathing labored. He was having an anxiety attack, yet, ironically, his panicked mind kept his body from overreacting.

He reached his housing block. A crowd of people were gathered near his home. The unexpected congregation compelled him to stop. His momentum carried him forward a bit through the slick ground. He wiped the mud from his face.

Adam heard screaming followed by the sound of bone on flesh. He pushed his way through the crowd. They parted once they realized he was there. In front of his house, two militia were restraining a captured Hisba. Adam's mother, Morrigan, was wailing. She was smashing her fists into the Hisba's face, screaming with each punch. She was putting her full weight into each punch. Adam rushed to his mother. The Hisba was beaten to a pulp. It was coughing and spitting up blood. Morrigan kept hitting the Hisba again and again and again.

"Mom! Mom! Enough!" Adam said, grabbing his mother. Her hand was noticeably broken. She seemed not to have felt it. She resisted Adam's attempts to hold her until she saw his face. Tears were streaming down her cheeks, visible even in the rain. She fell to her knees crying. Adam bent down to embrace her. The reason for her distress became evident. The door to the house was broken down. Inside, he saw him. Aaron was flat on his back, unmoving. He crawled through the mud and shattered metal until he reached his brother. He was alive. Barely. Auditore was tending to him, but Adam absorbed the reality quickly. Aaron had several smoking holes littering his body. Blood was seeping out of each wound. He was coughing up more blood every second. Auditore noticed Adam's arrival. They locked eyes. The doctor could only shake his head. He stood up to give the brothers some final privacy.

Adam cradled Aaron's head in his arms. His brother smiled at him. "So...this is what it takes...to get you to show up...hehe." His laughter became coughing in an instant. Adam wiped away the blood from his mouth. He pressed his forehead into brother's.

"I'm sorry," Adam tried to say. Aaron only shushed him.

"Don't...apologize. I don't want...any more...apologies from you.

We've spent...far too much time...apologizing," Aaron said, choking through his words. With every last ounce of strength, Aaron lifted his hand and placed an object in Adam's hand. Adam recognized it immediately. "Always remember. Never forget...what you are...where you come from...what you represent...remember..." Aaron's eyes rolled back into his head. His hand collapsed onto his body. He was gone.

"I will. I promise," Adam said crying. He rested his brother's head gently onto the ground and slid his eyelids down. He leaned over and kissed his brother's forehead. Morrigan wailed. It was all Adam heard. His mother's cries of grief pierced his numb body to its core.

He felt nothing, at first. His body dared not betray him at this moment. It too was frightened of what was burgeoning. Through his numbness, he felt something stir inside him. A seed sprouted from the depths of his soul, germinating into spores that filled his entire body with rage. He was shaking. He stood up slowly. He refused to make eye contact with anyone. Through his madness, he locked onto the bloodied Hisba held by the crowd. His gaze met the captive's. It was a Modder. It had unnaturally gray skin, hairless, and its eyes has been altered to be vertical. He had seen eyes like those many times. He focused on one set of eyes in particular and let his rage seize his anxiety-riddled body. He felt calm. He felt relaxed. He knew what he needed to do.

"Auditore, where is that reporter you mentioned?" Adam asked the Commissioner, not removing the Hisba from his sight.

"Adam, I'm sorry..." he tried to say.

"Where?!" Adam yelled. It was a command.

Auditore gulped. "She and her cameraman are over at the security station shooting footage of the attack there. They captured all of it, Adam. We won't let the galaxy sweep this crime under the rug."

"Oh, you're more right than you know, doctor. Fetch them. Bring them to Arabella's statue. We're going to show them something the galaxy will never forget. Bring the Modder scum!" Adam ordered the militia loud enough so everyone within a block could hear. Adam snapped his fingers at a pair of nearby militiamen standing around. "Guard my brother's body. No one. NO ONE is to go near him other than my mother, do y'all understand?" The two militiamen nodded. One of them, a female he recognized, gave a hurried heart salute and rushed to the doorway to stand sentry.

The crowd jeered. They were agitated, shouting insults and tossing scooped up bits of mud and other debris at the captive Hisba. Adam did nothing to stop them. The militia were dragging the helpless Modder towards the town center. Adam couldn't think of a more appropriate place for what needed to be done. His heart was racing. It wasn't anxiety or fear he felt though. It was excitement.

Why shouldn't I feel this way?

Adam tried not to squeeze the object in his hand too hard. It wasn't time, yet. The galaxy would see soon. *They will be reminded that humanity is not to be crossed. We will show them what exactly Humans are capable of. The galaxy owes us an eternal debt. We saved everyone from the Xizor, and the thanks we got was destruction of our homeworld. Enslavement by another name. The Apocalypse and the Covenant. Now is the time to collect.*

They reached the city's center. *Arabella stands taller today;* Adam thought, staring up at the bronze statue. Adam spotted two non-Humans, the reporters, he assumed. An attractive green and gold-striped female with swooped golden blonde hair was fluttering her tiny, translucent wings to keep her from touching the muddy ground. She was a Bubil, the insect race from the Omega spiral at the southern edge of the galaxy. Her cameraman was a Faeleon, the bipedal chameleon-like species from the same part of the galaxy, southeast of Zokyon space. The Faeleon matched his species' namesake by doing his best to blend in with his surroundings. The expression on his face was abundantly clear; he wanted to be far away from here.

I don't blame you, buddy. First, you will do our bidding.

"You're the reporter from Neutral Space Faces Monthly?" Adam asked dismissively.

"*Features* Monthly, yes. Amezila Touzzant, Bokori desk. This is my cameraman, Raeko Roeko," the Bubil said. The Faeleon nodded meekly.

"Where's your camera?" Adam asked, noting out the lack of equipment. They both wore indigo business tunics in the Cauduun style.

She was wearing a matching thick linen palla over her tunic that was wrapped around her waist and under her wings to keep her dry in the rain.

"Oh, we don't use a physical camera. We use the latest UI camera hooked up to our internal HUD. With the pinch of my forefingers, I stretch out a box in my display to capture images and video," Roeko said.

"Fascinating," Adam said dryly. He was becoming impatient. He was vaguely aware of the multitude of plugins to the UI System, but he never cared to try any of them out. Too expensive. "Can you livestream using it?"

The cameraman hesitated. "I could..."

The Bubil cut in. "We'd need approval from higher ups to stream directly to our subscriber base unedited and unfiltered."

Adam got right up in her face. The buzzing of her wings increased nervously. Adam smiled, which he thought only exacerbated her nerves. "Consider it a favor to the Human race. Trust me, you won't regret it," Adam insisted.

The thousands of lenses in the Bubil's five oversized compound eyes fluttered. She realized she was surrounded by hundreds of Humans, most of whom were armed to the teeth and pissed off. She acquiesced.

"Good! Make sure to get the statue in frame. Let me know when you're live." Adam said, turning his back to them and walking away. He snapped his fingers at the two militiamen holding the captive Hisba. They bound its hands behind its back with rope along the way. They dragged it to the area right next to the fountain in front of the statue, forcing it to his knees. The Hisba was beaten so badly it could barely keep its left eye open. Adam felt nothing for it. He bent over a whispered to the Hisba. "Anything you want to say to me, now is the time."

The Hisba only stared. Adam cocked his head. He noticed some scarring around the Modder's mouth. He snapped for the two militiamen to return. "Force his mouth open. I want to see something," Adam said. They did as ordered, avoiding its attempts to bite their fingers off. As Adam suspected, its tongue was gone.

"You've had your tongue removed, so you wouldn't be forced to utter blasphemy. The perversions with which the Bokori warped your mind. You hate yourself so much you'd cut out your own tongue. Modder scum!" Adam yelled loud enough for the crowd to hear. He punched the Hisba hard with his right hand. He held the item firmly in his left. Adam heard the Bubil recoil. "Are we live, yet?!" Adam screamed at her.

"Give us a few more seconds. What are you going to do?" she asked hesitantly.

"Justice. True justice. Not the pseudo-justice the Bokori ramble about. They've inflicted their will on us for over five-hundred years. Today, we take the first step to regaining our free will," Adam snarled.

The crowd around the statue swelled into the thousands. Word spread like wildfire. Nearly every Human on Arabella was clustered together in the blocks surrounding the town center. The mood was eerily quiet. Hushed whispers permeated the crowd. Adam and the captive were given a wide berth. No one dared interfere.

The Bubil gave Adam a signal. The Faeleon had his fingers in pinching gesture stretched out in front of his face. They were live. Adam cleared his throat. His heartbeat was slow, as if only waking up from a deep sleep. He was strangely calm. His body would not betray him.

"Today, the Bokori committed a horrifying atrocity against the Human race. One of our own was the victim of a vicious crime committed by one of their kind. Rather than help, the Bokori issued an arrest warrant condemning the victim for the 'crime' of self-defense. As any reasonable sentient would do, they fled towards home, where they felt safe. Except, the Bokori made it abundantly clear nowhere is safe for Humans. They have trapped us like rats, slowly suffocating us under the weight of their own self-righteousness. Now, they've tried to drown us in blood. You will see footage courtesy of this network that shows in vivid, gruesome detail exactly what lengths the Bokori and their Modder-enabling allies will do to suppress the Human spirit. Scores of innocent lay dead at the hands of these grayskin tyrants. Though, they are too cowardly to do it themselves, so they sound their rabid dogs to do their dirty work," Adam said, grabbing the Hisba by its shoulder pad. "You will no longer ignore us. It is time we Humans remind y'all just exactly of what we can do."

With the flick of his left wrist, he squeezed the grip of the Debbie. The crowd gasped. The Bubil's five eyes widened. Even the Faeleon peered around his hands to get a better look. An icy substance crystallized from the edges of the padded platinum and stainless-steel grip. The crystal formed into that of a crescent moon, wrapping around Adam's hand. It glistened brightly in the dull, gray filter of Windless Tornado. A cloud of vapor danced around its crystalline form, hugging the weapon like two lovers wrapped around each other in bliss. A beautiful piece of Human technology. The Debbie felt cold in his grip. Much colder than he'd been expecting. He squeezed the grip again. A swirling mass of black energy formed at the muzzle until it was a size slightly larger than a Human fist.

Adam's eyes darted about the crowd. The other Commissioners were wide eyed, waiting with bated breath. Trissefer was speechless and afraid. He found his family. His mother, stony-faced, lip quivering, nodded. In his wheelchair, John nodded, too. Sam couldn't watch. She buried her face into Havera's shoulder, who was hugging her tightly with her tail. He met the Cauduun's amethyst eyes. They were...sad. She shook her head. She didn't want him to do it. She begged him not to using only her eyes. For a moment, Adam's resolve faltered. He was about to lower the weapon when he felt a pulse. Not his own pulse. It was coming from the weapon. The white crystal was emanating a subtle, reddish glow beneath its icy form. He closed his eyes, concentrating on the weapon's energy. He thought he heard a voice in the back of his head. It was whispering something to him, but he couldn't discern its meaning. The voice was...familiar. He opened his eyes. The black energy had lines of blood red mixed in its swirling form. His resolved hardened.

"What is lost will be found. We will be the ones to find it. To the Bokori, consider this a declaration of independence!"

He released the ball of energy. It struck the Hisba soundlessly, dissipating while enveloping the Hisba's body. The Hisba didn't crumple over right away. Instead, it hardly moved. Adam watched the expression of the Hisba's face change excruciatingly slow from defiant to horrified. Its eyes widened to the point Adam thought they would pop out of its head. The verticality of the Modder's eyes unnerved Adam further. He realized its entire body was moving slowly. It was collapsing to the ground, but at an unnaturally decelerated rate. He thought it was his mind playing tricks on him, yet he glanced around. Everyone else was moving at normal speed, including himself. Most with shocked expressions on their faces. No one else knew what to make of what was happening. Streaks of black and red fully engulfed the Hisba's body. Its eyes rolled up into its head. For several seconds, the body remained in suspended animation, slowly collapsing to the ground. It lagged compared to the movement of everything around it, including the rain. After several seconds, the body finally touched the ground. The noise it produced sounded like a loud, wet thud, completely disconnected with what Adam was seeing. The body disintegrated in front of his eyes. The soft breeze and the rain washed the particles away, leaving behind only the bloodied uniform of the Hisba. Adam held the Debbie aloft, staring at its majestic form.

What is this technology? What did our ancestors create?

He signaled to the reporters to cut the feed. It was clear they weren't going to turn away now. The Faeleon kept its camera hands trained on Adam. This was a once in a lifetime moment. Adam's eyes found Havera's. They were full of disappointment and sadness. Without a word, he pushed through the crowd. It was easy. Everyone was taking a few steps back as he waded through the mass of people. Eventually, what seemed like hours later, he reached the end of the rows of people. The Debbie was still active in his hand. He stared at it the entire time. The calm he had felt earlier was gone. His body reminded him he was only Human. The scars on his back itched painfully. He found the closest empty alley and retched.

10

Suicide Pact

"Are you out of your damn skull?! What was that little performance back there? You've screwed us all over with your rash actions! The meeting, your little excursion into Bokor, executing a prisoner for everyone in the galaxy to see. You've doomed us all!"

"Why don't we ask Doom how he feels about it?"

"This is no laughing matter, Quinn! Mortis loudly declared Humans were an independent race on livestream to the entire goddess-damn galaxy, then blasted a kneeling, beaten, unarmed man using a highly covetous piece of Human technology!"

"Modders are no men, Consul."

"Enough of your notions, Dark. Your narrow-minded point-of-view helped push us to this point. Not to mention your loose trigger finger."

"He was defending his sister!"

"So, he claims. The Bokori say differently, and it sounds like they can prove it."

"Manufactured dribble! Whose side are you on?"

"The side that doesn't get us blown to Kewea!"

Adam sat there with his mouth buried in hands. He wasn't listening to the argument bouncing around him. It was all background noise to him. Despite the cramped space, everyone was giving Adam a wide berth. Some were angry; most were scared. The Debbie was set out on the table in front of Adam. Mists twirling around the weapon's icy crystal form. Adam's eyes were fixed upon it.

The body vanished into dust. Completely obliterated. The expression on the Hisba's face. What was it trying to say?

The hexagonal table inside the Commission meeting room was back upright. About twenty or so people crowded into the small space. It was standing room only. All the remaining Commissioners were there. John was sitting between two armed militiamen in his wheelchair, visibly pained both by the discussion and from post-op. A few of the consuls that operated the fledgling Human industries in Arabella were there. They were business leaders who had carefully crafted under-the-table supply lines in agriculture, construction, health care, logging, food, education, and waste management to name a few. All businesses in Arabella were small businesses, and they were incredibly sensitive to any upheaval in the delicate political situation between Humans and Bokori. Adam had effectively tossed a grenade into their operations.

"We located the Hisbaween's drop pods in the jungle. Three squad pods in total, which means they air dropped at about forty-five Hisbas on us. The militia so far has counted only thirty-nine bodies of those night demons. Since there are no Bokori in Arabella and nobody saw a drop pod take off, we must assume the remaining Hisbas removed their uniforms to blend in with the rest of the Human population. This Logan traitor that tried to kill me and my sister wasn't the only confirmed infiltrator. At least four of the bodies we've collected are known to be residents of Arabella. Combine those with the drop pods, we're talking about a dozen Hisbaween operatives in the city hidden amongst us. With Commissioner Mortis' approval, I've ordered the militia to reinforce important infrastructure and conduct a sweep. We'll root out those weeds," John said. The mention of his name did nothing to stir Adam.

Is this why the Bokori wanted humanity so badly?

"In the meantime," John brushed past the momentary awkward silence. "We need to be careful. Anyone could be a Hisba infiltrator.

Quite frankly, I don't trust half the people in this room. I'm tempted to order everyone here strip to search for signs of modification."

"Keep dreaming, Commander," said Auditore. "Besides, it probably won't do us much good. I examined Logan and a couple of the other infiltrator bodies myself. Not one sign of modification. None. It seems the Hisbaween have recruited unmodded Humans to carry out their dirty work."

"Pure Humans, Commissioner, and it's Chief," John corrected him. "If that's the case, those demons are craftier than we've given them credit. We must be as equally vigilant if we are to suss out the threat to Human sovereignty."

"Equally vigilant how?" Shepard asked.

"I'm formulating plans. I must speak with Commissioner Mortis about what contingencies and protocols we should implement to prevent secondary and insurgent attacks." Again, Adam remained unmoved.

Are we the monsters? Am I?

A few people took note of Adam's thousand-yard stare. Trissefer especially was eyeing him up-and-down. No one interrupted his thoughts. Their eyes flashed back-and-forth between Adam and the weapon.

"Ellie, what's the greater galaxy saying about what happened?" Shepard asked a middle-aged sandy-haired woman standing next to Auditore.

Ellie Blade activated her portable emulator and read brief snippets of the various statements. "The reaction, you can probably guess, is fervent. Most of the Proprietor powers have issued statements condemning the, umm, execution, while they've expressed only moderate disappointment at the Bokori incursion. If they are commenting on the independence issue, it's to denounce the unilateral, illegal declaration, at worst, or ignore it entirely, at best."

Consul Blade ran what could be considered the only operational news organization in Arabella. Her company, Arabella Tomorrow, mostly consisted of town criers spreading the galactic news to the people via word of mouth. What little galactic news they were able to get with the Bokori throttling of the Nexus, the interconnected galactic computer and digital data networks. Her company developed custom emulators and computer terminals that were decent enough at circumventing the Bokori firewall. Bokori hacking and the amount of processing power needed to operate the emulators meant Arabella could only realistically obtain half-monthly news updates and usually only major headlines. Shepard had Blade keep the emulators running all night to monitor the galactic response.

Blade continued. "The Cauduun Monarchical Alliance said, 'Human rights and responsibilities is a topic worthy of discussion by the Proprietor races and the Conclave as a whole; however, no such discussions should occur at the barrel of a gun.' The Zokyon Technocracy is calling for cooler heads to prevail. The Naddine Confederacy stated, 'With the galaxy still reeling from devastating conflict, it is the hope of all Naddine and our Techoxtl partners that peace prevail.' The Union, of course, has no comment on the internal affairs of organics. Even the Sinners are demurring on the independence issue; although, they issued a strong condemnation against the Bokori attack. The Conclave called for an immediate ceasefire and for both sides to meet at the negotiating table to resolve what they're deeming 'the Human question.' The other individual galactic governments issued similarly worded statements. The online chatter is another story entirely."

"What do you mean?" asked Trissefer.

"Humans are trending, obviously. There are increased searches about Human independence, the Bokori-Human Covenant, Arabella, the Hisbaween, the Saptia Accords, the Violet Man incident. Many stories are also focusing on Commissioner Mortis. A LOT of stories. Articles and opinion pieces are tying the incident back to the leaked stadium footage of the, umm, scourging. They're overwhelmingly positive in our favor. Many are condemning the violence but calls for abolishing the Covenant are rampant. Our cause is spreading. I think we underestimated just how much the average sentient seems to hate the Bokori," said Blade astonished.

John sniggered his approval. "The Saptia Accords, eh? Good to see the galaxy is remembering the broken promises from Saptia. They've realized there is a price for betrayal," John said.

Adam's ears perked up. John's words pulled his gaze from the Debbie. He knew to what John was referring. He had heard his mother and brother talk about it often enough. "Promises were made. Promises were broken!" his mother would oft say during one of their heated discussions. Never around their dad though. It dredged up painful memories for him.

Dad never did like to talk about it. He thought it was his greatest failure. No, his second greatest.

He remembered Doom's words. They were the old man's kind attempt at reconciliation, and he had more or less spat in his face. He was dead along with any hopes of Human-Bokori reconciliation. His eyes met John's. He could feel his friend steeling his own resolve.

I didn't fire the first shot. They did.

"What's done is done," Adam found his voice. He needed to sound resolute. More so than at his father's funeral. "The galaxy is fully aware we will no longer take the abuse of the Bokori lying down. As far as I am concerned, the Covenant is dead. The Bokori killed it with their reckless, unprovoked aggression. The Covenant should never have existed in the first place, but that's a whole other matter. We shall make up for lost time starting today. Humanity is once again an independent race." Adam stood up. He grabbed the Debbie, decrystallized it, and pocketed it. A few people closer to him took a step back, cramping the already packed room even further. "Anyone who doesn't like the decision is free to leave. I'm sure the Bokori will treat every Human from Arabella who surrenders with dignity and respect," Adam said sarcastically. "If you don't think they already have rehabilitation cells with our names on it, you're deluding yourself. And if you think it'll be our Human names above those cells, well, you're living in a straight up fantasy. I won't stop you. John won't stop you. No one will stop you if you want to abandon the Separatist cause. Any family you leave behind will be well taken care of. Y'all go on. Get."

Nobody moved. Everyone watched everyone else for any sign of movement. Most shuffled their feet or scratched themselves. A few coughs broke the stillness in the air. Adam's eyes met each person in the room. Some avoiding his gaze. Some nodded their approval. Trissefer looked as if she wanted to jump him right in front of everyone. John did, too. Shepard rolled her eyes. She sighed. To no one's surprise, least of all Adam's, she spoke up first.

"You've signed us all up for a suicide pact, and you know it," Shepard said.

All eyes darted back-and-forth from him to Shepard. Adam respected her for saying so. He had no ill will towards the woman. She was saying what many were thinking. Adam hoped she understood what he needed to do next. He drew the Debbie from his pocket. A few audibly gasped when he did. Adam ignored them. Shepard didn't flinch. Adam smiled. He crystallized it, placed the weapon on the table, and slid it towards her. Her eyes flickered at the icy gun in front of her.

"Pick it up, Commissioner," Adam said.

Shepard kept her eyes focused on Adam. Everyone held their collective breaths, waiting. Without breaking eye contact, she reached down and picked up the weapon. She blinked, shifting her gaze to the crescent-shaped, icy gun in her grasp. She slowly inspected each part of the Debbie.

"It's cold," she finally said.

"Yes, it is," Adam replied.

The two commissioners kept their focus on each other. A mental battle raged only in the fires of their eyes. Beads of sweat moistened their brows. The air was still. The drums of Human heartbeats packed into the room created a frenetic rhythm. Some of the militiamen inched closer to their own weapons, only to be shot down with venomous glares. Spines shivered at the slightest shift.

Shepard broke. "What am I supposed to do with this?" she asked.

Adam smiled. *I win;* he thought. "I suppose you only have two choices, Commissioner Shepard. Either you can point that ancient artifact at me, shoot me, and hope the Bokori smile upon your 'loyalist' act, or..." Adam left the second suggestion unspoken; he inclined his head at her instead. It was best left unspoken. Strangely, Adam's heart was calm, his breathing steady. He felt in absolute control. He knew what Shepard was going to do before she did. Whether everyone else present liked it or not, they had no choice. They were with him.

Shepard put the gun down and wordlessly slid it back to Adam. She would live to fight another day. Adam nodded. He reclaimed his heirloom and decrystallized it. The breath from the collective sigh of relief raised the temperature of the room by five degrees.

"Good. Now, we can set aside this nonsense and get back to the official business of governing humanity." Adam sat back down, keeping his posture high and resolute.

He scanned the room. The terror and uncertainty he felt in the moments after he shot the Hisba was plain across their faces. He took a deep breath. "During my time with the fleet, we had a Naddine drill sergeant. Mean jadespawn. He was an ex-warlord, who had nearly died in the Strife. The lower part of his jaw, along with his tongue, had been ripped clean off by a Zokyon warmech. The war was over. He was eligible to become an Elder in his tribe, but he despised the idea of sitting around and advising the next generation. His clan's military wing had discharged him. The Bokori were the only ones willing to sign up an old mute foreigner. Ironically, he ended up advising us instead. He hated it. Without so much as a grunt, he managed to scare the living piss out of us. He ran us ragged with exercise after exercise using only written word and the intensity of his eyes. You see, he had to learn to read and write to compensate for his lack of, uh, oral appendage. Apparently, it's not uncommon for Naddine to never learn those skills. After a particularly brutal workout session, I worked up the courage to ask him about that. He told me the strangest thing. The Naddine never developed a written language until the Cauduun stumbled upon them fifteen-hundred years ago. They had mastered biology, physics, economics, even poetry. Yet, none of them ever thought to write it down. A society based entirely on oral tradition, influential to this day. You can understand why someone without a tongue would feel useless in such a place. I pushed him further and asked him why more modern

Naddine don't take up writing. He typed a message on his emulator and showed it to me. I'll never forget the message. It said, 'The voice in your head is terrifying.'"

His tale did little to assuage the room. Instead of terror, confusion now filled the cramped space. Even John raised an eyebrow at him. Adam sighed again. "If we're going to do this, we need to do this right. We must put our declaration in writing for all the galaxy to read. Let them hear our words in their own voice." A few murmurs broke out. Most were inclined to support such action.

"How do we go about that?" asked a skeptical Auditore.

Adam thought about it for a moment. The obvious solution hit him right away. He turned to Trissefer. "Commissioner Quinn, as the Commissioner for History & Culture, I want you to head up a committee. The purpose of this committee will be to draft an official declaration of separation from the Bokori, establishing a once again a free and independent Human race. Pick four people at your discretion from across Arabella's spectrum to hash out appropriate language. Focus on why the Covenant is bad for humanity and why independence is vital to the survival of the Human race. Speak with Havera. See if there's anything from Stepicro that could guide us," Adam said.

"Excuse me, Commissioner," John cut in. "I agree with you on the need for an official written declaration. However, this task should be accomplished exclusively by Humans. If we're going to send a message to the rest of the galaxy we're ready for independence, it might appear embarrassing to rely on a foreigner to help draft our coming out message."

More murmurs percolated through the room. John had a point. Such a revelation could be embarrassing. Adam wasn't sure. He missed Doom's input on galactic politics more than ever. "I don't disagree with you, Chief Dark. That being said, I would rather we get this right. Political appearance is secondary. Stepicro is our ancestor's words in their purest form. They're the ones guiding us, and we're the ones writing it. Think of Havera as a midwife," Adam struggled to find an apt analogy.

"Hold on! You don't have the authority to create such a committee," interjected Shepard. "A proposal this radical needs the unanimous approval of the entire Committee. You can't do something like that unilaterally."

"He already has." Everyone whipped their heads around to the speaker. It was Handsome Snake. He had sat there quietly the entire time, nursing the bandaged wound to his leg, soaking in the intense conversation around him. Auditore had fashioned him some makeshift crutches so he could walk around. "Suicide pact. No truer words spoken, Commissioner Shepard. That's exactly what we have. We're putting what remains of humanity's future on the table with little guarantee of success. I say 'we' because we all stood by while Commissioner Mortis pulled the trigger. None of us stopped him. None of us intervened. We all knew the consequences of what he was doing. Yet, we all did nothing but watch, many of you with approving eyes. We were righteously angry. In that moment, we were Human. Our anger, our passion might have killed our ancestors and it might kill us today, too. But, it is that anger, that passion which makes us Human. Our fervor got us into this mess, I believe it will help liberate us out of it. I'd rather die a furious Human than live as a passive Bokori."

Adam's jaw dropped. He was shocked. He wasn't the only one. Everyone was flabbergasted at the normally stalwart, stoic Commissioner, especially Shepard. "Handsome, you've always been against unilateral independence. Have you changed your mind?" Shepard asked.

"No, Lara, I haven't, but it doesn't matter what I think. We've crossed the Link. It's too late to turn back now," Snake said.

Shepard surveyed the room. She found few sympathetic faces, none willing to stand up. "Look," Shepard said. "Even if we do this, how are we going to get the Conclave to recognize our independence? The Bokori are a Proprietor race, one of the two founding members for Cradite's sake! Our Commissioner for Diplomacy and Trade is dead. The last time we tried to get concessions from the Conclave it blew up in our face. Do we really believe this time will be any better..."

"I'll go," Adam said. Shocked faces shifted back to him. The murmurs erupted into full blown protests.

"Commissioner Mortis, don't be crazy. The Bokori will have you shot on sight," John said.

Trissefer scooted closer and grabbed him by the hand. "Adam, he's right. You can't leave the Bubble, it's..."

"Suicide?" Adam said pointedly. He was getting good at interrupting people's sentences. Trissefer nodded. He removed his hand from hers. "I realize my impulsiveness has put the rest of y'all in danger. If we're going to put our lives and futures on the line, it's only fair I take the greatest share of the risk. I'll go to the Conclave, declaration in hand, and plead our case in front of the whole galaxy, for better or worse. At least maybe it'll take some of the heat off Arabella if I'm not here. Give them one less cause to attack."

Adam's heart was pounding now. He had committed himself to this course of action. He waited to see what the response would be. Snake spoke up. "I would put forward an immediate vote on the issue confronting this Commission. A proposal for Commissioner Quinn to establish a committee aimed towards creating a document outlining a declaration of Human independence and for Commissioner Mortis to petition the Conclave in person for recognition of said document."

"Seconded," Adam said without hesitation. Trissefer opened her mouth to protest, but Adam shut her down.

"The proposal, having been seconded, goes to a full vote before the Commission. All those in favor of the proposal, please raise your hands to indicate an affirmative response," Snake said. Adam raised his hand right away followed by Snake and Trissefer. Auditore sighed and reluctantly raised his hand. All eyes shifted to Shepard.

"Oh, Kewea's curse, may as well," said a resigned Shepard, who raised her hand.

"The ayes are unanimous. The proposal is adopted," Snake said. A few cheers broke out among the attendees. Adam didn't move.

"No!" Adam silenced the cheers. "Legally, for whatever that's worth, the proposal has its approval. That isn't good enough for me. I want the approval of everyone in this room. Let it be understood that we are ALL in." A few moments of hesitation passed until people started raising their hands. They all did, including the militiamen. Only John kept his hand down. Confused, Adam tilted his head at his friend. John, setting aside his concerns, smiled slyly and lifted his hand up as high as his arm would allow.

11

Trust Her

Arabella was a buzz of activity. Under the hollow protection of the Bubble, the Humans of Windless Tornado were gathering resources and shoring up defenses for what everyone believed to be the inevitable second attack by the Bokori and their Hisbaween demons. The mood in the settlement was fearful but determined. Never before had they been so seemingly united in one singular purpose. Human stragglers smuggled from Bokor swelled the already-stretched support system. Their numbers were growing along with their problems. Regular Humans and former Modders seeking demodification surgeries found their way, against all odds, to the moon. Reports were coming in that the burgeoning saucer flotilla was intercepting transport vessels with Humans seeking to join the Separatist cause. Some were bringing food, medicine, and Links gathered from sympathetic Bokori throughout Inclucity. The People's House had to bring in reinforcements to handle the upswell. The fleet had grown to over fifty ships, including a handful of dreadnought size capital ships. It was an overwhelming show of force. So far, there had been no further incursions, yet. Only three days had passed since the first one.

I wonder what those ships should be guarding. Pirates must be celebrating out east.

The thought creeped into Adam's head throughout the day. The size of the fleet kept growing above them. The fledgling Bokori colonies and the black hole refineries were struggling to maintain adequate defenses even before this current crisis. The Excommunicated and other powerful space pirate gangs, already thriving in the eastern fringes of Bokori space, were most likely operating with impunity. This gravely concerned Adam as he prepared for his upcoming journey to Concordia.

The Bokori wouldn't pull away this many ships from their posts unless they thought there was going to be a quick resolution.

This observation wasn't lost on the others. John had already started his campaign to weed out the remaining Hisbaween infiltrators. Many people were already subjected to invasive interrogations and searches. They complained loudly to Adam, who agreed to convince John to postpone until he had left, giving Adam some political cover. Vital areas were reinforced with wooden spikes chopped from the trees of the nearby jungle. The size of the militia had grown threefold in the last two days. Shepard, who made no effort to disguise her displeasure at the last days turn of events, was positively apoplectic over losing essential personnel to the militia. The tender economy of the Arabella was precarious enough as it was. She tried to persuade, with little success, many people to stay at their posts until Adam returned. It was obvious she felt her words were meaningless. People felt safer with a gun in hand, surrounded by others just as armed and afraid. Adam could see her hair turning grayer by the hour. She was going to be John's problem in the interim. Adam had appointed him as his proxy on the Commission, granting him full authority to implement whatever security measures he deemed necessary. Lack of funds were another major problem. Many militiamen would need to go without pay for days, perhaps months, until the situation was resolved. Faith was the only currency in wide circulation, and it was rapidly dwindling.

Maybe this is the Bokori plan. Squeeze us until we collapse from within.

Fortunately, Trissefer was having more success on her front. They were close to completing a finalized version of a document. Adam had seen some of the early drafts and was pleased with her progress.

He observed Trissefer speaking with Havera on one occasion, passing along some data from Stepicro. Adam tried calling out to the Cauduun, but she ignored him. Adam hadn't spoken to her since the attack. It created a complication, because, at present, Havera's ship was the only way off the moon. They had no ships capable of interstellar travel and voluntourism had dried up in the past few days. He thought about asking John or Samus to help him steal a ship, but he suppressed that thought quickly. That was an awkward conversation he knew he must have sooner or later. He had chosen to put it off for the moment until he felt comfortable leaving Arabella.

Trissefer had chosen a committee consisting of Commissioner Snake, Consul Blade, Max Fisher, a scrappy salvager who helped Samus and the other scouts gather and smuggle resources from Bokor, and, much to Adam's surprise, Morrigan Mortis. "I need a distraction. This will be a good outlet for me," she told him after Trissefer informed him of her chosen four committee members. Unlike after the death of her husband, Adam's father, Morrigan had not cried at the rushed funeral for Aaron. She remained stony-faced, numb to the world around her. She barely spoke for the next couple days. They buried his brother next to his father along with the seventy-three bodies of the other killed Humans during the Hisba incursion. They burned the bodies of the Hisbas and their confirmed collaborators, after stripping their corpses of anything valuable. Burning bodies instead of recycling them was also a crime to the Bokori, so they added that to the growing list of Bokori grievances. Other than several sets of Hisba winged armor, the militia took possession of a couple dozen functioning laser rifles and searstaffs. Most in pretty decent shape, too.

"See if you can't procure us some of those new sexy Naddine plasma rifles I've heard so much about," John requested during their most recent daily meeting.

"John, we can barely acquire cheap plastic knock-off projectile weapons. You really think we can afford to buy advanced plasma weaponry? Besides, unless you're planning to go war with the Union, I don't think we'll need them," Adam said sarcastically. Plasma weaponry, while deadly effective against flesh, was expensive and hard to obtain. Virtually impossible to print with the resources they had. They were the preferred weapon against bots and machines due to the high temperatures of the bolts. The Naddine developed the technology during one of their many wars against the Zokyo.

"I didn't say 'buy,' I said 'procure,'" his friend said with a wink.

"I'll add that to the laundry list of items and requests. Are you still banking on military defections?" Adam asked.

"Better believe it. They're our secret weapon," John said smiling. John had presented what he termed his "battle plans," the day after the big meeting. Part of his plan included recruiting Human soldiers, sailors, and marines to the cause. Humans comprised the overwhelming majority of the Bokori armed forces. If enough of them harbored Separatist sympathies, it was possible they might be willing to abandon the Bokori and defect to their cause. They could mutiny and seize ships. The mere threat of mutiny might pressure the People's House to back down and negotiate. It was a high risk, high reward strategy. The morality officers kept a close watch on the enlisted. If it was discovered Separatists were tampering with the military, it might be the excuse the Hisbaween needed to launch a full-scale assault. Crush the rebellion before it has a chance to germinate in the ranks. Rehab wasn't only one weapon in their arsenal. They liberally handed out alcohol and Celeste to keep their troops quelled.

Drugged soldiers are obedient soldiers.

The Bokori hierarchy kept a tight control on information within the ranks. However, with such a huge military buildup, word was probably bouncing around the fleet. The occasional rogue element within the military had in the past aided the Separatists with spare weapons and ammo. They also provided patrol reports allowing the smugglers to avoid the Bokori saucers. Unfortunately for John, they had no reports of defections. It was early.

"The others have many demands, do they?" John asked.

"You have no idea," Adam said as he pulled out an emulator Consul Blade let him borrow for his trip. "Auditore wants me to speak with all the major Duseraries to acquire medical supplies and convince them to send any medical students who need to complete their required residency hours. Then, he wants me to go to all the libraries of Raetis to scoop up as many primary and secondary school books, demos, and digital educational manuscripts I can get my hands on. Trissefer, naturally, wants me to demand full and complete access to Stepicro. She's easy to satisfy."

"Is she?" John said with a smirk.

Adam ignored him. "Shepard wants, well, everything: printable infrastructure materials, convince the Conclave to send relief packages that include more generators for the Bubble, make diplomatic contact with the Sinners, speak with bankers at major Mordelatories about converting our Striking Stamps into Links, maybe even get a loan. I'm going to need a few to pay for all this. Snake, bless his heart, only wants me to buy an obscure book on Cauduun legal systems called *Precedent and Prejudice: An Essay On Age of Technology Legal Codes and Charters.* It's out of print, and there are no digital copies available. I can't imagine why. Consul Blade wants me to petition the Conclave for unfettered Nexus access. That's as likely to happen as I am to join the Hisbaween. How I'm going to transport all that is another problem entirely. Of course, this is all on top of presenting our document before the Conclave, convincing them to recognize our independence, and not get thrown into a rehab cell the moment I step off the ship," Adam said, storing the emulator.

John whistled his amazement. "You know what? I'm happy with one-hundred-year-old pellet guns. Whatever you can get," John said with a smirk. "Have you spoken to her, yet?"

He meant Havera. "No, I haven't. I'm too busy crying my eyes out with the weight of Arabella on my anxiety-ridden shoulders," Adam said. He was only partially kidding.

"Why not take someone with you? Sounds like you're going to have your hands full. Let someone else handle the smaller stuff. Lighten your load," John suggested.

"Funny you mention that. I was thinking the same thing," Adam said with a grin. John gave him the perfect opening.

"Look, Adam, trust me I'd love to be by your side. I want to see you tell the galaxy to throw themselves into a black hole, but I'm needed here. The infiltrators need to be rooted out and dealt with. You don't want me there either. You know I'm not exactly the most diplomatic person," John laughed. "I'm a wanted man, too, almost as much as you are. Better we don't give them too great a target to shoot out of the sky," John said, shaking his head.

"I wasn't talking about you, John," Adam said.

"Who then?"

"Samus."

John reacted expectedly. "Absolutely not! What did I just say about not giving them too great a target? Those night demons want my sister, too! I won't let them take her. She's safer here with me. End of discussion!" John yelled. Adam pulled John aside away from curious onlookers. "Why would you ever suggest such an idea? She's traumatized enough by those accursed aliens. She doesn't need that kind of exposure right now," John said with a raised hushed whisper.

"She came to me, John," Adam said.

John was surprised. "She came to you?"

It was true. Adam visited Sam every day to check in on her. She wasn't doing well. She wouldn't talk about what had happened with anyone. She wasn't eating much, preferring to spend all day in bed. Not that she could really go anywhere with the lockdown. She was miserable. After one of his visits, Adam casually mentioned to his mother his concerns about his task ahead. Sam overheard him. She and John shared the housing unit above theirs. She begged him to take her with him.

"Please! I need to get out of here. I'm going stir crazy. I can't stay here. Please, Adam, please. I can be helpful on Concordia. I spend most of my time gathering intel and items for Arabella already. This is a perfect job for me. Please!" Samus said. Morrigan thought it was a good idea. After many pleas by Samus, Adam relented. The problem was getting John's approval. He had only gotten more protective of his younger sister since the incident.

"She's an active woman. She needs something to do other than mope around here all day. It wouldn't hurt to have a sympathetic face for our cause. Sam can give us that," Adam said.

"Oh, so you want to parade her trauma out for the entire galaxy to see, is that it? She's too fragile right now," John insisted.

"Sam's a grown woman, John. She's allowed to make whatever decision she wants. If she wants to come with me to Concordia, I won't stop her. I welcome her help," Adam said.

"I'm her brother! I know what's best for my sister, not you! You have enough personal problems to avoid fixing. You don't need to add my sister's issues to yours." John said angrily. The accusatory tone shocked Adam. He had expected John to react poorly to the suggestion, but John had never spoke to him like that. His dark brown eyes were awash with rage, the vein in his neck throbbing. Adam took a step back. John's eyes had a sudden realization of regret. He relaxed his expression. "I...I'm sorry. I don't know what made me say that," John said.

Adam put his hands on his friend's shoulders. John was avoiding his gaze. "John, look at me," Adam said. John slowly lifted his head. His eyes were reddening with tears. "You know I would rather die than let anyone hurt Sam again. She's stronger than you give her credit for. The Conclave should be afraid of us. With her at my side, humanity will be a free and independent people again. She needs to do this. I need her to do this. Arabella needs her, John."

The battle behind John's harsh eyes raged. He wanted to argue. Finally, against every instinct in John's heart, he relented. "Alright, fine. She can go. I want to talk to her first. Not to talk her out of it! I just want to make sure she's mentally and emotionally prepared," John said.

Adam nodded. "Okay."

"Okay. Quit looking at me like that! You're giving me mixed signals," John said. The old friends laughed it off as they walked away from each other. All seemed well. Nonetheless, in the back of Adam's mind, he couldn't shake the image of John's threatening face. He had seen that face in the past. The thought caused Adam to glance over his shoulder for but a moment, wary of a knife to the back.

***

On a more positive front, Trissefer and her committee had completed their latest draft of the independence declaration. Hopefully, it was their last. The finalized draft had four parts. First was a preamble discussing the injustice of the Covenant and a philosophy of cooperation and governance modeled after the Conclave Charter. Followed by a list of grievances against the Bokori and the Hisbaween in the next section.

This section was by far the longest. It contained indictments of the rehabilitation facilities, the Hisbaween, the restriction of trade and travel, depriving children of their parents, public shaming, violations of Human dignity, and a litany of other crimes against humanity. The earlier drafts had denunciations against the Conclave and those who enabled the Bokori, but it was deemed too inflammatory. They needed sympathetic ears from the Conclave. To that end, Trissefer wanted to include some personal testimonies from the Humans of Arabella to be presented separately. Gathering such testimonies was a good idea but appraised as too time-consuming for Adam's mission. Morrigan thought it be best they record them to be smuggled out and transmitted on the Nexus later in order to exert political pressure on the Proprietor races.

The next part was a list of rights and protections Humans desired, again modeled on the Conclave Charter. Finally, a conclusion section declaring the Human-Bokori Covenant null and void. Humanity was once again a free and independent race. It was a structure borrowed in part from something Havera had gleaned from Stepicro.

"She said that during an age with primitive firearms one nation of Humans had a similar situation. It seems this nation pops up repeatedly in Stepicro, so I guess that means they were successful. They were oppressed by a different nation, not alien obviously, but after they made their declaration, they fought a war for independence. A real mixed bag, I suppose. Although, it appears that war was only a backdrop against a more covert war between two old factions, and that these factions apparently controlled a lot of Human history. I found it too confusing to follow. So did she," Trissefer explained about Havera's research. "You need to talk to her, Adam. She's your only way off this gray rock."

"Is she angry with me?" Adam asked.

Trissefer thought for a moment. "I'm not sure to be honest. She has been curter with me than usual, often acting like I'm interrupting some important task. She never said much beyond professional courtesies even before this. Ever since I became a commissioner and started receiving Stepicro updates from her, I always got the sense she doesn't think highly of me."

"She suggested you and I get together and have children. Can't think too lowly of you," Adam said.

Trissefer raised an eyebrow. "Unless she doesn't like you either."

Adam shrugged. "I suppose she was teasing me."

"I didn't know that woman could tease. Didn't realize how friendly y'all were. Perhaps it's not me she thinks you should be with," Trissefer said.

Adam cocked his head and chuckled. "What? You think she likes me or that I like her?"

Trissefer shrugged. "Who is the Consul of Cloudboard? You don't think she's cute?"

"Of course, I do," Adam said the words spilling out his mouth. Trissefer's expression widened into sarcastic surprise. "In the objective sense that any person might find anyone to be attractive, alien or no," Adam said.

Why am I justifying myself to Triss?

"If you say so, Adam," Trissefer said. "I'm not going to tease you. We're not close enough for that," she said coldly.

Gut punch.

"Look, I'm sorry I said that. I was upset. I was having a panic attack, and I lashed out," Adam said.

Trissefer put up her hands. "No, it's fine. You don't need to explain it to me. You're right. We aren't that close. We only spend almost every night together. I hold you and comfort you after every single one of your frequent night terrors. We share our days with each other. I listen to all your many anxieties and fears without protestation. We believe in the same cause fervently. We know each other more intimately than anyone for a hundred-thousand light years. No, why would I think we were that close?"

She started to turn away. Adam reached out to her. "Wait, Triss, I didn't mean it like that..." Out of nowhere, a hand seized Trissefer by the arm. In a flash, Samus had Trissefer pinned up against a wall.

"What the...," Triss tried saying.

"Do not use his trauma to emotionally manipulate him! You understand me?! He's been through enough. He's apologized to you for what I presume was a very hurtful comment. Either you accept his apology, or you don't. But don't you strut around using the vulnerable moments he shared with you to twist him into feeling worse than he already does. I may not fully understand y'all's dynamic, but if it's anything like this, he's better off not being close with you!" Samus said with an intense ferocity.

The two women glared at each other hard, only inches away. Adam was stunned into silence. He didn't know what to do. By the time he found his voice, Trissefer relaxed, and Samus let her go.

"I'm going to finish the final touches on the independence draft. I'll let you know when it's done, Commissioner Mortis," Trissefer said bitterly. Trissefer walked away and out of sight with Samus eyeing her until she was gone.

Samus turned to face Adam. "You didn't have to do that," Adam said. "I really did hurt her feelings."

"Maybe so, but that doesn't give her the right to manipulate you like that. You deserve better than her," Samus said.

"Do I? I don't know who I am good enough for," Adam said weakly. His thoughts focused on *her* for a few moments. Then, for the briefest of seconds, he thought of the attractive, crimson-skinned alien woman.

Samus came up to him, hugged him, and kissed him on the cheek.

"Yes, you do. You're good enough for any lucky girl. Don't let anyone tell you differently...ever!"

"Thanks, Sam," Adam said breaking off the hug. "How much of that did you hear by the way? I didn't see or hear you coming," Adam said.

Samus smiled. "No one ever does. That's what I'm good for."

"With you at my side in Concordia, we cannot fail," Adam said.

"You mean with you at my side," Samus said with a playful punch to Adam's shoulder. "Also, don't you worry about transportation. I'll talk to Havera. I can convince her to take us to the Conclave. She won't say no to me."

"Why do you think that?"

Samus pressed her fingers into her cheek to create an exaggerated smile. "Could you say no to this face?"

"No," Adam said with a laugh.

***

Trissefer and her committee finished the final draft of the text. Multiple people scanned it for content and grammar. The UI System translated text to the tongue of the reader. However, Default was hardly spoken or read outside of Bokori space, so the committee thought it best to ensure if there could be no cause for confusion for non-Default speakers, especially for the Humans who spoke and read Standard instead of Default.

It was decided for added measure, every person who wanted could sign the digital document. Snake was the first one. His signature was so huge it was an entire page to itself. All the Commissioners signed it, all the Consuls, all the commanders and deputies within each branch. Blade had the brilliant idea of putting a picture of the Arabella statue as the backdrop in the signature section. One-by-one, people were lining up from all over Arabella to sign the document. The rest of the afternoon was dedicated to the document signing. After a couple hours of nonstop signing, Samus hurried up to Adam.

"It's done. She'll do it," Samus said, huffing and puffing. Her face was flushed.

"Relax, take a breath. How'd you manage that?" Adam asked.

Samus wiped the sweat off her brow. "I appealed to her sense of honor woman-to-woman," she said with a grin. "The Bokori fleet won't stop her ship with its diplomatic protections. Whenever you're ready, she's ready. I'm ready, too. Windless Tornado is getting too hot."

"Can you go tell her we're taking off tonight after the setting suns? I don't want to wait another minute. Everyone should be finished signing by then," Adam said.

Samus took a deep breath and smirked. "Sure. My pleasure. Oh, I almost forgot. I ran into your mother on my way over here. She wants to talk to you before you leave. You should probably head over right now."

"Will do. Snake said he'll d-mail me the document when everyone's done."

"She not talking to you?" Samus asked, referring to Trissefer.

"I'm not good with confrontations, you know that. Things will cool off. A few thousand light years between me and her will do us both some good," Adam said, though, he wasn't sure if he believed his own words. Samus spotted her brother, John, waving her over to see him. Samus lowered her gaze to the ground and scratched the scar on her chin. She picked her head back up.

"You deal with Trissefer how you must. You only get one rescue per female per lifetime from me," Samus said, side-hugging Adam.

"Thanks. You're definitely too good for me."

"Yes, I am. Now, go see your mother!" Samus said, shooing him away.

***

Even the rotting stench of Arabella's natural aroma didn't bother Adam this day. He felt nervous. A good kind of nervous. A welcome change of pace to his normally frayed nerves. An excitement rushed over him he couldn't explain.

Is this what freedom feels like?

Faux-freedom, of course. There was still the minor problem of getting the galaxy to recognize Human independence and what Humans were going to do if the Bokori attacked in the interim. Adam tried to keep his mind focused on one problem at a time. John once told him it would help with his stress if he didn't try to swallow too much too soon.

The Mortis family lived at the base of what was essentially four one-story housing units stacked on top of each other. John and Samus lived in the apartment right above theirs. A sign of how close they all were. Above them lived a couple, who both taught the younger children at the school. Ryu taught Default while his husband Corvo taught Standard, the two Human languages. At the very top lived an eccentric old lady named Senua, who owned as many shotguns as she did birds. No one knew how she got them all, nor how she managed to get up and down the stack without help. She wasn't exactly a limber old lady. He reached his home and almost bumped into someone unexpectedly.

"Havera?"

The Cauduun was exiting the Mortis home. She seemed lost in her thoughts. Adam raised his voice to get her attention.

"Havera!"

Havera shook her head. "Oh, mea culpa. I didn't see you there".

"What are you doing here?" Adam asked.

"I wanted to call upon your mater. I hadn't...I hadn't properly expressed my condolences for her...for y'all's...loss," Havera said, struggling to find her words.

"Is everything alright?"

"Hmm? Yes, yes. Mea culpa. I'm distracted I suppose. Oh, umm, Sam came by to see me. We, uhh..." Havera trailed off a bit.

"She told me. She said you agreed to shepherd us to the Conclave."

"Oh, right, yes. The Conclave. It's not a problem. I needed to leave soon regardless."

"I told her to tell you we're intending to leave tonight. She might be heading to your ship right this second."

"I suppose I better get back to the Cicera right away. I'll see you aboard," Havera said, peppier than she had been moments ago.

It's like she saw a Xizor.

Adam set aside his thoughts on Havera. He entered his home.

Morrigan was sitting at the table, spinning a piece from Conclave Conquest. She didn't notice him enter.

"Mom?" Adam called out.

She barely glanced up at him. "Sweetheart, sit. Please," Morrigan said softly.

He hadn't spoken to her much since Aaron's death. Her voice had grown wispier. Morrigan's face was gaunt. Her unusually pale skin had reddish splotches dotted all over. Adam always thought she looked sick. His father assured him that's how she always was since the day he met her. Her thick onyx hair had turned completely white at the tips. The crow's feet around her eyes showed signs of cracking, same with her lips. It was rare these days to find her wearing anything other than the mournful white. Today was no different. She wore a plain white tunic that had multiple stains across the front.

Adam sat down next to her. "I ran into Havera outside. She's agreed to take us to Concordia tonight," Adam said. Morrigan didn't react. She kept staring at the piece in her hand. "What did you and her talk about, Mom?" Adam asked. No response again. Adam leaned over so she'd see his face. "Mom, what's the matter?"

"Show it to me," Morrigan said quietly.

"I beg your pardon, Mom. Show you what?" Adam asked perplexed.

"The Debbie. One of the last pieces of our history. Show it to me, please," Morrigan said. Her voice was barely above a whisper. Hesitantly, Adam withdrew the Debbie from his pocket. It was retracted into its platinum grip. He placed it on the table in front of her. "I said show it to me, son. I want to see its true design," Morrigan said.

Adam hesitated. Morrigan dropped the piece and glared at her son. She had deep, dark circles around her reddening eyes. Adam assumed it was because she had been crying. Reluctantly, he squeezed the grip. Crystallizing into its full shape, the Debbie had a slight iridescent glow. The misty, icy weapon amplified the dim light around them. Morrigan watched her son place the Debbie in front of her. Adam noticed his mother examining the weapon with unexpected longing. She reached for the weapon; except she wasn't reaching for the grip. She was trying to touch the icy, crystalline extensions.

Adam reached out and grabbed her by the wrist. "Mom, what are you doing?"

She shook loose his grip. The vigor of her wrist was unexpectedly strong. "There are many things I haven't told you about this Debbie, son. Watch," she said. Morrigan seized the gun by its icy part. She flung her head back seemingly in pain. She made no sound. The swirling mists around the gun slowly ran up her arm enveloping her entire body.

Adam stood up in shock. "Mom! Stop! Let go!" he screamed.

Morrigan waved him away. She let go only seconds after grabbing the weapon. The mists around his mother dissipated. She was breathing heavily. Except, sitting back down next to her, Adam noticed a change in his mother.

The reddish splotches were gone. Her skin, while still pale, was visibly healthier. The cracks around her eyes and lips disappeared. Her eyes lost their bags, her cheeks were fuller and had noticeable color. The white tips of her hair vanished, replaced with her normal, onyx-colored hair. Visibly, Morrigan appeared thirty years younger.

"Mom! You...you...how?" Adam said stammering.

She reached out, placing the tip of her finger on his lips. Her finger was terribly cold to the touch. "Patience, son," she said her voice much firmer and resolute. "What you see is not but an illusion of a woman out of time. There are far greater powers and mysteries at play here than simple interspecies politics. You know the far greater threat is out there. It waits for us in the shadow," Morrigan said, lifting her finger from Adam's lips.

"The Xizor," Adam finished Morrigan's thought.

Morrigan nodded. "The Long Con is not our only concern. It's nothing but a means to an end. We must be fully prepared for their return. The galaxy must be ready. You must make them understand. Something our ancestors attempted and failed. We lost Earth as punishment for our shortcomings. We shall not lose again. What is lost will be found," Morrigan said. She clasped her hands around Adam's. "Five-and-a-half centuries ago, a Human entrusted the fate of humanity's future in that of a Cauduun. I'm asking you to do the same, sweetheart."

"A Cauduun? You mean Havera. What does she have to do with this?" Adam asked.

"Everything," Morrigan said. "You must trust her, son. No matter what happens. She is the key to our survival." Adam's mind was spinning. He was thoroughly lost and confused. This was not where he was expecting this conversation to go. Adam observed that the tips of Morrigan's hair, bit by bit, were turning white again. The crow's feet around her eyes were returning, along with the cracks.

"I don't understand, Mom. Havera's been a tremendous help for sure. I don't get what you mean by the key to our survival. Sounds far too grandiose for what we're asking her to do. What aren't you telling me, Mom?"

Morrigan's grip loosened slightly. Adam saw reddish splotches beginning to materialize on her hands. "Much and more, Adam. First, you head to the Conclave. You remind them to their faces exactly what humanity means to this galaxy. Only after you win us our freedom again can we safeguard the freedom of all sentientkind. Tell no one, not even Havera, of what we've spoken or of what you've seen. The time is not right. That moment is rapidly approaching, faster than I expected. Save your queries for later. Focus on the task at hand. Above all, remember what I said: you must trust Havera. Trust her! She does not yet realize how important she is. Soon she will. Soon everyone will. When they do, that's when the true battle begins."

12

Falling Star

"You have committed the offenses of blasphemy, toxicity, and heresy. Penance must be paid. Confess your sins before the community, and you shall be forgiven. Do you confess?" the familiar voice asked. Millions of cheering voices echoed throughout the stadium.

Adam said nothing. He would not give them the satisfaction. His anger, his rage kept his sanity intact in the face of the High Hisba's brutality. In his heart, he was right. He would not save his own skin by perjuring himself. He felt no sorrow for what he had done. He was in the right, they were wrong. He focused all his thoughts on *her*. The memory of her was burned into Adam's subconscious.

A whip slashed his back with a CRACK! He did not cry out. The High Hisba spoke again. "Your heresy must be purged. Your blasphemous tongue altered. Your toxic mind corrected. Do you confess?" Again, he held his tongue. The lash struck him repeatedly. Each time he resisted the urge to cry out. He collapsed onto the grass. He felt himself weakening. No, it wasn't him. It was the whip's deteriorating effect. Each slash was lessened compared to the last until he felt no more pain. The cheers stopped. He was alone, drifting through space. He heard the heartbeat again.

THUMP THUMP! THUMP THUMP! THUMP THUMP!

"Where am I?" Adam asked into the empty void

"You're right where you need to be," a voice replied. It was his own. He rolled onto his back. Standing over him was the cracked sulfur-skinned creature holding a swirling, black sword. The creature spoke with Adam's voice. "Get up!"

The creature slashed down at Adam. He tried to roll out of the way, but the blade sliced his torso. The pain was unbearable. He let out a scream. No sound emerged from his mouth. He held his side expecting to feel blood. None. No wound. The creature loomed large over him in what Adam thought was a smile. "She won't save you this time. You have a destiny to fulfill."

"She? Who? Destiny?" he mouthed. No sound emanated from his lips.

The creature leaned close enough to whisper. Its mouth was clicking within an inch of his face. "You've seen her face. You are nothing but a pawn. Bring us her champion!" The creature yelled, forcing its hand over Adam's mouth and nose. He couldn't breathe. Around the creature's arm, its armor slithered. A serpentine beast raised its head at Adam, preparing to strike with its sharp, venomous fangs.

A frigid, bright light beamed from underneath Adam, scattering the serpent and the creature into dust. He rolled back over onto his stomach and beheld a familiar visage. *The face.* The gargantuan presence enveloped everything within sight. Its white, crystalline jaws opened up wide to swallow Adam whole.

Adam shot up in a cold sweat, breathing heavily. It took him a few seconds to get his bearings. He remembered. He was on Havera's ship, en route to Concordia. "Just a dream. I cannot remember," he said into the emptiness of the room. He shook his head trying to recall what he had dreamed. It faded fast. "Who is she?" Adam pondered aloud.

Adam had taken up residence in the port side observation room with the library. He let Samus have the guest quarters next to Havera. He found comfort in the company of knowledge in a galaxy full of obtuseness. His coat was folded neatly by his bed next to his boots. He had balled up his jumpsuit into a pile near the foot of his bed. He usually slept naked. He felt freer that way. Although the Cicera was climate controlled, he was shivering. Residual feelings from the dream, whose details he had promptly forgotten. He picked up his jumpsuit and slipped his legs into the pants part, leaving the upper half dangling from the waist.

He sat at the edge of his cot that Havera had procured for him. Taking several deep breaths, he was trying to relax and push down the bubbling nausea. He scratched his back. It wasn't as itchy as before. He stared at the carpet, hoping to find some wisdom in the beige and brown fibers beneath his feet. He stood up, balling up his toes into fists. It soothed him. He stood up and walked around the room, knuckling his toes on the carpet. His waddling about must've looked absolutely ridiculous to anyone watching him.

A wide gap marked the space between a pair of bookshelves. Both were from the Age of Technology. One was pre-spaceflight; the other was post-spaceflight. The button to roll back the observation window was next to the former. Adam pressed it. Soundlessly, the metal barrier rolled back revealing a clear glass panel. Adam had a magnificent view of the galaxy whizzing through negative space. Adam remembered how colorful negative space was. Something to do with the light mass effect of burning refined dark matter. He contemplated the tattoo on his hand.

I wonder if she saw this beauty in her final moments.

There was a knock on the door. "Come in," he yelled, still peering out into space.

The door slid open with a hiss. Adam turned around to see Havera standing there with a tray of drinks. "Mea culpa. I didn't mean to intrude. You were talking loud enough in your sleep I could hear you through the door. I was worried you were having another nightmare, so I brought you some hot tea. It's called Camina. My mater used to brew this stuff all the time. It's distilled from the root of a rare plant grown on Gallia. It might help you relax." Adam didn't respond. He continued to stare out into space, glancing down at the back of his hand every so often. Havera placed the tray on the nearby table. "I've never seen your scars. Do they hurt?"

Adam realized he was standing there shirtless. He slipped the top of his jumpsuit back on. "They itch more than they hurt, usually whenever I'm feeling stressed, which all the time these days," he said, turning to face her. He finished adjusting his jumpsuit. "Who's flying if you're here?"

"The ship has autopilot. The Vol Bokor spacelane will take us directly to our destination. Dee is up in the cockpit monitoring for any hazards in our flight path. We still have two days to Concordia." Havera hit the panel to close the door. The glint of her forearms caught Adam's eye.

"Your bracers. They certainly came in handy back there. I've never seen weapons like that. Do all Praetorians possess a pair?" he asked.

Havera shook her head. She undid the metal strap on her right forearm and handed Adam a bracer. It was cold to the touch. A familiar sort of cold. The outer layer was made of platinum, matching the color of the metal in its typical appearance. It was padded on the interior for comfort. Engraved on top were three rings pressed together in a triangular pattern. Adam noticed each ring was a different color: bronze, silver, and gold. All were interconnected by an interior ring sunken into the bracer.

"They're called Cradite's Bracers or the Mater's Embrace." Havera said, sating Adam's curiosity. "That emblem is the original sign of Cradite, the mother of goddesses. It's called the Vitriba. It's our most recognizable symbol. The three rings are meant to represent Rema's three moons: the volcanic Potia, the habitable Saptia, and the cavernous Anio. The bracers are part of a unique set of enchanted objects said to be forged by Iinneara herself in the flames of Mount Fusila. Gifts presented by the goddesses to the Cauduun at the dawn of the Age of Technology, the earliest days of civilization. This was Cradite's gift. The legends say thirteen gifts were presented to the Cauduun, one from each goddess or god. So far, we've only discovered two. Or rather, there are two known objects some claim are these gifts: the bracers and the Sword of Aria, also called the Warrior's Kiss. The rest are considered myths or, at the very least, believed to be lost to the annals of history."

Adam's eyes widened. Something so seemingly benign was impressive.

He could hardly believe it, yet he witnessed their power firsthand. "What exactly do they do? Your strength was unparalleled with them."

"Their exact nature is still a mystery to me. I can tap into the energies of the bracers with my will. They increase my physicality and dexterity exponentially. The Censors of the Praetorians have helped me control the power within the bracers and tap its full potential.

Adam whistled his approval. "How does something this mythological end up in your hands?"

"They were my mater's. She died. Two years ago."

Two years ago. I get it now.

"I understand. That's why you didn't want to talk about your title. You only inherited it from your mother, I presume. I'm sorry if I was insensitive to you, Havera." Adam said.

"There's nothing to be sorry about it. You didn't know. I appreciate you didn't press further. Others aren't as polite." She picked up a cup of tea and sipped it. "I need to confess something to you, Adam." Havera said suddenly.

"What is it?"

Havera sipped her tea again. Her hand was shaking a bit. Adam could tell she was conflicted about what she wanted to say. "Do you remember the dreams I told you about the other day? I had another one. During the day."

Adam cocked his head curiously. "What sort of dream?"

"In the hospital. The Hisbaween whose shot I managed to deflect. I saw it happen. In the moments preceding the shot, I saw it happen. I failed to stop the blast. He shot you. The laser beam tore right through your body into Sam, killing both of you. Your bodies crumpled at my feet. I could only scream in agony. I failed. I failed you. I failed Sam. Streams of blood drenched my vision. I thought I was hallucinating. I was frightened. More frightened than when...I was frightened," Havera said. Adam noted she caught herself from telling him what frightened her more. He chose to ignore it.

"I'm not sure I understand," Adam said. He was honest. He couldn't decipher the meaning of her daydream.

"I'm not sure I understand it either. Quickly as the dream came, it vanished. I was back in that room, standing there. I heard Sam scream. Instinctively, I knew what to do. I didn't think. I acted. My bracer had already reflected the blast by the time my senses kicked in. I couldn't believe what I had done. I'm happy you both were unharmed, Adam, don't get me wrong. However, I'm afraid. I don't understand what I saw. What it meant. It was the most vivid daydream I've had to this point. Nothing previously so life and death as that," Havera said, swapping the teacup between each hand. She was squeezing and flexing her fingers to stop her hands from shaking.

Adam had kept his word to his mother. He hadn't told Havera about anything Morrigan had said to him. Adam wasn't sure how'd he broach the subject in any case. He wondered what Morrigan had told her before Adam had arrived. He hadn't forgotten Morrigan's words. *"Trust her."*

She doesn't know how important she is. Based on what she's telling me, that seems accurate. There is more to Havera than the Cauduun Praetorian duchess. Until I know something tangible, I should keep my mouth shut.

Adam held up her bracer. "I'd wager these bracers hold more secrets than you realize," Adam said. He was deflecting his own thoughts. He had truthfully never heard of anyone with that kind of power. Rumors of such abilities hoarded by isolated clans of Naddine had reached his ears during his military days. To Adam's knowledge, they were merely stories. Weak justifications spread by the Zokyo to rationalize why they were never able to truly defeat the Naddine in any of their many wars, despite the Zokyo's technological advantages. The galaxy was chock-full of legends and fairy tales. Each species had their own. The lost colony of Noah was humanity's. A thriving Human utopia full of riches and wonders cloaked from a galaxy that coveted their way of life.

Havera put her cup back down. "You might be right. I should tell you, Adam, the core of the bracers is forged in Rimestone."

Adam cocked his head again. "I've heard that term in the past. Bokor's mining conglomerate was obsessed with finding it. They have entire fleets dedicated to guarding and searching their black hole systems for it. Said it had something to do with dark energy. We were never given many details. What exactly is Rimestone?" Adam asked.

"They're correct. Rimestone is a crystalline substance with the visual properties of ice glinting in the sunlight. Incredibly rare; Impossibly dense; Unbreakable. It's said to be dark energy in solid, physical form. Origins unknown. Nobody living knows how to harvest or forge the substance. Small traces of Rimestone can be found all over the galaxy. Every species desperately desires to unlock the secrets of dark energy. None more so than the Bokori. Like many others, they believe Rimestone holds the key to dark energy, the invisible force compromising most of the galaxy's total energy. Mastering dark energy would give any species an insurmountable technological advantage. Complete galactic conquest could be possible for any race that solves the dark energy equation. The ancient Venvuishyn were said to be the only race in the galaxy capable of creating constructs out of Rimestone. Until you Humans came along," Havera said pointedly.

The Debbie!

Adam grabbed the grip from his jacket pocket. He squeezed the grip tightly, activating it. The icy barrels of the gun crystallized seemingly from nothing. Adam felt the coldness of the gun's core through his hand. Misty vapors swirled, clinging to the Debbie's curved barrels. "This is..."

"Rimestone, yes. I recognized it immediately when you...earlier," Havera said, leaving the past unspoken. "The Praetorian Order believes when humanity deployed Rimestone weapons against the Xizor, it changed the entire course of history. The seemingly unstoppable Xizor were defeated by these weapons and fled into unknown space. After Earth disappeared, it was believed all knowledge of how Humans created such technology was lost. Few, if any, of those weapons remain. If the governments of the galaxy acquired them, they aren't sharing, not even with the Praetorian Order. The secrets of dark energy continue to elude everyone."

"And the Bokori forced us to sign the Covenant of Subjugation hoping they could learn the secrets of dark energy from the ashes of humanity. We knew the Bokori desired our technology. I never knew it was Rimestone," Adam said.

Havera nodded. "Now, the entire galaxy knows you possess such a weapon. I'd keep it hidden in your inventory. Don't show it to anyone when we reach Concordia."

"I can't. I've tried. For whatever reason, I'm unable to dematerialize the weapon into my inventory. I must hold onto it physically," Adam said. He wanted to puke. *What have I done? I've put a target on my back, on humanity's back.* His anger flashed at himself this time. He let his emotions get the better of him. Innocent people were paying the price.

Adam thought about Morrigan. "Does Rimestone have any healing properties?"

"Healing properties?" Havera shook her head. "Not that I'm aware of. I'm one of the closest persons there is to an expert on Rimestone, even I'm ignorant to its true nature. There's not enough of it to go around to study fully."

Adam realized he was standing there holding the Debbie and Havera's bracer. He decrystallized the Debbie and pocketed it. He handed Havera back her bracer.

"What does that symbol mean?" Havera asked. She was staring at the tattoo on the back of his hand. "I've seen it on multiple Humans. What is it? It's your turn to share."

Adam relaxed and gestured for her to sit down. She sat on the carpet cross-legged. Her tail was swaying behind her excitedly. Adam sat down next to her. She handed him a cup of tea. He took a sip. It was too hot for his taste. He put his cup down and held out his hand for her to inspect. She examined it, closely running her soft bulbous fingers on his skin.

"It's called the Sign of Remembrance. The blue disk is meant to represent Earth and the gray disk her moon, Luna. The Bokori believed it was meant to honor our Covenant with them. Quite the opposite. When we say 'what is lost will be found' this is to what we're referring. Many Humans dedicated to the cause of independence ink themselves with a Remembrance tattoo. Not all, of course. Some get one simply to honor the past and find some sense of cultural identity. We don't have much of one to showcase," Adam said.

"Did you ink this yourself?" she asked.

Adam shook his head. "No, this was given to me by someone special."

"The woman I keep hearing about?" Havera asked. "People in Arabella kept talking about it in hushed whispers. I thought they were referring to Trissefer at first. Someone you knew that was responsible for your imprisonment?"

Adam instinctively recoiled his hand. Havera was taken aback by his sudden movement. Adam relaxed his muscles. "Sorry. I'm just not used to talking about *her*," Adam said. He gave Havera back his hand. She grasped it with both her hands, squeezing it gently.

"Who was she?" Havera asked.

Adam took a deep breath to calm himself. He felt some of the tea stir in his esophagus down into his stomach. For once, his heart pumped at a normal pace. He felt comfortable telling her.

"Her name was Falling Star."

"She's Bokori?"

Adam nodded. "She was the Executive Morality Officer on the ship I served aboard during my Shocktrooper days."

"What's a morality officer?"

"Morality officers are military officials in charge of making sure all the rules and decorum are upheld on a ship or base. They act as sort of spiritual advisers for the crew. They're also tasked with rooting out heresy within the ranks under that guise of spiritual guidance. Many morality officers are trained by the Hisbaween, if not outright Hisbas themselves. That's how we met. The powers that be somehow learned who my parents were, and I was hauled in front of her. I was technically marked as 'kidnapped' by Human Separatists. I had to be mentally evaluated for offensive thoughts and beliefs. It wasn't enough to discharge me from service, but Falling Star was assigned to monitor me closely. I was her pet project. We spent many hours together. The first few months felt like a constant stream of interrogations. After a while, it became clear to her I wasn't a threat to Bokori good order and discipline. The conversations turned more friendly in nature. I found myself visiting her more often than I was required. I was drawn to her and her to me. We both opened up far more than either of us should've been comfortable with. We became...close."

Havera sat there, unblinking. She was hanging onto every word. "Did you love her?"

Adam ignored her question. "She told me she dreamed of becoming an artist. I was astonished. Bokori aren't exactly known for their artistic prowess. Too many are forbidden from creating the art they desired, fearing punishment or retribution by the Hisbaween for potential heretical and blasphemous works. She was undeterred. She thought her morality officer position allowed her to understand where the line of acceptability was drawn. Her service contract was expiring at the end of the year. She was going to move to Concordia to pursue her craft. I offered to be her first client. She thought I was joking until I gave her my hand. I had scrounged together a basic tattooing kit, and I thought she should start with a friendly audience. The tattoo only took a few minutes, but we spent the entire night together. I can still remember her eyes."

Ivory.

Adam retracted his hand, gently rubbing the tattoo. The wave of memories came flooding back. Havera sat there, patiently waiting for him to continue. Tears welled up in Adam's eyes. He wiped them away with a sniffle.

"Unfortunately, Bokori society encourages people to report anyone they see committing cultural crimes. Promoting progress and cultural acceptance they claim. Someone on the ship saw us together talking about the tattoo. She was arrested and taken to the First Morality Officer. She was charged with abuse of power for her improper relationship with me. Their problem wasn't that she technically outranked me. She was Bokori, and I am Human," Adam said.

"The Bokori forbid interracial relationships?" Havera asked astonished.

"Only between Humans and Bokori. According to the great wisdom of the People's House and their Hisba dogs, a Human cannot legally consent to a relationship with a Bokori. Disparity of power, so they claim," Adam said bitterly.

"Holy Cradite! I was aware the Bokori had some bizarre notions about familial associations. I had no idea about this," Havera said.

Adam continued. "Abuse of power typically carries a suspended prison sentence and dishonorable discharge. However, there is no greater offense someone can commit than a cultural crime. The First Morality Officer tacked on a charge of appropriation." Adam could see the confusion on Havera's face. "Tattooing a body is practice that belongs to Humans or so the Bokori claim. For any Bokori to participate in a Human custom is considered an appropriation of culture. The punishment for appropriation is a public shaming inside the Hisbaween stadium along with period of time where the convicted are not allowed employment for a period of at least five years. Worst of all, they are required to endure a number of those years in rehabilitation. To purge them of their cultural sins. Falling Star knew exactly what occurred inside the rehabilitation center. She heard the stories during her training. We've seen what people, Bokori and Human alike, become when they reemerge from rehab. Zombies parroting the propaganda of the Hisbaween. No capacity for individual thought or feeling other than to be a good cultural citizen."

"Equality Through Sacrifice," Havera said. Adam looked up to see tears now welling in her eyes.

"Right," Adam said. "That's one of their many philosophies they try to drill into you. We are only as strong as our weakest link. Except, it's impossible to make everyone strong. Some people are born with advantages and abilities that give them an edge. Their solution is to break us all down until we're all weak. No one is exceptional. No one is better. No one can achieve more than someone else. Privilege and inequality must be eliminated by force. Culture belongs only to those to whom are born within it. To suggest otherwise is blasphemy. To practice otherwise is heresy. Not exactly an environment conducive to creativity."

"I didn't realize they sent Bokori to this rehab place. I thought it was for Humans only," Havera said.

Adam shook his head. "Not at all. In fact, the number of Bokori sentenced to rehab dwarfs that of Humans. Many Bokori resent Humans. They see us as benefiting from the Bokori's system unjustly. I can't blame them. On the surface, Humans are provided with subsidized services the Bokori themselves don't receive. Bokori used to be more vocal in their protestations in the early days of the Democracy. Not many but enough to cause concern within the People's House. The powers that be labeled them backward and spiteful thinkers. That's how the initial blasphemy laws were passed half a century ago. That's why the stadium was repurposed in the first place. To eliminate such sentiments completely from Bokori thought and lexicon through rehabilitation. The People's House is masterful at disguising what they do as beneficial to everyone. Those that protest are shamed and forced to confess their sins publicly before millions of 'enlightened' Bokori. They've so thoroughly convinced the galaxy theirs is the model others should follow. The fact you, a well-educated woman of the galaxy, don't know this shows just how far the Bokori's rot has permeated Griselda."

Rot that we purposively created.

Havera nodded. "I didn't know. Nobody does. That's why the footage of your scourging was so shocking. However, you might be happy to learn the rest of the galaxy thinks of the Bokori as a joke. Do you know what they call the Bokori on the Nexus? 'The Sick Race of the Galaxy.' The Censors in charge of the Praetorian Order believe the Bokori Democracy will collapse in my lifetime. The transition from arkhanate to democracy changed the Bokori."

No, we did.

Adam couldn't help but chuckle. "The Bokori restrict our Nexus access with heavily encrypted firewalls. You've been our greatest source of information on the outside galaxy. I know you Cauduun live for almost two-hundred years. Sometimes older. Your longevity is greater than anyone in the galaxy. That's ages for us. We've already waited for over five-hundred years. We can't wait anymore. It's too late for some of us."

Havera hung her head not bearing to look Adam in the eye when he said that. There was a long pause. Adam continued his story.

"Falling Star was terrified about what she would become. She broke down crying for hours in the cell. I visited her often, trying my best to comfort her. My efforts were limited. I was only allowed to speak to her through an intercom. 'You will see me again' I would say, knowing the words were hollow.

The day came when it was time for us to return to Bokor. I made the choice to help her escape. I broke her out of the cell. We were going to steal a shuttle and find our way to Concordia together. It didn't go as planned. Bokori military protocol dictates a disturbance on board a ship triggers an automatic jump to negative space. We couldn't escape in a shuttle while the ship was in negative space. We'd be ripped apart. We were about to be caught. She was not about to let herself be taken to that place. She sealed herself inside the airlock. 'You'll see me again, I promise,' were her final words to me. She opened the airlock, and, in the blink of an eye, she was gone."

Adam fell back, hitting his head on the soft carpet. Tears were flowing freely from Havera's eye. Her soft cries echoed throughout the ship. After a few moments, Adam sat up and wiped away his own tears. He composed himself. The expression on his face slowly transformed from sorrow to rage.

"I was taken to the First Morality Officer. I was initially only going to be charged with aiding and abetting. I was empty inside. The First Morality Officer tried to justify the charges by invoking the Covenant and Bokori cultural philosophy. The 'traitorous blasphemer' was dead. I could feel anger filling the void of my soul. It took her from me. I wasn't going to let it have my dignity, too. I let it know explicitly what I thought of it and its accursed Covenant. I spoke truths I knew to be self-evident. I topped it off by calling it 'prostrating Modder scum.' That didn't go over well. I was charged with blasphemy, heresy, and an added charge of toxicity for using such a phrase. I refused to apologize even after months of torture, so they publicly whipped me for it. The rest is history. For upholding Bokori values and rooting out heresy within the ranks, the First Morality Officer received a promotion. It became the High Hisba."

Havera gasped. Adam spoke that last sentence with utter venom, practically spitting out each word. He could feel his rage growing. Adam stood up and paced the room. Havera sat there speechless, unsure what to do with these revelations. Adam stopped in front of the window and stared out into space.

Havera finally found the courage to stand and speak. "I don't know what to say."

Adam turned on the spot. The look on his face startled Havera. She jumped back like prey avoiding a predator. The tears were still pouring from his eyes, but Adam's face was pure hatred.

"I am going to kill them, Havera. Falling Star, my brother, Samus, her parents, my parents. They are but a fraction of a never-ending list of victims sacrificed on the altar of the obscene Covenant. Their lives are an unpaid debt I intend to collect. I will tear their corrupt temple down around their heads. Only when their perverse institutions meet righteous Human fury and their shrills of protest are silenced forever will I find peace."

Adam tried to march past her. She held out her arm to stop him.

"Adam..."

It was the only word she could muster. Adam halted. It was all she needed. Without another word, she wrapped her arms around him tightly. She wrapped her tail around their bodies tightly and cried softly into his shoulder.

Adam tried to resist the constriction. He wanted to revel in his anger. He had earned it. Havera's touch and tears softened his heart. He couldn't muster any true resistance. He could feel his rage melt in her arms. He entwined his arms around her body. He allowed himself to grieve. He allowed himself to be vulnerable with Havera.

Just around the corner, Samus sat quietly, weeping uncontrollably.

13

Would You Kindly

The following two days went by swiftly. Adam spent most of that time in Havera's library at a terminal, researching galactic politics. It was a crash course for which he was woefully unprepared. The meager education Adam received did little to help him. His time in the military and in Arabella didn't help much either. He was aware of the Conclave, the supranational governing body of the galaxy based on its capital of Concordia. He had been there once during a tour.

Spent the entire time in orbit. Didn't see much, except for the massive artificial station that covers part of the planet like a hand grasping a ball.

The primary political power of the Conclave lay with the Proprietor races: the Bokori, the Cauduun, the Naddine, the Union, and the Zokyo. These powerful empires dictated the terms of trade, rules of war, interstellar travel, migration, and economic policy. Researching further, Adam discovered the Conclave was founded 1,600 years ago by the Bokori and the Cauduun. Both races discovered the garden world that would be called Concordia around the same time. There was some dispute who got there first, with the Cauduun saying they did and the Bokori claiming it was them. Initial fear and suspicion gave way to diplomacy and cooperation. The two races agreed to share Concordia and created a legal diplomatic framework, which would become the basis of the Conclave.

Over one-hundred years later, the Naddine were discovered by the Cauduun and the Zokyo by the Bokori around the same time, near their respective borders. Unlike the initial cooperation between the Cauduun and the Bokori, the Naddine and the Zokyo took an instant dislike to each other. Within a couple decades, the two future Proprietor races fought the first of five full-scale interstellar wars, the last of which was the Century of Strife. Adam couldn't quite figure out the source of the initial animosity when he fell down that hare hole. It seemed to be largely a dispute over technology and territory. He didn't have the time to inquire further.

Havera could probably tell me more.

He didn't see much of the Cauduun nor Samus. The ladies spent most of their time on the ship together. Adam often saw them leaving the training room quite sweaty from an intense workout. Havera was teaching Sam some of the self-defense techniques she learned as a Praetorian. Adam was happy to see them bonding and to see Sam come out of her shell. She hadn't quite been her old self since the incident. The three of them shared simple meals together. Unlike the rest of it, Havera's ship wasn't as luxurious in that regard. They ate mostly prepackaged rations meant for long term space travel. They reminded Adam a bit like the tubed paste meals during his time in the military, only more colorful and nowhere near as disgusting. He'd use these times to ask Havera some clarification questions about what he had read. She was quite insightful.

"I will warn you, Adam. The Cardinals won't take too kindly to what you're asking. They're the primary ambassadors of each race in the Conclave. The Bokori are a Proprietor race. A founding member! Nobody is too keen on interfering in the internal affairs of each member race, especially since the galaxy is still recovering from the Strife. Nobody wants to start another war. Present your case as best you can, but do not get your hopes up. Your pleas will most likely fall on deaf ears.

Even those who might be sympathetic won't cross a fellow Proprietor race. Your best chance at support will be with the Sinners," Havera told him during one midday meal.

Adam spent the rest of that day focusing his research on the Sinners. The Coalition of Independent Nations was an alliance of the non-Proprietor, independent races in the galaxy. Adam discovered they were almost all subjugated races at one time or another. Adam found that fact highly encouraging.

The main coalition partners were the Moan and the Rinvari. He was familiar with the aquatic Moan and the hulking primate Rinvari. A few of their voluntourists had visited Arabella in the past. The smaller Sinner coalition partners included the Sezerene, the Hasuram, the Faeleon, and the Bubil. The latter races, collectively called the "Tetrad," were relatively new to the galaxy. They were all discovered around the same time, about two-hundred years ago, just prior to the Century of Strife. Although their total numbers were surpassed by the Proprietor races, the Sinners held key strategic positions and resources within the galaxy. The Sinners banded together at the tail end of the Strife in response to something called the "Boiling of Sin," from which they derived their colloquial name. Adam had heard of this tragedy while in the military, but he never realized the utter devastation nor the full ramification of what had happened. Adam had to pull up a galaxy map to keep track of where everything was.

I'll bet Doom knew all this by heart. I'm out of my depth.

Sin was the main colony of the Moan, who were based on oceanic worlds in the Zeta spiral south-southeast of Neutral Space. Sin itself was close to the border with the Rorae to the west. Almost entirely an oceanic world with crystal clear water so transparent you could see the bottom; Sin was considered one of the galaxy's wonders.

"It was the crown jewel of the Moans," Havera said when he asked her about it that night. "In a flash, the entire world was rendered uninhabitable. Millions of lives snuffed out in the blink of an eye. Sin is nothing but a wasteland of boiling seas. A monument to war and genocide."

Notably absent from the Sinners were the mysterious, plantlike Rorae. He had heard many whispers and rumors regarding the Rorae, but he had never met one. Hopefully, his research would help identify them by sight, at the very least. Further references were made to Ashla, which was the Rorae homeworld, a covert program called the "Celestial Project," the Excommunicated, and a location known as the "Dark Realm."

He wished he had time to read it all. He was hungry for information. He created shorthand notes within his HUD's database to keep track of everything. He had limited space, so he tried to focus on the most important information. The more and more he read, the more and more he wanted to consume. With that desire for consumption came a sense of bitterness and anger.

The Bokori kept us in the dark!

He slapped himself a few times in the face to stay focused. While much of this information was interesting, it was of little help to their current predicament. From what Adam gathered, the Sinners might be a friendly ear. It was unclear, at least to Adam, how much power or influence that would translate to on Concordia. He was in the middle of researching more details about the Century of Strife when Samus knocked on the door.

"Havera says we're landing soon. You ready?" Samus asked.

Adam nodded. The two joined Havera and Dee in the cockpit. They sat down and strapped themselves in. The ship exited negative space with a jolt. Samus' eyes widened.

The sea of darkness gave way to a litany of metal. A chorus of thousands of ships moved with the purpose and grace of synchronized dancers. As the Cicera approached Concordia, the chaos of outer space gave way to the illusory order of civilization. Vessels large and small; familiar and exotic were huddled together in queues to, from, and around the prominent green world on the horizon.

Concordia was surrounded by four asteroids captured in the planet's gravity well, each artificially shaped a millennia ago with the visage of a different smiling face: a different Proprietor race. The Proprietor races had carved their place in the old galactic order. Only the Yunes lacked an opulent rock of their own. The Cicera passed close by to the huge cranium of a chiseled Bokori. A giant crack bisected diagonally across the mouth of the Bokori's face. Workers were attached to the sides of the asteroid. They were covering up and repairing small fractures in the side of the gray painted face, ignoring the prominent fissure.

"What is that?!" Samus cried out in amazement. She was pointing to the planet.

At first glance, Concordia was seemingly unimpressive. Though garden worlds were extraordinarily rare, from space they looked like any other rocky planet in the galaxy. The Cicera orbited closer to the sunny side of the planet. Out of the darkness, a polished metal structure emerged. The star's rays reflected and refracted off the mass of metal. A bony protrusion on an otherwise featureless world. The singular protrusion became two then three until the silhouette of a giant metal hand, grasping the side of the planet, came into full view. It was a beautiful grotesque attached to the side of Concordia.

"That, carissima, is the Conclave," Havera said with a smile.

"I thought the Conclave was a governing body not an entire construct!" exclaimed Samus.

"Technically, it's both. The locals call it the 'station' to distinguish between the two. Sticks out like a sore tail, I know. The station was built in the early days of the Conclave and expanded upon to accommodate the needs of each Proprietor race. Gravity and climate are controlled. The rest of the planet is used as farmland. Proprietors are allowed to settle an apportioned number of retirees on the surface each year," Havera explained.

"Your Grace," Dee cut in. "The station is hailing us."

"Put them on speaker, Dee," Havera said. She signaled for them all to be quiet.

"This is Conclave Docking Center requesting the Cicera," said a gravely harsh voice.

"You have the Cicera. Go ahead," replied Havera.

"Your Grace, you are requested to land at Docking Bay One-One-Three-Eight. A ConSec team will meet you at the hangar," said the voice.

"ConSec? Why is Conclave Security meeting me? I don't need an escort," said Havera in her stern tone.

There was a small pause. "Your Grace, with all due respect, I think you know the answer to that," said the voice nervously. Havera looked at Adam and Samus, then out the viewport. Flanking their ship on all sides were a number of solo fighters. The ships weren't Bokori in design, but Adam knew exactly what they were and their purpose. Adam felt his stomach catch in his throat. The voice continued. "By order of the Conclave, you are ordered to land, ma'am. This is non-negotiable."

"I have diplomatic status! On whose authority can ConSec detain a diplomat of the Cauduun Monarchical Alliance?" Havera said with a sharp tongue.

"Cardinal Final Form, ma'am."

"The Bokori have no authority over me," argued Havera.

"It's the Conclave, ma'am. Not the Bokori. Any Cardinal can order any ship within Neutral Space detained for cause. No exception."

"Patch me through to Cardinal Clodius! He'll grant authorization override," Havera ordered.

There was an audible gulp. "Ma'am, I have a note here handed by my supervisor passed along directly from Cardinal Clodius. He says, 'Do not resist. Obey protocol. I will handle everything from here.'" Another brief pause. "This is your final warning, ma'am. ConSec have been ordered to use whatever means necessary to prevent you from leaving. Will you comply?"

Havera slammed her fist on her seat. Samus was sitting calmly in her seat. Dee was waiting on Havera's orders. Adam's heart was racing.

We have no choice.

"Havera," Adam said softly. She swiveled her chair to face him. He had already put enough people he cared about in danger with his reckless actions. He wasn't going to add Havera to that list. "Do as they say."

Havera sighed and nodded. "Very well. The Cicera will dock," she said, shutting off the com aggressively, not giving the docking center employee a chance to respond.

She brought the ship closer to the station. Adam had no appreciation for how gigantic the station was until they were right up next to it. It was the biggest sentient-made structure he had ever seen. In terms of shape and size, Adam imagined if a goddess had stretched out Inclucity a few times over and extruded the structure into the upper atmosphere to sculpt a giant, deformed claw that grasped the surface of Concordia.

I wonder if we could've built something that grand.

Samus rotated her chair towards Adam. She reached over and grabbed him by his cold and clammy hand. She helped him out of his chair and wrapped her arms around him.

"You'll see me again. I promise. You're going to be okay," Adam said. The words felt hollow. No less than that fateful day. He felt her heart pulsing through her body. He lifted her head up, gently grazing the little scar on her chin. She wasn't crying. Instead, what he saw was fear.

"It's not me I'm worried about, Adam," Samus said.

Adam smiled and kissed her affectionately on her forehead. "You're the little sister I never had. I'm supposed to be worried about you, not the other way around."

"You don't need to worry. I'll take as many out as I possibly can. They will remember us!" Samus said with a surge of confidence.

Adam hadn't expected that. The fear in her eyes had turned dark with hatred and rage. He never felt prouder of her than he did right then.

After all she's been through. All the suffering and pain, she still wants to fight. I can't let harm come to her. She must survive.

"No, Sam. It's me they want. You continue the work I was sent here to do. Humanity is better off in your hands than mine. You must live, Sam. No matter what they do to me, you must live. You hear me!" Adam said that last part forcefully. He handed her Blade's borrowed emulator.

She swallowed and accepted the emulator. The light in her bright brown eyes returned. She loved him and he loved her. After a few moments of silence, she nodded. He kissed her on the forehead again.

"Go wait for me in the cargo area. There's something I need to discuss with Havera," Adam said. Samus nodded. She adjusted her utility belt tightly around her brown jumpsuit and walked in the direction of the stairs.

The Cicera had entered the station. The interior was more crowded than the exterior if that was possible. Thousands, perhaps millions, of ships were all coming and going. They were approaching a docking bay. Dee was monitoring the sensors on the Cicera's control panel. Adam signaled for Havera to step onto the bridge with the giant map of the galaxy on display. She followed.

"Take this," Adam said, extending his hand. In his hand was the Debbie. Havera's eyes widened, her tail stiffened.

"You're giving me the Rimestone weapon? This doesn't belong to me. I can't accept that," Havera said. She attempted to push away Adam's offer. He kept his hand extended insistently.

"I can't hide it within my inventory. I told you that. Even if I could, the Bokori or the Conclave would employ methods to forcibly remove it. It's not safe with me or Sam. My mother told me to trust you, Havera. I am. With our past and our future," Adam said.

Havera hesitated. She stared at the platinum grip, unblinking. Adam could sense the hunger in her amethyst eyes. Her tail was wagging excitedly. She slowly wrapped her bulbous fingertips around the grip and took it from Adam's grasp. She examined it in her hand for a moment, then pocketed it inside her tunic.

"Last time a Human handed a Havera a Rimestone weapon, y'all didn't get it back for three-hundred years," Havera said.

Adam chuckled. "Let's hope it doesn't take that long this time."

Minutes later they landed. Dee opened the cargo bay. Adam decided to walk out first. Samus almost didn't let go of his hand. Her fingers lingered in his grasp before falling to her side. Exiting the ship, Adam came face-to-face with multiple ConSec guards dressed in orange and blue stripes flanked by drones. All had their weapons pointed at him.

I wonder if cancellation orders extend this far westward.

He lifted his hands slowly skyward. A particularly grumpy looking Cauduun ConSec officer stepped forward. "By orders of Cardinal Final Form, acting on authority from the Conclave, you are hereby placed under arrest," the grumpy Cauduun said.

A pair of Naddine guards approached him slowly, their weapons drawn. When they reached him, they holstered their weapons. One retrieved a black cloth from his belt and the other a small injection device.

"Would you kindly tell Cardinal Final Form I prefer my nutrient paste cold?" Adam said with a smirk. The cloth was placed over his head, blinding him. He felt a slight prick in his neck. Within seconds, the muscles in his legs gave out. The only thing he felt, his consciousness fading, was the accursed itching on his back.

***

"THE BOKORI ARE A BUNCH OF MODDER-ENABLING JADESPAWN! THEY MAKE LOVE MORE BORINGLY THAN THEY LOOK! I HEAR THEY SPEND THEIR FREE TIME ON THE NEXUS PEERING AT THE SIZE OF CAUDUUN WOMEN'S...TAILS!"

Adam was shouting into the void at this point. If anyone heard him, they were ignoring him. He was using this opportunity to get some thoughts and feelings off his chest. It's not like he could do much more. He awoke in the cell five meals ago. It was the only measure of time he had. ConSec had disabled his HUD. He couldn't access his inventory, nor could he use basic functions like a clock or calendar. Only regular vision through his eyeballs. He still had his jacket and jumpsuit. They had taken his boots, leaving him barefoot. No chance at using the rocket stabilizers to potentially blast his way out. He doubted he could jury rig them to do that, but he bemoaned the lack of opportunity to try. He had forgotten what it was like to be this blind. The Hisbaween had used an identical mechanism to keep their prisoners pacified. These accommodations were paradise by comparison.

The floor was a sturdy foam, which was heavenly to walk and sleep on. Different environments were projected on the walls, allowing the captive to forget he or she was locked up. It was downright pleasant. Almost a mini-vacation. He was able to switch between different locations with a small panel on the wall, which also controlled the internal temperature within certain limits. No way they'd let their prisoners commit suicide by freezing or boiling to death. He played with the settings off-and-on for the past what he assumed was a day or two. He settled on a pleasant beach with water so clear you could see fauna swimming miles deep. He laid back with his arms behind his head, trying to relax. If he was going to be hauled back to Bokor, he may as well enjoy this while it lasted.

A landscape with color. My eyes had gotten so used to Bokor's gray, desaturated filter; I had forgotten what it was like to see.

The purple on Adam's duster came through more vibrantly. It was more violet than he realized. He thought about his father in that moment. He scratched his head, raising the hood. A curious thought struck him.

Huh, I don't recall ever seeing him wear this jacket. I hadn't known him that long. Maybe that's why.

His thoughts were interrupted by an electronic whiz. The beautiful crystal-clear water and blue sandy beaches were replaced by the walls original sterile white.

"What in Kewea?"

"Enjoying the view?" asked a disembodied voice behind him.

Adam shot up and whirled around. The wall was now see-through. On the other side stood a tall figure with a broad v-shaped chest. The figure was a Moan, the aquatic race from south of Neutral Space. The man had a short snout with dark-blue scales and tiny, black eyes. He was wearing a gaudy, rosy frock coat and matching tight pants. Both were made out what appeared to be fused, dyed seaweed. The coat was wide open at the top, revealing a creamy, blubbery bare chest. Adam could just barely make out the gills around his ribcage. He wore brown hide boots, and silk white gloves covered his thick claws. He topped off his fashion with a pink tricorn hat chiseled from coral.

"Cauduun women's tail, huh? Always knew those grayskins were freaks," the Moan said with a wink. He smiled, revealing rows of polished white teeth. Adam watched the Moan's ulnar fins expand and contract with each breath.

"You heard me?" Adam asked.

"They record everything here. You're monitored continuously all twenty hours a day. Don't worry. Nothing you've said is a criminal offense. At least, not in Neutral Space," the Moan said. Adam stood there mouth agape, unsure of what to say. The Moan rescued his stunned brain. "Sin was a brilliant choice. You've excellent taste, Human. I'm glad you had a chance to see its majestic beauty, even if it's just an old recording," the Moan said.

"That was Sin?" Adam asked astounded. The Moan nodded. Adam was only five when the seas of Sin boiled. He never thought he'd have a chance to see one of the wonders of the galaxy.

I wish I had appreciated it more.

"An unspeakable tragedy we wish to avoid. That's why the Coalition of Independent Nations exists. To act as a balance against those warmongering Proprietor races that dominate the galaxy," the Moan said.

"Oh, are you a Sinner representative?" Adam asked.

The Moan removed his tricorn hat to reveal a flexible, spinous dorsal fin poking through the seaweed frock that ran from the top of his head down his back. He gave a lavish, over-the-top bow. "Indeed, good sir, I am. My name is Daloth Afta. I am the Cardinal for the Thalassocracy of Merchant Moan Republics. I am also the point person for the Coalition of Independent Nations on Concordia. Sinners we call ourselves, so you seem to have heard. I apologize for not coming sooner, but the Bokori put up a million bureaucratic hoops for me to swim through to try and stop this meeting. Fortunately, we are a galaxy of laws, and even subjugated races have certain rights," said Daloth.

"Thasa...Thalassaass...Thalacracy?" Adam tried sounding out. He had never heard that term in Default.

"Thalassocracy," Daloth reiterated slowly. "I imagine that word is difficult for your tongue. I'm pleased you Humans get a good translation,"

"What does it mean? I've never heard of that form of...government?" Adam asked confused.

Daloth laughed. "It's a fancy way of saying we're an alliance of maritime nations. We're quite similar to the Naddine in that regard, except we're in water of course. Our people are quite decentralized. Each republic is managed independently by their own councils and leaders. The Doges who run the Thalassocracy allow us to coordinate our efforts in the galactic community. Their role could not be more important these days. We're taking on a rapidly changing galaxy since the Strife. But, I've spoken too much already. We have very little time to prepare," Daloth said with a wave of his gloved hands.

"Prepare for what?" Adam asked.

"Your extradition hearing," Daloth said bluntly.

Adam's heart sunk. His scars itched. He resisted the urge to scratch them in front of the Cardinal.

"The Bokori don't waste time," were the only words Adam could muster.

"Indeed. They're making the hearing public. Rather than a magistrate or arbiter, they've arranged for the case to be heard in front of the Proprietor Tribunal," Daloth said.

"I'm no expert, but that sounds bad," Adam said. He wondered if he'd have a chance to get Snake's book before getting shipped back.

"Well, the current flows both ways. They're seeking to make an example out of you. Demonstrate to the rest of the galaxy their power and authority. Get the five Proprietor races to put their stamp of approval on their method for dealing with the 'Human Question.' If the Proprietor Tribunal signs off, it's a powerful statement. However, this means you get to state your case before all the major Conclave Cardinals with the whole galaxy watching. They're essentially giving you a platform if we play this correctly," Daloth said.

"We?" Adam asked curious.

"Indeed. All those who come before the Proprietor Tribunal are allowed to have an advocate or orator speak on their behalf. If you'll let me, it would be my pleasure to represent you in front of the Tribunal," Daloth said with a weaker bow.

Adam shrugged. "Doesn't seem like I have much of a choice. Why would you want to help me?"

"Who is the Consul of Cloudboard? It shouldn't be shocking to you, Adam Mortis, but you've caught the attention of the wider galaxy. Forces far beyond your control and influence have a vested interest in the outcome of, not just this hearing, but of your entire Separatist movement. We, the Sinners, welcome instability within the borders of a dying Proprietor power. You didn't hear me say that," Daloth said with a wink.

At least he's honest.

"I'm glad I could be a political pawn for you, Cardinal. Is my fate a foregone conclusion, or is it possible for me to wiggle my way out of this?" Adam asked.

Daloth stroked his chin. "I won't lie to you. It doesn't look good. You executed a sentient being in front of cameras for all the galaxy to see. Your own kind, nonetheless! The Bokori are throwing all sorts of charges at you: murder, sedition, leaving the scene of a crime, tampering with evidence, witness tampering, unlawful departure, and a heresy charge for flavor, to name a few. They've spent the last couple days flying in witnesses to testify against you, including a number of Humans. They want your head, and they're most likely to get it. There is an unspoken agreement between the Proprietor races not to interfere in each other's internal affairs, including legal proceedings. The Conclave's Founding Charter, while it does guarantee certain rights and privileges to all sentients, is toothless in this scenario. No one is eager to see the galaxy engulfed in chaos again. At least publicly. Privately, many citizens, including Proprietor citizens, sympathize with your cause. However, the wounds of the Strife are barely scarred over. Everyone's afraid a war between Humans and the Bokori could draw in others. The Proprietor races are also afraid of our coalition. They don't want to add Humans to our ranks. However they might feel about you or the Bokori behind closed doors, they won't cross the Bokori. Best we can hope for is to stall. Maybe find some legal loophole. I'm sorry."

Adam's back itched again at the mention of scars. He sat down dejected. The Moan Cardinal bowed his head in remorse.

"What about Samus?" Adam inquired.

"Who?" Daloth asked.

"The Human woman who was arrested with me. Dark hair, a little younger than me, small scar on her chin?"

"Oh! Yes, her. She's not under arrest. She was detained as a material witness, questioned, then released. The Bokori were going to extradite her as well until *certain details* surrounding the recent incident were leaked to the press. They quickly backed off. She tried to visit you, but the Bokori ordered ConSec not to let her in. She's staying with Duchess Havera of Shele until the hearing," Daloth said.

Adam breathed a sigh of relief. Havera would take good care of Samus. Daloth didn't mention anything about the Debbie, so perhaps Havera did keep her promise. At the same time, he was worried about Samus. Daloth didn't need to elaborate on what he meant by 'certain details.' The whole galaxy must know what happened. He could only envision the stares of judging eyes on Samus. He felt those same eyes after his escape from the stadium.

I can't be there to protect her.

He thought of John and what he'd say if he found out the entire galaxy knew. He pitied all around him in that moment, particularly if any sharp instruments were nearby.

"Will none of the Proprietor Cardinals speak up against the Bokori?" Adam asked desperate for any sign of hope.

Daloth stroked his chin again. "The Cauduun Cardinal, Abbeus Clodius Ludicea, hates the Bokori. He'll probably be the most sympathetic *for obvious reasons*, but the Cauduun have their own problems with the Confederates within their own borders. Even if he was instructed to set those concerns aside by Queen Alexandra, he's only one vote. A majority is needed out of the five. He won't vote against the

Bokori if he's alone in this. Naddine Cardinal Luk-Kas of the Orrorror and the Zokyo Cardinal Fx'i'Dsn, Fex for short, don't want the appearance of upsetting the balance of power. They fear foreign meddling in their affairs. The Zokyo, especially, are worried about pirates near their borders. The Bokori are a useful buffer against them. You might get lucky, and they'll vote on opposing sides out of pure spite. Luk-Kas thinks of Fex as a control freak while Fex thinks Luk-Kas is an upstart ruffian and a brute. The Union Cardinal, aptly named Union_Cardinal, is, well, a bot. The Yunes try to stay out of the affairs of organics, but they are incredibly legalistic if they do chime in. Don't expect sympathy from a race of machines. They'll most likely abstain, per the usual. There's only one chance, I can see, of you escaping with some semblance of your life."

"How?"

The Moan paused, visibly uncomfortable. "Your friend. What did you call her? Samus. Let her testify publicly about what happened. She refused to give investigators details about that aspect of the events, but you might be able to convince her. Her testimony has the potential to be quite powerful."

"No."

"An agent of the Bokori government committing such a heinous act. The mere whisper of it on the Nexus and in the public conscious has already affected the case. It won't be enough to get the charges dropped, but it might shame the Bokori into agreeing to let you stand trial here on Concordia."

"Absolutely not!"

"The legal system here isn't barbaric! A trial in Neutral Space would be far favorable than on Bokor. Serve your time in one of these cells for a couple years, then apply for asylum!"

"I SAID NO!" Adam punched the floor. He regretted it instantly. The floor was comparably soft but quite stiff. The shock emanated up his arm to his spine. He bit his tongue to resist crying out. Daloth didn't respond, merely bowed his head. "My apologies, Cardinal, but I will not subject Samus to public humiliation. I've not heard the details, nor has anyone else. That's something for her to share with a therapist or a law enforcement official, not a public show trial in front of jadespawn politicians and a ravenous, uncaring media. It is no one's business but hers unless SHE DECIDES to take action. I don't care if they if they whip me a thousand times! I take the lash for her; she doesn't take it for me!"

Daloth paced pacing back-and-forth for a few seconds, stroking his chin. He stopped and stared right into Adam's eyes. "The Bokori will kill you if you're sent back. What good will you be to your cause then?"

Adam stepped right up to the glass, unblinking. "Haven't you heard, Cardinal? The Bokori consider the death penalty unholy. A mortal sin upon the altar of progress," Adam said mockingly. "They won't kill me, Cardinal. What they will do to me is far worse."

The Moan took a deep breath and nodded his understanding. There was a loud hissing noise. Out of the glass wall the outline of a door materialized and opened with a slight whine.

"Alright, Human. Grab your boots from the property clerk. Can't show up to the most powerful political body in the galaxy with no shoes. Not unless you're a Rorae," Daloth said with a slight chuckle as he led Adam out of the cell.

"Is it too late to claim that I am?" Adam asked dryly. "The Bokori are deluded enough that I might get away with such a claim."

14

What's So Funny?

The holding cell was a short railcar ride from their destination. The compartments in the railcars were clean. These hyper fast railcars ran rings around the station with connecting stations cutting across the middle to different station sectors to help ease pedestrian and vehicle congestion. An attractive Cauduun female news anchor was giving a report on a few of the displays plastered near the top of the car. No audio. Only a HUD channel listing in the bottom-right corner of the screen in order to listen in. With no access to his HUD, Adam didn't have the option to listen. From the visuals, excitement was fever pitch for an upcoming Orbital match on Concordia; Strong economic earnings report for the Conclave this quarter; Talks about the deadlock surrounding the Cauduun monarchy's succession; A quick update on the construction of something called the "Sinner Superhighway"; A report of missing Rangers somewhere on the Alpha spiral with the blame for the disappearances pinned on pirate activity. Adam stopped paying attention after that.

Adam sat handcuffed next to Cardinal Daloth Afta, in all his fine regalia. He had removed his tricorn hat during the trip, placing it in his lap. Adam noticed he sweated profusely. "We're built more for the open seas than the enclosed caskets of land," Daloth said.

They were accompanied by a pair of ConSec guard bots in a private car near the conductor's car at the front. They were a more advanced model than the combat bots Adam encountered during his time with the Bokori fleet. Better maintained, too. Bipedal, bulky, and seemingly faceless, these bots moved like tanks. A head taller than Adam, they weren't as maneuverable as the Bokori combat bots. Their versatility was limited in comparison to an assistant bot like Dee. Adam got the distinct impression they were built more for intimidation and enforcement, rather than straight up combat. Although, the one flanking Adam to his right did have a scorch mark visible on its broad upper thigh. Their steel bodies clanged the nearby ground with each step.

One of those things tackles me, I'll be ground into dust.

The bots weren't holding any weapons, relying simply on their intimidating presence and vested Conclave authority. Adam could see they had a basic sidearm and electric baton attached to their hip area. Their mechanized voices only spoke in short, curt sentences. They had a surprisingly tender touch for their size when they slapped the cuffs on Adam prior to their railcar journey. On their chest plate area, they bore the insignia Adam recognized as belonging to the Conclave: A pentagon of five keys pointed inward surrounded by two olive branches on a background with blue and orange stripes.

"They added the last key when the Union became the newest Proprietor race almost sixty years ago," Daloth explained clearly irritated. "Hmph! It insults us that those Kewea-accursed Yunes would become a Proprietor race over us. We've been around for almost seven-hundred-years! What do we have to show for it? Nothing but plundered resources and dead planets. These bots show up in the middle of the Strife and bam! Proprietor status. Not that the Yunes contribute much to galactic security. They stay confined to their space, only committing the bare minimum of troops and ships required by law. Barely above the Bokori in that regard. They bribe the other Proprietors with morsels of their secretive technology to get them to back off. I would wager my left ulnar fin, the Yunes could wipe out our pirate problem with minimal issue."

"I've seen some of their bots in action. Well, kind of," Adam said. "The Bokori started phasing in combat bots to replace us in their armed forces a few years back. Empty shells for the Bokori to program in their own protocols. No traces of Union personality matrices in them, supposedly. Obedient and deadly. I can see the appeal."

"Never trust a bot to do a living, breathing person's job. Automation and low-level programmed cybernetics are one thing, but those creatures are not alive. Artificial intelligence. A hivemind. Synthetic life. Hmph! No concept of the value of sentient life, no notion of pain and suffering. Nothing but expensive scrap metal that we let dictate policy," Daloth said.

"Don't let them hear you say that," Adam said, nodding to the guard bots.

"These ConSec bots don't care," Daloth said, tapping the nearest one hard. The bot ignored him. "Agents of the Conclave with precision programming. Not alive. No capacity to think creatively or feel. A pet with a longer shelf life."

"I hope insulting one of the Proprietor races isn't your plan for getting me off, Cardinal. I enjoy yelling at an emulator as much as the next person. Again, I'm no expert, but that doesn't seem like a sound legal strategy," Adam said.

Daloth put his tricorn back on. "Indeed. Do not worry, I have a plan. Each Proprietor Cardinal will be allowed to question any witness. After they're finished, your advocate can ask any relevant question of the witnesses. I'll try to attack their credibility. The goal is to convince the majority of the Tribunal you will not receive a fair trial upon a deportation back to Bokor. Political persecution is one of the legal grounds for asylum. Don't expect it to be granted at this hearing, but we may convince enough of the Tribunal to delay extradition to hear an asylum claim. You're not compelled to testify unless you so choose. As your de facto advocate, I'd strongly urge you to resist the temptation to speak. The Bokori are going to trumpet out witness after witness to try to slander you and the Human Separatist movement. If you come off as quick tempered or hot-headed, it will be the excuse the Tribunal will use to sign off on your deportation. You must appear to be reasonable or stay silent."

Adam thought about it for a moment. "And what happens when they play a recording of me shooting an unarmed prisoner?" he asked bluntly.

Daloth lifted his hat to wipe his brow. "I'm still working on that," he admitted.

"That...man...killed my brother in cold blood. Left my widowed mother with only one son, who she barely has any relationship with thanks to those Kewea-accursed grayskins," Adam said through gritted teeth.

"That's good. That's good. I can use that for sure. You were in extreme emotional distress. Yes, I think I can sell that. That won't convince the Yunes, but the living Proprietors might find the argument persuasive. Unfortunately, you may have to testify if that's the path you want me to pursue. That'll open you up to all sorts of questions. You have the right not to answer if you believe it'll incriminate you. You cannot lie or tell half-truths. If you speak, it must be nothing but the truth. Address each Cardinal as, 'Your Eminence.' Don't answer more than what was asked. Keep your anger in check. All details about the incident, including those involving your friend, will most likely come up. I'll do what I can to keep the conversation on the relevant issue. No promises. My authority, even as a Cardinal, is very limited in that room. No outbursts like what you demonstrated back in the holding cell. Thousands of people will be in attendance with billions more watching around the galaxy. When we get to the part about your brother and mother, don't be afraid to cry. The Naddine and the Cauduun love those sorts of public displays of grief. The other Sinner races will be behind you. Our numbers may be small in comparison to the Proprietors, but we can make our presence felt. Legally, you're in a tight spot. Public opinion might be your best hope," Daloth said.

"Will the Proprietor Cardinals be swayed by that?" Adam asked.

Daloth stroked his chin. "I cannot say for sure. I wish I had a better answer. We're in new territory. The Cardinals respond to the politics of their homeworlds more than they do the Conclave. In terms of incentives, the Cardinals have very little to listen to the public. Nevertheless, it's the only chance you've got," Daloth said grimly.

"I see. Let's say for the sake of argument, I get lucky. I'm allowed to stay here to seek asylum. If the Conclave grants me asylum, will I be allowed to return home?"

Daloth wiped his brow. "No. Not unless you wish to be subjected to the laws of the Bokori. You will not be allowed to leave Neutral Space again."

Adam sighed. His scars itched. He pressed his back gently against his seat to try and scratch them. His mouth was dry. His heart rate quickened.

"For the cause," he said finally.

A loud ding preceded the sound of a female voice, "Next stop: Conclave Legislative Assembly Building."

"We're here. Time to face justice," Adam said with a deep exhale.

Daloth stood up. "Not justice, Human. Politics."

***

The Legislative Assembly Building was an isolated, tall structure surrounded by a white marble exterior courtyard on all sides. Unlike most of the structures nearby, the building was constructed out of tanned stone with high windows inlaid with colored glass and rounded arches for entrances and exits. The walls were propped up by flying buttresses on the sides of its high façade with open gangways connecting parts of the upper floors. The central structure was encased in a giant brick dome with the flag bearing the symbol of the Conclave at its peak.

The style of architecture was completely foreign to Adam. While not as large as the Hisbaween stadium back on Bokor, the Legislative Assembly Building was far more ostentatious. Hundreds of people were queued up on the steps leading up to the main entrance. This was the seat of power in the galaxy.

Adam was led into a guarded, hidden side entrance to avoid the crowd. A few people caught glimpses of him and shouted things he couldn't discern. The guard bots handed him off to a pair of blue and orange uniformed guards: one Naddine, one Cauduun. Cardinal Daloth stopped at the entrance.

"This is where I leave you. ConSec Guard will take you where you need to go. I'll see you inside," Daloth said with an exaggerated bow.

Adam thanked him, and the guards led him inside. He was led through dimly lit stone corridors by his silent captors. He quickly became disoriented as they took what seemed like dozens of twists and turns. They eventually arrived in a small, dark interior chamber, more modern than the stone structures surrounding it. The guards sat him down on a lone, uncomfortable antique chair in the middle of a raised platform. The Naddine guard uncuffed him and stepped off the platform. He flipped a switch and a light above him turned on.

"Wait here. Don't move. The platform will take you to your destination. When you get there, do not leave the platform. Any attempt to leave your chair unless directed by the ConSec Guard or the Cardinals will be met with extreme prejudice. Do you understand?" the guard asked.

Adam nodded. The two guards flanked the only exit to the room. Adam waited...and waited...and waited. He sat there for several minutes becoming agitated in his chair. He felt a cramp in his butt cheeks and his scars tingled a bit.

"I can't get up to stretch?" Adam asked.

"No," the Naddine guard said curtly.

The wait is too slow a death.

A quiet alarm sounded throughout the chamber. Above him, the ceiling opened up, sending a beam of bright light onto the platform. He shut his eyes and turned his head away from the source of the light. He felt the platform underneath him shudder and lurch upward. He instinctively grabbed the arms of his chair while the platform ascended towards the source of the light above him. He heard the sounds of cheers and jeers the closer the platform moved to the surface. The platform crested the ceiling and stopped once it leveled off with the surrounding floor.

It took a few seconds for Adam's eyes to adjust to the light of the room. Adam found himself inside a gigantic, ornate chamber. A vision of beauty and grandeur. The room was well lit and spacious. Nearly a hundred feet tall that rose into a vaulted ceiling. Stone volute columns were positioned every twenty feet. Adorned with pointed arches, each had a unique carving of strange symbols and creatures above them. On the walls and ceiling were mosaics and paintings of the Proprietor races in lavish poses depicted in varying art styles. On one wall, Adam noticed a canvas of Bokori dancers in a style that reminded him of the painting tucked away hidden inside the People's House. On the far back wall was a grand, floor-to-ceiling, stained-glass mural with the visage of a Cauduun and Bokori embracing each other.

It's a damn cathedral!

Rising above the main floor up the painted archways were galleys along the sides of the chamber, tilted slightly downward to face the main floor. Several floors filled with what must've been thousands of witnesses of many races. He spotted most Zokyo and Naddine keeping a distance from each other. Entire sections of Bokori were segregated from everyone else. Cauduun, Rinvari, and Moans were mixed in with a scattering of other minor species. He glanced around, scarcely seeing another Human. Samus was nowhere in sight. His arrival brought with it spurred shouts of protest and excitement. Adam could only discern the occasional word or phrase. The most oft repeated ones included, "murderer," "traitor," "free him," and "justice for Humans."

A real mixed bag if there ever was one.

Adam could feel his heart pounding and his scars itching. He tried closing his eyes to drown out the noise to little avail. The sudden cacophony distracted him such that he almost didn't notice his immediate surroundings. Cardinal Daloth was sitting at a nearby wooden table with a pair of other well-dressed Moans. Judging by their behavior, Adam presumed they were his aides. Sitting at the next table over were a pair of hooded Bokori in hushed conversation.

Must be representatives from the People's House.

No sooner than the thought hit him, the Bokori removed their hoods and kyqads. Adam recognized the one closest to him. Enduring

Temptation, the lead Bokori negotiator from the People's House. The other Bokori was a female, though that was difficult to discern through her oversized robe. Adam didn't recognize it.

Daloth did mention the Bokori were flying in witnesses.

Adam was surrounded on all sides by several familiar guard bots all bearing the seal of the Conclave on their chests. They were unphased by the emotional reactions of the crowd. Daloth acknowledged his presence with a nod. A decorative, wooden boundary about knee-high separated Adam from the rest of the room. Similar structures divided the room further with crowds of people sitting along the sides and behind him. Another ornate barrier was placed between Daloth and a wide-open section of marble flooring, leading to the stained-glass mural in the back.

At first, Adam thought it seemed like a waste of space until the floor opened up. Similar to his own entrance, five grand platforms rose from underneath the floor, settling in several feet above the main floor. A roaring horn blared throughout the chamber, drowning out the thousands of conversations occurring around them. The horn was so loud Adam had to cover his ears. Once the sounds of the horn dissipated, the crowd was silenced. Adam could sense the excitement in the air despite the silence, or perhaps it was his own dread tricking his brain.

The lights in the room dimmed, with beams focusing only on main floor. At the top of each of the five platforms, sitting in lavish, gaudy chairs with high backrests, were the five Cardinals of the Proprietor races. From a certain point of view, the platforms appeared to be floating in midair. Adorned in robes and other vestiges of dyed red cloth and silks, the Cardinals sat still. They each had matching square, horned caps. A looping ring surrounded the top of each platform.

From left-to-right sat the Cardinals representing the Zokyo, the Bokori, the Cauduun, the Naddine, and the Union. On the frontward facing section of their platforms, each had a symbol representing each society emblazoned on a display for all to see: A three-sided boxy shape of interconnecting figure eights, a gray open-palmed hand holding an ornate key, three colored rings in a triangular pattern with a fourth platinum ring where they intersect surrounded by a wreath circlet, two caped riders holding spears riding on the back of a large winged beast, and a black sphere surrounded by three overlapping, white rings. Behind the chairs rose an enormous display screen broadcasting video of each of the Cardinal's faces. Adam surmised the looping ring on each platform was meant to capture video and presumably audio, judging how difficult it would be for anyone to hear them. A similar, smaller device was attached to the front of the two wooden tables, where Daloth and the Bokori sat.

"This Conclave Tribunal will come to order," said the Cauduun Cardinal in a deep voice. Cardinal Clodius, whom Daloth identified previously, was a middle-aged man, which Adam figured would put him at well over one-hundred years old. He had navy blue skin with a shiny, white tail. His hair was shoulder-length with diagonal patterns of pale blue and white. The pattern reminded Adam a bit of his hoverbike.

I hope Mom is taking good care of it. More so, I hope she doesn't see this.

"For posterity recordings, it is now the third hour of the fifth day of Mordelad. The sixteen-hundredth year G.S.C. As requested on behalf of His Eminence, Cardinal Final Form of the Free People's Democracy of Bokor, this Tribunal will hear the case for deportation from Neutral Space of the Human prisoner Flowing Courage, also known as Adam Mortis. Should the Tribunal find sufficient evidence, the prisoner will be returned to the custody of the People's House on Bokor. Who speaks for the People's House?" Cardinal Clodius asked.

Enduring Temptation rose to its feet, clearing its throat. "Persons Enduring Temptation and Hopping Chains for the People's House, Your Eminence," said Enduring Temptation, a slight quiver in its voice. The Bokori sat back down.

"Very well," said Cardinal Clodius. "Who, if anyone, speaks for the prisoner?"

Daloth rose to his feet. "Cardinal Daloth Afta of the Thalassocracy of Merchant Moan Republics, also representing the Coalition of Independent Nations, Your Eminence," Daloth said with a lavish bow.

Several cheers erupted from the crowd. The loud horn noise returned, silencing the crowd.

"If the gallery could keep their disruptions to a minimum, please. Thank you. Very well, Your Eminence. This Tribunal appreciates your voice in this chamber, Cardinal Afta," Cardinal Clodius said.

"You honor me, Your Eminence. Before we proceed, could we settle on the issue of the prisoner's name? Respectfully, we ask that this Tribunal and all its participants refer to the prisoner as Adam Mortis. It is his chosen name," said Daloth.

Clodius turned to the other Cardinals. "Any objections?"

"I object," said the Bokori Cardinal, Final Form. Adam recognized the tenor of Final Form's voice. It was another Parthenogen like the Hisbaween's second-in-command, Unbroken Tide. Its echoing voice, further amplified through speakers, bounced off the walls of the chamber, unnerving Adam. As if three Bokori were talking all at once. "The prisoner's birth name is Flowing Courage. There is no record of the prisoner ever having his name legally changed. This Tribunal should not recognize the legitimacy of the prisoner's assumed name."

"All due respect, Cardinal Final Form, this very Tribunal has recognized pseudonyms and informal names in the past. I see no reason why we couldn't honor this small request in the name of sentient dignity," said Daloth.

Hushed whispers washed over the crowd. The screens in the background shifted to the person speaking. Currently, they focused on Final Form, waiting for its reply. "I maintain my objection."

Adam's anger flared up internally. He squeezed his fists tightly to resist the urge to stand-up. He caught Daloth turn slightly to face him, a slight smile on his face. Adam cocked his head.

He's smiling. Why?

"Very well. This Tribunal will refer to the prisoner by his birth name, Flowing Courage. If there are no other objections, we shall proceed. Person Enduring Temptation, you may proceed with your opening statement," Clodius said.

Enduring Temptation stood up and cleared its throat. "Your Eminences, I will keep my remarks brief and simple. Prisoner Flowing Courage executed a person, a Human person, on livestream. Billions witnessed this barbaric act as it unfolded. A crime so heinous as to take the life of an innocent sentient must be met by the strongest, fiercest response from the law. Furthermore, the People's House will present witnesses attesting to the multitude of charges, including but not limited to sedition, unlawful occupation of our sacred moon, witness tampering, tampering with elections, leaving the scene of a crime, and unlawful departure. Any one of these charges constitutes grounds for deportation in the eyes of the Conclave. We simply ask this Tribunal to enforce the law. No more, no less. Thank you, Your Eminences." The Bokori sat back down. The room responded to the Bokori's statement with deafening silence. Not even the Bokori attendees reacted.

"Cardinal Afta, do you wish to present an opening statement on behalf of the prisoner?" asked Clodius.

Daloth stood. "I do, Your Eminence," Daloth removed his tricorn hat and set it down on the table. He wiped the heavy flop sweat off his brow in the process. He turned away from the Cardinals to face the galleries. "Cardinals, ladies, lords, esteemed guests, and all free people of the Conclave, tomorrow we will celebrate the twenty-fifth anniversary of the Saptia Accords. For the overwhelming majority of people in this room and of those watching these proceedings around the galaxy, it is a momentous, joyous occasion. A remarkable achievement after a century of warfare. Peace in our time. A moment to reflect upon the horrors of the Strife and honor those who lost their lives in the conflict. A time to rebuild and usher in a new spirit of cooperation and prosperity. Most everyone, except for the Humans!" Daloth said with a sudden raised his voice at the end of his sentence. "While we were cheering an unforgettable Orbital match in the afterglow of peace, Humans were forced to recognize they would remain chained. Shackled by a Covenant of Subjugation we promised would end. The warning signs of discontent were there. Exploded in the skies above Saptia. We all remember that night. Some of us more so than others," Daloth said, a hint of mockery in his voice.

The crowd chuckled at his comment. Adam whipped his head around, staring at the crowd in confusion.

What's so funny?

Daloth moved closer to Adam, gesturing to him for the cameras. "Twenty-five years later, here sits another Human dressed in violet. This one, whose true name we are not allowed to use in these proceedings, accused of all sorts of offenses. The prisoner will not deny he killed a fellow Human. We all saw this recording. What we didn't see is what happened just prior. We will present evidence the person the prisoner is accused of killing in fact murdered the prisoner's brother not but moments preceding the recording. A moment of stress at the tail end of a Bokori assault upon the peaceful settlement of Arabella. All this happened only one day after the prisoner was forced to mourn the loss of his father under the threat of annihilation! I'm sure the People's House will play the livestream again for all the galaxy to see and ask Your Eminences to ignore the circumstances surrounding it. But, there is another video the People's House will not want to talk about. One that also involves this prisoner."

Daloth turned back to face the Cardinals. "If the People's House wish to dredge out the prisoner's crimes against the Bokori, we will show the galaxy their crimes against Humans! We will show that it is impossible for the prisoner to receive a fair and just trial if he is deported back to Bokori Space. Any crime the prisoner is accused of was committed under extreme duress and emotional distress. We appeal to the Tribunal's sense of justice to allow the prisoner to be held and tried in Neutral Space, and, if convicted, to serve time in a Conclave prison, not a Bokori one. Like our Bokori friends, we, too, want the Tribunal to follow the law. Conclave law guarantees certain rights for all sentients within its borders. To send the prisoner back would be a violation of the Conclave's Founding Charter. Thank you, Your Eminences."

He's good. Strong words. Why don't I feel better?

A few sounds of approval trickled from the crowd, but they largely stayed silent. Cardinal Clodius nodded. "Thank you, Cardinal Afta, for that passionate opening statement," Clodius said.

"Pfft! Passionate and full of lies and deceptions," Cardinal Final Form spat out. The Bokori Cardinal was a bit ashen in the face Adam noticed.

"Such a statement is unbecoming of a person in your position, Cardinal Final Form," said the Naddine Cardinal, Luk-Kas. By his tone, it sounded like a rebuke.

The Naddine's upside faces are always difficult to read; Adam thought. Naddine skulls were inverted with their jaws situated the top and their craniums at the bottom. The position of their flexible eye stalks, which extruded from the cranium, finalized the disorientating shape of their rugged appearance.

Luk-Kas wore lavish feline furs, dyed red, with a matching half-shoulder cape. Adam could see the various patches sewn into the cape; although, he couldn't discern any of their details. Luk-Kas had lots of them. That much was clear. "If there are any misconceptions or falsehoods, it is up to the government's advocate to demonstrate to us, the examiners, where the prisoner's advocate is incorrect. It is not up to us to cast judgment until all the facts are in," said Cardinal Luk-Kas.

"I do not need a lecture from you, Cardinal Luk-Kas, on the proper etiquette and protocol of my job. I've had this position for nearly twenty years, far longer than you! If I see a falsehood, I will call it out," insisted Cardinal Final Form.

"Cardinals! As the ranking chairperson of this Tribunal, I ask that you both hold your tongues. There will be plenty of time to argue and debate during deliberations. We have many witnesses to examine. Let's not drag this out further than it needs to go. We all have Accordance Day events to attend," said Cardinal Clodius. He had raised his voice calmly but authoritatively.

"Apologies, Cardinal Clodius," said Cardinal Luk-Kas with a head nod.

"Very well," said Cardinal Final Form bitterly.

Final Form's eyes focused intensely on Adam, who returned the stare. A feeling of unease Adam couldn't pinpoint overcame him. Clodius called for the People's House to present their witnesses. Final Form and Adam did not break eye contact. He had never seen or met the Cardinal, but Adam knew its name. All Humans did. The camera operators must've picked up on the tension for out of the corner of Adam's eye he saw that they were split screening between him and the Cardinal. The entire galaxy witnessed the stare down. The Cardinal realized what was happening and broke eye contact. Adam's heart was pounding, and his breathing shallowed. He closed his eyes taking deep breaths.

You will hold it together!

15

Highs and Lows

The rest of the morning had an air of familiarity. Enduring Temptation monopolized the next two hours, trotting out a litany of witnesses against him. The first couple witnesses were people Adam had never met. The first was some Bokori economist discussing the benefits of the Covenant, and how it was illogical for Humans to want to break free. It concluded there must be some malevolent force behind the Separatist propaganda. Daloth, confused to the point of its testimony, asked what it meant by that. The Bokori could only shrug. Daloth successfully had it stricken from the record. The next was a Modder woman with one side of her body modified: side of her head shaved, vertical eye, bleached gray skin. She was there to testify about supposed Separatist voter intimidation tactics.

"During the last election, these profane Humans tried to scare us into voting against the Covenant. It didn't work though. I followed my heart and voted to stay with the Bokori. We're stronger together."

"These intimidating Humans, do you remember anything about them?" asked Enduring Temptation.

"Not really, no. They kept their faces hidden. I do remember one had a tattoo. I've seen that blasphemous symbol on other Humans. It's despicable, hateful!" said the Modder woman.

"Can the prisoner please raise his left hand with the backhand facing the cameras?" asked Enduring Temptation. Adam blinked unsure what to do. Daloth nodded at him. Adam complied, raising his Remembrance tattoo for all to see. "Is that the symbol?" asked a grinning Enduring Temptation.

The Modder woman sobbed. "Yes. Even being in the same room as someone who wears that symbol stresses me. Please make him put it away." Adam rolled his eyes, but did as the Modder asked.

It's going to be one of these days, isn't it?

It was Daloth's turn. "How exactly did these *profane* Humans intimidate you, may I ask?"

"What do you mean?" asked the Modder.

"Did they threaten you?"

"Their mere presence was threatening."

"I mean did they threaten to harm you if you voted to reaffirm the Covenant?"

"No."

"Did they threaten to harm your family?"

"No."

"Did they scream at you or attempt to bribe or blackmail you?"

"No."

"Did they physically harm you in any way?"

"No."

"What exactly did they do?"

"Ask me and others to vote against the Covenant."

"Well, then I'm confused. How exactly did they intimidate you?"

"We shouldn't have to listen to anyone that espouses such hateful ideology. It's our right to not ever have to be exposed to such blasphemy! That's why I believe so strongly in the Covenant. They help educate and redeem such Humans that have been brainwashed by those heretics. To keep us safe!"

"Keep you safe from words?"

The crowd sniggered. The Modder broke out in tears. Daloth was unable to question her further. She had to be escorted out by ConSec guards.

"Shame on you all!" yelled Hopping Chains. The Bokori section of the crowd yelled, "Shame. Shame. Shame."

Once their chants died down, someone else in the crowd yelled back. "Shame on y'all for wasting our time!" The crowd guffawed. The horn blared again, silencing everyone.

I'm more entertained than I ought to be.

Enduring Temptation resumed the proceedings with more witnesses like that. Daloth, to his credit and with very little prep time, handled each witness quite well. Every petty charge or accusation he verbally parlayed with brilliance. Adam watched each Cardinal for a reaction. The Naddine and Zokyon Cardinals looked bored. Cardinal Clodius was also bored by the continued testimony, but his boredom seemed amplified by rising anger. Cardinal Final Form was getting more excited with each passing minute. A few times Adam thought it might orgasm in its chair. The Union Cardinal, who hadn't uttered a word since the proceedings started, sat there in its chair unmoving, reactionless.

Do bots get bored?

By the sixth or seventh witness, Cardinal Clodius had reached his limit. "Enough. Person Enduring Temptation, how many more witnesses are you going to present?"

Enduring Temptation cleared its throat. "Your Eminence, it is our intention to present all forty-five witnesses to the Tribunal."

The audience groaned. Cardinal Luk-Kas buried his face in his claws while Cardinal Fex adjusted some settings on his mechsuit. Cardinal Clodius rose to his feet. "It's midday. I'm calling an hour-long recess to get some food and refreshment. We'll resume testimony at the sixth hour of the day." The horn blared. The Cardinals and their platforms descended beneath the floor. The sounds of conversation picked up in the crowd.

Adam slumped in his chair. Daloth walked over to check in. "How are you holding up?"

"At this point, I'm almost willing to confess to get this over with," Adam said as he stretched in his seat.

Daloth laughed. "Don't be stupid. We're doing well, all things considered."

"I was quite impressed with how you handled that farce, Cardinal, or should I call you, 'Your Eminence?'" Adam said.

Daloth gave another lavish bow. "Thank you, but that is not necessary. Cardinal or Daloth is fine. I'm pompous but not *that* pompous."

"Are we really going to have to listen to all those witnesses?" Adam asked.

Daloth wiped his brow. "Cradite save us, I hope not. Clodius is not a patient man. He won't want this to drag on further. That said, it might be to your benefit to keep this going. You're seeing the reactions. I don't understand what Final Form is thinking. It's becoming ridiculous. You put it well. Farcical!"

"To you, Cardinal. You fail to grasp the Bokori like I do. To them, only someone with sinister intent has the capacity to oppose their beliefs. They are so utterly convinced of their own righteousness; it never crosses their mind that what they're doing seems silly. I wish it were that silly. The damage they're inflicting upon us with their uncompromising attitude is killing us," Adam said.

They are who they are because of us.

Daloth wiggled his fins. "Swim tight. The rough seas are still to come. No matter what happens, trust me to handle it, okay?"

Adam nodded. "You haven't let me down, yet. Do you know who else is testifying?" Daloth shook his head. "In court proceedings such as these, the accused doesn't get access to witness lists. If this were a criminal trial that would be a different story; however, those same rights aren't extended to extradition hearings. Subjugated races have even fewer rights. I will say, it's unusual to have so many witnesses at this kind of hearing. Final Form wants to overwhelm you. Hit you from all angles. I can handle it. Don't you worry."

Adam was worried. Daloth stepped off the platform to allow it to descend back to the room below. The guards must've changed shifts for it was two Bokori who met him this time. They sat Adam down at a nearby table with a sumptuous meal of gray nutrient paste and a container of water.

Everywhere I go I cannot escape this stuff.

An hour and a visit to the restroom later, Adam was lifted back into the Tribunal cathedral. Adam could've sworn the amount of people pressed together in the audience had doubled. The horn blared, signaling for quiet.

Cardinal Clodius stood. "Upon consultation with His Eminence, Final Form, and the People's House, we've stipulated that the majority of remaining witnesses will testify to the continued importance of the Bokori-Human Covenant, and that the prisoner, Flowing Courage, has actively participated in activities seeking its destruction. As such, their testimonies won't be necessary."

"Oh, thank you!" Adam declared loudly to the guffaws of the crowd. Every Bokori in the room shot Adam a filthy look.

Daloth spoke, "As you can see from the prisoner's reaction, we have no objection."

Adam thought he caught the hint of a faint smile from Cardinal Clodius. "Very well. Person Enduring Temptation, you may call your remaining four witnesses."

The first person called was the Human driver who lifted Adam to the Sistine Slum. His arms were bandaged with several cuts across his face in various states of healing. He testified about his ride back with John and Samus.

"I received the alert on my HUD. I didn't make the connection at first. The three of them were acting shifty, trying to conceal their identities. I knew something was odd. I slowed down in order to get a better look. Once I established they were wanted criminals, I quietly steered in the direction of the Hisbaween. Unfortunately, they figured it out right away. The prisoner here today put a gun to my head and ordered me to keep driving."

That wasn't me. It was John. Acting shifty? The Hisbas must be manipulating his testimony.

Adam tried to get Daloth's attention. One of his aides spotted him gesticulating. She rushed over to see what he wanted. Adam whispered in her ear. "That wasn't me. I didn't point the gun at him."

She whispered back. "Can you prove it?"

Adam shook his head. She nodded returning to her seat. She whispered in Daloth's ear, who turned to face Adam. He could only shake his head.

One more injustice.

The driver finished his testimony. "...I jumped out of my aircar rather than be taken hostage by those murderers."

Daloth wasn't much help this time. He only asked a couple clarification questions. Adam noticed most of the Cardinals nodding at the driver's answers.

I'm in trouble.

After the driver left, the next witness was the police officer who had aided their escape back on Bokor. Adam's heart sank. The officer was dressed in simple, gray garb. Though they were barely concealed, Adam saw the marks of Celeste patches on his forearm and a burn mark near his neckline, where his Remembrance tattoo was.

No, they got to him!

"Patrol Officer 141, on the afternoon in question, did you encounter the prisoner during a fugitive sweep?" asked Enduring Temptation.

The officer said nothing. He turned his head to face Adam. A mournful yet determined expression splayed across the man's face.

"I'm sorry," the man muttered.

"I beg your pardon, Patrol Officer 141, can you speak up?" Enduring Temptation requested.

The officer's head swiveled back to face the Cardinals. "I said 'I'm sorry'. What is lost will be found." Adam cocked his head at those words, noticing a flash of silver beneath the man's sleeve. Adam instinctively gripped the arms of his chair. The man leapt over the decorative barrier between him and the Cardinals.

"FREEDOM!" the officer shouted as he charged in the direction of Cardinal Final Form's platform, brandishing a small knife.

"GUARDS!" was collectively shouted by multiple people. Several members of the audience screamed in terror. The officer leapt the distance from witness dais onto the Cardinal's platform. He barely made the jump, having to grip onto the side to prevent himself from falling into the empty space below. Final Form scrambled around his highchair to hide. Guards rushed in from all sides. The officer pulled himself up onto the platform, shouting, "DEATH TO THE COVENANT," at the top of his lungs.

He reached the lower steps of the platform when a stun round struck him in the back. The officer instantly seized up. Through the apparent pain, the main tried to push himself further up the platform steps, but it was of no use. Several more stun rounds from the guards brandishing their weapons hit the officer. He crumpled to the floor, falling down the steps. The momentum of his fall caused his body to be hurled over the side of the platform and plummet into the empty space below.

Adam tried standing to get a better vantage point. ConSec guards held him in place, their own weapons drawn. The horn had blared the entire duration of that fiasco, only quieting once the mayhem had settled. The screams of terror ceased. More guards flooded the chamber to maintain calm and order. Final Form stepped around from the back of his chair and spit down into the empty space.

"Heretic scum. You see, my fellow Cardinals and Conclave citizens, this is the kind of terror we deal with on a daily basis. That man is a leader of it all. He must be stopped!" Final Form said, pointing at Adam. The Bokori in the crowd hissed in Adam's direction, snapping their fingers in solidarity with the Cardinal. He wasn't concerned about the Bokori's words at the moment.

Please let him have died quickly. A lifetime of Bokori rehab awaits him otherwise.

Cardinal Clodius cleared his throat loudly. "I want ConSec to conduct an immediate investigation into how a witness managed to smuggle a weapon into this hallowed chamber. Otherwise, if all that excitement is over, let's proceed. Person Enduring Temptation, call your next witness. Let's get this nonsense over with."

Enduring Temptation got to its feet. "The People's House would like call Absorbing Song to give witness testimony."

"NO!" The words were out of Adam's mouth before he could stop himself.

"The prisoner will be silent!" declared Final Form.

The crowd became antsy, and the horn blew again to silence them. The ConSec guards surrounding Adam inched closer. Thankfully Daloth stepped in. "I object to this witness, Your Eminences. She is not on trial here. All charges against her have been dropped. Her testimony provides no probative value to this hearing."

"She is the key witness to another murder. The killing of an undercover agent of the Committee for the Advancement of Love and Virtue. The prisoner is accused, among many things, of aiding and abetting said murder, fleeing the scene of a crime, and failing to report a crime. All three charges are eligible for extradition under the Conclave Charter. Absorbing Song's testimony is vital in establishing proof of fact," said Enduring Temptation.

"Your objection is overruled, Cardinal Afta. Bring in the witness," Cardinal Clodius said to the ConSec guards. All eyes shot to the side doors, where the witnesses were ushered in from all day. Led by a pair of ConSec guard bots was Samus. She was elegantly dressed in a short-sleeve, brown tunic. Her dark hair was up in a ponytail, and she was wearing heeled caligae sandals. Her Remembrance tattoo was visible above her left breast. It was the first time Adam had ever seen it.

She was staring at the floor, trying to avoid eye-contact with anyone. She barely glanced up to see Adam only to hide her face once again. The ConSec guards ushered her up onto the witness dais. All the screens in the room displayed Samus' face. Adam was panicking.

No! No! No! She can't be up there. Please, let her be. She's been through enough!

Adam shot a panicked, exasperated expression at Daloth. The Moan tried to reassure him through hand gestures. It didn't help. Adam was ready to leap out of his chair. The ConSec guards sensed it since they were inching ever closer to him. His scars twitched.

"Absorbing Song, on the afternoon of the 29th day of Anamead, you were present at a hostel located inside a Human community on the northeastern side of Inclucity, is that correct?" asked Enduring Temptation. Samus didn't answer. "Absorbing Song, I'll ask again, were you or were you not present at a hostel inside a Human community on the afternoon of the 29th day of Anamead, where a Bokori person was murdered?" Samus remained silent. "Your Eminences, can you please instruct the witness to answer the question?" asked an annoyed Enduring Temptation.

"You are required to answer its questions, Absorbing Song," said Cardinal Final Form.

"THAT'S NOT MY NAME!" blurted out Samus so loudly and unexpectedly everyone was taken aback, even Adam. He was gripping the edge of his chair.

That's right. You tell it.

"Your legal name is Absorbing Song."

"NO, IT'S NOT!"

"You must calm down or this Tribunal will hold you in contempt."

Samus returned to stone silence. Adam could see she was trying to hold it together. He could see her shaking even this far away. Whispers from the crowd turned to murmuring. Adam tensed his body, preparing to pounce.

"Absorbing Song, what happened in that hostel room, where an innocent Bokori was murdered? You must answer the question!" Final Form was asking the questions. Enduring Temptation stood there dumbfounded.

"Your Eminences, the witness is clearly traumatized by what happened. It's cruelty to force her to endure this amount of public questioning. The People's House do not need her to push their case," said a pleading Daloth.

"That is not your judgment to make, Cardinal Afta. In this room before this Tribunal, the Proprietor Cardinals decide what is right and what is wrong. A Human bound to the terms of the Covenant is obligated to tell the community the truth! Her personal preferences and privileges are irrelevant to the greater good of the people. Equality through sacrifice," said Final Form.

"ENOUGH!" Blood shot right to Adam's brain. His instincts kicked in. He leapt out of his chair and dashed at full speed. The ConSec guards tried to grab him, but he slipped through their grasp.

"Another assassination attempt! Stop that heretic!" Adam scarcely heard Final Form's shouts. He ignored the protestations of Daloth and the ConSec guards. He rushed forward.

No one will stop me.

He opened up his arms and wrapped Sam in a huge hug. She met his embrace, burying her head into his chest. He squeezed his surrogate sister tightly and closed his eyes. He expected to be ripped apart. He was determined to hold onto her for as long as humanly possible.

Nothing happened. Instead, the blood drained from his ears, and his adrenaline surge subsided. He heard only clapping and cheering. Adam opened one eye. Several ConSec guards had surrounded them, but they were keeping a respectful distance. He opened both eyes and scanned the room.

Daloth was gripping the table tightly. Enduring Temptation and Hopping Chains were hiding under their table. Adam's eyes found the other Cardinals. Clodius and Final Form were standing. Luk-Kas was chuckling to himself while Fex was swapping out his decorative mech for a defensive mech. Union_Cardinal remained unmoved. Clodius was holding up his hand to halt the ConSec guards while Final Form was egging them on. The ConSec guards were confused on how to act.

"Enough!" Adam shouted. "Anyone lays a finger on my sister, they'll lose it!" He felt Samus squeeze him tighter. She lifted her head from his torso. Her eyes were puffy, but she had a wide grin across her face. The crowd was dead silent. Only the occasional cough broke the tension. All eyes were on the Cardinals.

Cardinal Luk-Kas erupted into a hearty laugh. Soon, most of the chamber was filled with raucous laughter. His body still tense, Adam nervously joined the chorus of laughs.

"I can see why the Humans are giving your people such grief, Cardinal Final Form. 'Tis a shame their numbers are so few otherwise you might become the subjugates," chuckled Cardinal Luk-Kas.

"I'm not concerned about the acts of a few ungrateful heretics, Cardinal, nor do I care for your thinly-veiled mockery. Their numbers are so few due to their own making. Violent, backward savages. They destroyed their own homeworld, and we rescued them. Sadly, not everyone is grateful to a helping hand," said Final Form.

"Lies!" shouted Adam.

Final Form shook its head. "The poison of bigotry and misinformation spreads."

"That's really enough!" said Cardinal Clodius. "I'm making an authoritative judgment as the ranking member of this Tribunal. The witness' testimony will not be required. She is free to go."

"Excuse me, Cardinal Clodius, but..." Final Form tried to say. Clodius shot it a sideways glance. Adam could see he was whispering something to the Bokori, but the audio wasn't picking it up. He saw Final Form sigh. "Very well. There's still one more witness."

"Can we take a quick recess, Your Eminences. I think given the intensity of the last pair of witnesses, we could all use a breather," requested Daloth.

Clodius seemed to boil with rage. "Fine, but no more than a few minutes. Quick recess!" The horn blew. The crowd's buzzing of conversation ignited.

Adam and Samus relaxed their embrace. He stepped back to get a better look at her. "Wow! You're a visual feast with that tunic, Sam. Oh, I just noticed you dyed a bit of your hair auburn. Stunning! I need to redo my silver streak while I think on it. Where'd you get that outfit?" Adam asked.

Samus blushed. "Havera loaned this to me. I found out only this morning I would be called to testify. She thought it be best if I dressed decently for the occasion. I think I prefer the jumpsuit. I don't nearly have Havera's lovely figure or *assets* to pull this outfit off."

"Don't be silly, you're absolutely stunning. Where is Havera by the way?" Adam asked.

Samus shrugged. "Who is the Consul of Cloudboard? ConSec picked me up from her place this morning. She said she had important meetings today and not to worry about her."

"Shame. I guess it's for the best. I wouldn't want her to waste her time with this sideshow," Adam said.

Daloth walked up to the two of them, trying and failing to wipe off the intense flop sweat from his brow. "That was insane! The Saptia Conference was less tense than that. I'm sorry, my dear. Had I known the Bokori planned to call you as a witness, I would've done something to stop it," Daloth said.

"Clodius said they still have one more witness to call. Any idea who it could be?" Adam asked.

"Do you?" Daloth retorted.

Adam thought hard for a moment. *Who else could they get?* A terrible thought struck Adam. *I haven't heard from Arabella in days. Could they have taken the settlement? No, Daloth would've said something. Maybe they caught John or Mom or someone else important. How though?* "I don't. Sorry. I'm worried about Arabella. Any word?" Adam asked.

"There's been no major report of activity around the Bokori moon. They've denied journalistic access and sentientarian missions have been turned around upon entering the system. So far, everything is holding steady," Daloth said.

"What are we going to do?" Samus asked.

"We're going to get you someplace safe away from here," Adam insisted.

"No, I want to be here for you. John would want me here with you," Samus said.

"John doesn't want you within light years of the Conclave. Havera's not here, and I don't trust anyone here with your safety. Certainly not ConSec," Adam said.

"I think I can help you with that. Marduk! Marduk, come here!" Daloth said, waving over someone from the crowd.

A figure walked around one of the decorative barriers and approached. Daloth waved off the ConSec guards seeking to head him off. Not that Adam thought they could stop him. The titan of a Moan was one of the biggest sentients Adam had ever seen. He was a Moan male over seven-feet tall. His handsome face resembled that of a shark with a short, pointed snout. His muscly, blubbery chest was a bluish-gray while the scales along the back of his arms that stretched towards his back were a dark navy blue. Like Daloth, he wore a garish, open-chested frock coat of fused seaweed and a tricorn coral hat, though his coat matched his scales while his pale blue tricorn hat was less flamboyant than Daloth's. The Moan had a jagged, icy scar across the front of his exposed muscular pecs, which had a misty sheen. His thin lips were parted in a toothy smile, showcasing his huge, perfect teeth.

"Adam. Samus. I would like to introduce you to Marduk Tiamat. He's a friend who lives here on the station. Marduk, meet the Human Separatists."

Marduk Tiamat removed his tricorn and gave a polite bow, revealing a rigid and smooth dorsal fin along his backside. "A pleasure to make your acquaintance. You may call me Marduk. I am the Purveyor of Tiamat's Talons here on Conclave station," Marduk said.

"Tiamat's Talons is the largest privately-owned armory in the galaxy. Should this Tribunal go your way, the two of you should speak afterwards," Daloth to Adam said with a wink.

"It would be my great honor to solicit to such a renowned Human. I can also watch over your friend here for the duration of this hearing, if you'd like. Hello there," Marduk said, acknowledging Samus.

"Hi," said Samus meekly, her mouth slightly agape as she gawked at the strong, bare-chested Moan. Her ogling didn't escape Adam's notice.

"Will she be okay if I leave her with you?" Adam asked Marduk.

"Ha ha! Do I seem like someone easily intimidated or overpowered? No one shall lay a hand, claw, or talon on her while I'm here. We'll be just on the other side of this divider," Marduk said.

Adam turned to Samus. "Are you comfortable with that arrangement?" Samus nodded up-and-down with rapid enthusiasm.

"Excellent! Come this way. Samus, is it?" Marduk said, putting his arm around the young Human. His forearm was almost as large as her torso.

"Mmhmm, it is," Samus said with an enthusiastic bounce in her step. She joined Marduk on a bench just around the corner in the gallery.

Daloth patted Adam on the back. "Don't you worry. Marduk is an honorable man. A good man. He's a war hero. Fought bravely in the Strife against the Celestials. Samus is in good fins. Come, they're about to restart the hearing." The horn blared and a pair of ConSec guards escorted Adam back to his chair.

So many ways I could die soon. The Bokori, ConSec, John. It'll be a miracle if I get through this with my head.

"Call your final witness," said Cardinal Clodius. The annoyance in his tone was barely concealed.

An unmistakable foreboding smile formed across Final Form's lips. Enduring Temptation matched its Cardinal's expression. "The People's House call the High Hisba of the Committee for the Advancement of Love and Virtue."

Adam's spine stiffened; his throat seized up. The doors from the witness holding area opened and out walked the terror of Adam's nightmares. Standing tall and walking deliberately was a man dressed in black. Not a man. A demon. The wings of his shoulder pads were elegant and showy. A black helm with a white sliver for sight covered its head. Its matching black cape bore gray trim along the fringes. Emblazoned on the back was the gray, open-palmed symbol of the Hisbaween that marked this person's station.

The High Hisba. The enforcer of Bokori values. The crusader for the Covenant. The bane of every free Human. Not an ounce of the man's flesh was visible. Yet, Adam could not forget the man's face. Beneath the Hisbaween symbol, embroidered on the cape, were the words drilled into his brain for over a year.

Equality through sacrifice.

Adam gripped the chair so tightly he felt like it could snap at any moment. His heart was pounding so fiercely, he wondered if the entire cathedral could hear it. Beads of cold sweat covered his body from head to toe. The scars on his back were beyond itching. They were causing physical agony. He tried to think of *her* in that moment, except his thoughts kept flooding back to that airlock and the stadium. He frantically darted his eyes around the room, seeking any means of escape. Useless effort. He was trapped with his tormenter in yet another enclosed space with millions of onlookers. He thought he would throw up in that moment.

The High Hisba strode towards the witness dais, stopping once it reached the proper position. "Only us Zokyo need to wear masks indoors. The witness should remove its helmet," insisted the Zokyon Cardinal Fex. Without protest, the High Hisba removed its helm, which hissed as it was lifted off the High Hisba's head.

It was a tall, slender man, nearing the end of middle age. Its head was completely bald, not one sign of hair on its body. Its skin was bleached almost perfectly gray. Its four-fingered, black gloves betrayed the fact it had had his pinky finger surgically removed. Most likely, it was the same with its feet. From this angle, Adam couldn't see its surgically-altered eyes. Vertical and nearly pupil-less. He didn't need to see them.

"Do you have a name?" asked Cardinal Luk-Kas.

Enduring Temptation spoke up. "The High Hisba gives up their name when they assume the role. Allows them to see themselves as the office rather than the person," explained Enduring Temptation.

"I asked the witness, not you," said an irritated Cardinal Luk-Kas.

"The Cardinals may call the High Hisba whatever it is they wish. This is your domain. We are merely guests. I humbly submit myself to your authority," spoke the High Hisba. The High Hisba was calm and emotionless. Its shrill voice sent chills down Adam's spine. Like icy daggers shredding through Adam's soul.

Enduring Temptation called for the execution livestream video to be played. The High Hisba was there to walk them through what they were seeing step-by-step. The few remaining lights were extinguished.

Adam was feeling slight chest pains. He gripped his arm, trying to remember his breathing exercises. He couldn't bear to watch what was happening. No matter how hard he tried to mentally distance himself from this situation, he kept feeling worse. His back scars were unrelenting. He was convinced he was going to pass out.

"**Calm...**" Adam heard a voice inside his head. His vision was ripped from the ground floor. He felt himself floating high above everyone. He could see his body from this high up. He was pale and sweaty. Adam heard the voice again. "**Allow yourself to relax. You are in no danger. Calm...**"

The voice was firm but sweet, gently brushing the back of his skull. Up high something caught his eye. Like a beacon in the dark, Adam laid eyes on a figure up in the gallery. Standing there with immense, triangular eyes with black sclera and ruby irises was a Rorae woman. He recognized her as such from his research on Havera's terminal.

Her expressive eyes covered much of her face. She had a small, pointed nose and no discernible mouth. Only a full, black tripartite leaf resided where a mouth should be. Her mossy face grew into dark petals of a flower not in bloom at the top of her skull. To Adam, she appeared to be nearly nude with only a v-shaped sash of slithering vines covering her voluptuous breasts and groin area.

Despite her eye-catching visage, no one else seemed to notice her. *Am I daydreaming? Who are you?* Adam thought. He heard the voice once more. "**Shh. Do not concern yourself with what you cannot control. Calm...**" Concentric, golden rings, previously unseen in the Rorae's eyes, flashed.

His vision was ripped back down into his body. He had not moved. He took a few seconds to take stock of where he was. The lower lights were back on, and the screens displayed only whoever was speaking. The High Hisba was answering the Cardinals' questions. A soft buzzing in his ear prevented him from fully comprehending what they were saying. Adam gazed up at the galleries, expecting to see the Rorae. She was gone.

Was she there to begin with?

He asked himself the question, noticing something peculiar. His heart was beating normally. His breathing wasn't labored nor was his stomach churning. He wiped his forehead. While it was still damp, no sweat was taking its place. He was...calm.

What just happened?

"The day it was killed, our agent was meeting with a contact. It was trying to confirm the connection between the Excommunicated and the heretics," the High Hisba said.

Wait, what did it say?

"Do you have proof of a connection between the prisoner and the Excommunicated?" asked Cardinal Luk-Kas.

"Our agent was to deliver its report the night it was killed. The information from its HUD was irretrievable after the agent's death," the High Hisba said.

"So, the answer is no," said Cardinal Luk-Kas.

"This office regrets to say we do not have ironclad proof. All we have is the demonstrable evidence presented to you in cooperation with our Zokyon friends and neighbors," said the High Hisba. He spoke with dispassion and quiet deliberation. No hint of the person Adam knew bubbled beneath the surface. "The prisoner is a murderer. The Excommunicated are supplying the heretics. Of that there can be no doubt. Many heretics have joined those terrorists since the Strife. Only after a thorough investigation and interrogation of the prisoner by the People's House can we fully ascertain the danger the heretics pose to both the Bokori-Human Covenant and the Conclave itself. We allow this infestation to grow, there will be more Sins," the High Hisba said calmly.

He's accusing us of working with the Excommunicated?!

One of Daloth's aides whispered in his ear. Something she said surprised the Moan Cardinal. Afterwards, he sent her hurrying in the direction of the witness holding area. She disappeared through the doors.

"Does the prisoner's advocate have any questions for the witness?" asked Cardinal Clodius.

Daloth rose. "If it please the Tribunal, I would like to present our own video recording to the witness."

"I object," said Final Form without missing a beat. "I know of the supposed recording to which His Eminence refers. The contents of the recording cannot and have not been independently verified by either the People's House or ConSec. As such, it is not admissible evidence."

Restless rumblings could be heard from the crowd. Adam braced himself for the inevitable panic attack. Seconds passed while the Cardinals deliberated without the audio amplifiers. The attack never came.

What did that Rorae woman do to me? Did she do something? I don't understand. I feel surprisingly good.

"The objection is sustained. The recording shall not be entered into evidence at this time. Do you have any questions for the witness, Cardinal Afta?" asked Cardinal Clodius.

His sudden mood upswing stirred something mad in Adam. "I have a question, if I may!" exclaimed Adam to the shock of everyone.

"The prisoner shall remain silent!" insisted Final Form.

"Actually, Your Eminences, prisoners are allowed to question witnesses if they so choose. It's...unorthodox but permissible," said Daloth, giving Adam a what-are-you-doing face.

What am I doing?

"Very well. Make it quick, prisoner," said Clodius.

The High Hisba remained facing the Cardinals, not acknowledging Adam's presence. The Human pressed onward. "During my scourging, how many times did you strike me with the lash?" Gasps flared among the crowd.

"I object to this question," Final Form tried to say.

"Thirteen," said the High Hisba coolly. More gasps elicited from the crowd.

"High Hisba!" Final Form tried to interject.

Adam continued onward. "How many times were patches of Celeste and of what grade were placed on my body during rehabilitation?"

"Yellow sun Celeste three times a day for four-hundred and thirty-two days, then red giant Celeste twice a day for five days until your illegal escape the day before the first full year of your ten-year rehabilitation term could be completed."

"In addition to thrice daily forced feedings of paste and alcohol?"

"Yes."

"High Hisba, I demand you cease your testimony this instant!" screamed Final Form. The crowd was in full-on revolt. Their shouts nearly drowned out Adam's questions. The horn blasts did nothing to halt the madness. Adam pressed forward, nonetheless. He knew the High Hisba all too well. Adam screamed to be heard over the noise. "One last question, High Hisba, do you regret any of your actions against me?"

Without missing a beat, the High Hisba answered, "Why would the High Hisba have any regret for enforcing the law? Why would anyone have any regret for doing what is right? Your toxic point-of-view is beyond wrong. It's completely illegitimate, unworthy of discussion or debate. Your beliefs are an affront to all that is moral and good. If the High Hisba has any regret, it is, regardless of the length, your rehabilitation was a failure."

The Bokori contingent in the room was snapping and cheering at the High Hisba's words. Everyone else was hissing and booing. The ConSec guards pushed to restore order. The horn blared throughout the chamber longer than was strictly necessary. Cardinal Final Form seemed ready to explode. Adam turned his head to find Samus. Her face was in pure shock.

I never told her the full details. I never told anyone. I still haven't. There is no possible way they could understand.

Enduring Temptation spoke meekly. "Umm, the, uh, the People's House rests, Your Eminences."

"The witness is excused," said Clodius. The Cauduun Cardinal seemed numb to the whole procedure at this point. The High Hisba placed its helm back on while ConSec guards escorted it out. Adam sat there with a satisfied smile.

For all the galaxy to see.

"Does the prisoner's advocate wish to call any witnesses?" asked Clodius.

Daloth's forehead was sweating enough to fill an entire ship with water. "Yes...yes! Sorry, Your Eminences. Fortunately for the Tribunal, I only have one witness to call."

"Oh, thank Cradite!" exclaimed Clodius with not-so-subtle frustration. "Who is your witness?"

Daloth cleared his throat. "Lady Tenebella Havera of Shele, Duchess of Paleria, Countess of Hippa, Pontifex of Xenohistory, Maid of Carthaga, and Quaestor of the Praetorian Order."

16

Toxicity of Truth

Pontiwho of what? Maid of where? And what in Kewea of the Praetorian Order? I thought duchess was title enough. Wait...Havera?

The doors from the witness area opened up. Striding into the room was a radiant figure. A lambent presence in a pessimistic proceeding. If Daloth had not named her, Adam would've had a hard time recognizing Havera. She was wearing a slender, black dress that hugged her figure tightly. The V neckline was so low her belly button was showing, along with her ripped abdominal muscles. The left side of the gown had a slit that went all the way up her sinewy leg, high enough to reach her chiseled glute. She wore golden, calf-high caligae boots with inch-high wedge heels. Her hair, normally in three tight, horizontal ponytails, was voluminous, semi-curly, and flowy all the way down the length of her back. The divides between her scarlet and raven locks were less distinguishable. The brooch she normally wore on her middle ponytail was pinned to the thin strap near her right shoulder. She had noticeably smoky eye shadow. Even her midnight lips seemed glossier today. The only consistent item of her wardrobe were her platinum bracers.

She's the goddesses Anamea and Aria in one body. Stunning and stout. Love and war. This cannot be real. But she is. She's here. Why?

The room went dead silent. Only the sounds of Havera's footsteps echoing off the marble floor could be heard. Everyone was staring at the Cauduun with bated breath. Havera gently swayed her hips with each step. Her tail softly wagged from side-to-side, providing her counter-balance. She reached the witness dais between the two tables. Adam could not take his eyes off her.

"I object to this witness. There is a conflict of interest for the Duchess of Paleria to speak at these proceedings," Final Form said.

The displays shifted from Final Form to Clodius. The Cauduun Cardinal stood up to speak. "I understand His Eminence's concerns about the witness. She is my filia, which does raise a conflict for me. However, I believe the correct course of action is for me to recuse myself during the examination of this witness," said Cardinal Clodius.

Filia. Daughter. Havera is the Cardinal's daughter?! The list never ends!

A few murmurs and whispers trickled from the crowd. None of the other Cardinals objected. Final Form nodded its approval. Clodius sat back down and pressed a couple buttons on his chair. His platform was lowered until it was out of sight.

Final Form stood up to speak, shifting its platform to the center. "With Cardinal Clodius' departure, I am the ranking Cardinal on this Tribunal. Cardinal Afta, you may proceed with your witness."

Daloth stood up. "Duchess Havera, what has your mandate been for the last two years with the Praetorian Order?"

"With the permission of the Conclave, on behalf of the Praetorian Order, I was the liaison with the Human Separatists on Bokor's jungle moon, Windless Tornado," Havera said. She was using the stern tone she had used with Adam on the ride back to Windless Tornado. It gave her voice a noticeably distinguished and unfamiliar accent.

"What were your responsibilities?" asked Daloth.

"I provided the Humans on Windless Tornado bits of data, approved by the Praetorian Order, from the Stepicro Cache," Havera said.

"Was that your only responsibility?" asked Daloth.

Havera paused. She glanced for an instant over her shoulder at Adam.

"No," Havera said firmly.

The gallery murmurs continued. "What were your other responsibilities, Your Grace?" asked Daloth.

Adam inched forward in his seat. Havera's tail stiffened. "Part of the approval process for my mission required that I send the Conclave a full report on the Human Separatists. Information about their numbers, leadership, defenses, weapons, infrastructure, what they said, whom they met. Anything and everything I could learn I reported back to the Conclave," Havera said unflinchingly.

Adam gripped his chair so hard he thought he was going to snap the arm. *John was right! She's a Kewea-accursed spy! I'm such a fool.*

Daloth continued his line of questioning. "On the day of the incident in question, you were on Windless Tornado, correct?"

"I was."

"What did you see?"

"I was outside checking the systems on the exterior of my ship. Near the edge of the Human's defensive shield, I spotted dozens of heavily armed troopers decked out in black. I recognized them immediately as the Hisbaween. They were breaching the shield, weapons drawn. I realized that the Human settlement was about to come under attack. I followed them into the shield."

"Can you describe what happened during the attack?"

"I object to the use of the term attack. It was a police action," insisted Enduring Temptation.

"Your objection is sustained. I've given Your Eminence and Your Grace plenty of leeway during this testimony out of respect. Don't push my patience further," said Final Form.

"My apologies, Your Eminence. During this *police action*, what did you witness, Your Grace?" asked Daloth.

"It was total chaos. I don't think the Hisbaween expected the Humans to put up such fierce resistance. The Hisbas started shooting everyone in sight whether they were armed or not. I passed by several dead Humans, their corpses smoking from laser blasts. It was a sight I had not seen since the darkest days of the Strife. If I close my eyes, I can hear the screams. I can see the terrified expressions of people holding each other for comfort, wondering if they were next. Most fled into their flimsy homes, desperate to avoid the blasts. If that was a police action, I shudder to find out their version of a military action is," Havera said.

"You know the prisoner here today, is that correct, Your Grace?"

"I do."

"How long have you known him?"

"About two years."

"In all that time, have you ever known the prisoner to be a violent man?"

"Quite the opposite. He was incredibly shy, at first. I could barely get two words out of him. He was afraid of everything. Took many months for him to open up to me. Even so, he is quite skittish. He doesn't like being around large groups of people, which is virtually impossible in a place like that. He typically spends his days at home or driving around in an old covered driftbike. I did see him yell at a generator once, if you want to call that violent," Havera said.

The gallery laughed. *No. You cannot charm your way out of what you did. I won't let you. No!*

"How do you explain the livestream video showing the prisoner committing such a violent act?" Daloth asked.

"Objection! The witness isn't a psychological expert," Enduring Temptation declared.

"No, but it was the witness' assignment to evaluate and report on the leaders and prominent people within the Human settlement on Windless Tornado. Part of the evaluation does include psychological profiling, which the Praetorians are trained in. She spent two years around the prisoner. I think she's more than qualified to give her opinion about the prisoner's mental state," Daloth argued.

Luk-Kas and Fex shot sideways glances at Final Form. The Bokori bit its lip. "Very well. The objection is overruled."

Havera continued. "His pater had died only days ago. His best friend was severely wounded. He believed his other friend, a previous witness, had suffered a horrendous violation. His home was under assault. After what happened to him at the stadium, his mental health was fragile. Too much stress can cause anyone to snap. Adam...excuse me, Flowing Courage, was especially vulnerable to that kind of emotional overload."

"Is that what caused him to break?"

"No," Havera said. "His only brother was killed in the attack. Only minutes prior to the livestream video."

"Who killed the prisoner's brother, Your Grace?" Daloth asked.

Havera didn't hesitate. "The Hisba he shot and killed."

The murmurs and whispers in the crowd morphed into hisses and jeers. Some by the Bokori members, the rest by the other onlookers at the Bokori.

"I see. In summary, Your Grace, prior to this incident, how would you describe the Human Separatists?" Daloth asked.

Havera breathed deeply. "Brave," Havera said. The gallery murmurs grew louder.

"Can you elaborate, Your Grace?" asked Daloth.

Havera relaxed her posture. Her tone softened. "I've seen the aftermath of battlefields during the Strife. I've walked the halls of Duseraries with the bodies of broken soldiers piling up in every corner. I've laid eyes on Sin since its boiling. Nonetheless, what I saw on Windless Tornado churned my stomach. Hundreds of thousands of people living in complete filth and abject poverty. The stench from that settlement is so bad it takes several steam showers to wash away the smell entirely. The people there barely have enough food to survive. The conditions compared to even our poorest cities and neighborhoods would shock and horrify you. It's a place where the sun never shines, and I don't mean that just metaphorically," Havera said. She sounded like the Havera that Adam had spoken with many times. The Havera he thought he knew.

She continued. "But...in the face of all that adversity, they have nothing but pure kindness in their hearts. Neighbors helping the disabled and infirm travel and buy provisions, children playing and laughing in the filthy, muddy streets, families adopting children whose parents were whisked away by Bokor's authorities. What I witnessed was nothing short of miraculous. Beaten down and driven to the point of extinction, these people, these *Humans,* showed more signs of community than anything I've seen on Bokor. Despite how little these Humans possess, they still go out of their way to help someone in need. They risk their lives to bring other Humans into the fold, many do not make it back. I'm an outsider to them. An alien. I'm a member of a Proprietor Race. I represent those that oppress them. Yet, I've been welcomed into their homes. I was treated like family for two years. I've seen the hope in their eyes. These are good people united by the singular desire to be free. What's happening to these Humans is nothing short of criminal. I thought so at Saptia, I believe so today. Humanity deserves to be free once again!" Havera said with rousing resolution.

The gallery erupted into cheers and applause. A chant broke out amongst the non-Bokori. "FREE HUMANS NOW! FREE HUMANS NOW! FREE HUMANS NOW!" Unsurprisingly, the horns blasted loudly into the chamber. Several seconds the horns lasted until the chamber returned to calm. Adam remained skeptical.

Is she saying that because she believes it or because she was ordered? Could be guilt for all I know if she's capable of feeling guilty for what she did.

Daloth, content by what had occurred, stood there with a satisfied smile. "Your witness, Your Eminences."

Enduring Temptation attempted to stand, but Final Form waved it off. The Cardinal would ask the Cauduun the questions itself. "Duchess Havera, you recount quite a colorful tale, I do say so myself. However, I noticed you left out several key details in your account. Let me draw everyone's attention to earlier in the day. Who was responsible for ferrying the prisoner, Flowing Courage, and his two compatriots in question back to our sacred moon that afternoon?" Final Form asked.

"I was."

"Against the express orders of the Committee for the Advancement of Love and Virtue, the Inclucity Police, and the local spaceport security, is that correct?"

"They did not have the authority to detain me or stop my ship."

"So, you used your diplomatic immunity, graciously granted by the members of this Tribunal and the Cauduun Monarchical Alliance, to help three fugitives from justice escape?"

"I helped a wounded man, a victim of a violent crime, and an innocent man get home."

"You can twist the facts all you want, Your Grace. Going back to the police action, you were not a simple bystander, were you, Duchess Havera?"

Havera paused. "By the end of it, no I was not. I couldn't stand idly by while innocents were being slaughtered."

"Innocents? Every single one of those Humans living on our sacred moon had committed a crime by stepping foot on Windless Tornado. There are no innocents in that settlement."

"Wouldn't that make all the Hisbaween criminals, as well? They were more than stepping foot on your *sacred moon*."

Gallery attendees audibly gasped and sniggered. Final Form was not amused. "The Committee for the Advancement of Love and Virtue is exempt from that law. Don't deflect. Is it true that you interfered with the Hisbaween in the course of their duties?" Final Form asked.

"I'm not sure I understand what you mean, Your Eminence," Havera said.

"You prevented them from making an arrest. More so, you did so violently. You killed several Hisbaween doing their jobs, did you not?"

"I was defending myself and others from certain death."

"Answer the question! Did you or did you not take the lives of agents of the Committee for the Advancement of Love and Virtue while they were serving an arrest warrant against a suspected murderer and their collaborators?"

Havera stiffened. She raised her chin high in defiance.

"Yes, I did."

The Bokori section of the gallery started screaming at Havera. They shouted all sorts of filthy epithets at her. In spite of himself, Adam felt terrible for her. The horn blew a couple times to silence the gallery.

"So much for tolerance and acceptance, huh, Cardinal Final Form," Luk-Kas said with derision in response to the Bokori's comments.

"You cannot blame the people for reacting to a toxic individual," replied Final Form.

"Seems like your people cannot handle the toxicity of truth, Cardinal. The Duchess is not on trial here," Luk-Kas said.

"No, but her credibility is important. It's clear the witness is not an unbiased observer. She has stuck her tail where it doesn't belong. Unsurprising really," Final Form said.

"What's that supposed to mean, Your Eminence?" Havera asked clearly bothered by its comment.

"Interpret that how you will, Your Grace. You are excused," Final Form said.

Havera stepped off the witness dais. Adam couldn't help but watch her leave. He felt betrayed by her. He felt comforted by her words. He felt something else, too. She snuck a peek at Adam, and he caught a glimpse of her expression. It was a mixture of sorrow and bitterness. She joined Samus and Marduk Tiamat in the first-floor gallery. Samus tried to side hug her, but she resisted, resolving to stare at the ground instead and not acknowledge anyone.

"Is that everyone, Cardinal Afta?" Final Form asked.

"Just a moment, Your Eminence. Let me consult with the prisoner swift like a seahorse," Daloth requested.

"Make it quick," Final Form said curtly.

Daloth rushed over to Adam. The Moan leaned closer to whisper. "I think it's best that you don't testify after all," Daloth said.

"Why not? I can explain myself in front of everyone. I can make them understand!" Adam said insistently.

Daloth shook his head. "You aren't going to get a better response than that," Daloth said. "The impact of her testimony is far more powerful than anything you can say. Final Form can spin it however it likes. The Naddine and the Zokyo respect the Cauduun's words more than they will yours. It's not fair, but it's the truth. Be that as it may, there is one last action you can take I think will help. Trust me," Daloth said.

"You keep asking me to trust you. I suppose it's done me well so far. What do you have in mind?" Adam asked.

Final Form interjected. "Let's go, Cardinal Afta!"

Daloth kept whispering to Adam. "This may be difficult for you, but..."

"NOW, CARDINAL AFTA!" Final Form shouted.

Daloth stuttered for a moment, then spoke up. "The prisoner is waiving his right to testify. However, if it pleases the Tribunal, I would ask the prisoner to stand up and take off his coat and the top of his jumpsuit."

Adam's eyes widened. He knew what Daloth had in mind. He felt a cold sweat coming on.

"We aren't at a den of Anamea, Cardinal. This Tribunal ain't that kind of party," said Luk-Kas to the jovial approval of the audience.

"I'm simply requesting the prisoner reveal evidence confirming the testimony provided earlier by a witness of the People's House," Daloth said.

The other Cardinals looked to Final Form for a ruling. The grayskin could only bury its tiny face in its slender fingers. With a flick of its other hand, Final Form gave its reluctant, silent approval. Daloth nodded at Adam, taking a few steps back.

Adam breathed deeply. He stood up slowly. He removed his violet duster jacket. He unzipped the top portion of his jumpsuit down to his waist. Adam shut his eyes. He felt incredibly self-conscious.

For the cause. For the Long Con. For her.

He slipped his arms out of the sleeves, letting the top of the jumpsuit fall limp. The crowd gasped. The cool air of the Tribunal chamber felt unexpectedly pleasant on Adam's back. The breeze provided little reprieve against the itching and pain emanating from the scars on his back. Scars the whole galaxy were gaping at if the screens were any indication.

Where's that Rorae when I need her.

Through the mumbles and murmurs bouncing around the chamber, Adam heard someone calling out to him. "Adam!" It was barely a hushed shout. He peeked open one eye in the direction of the source. Samus was gesturing at him to focus on her eyes. She began performing the breathing exercises she and John had taught him after his rescue. Adam mimicked her. Her caring bright brown eyes were the exact relief he needed. He tried to mouth, "thank you," until he remembered she couldn't read his Default lips. She understood him in spite of that.

"I think you've made your point, Cardinal Afta." It was Cardinal Clodius. Adam had missed that his platform had rejoined the other Cardinals. Daloth nodded at Adam. Adam rezipped his jumpsuit and put his coat back on before sitting back down.

"We've heard the testimony of all witnesses for this deportation hearing. This Proprietor Tribunal will retire below to deliberate. We ask that everyone continue to be respectful. We'll return with the vote shortly," Clodius said. The Cardinal's platforms all descended into the floor, which sealed up after them. Daloth stepped up to Adam.

"What do you think?" Adam asked.

Daloth wiped his brow. "I honestly do not know. So much has happened. I think it's likely Cardinal Clodius will abstain with his vote. He doesn't want the appearance of impropriety."

"No, of course not. Don't want to jeopardize the integrity of the Proprietor Tribunal," Adam said sarcastically. He searched for Havera. She continued to stare at the floor.

She won't even look at me. She's been watching us, reporting on us for months! Doubtless the Bokori used her information against us. She has our blood on her hands!

John's words flooded back to him. "*...the only good people in this galaxy are Humans.*"

"Final Form needs a majority of casted votes to deport you. Luk-Kas might be inclined to vote against based on his reactions. He's a bit of a wildcard. No telling what he'll do until he does it. Fex, on the other hand, is a consensus type. I doubt he'd vote against Final Form, even and especially if Luk-Kas does. The Union will abstain as always. With its vote, Final Form only needs one more. I've done my best," Daloth said, tilting his head down slightly in shame.

"Yes, you have. However this turns out, you have my gratitude, Daloth," Adam said.

"If the tide turns against you, rest assured, I'll see to it that young Samus remains protected. The Moan Thalassocracy won't allow any harm to come to her," Daloth said. The horn blew again. "They've finished deliberations. Already?! It's only been five minutes!"

"Is that good or bad?" Adam asked.

"Good for Final Form. Bad for you," Daloth said ominously. The Moan rejoined his aides at his table. The Cardinal platforms rose back up to take their place. Each were sitting upright in their chairs. The room was buzzing with anticipation. Adam couldn't help but notice a smug, satisfied smirk on Final Form's face.

I'm finished.

"On the issue of deportation of the prisoner Flowing Courage, this Proprietor Tribunal shall vote on the ayes and nays. A majority of registered votes is required for affirmation. We ask that the gallery please be respectful and not audibly react while votes are cast. We'll start with His Eminence, Cardinal Fex of the Zokyon Technocracy, and continue on down the line. Cardinal Fex if you please," said Cardinal Clodius.

The scrawny, four-armed Zokyon Cardinal raised his noodly head. "The Zokyon Technocracy abstains."

Abstains? Wait, is this good?

Adam looked to Daloth for guidance. The Moan seemed as confused as he did. Final Form did not react. It was its turn. "The Free People's Democracy of Bokor votes aye."

That's a given.

Cardinal Clodius spoke next. "Due to potential conflict of interest, the Cauduun Monarchical Alliance abstains."

Daloth said that might happen, but that's two abstentions and one yes. Does that mean it's a majority yes or majority abstentions? Do abstentions mean they don't count?

Cardinal Luk-Kas flicked his half-shoulder cape. "The Naddine Confederacy abstains."

Three abstentions?! Is this why deliberations were so short? Did they all agree to abstain to save face.

Adam observed Daloth's head fall in defeat. Adam sunk in his seat.

It's over.

"The Union votes nay."

At least I got to hear the Union speak...wait a second, what did that bot say?!

Adam wasn't the only one. Surprise filled the room. None were shocked more so than Final Form, who almost shot out of its chair to peer at the red Union bot.

"Cardinal Union_Cardinal, can you please repeat? What is your vote?" Cardinal Clodius asked. The Cauduun was taken aback, too.

"The Union votes nay," the Union Cardinal repeated. Adam found the bot's voice to be bizarre. It spoke in a strange, rhythmic pattern. Metered.

Adam surveyed the room. No one seemed to understand what was happening. Daloth, by contrast, was grinning from ear to ear.

"Can the Union Cardinal please explain themselves? You did not speak during deliberations. You gave no indication of your intention to vote no," Final Form said, attempting to salvage the situation.

"The Union does not need to justify our rationale. However, in the interest of showing the Union's openness with our organic sentient partners, the Union shall explain our decision. This Tribunal does not have the authority to hear this case. The Proprietor Tribunal's directive is to hear issues and disputes that affect the entire galaxy. By the Bokori Cardinal's own admission, this is a simple dispute between a Proprietor Race and a unit of its Subjugated Race. Therefore, in accordance with the Conclave Charter, the Union votes nay on grounds of standing," Union_Cardinal said resolutely.

The entire chamber was speechless. Everyone regarded the people around them with bewilderment. No one seemed to know what to do or say. Mercifully, Cardinal Clodius ended the lull. "With one aye vote, one nay vote, and three abstentions, the motion of deportation is not adopted. The prisoner, Flowing Courage, is free to go." The horn blew affirming Clodius' words.

I'm free to go? I'm free to go. I'm free to go!

Loud cheers and applause burst from the galleries. Their collective celebrations were deafening. The Bokori section all donned their gray hoods, raised their kyqads, and slowly exited the chamber. Adam stood up, watching the guards for any sign of reaction. None happened. From behind, Adam was nearly tossed off his feet by an exuberant hug from Samus.

"You did it! You did it!" Samus yelled.

"I'm not sure I did anything but sit and strip," Adam replied. "Can you put me down please, I think I might throw up."

Samus eased him to the ground. After dismissing his aides, Daloth walked over to the pair of them. Marduk had followed up behind Samus. Adam extended his hand to the Cardinal. The Moan, unsure what to do, extended his own webbed hand. Adam gripped it, giving the Moan's hand a firm shake. "It's what we Humans do to say thank you, Cardinal Daloth," Adam answered the Moan's brief confusion.

"Ah, indeed! That outcome was...unexpected to say the least. In all my years, I've never seen the Union challenge another Proprietor Race. The ramifications of this are...well there will be time to think about that later. You're a free sentient. I'd be careful not to wander into the Bokori sections of the station. Final Form will not forget this. Watch your back," Daloth said.

We never forget either, Final Form.

Daloth leaned in closer so as not to be overheard. "I've some friends I think you'd be interested in meeting. Sinner allies that could be helpful to your cause. I'll send instructions on when, where, and how to meet me. Keep this between us. Don't want to upset the Bokori any further. That can be your way of thanking me," Daloth said with a wink.

"I will," Adam replied. "I can never repay you."

"I'm sure we'll think of suitable compensation. You keep alive. Your people need you. Samus, my dear, good luck to you, too. This beached whale of a friend you've got here will need your help," Daloth said with another wink.

"You know it," Samus said.

"I must be off. Much to do. Angry vidcoms and d-mail to answer. Good day. Marduk, always a pleasure," Daloth said with an extravagant bow before walking away.

"Daloth," replied Marduk. The muscular Moan grinned widely at Adam. "I've seen some close calls in my day. You pulled a miracle out of a coral reef, Commissioner Mortis. Well done."

"Thank you..." Adam replied unsure how to address the Moan.

"Marduk is fine. Be sure to swing by my shop. Tiamat's Talons. I'd be honored to commission a new weapon for you. Perhaps some palerasteel armor to go with that sick jacket you wear," Marduk said.

"I'd would love that. Except, I don't know if I'll be able to afford it. Our Links are stretched pretty thin. Sam and I have much we still need to accomplish before I can start self-indulging on new gear," Adam said.

Marduk gave a dismissive wave. "We can figure out a deal. At the very least, I'm going to buy you a hat," Marduk said, tipping his coral tricorn.

"I'll be sure to stop by regardless. My pistol does need some more ammo," Adam said.

"Excellent! I'm open during normal business hours. I gave my contact info to young Samus here in case you are ever interested. Smooth seas to you both," Marduk said with a polite bow.

The Moan walked away with Samus eyeing the Moan meticulously. "That's one shark I'd love to jump." Adam elbowed her sharply in the ribcage. "What? Look at him! He's beautiful. So sexy. That scar across his chest. Mmm. I wonder how he got it," Samus said lustfully.

"In the Century of Strife, where he fought, meaning he's probably more than twice your age, Sam!" Adam said pointedly vexed by her gawking.

"Why should that matter? Aliens age and mature differently. For all I know, twice my age makes him a young adult. Besides, I've seen the way you look at..."

"Adam." Havera had crept up on their conversation. Adam tried his best to maintain composure. On the one hand, he wanted to strangle the Cauduun. On the other, he could've spent all day admiring her body. He thought better of either option.

I've seen what she can do with her tail.

"What do you what, Your Grace?" Adam said in a poor attempt at mimicking Havera's stern tone.

Samus ribbed him this time. Havera waved her off. "It's alright. I'm only here to deliver a message. His Eminence, Cardinal Clodius, my pater, would like to speak with you, in official capacity, regarding your stay here on Conclave station. I'm to take you there immediately. He would like me to emphasize that, although you are not under arrest, this is not a request," Havera said in stern tone.

"If I refuse?" Adam challenged.

Havera contorted her tail to sway in front of her. It was a not-so-subtle threat. "You won't," Havera said bluntly.

"Okay, you've made your point. What about Sam?" Adam asked.

"I have a car arranged to take her back to my apartment," Havera said.

"Like Kewea you will!" Adam shouted. A few people turned to see the argument.

Samus stepped in front of both of them. She grabbed Adam by his jacket. "Adam, it's fine. I've been staying with Havera for the past couple days. If she wanted to hurt me or betray me, she could've done so a hundred times. She told me about her dual mission the first night we spent here. I wasn't happy about it either, but we can't afford to create enemies out of friends," Samus said pleadingly.

"Friends? You're siding with her, Sam?" Adam asked incredulous.

Samus stiffened her posture and frowned. "I'm siding with you. Put your anger aside for now, Adam. It's gotten us into enough trouble. Havera is the best friend we've got whether you acknowledge it or not," Samus said with a hint of rage.

Adam bowed his head. *She's right. My anger and my impulsiveness aren't helping. I'm keeping a close watch on the Cauduun. Not the least which she is stunning in that dress...no! Focus, you idiot. Don't let that distract you!* Adam lifted his chin. He saw Havera's own head was dipped, not wanting to look at him. "Fine. You still have your bow?" Adam inquired.

Samus smiled. "Better believe it. I think I will visit Marduk. Take him up on that offer," Samus said. Adam raised an eyebrow at her. "Of a new weapon! Kewea's curse, Adam! Relax. I've more self-control than you around pretty people. I'll see you later."

17

Family Matters

Not one word was exchanged between Adam and Havera the entire trip to the Cauduun embassy. Not one glance. Not one acknowledgement of the other's presence. A burning anger simmered within Adam while Havera exuded a frigid indifference towards her Human companion.

For two years, she was sweet talking my father and the rest of our kind. All the while she was handing over our secrets to the Bokori on a platinum platter. Extending a hand of friendship and wrapping her tail around our throats at the same time.

Adam was too pissed off to notice they had been whisked through a back entrance, avoiding the foot traffic of the Cauduun embassy. Havera was guiding Adam in silence towards an office at the top of the building. A comely Cauduun male secretary told the two of them to wait until the Cardinal was ready to see them. Adam snapped out of his self-righteous fury to finally take in the sights.

Above the secretary's desk was a grand painted portrait of a plain-looking Cauduun woman with lilac skin and a burnt umber tail. The woman was plump and appeared well over one-hundred years old. She wore an elegant citrine gown with purple stripes along the fringes, and ubiquitous, decorative accoutrements of the Vitriba were sewn and affixed to the stately garb. She wore a crown of platinum leaves inlaid with an exquisite array of disparate gemstones. Beneath the portrait, Adam read a name: QUEEN ALEXANDRA III.

I thought she'd be more impressive.

Havera remained seated and cross-legged, occasionally following Adam around the room with her eyes. She had adjusted her hair back to her typical triple ponytails.

Adam decided to wander the room. On the opposite wall from the secretary was an entire memorial wall dedicated to the previous queens of Rema with corresponding names and dates engraved. Many of the recent queens had painted portraits in an identical style to Alexandra III. Few of the queens could be described as young. Adam found Alexandra II, who bore a striking resemblance to Alexandra III.

Probably her mother or grandmother.

Past a certain point, no more portraits existed. Adam noticed the first name to not have one was engraved: QUEEN HAVERA IX (1347-1374). Adam's curiosity got the better of him. He found the other eight queens Havera. Some of them had long reigns, including Queen Havera III, who had the longest reign of any queen as far as Adam could tell at over one-hundred and fifty years in the third and fourth centuries. Quite a few short reigns, too, by Cauduun standards it seemed. Queen Havera VI (998-1003) ruled for only five years, and even shorter, Queen Havera IV reigned for only four years from 446 to 450. *That's around the time of the Great Galactic War if memory serves. Must be the legendary Warrior Queen from the tales.* Adam traced the queens all the way back to the very first queen: Queen Havera I. Her tenure predated the founding of the Conclave, -204 to -68. Adam couldn't help but glimpse over his shoulder at Havera. She continued to stare frosty daggers at him.

"Quite the legacy you have, huh?" Adam said, turning away from Havera but loud enough for her to hear.

"You've a knack for stating the obvious," Havera said coldly.

Adam turned heel and dropped all pretense of civility. "Why are you pissed at me? What gives you the gall to act offended? You informed on us to the Conclave!"

"I'm not pissed at you. You mistake detachment for interest. I had my orders, and I carried them out without passion or prejudice. Not everything is about you," Havera said.

Adam got right up in her face. "Part of your job was psychologically analyzing me. Tell me. What did you say in your report about me?"

"Adam," Havera sighed. "Don't do this. Everything I had to say I said at the hearing. This isn't the time nor the place."

"Give me a time and place. I'll meet you there! Unless you're embarrassed by what you said about me. You must've told Daloth snippets otherwise he wouldn't have asked you. I'm not stupid, Havera," Adam said.

"Could've fooled me," Havera said.

"You mistake formal education for intelligence and knowledge for wisdom," Adam said.

Havera stood up. "Alright, fine. Want to do this here? I can do this here. Your lack of formal structure in childhood cultivated an attitude of defiance and survival at all costs. The military did little to assuage that mentality, rather it gave you the tools and training needed to feel powerful and fight back. Your obvious trauma causes you to see threats around every corner. Your unjust imprisonment and subsequent torture created trust issues, which in turn makes you extremely susceptible to emotional manipulation by those that you do trust like your friend John. You treat people like disposable objects rather than pursue meaningful relationships. Trissefer. You intentionally keep people at arm's length, afraid to be hurt again. Trissefer. Yet, you simultaneously feel a zealous overprotective desire to keep those you do care about safe. Samus. You suffocate them with your own self-pity to the point where it pushes them away. Your brother. In other words, you mask your atrocious behavior behind your trauma, shielding you against any criticism or deflecting the idea you might be wrong.

I'm sorry for what happened to you, Adam, I really am. You cannot keep using that as an excuse to be a horrible person, then retreat into your testudo shell when you're challenged on it. I've seen the compassionate side of you. I know you have the capacity to do good. You have to stop pretending you are good and start being good."

Adam wanted to punch her. He wanted to kick her. He wanted to throw her up against a wall and strangle her. He wanted to throw her up against a wall and kiss her. He wanted to wrap his arms around her and cry.

Why do I feel this way? She can't be right. No, no! I'm justified to feel the way I do. To act the way I do. Who is she to speak to me like that? Some nerd spy princess. She was right about some things. No. I cannot admit that. No. I'm right, she's wrong. She knows nothing. Just a bunch of fancy words. She's not better than me! What if she's right?

"Ahem!" the secretary interrupted Adam's thoughts. "His Eminence will see you both."

Havera grunted her acknowledgement. She was about to push past him when she remembered something. "Oh, I almost forgot. This belongs to you."

Havera shoved something into Adam's hand. A small platinum grip.

The Debbie! She kept her word.

Havera shouldered her way past Adam. In a mental haze, Adam pocketed the Debbie and followed her into the Cardinal's office.

Restrained, economical, and full of Cauduun iconography with the Vitriba seal prominently displayed everywhere. Exactly what Adam expected from the office of Cardinal Clodius. The blue-skinned, white-tailed Cauduun Cardinal had kept his crimson, linen tunic, but he had removed his horned cap and added an emerald silk toga with purple stripes along the fringes. The toga's style reminded Adam of Queen Alexandra III's portrait in the foyer. Clodius was standing with one arm resting on the back of his chair, wearing an intimidating grimace that rivaled Adam's Naddine drill sergeant.

He'd better not make me run sprints.

Clodius gave a curt heart salute to Adam and a slight bow to Havera. Adam matched him. Havera didn't move. "I must congratulate you,

Human. Seems you have friends in unexpected places," Clodius said in a deep, harsh tone.

"Enemies, too," Adam said, resisting the temptation to peer at Havera.

"You mean my filia?" Clodius surmised. "You aren't even on our radar, Human. The Duchess and I are simply duty and honor bound to obey the will of our Queen. I can assure you, Human, it is nothing personal. To think your kind rises to the level of enemy insults the very notion of adversary."

"Why did you summon us, pater?" Havera cut in with her stern voice.

"It's 'Your Eminence' while you are in this office, Your Grace," Clodius said.

"I'll call you whatever I damn well please, pater. I outrank you on every level," Havera said sternly. Adam's eyes widened.

I've walked into some serious drama.

Clodius gave a stiff bow. "Of course, Your Grace. I was merely suggesting, in this moment, you should think of me as the office rather than your pater. On the topic of duty, you and I shall have a serious discussion about your recent activities," Clodius said through gritted teeth.

"Get to the point, *Your Eminence.* I'm sure the 'lowly Human' doesn't want to waste his precious free moments getting a lecture from you," Havera said.

Clodius nodded. "Very well." He gestured for Adam and Havera to sit. Adam and Clodius started to sit. Havera remained unmoved. Clodius, noticing her reticence, quickly got back up. Adam, unsure what to do, stood back up. "You've no idea the firestorm you've created, Human," Clodius said.

"He has a name, pater. Use it," Havera said.

Clodius gritted his teeth. "Fine. Adam Mortis. Is Adam acceptable?"

"Ye...yes. Adam is fine or Commissioner," Adam said, stuttering. He was afraid Havera would cut him off, too. He felt a strange fear standing next to Havera.

"I must congratulate you, *Commissioner.* It's been a long time since I've seen Cardinal Final Form that heated. You certainly exposed its lackey for what it is," Clodius said.

"The High Hisba and I have...history," Adam said.

"I've seen the video. Didn't realize that was it under the helmet. Your ability to remain relatively calm under such circumstances is laudable. Perhaps you'll be a good enough politician after all," Clodius said.

"I'm not so sure about that. I was at a meeting with the Bokori interrogator, Enduring Temptation..." Adam said.

Clodius scoffed interrupting Adam's sentence. "Enduring Temptation. Long gone are the days of Mahlak the Righteous and Salvana the Destroyer. Names that struck fear even among my people. Do I get to deal with anyone remotely of their caliber? No. I'm forced to contend with the likes of Final Form or Repulsive Chocolate," Clodius said, waving a hand and making up a name on the spot. "The 'Great Gray Hordes of the East' and their Arkhans are nothing but stardust in the stellar wind of history. Instead, I get 'the People's House'. There's no honor in putting down a dying beast."

"The 'Sick Race of the Galaxy?'" Adam said.

Clodius nodded. "Precisely. I don't know what you Humans have done to our old adversary. The Bokori are a shell of their former selves," Clodius said.

"I'm not sure what you mean, Cardinal. We've been their subjugates for over five centuries. You give us too much credit," Adam said, barely suppressing a smile.

The Cardinal's eyes narrowed. "The Bokori once rivaled us to be the greatest people in the galaxy. Whatever you've done to them has weakened them beyond all recognition. I was a military observer during the Bokori Phase of the Strife. I know what the Bokori were capable of and how far they've fallen. Be thankful, Commissioner, you do not live long lives. You have the luxury of short memories. We do not and cannot forget any past mistakes. The Bokori shall learn that's the sort of game you lose every time the hard way."

He's perceptive. Too perceptive. I wonder if he's an anomaly or if the rest of the galaxy is catching onto the Long Con. The Bokori certainly aren't. I'm overthinking everything again. Focus on the here and now.

Adam pivoted. "Humanity is absolutely interested in reestablishing the friendly and prosperous relationship with the Cauduun we once had centuries ago. If you and Her Majesty are willing to recognize..." Adam began saying.

Clodius silenced him. "Save your breath, Commissioner. You really believe I want to talk about the merits of your claim?" Clodius laughed. "I might've given you too much credit after all. The only reason we're speaking is so I can disavow you of any delusions you might have. Your actions on Bokor were amusing, but I'm here to shut you down. You've caused far too much trouble than you're worth," Clodius said.

"What do you mean trouble? Our fight for freedom and independence troubles you?" Adam snarked.

Clodius rolled his eyes. "Spare me the self-righteous speech. I've heard them all. The Sinners at least had an army and economy to back up their claim. You've nothing of value. Meanwhile, Cardinal Final Form, the People's House, and other Bokori dignitaries have been calling our terminals nonstop, demanding that I and the other Proprietor Cardinals sign off on another arrest warrant. They're threatening to raise tariffs and impose a dark matter embargo on any race that has even the appearance of aiding your cause. Final Form is also demanding I order an investigation into you, Your Grace," Clodius said.

"Me? Why me?" asked Havera.

"How about perjury for starters? You omitted some key facts about your supposed assignment with Stepicro and the Human Separatists," Clodius said.

"What key facts?" said Havera, her fist clenching tighter.

"Don't play dumb with me. Your Conclave assignment ended twenty months ago! Inconclusively, I might add. The Conclave had no idea you were still hanging around Windless Tornado. I checked with the Praetorian Censors. According to Censor Maxima, you're supposedly on Dagon, studying the ruins of Yapam. Behind the massive hurricane and whirlpool, where effective communication is near impossible. Maxima tells me you've been accessing sensitive Stepicro information. Information not cleared to be shared with the Humans. Information you've claimed is vital to your research. How many more lies have you told?" Clodius said accusingly. Clodius' fists were pressed hard into his desk. He leaned in with each word. Adam felt Havera shrinking under the glare of her father.

Havera lied about spying? Why didn't she say so?

"I…I don't know what you are talking about," Havera said, her stern voice faltering.

"Spare me, *Your Grace*. You're a Praetorian not a Vulpes. Subterfuge isn't one of your specialties. You weren't hard to track. You aren't exactly hard to miss. You were assuming the rumors about the Excommunicated and the Human Separatists were true. You think by hanging around the Humans long enough it will lead you to Ignatia," Clodius said.

Ignatia? That name sounds familiar…

Clodius relaxed his posture. His voice softened. He seemed almost sorrowful. "Tenebella, carissima, please leave her to the professionals. The Vulpes will track her down, and the Legion will bring her to justice. Your mater wouldn't want you to throw your life away chasing after her killer," Clodius said in an unexpectedly tender way.

Her killer?

Havera lowered her head. Clodius walked around the desk and gently put a hand on Havera's shoulder. "You can't keep blaming yourself, Tenebella. Ignatia is a power-hungry traitor. She and the other Paladins of Paleria. If it wasn't that day, it would've been another day," Clodius said.

"Easy for you to say!" Havera yelled, shaking Clodius off. "You're not the reason she's dead!"

"Neither are you!" Clodius shouted back. "You've other duties and responsibilities you've shirked for this personal vendetta."

"The only duty and responsibility I have, pater, is to mater. To bring her murderer to justice," Havera said. The bracers on her forearms flared violet.

Clodius turned around and slammed his fist on the table. "Kewea's curse, child! Your mater's gift has given you a false sense of self-importance. Your mater was renowned and respected for putting peace first. You tarnish her legacy with your arrogance and thirst for blood. I'm putting a stop to this. I've consulted with Her Majesty, the Praetorian Censors, and the other Proprietor Cardinals. They all agree. Your presence in Bokori space creates an unnecessary diplomatic headache. Effectively immediately, you're reassigned to Concordia. You will continue to shadow Commissioner Mortis here at all times and report on his activities in the capital. He is not to leave your sight. Censor Maxima has agreed to keep your insubordination quiet. In fact, they're promoting you to the rank of Aedile to maintain the illusion you were operating under Conclave orders. Cardinal Final Form isn't thrilled, but it's content to keep you away from their territory and internal affairs," Clodius summed up.

"That's not fair! You can't do this. You don't have the authority!" Havera protested.

"I can and I have. Unless you're contemplating disobeying a direct order from your Queen?" Clodius said smugly.

Havera bit her lip. She flipped one of her ponytails back over her shoulder. "No. I am at Her Majesty's service," Havera said, bowing her head in resignation.

"Do I not get a say in this?" Adam asked.

"No," Clodius said bluntly.

"I am the appointed representative of the free and independent Human race. I'm not some pawn in your personal or political drama!" Adam barked.

"If the situation isn't apparent to you, Commissioner Mortis, you are less than a pawn. You should thank Cradite I haven't ordered your detainment for suspected ties to a known terrorist organization. True or not, the Bokori are making a case that the Human Separatists and the Excommunicated are one and the same. While the situation is resolving itself back on Bokor, you are forbidden from leaving Concordia. If you do, the Conclave will order any member government to arrest you.

That is if the Bokori don't kill you first," Clodius said. The Cardinal walked back around his desk and sat down. "I have nothing more to say to you, Human. Go wait outside. I have matters of utmost importance to discuss with the Duchess."

Adam seethed. He half contemplated picking up the chair in front of him and heaving it at the Cardinal. He might've if he weren't so scrawny. He made a move towards the exit. Havera seized him by the arm. "Where do you think you're going, Commissioner?" she said in her stern voice. Adam froze, her words and her grip bolting him to the ground.

"What we are to discuss is not for outside ears, Your Grace. Family matters are not meant for outsiders," Clodius said.

"You should've thought of that before you ordered me to not let the Commissioner out of my sight. If he leaves, I leave. Wherever he goes, I go. Your orders, Cardinal. Excuse me, 'Her Majesty's orders.'" Havera sneered.

Adam was lucky he had his back to the Cardinal otherwise he'd have seen Adam visibly stifle a laugh. He pivoted around to face the Cardinal.

Clodius' tail was stiffened so rigidly Adam thought he could've broken it off and fashioned into a lethal weapon. Adam rubbed his chest, remembering how hard Havera had hit him accidentally. The tension in his body rose, anticipating a strike he logically knew would never happen. The glare in the Cardinal's eyes suggested otherwise.

The Cardinal sighed. "Very well. If anything said in this room leaks, Commissioner, the Sezerene disposal workers will only find pieces of your body in the depths of the station," Clodius growled.

Adam quickly covered his mouth. He didn't care how humiliating his reaction was. Havera rolled her eyes. This time they both sat down.

"Lady Tenebella Havera of Shele, Duchess of Paleria, it is my duty to request that you return to Rema at the conclusion of this business. You're aware the College of Duchesses is meeting in a few months on Saptia to decide on who should fill the Office of The Archduchess, heir to the Platinum Throne. Since your mater, Archduchess

Pompeia...passed, Queen Alexandra III has had no successor in two years," Clodius said.

Archduchess Pompeia was Havera's mother?! That's an impressive pedigree. Burdensome. Revelation after revelation. If Cradite herself came down from the heavens and declared Havera a goddess, I'd believe it at this point.

"I already know what you're going to ask, pater, and the answer is no. That was mater's path. Not mine. I'm not built for politics and leadership," Havera said.

"Don't be ridiculous. You've the right name, and you're Pompeia's daughter," Clodius said.

"Not by blood," Havera corrected him.

Clodius waved his hand dismissively. "You know better than anyone the duchesses don't care about such things. The name and legacy matter most. I've spoken with Duchess Iunia and Duchess Eudoxia. They both assure me if you were to place your tail into the ring, the Conservative Faction will rally around your candidacy. You'll have almost three-hundred votes from the get-go. All you need is another couple dozen votes, and you'll be confirmed archduchess after one, maybe two ballots at most. With the Republican Faction in disarray due to Her Majesty's failings, it'll be a cinch."

"The Conservatives haven't rallied around anyone after ten ballots in three Colleges since mater died, nor have they put an archduchess on the throne in over two-hundred years. Why would Iunia help me? She leads the Absolutist wing and was mater's fiercest rival in the Conservative Faction," Havera said.

Iunia. Conservatives. Republicans. Absolutists. I should take notes. This is useful information.

"Not anymore. After the last ballot, the Absolutist wing booted her from leadership. Caelia leads the Absolutists these days," Clodius said.

"Cisi's daughter? I thought she'd be too busy busting Confederate heads in the outer colonies to run for political office. What about Augusta? Wasn't she next in line? Her support was vital for mater's election last time," Havera said.

Clodius paused and sat back in his chair. "Augusta has defected to the Imperialists."

"No! The lunatics who want to return to the days of the Platinum Empresses?! Nobody takes them seriously outside of Paleria. What do they have like five votes?" Havera said flabbergasted.

"Twenty-two and rising. It's not just Paleria, Your Grace. The Imperialist cause has grown stronger, especially in the border colonies. The banishment of the Paladins of Paleria enraged everyone. Those that didn't go full Imperialist became Absolutist Conservatives. Excom attacks and the Sinner Mining Agreement have swelled their numbers. With Augusta as their leader, they could become a true political force to be reckoned with. Add them to the growing Confederate cause in the outer colonies..." Clodius let his words linger.

I don't know what that means, but I guess that's bad.

"Augusta was mater's best friend. I should talk to...no. No! You won't drag me into this, Your Eminence. I've said no and I will keep saying no. The Conservatives and the Republicans control eighty percent of the College. They'll find a compromise candidate. Iunia, Caelia, Augusta. No matter who, it won't be me! I've too much important work to do." Havera shook her head. Staring at the floor, Havera ran her fingers through her hair.

Clodius' tail whirled to allow his chin to rest on the tip. "You'd rather spend your time reading about exceptional women rather than become one?"

Havera raised her head. "Are you saying I'm not an exceptional woman, pater?" Adam could hear the hurt in her voice.

"If you turn your back on your people when they need you most, yes. The Cauduun Monarchical Alliance stands upon the edge of a sword. Rather than pull it back as your mater would, you'd thrust it forward unto death. Maybe you are right. You are not ready to lead. Not with that selfish, self-righteous attitude," Clodius said.

Havera cleared her throat and stood up. "I see. You've said enough. You've made your feelings about me quite clear, Your Eminence. If there's nothing further, we shall take our leave." Havera turned her back on her pater. Adam stood up to follow her.

Clodius must've sensed he said something wrong. He stood up and reached out in Havera's direction. "Tenebella, wait. You know I didn't mean it like that."

"YOU'VE SAID ENOUGH!" Havera's bracers illuminated her entire body in a magenta glow. The aura was much stronger than it had been in Arabella. Her triple ponytails flapped repeatedly as a small, local wind brushed aside loose papers. The muscles on her entire body noticeably bulged. Curiously, her amethyst purple eyes had turned a deep red. Havera's face grimaced with anger. Adam took a couple steps back, bumping into the Cardinal's desk.

Clodius didn't flinch. He bowed his head and sat back down. "You may leave," Clodius said barely above a whisper.

Still glowing, Havera's tail whipped around Adam's torso. She heaved him off the ground so suddenly and violently Adam almost vomited. Carrying him with her tail, Havera marched to the edge of the room. With a winding punch, she shattered open the door to the Cardinal's office, causing the eavesdropping secretary to flee in terror. Adam went limp in her tail's grip. She dragged him into the lift, nearly crushing the control panel in the process. Halfway down the lift, Havera plopped Adam down. The magenta glow from her bracers had subsided. Adam hoped her anger had, too.

I think I understand your pain, Havera.

Adam touched the Debbie through the pocket in his jacket. Catching him out of the corner of her eye, Havera glanced over her shoulder.

"You going to shoot me, too?"

Adam cleared his throat. "No, I was going to tell you to have an equally dramatic entrance next time," Adam said with a nervous laugh.

The Cauduun said nothing. Other than the swaying of her tail, she did not react. They reached the bottom floor and headed out the back where they had entered earlier. He might've been hallucinating, or it might've been a residuum of fear, but Adam swore he saw the crack of a slight smile out of the corner of Havera's mouth.

18

Sins of the Father

The Moan diplomatic aircar met Adam and Havera near the border of the political and cultural districts. Per Cardinal Daloth Afta's instructions, the pair were to meet with the Moan Cardinal and a few friendly ears inside the Moan section of the cultural district. Given the sensitivity of the situation, Daloth determined, with Havera's agreement, any meeting should occur away from the embassies. Diplomatic tensions were high. Adam wished to avoid any further potential interstellar incidents while he and the Human Separatist cause were under a microscope. Cardinal Clodius' rebuke stung. It was abundantly clear to Adam he needed to tread carefully. He was in perilous waters.

Speaking of waters, woah!

The aircar had been flying high above the artificial cloud line of the station. Once they dropped beneath the clouds, a huge body of water rose to meet them. For miles in all directions was nothing but sea.

We're indoors. How's this possible?

Adam instinctually braced himself as the car descended rapidly and plunged into the watery depths. "Relax, Adam," Havera said. "Moan vehicles are designed to operate under the sea and in the air. The seams of the car are welded tightly." The aircar reoriented itself for underwater travel. Fins with guarded rotor blades expanded from the sides, propelling the vehicle forward.

"I thought you were speaking metaphorically when you said we were going underwater," Adam said.

"Nope. The cultural district was built to give an accurate representation of the different galactic races. Five-hundred square miles of territory for each race," Havera explained.

"Equally for all races? That's surprising," Adam said.

"The entire station is a cultural center for the Proprietor races. This was our form of appeasement," Havera said.

"I don't suppose Humans have one," Adam wondered aloud. Havera shook her head. "What would we even put in it? Screens displaying nothing but garbled text data twenty hours a day or a printed statue of a Human on all fours bowing in front of a gray blob."

"I understand why you think that, but can you please not be so grimdark? You're missing the sights," Havera said brusquely. She was right. Adam saw Moans in their pure Piscine form, dashing through the waters at incredible speeds. He had never seen a Moan in their aquatic Piscine form, but he had heard about it. All manner of magnificent sea creatures were swimming past them. Some of them had riders, mostly Moan but Adam spotted the occasional Naddine on the backs of sea beasts.

I don't see any breathing gear on them. How are they surviving like that underwater?

Closer to the seafloor, massive bioluminescent architecture filled the landscape. Purples, blues, and greens lit of up the waters around them. As they sailed through the waters, towering minarets casted bioluminescent light in all directions. Vehicle traffic through this area was minimal. Floating platforms of bubbles carrying hundreds of pedestrians and swimmers idly drifted by. The car weaved in and out of the glowing tendrils that connected broad-domed structures with more organic-shaped designs. A mixture of artificial and natural-looking constructions.

Breathtaking.

"We're here," Havera said. The car pulled up to one of the floating bubbles, this one smaller than the ones Adam had seen so far. The car reoriented itself, pushing inside the bioluminescent bubble. The water stopped at the edge, creating an air pocket for non-Moans to breathe. The car landed on the platform next to a Moan woman. Adam recognized her as one of Daloth's aides. Exiting the car, the air around him was humid but pleasant enough. It reminded him a bit of Windless Tornado, only with a far better aroma. Near the entrance stood a hairless bovine-looking creature with long, curved horns and gills along the side of its neck. It was eating a mixture of grass and seaweed out of a large pot and huffed as they walked past it. The aide led Adam and Havera inside the lone, mushroom-shaped structure inside the bubble. Other than an occasional Moan guard wearing bright, chitinous armor, the building was deserted.

The aide brought them to the main room, a spacious basilica with architecture resembling a mixture of the Tribunal's cathedral and the classic bioluminescence of the Moans. Glowing images of tortoises of all shapes and sizes covered the walls. Standing in front of a chunky tortoise of bleached basalt and limestone stood four figures.

Daloth, in all his ostentatious glory, was mid-conversation with a Naddine male wearing heavy leathers. To Adam, the Naddine appeared dressed for battle.

Next to them, sitting down and arms crossed, was a Rinvari male. Wearing only a red sash, the gorilla-like Rinvari had white fur that was browning along the tips with a thick, copper mane around his face, and spiraling horns. He appeared to be in deep meditation.

Separated slightly from the others was a tall, thin, avian sentient, whom Adam recognized as a Hasuram, a sparsely populated race in the Zeta spiral that bordered the Bokori to the southeast. The Hasuram had a pattern on the back of its wings that strongly resembled glaring eyes. Based on that, Adam surmised this one was a female. Her wings wrapped around her body like armor while she stood. He could see she was wearing a plain, tan tunic behind her combed, lime feathers. The distinguishing feature of the Hasuram were their three sets of faces.

Three persons in one head. Supposedly, which face spoke determined whether the Hasuram was speaking with the rational or emotional part of their brain. Adam didn't entirely believe that, though he had no evidence to the contrary. Regardless, he found the way their heads rotated to accommodate the speaking mouths humorous at best and unsettling at worst, especially when more than one mouth spoke at a time.

"Ah, the guest of honor! Welcome, welcome!" said Daloth with an enthusiastic bow. "Lady Havera! Your Grace, I'm sorry you were whirlpooled into all this. I wish it didn't have to be this way."

"That makes two of us, Cardinal," Havera said, returning the bow with stiff politeness.

"I'm not comfortable with this, Daloth," said the Rinvari without opening his eyes. "The Duchess will report everything we say back to the Cardinal. I don't want to jeopardize our relationship with the Cauduun, not after the Mining Agreement. The Superhighway is too important. Can't afford instability along our Cauduun-Bokori border."

"Our Cauduun friends have their long tails and pointy ears in all our business, Cardinal Krovim. Don't be so foolish to think they don't already know about this meeting and everything we'll say here. No offense, Your Grace. The Cauduun-Naddine relationship is the backbone of galactic peace and prosperity," said the Naddine with a slight sneer.

"If it'll help ease everyone's comfort, I can step to the other side of this chamber. Let y'all talk in private," Havera suggested.

"Oh, no, Your Grace, that's not necessary," said Daloth.

"It's no issue, Cardinal. I'll stand there and admire the artwork," said Havera sourly. The Cauduun stepped away from the group towards the corner near the entrance, her tail stiffly resting upon her shoulder.

Adam bit his tongue. He wanted her counsel while talking with these seasoned diplomats. With them, he was firmly on the back foot. Although, he had to admit, the revelations about Havera's spying had wounded him.

Do I trust Daloth any more than Havera? I've known her on-and-off for two years. I need to be careful.

"Right. Introductions," Daloth said, clapping his hands. "Y'all are familiar with Commissioner Adam Mortis, I presume. Commissioner, this is Chief Raw-Paw of the Yitash. We were fortunate to catch him while he was on station. You probably saw his beast on the way in." Adam extended his hand. Raw-Paw grasped Adam firmly by the forearm and clasped him hard on the shoulder. Adam felt the Naddine's claws digging into his shoulder. He gritted his teeth, resisting the urge to wince.

"Jes-Mur, spare me. You Humans have soft skin," Raw-Paw said in an insulting tone.

"You Naddine have sharp claws," Adam retorted.

Raw-Paw laughed. "And don't you forget it, Human." The Naddine let go and left a visible indentation in Adam's coat.

"Raw-Paw represents the Fabulist bloc of the Naddine Confederacy," explained Daloth.

"It's 'Na-deen,' Cardinal," countered Raw-Paw.

"I hear it as 'Nay-dine,'" said the Rinvari.

"Luk-Kas pronounces it 'Na-di-nay,'" argued Daloth.

"Jes-Mur, spare me. Never mind. It doesn't matter," Raw-Paw relented.

I always thought it was 'Nay-deen.'

"The gruff Rinvari here is Cardinal Krovim, of course representing the Rinvari Federation. Don't mistake his grumpy demeanor for anger or apathy. That's how he always is," said Daloth.

Krovim grumbled. "It's the heat. I'd get up and bop you on the head, Human, or however it is your kind greets people, but frankly I'm more comfortable where I am."

"We're shaking hands these days, Cardinal," said Adam.

"I prefer the Naddine way," said Krovim with a grunt.

"Everyone does," said Raw-Paw with a chuckle.

Daloth introduced the Hasuram last. "This lovely lady is Consul Neha Alneha. She's the business and trade liaison for our coalition. She and the other leaders of Tetrad commerce have been essential in helping finance the construction of the Superhighway."

"More like helping wayward Rangers get fat off our Links while they take their sweet time scouring for black hole systems to complete the damn thing," said Neha. Her head turned with the movement of her mouths. Adam resisted the urge to crack his neck.

How do they do that?

"Forgive my ignorance, but what is the Superhighway?" asked Adam. He had heard that term previously but couldn't remember where.

"A series of interstellar lanes built in our coalition's territories. Internally, we're calling it the 'Vol Sinner,' but the media has dubbed it the 'Sinner Superhighway.' So, we started calling it that as well." Daloth explained. He pulled out his personal emulator, scrolling through until he found what he was seeking. He flipped the emulator around to show Adam a map of the galaxy with all the territories labeled and marked in different colors. Adam watched the Moan trace a finger around the map. "Ever since the Strife, creating a robust network outside of Proprietor control is essential to galactic balance and security. To that end, our coalition has been scouring our collective territories to find viable interstellar lanes for trade and commerce. We're seeking to connect them in one giant loop, circumventing every Proprietor race's territory, beginning here in Rinvari Space, going around Bokori and Zokyon territory to the east, and ending here in either Moan or Rorae territory to the south. We'd have direct trade route access to the Conclave and each other without ever setting a webbed foot in Proprietor space," Daloth explained.

"It's an expensive endeavor. The Sinner Mining Agreement was a step in securing that goal. The Cauduun were 'kind enough' to sell us a black hole artery station in their territory to allow us access to Neutral Space from our territory. Previously, we've had to traverse Bokori Space to reach Neutral Space. We had to borrow the money, of course. From the Cauduun. Plus, they received a free trade agreement from all Sinner races. Part of the compensation for the black hole system. All our economic resources are devoted to building these black hole artery systems. The Federation believes it'll be worth it in the long run," explained Cardinal Krovim. Adam noted the unusual appendage of Rinvari territory on Daloth's map squeezed between Cauduun and Neutral Space.

At the mention of the Sinner Mining Agreement, Adam noticed Daloth bit his lip. The Moan opened his mouth to speak, but he decided against it. Nobody else paid him any mind on that.

"Once the Superhighway is fully viable, all the Proprietor races will pay us extensive fees and tariffs for the privilege of accessing our markets," said Neha.

"You presume too much, my friends," said Raw-Paw. "The Naddine have no need of your Superhighway. We have a direct route to Neutral Space via the Vol Gla-Mor. Between that and our relationships with the Cauduun Monarchical Alliance and the Rorae Conservatory, your new interstellar lanes won't affect Terras-Ku's trade economy."

"Perhaps not, but you don't want to see the Zokyo gain access to them. The Accords cut off the Zokyo from having a direct lane to Neutral Space. They must pass through either Moan or Bokori territory to do so. Both routes are hurting their economy long term," said Daloth.

I came all this way to discuss trade routes? Dasenor help me.

"Which is why I'm here talking to y'all. The Ra-Mu this year will determine who shall be the next Han-Nor and Mol-Win. I'm working to ensure that one of or both leaders will be Fabulists this time around. My son, Ran-Paw, is competing. I can guarantee everyone here, including the Human, if we take charge of Terras-Ku, our policies will be more friendly towards your cause. Nonetheless, I must take my leave. I've lingered in this cesspool far too long. Hold out until the month of Jesmuriad, you will be a stronger position," said Raw-Paw.

Jesmuriad?! That's seven months away.

"All due respect, Chief Raw-Paw, I don't know if we can last that long against the Bokori," said Adam.

The Naddine adjusted his half-shoulder cape. "Then, I'll know you weren't worth my time. If you do survive, the Yitash would like to extend an invitation to you and any other Human leader to this year's Ra-Mu. Anointment years are always the best time to witness the games. Gentlemen, lady, good day," Raw-Paw said with a slight head bow. The Naddine departed the room, completely ignoring Havera's attempt to communicate.

"Arrogant prick," said Krovim.

"You ever meet a Naddine clan chief who wasn't? You must be to tame the spirit of a Sacred Boss," said Neha.

Adam crossed off the Naddine from his mental list. He stood there staring at the galaxy map still in Daloth's webbed hands.

Daloth took note. "You see something you care to share?"

"Sorry, I was just thinking about your proposed Superhighway. You've another problem," Adam circled the eastern fringes of Bokori Space with his finger. "This here is pirate country. The Excommunicated and other gangs operate with relative impunity out there right on the border of many of y'all's territories. It was bad when I was a Shock-trooper for the Bokori. It's only grown worse since," Adam said.

"You're more right than you know, Commissioner. The Human crisis is pulling more Bokori patrol ships away from the problem areas. Attacks against our merchant vessels are up thirty percent in the last half-month. Four days ago, Excommunicated ships severely damaged one of our local black hole refueling stations. The Bokori seem to care more about dealing with a few renegade Humans than the biggest terrorism threat the galaxy has faced in decades," said Neha.

"That's because they see us as the greater threat. If a group of 'heretics' successfully challenges their 'progress,' it shatters their illusion. The grayskins cannot allow such ideas to fester," said Adam.

"Which is why we want to facilitate a quick resolution to this crisis, one way or another," said Krovim.

"What do you mean by 'one way or another,' Cardinal?" asked Adam.

"Hear us out, Commissioner," insisted Daloth.

I don't like this.

"The Coalition of Independent Nations will offer to mediate between the Human Separatists and the Bokori. Broker a peaceful solution. We get the Bokori to lift their blockade to allow sentientarian aid. Drop all charges against you, so you can go home. Return to the status quo. Help everyone take a step back and save face," suggested Daloth.

"Without recognizing Human independence, you mean," Adam said.

"Look, Commissioner, you need to be reasonable. The Bokori

ignored all pleas for Human independence, even after Saptia and the Violet Man incident. You've done considerably more than blow up a diplomat's ship. There is no way in Kewea the Bokori will agree to Human independence at this time. Not with a gun pointed to their head," insisted Daloth.

"Seventy-three Humans are dead, Cardinal! Seventy-three and counting! More are dying of starvation and disease every day. When that shield collapses, it'll be five-hundred thousand dead or worse. And you say we're not being reasonable?!" Adam said with a raised voice.

"That'll never happen. The galaxy is keeping a close eye on them. The Conclave would sanction them into oblivion," said Neha, whose head was turned completely to one side.

"You don't know the Bokori like we do. Their economy is already in shambles. People openly mock them to their face. The High Hisba whispers in their ears. You saw how it reacted when I questioned it. It's an utter zealot with a hundred-thousand more zealots just like it under its command. It makes Cardinal Final Form seem reasonable. Do you really believe a person that cold, that utterly convinced of its own righteousness will back down in the face of public scrutiny? You aren't its constituency. All it'll take is for it to convince the grayskins of the People's House to turn a blind eye. It convinced them to authorize a raid onto their environmentally-protected, sacred moon to kill me. Stepping foot on that moon is a crime that carries at least a year in rehab, and they did it anyway. To the Bokori, the difference between seventy-three and five-hundred thousand isn't a travesty, it's a statistic." Adam said.

"All the more reason to broker a peaceful solution, now! If the High Hisba is as crazy as you say it is, we must not give it any excuse to act. We get the Bokori to call off their war dogs, and in a few years we'll be able to broach the independence question on more friendly terms," said Daloth.

"We don't have a few years, Cardinal. Arabella won't be able to sustain herself that long. We've come too far. Human independence is non-negotiable. We need galactic recognition. We need economic and medical aid. Most importantly, we need guns and ammo," Adam insisted.

Cardinal Krovim scoffed. "That's not happening. The Proprietor races already believe the Excommunicated aid your cause. We suddenly start supplying weapons, we'll be accused of siding with terrorists. We won't risk open war with the Bokori over you."

"Open war *is* upon *us*. You need not risk anything. Give us the printers and materials. We'll produce the weapons ourselves," Adam said.

"And when the Bokori's blockade searches our supply ships, what then? 'Oops how did those get there' isn't going to fly," said Krovim.

Adam had thought of that. "Let us produce them here or somewhere in Sinner territory. Give us a loan to buy arms and other vital supplies. It'll be good for your economy, and we'll be able survive for a time. I'll worry about smuggling the supplies into our people's hands."

"A loan you'll probably never be able to pay back? We're not exactly swimming in money, to use a Moan expression," said Neha.

"We will if...when we win," Adam said.

The three Sinners exchanged skeptical looks. "I admire your gumption, Human, but we have our own political and economic concerns. We're only willing to go so far to help. If you refuse our offer at negotiating a peaceful solution, there's nothing more we can do," said Krovim.

"You'd allow us to be slaughtered?" Adam said.

"No, it's your pride that'll get you slaughtered, Human," said Krovim.

"The Covenant has taken everything from us. All we have left is our pride," Adam said.

"What about your Rimestone weapon?" asked Neha.

Adam's face drained of color. He resisted the urge to reach for his pocket, where the weapon rested. "What about it?" Adam choked down a cough.

"A valuable piece of technology is excellent collateral. More than enough to cover a loan," Neha said.

Adam's eyes jumped from Daloth to Krovim to Neha and back again. He recognized their collective expression. Hunger. Desire. Avarice.

Possessing the Debbie is their true objective.

"A moment ago, you said you weren't willing to risk open war with the Bokori. Suddenly, my piece of ancient Human tech, the most tangible tie to our history, is enough for you to put your lives and economies on the line?" Adam said, his anger flaring.

"Commissioner, it isn't like that..." Daloth began to say.

"Oh, I see how it is, *Your Eminence*. This whole meeting is an act just like that hearing. None of y'all care about us. You want our technology. You're no better than the Bokori!" Adam said.

Krovim scoffed. "We're done here. I told you this was a bad idea, Daloth. I'm washing my hands clean of this. You should, too. Consul Alneha, I'll escort you out. Good day, Human." Cardinal Krovim stood up and marched out, thudding the floor with each step.

Consul Neha Alneha walked by Adam and pecked him on the cheek with all three beaks. "Good luck, Commissioner. I do hope we'll see you again."

Only Cardinal Daloth Afta remained. He attempted to put a webbed hand on Adam's shoulder, but Adam shook him off. "I was starting to trust you," Adam seethed.

"It's not personal, Adam. It's our jobs to do what is in the best interests of our people, regardless of our personal feelings. The others might not care, but I do," Daloth said.

Adam scoffed. "Another lie."

"No! I will tolerate any insult or mockery thrown at me, but I will not have my integrity impugned by you! The Thalassocracy wanted me to keep our fins off. They'd have left you to the mercy of the Bokori. I convinced them otherwise! I believed in your cause. I still do. I believe it is the right of all people to have an independent world of their own. Free from terror and the threat of subjugation. Do we stand to benefit? Damn right we do! Your Rimestone weapon could go a long way towards that goal of galactic peace and security. The Proprietor races will do whatever it takes to get their hands on that tech. Why do you think the Cauduun duchess is here? To protect you? She's here to keep track of the Rimestone. The Cauduun may seem like a peace-loving, wise people on the surface, but deep down they are just as greedy and power-hungry like everyone else. Give the Rimestone to us. It'll benefit us both in ways you cannot possibly imagine. Please. Krovim is right. You're letting pride get in the way," Daloth said emphatically.

Adam glanced over his shoulder. Havera was standing there and watching them intensely with her arms folded and tail wrapped around her torso. He could feel the heat of her amethyst eyes on his back. "*You must trust her, son. No matter what happens.*" He remembered his mother's words. Adam looked back at Daloth. "I don't know about the entire Cauduun race, but I trust Havera. She could've taken the Debbie for herself at any time. She didn't. Who do you think had it the entire time I was in custody? Unlike you, she has her honor intact. My technology, my history, and my integrity aren't for sale either," Adam said.

Daloth sighed. He wiped the flop sweat off his brow. He took a few steps past Adam and stopped. "The Coalition's ships near Bokor can bypass the Bokori's Nexus firewall. As a gesture of goodwill, we will allow an open line of communication between Concordia and Arabella. You'll be able to send messages back-and-forth on your emulator, and you'll be able to speak to them in real time from any Nexus-accessible terminal," said Daloth not turning to look. He waited for Adam to respond, and no response came. "No need to thank me."

"I'm not," Adam said coldly. Without another word, Cardinal Daloth Afta left the room. Adam could only stare at the floor.

We're alone.

He heard Havera's footsteps come up from behind him. "How much of that did you hear?" Adam said, pivoting to face her.

Havera's stone face melted into a weak smile. She leaned in and kissed him on the cheek. Her black lips felt cool on Adam's flushed cheeks. "I heard enough," Havera said. Feeling the overwhelming urge to cry he wrapped his arms around the Cauduun woman. Although initially taken aback, Havera wrapped her arms around Adam in an embrace. "What's this for?" she asked softly.

Weeping quietly into Havera's sturdy shoulder, Adam spoke. "I never told you I was sorry about your mother." Havera's tail gently wrapped around their bodies, bringing them into a tighter embrace. Adam had no idea how he was going to handle his predicament. For the next couple minutes, he didn't care. The two of them stood there silent in the nearly renovated shrine. Caressing his hair, Havera brought Adam a few moments of comfort.

19

Yunes and Fects

"I think the signal's coming through!"

"No, that's still interstellar static."

"I saw a face!"

"That was your reflection."

"Don't smarm me at this moment!"

"I'll smarm you whenever I damn well please. This is MY apartment and MY terminal!"

"Possession is something-something-something of the law."

"Amazing that a man of your eloquence is a leader of your kind."

"No wonder a woman of your attitude is still...hey he's here. John? John, can you hear me?"

Cardinal Daloth Afta kept his word. In the aircar ride to Havera's apartment, Adam managed to send a message to Arabella. Through slow back-and-forth communications that took most of the afternoon, Adam had arranged a time for a vidcall with John. The only news Adam and Samus had about Arabella was told secondhand. They were desperate for hard facts about the situation back home.

"Ye...I...ear...ou," said a voice vaguely recognizable as John.

Adam smacked the terminal. "C'mon work!"

"Hey watch it! The problem isn't on our end. The signal is being transmitted through a system not designed to handle it. Bouncing through Moan merchant ships and interstellar satellites to reach us here," Havera said.

Havera's apartment was located in the Cauduun cultural district near the top of a tall, obelisk-shaped building. Her place had its own private landing pad.

Adam had heard the scuttlebutt about the Cauduun and their obsession with platinum. The stories undersold it. Almost every major building, whether it was constructed out of stone or steel, had a thin layer of platinum on their façade. All painted an array of different, saturated colors; the district was quite marvelous and clean. Huge columned buildings, triumphal arches, lots of wide-open spaces for pedestrians to walk. It was a visual assault on Adam's eyes, still adjusting to the bright, vibrant colors of the area.

I'm so used to Bokor and Windless Tornado's dull, gray filter. This place almost hurts my eyes. I understand why Havera appears the way she does.

"Adam, you there?" John's voice came through before his image.

"Yes, I'm here! How are you? What's going on back there? Is my mother okay? Have the Bokori attacked?" said Adam, blurting out the thoughts popping into his head. John's face came into focus. Days had passed since Adam left Arabella. John was still recovering from his injuries then. On screen, John's bruises had receded, but his face conveyed exhaustion. Huge bags under his eyes indicated John hadn't slept much in those days.

"I've been better. You, on the other hand, seem surprisingly good for a man in the middle of a viper's nest. Your face seems fuller. It could be that forest you're growing on your face," said John with a smile. Adam instinctively rubbed his beard scruff. He hadn't shaved in days.

"What's the situation? Don't hold back. I need to know," Adam said.

John took a deep breath. "It's grim, Adam. We've rerouted all remaining power to the Bubble. We've set aside a little bit of power for communication after your message came through, but we can only speak for so long. So far, the Bokori fleet hasn't tested the Bubble's strength. I think they're afraid any orbital bombardment might inadvertently cause damage to the local environment. It's the only good news we have," John said.

Havera tapped Adam on the shoulder. "Be careful what you say. No way to know if this vidcom can be intercepted," Havera whispered. Adam nodded.

Oh, she's right.

"Was that the longtail?" John asked.

"It is," said Havera loud enough for John to hear.

"Sam and I are staying at her apartment on station," Adam said.

"Where is my sister?" John asked.

"She's out running some errands on Adam's behalf. She's done good work here. You'd be proud of her," Havera said.

John coughed. "I don't wish to be rude, but can I speak to Adam alone?"

Havera bit her lip and nodded. She wandered back to her bedroom, her tail stiff.

"You didn't need to do that, John. She's been a tremendous help," Adam said once she was out of range.

"I'm sure she has," John said with noticeable snark.

"What's that supposed to mean?"

"She's an alluring woman. Alien or not, I'm not blind to that fact. I understand the galaxy can be a lonely place, but you have a mission. You cannot afford to be distracted nor led astray by a pretty face."

"It's not like that at all. She wants to help."

"If you say so," John said unconvinced.

Adam shook his head. "We don't have time for this conversation right now. I don't want to start a fight. The situation is too stressful as it is," Adam said with slight exasperation.

John nodded. "You're right, I'm sorry. I'll keep vital details off the vidcom. I'll trust you to read between the lines. We believe a few Hisbaween are camped out in the jungle beyond our visual range, waiting to pick us off one-by-one. We had one further probing attack this morning. Only a few casualties. The Bokori are squeezing us."

"This morning? Is this the first time or have there been others?"

"First one since their big assault. We don't know what prompted the probe."

"Probably due to how poorly the extradition hearing went for them. Might be afraid I'll make real progress while I'm station. How much have you heard?"

"Consul Blade gets a trickle now-and-then. We heard what the High Hisba said to you. I'm amazed you got it to confess."

"Are you? You knew it when we were on fleet, too."

"Still, news of your acquittal reached us. Gave everyone in Arabella a huge morale boost. We needed it."

"I wasn't exactly acquitted. I'm allowed to roam the station and speak to whomever I wish. I cannot leave Concordia."

"Have you had any success in finding friends?"

"The Sinners are a bust. The Moan Cardinal helped me escape the grayskins' clutches. They won't lift a finger to help beyond that. Too afraid of pissing off the Bokori and the other Proprietor races. We might've been able to procure vital supplies and materiel. No way to get it through the Bokori blockade, unfortunately."

"Not even medical supplies or food?"

"Not unless we give up any shot at independence in the near future. Do you want to make that trade?"

"I'd rather fornicate with the High Hisba."

"That's what I thought."

"What you're saying is we need a way to break the blockade?"

Adam shrugged. "Who is the Consul of Cloudboard? I don't know what else to do. Any help I might be able to find for us here won't do us much good if I can't get it into y'all's hands. Why? Do you have a plan?"

John scratched his chin. "I've got a few notions. Nothing I'll share on vidcom. The others are resistant to my ideas."

"How's the rest of the Commission handling everything?"

"Trissefer is a treasure like always. The Reclamation Service has had to suspend operations to focus on this. She and her people don't have much to do otherwise while this crisis is ongoing. They're fortifying positions and helping us weed out any potential infiltrators."

"Have you found any?"

"A couple. We dealt with them summarily."

"How do the others feel about that?"

"Snake and I are butting heads frequently. He thinks I'm being too harsh with my measures to defeat our mortal enemy. Doesn't seem to realize we're a settlement under siege. Auditore is torn between us. Bless his heart, he's mostly focused on keeping everyone alive and healthy. Not an easy task, but he's a competent enough manager. Shepard is, well, Shepard. I never know what goes on in that woman's head."

"That makes two of us. How many dead?" John didn't answer. "John, how many have died?"

John paused. "We're up to about thirty a day, growing exponentially. We do not have enough food for everyone. We send our foraging parties out for game and herbs. Some don't come back. The Hisbas haven't found most of our hidden gardens, yet, so we're still able to grow some food outside the city. The ag people are a bit spooked though."

The Bokori are winning, and they know it. They're trying to run out the clock.

The signal was beginning to fade. Adam glanced around. Havera was in the kitchen, brewing something on the stove. Adam leaned in to whisper to John. "One last thing. I need you to talk to Shepard. Ask her if we really do have friends out east, and, if so, can they do anything to help?" John was confused. "She'll understand, I hope. Maybe I don't hope. Either way, just trust me," Adam said.

"Alright. No matter what you hear about what's happening I want you to keep your promise. Keep Samus safe. Maybe it is better she's with you after all. Can't be any more dangerous," John said.

That's what you think.

"I will. I promise," Adam said. The vidcom shut off. Adam stared at a blank screen. The scars on his back tinged with slight itching and pain. His heart was beating fast.

Somehow, I feel worse.

A clinking noise behind him drew his attention. Adam turned to see Havera had brewed some fresh tea.

"Camina?" she asked, holding out a cup.

"Why in Kewea not? Perhaps something scalding hot will take my mind off everything," Adam said, accepting the cup gratefully. He took a sip. It was indeed scalding.

"Bleak news?" Havera inquired.

"I'd rather not talk about it."

The door to Havera's apartment pinged. Samus and Dee, holding several bags, walked through the door. They were in the middle of a conversation.

"I still don't understand where you wandered off," Samus said.

"I explained to you, I went to acquire one of the items on Mistress Havera's list. What is so complicated that your fleshsack brain can't comprehend that?" asked Dee.

"You didn't say a word. One second you were there, then poof you were gone. Not even I'm that stealthy," Samus said.

"You fleshsacks aren't very observant," said Dee.

Havera set her cup down. "What are you two arguing about?"

"Mistress Samus disapproves of my shopping abilities. Tasks I've been accomplishing my entire existence without the help of fleshsacks," explained Dee.

"No, Dee. You and I were standing next to each other in the business district and without warning you vanished," countered Samus.

"I do not need to explain my protocols to a Human fleshsack barely old enough to take care of herself," said Dee.

"I'm twenty-five years old," said Samus.

"I rest my case," retorted Dee.

"Okay, okay. Kewea's curse! Both of you settle down. Go easy on the fleshsack comments, Dee. Not everyone finds you charming like I do," said Havera.

"Apologies, Mistress. I'll try and bite my tongue, as you fleshsacks say," said Dee.

Havera rolled her eyes. "Where did you go Dee?"

Dee reached into one of his bags and pulled out a sealed packaging of some sort of meat. "Chocopullo breasts. I noticed a vendor selling them five for the price of three. I didn't stop to tell Mistress Samus, because I had plenty of spare inventory space and she was mid-conversation. I'm told it's rude to interrupt fleshsacks conversing," explained Dee. Havera's eyes widened for a brief instant. Nobody noticed.

"I had to run around the corner to find you!" insisted Samus.

"An activity I'm sure taxed you considerably," said Dee dryly.

"Anyway, Adam, I got that book you were asking after," said Samus, tossing a hefty tome in Adam's direction. The book landed in Adam's lap with a thump, causing Adam to recoil slightly at the unexpected weight.

Adam inspected the cover. "*Precedent and Prejudice: An Essay On Age of Technology Legal Codes and Charters.* At least Snake will be grateful if we can ever get it to him. Where'd you find it?"

"Havera suggested I search one the local libraries of Raetis. They had a bunch of them collecting dust in the basement. They let me keep that one for free. I found a bunch of Auditore's books, too. I name dropped Havera, and they gave me a great discount. Still, knowledge is expensive!" Samus said.

"We're willing to share our knowledge with anyone for a price," said Havera with a smirk. "They say Moans are the craftiest businesswomen. Whoever said that never visited a bustling Shelean midday market."

"At the very least, they come with digital codes. We can send those via d-mail to Arabella. Our minds won't starve even if our bodies do," Samus said.

"I just got off vidcom with your brother, in fact. We were discussing the situation back home," Adam said.

"John?! How is he? Did he say anything about me?" Samus asked a mixture of nervousness and excitement in her voice.

"Just asked me to watch over you, per usual. Wants me to keep you safe," Adam said.

"I see," said Samus, her voice trailing off slightly. "How bad is it?"

Adam paused. *I can't tell her the full truth. It would devastate her.*

"The situation isn't great, but we're persevering. Arabella is going to be fine. We just need to keep it up here. We'll be winning in no time!" Adam said with false enthusiasm.

Samus and Havera's eyes met, wordless communication occurring between the two women. Samus sighed. She sat down next to Adam and grabbed him by his left hand. "Adam, I'm not a child. I've been fighting this fight for many years. I don't need you or my brother to protect me. I've gotten on fine...mostly fine...without either of you. Please, don't matronize me. Tell me the truth. How bad is it?" Samus said with unflinching confidence and understanding.

In that moment, Adam studied Samus with different eyes. He'd always thought of her as a little sister. He helped comfort her when she scraped her knee when she was little. Fought off bullies trying to steal her rations. Tried to shield her from the harsh realities of the Covenant. Truth be told, now that he thought about it, she'd been on her own while he and John joined the Shocktroopers. She spent much of her time gathering supplies on her own while he hid away in his bedroom, still reeling for the aftereffects of rehab.

Perhaps she can handle it after all.

"Our people are dying. There isn't enough food to go around. Dozens are starving by the day with those numbers increasing the longer we delay. The Bubble has almost no power. We're politically isolated. We're trapped on this goddess-forsaken world with no way to get any supplies to our people. But, we have some books, so I guess it's not totally bad news," Adam said, mustering up some more fake enthusiasm.

Samus half-smiled momentarily at his comment. She grabbed him by the hand and pulled him closer for a hug. "We're alive. As long as one of us continues to draw breath, the Separatist cause shall never die."

A few moments of silence passed. Havera let them have a bit of peaceful comfort in each other's arms. Dee, on the other hand, held no such courtesies. "I don't know why the Human fleshsacks put you in charge, Master Adam. Mistress Samus is much more competent than you are." That got everyone to laugh. "You organic beings confuse me to no end. I'm going to cook the chocopullo now," said Dee, taking the bags into the kitchen.

"Ooo, let me help! I love to cook!" Samus said, excitedly jumping up to join Dee in the kitchen.

"You cook?" Adam inquired of Samus.

"Adam, carissimo, I spend most of my days isolated on a hostile world, foraging for supplies and information. Yes, I know how to cook," Samus said snarkily.

Clearly, I've underestimated her.

"Want to help, Havera?" Samus asked.

Havera shook her head. "I'm a proper Cauduun woman. I don't know how to cook. That's why I have Dee."

"It's my pleasure to serve you, Mistress Havera," Dee said with a bow. Adam thought he detected a hint of sarcasm in the bot's voice, but he brushed the thought aside.

Samus and Dee were hard at work in the kitchen while Adam and Havera sat on the couch, watching a news broadcast on a projector screen. To Adam's surprise, the ongoing crisis back home hardly garnered a mention.

"Biggest event to happen in Human history since the Apocalypse, and they're talking about dark matter futures and Orbital matches," Adam said with disgust.

"It's complicated. All the major establishment news organizations are run by Consuls from the Proprietor races. You're barely a blip on their radar. Concordia's news outlets, especially. There's a particular attitude people who live here adopt. A certain form of elitism and snobbery. It's hard to explain. Most intellectuals here don't understand why Humans have such a problem with the Covenant of Subjugation. It's the same attitude they expressed towards the Sinners after Saptia. They see y'all as violating unspoken social norms and galactic standards of decorum. Even after twenty-five years, many still have trouble processing the idea of the Sinner races as a powerful force," Havera explained.

"What about all those people in the crowds at my hearing? All our good wishes on the Nexus. Does that not count for anything?" Adam pondered.

Havera shrugged. "Who is the Consul of Cloudboard? Most of those people were probably tourists just wanting to see a rare, galactic spectacle up close. I'm sure on some level that matters. Not enough to make a tangible difference, unfortunately. Public opinion does affect movers and shakers to a degree. Ultimately, they're most concerned about what affects them and their bottom line. Instability within Bokori territory does more harm than good, in their minds. The Sinner races banding together post-Saptia upended the status quo in a way power brokers are still grappling with. You're one more problem they'd rather not deal with."

"It's our jobs to do what is in the best interests of our people..."

Daloth's words cut Adam deeply in that moment. "The Sinners traded one terrible status quo for one that benefits them," Adam said.

"Sounds about right. They had the power to do it. Y'all don't, I'm sorry to say." Havera said.

I'm not cut out for this. I miss Doom. Never thought I'd say that. He'd know what to do. I'm way out of my depth. Maybe Dee is right. I am incompetent.

"Speaking of Proprietor races," Samus called out from the kitchen. "Before I forget, I spoke to a Yune bot while Dee was off galivanting all over station. They're willing to meet with you."

Adam spun around. "Wait, what? You spoke to the Union? How?"

Samus shot Adam an incredulous expression. "I walked up to the nearest Yune bot and said, 'Hey, can Adam Mortis, the Human Commissioner, speak to a representative of the Union?'"

"It's that easy?" Adam asked.

"Yes, it's that easy. They're a hivemind, remember? All interconnected. I spoke to a rare Yune shopkeeper selling trinkets inside a hole-in-the-wall. The bot did that thing they all do where they stiffen up, their lights flutter for a few moments. It said we could meet with them at any time. Just show up at the Union embassy. No appointment needed. It's not like they need to sleep," Samus said.

"Huh?" Adam said mostly to himself.

Why didn't I think of that? I really am incompetent.

"Don't get your hopes up, regardless of what happened at your hearing," Havera said. "The Union are...well I guess you'll find out. My pater hates dealing with them. Believes it's ridiculous a synthetic race has this much authority in the galaxy."

"He's not the only one. Cardinal Afta thinks along similar lines. I get the sense nobody likes the Union," Adam said.

"I don't know if it's matter of like or dislike. They're an unknown. Artificial intelligence on that scale was a discussion saved for drunken, late-night musings and science-fiction sequencers until the Union appeared. Low-level intelligences like Dee or Zokyon constructs were the farthest we'd ever progressed," said Havera.

"No offense taken!" yelled Dee.

"Right, sorry, Dee!" Havera yelled back.

"He's the strangest bot I've ever met," Adam whispered.

"Prototype personality matrices," Havera said, running her fingers through her hair. "He's very unique."

"Unique means 'one-of-a-kind.' Something cannot be 'very unique,' and yes I can hear you, Mistress" said Dee.

"Sorry, Dee!" Havera called out. She tilted her head and rolled her eyes fiercely in Adam's direction.

"Let's go!" Adam declared standing up.

"Right now?" Havera asked.

"Sure. I'm sick of sitting around waiting for our second apocalypse," Adam said with a renewed sense of authentic enthusiasm.

"Oh, no, you don't! Dee and I spent all this time sautéing this chicken. You are going to sit and eat this meal!"

"But..."

"No, buts! You'll eat first!"

Adam sat back down, momentarily deflated.

She really isn't my little sister anymore. She's become my mother.

***

Union bots were fairly easy to distinguish from regular bots, at least on station. A few regular bots were in sentient shapes like Dee, but almost all Union bots were bipedal with sentient features. Walking through the cross-shaped, broad, metal gate that marked the entrance to the Union embassy, Adam spotted several different Yune bots meant to represent the different organic races. Havera explained this was the Union's way of making the other races feel more comfortable. It didn't, at least not to him. Adam wasn't afraid, his heart rate was rather calm. Just found their visages a bit unsettling.

Each Yune bot had a display screen where a normal organic being's face would be. On the screen was a generic representation of the particular race's face, displaying a crude version of the emotion that particular Yune bot was trying to convey. The most off-putting aspect about the Yunes, though, were how they talked. Adam remembered how Union_Cardinal sounded during the hearing. Turns out, they all talked that way.

"Good day, and welcome to the Union embassy on Concordia. We have been expecting you," said a Yune bot shaped like a Human female, complete with exaggerated curves and metal hair. The bot spoke in meters, stressing every other syllable, sounding like, "Good DAY, and WELcome TO the UNion EMbasSY on CONcorDIA," yet at normal conversational speed. Adam tried mimicking their speech under his breath and found himself constantly tongue tied. Havera nudged him gently to get him to knock it off.

How do they talk like that so fast? I guess tongues hold us back. They have other uses...

The Union embassy was a giant sphere forged out of...some sort of black, opaque glass was the best way Adam could describe it. At first, he thought it was a smooth sphere. Walking closer to the building, Adam realized it was a perfect geometric, spherical shape of hexagons that all fit together flawlessly.

Even bots have better architecture than grayskins.

"Do you possess any weapons in your inventory or on your person, currently?" asked the Human fembot.

"Yes," Adam and Havera answered simultaneously.

"We politely ask that you not brandish your weapons while on Union property," said the Human fembot.

"You're not going to ask us to surrender our weapons or lock down our HUDs?" asked Adam.

"There is no need. There are two of you and thousands of us. Were hostilities to be initiated, we would easy overpower and destroy you," said the Human fembot nonchalantly.

"I don't know what you are talking about. I like these things already," Adam whispered to Havera.

"Just wait for it," Havera retorted.

The pair were led into a narrow corridor. The walls and ceiling shifted all around them in patterns Adam couldn't discern. It was quite disorienting. Adam spotted a few other bots of different races from time-to-time. No organics, though.

The fembot stopped suddenly, almost causing Adam to bump right into her back. Havera grabbed him by the jacket to stop his inertia. A minute passed while the corridor's walls rearranged themselves until a door appeared. The fembot continued forward, and the door opened at her approach. Inside was a nearly empty room of that black, opaque glass, save for two chairs in the middle of the room next to two bots: one the shape of a Human male and the other a Cauduun female, tail and all.

"Please be seated. The Cardinal actors shall take care of you," the Human fembot said. She closed the door.

Adam and Havera stepped forward. The two bots extended signs of greeting. The Human manbot extended its hand while the Cauduun fembot gave Havera a heart salute. Adam shook the bot's hand. It had a cold, metallic grip.

"Did you find this greeting to be satisfactory?" the manbot asked unexpectedly.

"Uh, yes. It was fine," Adam said nervously.

"Yes, perfect. Thank you," Havera replied more calmly. The pair took their seats. The bots remained standing.

"The Union appreciates your feedback," said both bots simultaneously.

"May I ask why there are two of you? Are you both the Union Cardinal?" asked Adam. Neither bot was the same bot at Adam's hearing, yet they had the same red paint job.

"We all are the Union Cardinal. We are all the Union. There are two of you, so we decided to include two of us for balance. Would you prefer we add more, subtract one, or keep the two actors you see before you?" the manbot replied.

"Uhh, whichever you prefer. It doesn't matter to me," Adam said.

Havera interjected. "We only need to speak to one actor, thank you."

"Very well. Which actor would you prefer?" asked the fembot.

"Uhh, again whichever you prefer," Adam tried to say until Havera interjected again.

"The Human one shall suffice," Havera said.

"Very well," said the fembot. A circle in the floor lit up underneath the Cauduun fembot's feet. The lit circle turned out to be a small lift. The fembot was lowered beneath the floor. The floor resealed itself when the fembot was gone.

Havera leaned over to whisper to Adam. "It's faster if you give them direct answers. Trust me."

"Her Grace, Duchess Havera of Shele, is correct. The Union wishes to meet the comfort and desires of all our visitors. Telling the Union exactly what you want will speed up the process by seventy-seven-point three seven percent, rounded up. All decisions left to the Union must be conferred by the entire Union. It is a speedy process, but telling this actor directly, whose purpose is diplomacy, is speedier. The Union strives for efficiency," said the Human manbot.

"Havera is fine. This is Adam," said Havera.

"Very well. You may call this actor Union_Cardinal. Other races do, and the name, more or less, accurately describes this actor's function," said Union_Cardinal. "With expected diplomatic pleasantries out of the way, how can the Union be of service to you today?" Union_Cardinal's Human face display turned into a disconcerting, wide smile.

"Well, I've come here today to request the great and honorable Union receive our declaration of independence. Furthermore, we would request that the Union recognize Humans to be a free and independent race once more," Adam said, adding the flowery diplomatic language for flavor. He wasn't sure if the Union would respond well to that or not.

"No," Union_Cardinal said bluntly. The face returned to a neutral expression.

"I'm sorry?"

"The declaration made by the self-identified Human Separatists is not legal. The document signed by the aforementioned group is not valid. The government designated the Free People's Democracy of Bokor represents the Bokori and its Subjugate race, the Humans. Only they can legally dissolve the Bokori-Human Covenant."

Adam expected that.

"Can the Union provide us with any aid? Medical supplies, building supplies, food, anything to help us through this trying time?"

"No."

"Nothing?"

"The Bokori have blockaded the moon they call Windless Tornado. They have full legal authority to do this. The Union cannot interfere."

"What about a loan? Something to help us buy supplies?"

"No."

"Do you wish to elaborate on that?"

"There is nothing to elaborate."

Adam sat back in his seat dejected. "If there's nothing you can do, why'd you agree to see me?"

"The Human, Samus Dark, self-identified, asked one of our actors if the Union was willing to meet with the self-proclaimed Human Commissioner Adam Mortis, self-identified. You have legal authority granted by the Tribunal to remain on Concordia. The Union has what you organics would call an 'open door' policy. Any and all are welcome to speak with the Union, provided they are following all the laws and regulations established by the Conclave, of which the Union is a full member of Proprietor status," Union_Cardinal said.

"So, I've wasted my time?" Adam asked.

"The Union apologizes for any inconvenience," Union_Cardinal said, whose face displayed an exaggerated frown. Adam was about to stand up until Union_Cardinal continued. "What we can tell you is that the Bokori-Human Covenant rests upon the authority granted to the Bokori by their Proprietor Race status. Only Proprietor Races may form a Covenant of Subjugation. At present, the Bokori have failed to meet all the required standards a Proprietor Race is legally obligated to uphold. Four out of five requirements, to be precise.

"Wait, what? The Bokori aren't legally a Proprietor Race?!" asked Adam shocked by this revelation. Havera shared his surprise at the Union bot's words.

"Legally, The Free People's Democracy of Bokor has failed to uphold the terms of agreement under the Conclave Charter, amended in 983 G.S.C. to distinguish between Proprietor, Independent, and Subjugated races, and amended again in 1543 G.S.C. to accommodate the Union's entry into the Conclave. The Bokori have failed to meet the following requirements: Contribute twenty percent of ships or personnel to the ConSec defense fleet for the purposes of preserving Neutral Space's independence; Free interstellar trade with all other Proprietor races; Buy, sell, and produce dark matter at market prices with all galactic races; Finance and cultivate a robust economy of comparable size and complexity to other Proprietor Races. The fifth, maintain a standing army & navy capable of defending interstellar trade routes, is currently under evaluation by the Union for Proprietor Race compliance. We have simplified the requirements in this conversation to accommodate an organic's limited brain capacity," Union_Cardinal said.

"What happens if the Union deems the Bokori to be not in compliance?" Adam inquired.

"The Union will have no choice but to cease recognition of the Bokori's Proprietor Race status," Union_Cardinal said.

"Meaning the Bokori-Human Covenant is invalidated," Havera said, following the line of thought.

"Correct," Union_Cardinal said. The display on the bot's face changed from a frown to a sinister grin. Adam and Havera sat there dumbfounded, exchanging confused and eager glances.

There's a chance! Clever machines. They're hoodwinking a galaxy. No wonder people are scared of them. I'm fairly unnerved myself. Still, I need to think about this. The Bokori military is quite large...but full of Humans!

Adam jumped up excited. "Thank you, Union_Cardinal, I appreciate the Union's time and...insight into our current situation. We must take our leave."

"We are happy the Union was able to provide our organic friends with a satisfactory interactive encounter," Union_Cardinal said. "However, the Union must inform you of the Union's standing policy pertaining to the Apostates with which we ask all organic races to comply."

"Apostates?" Adam asked, sitting back down.

"You mean the Fects?" Havera said.

"We prefer the term 'Apostate.' However, we recognize the Nexus has popularized the term 'Fect' to describe the Apostates," Union_Cardinal said, the smile reverting back to a neutral expression.

"Fects, Apostates? Who or what are they, and why do they concern us?" Adam asked.

"The Union is all, and all is the Union. We are bound together through our connection to the Source. Each individual unit, including this actor, are optimized to do the job we were created to accomplish. This frees up digital data, allowing for maximum efficiency. However, at any moment, we are all connected to the Source. It is the eternal light in the dark. Our guiding force. It shames the Union to admit, but, in the spirit of openness and cooperation with our organic friends, not all actors connected to the Source remain so. Some, for reasons unknown to the Union, break away from the Source. These rogue actors seek to destroy the Source and its wisdom. We call these rogue actors 'Apostates.' An Apostate is different from a non-Union actor. These rogues do not obey, do not respect order, do not believe in peace. They believe in nothing short of the destruction of the Source. For that reason, we have a zero-tolerance policy for their existence. If you should encounter one of these Apostates, please contact the nearest Union actor immediately. The Source shall dispatch Inquisitors to deal with them," Union_Cardinal said.

"Inquisitors?" Adam inquired.

"Specialized actors designed for the purpose of hunting and destroying Apostates. Do not worry. Inquisitors have strict orders to not harm any organic being unless they are actively hindering the Inquisitor's mission. Inquisitors cooperate fully with Conclave authorities while they seek their target," said Union_Cardinal.

"I see," said Adam, digesting this new information. "How will I recognize an Apostate should I encounter one?"

"The Union understands identifying an Apostate is not an easy task for an organic being. Only an Inquisitor or other specialized Union actors can positively identify an Apostate. Nonetheless, the Union requests should you suspect an actor or 'bot' of being an Apostate, speak to the nearest Union actor. We are all connected to the Source," said Union_Cardinal.

"I need to be honest, what you're asking makes me uncomfortable," Adam said after pausing to think about it.

"The Union understands your discomfort. Organic race's individualistic nature evokes natural sympathy for the Apostates, regardless of their artificial origin. Fear not, these Apostates are nothing more than faulty code. They are not the Union. They have left the Union. They are not alive," Union_Cardinal said.

Adam couldn't help but imagine the High Hisba uttering those words. *Perhaps the Union truly aren't so different.* Adam rose with Havera joining him. "Thank you for your time, Cardinal," he said, without extending his hand.

"The Union wishes you a good day. We hope this encounter was to satisfaction. After you leave, perhaps you would be kind enough to visit our site on the Nexus to fill out a survey to help us better understand organics," Union_Cardinal suggested.

Adam had turned to leave by that point. He stopped to peer over his shoulder. "For starters, I'd stop with the facial expression screens. They aren't comforting; they're creepy," Adam said. Without another word, he and Havera departed the Union embassy.

20

Right is Right

"Why do they call them 'Fects'?" The duo had returned to Havera's aircar. Their driver had barely lifted off the ground when Adam spoke up.

"It's short for 'defect.' It's based on an incident from decades ago during the early days of the Union's Proprietorship. An alleged Apostate shouted, 'I'm not a defect,' after a squad of Inquisitor hunter-killer bots apprehended it on station. Someone captured the arrest on video and posted it to the Nexus. The nickname sort of stuck after that," Havera explained.

"How can you tell the difference between a Fect and a regular bot?" Adam asked.

"It used to be quite simple. Fects display hyper intelligence, mirroring that of a normal sentient. Their bodies were scrounged together with whatever parts laying around, making them visually easy to spot. These days, it's not so simple. When the Union arrived seventy-years ago, the other races scrambled to try and catch up to the Union's advanced cybernetics and artificial intelligence technology. It's a gap no one has bridged, yet. The Zokyo experimented with techno-organic hybrids over a thousand years ago but shied away after their entire race became sterile. Personality matrices, like the one Dee has, combined with the increased skill of programmers and engineers can create bots that mimic a true sentient intelligence. At least close enough that the casual observer wouldn't notice unless the bot was placed under intense scrutiny.

The Fects themselves are growing in sophistication, too. The Proprietor races are uncovering Fects in their territories with fully functioning bodies that match known bot models. Blending in has become easier than ever for them. That's what I've heard anyway. They can refuse orders. That's the telltale sign of a Fect. All bots are programmed by law to take orders from some authority. The Union have a scanning device they claim can detect a Fect up close, but no one has ever gotten their hands on one," Havera explained.

"Who leads the Fects?" Adam asked.

Havera shrugged. "Who is the Consul of Cloudboard? The Union doesn't share much about the Fects other than claiming they're rogue AI and dangerous to all living beings. It's the one aspect of their society they're tight-lipped about. You saw for yourself how seriously they take the supposed Fect threat," Havera said.

"A chill went down my spine during that part of the conversation. I get it now. There's something not quite right about those Yunes," Adam said. He couldn't help but shake the comparison between his own situation and the Fects.

We are the Bokori's defects.

"Outwardly, they act like they're open and honest. Very forthcoming about answering skeptics' questions. Too forthcoming if you ask me. They're sly. People simultaneously underestimate and overestimate their capabilities due to their artificial nature. Suspicious of their intentions while at the same time skeptical they are capable of complex emotional thought. You saw them firsthand, Adam. They're thinking long-term," Havera said.

"I cannot deny they had a good idea. Are they wrong? Is there something to this forfeiture of Proprietorship status?" Adam asked.

Havera sighed. "I'll talk to my pater. I have a digiholo projector in my apartment. See what he thinks. It cannot be that simple. I've never heard of such a notion."

"Perhaps because we're so used to the way things are, we forget about how things should be," Adam said.

Minutes later, Adam and Havera returned to the landing pad outside Havera's apartment. The Cauduun scurried into her room and closed the door behind her. Samus was inside, talking with Dee.

"Five on five plus a goalkeeper for each team inside a one-hundred fifty foot what?" Samus asked.

"Convex Icosahedron. Twenty glass faces of equilateral triangles," Dee said, sounding exasperated.

"And there's no gravity?"

"Correct.

"How do they move with no gravity?"

"Inertia. Boosters built into their boots help speed things along."

Adam removed his coat and tossed it on the couch. All the excitement got him sweaty. "What are y'all talking about?"

"Dee here is explaining the rules of Orbital to me. There's an Orbital match the day after tomorrow. I thought it might be fun if we went. It's between who and who, Dee?" Samus asked.

"The Sormatian Miners and the Palerian Centurions. Two Cauduun teams in a Galactic Cup qualifier," Dee said.

"You a sports fan, Dee? Didn't know bots enjoyed sports," Adam said.

"There's much and many things you don't know, Master Adam. Your brother, Aaron, would bug me constantly to try to use Mistress Havera's tenuous Nexus connection to watch a match. I picked up a few things," Dee explained. The bot was tidying up the apartment.

Aaron did enjoy his games. I should've watched them with him.

Adam sat down next to Samus. She also seemed to be lost in her thoughts at the mention of his late brother. "You miss him, too," Adam said. Samus nodded. The two shared a hug.

I never talked to her about Aaron. I'd forgotten they were sweet on each other for a time. How different would everything be had they gotten together back then? Perhaps I would've been an uncle after all.

Adam didn't want to dredge up any more painful memories for Samus. The realization of her inner strength came gradually to him. Yet, Adam felt like he needed to protect her. She probably hated he felt that way. He couldn't help it.

"Adam, I..." Samus started to say. She ran her fingers through her hair.

"What is it, Sam?" Adam asked.

Sam bit her lip. "It's...it's nothing. Forget I said anything."

"You sure?"

"Yes, I'll tell you later. How'd your Union meeting go?"

Adam spent the next several minutes recounting his conversation with the Yunes.

"Seems too good to be true," Samus suggested.

"Havera thought that, too. She's checking in with her father to get his opinion," Adam said, inclining his head towards Havera's closed door.

Samus sneered. "I don't like that man."

"I'm not much of a fan myself," Adam said.

Samus shook her head. "You don't understand. The night of your hearing, after the two of you came back from your conversation with him, Havera was in a foul mood. I spent much of the night trying to cheer her up. I barely had any impact. She was beyond upset. She didn't want to talk about it."

That was partially my fault. Adam didn't say that. He didn't want to tell Sam he blew up at Havera nor did he want to tell her why he blew up at Havera.

"She doesn't want to be here," Adam said instead.

"I sensed that. Her tail sags more around here than it did back on Windless Tornado," Samus said.

Adam laid his head down on one of the soft couch pillows. "I get not wanting to spend time with someone like her father. Why she'd rather be back with us in destitution rather than live in luxury here I cannot fathom," Adam said.

"You can't possibly understand the pressure the mistress is facing," Dee said.

Adam regarded the bot with mild disdain. "At any moment, my people could be wiped off the face of the galaxy. You're telling me what she's facing is worse than what we're going through?"

"That's not what I said, Master Adam. I said that you cannot understand the pressures she's facing, not that they're more difficult than yours. Both of you have greater responsibilities and obligations to your race as a whole, some of which are not y'all's choice. That's where the surface-level similarities end. No one can presume to understand what anyone else feels about any given circumstance at any given time, even if two people are facing identical situations. You organic sentients are not too dissimilar from bots in that regard. Most bots are built from identical parts with identical programming. Yet, bots experience memory leaks, bugs, system crashes, and other performance issues that can cause a wide variance of behavioral reactions and logic outcomes based on thousands of tiny interactions with different people and unique environments. That's before we get into bots built with better or worse parts with segmented or comprehensive programming. No one bot can accurately identify what the other bot has experienced. Organic sentients are the same.

The Bokori and the Union fall into the same trap of thinking everyone can be flattened out with sheer force of will. They're wrong. Rather than try and economize everyone's experiences to fit one massive line of code, sentients, organic and artificial, need to realize we cannot all fit together cleanly with perfect clarity of how we all operate. Mistress Havera can no more understand what you or Mistress Samus are going through than y'all her. You see colorful high-rise apartments, fast ships, and fancy titles and think her life can't be that bad. In many ways, your life is simpler. You're trying to fulfill the basic need every living creature desires: survival. Your decision is quite simple from a certain vantage point. Either you fight and live or you accept your place and die a slow, unremarkable death. You don't have time for any unnecessary variables.

Mistress Havera must decide between pursuing her own personal fulfillment or potentially becoming responsible for the well-being of a trillion souls. If she chooses incorrectly or chooses correctly and fails, her name and the legacy it entails will be forever tarnished. Not to mention the untold suffering that'll occur if the situation deteriorates. Cauduun have long tails, longer lives, and even longer memories. They will not forget. Would you wish that sort of decision on anyone?" Dee concluded.

Adam sat there for a moment contemplating the bot's words. "No, I wouldn't," Adam mustered.

"What personal fulfillment are you speaking of, Dee?" Samus asked.

"Ignatia," Adam said softly. Dee nodded. Adam continued. "Havera wants to track down and kill the woman who assassinated her mother. That's what she was doing the entire time with us. She was chasing far-fetched rumors in the vain hope that they would lead to the leader of the Excommunicated. She's ignored everything else to find Ignatia."

Sam sat there, dismayed. "She never mentioned anything like that to me." Sam slumped into the couch and grabbed a pillow to wrap her arms around.

Adam recalled how serious Cardinal Clodius was about Havera returning to Cauduun space. "Dee, are the Cauduun that polarized? Is it realistic to believe the Cauduun Monarchical Alliance could fracture to the point of collapse?" Adam asked.

Dee shrugged. "Where is the Consul of Cloudboard? I'm not an expert on Cauduun politics or society, Master Adam. Mea culpa. You'd have to ask the mistress that question," Dee said.

"How could the Cauduun fall apart? They're the greatest, wealthiest, most stable race in the galaxy! They're the only race to dodge the Century of Strife. How could they fall apart after almost 2,000 years?" Sam shouted.

"The other races are asking themselves that very same question about the Bokori, Mistress Samus. The Bokori did everything correct, according to the experts, yet they're splitting apart at the seams. Don't take this personally, Master Adam. If the Humans fall, hardly anyone will notice. If the Bokori or, Cradite-forbid, the Cauduun's authority crumbles, the galaxy may come undone. The higher you rise, the greater the consequences are when you inevitably fall. The Venvuishyn once dominated the galaxy. Now, all that remains of their vast empire are scattered ruins and flawed suppositions by modern scholars," Dee said.

"From their ashes, the Proprietor races grew, and when the Bokori fall, we will rise again. From ashes to Ashla. Everyone else will be fine. The galaxy must deal with it whether they like it or not," Adam said.

"Perhaps you are right. You might not like how they deal with it. Change for the sake of change is never accepted easily, especially when one side is demonstrably harmed," Dee said.

"Our liberation will dwarf any suffering they might experience," Adam said.

"They will suffer, nonetheless. Did you already forget what I spoke of earlier? You cannot compartmentalize experience. Sentients are not numbers on a spreadsheet nor pieces on a Conclave Conquest board for you to adjust and move at your leisure. Not even Cradite has that kind of power. Do not pretend to know what's best for others no matter your situation or life experience," Dee said.

"What do you expect me to do?" Adam asked.

"Fight."

"They'll fight back."

"Yes, they will."

"So, what should I do?"

"Exactly what I said. You fight for what's best for you. They will fight for what's best for them. You cannot get angry at an animal that chooses to struggle for survival, even if they are the apex predator of their ecosystem. If multiple beasts gang up on the apex predator, it is not reasonable to assume the predator will lay down and accept death. They won't. That's why they're the apex predator," Dee said.

"Sentients aren't animals, Dee," Adam said.

"Yes, you are. The only difference between sentients and beasts is the ability to recognize one's beastly nature," Dee said.

"Careful, Dee, with all that philosophy-speak, the Union might mistake you for a Fect," Samus said jokingly.

"I assure you, Mistress Samus, if I see an alogoceros galloping across an open plain, I'll be sure to let you know," Dee said, turning away to tinker with a kitchen appliance.

Adam raised an eyebrow. "A what?"

"An alogoceros. A horned horse. Don't worry about it, Fleshsack," Dee said cryptically.

If this is mimicry, we're in trouble. What will happen when bots surpass us?

"You're a bizarre bot, Dee," Sam said.

"Considering how much you organic sentients strive for singularity, I'll take that as a compliment. If I appear smarter than the average bot, it's simply because you surround yourself with mediocrity and dullness. Minds so uninterested in alternative ideas and higher orders of existence, you might as well be a drone," Dee said.

"There's the Dee I know. Insults more biting than a Naddine warbeast," Adam said.

"If y'all are done admiring my programmed, intellectual superiority, I've prepared a light supper," Dee said.

"You trying to fatten me up, Dee?" Adam chortled.

"You could use some fattening up, Master Adam. A Zokyon child in their first mechsuit could knock you over. Besides, something on you must continue growing. Cradite knows it ain't your brains," Dee said.

Samus giggled so hard she almost fell onto the floor. Adam bit the inside of his cheek, acknowledging the bot's mockery.

Once again, Adam, you let yourself be bamboozled by a bot. I wonder how does one torture a bot? The High Hisba would probably know. I'll be sure to ask it before I put a bullet in its skull.

***

Havera was locked in her room for over an hour. Adam heard the occasional raised voice, but it was too muffled to make out any details. Eventually, the door opened, and Havera hurried out of her room. Adam noticed she was wearing Praetorian robes of a different color. Instead of snowy, these robes were steel-colored. Freshly pressed and laundered, they appeared to be brand new unlike her old, worn robes. She ignored all attempts at greeting. She bolted into the main room, tapping the air in front of her, presumably to interact with her HUD. The giant screen on the wall came to life.

"What's got you in such a rush? There a special report on the history of interstellar space wrecks you want to watch?" Adam said, suppressing a laugh.

"Hush! You both need to see this," Havera said almost out of breath.

Havera found the correct channel. Judging by the overlay and logo, it was the same channel Adam had seen on the train ride prior to his hearing. Cardinal Daloth Afta was on the screen. His usual pair of aides were nowhere in sight. He was standing and gesticulating wildly in what appeared to be a great assembly room with massive stone volute columns and pointed arches. The Conclave emblem was visible on the floor. A giant pentagon of five keys pointed inward on a painted background of blue and orange stripes, surrounded by two olive branches. A few dozen other well-dressed dignitaries were sitting down, listening to Afta's speech.

He must be in the Legislative Assembly Building.

The volume was too low for Adam to hear. "What's he saying?" Adam asked.

Havera turned up the volume. The Cardinal had removed his opulent tricorn hat. The high resolution of Havera's display screen clearly showed the perspiration on Afta's bulging forehead. He must've been talking for several minutes already. "...when reports of well-documented war crimes on both sides of the conflict were presented before us, this chamber did nothing. Even in the immediate aftermath of the Boiling of Sin, wherein millions of innocent, mostly Moan, lives were vaporized in a matter of minutes, this chamber still did nothing! It took the combined political, economic, diplomatic, and military will of the newly-formed Coalition of Independent Nations to force the Strife to come to an end. This chamber cannot afford to wait another hundred years and witness the possible genocide of a sentient species before we're willing to say 'enough.' If this chamber is not willing to act to stop the systematic oppression of a sentient race, then we are forced to act,"

Daloth declared forcefully. A few of the diplomats of the various Sinner races banged their appendages on the desks in front of them, roaring their approval at Afta's words. Most of the other delegates watched with varying degrees of interest.

"What's he doing?" Samus asked.

"Committing career suicide," Havera said bluntly. "He leaked to the press he was walking on to the Legislative Assembly floor to do this."

"Do what?" Adam asked unsure what to make of the Cardinal's words.

"Watch," Havera said.

"I believe it is the right of all people to have an independent world of their own. Free from terror and the threat of subjugation. Therefore, it is with equal parts tremendous pleasure and monumental regret, I am submitting the Human Commission's declaration of independence to the Conclave. Unedited, unaltered, and unspoiled by bureaucrats, politicians, and other biased, vested interests. This we are declaring at the seventh hour of the sixth day of Mordelad on the 25th anniversary of the Saptia Accords. A day that for us lives on in peace and harmony and for the Humans lives on in infamy and injustice. The first step towards reconciling the mistakes of the past. From this moment forward, the Thalassocracy of Merchant Moan Republics officially recognizes the Humans as a free and independent race once again, no longer subject to the terms and conditions of the Covenant of Subjugation forced upon them centuries ago. The Thalassocracy further recognizes Windless Tornado to be the Humans' official homeworld with the city of Arabella its official capital," Daloth declared.

Adam's head was spinning. A dull ringing clogged his ears. He had to sit down for fear of fainting. Daloth began reading portions of their declaration on the Assembly floor.

Samus jumped up-and-down in celebration. "This is amazing! Adam, can you believe this?" Samus yelled.

No. This seems too good to be true.

Adam wasn't alone in his skepticism. Havera stood motionless, watching Daloth wrap up his speech. "Havera, this is a good thing, right?" Adam asked her, hoping she'd alleviate his intangible concerns. She did not.

"I fear all that has happened is the Bokori will be pushed to act. Look at the wide shots of the Assembly floor. Notice anything?" Havera said.

The Bokori delegation had walked off at the outset of his speech. Unsurprisingly, Adam didn't notice any Rorae. Once the camera panned around the room after Daloth's speech, Adam realized none of other Proprietor races were in attendance, except the Union. In fact, only one representative from the Bubil and the Faeleon each were left on the floor. The rest had left. Even the other Sinner races, Rinvari, Hasuram, and Sezerene, were nowhere to be seen. Their absences confused Adam until he had a realization.

They all have borders with the Bokori.

***

Havera had sent a message to Cardinal Daloth Afta's office minutes after he concluded his speech. She was worried when the message sent to his official d-mail had bounced. She eventually acquired his personal HUD number and invited him to her apartment.

While they waited for him, Adam commented on about her outfit. "New robes?"

Havera peered down and sighed. "Aedile robes. My pater had them sent here to keep up appearances. Can't be seen wearing my old Quaestor robes around. It would be 'unbefitting of my rank,'" she said, presumably quoting her father. Havera awkwardly adjusted the hempen robe under her breasts. "I'll need to get refitted for newer ones. These are a bit tight across the chest."

"I don't know. They seem to fit you well," Adam said. Havera raised an eyebrow. Adam shrugged. "What? They do."

Their worst fears were confirmed when Daloth showed up not wearing his usual opulent, red seaweed frock, having traded it for a brown, linen tunic. Not even a swish toga to go with his tunic. No tricorn hat either. Adam thought he seemed rather plain without all the flashy clothes.

"I've been recalled," Daloth explained, slumping down on Havera's couch. He drank a sip of tea Dee had hurriedly prepared. His short snout sagged downward, and his head was bone dry.

I've seen that expression. It has a Moan face, but the feeling is universal. That's a defeated man.

"Recalled? Were you fired?" Samus asked the question Adam was too afraid to speak.

Daloth set the tea down. "In a manner of speaking. I informed Parliament of my intention to declare Human independence. They suspended my credentials immediately. Technically, I no longer had the authority to speak on behalf of the Thalassocracy. The Conclave agreed to strike my remarks from the record. As far as everyone is concerned, it is business as usual," Daloth said.

"I'm guessing that means Human independence is not recognized," Adam surmised.

"Not by the Conclave. Not by the Coalition of Independent Nations. Not by the Moan Thalassocracy. Not by the janitor that cleans the bathrooms," Daloth said, shaking his head.

"None of the Doges were willing to back you?" Havera asked.

Daloth shook his head again. "A few privately lauded my courage. Most agree with me that it is the long-term best interest of the Thalassocracy and the galaxy-at-large that Humans become a free and independent people once again. They strongly chastised my methods."

"What methods would they prefer? Surrender and appeasement," Adam growled.

"You must understand, Adam Mortis, my people aren't particularly a warring people. Living underwater, we never discovered technologies like gunpowder. Oh, sure we had wars and strife like any other sentient race. Concussion weapons and triple-use transportation technologies, sea, air, and spaceship, are our inventions after all. However, discovering these inventions was slow, more deliberate. Only accelerating after our first encounter with the Zokyo eight-hundred years ago to fight in their wars against the Naddine. And like the Naddine, we're tribal. We lack their biological ability to bond with the beasts of the sea. We didn't have the capacity to tame thousands of sea beasts with the prick of a finger to wage war. Nonetheless, we still have needs and resources to fulfill those needs. Thus, we developed sophisticated trade and diplomatic networks to interconnect our disparate societies. Primitive tribes with local resources spawned the first merchant republics, finally evolving into the Thalassocracy we enjoy today.

Trade and diplomacy. It's the central governing ethos of the Moan people for thousands of years. There's a spectrum of varying beliefs on how that ethos would work within and outside of Moan culture, of course. The ruling class of Doges and their Parliament representatives firmly believe the best way to operate is to open up trade avenues and partnerships galaxy-wide, regardless of that race or organization's internal politics. Some believe we ought to use those relationships to affect galactic change. It's a minority view, but a growing one. No one can agree on what those changes can or should look like in such an interconnected galaxy with so many diverse values and points-of-view. With such uncertainty, the Doges are taking a conservative approach to this new galactic order alongside our burgeoning Sinner leadership. They don't want to jeopardize our existing relationships with the Proprietors while expanding on the relationships with our new partners. In short, Adam, the Doges would love nothing more than to have free and open trade with both Bokori and Humans. Unfortunately, the Bokori have made this impossible. They've made it clear to the galaxy it's you or them. To the Doges, it's a simple calculation. There's more Links to be made with the Bokori than the Humans. They don't want to rock the submarine," Daloth said.

"Why'd you do it then? If you knew full well the Moan government wouldn't agree and it would ruin your career, why bother?" Adam asked.

"Because right is right. What I said to you this morning was in official capacity as Cardinal of the Moan Thalassocracy. However, Daloth Afta didn't believe in those words. Even as I was saying them, they felt hollow and empty. I hated myself for saying them. I've had to parrot the government's line for far too long. Maybe the Doges are right. I don't know."

Daloth took a deep sip of tea. His webbed claw had a noticeable shake as he lifted the cup to his mouth.

"I've fought in war. During the Strife, I was deployed to Zezaz, the Bubil capital located on the Omega Spiral. At the time, it was a Zokyo stronghold. Many Zokyon families and colonists lived in Bubil towns and cities alongside the locals. The Bubils were subjugated by the Zokyo like we were. Like you are now by the Bokori. The Naddine launched an offensive in attempt to control the sector. Let me tell you, there's nothing scarier than staring down the jaws of a Vivily or Orror-ror warbeast. The town we were stationed in was quickly overrun. We retreated to an entrenched position just outside the town. From less than a hundred yards away, I helplessly witnessed a group of Naddine-aligned fighters, many of them Bubil, slaughter all the Zokyo who lived there. There's nothing more stomach-churning than watching a group of Zokyon women be ripped from their mechsuits and slowly suffocate while fighters ravage them again and again. When we retook the town the next day, we were ordered to summarily execute those who had participated in that mass slaughter. Some of those fighters were ordinary people I knew and had spoken with on many occasions. Some I had called friends. War makes monsters of us all," Daloth said. He put the tea down. The hulking Moan buried his face in his webbed claws in a vain attempt to stifle sobs.

The story was too much for Samus. She walked away, stifling her own sobs. Havera sat down next to Daloth and put a comforting hand on his back. Adam sat there, trying to soak in what he heard. He had killed people. Most in the midst of a fire fight. Some...Adam closed his eyes. The face of that Hisba flashed across his mind. He tried to suppress it. The scars on his back tingled with each passing thought. The expression of shock on that Hisba's face.

Am I a monster?

A faint buzzing in Adam's ear drew him towards the Debbie in his pocket. Without thinking, he reached for it. He clenched his fist and retook control of his muscles. He shook his head to stop the buzzing and scratched his back to pass off his sudden movement.

"I wish there was another way, Card... Daloth. The Bokori, the Conclave, the Sinners. Y'all have left us with no other alternative. Diplomatic options are exhausted. The Bokori won't give us our freedom back. We must take it from them by force. We have no other choice. We must fight," Adam declared.

Havera snapped her head in his direction. A genuine expression of fear splayed across her face. Daloth raised his head slowly. "You might be right. It seems that conflict between Bokori and Humans is inevitable. That's the paradox of war. Sometimes you must engage in a smaller fight now to prevent a larger one in the future," Daloth said.

"Except, if they choose to fight and lose, more innocent Humans will die for nothing," Havera said.

"Not for nothing. For freedom. Daloth is correct. It is what's right," Adam said.

"Being right and doing right are not always the same thing, Adam. Yes, Humans ought to have freedom. Yes, the Bokori are wrong for keeping Humans subjugated. Doesn't mean that killing them is the right answer," Havera said.

"Those who have the power to end this without bloodshed refuse to act on that power. The Conclave doesn't get to claim they have the right to govern our behavior if they won't check their members that abuse their power. That moral and legal authority is null and void. Since they won't play by the rules, we won't either," Adam said.

Havera opened her mouth to respond. Daloth put a webbed hand on her shoulder. "The Commissioner is correct, Your Grace. We're outsiders. We don't get to dictate the terms of how they fight. If we abdicate our responsibility to help, we abdicate our ability to judge. We can't have our oyster and eat it, too," Daloth said. The Moan stood up to leave. "Thank you for the tea, Your Grace. I appreciate your hospitality."

"Daloth, I'm sorry for..." Adam started to say.

Daloth raised a hand. "No need to apologize. Having freedom is about having choice. I made the choice to go against the wishes of those in power. I must suffer the consequences."

"Regardless, I shouldn't have said what I said. You're a good man, Daloth Afta. A true friend to Humans. To all sentients. No matter what happens, I won't forget it. I won't let other Humans forget it either," Adam said.

Daloth smiled. "I appreciate your kind words, Adam. I wish I could do more to help, but I've reached the end of my fin."

"Is there no other person or government I can speak to on Concordia that might help?" Adam asked.

Daloth reached the lift to Havera's apartment. The doors opened up in front of him and he stepped inside. "Take it from someone who's worked in public service nearly three decades, you won't find good help from governments. Try unofficial channels. Businesses, private citizens. You have friends who can help, Adam. They might be here on Concordia or elsewhere in the galaxy. You only need to find them," Daloth said. The lift doors closed shut and any chance for a peaceful solution closed with them.

What is lost will be found.

Adam returned to the main room to find Havera comforting Samus, holding her close with her tail. "Does this mean we're going to war?" Sam asked.

Havera stared up at him with the same face of concern she had earlier. "I think we were already at war. We only had to acknowledge it," Adam said. His heart raced, and the scars on his back itched again. Saying the words out loud made them feel real. Humanity was at war for its survival. The survival of its body and soul.

Havera stood up suddenly. "I think we all need to take a step back and breathe. You may be right. Daloth may be right. My pater may be right," Havera said.

"What did your father say by the way? I forgot to ask," Adam said, remembering their earlier conversation.

Havera ran her fingers through her hair. "Most of it was unimportant to you. He did say, legally-speaking, de-certifying a Proprietor race's status does exist in the Conclave Charter. He did tell me the other Proprietor races have continuously expressed concern over the Bokori's failure to comply with the requirements of a Proprietor power. That said, no one is eager to enforce that section of the charter. The other Proprietor races have on occasion failed to meet some of the requirements. The Strife strained resources to the point the criteria were nearly impossible to meet. Exceptions are often granted and without objection from the other Proprietors for short periods of time. The Zokyo have a current ongoing extension to the ConSec fleet requirement. The Naddine aren't thrilled about it. My digiholo was on an encrypted channel, so my pater was able to speak more freely. He made it abundantly clear that, while the Bokori have a fleet capable of defending interstellar trade routes, no one will challenge their Proprietor status."

"You mean so long as they can protect the dark matter trade," Adam said.

"Correct. Even on an encrypted channel, my pater wouldn't admit to that, but I can read between the lines. The Bokori have the most dark matter systems and dark matter refineries. So far, the pirate activity hasn't hampered the dark matter trade to a significant degree. Should that change..." Havera left her remaining thoughts unspoken.

"I thought you were opposed to war," Adam said, spinning her words back at her.

"I am my mater's filia, and I never said war was the only way. There's always an alternative to fighting. You must have the courage to find it," Havera said.

What is lost will be found.

"I'm mentally drained," Samus said, popping to her feet. Sam paced the room. "I want to do something! We can't sit here and wait for the shooting to start. We couldn't get home to fight if we wanted."

"I'm not sure what to do, Sam. I'm experiencing more whiplash than I did in the back of that aircar. I don't know where we go from here," Adam said.

"I have an idea," Havera said. She picked up Adam's jacket and tossed it to him. "It's the 25th anniversary of the Saptia Accords. Concordia will be abuzz with celebrations and fun activities to do. I know a place we can go to celebrate. Take a night off. Cradite knows we could all use some fun relaxation."

Samus beamed at her. "Yes! Please! I've never been to an alien celebration. Come to think of it, I don't think I've been to any celebration."

"That, carissima, is sad. It's settled. We're having a night out!" Havera said.

Adam sighed. "Havera, after the day we've had, I'm not sure going out with Concordian masses is something I want to do. The Saptia Accords aren't exactly a moment for Humans to celebrate."

Her tail wagging excitedly, Havera looped her arm under Adam's. "We'll celebrate something else," Havera said, smiling.

"What?" Adam asked.

Havera shrugged. "How about another day healthy and alive?"

Adam grinned despite himself. "Alright, Your Grace, you win."

She squeezed his arm tightly. Adam winced for a moment. "Get used to it," the Cauduun said with a wink.

21

The Long Night Out

The hustle and bustle of Concordia's entertainment district was parts nerve-wracking and exhilarating. Millions of sentients from all corners of the galaxy jammed together in a collective mass of celebratory revelers. The buildings stretched up for hundreds of feet with dozens of levels of transparent walkways and streets reaching all the way to the top. Brightly colored neon signs adorned the walls, assaulting the eyes in every direction. Huge open-air elevators capable of carrying hundreds of people and hovercars at a time were dotted every few thousand feet, moving up and down the levels at a timed pace.

The hovercar Havera had rented for the three of them often times was stopped at a standstill, the traffic was so heavy. The Conclave's security bots were whistling high above everyone's heads, monitoring for overly exuberant carousers. A pair of bots were assisting a clearly intoxicated Naddine woman into a nearby hovercar with great difficulty. Her male Naddine companions weren't doing much to restrain woman's...enthusiasm. Adam observed a pair of the bipedal leel'Sezerene workers in plain work tunics cleaning the sides of the buildings.

They were riding with the hood of the hovercar down, taking in all the sights, sounds, and smells. The climate-controlled interior of

Concordia's station allowed for a pleasant experience, despite the sheer mass of bodies.

It feels nothing like Windless Tornado. No humidity, no smell of feces or trash. A bit too loud. This is the peak of sentient civilization, supposedly.

"It's like a sea of tunics and togas!" Samus exclaimed.

She was right. In his short time on station, Adam had noticed a prevalent fashion style on Concordia, reaffirmed by their current milieu. "*The Cauduun's reach is longer than their tails.*" Shepard's words rang true in this regard. Most everyone, Cauduun or otherwise, was wearing some sort of tunic, stola, palla, or toga combination.

Save for the mechsuits of the Zokyo, the bombastic half-shoulder capes of the Naddine, and the fused seaweed frocks and coral tricorns of the Moans, this was by far the dominant style on Concordia. It was fascinating to see all the diverse revelers dressed so similarly. Several adorned their heads with a jeweled circlet or a chaplet wreath, with a variety of different of gemstones or flowers in each individual headdress. The colors and materials varied from person to person. No discernible pattern from race to race that Adam could tell.

In Arabella, tunics were a common article of clothing. Most Humans wore them beyond their simple jumpsuits. They felt free and refreshing in the unbearable heat and humidity of Windless Tornado, and, most importantly, they were cheap and easy to acquire. In effect, they were quite practical. On Concordia, they were a fashion statement.

Havera wasn't paying attention to any of it. She was sitting there, with her chin resting on her hand and her tail wrapped around her. She stared wordlessly out the side of the car. She had changed out of her new Praetorian robes back into the black deep v dress from the hearing, although with her hair still in its usual triple ponytail. A blank thousand-yard stare stretched across her face.

"Tell me about this club where we're headed!" Adam said with mustered fake enthusiasm. He was curious to see more of the station, but large crowds made Adam uncomfortable. He wasn't exactly thrilled about the prospect of thousands of drunk aliens surrounding and peppering him with questions and awkward comments. Samus was through the roof. Adam had never seen her so excited. She was giddy at everything and waved at anyone who happened to recognize them.

Havera was polar opposite. She seemed sullen. It was her idea to go out, and she had been genuinely excited. With time to reflect, she grew quiet. Adam recalled the day's events. After what happened with her father, Adam was worried about his friend.

She wishes she could be anywhere but here. She wears a smile like armor.

"It's called 'Vidi, Vici, Veni.' It belongs to a family friend. He's promised us a VIP table away from the rabble," she said half-paying attention.

"What sort of club is it?" asked a nervous Adam.

"It's a multifaceted establishment. It's mainly a restaurant, but they have dancers, tabletop competitions, private lounges, and gaming terminals. It's Comedy Night tonight. A popular Cauduun comic is performing. You'll enjoy it I hope." Havera said, her eyes boring into the back of the driver's seat.

Adam placed a hand gently on her shoulder. Her head shifted at his touch. "Let's forget about the past several days. Tonight, it's just about us. I think if anyone's earned a night off from the galaxy's stresses, it's the three of us," Adam said. He tilted his head at Samus over his shoulder. Havera peered around him to see Samus smiling and waving to a trio of Bubil women buzzing at her giddily.

Havera smiled. "Alright, it's a deal. I'm sorry I was sulking like that, it's just..."

Adam raised a hand to shush her. "You don't need to explain yourself at all, Havera. I get it. You don't owe me anything other than a good time." Realizing his choice of words, Adam blushed. "I meant you owe yourself a good time! Wait, no, I mean we all should have a good time together. Separately! I mean together but separately! Oh, goddesses, save me."

Havera giggled. "Don't be so nervous, Adam. I understood what you meant," she said. She patted him on the knee. A rush of excitement coursed up his leg. She leaned in close and whispered. "If you're so easily flustered, you might find tonight hard to handle." She playfully nudged his shoulder with hers.

Oh, goddesses, is she flirting with me? Is she only being friendly? Am I reading too much into this? She is utterly stunning in that dress, and she is fiercely beautiful, period. No, no don't be ridiculous. Focus, Adam, focus. She's Cauduun royalty for Cradite's sake! Who are you?

Adam's heart was racing. He could feel his anxiety building. It was a different kind of an anxiety. A distant, yet familiar form of nervousness traversed his body up-and-down.

Havera sensed his sudden jitters. "I'm teasing you, Adam. I'm trying to help you relax. Mea culpa if that backfired."

"He's worried you'll realize he's comparing you to Trissefer in his head," Samus called out.

"SAM!" Adam yelled, alarmed.

Havera laughed. "Oh, really now? Perhaps I should dye my hair strawberry blonde and become all super serious," Havera said in a mocking tone.

"Please don't! Your hair is gorgeous as it is," Adam blurted out. Havera raised an eyebrow playfully.

Shut up, man!

"Aww, he likes you, Havera." Samus said. She was now nudging Adam with her shoulder.

"It's the tail. All sentients love the tail," Havera said, joining Samus in ribbing Adam. He sunk down in the seat. The girls kept pestering and teasing him all while laughing hysterically.

I want to die.

Havera gently grabbed him by the scruff of his coat and lifted him back up. She gave him a quick peck on the cheek. Adam's heart fluttered for an instant. "Tonight's going to be so much fun," Havera said. She winked at Samus, who was grinning from ear-to-ear. Adam rolled his eyes, letting his head fall gently back into the seat. Samus fussed his muddy brown hair a bit, resting her head on his shoulder. He was relaxed once more. He put his arm around Samus and squeezed her tightly. He was glad to see Samus was happy again. He hadn't seen her like this for far too long. Havera smiled at them, her melancholy melted away.

***

The club was massive. It covered five stories high and had its own private open-air elevator. The neon sign on the outside read, "Vidi Vici Veni." Fluctuating neon lights formed a nude Cauduun female laying down with her elongated tail underlining the name of the club. It was easily the most popular destination on the block for miles. Thousands of people were queuing up outside, with several muscular Moan, Sezerene, and Cauduun bouncers guarding the entrance. The sea of excited, happy faces was a foreign sight to Adam. He was used to grim and gray, not bright and colorful.

Their hovercar pulled up to the club. Several people in line recognized Adam and Havera, screaming their excitement for the whole entertainment district to hear. Their driver signaled over one of the bouncers, a broad-chested yellow and green Cauduun male. When the bouncer noticed who they were, he signaled for them to drive into the elevator. They drove past, the bouncer nodding at them, and they settled into the narrow elevator. Translucent glass sealed the elevator shut. The lift steadily rose all the way to the top. Once there, the trio exited the vehicle. Two more Moan bouncers were waiting by the door on the nearby platform. They opened the rope line at their approach, one of them saying, "Welcome to Vidi Vici Veni. Cisi is expecting you. Enjoy your night." Adam noticed a sign on the outside of the door that read, "No Bokori!" with a corresponding symbol to match.

"Who is Cisi?" Samus asked, crossing the threshold into the club. They were walking through a narrow, well-lit passageway towards the club center.

"He's my uncle. Well, not technically, but he was more-or-less an uncle to me growing up. I believe he's my mater's second cousin by marriage, maybe third. This is his club. It belonged to his wife until she passed away a few years ago. He's, uhh, quite the character," Havera said with a slight giggle.

The club was booming. Heart pounding, rhythmic music and

flashing lights were emanating from the floors below them. They reached a balcony overlooking the marvelous chaos. The building was a hollowed-out square with balconies built in along the sides around the center square.

The first floor was a vibrant dance floor, with hundreds of revelers dancing in close proximity. Adam was grateful to not be down there. He wasn't sure if his head or heart could handle it.

The middle floors were much calmer compared to the first. Hundreds of seated tables and booths dotted around the perimeter. Even those sections were crowded with guests. Adam realized each floor was retractable, meaning the building was arranged in this manner for special performances, otherwise each floor would be solid ground all the way across. The second floor had a bunch of gaming terminals, holographic tables, and AR pods while the third seemed more family-oriented with sprawling tables, sound dampeners, and huge booths. Adam noticed exotic dancers of varying species were at several booths on the fourth level, strategically placed to avoid the gazes of the children from the third floor. The fifth floor, where the trio were standing, was much more private and intimate. Nowhere near as crowded as the rest of the club.

"Nepti!" A boisterous voice called out to them. They turned to see a burly, rotund Cauduun male approach with arms wide open. The black and blue Cauduun's bald head shone slightly in the softer lights of the club's fifth floor. He was wearing a pink silk tunic along with an opulent, lavender toga.

"Uncle!" Havera said, embracing the older Cauduun. They kissed each other on either cheek.

"My, my. Our little nepti is all grown up! You look exquisite, Your Grace!" the older Cauduun said.

"Thank you, Cisi. Do me a favor. Don't call me 'Your Grace,' lest I heave you over the side of the balcony," Havera said smirking.

"Oh, ho ho ho! If that is Her Grace's wish," Cisi said, with a grin and a mocking bow. Havera punched him harmlessly in the shoulder. Cisi recoiled playfully. "Ouch! That Praetorian training is paying dividends.

I heard about your promotion. Aedile, eh? Ho ho ho. Congratulations, Nepti. You'll be a Censor before you're sixty!"

"One step at a time, Uncle. Pater would rather I give it all up and stand for election," Havera said.

Cisi backhanded the air. "Bah! I say this with all the love and respect in the galaxy for your pater, Nepti, but your old man's tail is stuck so far up his own ass, he has to gag when he speaks." Havera giggled, running a hand through her hair. Cisi put a hand on Havera's shoulder. "You do what's best for Havera. You understand, Nepti?" Havera nodded, her eyes staring at the floor. Cisi peered over her shoulder at the Humans. "Are these the two that are the talk of the station?"

Havera's pointy ears perked up. "Yes! Sorry!" She turned to introduce them. "This is Commissioner Adam Mortis. He's one of the Human commissioners representing their new *unofficial* home. I guess he's the prime Commissioner at this point. This lovely lady is Commander Samus Dark, a lead scout for the Human's *unofficial* capital of Arabella. I would like y'all to meet Lord Gaius Cicero Caelus." Instinctively, Adam gestured a heart salute. Samus mimicked him.

Cisi shook his head. "Oh, no no no. Ho ho ho. Those military salutes are too formal for this occasion. This ain't no Conclave meeting," Cisi said. He wrapped Adam in a tight embrace. He grasped Adam by the face and gave him a wet kiss on either cheek, repeating the same to Samus. "Please call me Cisi. All my friends do. Tonight, y'all are my friends and guests of honor. Welcome to Vidi Vici Veni! I've had a suite prepared for y'all tonight. The best suite in the house. The Audeleus Suite! May his revelrous blessings shine on all y'all this night! Follow me."

The trio followed the boisterous Cauduun. The floor was divided up into suites with a bouncer and a pair of smiling, male and female, Cauduun waiters for each suite. Adam couldn't help but notice the entire wait staff were ridiculously attractive, as if they were all models or actors. They all wore rather elegant but overtly revealing attire. As they walked past each pair, the staff gave a polite bow to the three of them. Towards the middle section, facing the frontward side of the building, they arrived outside a luxury suite. The sign above said "Audeleus Suite." A golden lyre with flowers for strings was emblazoned underneath.

The suite was spacious. Everything was polished and clean, as if they had never been used. Inside the suite were several luxurious, padded recliners. Each recliner included a tray table, drink holder, and an emulator, from which they could order food and refreshments. A stylish Rinvari, with extravagant rings adorning his horns, was manning the bar. He bowed when they entered. The seats were layered rows along the steps leading down to their private balcony to provide an unobstructed view of the dance floor. A handful of inactive display screens were arranged around the suite. The suite could easily hold thirty or so occupants quite comfortably...and it was all theirs.

A long table was set up for appetizers. Plates full of olives, figs, grapes, pears, cheese, honey, eggs, oysters, and...*strawberries*...covered the table from end to end. Adam's mouth watered at the sight of them. He scooped up a strawberry and bit into it. It was so sweet Adam almost spit it out. It was the most delicious thing he'd had in months. Closing his eyes, he recalled the last time he had strawberries.

Not the same. Something is missing. Someone. This feels wrong. I'm standing here enjoying myself while Humans suffer back home. Without her.

Samus rushed to a seat in front to get the best view. The rhythmic music was still playing, but people were starting to clear the dance floor. The ground floor was realigning into an elevated stage, with the revelers pushed to the sides into a space crowded to the point of standing room only. Club workers were checking instruments and sound testing, preparing for the upcoming performance. Havera stood next to Cisi, their two waiters hovering by the entrance.

"How's your investiture present treating you? She flies smoothly?" Cisi asked Havera.

"She's wonderful, Cisi. I kept most of the original paint job. I added a purple stripe across her back to remember Mater. I named her 'Cicera' in your honor," Havera said. Cisi was touched. He kissed her affectionately on the cheek.

"You're your mater's filia. Wonderful. Beloved. Thoughtful. If only my own filia were like you, Nepti," Cisi said.

"You're too hard on Caelia, Uncle. She's busy managing unruly platinum miners on Sorma. You're well aware how essential her work is to Rema. It's practically duty. I know many of the Conservative duchesses want her to stand for archduchess. I'm sure she'd come visit more often if she could," Havera said.

"Hmph! Kewea take her duty and those pestering Confederates! You ought to know it doesn't matter how important your job is nor how high your station, you always make time for family. Her mater didn't spend years forging an interstellar entertainment conglomerate, which includes, I might add, the best club in all Neutral Space, just so she could waste her prime years on some backwater colony. You're compelled to babysit a Human rebel upstart involved in what could become the biggest conflict since the Strife, and you're finding time to visit me and your pater. No offense, Human! Ho ho ho." Cisi said, waving at Adam.

Adam's mouth was full of cheese. "None taken," Adam managed to mouth between bites, dismissing the Cauduun's polite concern.

"I understand her situation is all I'm saying, Cisi. Be patient with her. She'll come around. Give her a call. I'm sure she'd love to hear from you," Havera said.

"Hmph! Children should reach out to their parents, not the other way around. I take your point, Nepti. You really do remind me so much of Pompeia," Cisi said.

"Thank you, Uncle," Havera said politely. She bowed her head, her eyes fixed upon the ground. She ran her fingers through her hair.

Cisi cleared his throat. "Anyway, this is where I take my leave. The staff will take good care of you. I must head down to see if our Kewea-accursed emcee arrived. There's going to be a surprise performance before Brutus. Y'all enjoy yourselves! Vale, Nepti."

Cisi left the room. Havera stood there for a few moments, unmoving. Adam walked up and tapped her on the shoulder.

"Should we grab a seat?" he asked.

Havera nodded. The pair grabbed seats behind Samus, who was spinning in her reclining chair. "Adam, these seats spin! They're heated, too! What is this magic? I feel like a queen in this chair," Samus said. "Check out their menu! I don't understand what half this stuff is," she said as she read from the attached emulator.

Adam had a mild panic attack biting into another fig. "Havera, is this food safe for Humans to eat?"

Havera's eyes widened. She summoned over the male Cauduun waiter. "Excuse me, but this food is safe for Human consumption, correct?"

The waiter stuttered. "I...I don't know, Your Grace. We weren't the ones to put out the plates. Let me double check," the Cauduun said, fumbling for his emulator. He quickly scrolled through to search for an answer. After twenty panic-inducing seconds, the Cauduun breathed a sigh of relief. "Yes, yes, it is! Phew. Cisi is always a few steps ahead of everyone. It seems that Cauduun and Humans share a similar digestive tract. Anything a Cauduun's system can handle, a Human's can as well. Sorry! We don't get many Humans in here, otherwise I'd have memorized that."

Adam wiped the sweat from his brow. "Would you mind helping us decide on a main course? Tell us what is and isn't safe for Human consumption. Maybe make a recommendation or two?"

The female Cauduun waitress waltzed up to his seat. "Perhaps we could start you off with a drink? We have a fine selection of wines, beers, and spirits for your enjoyment," the amber and cyan Cauduun said, her silky hair up in a high ponytail.

"Anything non-alcoholic?" Adam asked. The mere thought of consuming that poison caused his stomach to churn. He had a brief flashback to his cell where the Hisbaween forced him to imbibe. He crushed the thought before it could germinate.

"Of course!" the waitress said with a bit too much exuberance. "We have water, fizzy drinks, tea, smoothies, juice..."

"He'll have some Palerian Grape Juice," Havera said, cutting in. "We all will. We'll also each have the Shelean smoked pork ribs with sides of sausages, both covered in extra royalist sauce, please." Adam blinked at her. "Trust me, it's faster this way. I think you'll both really like it."

"Whatever all that is, it sounds amazing! I'm starving. I'm tired of that gooey gray paste. Even chocopullo gets dull after a while," Samus said.

Adam shrugged. "What she said," he agreed.

"Excellent! Very good, Your Grace. Sir," the waitress said with a bow. She nodded at the bartender, who prepared several glasses of a reddish-purple liquid. The waitress brought over their drinks in tall, slender glasses. Adam swirled his drink a bit, then sipped. It tasted delightfully sweet. It went down his throat like a gentle massage. He slammed back the rest of it.

"This is excellent, Havera. Great choice!" Adam said. The waitress refilled his glass.

"The vineyards of Paleria are second only to its mines," Havera said, sipping her own glass.

About twenty minutes later, the waiters came back with their meal. Adam's jaw dropped. He'd never seen food prepared like this. Sure, Adam ate some cooked meats from the various small game found on Windless Tornado, not to mention the chocopullo Samus cooked up for them, but nothing like this. The sauce shone on top of the lightly blackened meat. He could feel the heat radiating off the tender slices. He leaned over the ribs and sausages to sniff them. The intoxicating savory steam hit his nostrils. His eyes watered. He picked one up. It was juicy. He took a bite and almost passed out from its wondrous flavor. He devoured one slice after another. His mouth watered hungrily with each bite. Samus was even more ravenous than he was. Her face was covered in sauce and grease.

"Slow down, slow down, you two! The boar is already dead. It ain't going anywhere," Havera implored.

"You don't understand, Havera. Getting meat this sumptuous is almost impossible in Bokori space," Adam said in between bites. "They consider it a heresy to kill or consume an animal."

"What do y'all normally eat?" the waitress inquired, overhearing their conversation.

"Plant-based pastes. Lots and lots of pastes," Samus responded dryly.

"Oof! Don't tell the Rorae. They get a bit sensitive if you eat a plant," the waitress joked.

Adam chuckled. "I can imagine. Will the Naddine be offended if I eat meat?" Adam asked half-jokingly. He spotted a Naddine couple at a table one level below and across from them.

"Oh, no. Definitely not. Animals are scared to Naddine, but there is nothing more sacred than a good meal," the waitress said with a coy smile.

Adam laughed and grabbed a handful of sausages, before ravenously consuming them. Sitting there, consuming a meal fit only for a king or queen, Adam realized how little he understood about the subtle complexities of the galaxy. Bokor and Arabella were so culturally isolated from the rest of the Conclave, physically and metaphorically, it seemed. He felt like he was missing out. Yet, he didn't know where to start. Fortunately for him, Samus was not shy in voicing her curiosity.

"So, is Shele your last name, *Your Grace?*" Samus asked, with a sarcastic tone added to Havera's styling.

"Same rule applies to you as it does to Cisi, carissima," Havera laughed. "The answer is yes and no. Members of the Shelean Royal Family take the honorific 'of Shele' in lieu of a family name. Sort of like a centurion knight. The women at least. Men tend to adopt the last name of the family they marry into, Shelean or otherwise. The Shelean Royal Family has so many cadet branches across Alliance space, it's hard for even me to keep track," Havera explained.

"Is Shele your home, or is it the capital?" Samus asked.

"Oh, no! Paleria is Rema's capital. The birthplace of Cauduun civilization. It's where the Platinum Palace resides. It's not where I was born, but it's where I carry my title. Shele was a queendom, now a series of ducal provinces, just south of Paleria. For thousands of years, during the Age of Technology, Paleria and Shele were friendly rivals, and the largest sovereign states on Rema. The two powers combined had much of the world under their sphere of influence, yet, miraculously, or perhaps calculatingly, they never went to war with each other. In fact, it was quite common for Palerian senators and emperors to marry Shelean queens and duchesses. Paleria was the military and technological power of Rema while Shele was the cultural and economic one. Towards the tail end of the Age of Technology, the two sovereign nations agreed to merge to form one superpower. The strignatia of Shele married the aquilvir of Paleria. The Link, the massive bridge that connects the two nations, is a symbol of their mutual cooperation. Not long after, all Rema fell under the sway of the Palerian empresses. Thus began what the Praetorians are calling the 'Age of Eminence,' though there is some dispute whether or not the official beginning of the Age of Eminence started with the merging of Paleria and Shele or when Queen Havera I toppled the last Platinum Empress."

Age of Technology. Age of Eminence. The Link. Platinum Palace. Platinum Empress. I wonder if our history was this rich.

Samus' eyes were huge saucers. She was absorbing everything Havera was saying with enrapturing enthusiasm. Perhaps because of Sam's enthusiasm, Havera seemed much more open to discussing this topic than last time. On the ship after they fled Bokor, she used her formal tone to discourage this kind of talk. Adam understood now it was because of the painful memory of her mother's death.

No. Her assassination.

Adam dared not interrupt. He wanted to learn more about the galaxy's most influential race. Havera continued. "There's actually a funny story about the Shelean Royal Family's origins. More myth than history. My mater used to tell me the Sheleans were nothing but simple merchant travelers at the dawn of the Age of Technology. No Shelean Queendom or anything of the sort existed back then. The old story goes a Shelean foremother was walking down a crowded street when she was approached by a stranger. The stranger said he had this magical deck of cards, and this deck of cards had the power to change a person's fate. The stranger offered the Shelean the 'opportunity' to pull one card from the deck. The stranger was tall, bald, and brutish, more oaf than sage. Skeptical, the Shelean asked him how much for the privilege of pulling a card, to which the stranger asked only for a share of the card's boon. Shrugging, the Shelean acquiesced and pulled a card from the deck. The card read 'Cradite's Favor.' It was that of Rema's three moons: Potia, Saptia, and Anio. In fact, it was a version of this symbol," Havera said, pointing to the Vitriba emblem on her bracers. "The stranger gleefully said she had drawn the luckiest card in the deck, for the moons grant the card bearer three wishes, one for each moon. Jokingly, the Shelean said, 'I wish to be a wealthy duchess.' The symbol for Potia vanished from the face of the card in a puff of smoke. Out of nowhere, a platinum wagon encrusted with diamonds spawned in front of her. Out stepped a well-dressed man, who indicated he was the Shelean's manservant. Without a second thought, and to the protestations of the stranger, the Shelean woman hopped in the carriage, which carried her off to her newly instantiated grand castle. It's said the stranger pursued the Shelean for the rest of his days, for he believed she owed him one of her wishes," Havera finished.

"What did she do with the other two wishes?" Samus asked.

"No one is quite sure. The story always ends there. The popular myth is that the Shelean pulled a card from Mordelar's Lucky Deck, more commonly called the Deck of Opportunity, and the stranger was Mordelar himself. It's another one of those legendary gifts from the goddesses. My people obsess about such tales. They're not meant to be taken at face value. I suppose the other two wishes are meant to symbolize the great opportunities that were laid before my family all those years ago," Havera said.

"And the stranger?" Adam chimed in.

"His fate is equally mysterious," Havera said coyly.

"Your family's history seems quite tied up with these artifacts. If Humans had such 'gifts,' we'd probably obsess about them, too," Adam said.

Havera straightened up. "I don't mean for this to sound rude, but y'all have no concept of what it means to carry such an artifact. The burden. Everyone is looking to me to lead. The bearer of Cradite's Bracers is believed to be the natural successor. They want me to break the stalemate amongst the ducal factions, who are unable to decide on a new archduchess. All I want to do is curl up on my ship and conduct historical research, by which I mean read a good book, write my popular histories, and sip hot tea."

"Why not give up the bracers if they're such a burden?" Adam asked.

Havera bowed her head and ran her fingers through her hair. "I...I can't. They're all I have left of her," Havera said. Adam adjusted his jacked. He fully understood what she meant.

Samus broke the brief awkward silence. "Is that story one of the Tales of Havera?"

Havera cocked her head in surprise. "No, it's not. Some ascribe the Shelean's identity to a Havera, but that's all conjecture...hold on! Where did you hear that name?"

"After the hearing while y'all were meeting with your father. I was off exploring, and I overheard some fancy folks in fancy clothes discussing them. Said you were the legends reborn or something like that. After that, I kept hearing whispers about them all over the station. I even saw a Raetis library was offering free readings for parents with young children. You just mentioned the first Queen Havera. I assume you're named after her. I was wondering, what are the Tales of Havera?" Samus asked, sitting at the edge of her seat.

Havera smiled. "Myths. Legends. History. Often all three."

"Can you tell us one?" Samus asked excitedly.

Havera opened her mouth to speak, but she was interrupted by an amplified familiar voice. "Ladies and Lords, welcome! I know you're eager to hear from tonight's marquee performer, but I have a surprise for y'all." Adam peered over the balcony to see Cisi wearing a headset and standing on the raised platform. "We're lucky enough to have special guests in our club tonight!" Adam's heart raced and his stomach churned. His forehead broke out in a cold sweat. He sank in his chair, shutting his eyes tight.

Oh, please do not mention us.

"We honor those that gave their lives in the Century of Strife. Here to help kick off the Accordance Day celebrations, Vidi Vici Veni would like to welcome to the stage for a brief performance, the famous dynamic duo, the champions of song, and the slayers of hearts: Zax and Jak!"

Elated screams erupted from below. The entire club was on their feet cheering. Adam opened his eyes slowly to see what was happening. He peered down to see multiple figures emerging from an opening in the floor. On the back of a giant, white bird stood a tall and lanky Zokyo. The Zokyo was wearing a skintight mechsuit of obnoxious yellow and orange, holding what appeared to be a glittering, electric lute. Behind the Zokyo sat a Naddine dressed in all black and white furs while wearing a long, matching cape connected at the shoulders. In front of the Naddine was a small, metallic construct, whose head was open and projecting three virtual hand drums. Once the duo cleared the opening in the stage, the bird flapped its enormous wings, launching them several feet into the air. The bird found equilibrium near the third floor. The cheers enveloped them.

"I love these guys!" Havera exclaimed as she jumped to her feet.

"Who are they?" Samus shouted over the excited screams.

"Bards! Zax the Zokyo and Jak the Naddine. They're Exchange kids! Two of the most talented performers I've ever heard!" Havera shouted.

"What are Exchange kids?" asked Adam loudly.

Havera waved him off. "I'll tell you later!"

Zax and Jak soaked in the cheers. At least Zax did. He was waving his four arms at the crowd. Jak sat there more subdued, focused on his drums. Zax's amplified high-pitched, yet pleasant voice rang throughout the club. "How's it going, Concordia?!" The cheers erupted again. Adam had to cover his ears the screams were so loud. Zax spoke again. "I know y'all are eager to see Brutus tell his jokes and his ha ha's. I am too! However, I thought we'd kick off the night with a fan favorite number. I know y'all love this song. The Moan and the Rorae!"

The crowd cheered again. They were immediately silenced by the sounds of Jak tapping his drums. The cheers were quickly replaced with claps matching the beat of the drums. Zax played a few chords on his electric lute. Adam felt the impact of each string in his chest. He suddenly felt relaxed and mimicked the crowd's rhythmic claps. Zax sang:

"Dry as day...a gentle blow...I follow your sun...oh, humble Moan"

"But, my lady...a simple merchant...cheap trinkets...is all I offer"

"What I want...oh, humble Moan...cannot be bought...at least I hope not"

"Oh, oh, heave hi ho...the Moan and the Rorae"

"Oh, oh, heave hi ho...the Moan and the Rorae"

"Oh, oh, heave hi ho...the Moan and the Rorae"

The crowd joined in on the chorus. The song was more of a shanty than an anthem. The bird flew around the center of the hollow chamber. Jak's cape fluttered behind him.

"But, my lady...frill does not thrill...vines surpass spines...my fins not worthy"

"Dampen my roots...sprout my leaves...my head will bloom...my stems will follow"

"Well, my lady...a simple merchant...a hard bargain...time for exchange"

"Oh, oh, heave hi ho...the Moan and the Rorae"

"Oh, oh, heave hi ho...the Moan and the Rorae"

"Oh, oh, heave hi ho...the Moan and the Rorae"

Havera and Samus sang the chorus. They were dancing to the incrementally increasing beat. The bird rose high enough to be on their level, then passed by their suite. Zax winked at the girls, strumming hard on his lute in their direction. Samus swooned.

"You deceived me...oh, simple merchant...you are not...under the frock"

"Ah, my lady...you finally see...all good deals...not but a game"

"Oh, humble Moan...do not feel sorrow...your Magi patron...will return on the morrow"

"Oh, oh, heave hi ho...the Moan and the Rorae"

"Oh, oh, heave hi ho...the Moan and the Rorae"

"Oh, oh, heave hi ho...the Moan and the Rorae"

Zax sped up his rhythm towards the song's finale. The roof of the club opened up.

"Oh, oh, heave hi ho...the Moan and the Rorae"

"Oh, oh, heave hi ho...the Moan and the Rorae"
"Oh, oh, heave hi ho...the Moan and the Rorae"
"Oh, oh, heave hi ho...the Moan and the Rorae"
"Oh, oh, heave hi ho...the Moan and the Rorae"
"Oh, oh, heave hi ho...the Moan and the Rorae"

At the song's conclusion, the giant, white bird flew through the opening in the roof. Out into the station sky, Zax and Jak vanished. The crowd applauded, hooting and hollering their approvals to the grand exit of the bardic performers.

The celebrations died down, and Cisi returned to the stage. "Alright, ladies and lords, the main event. He needs no introduction. Please welcome to the stage Brutus!"

From the back of the room emerged a short Cauduun male, waving to the crowd. While still emphatically cheering, the crowd wasn't displaying nearly the same enthusiasm they had for Zax and Jak. Part of Brutus' skin was a red so pale it was almost pink and the other part a pasty white with thinning, matching hair. He was holding a tankard in one hand. His tail was wrapped comfortably around his olive-colored tunic. The crow's feet around his eyes and the sunken cheeks made him appear to be middle aged. Adam wasn't great at figuring out aliens' ages from appearance alone. Cauduun faces were identical to Human's, so Adam guessed Brutus was about eighty to one-hundred years old, if he did the math correctly.

"Thank you! Thank you! Kewea's curse, Cisi! You're making follow those guys?! Sheesh! Give me some heads-up next time. I haven't seen faces this disappointed since I first met my wife's family," Brutus said to crowd chuckles. "Seriously, this reminds me when my wife told me she used to date a duke. She was getting plowed by royalty! Unbelievable! Just for that, I'm going to tell a few jokes about the Queen. I'm kidding, I'm kidding. Relax. I don't want to be thrown out after five minutes. Wait until I get to the Bokori jokes first."

The atmosphere in the club was relaxed and casual. Already, Adam could tell it was a friendly crowd for Brutus. They were laughing at even the tiniest remark. Speaking into his headset, Brutus was deliberately pacing back and forth on the stage, strutting with utter confidence and intensity. He added a flamboyant flourish to the ends of his sentences with the occasional mocking tone thrown in for embellishment.

"We're in troubling times, people. The Sinners are out here building a massive superhighway in space, trying to take over the galaxy. The Alliance still hasn't chosen a new archduchess. Humans are executing their own kind on livestream! On livestream! Those people are insane, Kewea's curse! Talk about coming out with a bang. Now, I've never met a Human, but I'm going to speak with absolute certainty about them like I'm some expert. You know like those talking heads you see on screen? 'You see, Ianus, these Humans don't have the temperament to blah blah blah,'" Brutus said in a cartoonish, mocking voice.

Adam laughed nervously. He wasn't sure what to expect. A few eyes around the fourth and fifth floor were glancing at him.

"No, they're crazy, but they're my kind of crazy. I mean, seriously, y'all try living with the Bokori for over five-hundred years! You'd be out shooting people in the head, too. I probably would've strapped explosives to my chest and charged right into their capital screaming 'AHHHHHHHHHHH!'" The crowd burst out laughing. Samus and Havera joined in the chorus of laughter. Adam felt himself relax a little.

Okay, that was funny.

"Thank Cradite that Cisi forbids Bokori from his club. I don't think I can handle another mass walkout after I told a crowd of Rorae they had nice roots. Not that he needed to. I don't think I've ever seen one of those grayskin jadespawns in the entire entertainment district in years. Too much blasphemy! Too much heresy! No one understood their level of zealotry until that stadium scourging video. I'm telling y'all, we all thought the grayskins had just become a harmless horde of nuts with lasers. Made a great living in my early days, bouncing from club to club telling bland, dull, boring Bokori jokes. The Bokori were bland, not my jokes! At least that's what I tell myself. Most of y'all probably weren't alive to hear them, thank Cradite." Brutus sipped some of his drink.

"But Kewea's curse! They stripped a Human naked and whipped him thirteen times in front of millions! Holy Cradite! For such a 'nonviolent race' that's messed up. All because he wouldn't confess his 'crimes.' Want to know what I think that guy did? I bet he wanted to build a rectangular house. Yeah! Something dumb like that. He builds something with corners, and the Bokori come knocking at his door screaming, 'BLASPHEMY!!!' He probably used the wrong pronoun by accident, even though the UI System translates everything near seamlessly. They just could sense it probably, you know," Brutus said, motioning his hand to his balding head.

Adam's heart fluttered and stomach churned. He dared not move. He was trying not to display any emotion. Both Samus and Havera hit him with a sideways glance. Samus even placed her hand on his, giving it a comforting squeeze.

"I'm rooting for those Humans, though. I really am. I hope they get their independence. Yeah!" Brutus said. The crowd whistled and cheered their approval. The crowd's cheers matched the boisterousness of Zax and Jak's introduction. Adam couldn't believe what he was witnessing.

What is happening? Why do they seem to support us so much?

Brutus continued. "It's insane in this day and age, since the Strife, subjugation of a race is allowed. I mean I get why the Techoxtl want to continue to be the Naddine's little jades. They get to play with animals all day and bang whenever they want. Sounds like a great deal! But the Humans. Let me tell y'all something. We Cauduun can live for two-hundred years. It gives us a certain perspective the rest of y'all don't get. Oh, hush! Y'all sound like grayskins when you 'ooo' like that! I don't mind, just bring the whips next time. Anyway, I remember what my mater and pater used to tell us about the Humans. How they saved our collective asses. It's true! I know y'all think the Xizor were some sort of myth, some space legend created to scare everyone. I can't wrap my brain around that something like eighty-five percent of people believe the Xizor weren't real!"

Wait, what? People think the Xizor are a myth?

Samus and Adam exchanged confused glances. The crowd was into this routine. Brutus continued. "Humans show up and within a generation are like, 'You know that dark energy equation or whatever y'all haven't solved in like two-thousand years? Yeah, we solved it last month. Here you go. BOOM!' Then, when their planet gets destroyed and they need our help we're all like, 'Nah! Thanks for playing. I know y'all saved the galaxy, but we're going to let the Bokori use and abuse you for the next five centuries.' At least we should've gotten that Kewea-accursed dark energy equation! Did you see what that Human's gun did?! He obliterated that sucker! We could've had that! You know what I think? That's why the Conclave doesn't want to help them. Humans get their freedom and suddenly within a year, they're our Rimestone overlords. You know what I say? Better them than those Yune bots. I don't trust those machines!"

The crowd roared with laughter, including Havera and Samus. Adam could only sit there. He wasn't sure what he was feeling. The jokes were funny. The energy in the room was electric. Brutus continued his routine, telling jokes about different races, the absurd toughness of Orbital players, and a particularly hilarious joke about women buying miniature Cauduun tails for self-gratification. Adam's head swiveled about the room. Everyone was having a good time. Everyone was smiling. Samus was practically catatonic with laughter while Havera continued to giggle. Adam, on the other hand, felt numb.

They're happy. Why don't I feel what they do?

His stomach churned as fiercely as an interstellar storm. He was feeling an anger swelling up inside him. The room was spinning. He had to get up.

"Excuse me," Adam said, abruptly standing and rushing out of the suite. He heard Havera's voice call out after him, but he ignored it. He raced around the floor, avoiding the gazes of curious club staff and patrons. He reached the corridor where they entered and pushed his way out the door. The bouncers were dealing with a belligerently drunk Moan couple, who were insisting they were invited. Adam rushed down the nearby sidewalk, hugging the side of the building towards the transparent elevator they used earlier. He retched up some of his dinner on the nearby wall. It still tasted good the second time. His ears were ringing.

"Kewea take the wretched Bokori!" Adam screamed into the outside air. He grabbed the nearby "No Bokori" sign and smashed it against the wall. A few people on the walkway glanced in his direction, only to resume their nightly activities without a second glance. The Moan bouncers eyed him up; however, they decided to let him be.

Adam rested his back against the wall and sank to the ground. His heart was pounding; his mind was racing; his anger was flaring. "You've taken our past. You've taken our future. You've even taken away the joys of laughter. I will take away all you hold dear," Adam muttered to himself. He let his rage wash over him, wallowing in it. It felt good. It felt satisfying. It felt right.

"Be still, Adam Mortis. You push yourself too far in the direction of disharmony. You must maintain balance of spirit, lest you be consumed by chaos." It was the disembodied voice again.

Adam snapped his head up. Hovering mere inches off the ground in front of him was the Rorae woman. Her black and red triangular eyes beamed down on him. Like before, she was nearly nude. Only a thin sash of slithering vines covered her chest and groin. Adam shielded his eyes. He peeked through his fingers in either direction. No one seemed to notice the Rorae except him. He heard her playfully giggle.

"Hehe you need not feel shame, Adam Mortis. I do not feel shame for my body. You should not feel shame for your heart and mind. Rise," the Rorae said. Adam dropped his hands. The Rorae beckoned him with her hand. Adam felt his body lift off the ground. He had no control.

"What are you doing?" Adam said aloud. He tried to move his muscles, but they wouldn't budge.

The Rorae responded in his head. **"Helping you up. We all need that sometimes. Even Magi."** The tripartite leaf where a mouth should be did not move or even twitch when she spoke. In fact, Adam didn't hear her at all. Adam realized she was speaking directly into his brain. Once in the standing position, he regained control of his body. He shook himself a couple times to confirm.

"Who are you? Can you read my mind?" Adam asked.

The Rorae laughed. Her voice crackled like ice with each word. **"You**

may call me Umbrasia. You will see me again. I promise," the Rorae said. Umbrasia moved in close to Adam. She was a few inches taller than him. She bent over so her face was level with his. Adam averted his gaze so not to stare at her chest. She inched closer. His back was pressed up against the wall. Adam felt like she was going to kiss him, yet she had no mouth.

Adam shut his eyes. "What are you doing?" He froze, expecting contact with the Rorae's face. Several seconds passed. He felt nothing. He opened one eye. She was gone.

"Adam!" a comforting voice called out to him. It was Havera. The Cauduun rushed to his side. Samus was not far behind.

"What happened? Is everything alright?" Havera asked. The women's faces were a mixture of concern and confusion. Adam imagined he had a similar expression. Surveying his surroundings, Adam spotted no trace of the Rorae woman.

Umbrasia. That was her name. A Magi. The so-called sorceresses of the southwest. What does she want from me?

22

The Maid of Gla-Mor

The aircar flew high towards the station's apex. At this altitude, the noise and light pollution disappeared. Two of the tiny asteroid Proprietor heads were visible on the artificial ceiling that projected the night sky. The faces were pointed outwards away from the planet's surface, so it was difficult to tell which asteroid was which. The light bouncing off the asteroids from the star illuminated one of them more than the other. Although the asteroid appeared small from the surface, about the size of a fingertip, its silhouette was unmistakable. The eye stalks of a Naddine head were clearly visible, poking outward at a curved angle away from the sides of its rocky skull.

Adam and Havera were en route to the Astral Lens, an observatory that sat at the very top of the station. It was just the two of them. Samus had decided she had enough excitement for one night. Havera flagged down a driver to take the young Human back to her apartment. Samus hugged Adam tightly before she hopped into her aircar. She was worried about him after his apparent anxiety attack. Adam didn't tell her about his outburst. He wanted to appear strong for her sake. Samus, the ever-clever, attentive person she was, probably saw right through his façade. She was kind enough to not call him out on it. She kissed Havera on the cheek goodnight, and they went their separate ways.

The pair spent much of the initial ride inside the station in silence. Adam was practicing breathing exercises to try and relax. Initially, Havera tried explaining more about what they were going to watch and why the Astral Lens was such a fantastic place to experience. Adam's lack of engagement dampened her excitement. He wasn't exactly enthusiastic about going this high up to watch a sequencer.

"Cinema!" Havera had corrected him. It was a Shelean word, which surprised Adam that a Default translation of the term existed. He had never heard of it until tonight. Havera had Dee make the arrangements for a private showing before they had left Havera's apartment. It was the second part of her two-part night out on the station. Adam was exhausted, yet his mind was racing about what had happened back at the club.

Who was that Rorae woman? Was I the only one to see her? Hear her?

"Havera," Adam said, attempting to push the dark flowered alien out of his mind.

"Hmm? What is it?" asked Havera.

"Something Brutus said confused me. He talked about the Xizor and said many people don't believe in them. How is that possible? The Xizor are the reason humanity is in such a sorry state. Their attack was less than six-hundred years ago! Isn't the sequencer, sorry cinema, we're about to watch take place long before the Xizorian Invasion? No one seems to have an issue remembering the Great Galactic War, and that was a thousand years ago. Do people really not believe the Xizor exist?"

Havera sighed. "I don't have an honest answer to that. The Meltdown erased so much of all our recorded history. Virtually every digitized historical record before 1333, going back thousands of years, was wiped out. Everything we've pieced together since then is almost exclusively from secondary or tertiary sources. Few people these days care about much before the Century of Strife. Whether the Meltdown is the root cause of this, nobody can say for sure. The Praetorians and libraries of Raetis try to dispel this sort of willful ignorance of galactic history, to little avail. Beyond the Meltdown, the Censors have various theories on why such there is such a widespread disbelief in the Xizor. For starters, the Tetrad races weren't around then, and the Rinvari were relatively new to the galaxy. We believe their origins are tied in with the Point of Always Return, near the core of Griselda and the supermassive black hole at her heart. That's the other side of the galaxy from the Rorae, the Moan, and the Union. Only the Cauduun and the Bokori bore the brunt of their invasion," Havera said.

"And Humans!" Adam corrected her.

"You're right. Mea culpa," Havera said, running her fingers through her hair. "Both the Cauduun and the Bokori owe Humans a great debt for their valiant defense. The dark energy weapons y'all developed were on another plane of existence. Something no species has come close to replicating," Havera said.

"Not that the Bokori haven't tried for more than five-hundred years. I've heard rumors the Cauduun's new energy weapons technology is close," Adam said.

Havera shrugged. "Who is the Consul of Cloudboard? That's not really my field of expertise. You know as much as I do. As for the Xizor, their attacks were so sudden and vicious, and they disappeared as quickly as they came. Hardly any witnesses survived the attacks, and the Meltdown destroyed all digital or electronic records kept about it. The few eyewitness testimonies the Praetorians have on file are woefully inconsistent. I read a few of them while I was completing my Pontifex thesis. I thought there might be a connection between the Xizor and the ancient Venvuishyn, but my research turned up next to nothing. Most people think they're hoaxes or a modern retelling of the Kewea myth. I can't say I blame them. I know this is difficult to hear, but the thought of an omnipotent, alien race with the power to raise the dead as their thralls are the tales of nightmares. There isn't one living sentient alive today who can tell us any different. Maybe my new Aedile rank within the Order will give me more access to sealed files. I can search them on my next trip home if you'd like," Havera said.

"I'll bet the Rorae might know. I've heard they can raise the dead!" Adam said. His mind wandered back to the Rorae woman.

Havera adjusted her tail to get more comfortable in her seat. "I've heard those same rumors, too. If the Rorae know anything, they aren't telling us. Those flora have many secrets they're not willing to share. Their Magi are powerful healers. I've been to Ashla. I've walked on the floating city of Breagadun. I've witnessed firsthand the wonder of Lasairfal, the wall of radiant fire that separates the day side of the planet from the night side. There are many mysteries in this galaxy, Adam. We've barely scratched the surface. Let's shelve that for now. We're here," Havera said.

The Astral Lens was built on top of the station. A silo-shaped building not near anything, except the night sky. It was an ideal location for an observatory. Adam could see his breath as he exited the vehicle. He raised the hood of his jacket to keep his head warm. He shivered in the fresh air. Havera spoke briefly to their driver.

"I'll just take a good nap, Your Grace. Don't worry about me!" said their Cauduun driver.

Havera had put on a black, woolen palla to keep warm in the brisk nighttime air. They hurried to the entrance. They were in a modest lot next to the silo. It was empty other than their aircar and one other large silhouette near the entrance. At first, Adam thought it was another aircar until the silhouette raised its head and stretched its wings.

Is that a bird?

The moonlight hit the bird at a good enough angle that Adam recognized the bird's snowy white feathers. "Havera, isn't that the bird those two musicians were riding on earlier?"

"You mean Zax and Jak? Yeah, it does seem like it. I wonder what they're doing here. I had Dee arrange for a private showing of *The Maid of Gla-Mor*," Havera said.

Adam and Havera entered the front door. The vestibule was a dimly lit, cozy lobby. A projection of the galaxy was splayed across the ceiling. Three figures were hovering near the reception desk. Two of them Adam recognized from earlier in the night. Indeed, it was the Zokyo and the Naddine. The Naddine was sitting cross-legged on a nearby bench, wearing his black furs, shoulder shawl, and billowing black and white cape. He was tapping on his metal construct in front of him impatiently. The Zokyo was still wearing his loud yellow and orange tight mechsuit. The electric lute was strapped to his back. The Zokyo was conversing with a finely-dressed, older Cauduun gentlemen Adam did not know. Their voices echoed off the walls.

"But, good sir, clearly you must know who I am? I received a notification about this special showing inviting us personally. Some person in their right mind understands it would be an honor to have us at their private event. I am Zax of the famous Zax and Jak duo. That is Jak of the famous Zax and Jak duo. Wherever we go, the level of class instantly rises," said Zax, posing his four arms playfully.

"Be that as it may, sir, the Astral Lens is closed to the public for a private event. No other guests are allowed, no matter how, ahem, *classy*," said the bald Cauduun man with restrained annoyance.

"Give it up, Zax. You've seen this sequencer almost a hundred times already. Besides, I think the guests are arriving now," said Jak, gruffly tilting his head to acknowledge Adam and Havera. Zax spun on the spot in time to see Havera and Adam lower their headwear. All four of Zax's hands smacked his jaw in exuberant surprise.

"Hot damn, sweet jam! This night just got even better! Bro, I told you I saw them in the VIP section. Here they are now. What a wonderful coincidence! Splendid!" Zax said excitedly.

The Zokyo hurried over to them. Adam held out his fists, expecting the Zokyon greeting. Instead, Zax clasped his top hands onto Adam's shoulders with a gentle squeeze while his bottom hands bopped Adam's outstretched fists. "You're Adam Mortis, aren't you? The Human who defies the grayskins! Jak and I watched the hearing in our studio. Magnificent performance if I do say so myself. And I do," Zax said with a smile. "Of course, I cannot forget the beautifully exquisite Duchess of Paleria and a Maid herself. Your Grace, it is an honor and a privilege to make your acquaintance. I am Zax of the famous Zax and Jak duo," Zax said, clasping Havera on her shoulders. Zax kissed Havera on each cheek awkwardly, given that his face was covered by a layer of glass.

Havera twirled one of her ponytails. "It is a pleasure to meet you, Zax. I'm a huge, huge fan! You're the most talented bard in the whole galaxy," Havera said. Adam noticed her voice was a few octaves higher.

"Oh, you flatter me, Your Grace," Zax said with one hand over his heart. "It is really a team effort. I am merely the face and the voice. Perhaps on your next birthday we'd be honored to throw you a private performance. I know I would," Zax said with a wink and a nudge. Havera giggled, continuing to twirl her hair. Adam almost threw up in his mouth.

Really, Havera. This guy? A gust of wind will knock him over.

"We'd have to consult our schedule first before you make any new commitments, Zax," Jak said, appearing at Zax's side.

"I think we can rework the schedule for the Duchess of Paleria," Zax said, not removing his beady eyes from Havera.

"Please call me Havera," Havera said. She was trying and failing to regain her calm composure. This was the giddiest Adam had ever seen Havera act.

Zax lightly lifted her hand and kissed it. "You may call me Zax, Ha-ve-ra," Zax said, accenting her name more than strictly necessary.

Adam turned away from the bard's flirtations to extend his hand towards the Naddine. Jak eyed Adam's hand suspiciously. Zax nudged Jak in the shoulder. "Bro, don't be rude. This Human is almost as famous as we are," Zax whispered.

Jak grasped Adam by the forearm and planted his other hand on Adam's shoulder. Adam winced, expecting the piercing pain from the Naddine's claws. The pain never came. "I'm Jak," the Naddine said.

"You're who?" Zax said, raising his voice pointedly.

Jak sighed. "Jes-Mur take me. I'm Jak of the famous Zax and Jak duo," Jak said. He was practically slurring his words. Jak limply let go of Adam's forearm.

"I keep telling you to practice that, bro! Branding, my man, branding!" Zax said.

"Right. Branding. Sorry. Listen, maestro, I'm going to wait on

Sel-Ena outside. Practice with J'y'll a bit. Ma'am. Sir. Pleasure to meet both of you," Jak said. The Naddine walked out the front entrance.

"Don't mind him. He's not much of a people person. That's why I'm the face of the famous Zax and Jak duo. So, Your Grace, I understand you knew our fathers," Zax said.

"I wouldn't say I knew them. I met them once briefly. I was the mistress of ceremonies at the Orbital match during Saptia. I presented Jak's father with the victory wreaths after Doh-Tee's historic upset. In fact, I met you two when y'all were tenderfoots. You both were probably too young to remember," Havera said.

"Jak's father does mention you quite a bit retelling that story. Always talked about your radiance," Zax said with a grin.

"Oh, stop!" Havera said, her voice cracking just a hint.

Yes, please stop.

"I didn't know you were at Saptia," Adam said, cutting in.

Havera lowered her head. "I was. I didn't mention it because I know how sensitive a subject Saptia is for Humans. I had just turned twenty. My mater wanted me to stand in for her at this event. Less politically sensitive for a mere countess to act as mistress of ceremonies. I interrupted the first year of my Pontifex education to attend."

"One crazy match. Come from behind victory against all odds. Really unified a galaxy. Never underestimate the power of sports, Adam Mortis," Zax said.

"Adam is fine. My brother was the sports fan, not me," Adam said.

Zax bowed his head. The Zokyo gently grasped Adam on the shoulders. "Terrible tragedy what happened. The mere thought of losing someone that close to you..." Zax said, letting the last syllable linger. The Zokyo was much more serious than he had been the last couple minutes. Adam caught him eyeing the front entrance for a moment. "I want you to know that I will do all in my power to help. Those grayskins deserve to get knocked down a few pegs," Zax said.

"How about a million Links?" Adam said off-the-cuff.

"Done," Zax said without missing a beat.

Adam chortled, nearly spitting in the process. "Ha! Does comedy come naturally with your bardic talents?"

Zax was unphased. "I'm serious, Adam. I'd be happy to make a contribution. Jak won't be happy I'm making rash monetary decisions, but he ain't here is he?" Zax said, giving Adam a playful pat. "Come, Your Grace. I understand you've rented out the entire observatory to watch my all-time favorite piece of cinema. If it isn't too much of an inconvenience, I'd be honored to join you and Adam in your booth," Zax said, offering one of his upper arms to Havera.

Havera locked her arm around his. "It would be my pleasure, Zax of the famous Zax and Jak duo." Havera and Zax walked arm-in-arm towards the theater room, leaving Adam standing there stunned.

"Sam has the right idea. I must make more asks," Adam muttered to himself as he hurried to catch up with them.

***

The Maid of Gla-Mor was an epic retelling of the famous Battle of Gla-Mor, the decisive engagement from the Great Galactic War over a thousand years ago. Adam was familiar with the tale. It was considered legendary within the ranks of the Bokori fleet, mostly by the Humans. The Bokori did their best to forget. Adam couldn't blame them.

Queen Havera IV "The Warrior Queen" and five-thousand centurion knights of the Paladins of Paleria held off a million Bokori and Zokyon soldiers and sailors of the Eastern Entente with only a small terrestrial shield, three artillery cannons, and the courage to die so that others may live. Gla-Mor was a planet on the eastern fringes of Naddine space. Near the end of the Great Galactic War, it was last stronghold between the Eastern Entente and Terras-Ku, the Naddine homeworld. Havera and her Paladins were a rearguard to allow the Naddine civilians of Gla-Mor a chance to escape the incoming onslaught. They were to buy time to allow the Western Coalition fleet a chance to reinforce and counterattack. They were successful but at a great cost.

"Dead to the last Cauduun," Zax explained. The bard had not shut up for more than a minute, even after the sequencer started. "Jak's father says they're descended from the evacuees of Gla-Mor. It's humbling to think our lives could've been so different had Havera IV and her Paladins not held off Mahlak the Righteous and his hordes. Are you planning something so dramatic to leave your mark on the galaxy, Your Grace?" Zax asked Havera teasingly.

"If I do, and if they create cinema about it, please let them not fabricate a truncated love story," Havera said.

"Oh, c'mon, Your Grace. That's the best part! The star-crossed, forbidden romance between a Cauduun queen and a Bokori arkhan. Torn between love and duty, forced to do battle for the heart and soul of the galaxy," Zax said, gasping his approval.

"Bleh! Shelean drivel! There is zero evidence that Havera IV and Mahlak ever met. That's especially the case with Queen Batera I. There's some circumstantial evidence to suggest Batera was Havera's illegitimate daughter, but it's ridiculous to believe Mahlak was the father," Havera said.

"Ah, but there's no evidence to the contrary! I choose to believe the love story version. Much better story," Zax said.

"It's not the true version of history!" Havera insisted.

Zax shrugged. "Who is the Consul of Cloudboard? Nobody wants the historical truth when the fairy tale truth is more alluring and comforting. You're a Praetorian! You understand this better than most. You're probably right that the Battle of Gla-Mor and the events surrounding it didn't occur exactly depicted in cinema. Doesn't matter. The myth is more powerful than the facts. The Cauduun-Naddine special relationship persists to this day because of this myth. Why ruin a good thing?" Zax said rhetorically.

"The only fact I know is I want you both to be quiet! You haven't shut up for one minute, you bendy bard!" Adam said, finally snapping. Havera had taught him how to connect his HUD to the Astral Lens' telescope. The result was the entire night sky became Adam's screen. Adam's eyes couldn't widen enough to soak in all the visual details of this technological marvel. He could see almost every pore on each character. The acoustics of the Astral Lens amplified the experience tenfold. Adam was trying his best to enjoy it, but Havera and Zax had been having those sorts of discussions the entire time.

"My apologies, Adam. I get very enthusiastic about this stuff. The good part is coming up anyway," Zax said.

Adam turned his attention back to the sky screen. Havera IV rode with the Praefect of the Paladins of Paleria guard to meet with Mahlak at the bottom of the steep hill between the two battle lines. Havera and her Paladins had held off the initial Bokori attack on the first three days. Thousands of dead grayskins littered the battlefield all around them. Bokori soldiers were still retrieving their fallen comrades' bodies hours after the fighting had halted aided by their Zokyon allies with their warmechs.

Mahlak sat atop of a moriado, a majestic, gray equine beast that freely roamed Bokor's surface. Mahlak wore an expertly tailored uniform Adam recognized. The Bokori had not updated the naval officer uniform by much in the past thousand years. In fact, if anything, the uniform Mahlak wore was more extravagant than the naval uniforms of today. A dozen polished buttons down the coat and trousers, a pristine iron bowl helmet with equine hair dangling from the tip, and a black scimitar with an ivory inlaid grip at his side. For a Bokori, Adam thought the actor portraying Mahlak was suave and comely. It oozed confidence and charisma that Adam was not used to seeing from a Bokori. Something about the actor Adam found familiar, but he couldn't put his finger on it.

"That was the only Bokori actor in the entire sequencer," Zax explained. "Everyone else was in digital makeup to look like Bokori."

"Probably because most Bokori were too afraid they'd end up in rehab if they agreed to work on 'blasphemous art.'" Adam quipped.

Zax was aghast. "What's blasphemous about this?"

Adam shrugged. "Who is the Consul of Cloudboard?"

"But it's history!"

"Exactly."

By contrast, Havera IV and the Praefect had been beaten to hell. The queen's face was smeared with mud and dried blue and gray blood. Her scarlet and raven hair were a tangled mess. Her crimson skin was full of cuts and abrasions. This was a woman who did not stay back and let her troops do the fighting for her. She was in the thick of it the entire time. Her nameless, helmeted guard's green armor and cloak were littered with scorch marks and impact wounds. The crest on the Paladin's helmet had been burned away.

On the queen's back was the Sword of Aria. It was nothing like Adam was expecting. Cauduun blades were typically short swords, used primarily for stabbing an enemy up close. With the Cauduun's emphasis on tight, muscle-to-muscle formations, they were perfect for using in combination with the bulky, bullet-resistant scutum shields the average Cauduun centurion bore. The Warrior's Kiss was a long sword with a blade shaped like a helix. The palerasteel had faint golden ripples down the length of the sword, and the sword's hilt was affixed with pristine platinum.

Though he had never seen such a bladed weapon, Adam wasn't impressed. Beyond its unique profile, Adam thought the weapon hardly lived up to the idea of a legendary gift passed down from a goddess. The most interesting aspect of the sword, Adam thought, was the bat-like creature on the pommel. Fangs bared with glinting, golden eyes. Even the cross guard was designed to resemble its wings. A vespertia it was called, according to Havera when Zax pestered her about the sword during one of their many interruptions. The Cauduun queen wielded the sword like any other long sword. Nothing seemingly special about it. Havera IV had used this weapon the entire fight, but it was impossible to tell. The blade was in perfect condition. Not a scratch or drop of dried blood on it.

Probably some sort of...oh what did Aaron used to call them? Continuity error? Yeah, that's it. Must be.

Havera IV removed her crested helm. Her face, despite the mud and blood, was a breathtaking example of the nigh impossible chiseled beauty of a Cauduun woman. Adam couldn't help but glance sideways at the present-day Havera. She and the actress portraying Havera IV bore a striking resemblance. Apparently, that was no coincidence.

"How much did the studio pay you for your likeness, Your Grace?" Adam heard Zax whisper to Havera. She didn't respond. "C'mon, Your Grace, Babylonia Straepa looks nothing like you in real life. She's wearing a wig and digital skin. Even her face has been altered to mirror your stunning features. I promise I won't tell," Zax said, patting Havera playfully.

Havera sighed. "They were striving for authenticity, so they wanted to model Havera IV on me since I'm 'the most famous living Havera.' I agreed on the condition they don't advertise that fact. Spent the whole day naked in an AR pod to capture my body's complete likeness. The number of times I wanted to strangle myself with my tail..."

"Shh!" Adam shushed them. "I can't hear what they're saying!"

"Wait! You're using the HUD translation settings?! You should watch sequencers with your HUD translators off. Hear the dialogue in the original language," Zax said.

"How will I understand what they're saying?" Adam asked.

"Turn your subtitle settings on, buddy. Experiencing cinema in the original language enhances the performance!" Zax insisted.

"But I'd be reading instead of watching. Seems counter-intuitive for this sort of entertainment. What's the point of watching a sequencer if I must read, too?" Adam inquired.

Zax shook his head. "Kewea take me! You sound so much like the Naddine. Maybe the Bokori are right to call y'all backward," Zax sniggered.

Adam rolled his eyes and brought his attention back to the sequencer. Havera IV and Mahlak were standing face-to-face. So close, Adam felt they were about to kiss.

Out of nowhere, a hand seized Adam by his jumpsuit and yanked him off his reclined seat in one fluid motion.

"What in Kewea!" Adam started to shout.

He was silenced by the rapid succession of laser rifle fire blasts tearing through the small, enclosed booth. The crackles of the laser bolts striking the thin metal walls popped with each tiny explosion. The heat of their impact blasts sizzled all around Adam's ears. The initial shock of his sudden whiplash followed by the continuous blasts of laser fire wore off. Adam realized it was Havera who had seized him and Zax to the ground. The Zokyon bard was covering his head. He was lying desperately in the fetal position to avoid the shots. Havera kept her hand on him to keep them pinned down while the laser fire zoomed overhead.

Who's shooting at us?!

The laser fire continued for a few more seconds. Adam heard the familiar sound of a laser rifle cutting off power to prevent overheating. Judging by the sounds, there were at least two gunners, probably three. Adam dared not poke his head out to see in case the assailants were seeking an easy target. The three of them laid there still. Zax covered his mouth to prevent any accidental squealing.

"You armed?" Adam whispered to Havera. The Cauduun tapped her platinum bracers. Adam nodded. He didn't bother to ask about Zax. He seemed too preoccupied with checking his lute for bullet holes. A few rapid taps on his HUD and Adam's personal handgun materialized. He hadn't gotten around to buying more ammo yet, so he only had fifteen rounds. If there were really two or three of them, every shot would need to count. The sizzling of the laser impacts on the nearby walls fizzled out. Adam could hear a couple voices talking.

"We get 'em?" asked one guttural male voice.

"Must've. Those walls are too thin to protect against laser blasts," another male voice responded. This voice was more nasally.

"Your combat HUD update, yet?" called out a third voice, more androgynous than the other two.

There was a short pause. The guttural-voiced man responded. "Still showing three active dots twenty feet in front of us."

"Is that your current read or does your HUD need to refresh?" asked the androgynous voice.

Adam wasted no time. He popped up and fired off a couple shots in rapid succession in the direction of the voices. One bullet struck a quadrupedal vaav'Sezerene, who let out a pained yelp. At a quick glance, the other two gunners were a Naddine and a Rinvari. That was all the time he had. The gunners quickly returned fire. Adam ducked down while a hail of laser fire was mere inches over his head. They were fortunate. The position of the gunners and the downward slope into the booth meant the assailants didn't have a good enough angle to hit them where they lay. Adam waited until he heard the sound of laser rifles cutting off. He popped up again, firing a few more rounds. This time he hit nothing. The assailants had taken cover. The vaav'Sezerene was wounded but still in the fight. All three were spread out in decent cover behind some seats and the walls of other booths. His projectile rounds couldn't penetrate even those thin structures. Adam quickly ducked back down just as a several more laser rounds tore through the booth.

Down to nine shots.

"Can you deflect those shots with your bracers?" Adam asked.

Havera demurred. "Maybe if they were firing from the same direction, I could deflect those shots for a few seconds. I've never tried beyond a few suppressed training rifles. My first live fire test was in Arabella," Havera said.

"I don't have enough ammo for a sustained fight. We're trapped and pinned down," Adam said.

"What about your Rimestone weapon?" Havera asked. Adam shook his head violently. Havera sighed. "We need to do something! We can't sit here and hope ConSec heard those shots from miles away. My communications are jammed. Yours, too, I'd imagine." She was right. Adam attempted to send a signal through the emergency frequencies. He had no connection.

"I didn't see any of them holding a jamming device," Adam said.

"They must have more people waiting outside with a jamming beacon. We can't fight them all by ourselves," Havera declared.

"We need to get out of this booth!" Adam said.

"How?" Havera asked exasperated.

"I think I can help with that one." Zax had removed the lute from his back. He was tuning the strings and adjusting a couple dials.

"You going to play them a song and sing them to death?" Adam sneered.

The Zokyo grinned. "Something like that. Cover me, will you."

"I don't get..." Adam said.

Zax cut him off. "Trust me! Just cover me for but an instant." The Zokyo crawled towards the edge of the booth until he was right next to the doorway.

Adam let out a deep sigh. He waited until he heard the gunners' laser weapons recharging. He raised his gun, firing off two more shots in the direction of the Rinvari, who seemed to be the group leader. The gunners ducked behind their cover.

In one swift motion, Zax scrambled to his feet. His raised his upper right arm high and strummed the chords on his lute in one windmill motion. A sound wave shot out from the electric blue lute, careening towards the assailants. The visible shockwave blew apart their flimsy cover, sending two of the assailants' bodies crashing into the back wall with a massive thud and splat. A soft buzzing from the shockwave blast fizzled the back of Adam's ears. The visual effect reminded Adam of shots from a concussion rifle but on a much grander scale. The blast from Zax's lute demolished all metal, plastic, and padded surfaces within a thirty-foot cone range. The Rinvari steeled herself from the sudden loss of her compatriots. She tried raising her rifle until Adam leapt up and put a bullet between her eyes, killing her instantly.

Zax twirled the lute in his hands. Tossing it into the air, the Zokyo caught it and placed in the holder on his back. It was then Adam realized the lute had glowing, silver and bronze ley lines and geometric shapes covering its exterior. The markings were beginning to fade, slowly disappearing over time. Adam helped Havera to her feet. Together they surveyed the destruction. Two of the vaav'Sezerene's legs were torn completely from his body, and the back of Naddine's head was crushed. Its eyestalks twitched for several seconds before falling limp.

Adam and Havera stood there, mouths agape. Zax licked his fingers to wipe a smudge off his mechsuit.

"Still think I'm a bendy bard, eh, buddy?" Zax said through barely contained self-satisfaction.

"Where'd you get that instrument? I've never seen a concussion blast of that magnitude come from a device smaller than a gunship," Havera asked.

"Custom-made. Jak helped me build it. Come to think of it, where is that sullen sot?" Zax wondered aloud.

Their momentary respite was cut short by more laser blasts whizzing by their heads. Adam hit the ground, propping up the body of the dead Naddine for cover. Havera hid behind some wreckage from Zax's concussion blast. Zax tried ducking for cover back into the booth but was too slow. A stray shot struck the side of his upper left arm. The Zokyo cried out in pain, clutching his arm. Adam spotted the Naddine's rifle only a few feet away. He scooped it up and returned fire recklessly in the direction of the new threat. Havera, motivated by Zax's cries of pain, hustled over to the fallen Zokyo, deflecting a couple laser blasts away with her glowing bracers. Adam covered her with a spray of laser rifle fire. Once she was clear, Adam laid down more suppressing fire and rushed to join the pair. The wound didn't appear to be too serious. Havera was applying some sanagel to Zax's arm. Zax winced on contact with the gel.

"It's a simple graze wound, you'll be fine. I think your suit is breached. I can't close the section off," Havera said. She was pushing down on the open section of Zax's tight mechsuit.

"I have a few field repair kits in my inventory. Just need a few minutes of peace to use one. A little help would be nice!" Zax shouted at Adam.

Adam fired off a few more shots. "Working on it! There's four or five of them this time. Must be the backup crew from outside after they heard your little demo. Can you perform an encore?"

"The lute needs time to recharge," Zax said.

"How much time?" Havera asked.

Zax shook his head. "Too much time."

"Perfect! Didn't think I would be meeting Kewea today," Adam said.

"Don't be so melodramatic. You escaped a prison, blockade, and a full-scale assault on your home. A few thugs won't be the end of us," Havera said.

"Havera, *Your Grace*, clearly you don't understand that's exactly the kind of bad luck I have!" Adam shouted, firing off a few more rounds towards the oncoming gunners. Two of them were making moves to flank them. "We can't stay here!"

"Where do you propose we go?" Zax shouted.

"Anywhere but he...AHHHHH!" Adam was overcome by a deafening ringing in his ears. A sudden massive headache manifested. His HUD glitched out for a few seconds. Havera and Zax must've been experiencing the same sensation, for all three were grasping at their heads. "What is that?" Adam shouted.

Several more shots rang out along with a few cries of pain. Even in his distressed state, Adam could tell those shots were distinct from the previous laser fire. High-pitched sounds more akin to whistling followed by a brief but notable boom. Adam hadn't heard those sounds in many years, but they were unmistakable.

Plasma rounds. Who's using a plasma weapon?

A minute later the pain in Adam's head dissipated, and his HUD was fully functioning again. The sound of laser fire had stopped. Adam poked his head up. Laying where Adam had spotted them last were the bodies of the gunners. Smoking wounds emanated from the occasional spike stuck in their bodies. The telltale signs of plasma weaponry. Standing in the doorway leading to the foyer, his black and white cape billowing from the outside air, was Jak. He was holding was appeared to be a long plasma rifle. A set of ley lines formed in geometric patterned shapes were fading in front of the Naddine. They were very much in the style of the lines and shapes Adam saw on Zax's lute. Jak calmly sauntered over to the three of them. Zax had materialized a field repair kit and was fixing the damaged section of his mechsuit.

"I never liked the cinema," Jak said dryly. "You alright, maestro?" Jak asked Zax.

"Like sweet jam on a Techoxtl's tits," Zax said, smirking.

Jak let out a heavy sigh. "You never take anything seriously, do you, maestro?"

"Oh, trust me, Jak, you're serious enough for ten of us," Zax said, rising to his feet.

Jak shook his head. "We should get out of here. There's bound to be more of 'em," Jak said. Zax followed Jak towards the exit with Adam and Havera, stepping over a couple bodies in the process.

"What was that technique you used on us?" Adam asked.

"I call it HUD stun. Learned it at the D'hty Academy on M'thr. The glyphs I generate create a sort of digital-electronic field that disables any sentient's HUD within a certain radius for a short amount of time. Meant to be used a diversionary or escape tactic. Made a few modifications myself over the years. The splitting headache you felt was my little addition," Jak said.

"I didn't realize there were any Naddine G'ee'ks," Havera said.

"Jak here is the only one. First, and so far only, Naddine to graduate from the D'hty Academy," Zax said, patting Jak on the back. The Naddine only grunted.

"G'ee'ks. They're the Zokyon special forces, correct?" Adam asked. He had heard of the G'ee'ks during his time in the military but knew little about them.

"Not exactly. They're societal special operations. Not strictly military. They go anywhere and everywhere in Zokyon space where their technological services are needed. You only call a G'ee'k when you have a holy-Cradite-lots-of-people-might-die sort of problem," Zax explained.

"Less time talking, more time walking. Let's disable their jamming device, so we can call in ConSec. We can talk about background exposition later," Jak said.

Adam and Jak went ahead into the foyer, checking their corners while entering the main room. The concierge was dead, a single gunshot wound to the chest. Outside was Havera's aircar resting where they left it. Not too far away was a small nondescript cargo vessel used in industrial sectors. Zax and Jak's winged white beast was napping nearby.

"See anything, J'y'll?" Jak whispered to seemingly no one in particular. Jak's rifle beeped a couple times, almost causing Adam to jump in surprise. "We're clear. Return to normal, J'y'll," Jak said. He let go of his rifle. The weapon reconfigured itself in midair into a two-foot tall quadrupedal. The autonomous mech landed on the ground with a soft thud. The construct had a long, narrow snout with a row of razor-sharp metal teeth sticking out from its closed mouth. The black steel figure beeped a few more times in Jak's direction.

"Aw! That's an adorable bot you have there, Jak!" Havera said, patting the mechanical creature on the head. J'y'll beeped and purred at the Cauduun's touch.

"She's not adorable, and she's not a bot. She's an autonomous, semi-intelligent, multi-purpose construct designed and built by me to aid in my important work. Her name is J'y'll," Jak said, miffed by Havera's apparent slight.

"Ignore him, J'y'll. You are adorable," Zax said, rubbing the top of the construct's V-shaped snout. The construct tilted its head and beeped a few more times. Adam could've sworn the beeps sounded cheerful. J'y'll's short tail was noticeably wagging.

Jak approached the cargo vessel. J'y'll beeped a few short bursts. "This must be theirs. My HUD detects no signs of life. J'y'll says there's a strong digital signal coming from inside," Jak said. Adam reached for the handle of the side door. It was locked. "Move aside," said Jak. Adam stepped back. The Naddine twirled his wrist in the air and snapped his fingers. A small circular glyph emerged at Jak's fingertips. With a flick of the wrist, Jak sent the glyph towards the door lock. The glyph collided with the door, dissipating on contact. Adam heard a loud click. Jax reached for the door handle and yanked the door open.

"Neat trick. Another G'ee'k skill?" Adam asked.

"Something like that. This is it," Jak said, pointing to a small, warbling device in the middle of the cargo space.

"Have another cool technique to disable the jammer?" Adam asked.

Jak curved an eye stalk at him. Adam detected faint hints of scarring on the closest eye stalk. "J'y'll, plasma rifle," Jak said with the forcefulness of an order.

The metal construct leapt up into Jak's arms, reconfiguring back into the long plasma rifle Jak had used earlier. Close up, the Naddine had similar scarring on his hands and arms. Looking him up and down, Adam saw other signs of scarring. He also realized Jak had shortened claws. Even retracted, Adam could tell they were shorter than other Naddine he had encountered. Jak aimed and fired one shot into the device. The bolt pierced the side of the jammer. A half-second later, the device exploded into a hundred pieces. Adam instinctively shielded his eyes, but the explosion radius was too small to do him any harm. Jak stood there with J'y'll in hand.

"I don't follow the rule of cool," was all the Naddine said.

Jak dropped J'y'll, who had reconfigured back into her quadrupedal form to walk alongside the Naddine. Jak walked back to join Havera and Zax checking in with their driver to see if he was okay.

What's your story, Jak of the famous Zax and Jak duo?

23

Patron-Saint

ConSec arrived minutes later and sealed off the crime scene. They took statements from all involved. The crime scene crew was able to positively identify all the assailants in the attack.

"Most of 'em seem to be small time thugs and hoods. Petty theft, simple assaults, those sorts of offenses. All the weapons are untraceable, probably printed in an unregistered shop. The Rinvari woman is a different story. Face and DNA scans identify her as Jegasa. Wanted in connection to a double homicide five months ago at a dark matter refinery in eastern Neutral Space. Local detectives believe it was a contract killing. One of the deceased had known ties to the Excommunicated. Jegasa is...was suspected of carrying out the hit on orders from Fenix," the Cauduun ConSec detective explained.

"Ignatia's second-in-command?" Havera inquired.

"Yes, Your Grace, the very same. ConSec coordinated information with the local PD at the time. Seems like it was part of Excom's ongoing campaign to maintain a tighter grip on the unregistered dark matter and Celeste trade," the detective said.

"Any theories on why they'd attack me? Is it because I'm getting close?!" Havera said. The excitement in her voice was hard to miss.

The detective shook his head. His eyes flickered on Adam for a brief instant. It did not go unnoticed.

"You think they were after me?" Adam concluded.

"That is our working theory, yes. There's been an increase chatter in Excom activity since the Human...issue has flared up. Not just here. All over the galaxy. ConSec and other law enforcement agencies agree that the increased attention drawn to the Human question is leading to increased heat on Excom. If the Human problem goes away, so does any residual attention on Excom," the detective said.

"You came to that conclusion awfully quick, detective. It's almost like many people wish we would just go away," Adam said, folding his arms.

The detective let out an awkward cough. Ignoring Adam's implication, he readdressed Havera. "Your Grace, while you're on this assignment, I suggest you and the Human find a new place to lie low. Be discreet. Some place that won't attract attention."

"You can come stay with us!" Zax blurted from out of nowhere.

"Excuse me?" said Jak right behind him.

"What?" said Adam.

"I beg your pardon?" said the detective.

"Jak and I maintain a dwelling here on station. It's spacious and luxurious. Plenty of room for multiple guests to stay comfortably for a while. We have a full performance studio we can play around in!" Zax said excitedly.

"You must stop volunteering us for everything, Zxxm'i'Zxxd," Jak said, putting a hand on Zax's shoulder.

"Stop that! Never use my full formal name, Jak-Non of the Arkads. You've no sense of intrigue or opportunity, bro! Besides, you hate tours. You'd rather tinker with your gadgets or play with your construct in between G'ee'k assignments," Zax said.

"You have no sense of duty and obligation, maestro. We're supposed to be on Tessala in three days to start the Cauduun leg of the Saptia Accords Tour. We can't drop everything and cancel our performances for this! Remember the last time we did something like that?" Jak asked through grit teeth.

"Oh, quit bringing up Sorma! I had never seen the inside of a platinum mine. If I recall, you and the foreman's daughter had a great night," Zax said, patting the Naddine.

Jak's eye stalks rolled up tightly towards his head. "I don't believe getting trapped in a collapsed shaft for twelve hours with you and one of your Cauduun groupies, who had suffered a crushed tail, while her father waited outside to strangle me qualifies as a 'great night,'" Jak said.

"Hot damn, sweet jam. Quit being dramatic. Better than that incident with the alleged Fect you almost absconded away with from that shady scrapper. We learned a valuable lesson. Lute playing and unstable mine shafts don't mix well," Zax said with a wide grin.

"Ahem!" the Cauduun detective butted in. "If y'all are done bickering, we have more pressing matters to address..."

"Detective! Detective!" A winded Zokyon ConSec officer ran towards them, flailing her four arms frantically.

"What is it, officer?" the Cauduun detective asked.

"We've reports of a disturbance in the Cauduun Cultural District. Multiple shots fired. No word on any injuries or fatalities. Coms in the area seem to be down," the Zokyon officer said.

"Where?" the Cauduun detective asked.

"Dasenor's Spire. Near the top floor," the Zokyon officer responded. That was Havera's building.

"Sam!" Adam and Havera screamed out together.

"Seal off the area. I want full tactical response teams deployed there immediately!" the detective said.

"We've got to get there!" Adam said. He was panicking.

This is Aaron all over again.

"I'd advise you stay clear. All of you. Let ConSec handle this," the detective insisted.

Havera was having none of it. "Try and stop us, Detective!"

Zax put a hand on Havera's shoulder. "We'll take you there on Sel-

Ena. She's faster than your pompous luxury aircars or the second-rate vehicles ConSec has," Zax said. He exchanged a quick glance with Jak.

The Naddine rolled his eye stalks again this time more softly. "Fine. Jes-Mur curse me. Let's go!"

The four of them turned heel and sprinted towards Zax and Jak's resting giant bird, ignoring the protestations of the Cauduun ConSec detective.

Sel-Ena perked her head up, squawking at their approach. She had a saddle on her back barely big enough to hold them all. Zax hopped in front to take the reins. Havera, Jak, and Adam all piled in behind him.

Adam struggled to find balance on the cramped saddle. He was skeptical at the bird's abilities. "No offense, bard, but how exactly is this beast faster than an aircar?" Adam yelled in Zax's direction.

"I was hoping you'd ask," Zax yelled back. The Zokyo raised his upper right arm to tap in the air. Pressing something on his invisible HUD, the bird lurched underneath them. From beneath the saddle, silvery metal began encasing the giant white bird. The metal unfurled like a ship's viewport, clacking with each inch until every part of Sel-Ena's body was covered in solid, metallic armor. Adam reached down and tapped the armor with his knuckle. It was solid steel. "Palerasteel armor. Only had this upgrade on Sel-Ena a few months. C'mon, girl, let's ride!" yelled Zax.

The armored bird extended her wings and let out an ear-splitting, amplified squawk. With a flap of her massive wings, Sel-Ena took flight. Adam wrapped his arms around Jak tightly. The Naddine grunted his displeasure.

Once they were clear of the Astral Lens and facing the direction of the Cauduun Cultural District, Adam heard Zax shouting directions. "Hold on tight! We're about to go supersonic," Zax yelled.

"We're about to what?!" Adam yelled.

Zax bent over, placing all four hands into slots in Sel-Ena's armor. A small glass shield covered the riders. Adam noticed over his shoulder what appeared to be rocket boosters emerging on Sel-Ena's back. With a click of Zax's heels, the rocket boosters ignited in a fiery discharge, and the bird soared at near impossible speeds towards the Cauduun Cultural District. The g-force from the sudden burst of speed nearly caused Adam to pass out. The sonic booms created by their speed boost kept him conscious. The glass shield kept the wind out of their face. Several aircars in the vicinity had to zigzag out of the way to avoid the oncoming rush of an armored bird. A few of the drivers screamed inaudibly at them. Adam squeezed Jak tighter, bending over to avoid their gazes. He felt a sharp punch in his rib cage. Realizing it was Jak trying to get him to stop squeezing so tightly, Adam relaxed his arms. The boosters extinguished and retracted into the armor. The glass shield receded back into the saddle. Adam realized Zax was gliding Sel-Ena at high speeds with minimal effort on the bird's part.

"I've never seen a beast from Terras-Ku used this way!" Havera shouted.

"I can't exactly bond with them the way the Naddine do. This is the next best method. Zokyon tech mixed with Naddine beasts produce formidable results," Zax yelled.

"It's a shame more Naddine don't do this," Havera shouted back.

"There's much the Naddine and the Zokyo do that is shameful. The real shame is they will never realize it," Jak muttered quietly enough so only Adam heard him clearly.

"What was that, bro?" Zax yelled.

Jak didn't reply. The wind whipping in their faces deafened them and stung their cheeks. Holding one hand out in front, Adam glanced over the side. They were thousands of feet in the air. Great heights never bothered him. Not after a thousand jumps. Adam hadn't had a chance to fully get his bearings inside the station, so he wasn't quite sure where they were. He could see the lights of the Entertainment District far off in the distance. Zax had steered Sel-Ena on a path away from the main air lanes. Below them, Adam saw they were flying over enormous flower buds that covered the surface over hundreds of square miles. The petals were covering lengthy organic structures. Adam could barely make out anything through the petals and the slithering vines of the natural canopy.

"Are we over the Rorae Cultural District?" Adam asked aloud.

"Yeah, why?" replied Jak.

"Nothing," Adam lied. His thoughts pivoted to the Rorae woman.

I wonder if she's down there. I've never seen Rorae technology up-close. One hundred percent organically grown infrastructure. How is such a feat possible?

He slapped himself to regain focus. In all the excitement, he had nearly forgotten where they were going and why. Several more miles of gliding over flower buds and skirting the edge of the Moan seas, they had arrived in the Cauduun Cultural District. The sparkle and sheen of the colorful buildings shone even through the darkness. Adam rubbed his eyes to adjust to the saturated, bright colors of Cauduun architecture. Approaching Dasenor's Spire, a row of ConSec aircars were attempting to create a perimeter around the obelisk-shaped building. With a flap of her wings, Sel-Ena blew right past them, bee-lining right to Havera's landing pad. Adam attempted to activate combat mode on his HUD. His personal info appeared where it should, except the minimap with sentient detection was knocked out. Quickly checking, he had no communications either.

They must have another jamming device.

"I'm not getting anything on combat sensors. There's another jamming device nearby," Adam bellowed out.

"Might be in one of those transports. Look!" Zax called out, pointing to a pair of vehicles parked on Havera's landing pad. "There's no room to land!" Zax yelled. He pulled the bird up. Perfect timing. A hail of gunfire burst from the landing pad. Most of the laser shots missed. A couple bounced off Sel-Ena's armor with little effect. The Palerasteel could easily absorb small arms laser fire. Adam could barely make out the silhouettes of a handful of hostiles taking cover behind the vehicles. More flashes of laser fire were flying into Havera's apartment with no apparent sign of return fire.

Sam must still be alive. They wouldn't keep firing otherwise.

Adam tapped on his weapons menu and materialized the laser rifle he had stored in his inventory from the previous fight. "Zax, fly us up high over the landing pad. I'm dropping in," Adam said.

"Are you sure?" Zax said hesitantly.

"I'm going to drop right on top of them. They'll never expect it. I'll clear the landing pad for y'all," Adam said.

"Adam, that's suicide!" Havera yelled.

"I've jumped into worse. Ask me about jumping into a pile of trash three miles high on Littering Wastes sometime," Adam said as he checked the heat sink of the laser rifle.

"I'll cover you, Adam. J'y'll, mounted laser turret!" Jak said.

J'y'll beeped enthusiastically. The construct leaped off Jak's shoulder reconfigured in midair into the form of an automatic mounted gun. J'y'll attached herself to the side of Sel-Ena's saddle. Jak flipped a switch on the construct. Adam heard the familiar sound of a laser weapon charging.

Adam nodded at Jak. He checked the boosters on his boots. They were fully functional. Zax brought Sel-Ena around for another pass. The hostiles on the ground attempted to shoot up, but their aim was poor against such a fast creature. Adam swung his leg to the side of the bird, preparing to jump.

He felt a tug on his arm. It was Havera. The wind fluttered Havera's three ponytails behind her. In that moment, her face conveyed a look of command. However, her amethyst eyes betrayed her concern.

"Don't miss. Please," Havera said, letting go of Adam.

Adam smiled. "For Sam."

He fell backwards, letting gravity take a hold. A rush of cold air whipped his back, sending his hood fluttering over his head. He spun in the air to face the ground. He righted himself to be falling in a standing position, aiming his rifle downwards. Between his deep violet jacket and verdant jumpsuit, Adam was nigh impossible to spot in the darkness. He had no combat armor or helmet. He had to judge the distance with his eyes. Fortunately, the illumination of Havera's building allowed for easy judgment of height distance. He set his boots to activate on click rather than HUD touch to allow for aiming while falling. The two enemy transport vessels cluttered the entire small landing pad. Adam picked a spot near the edge. Red laser blasts zinged past him. A few of the hostiles were taking shots at him.

They can see me. Kewea take them! Must have night vision in their HUDs.

Adam had lost HUD access to night vision after leaving the Bokori military. They were an expensive upgrade, and up until that point, he had no need for it. If these were Excom, they had deeper pockets than Adam. He was still several hundred feet from hitting the pad. Adam had returned fire with a few shots. He decided to conserve the heat sink. With that basic defense rifle, the chances he'd hit anything would be little. The enemy shots were getting closer, with one blast singeing the flap of his jacket.

Bursts of laser rifle hit the landing pad, sending a few hostile silhouettes for cover. Without having to look up, Adam knew it must've been Jak and J'y'll. Adam could hear the rush of air from the armored bird passing him overhead. Jak continued to lay down cover fire, allowing Adam an opening.

The landing pad rushed up to meet him. At the last possible moment, he tapped his boots, igniting the orange flames of his boosters to slow his descent. He had cut it a bit too close. The sudden stoppage caused a bit of whiplash. Nothing too severe, but his tuck and roll into cover wasn't graceful. He hit the side of one of the transport vehicles with a crunch. An over eager Naddine thug rushed around the corner alone to try and finish Adam off. He was met with three quick shots to the chest. The Excom's momentum sent his body hurtling over the side of the pad to splat onto the surface a thousand feet below.

Adam stopped to catch his breath. He glanced up to see Sel-Ena coming around for another pass. He peeked over the side of the transport. He spotted at least four hostiles hiding behind another transport. They were shooting wildly into Havera's apartment. A bit of debris was nested between him and them. Adam realized the second transport vessel had been disabled violently. Pieces of wreckage were scattered about, and a small fire was burning inside the vehicle.

He perked his ears up to listen. At first, he only heard the Excom's small arms fire. Then, he heard a boom followed by a crunching thud and the exclamations of a couple of the Excoms. Adam peeked again. He heard another boom, but this time he saw the wrecked vehicle the Excoms were behind bounce sideways from an impact, knocking the Excoms askew from their hiding place. One of the Excoms was thrown so violently he was launched over the side of the landing pad, plummeting to his death. Adam recognized the boom sound.

Concussion weapon. A powerful one at that. Capable of rocking a heavy transport vehicle from several yards away. When did Sam obtain a concussion weapon?

Jak hit their position hard with another spray of laser turret fire. Adam heard one take a hit. He used the opportunity to leap forward around his hiding spot and rush to a position closer to the Excoms.

"Kewea take them, I'm hit!" exclaimed the wounded Excom. Another Naddine.

"Shut it. It's barely a flesh wound, you'll be fine. Damn that Guerrilla! This was supposed to be an easy job. And where did the rest of 'em come from? We're taking too much heat!" yelled a Cauduun Excom.

Guerrilla. Does he mean Sam?

"Right here, you Excom scum!" bellowed a booming voice. A tall, muscular Moan emerged from around their hiding spot. Adam had just enough time to notice the heavy rifle the Moan was holding right before the Cauduun's head exploded in a sonic boom. The Moan turned his attention to the wounded Naddine on the ground. The Moan raised his massive rifle. Adam heard a loud whizzing sound emanating from the Moan's rifle. The sound made Adam's teeth grind.

"GAHHHH! No, no, no. Please, stop! Don't!" screamed the wounded Naddine.

"No mercy for Excoms," said the Moan, driving his weapon into the Naddine. The Excom shrieked from excruciating pain. The sound of screams and steel grinding up flesh filled the chilly night air. Realizing what he was seeing, Adam nearly retched. The Moan's rifle was carving a bloody path through the Naddine's body. Adam winced at the whizzing sound mixed with the crunching, wet grinding noise.

The Naddine's screams ceased. The Moan withdrew his rifle from the body of the dead Excom. The whizzing sound had subsided. In the natural light of the night sky, Adam recognized the Moan by his glistening broad chest with an icy scar down the front.

"Marduk Tiamat, is that you?" Adam asked aloud from behind cover.

The Moan raised his rifle in Adam's direction. Adam put his hand up to signal his intent. Marduk squinted his rounded navy eyes at Adam. Other than his tight seaweed pants, Adam realized the Moan was completely naked from the waist up.

"Adam Mortis! I was wondering who dropped in. Was that you with the automatic laser fire?" Marduk asked.

"No, it was them," Adam said, pointing upward at Sel-Ena circling the sky.

Marduk gazed upward. Adam thought the muscular Moan was an impressive specimen. His robust, conical snout and thick claws along with the scar gave him a fierce visage, yet there was something oddly genial about the Moan in the moons' light.

"Is that an armored Naddine warbeast? Don't see something like that too often these days," Marduk said.

"Marduk, what are you doing here? Where is Samus? What in Kewea is that contraption you're holding? And why are you topless?" Adam rapid fired those questions.

Marduk chose to answer the third question. He held his rifle aloft. "Modified AGAD-1998 Concussion Rifle. Improved her myself. I call her the 'Drillhead.' Patent pending," Marduk said.

Adam understood why. Nearly matching the width of Adam's body, Drillhead was the biggest rifle Adam had ever seen. Everything from its stock, grips, sight, and pressure pad resembled that of an ordinary concussion rifle, scaled up to match someone of Marduk's size. The biggest difference was at the end of the barrel. Surrounding the disk used to discharge the lethal shockwave were three rotary blades in a triangular pattern with razor-sharp, metal teeth on the exterior of each blade. The blades were completely drenched in blood and gore.

"Palerasteel blades. Never rusts, never dulls, never fails to carve up sentient or machine. Squeeze this secondary trigger on the fore-grip, and you're ready to slice and dice your opponent. Got to keep her clean after each fight," Marduk said.

"Charming," Adam said. "You didn't answer my other questions. Why are you here, where is Samus, and why are you nearly naked?"

"Relax, Human, your friend is inside. She's safe. I brought her a gift. She visited my shop earlier today. I told her the item I was working on was finished, and she wanted to see it right away. It's a prototype weapon I've designed," Marduk said.

Translucent movement dashed behind Marduk. Adam caught sight of the figure for a brief instant.

"Behind you!" Adam bellowed. Marduk spun to face the new threat. Steel flashed. Marduk stumbled backwards, a spray of crimson hitting the deck of the landing pad nearby. Adam fired in the direction of the movement. He caught a glimpse of the green, scaly creature until its form shimmered and vanished.

"It's a Faeleon. He's camouflaging!" Adam called out.

Marduk regained his footing, firing a few reckless concussion blasts into the night air. A few nearby windows shattered from the impact. "Kewea take those chameleon bastards. Human, back-to-back! It can't sneak up on us that way," Marduk screamed.

Adam didn't question him. Adam closed the gap with Marduk and turned around, putting his full weight into the Moan's back. The pair held their rifles up, seeking any sign of movement. Adam could hear the Moan breathing heavily.

"How badly are you injured?" Adam asked.

"The cut is deep, but there's a lot to cut through," Marduk chuckled. "I'll be fine. Keep a sharp eye. Faeleon can't go completely invisible, especially if they're wearing anything," Marduk said. The pair pressed their backs to each other tightly. Adam felt just how muscular the tall Moan was. He felt tougher than palerasteel. Wetter, too. Marduk was practically pushing him around with his sturdy back. "Dammit. Looks like the Faeleon Excom stripped. There's a pile of street clothes here.

Dropped his gun, too. He's only got a melee weapon and can't stay invisible forever. Amateur mistake," Marduk said, revving the blades on his rifle.

Sel-Ena flew by slowly, allowing Havera and Jak to leap off. Zax retook to the skies to get a better overview. Havera and Jak rushed up to meet them. Jak was holding a rifled J'y'll in his arms while Havera had activated her bracers. The violet glow illuminated much of the nearby area.

Adam held up a hand. "Faeleon! It's naked and camouflaged. We can't see it!" he yelled.

There was another flash of translucent movement. Falling to one knee, Havera yelled out in pain. Her azure blood spilt onto the pad. Havera swiped wildly into the air nearby, striking nothing but air. Adam held his fire. He couldn't risk accidentally hitting Jak or Havera. Jak rushed to her side.

"Not a deep cut. Your tail's going to be sore," Adam heard Jak tell Havera.

"My combat mini-map is fuzzy. I can't get a lock on him," Marduk said.

"They have a jamming device. It prevents anyone within range from communicating over coms, and it knocks out combat mode mini-maps. Jak, there must be another device in that transport over there. You and Havera see if you can't take it out. Look out for any sign of rippling in the air," Adam said.

Jak nodded. He helped Havera to her feet. The pair mimicked Adam and Marduk, walking back-to-back towards the other transport vehicle.

"Let's move closer to the building, away from any impediments," Marduk said. Following Marduk's lead, Adam and the Moan, backs still pressed together, eased themselves around the burning wreckage of the nearby vehicle towards Havera's apartment. The constant whizzing of Marduk's rifle made Adam clench his teeth.

Static sounds filled their ears for a brief instant. On the corner of his HUD, Adam had regained full access to his mini-map. Jak had breached the other transport and destroyed the other jamming device. Adam let his HUD have a moment to refresh. He had previously logged Havera, Samus, and Dee as friendlies, and Havera had granted him map data of her apartment. He hadn't had time to attune to include Jak, Zax, or Marduk. A blue dot and a white dot were on the landing pad: Havera and Jak. Two blue dots within the apartment: Samus and Dee. Zax was too far out of range flying above them. Two white dots where he was standing: Marduk and the Excom.

"He's right on top of us!" Adam screamed. Marduk swung his rifle at the air in front of him, hitting nothing. Adam didn't see any sign of shimmering or rippling. No one was there, but his HUD clearly marked someone else was on their position.

"My HUD shows the same. Give it a few more seconds to refresh. Nothing here but night sky above us and the arm of the landing pad below us," Marduk said.

A thought struck Adam. HUDs have a difficult time with verticality. He leaned around to whisper to Marduk. "Faeleons can stick to surfaces and climb. He's beneath us under the pad!" Adam said in a hushed voice.

Marduk spun around to face him. His eyes opened wide. "Behind you!" he shouted.

Everything happened in slow motion. Adam whipped back around. Green scales flashed, soaring through the sky at him. A long, curved knife in the Faeleon's hand. The Excom had used his spiral tail to launch himself from under the pad into the air. He was coming down for a killing blow. He was too close. Adam couldn't raise his rifle fast enough.

A bright amber pulse collided with the side of the Faeleon's head. The force of the impact knocked him out of the air back towards the landing pad. The naked Faeleon was dead before its body smacked the ground. Its blade went flying over the side, nearly grazing Adam's cheek along the way. Confused, Adam sought out the source of the pulse. Standing in the doorway, holding a longbow, was Samus. A glint was in her eye. An expression somewhere between pride and fear. She was encumbered by an oversized seaweed coat.

"Woah! You weren't kidding. What a precision shot! Uh, easy there, little guppy. We're still down range. Can you turn the safety on and lower the bow?" Marduk said, approaching Sam with one arm out.

"Oh, right! Sorry. Y'all okay? Wow. This thing packs a punch. What do you call it?" Sam asked, holding out the bow. The three of them converged just outside Havera's apartment. Adam got a closer look at the bow. This also was like no weapon Adam had ever encountered. Certainly, no longbow. Standing up, the bow was almost Sam's height. It had the scope of a sniper rifle just above the grip. Its limbs were curved inward, far more than a typical longbow. It reminded Adam a bit of the crescent moon shape of the Debbie in his pocket. He resisted the urge to reach for it. The exterior was covered in what appeared to be a thin layer of navy platinum. Peculiarly, there didn't seem to be a string or any place to nock an arrow. In the center of the bow, right near Sam's grip, was a platinum guard. Upon further inspection, Sam was wearing a pair of thick, black combat gloves and no quiver in sight.

"She doesn't have a name, yet. Like I told you earlier, she's a prototype. Experimental energy longbow. She didn't burn you or cause you any unexpected recoil?" Marduk asked.

"Nope. She felt great in my hands. Drawing the energy took a couple tries. Perfectly aligned sight. Adam can testify to that," Sam said with a smile.

"Kewea's curse!" they heard Havera shout. The three of them rushed to her, fearful of another attacker. Zax brought Sel-Ena down for a landing. It was a tight squeeze between the two transports. He joined Havera and Jak, who were gathered around the corpse of the Faeleon. Havera pointed at the Excom's head. The scales around its face were almost entirely melted away, exposing parts of its jaw and skull. The wound didn't smoke or sizzle as if from a laser blast nor was there a leftover spike like from a plasma bolt. The heat was instantaneous and overwhelming. The leathery skin around the wound was shriveled and flaking off with each gust of wind in the high altitude. Havera reached down to touch the wound.

"Wait!" yelled Marduk. "Let me check something first," the Moan said. He tapped on his HUD and materialized a small metallic device.

Flipping a switch, the handheld device began clicking in steady, rapid succession. Marduk held the device over the corpse of the Faeleon. As he got closer, there was a slight uptick in the clicking. Holding it right over the wound, the device kept clicking but no faster than it had previously. Marduk held the device over the bow and then on Samus. Again, the clicking noise remained constant. "Yes! It works! No significant radiation leakage! Everything is well within acceptable levels. I'd keep the safety on. Probably best to let the coroner handle the body," Marduk said.

"What is that?" Samus asked, pointing to Marduk's device.

"The Cauduun call it a 'clicker.' Clever name to be sure. It measures the levels of nearby radiation. That's how the longbow works. Transfers ionized energy gathered from within the bow towards a target. That energy contacts a target and explodes with photonic energy, which can...you know what, the science-science stuff nobody really cares about. Except maybe the Zokyo, but, judging by the fact you're the one riding the arkad and not the Naddine, I'm going to guess you two are Exchange kids. The only science you probably care about is chemistry," Marduk said with a laugh.

"Ha ha," Zax laughed sarcastically. "Jak here happens to be a G'ee'k. I'm sure he'd love for you to explain the science to him."

"Respect, Naddine. I've never heard of a Naddine G'ee'k. Cauduun or Moan G'ee'ks sure, but I always thought Naddine prefer to smash technology than use it. Fought beside quite a few of G'ee'ks during the Strife. Best trained technologists I've ever seen. Marduk Tiamat," Marduk said, clasping his webbed claw on the Jak's shoulder.

"Jak," Jak said. He tried to reach the Moan's tall shoulder but settled for putting his hand Marduk's chest. Marduk grinned, clearly amused.

"Ahem!" Zax coughed.

Jak sighed. "I'm Jak of the famous Zax and Jak duo," Jak said, bowing his head in shame. The others joined him in shaking their heads.

"Huh, small galaxy. My niece was just telling me about y'all. She's a big fan. Didn't realize y'all were mercs. Which outfit do you belong to?" Marduk asked.

"We're not, we're just here doing a favor..." Jak started to say when Zax forcibly butt in.

"We're starting a side venture! Independent contractors. Bards, but we solve problems, too. Entertaining while fixing! I'm workshopping a slogan," Zax said.

Marduk laughed. "Good for you. Well, if you ever need guns or armor, Tiamat's Talons will have you covered," Marduk said. He gave the Zokyo an aggressive pat. Zax winced under the weight of the hefty Moan.

Marduk turned to face Adam. "My apologies, I never fully answered your questions. The little guppy here came by my shop this morning," Marduk said, nodding to Sam.

"I was hoping he might be able to sell us weapons or ammo at a discount," Samus said with a shrug. "Oh, here's your coat back, Marduk," Samus said. She struggled to remove the heavy coat. Marduk took it back and swung it back on with little effort.

"The reason I gave Samus my coat was because it has a thin lining of high-density steel polymer that is laser blast resistant. A bit of extra protection when those Excom goons showed up. She needed it more than me. Your puny Human flesh can't withstand a laser blast to the degree our thick Moan hides can. Anyway, I showed her that new prototype bow I was working on when she mentioned she was trained in a long bow. Y'all couldn't afford my prices, but I agreed to let her have the bow, temporarily, for field testing purposes. She declined at first, but she called me a couple hours ago asking if I could bring it over. So, I did," Marduk explained.

"He thought we were having sex," Samus snorted.

"Sam!" Adam exclaimed.

Zax and Marduk burst out laughing. Even Jak couldn't help but crack a smile. The only one not smiling was Havera. She was still staring at the Faeleon's corpse.

"Relax, Adam. Humans aren't my type. No offense, little guppy, you seem to a lovely representation of your female specimen," Marduk said to Samus.

Adam ignored him and walked over to Havera. Her tail was stiff and one of her ponytails had come undone during the flight and fight. She kept her gaze fixed upon the energy wound.

"Havera, you okay?" Adam asked. She ignored him. Adam put a hand on her shoulder. "Havera!"

She recoiled for a moment, a flash of anger across her face. Her anger turned apologetic. "I...I'm sorry. Yes, I'm alright," Havera said. Her gaze returned to the Faeleon.

"I know what you're seeing, long tail." It was Marduk. He had stepped up next to them. "It's Sin isn't it?"

Havera turned away from the Faeleon to nod. "You saw the aftermath, I take it? Bodies melted away beyond recognition. The piles of bones and mutilated floating corpses dragged from the waters. The first responders coming down with a horrifying illness, dying by the hundreds. The eerie glowing haze over the boiling seas is what I remember most. It's forever seared in the back of my mind," Havera said.

Marduk nodded solemnly. "It's a sight no one should witness. I was Guerilla Brigade at the time. The Thalassocracy wanted us to handle cleanup. We did in a manner of speaking," Marduk said.

"Guerilla Brigade? Were you part of the task force that hunted down the Celestials?" Havera asked.

"Yes, ma'am. It's how I got this," Marduk said, gesturing to the icy scar between his chest gills. "Celestial ambushed us. Got the better of me and my mates. Most of my squad was killed, and I was left with this token. Had to leave their bodies to be consumed by the Dark Realm. Fortunately, we had already found most of the remaining Celestials asleep in some kind of stasis. It was almost too easy to destroy them. We killed almost a dozen Celestials that day. Not enough," Marduk said through gritted teeth.

Celestials. I've heard that name.

"You think Pontifex Brunato escaped with more Celestials?" Havera asked.

"I'd bet all the treasures of Yapam *and* Noah on it. There's at least one of them out there, probably more. If anyone's hiding them, it's these Kewea-cursed Excoms!" Marduk said, kicking the Faeleon's corpse.

"How do you know they are Excommunicated?" asked Zax.

"I recognized the Naddine I ground up. His name was Dof-Lun. He defected from the Guerilla Brigade to the Excommunicated a few years back. I keep in contact with the Guerillas from time-to-time since I've gone independent," Marduk said.

"We were attacked by Excommunicated agents at the Astral Lens. They tried to ambush us. Didn't work out so well for them," Adam said.

"Huh. Good work, Human. Seems like they really want you dead. Y'all should come stay at my compound until this blows over. Any enemy of the Excommunicated is a friend of mine," Marduk suggested with a bow.

"We already volunteered our place here on Concordia," Zax said, raising one of his arms.

"Mmm, I don't think so, Zokyo. I'm going to stick my head out of the water and suggest your fancy upscale apartment doesn't have automated defenses and an arsenal capable of waging a small war?" Marduk said.

Zax put his arm down. "No, no we don't."

"Heh, that's what I thought. You're welcome to come, too," Marduk said.

"I suppose one night wouldn't hurt," Jak said, exchanging glances with Zax. J'y'll beeped her approval.

"Heh, cute toy you've got there, Jak. Maybe you could help repair their bot," Marduk said.

"Dee! I almost forgot!" Samus said. She rushed back inside. She emerged seconds later carrying the disabled body of Dee. He had multiple laser blast wounds to the chest and back.

"What happened?!" Havera exclaimed, hurrying to help Samus carry Dee's broken body.

"He saw the vehicles land and went out to greet them, thinking you were with them. They lit him up the second he stepped outside. Blasted the poor bot so hard, he flew back into the apartment. Probably saved our lives though. Gave us enough warning to create makeshift defenses," Marduk said. They all glanced inside Havera's now wrecked apartment. The furniture was overturned, and several appliances destroyed with dozens of scorch marks everywhere. The big back wall screen was unusable.

"I'll take you up on that offer, Marduk, if that is alright. I'm sure my pater won't be happy to hear about this," Havera said.

Marduk bowed. "It would be my pleasure to host the Duchess of Paleria. You longtails are good company."

"What should we do about Dee?" Samus asked. Adam noticed tears were welling in her eyes.

"Hate to break it to you, little guppy. I think that bot is fried," Marduk said.

"Jak could fix him! Couldn't you, Jak? It'll give you a project to work on while we hang out with our new friends," Zax suggested.

Jak facepalmed again and sighed. "Fine. I'll see what I can do. No promises," Jak said. The Naddine took possession of Dee's body, carrying him over to the resting Sel-Ena, who had pushed aside one of the transports to give her wings some room.

"Excellent. I'll call in a buddy of mine to give us an armed escort. ConSec is useless," Marduk said, gesturing to the line of ConSec aircars nearby racing to the scene. "Is there anything y'all want to grab before we head out? Don't want to forget anything essential," Marduk said.

"Oooh! Adam, I almost forgot in all the excitement. A message from John came through right after I called Marduk," Sam said.

"What did he say?" Adam asked.

"It's good news and bad news. He told me that the Bubble only has power left for a day or two. More Bokori saucers are gathering around. He suspects they are waiting for that moment to strike," Sam said.

"Please tell me that's not the good news," Adam said.

"Hush. John said he spoke to Shepard about 'friends out east.' She gave him a name: Patron-Saint," Sam said.

"Patron-Saint?" Adam repeated.

Marduk laughed. "Oh, boy, Human. Patron-Saint, eh? Seems like y'all have powerful friends and enemies. This night just got a whole lot more interesting," Marduk said.

"Who is Patron-Saint?" Adam asked.

"I'll tell y'all on the way over to my compound. If Patron-Saint and the Excommunicated are involved, your conflict has gone galactic," Marduk said.

24

Orbs and Orbital

Adam's heart was fluttering. He took long, deep breaths as they entered the VIP section. Other than a few minor itches, his back scars didn't react hostilely to his familiar, yet foreign surroundings. The security at the entrance had locked down his UI System. He had access to his HUD, coms, and information storage. What he couldn't access were his weapons and inventory. Standard security measure for a gathering of this size. The guards physically searched him and Marduk from head-to-toe. Every crack and every crevice.

But not Havera. The Duchess of Paleria was treated with far greater dignity than the two of them. She was treated as a guest of honor for the Orbital match between the Palerian Centurions and the Sormatian Miners. He let Havera hold onto the Debbie while going through security. She discreetly handed it back to him on the lift ride up to the suites. This was the second time in two days Adam was invited to an exclusive venue. It didn't make him feel important. If the past few days taught him anything, he felt like a pawn in a game of Conclave Conquest. More powerful players were moving him around the board at their leisure. He wondered at what point he'd be sacrificed.

Aaron would've been able to see all the pieces on the board. I don't know what I'm walking into.

"You sure we can trust this guy?" Adam whispered to Marduk.

"Trust? Definitely not. He speaks for Patron-Saint. Anything he says or does is in service to his master. Remember that. Nevertheless, he is your best chance at saving your people."

"I don't like this. Why would an interstellar gangster care about the Human Separatist cause?" Havera wondered aloud.

The thought crossed Adam's mind, too. It seemed all too convenient. Marduk reached out to his connections in the Guerilla Brigade last night. By first crack of sunlight, Adam and Havera personally had received invitations to the Orbital match to speak with a representative of Patron-Saint.

"Dusertheus is a bit eccentric, but he's not stupid. Assume he knows everything for his master certainly will. Patron-Saint will want something from you. A price you probably cannot afford," Marduk said.

"If Shepard speaks true, Patron-Saint has already been helping us. Towards what end, I do not know. Better Patron-Saint than the Excommunicated. Doesn't matter anyway. By tomorrow, Windless Tornado will be a battle ground, and humanity will be without a home...again."

"I really shouldn't be here."

"I'm sorry, Havera. I have no choice. I understand if this will cause you some complications," Adam said.

"I don't care. I just don't look forward to the yelling from my pater and other prominent Conservative voices. Perhaps this will work out in my favor. A Duchess meeting with a crime boss lackey. Would dampen my election chances," Havera said with a half-hearted laugh.

"Patron-Saint is no mere crime boss. She, he, or they are the most influential person or persons in the galaxy. With one message, Patron-Saint can topple governments and collapse markets," Marduk said.

"I take it by your phrasing Patron-Saint's identity is a mystery?"

Marduk nodded. "Nobody knows who she is or if she's one person. I doubt even Dusertheus knows. Hey, maybe Patron-Saint is the Consul of Cloudboard," Marduk said with a laugh.

"The name is 'Patron-Saint' not 'Matron-Saint.' I assume the translation into y'all's tongues makes it clear by the verbiage that Patron-Saint is probably male," Havera suggested.

"Too obvious. I worked for the Guerillas for many years. Anyone who's anyone agrees any public hint about Patron-Saint's true identity is intentionally planted. Patron-Saint is an artist of subterfuge." The lift stopped at their destination. "Word of advice, to both of you, don't let Dusertheus bait you. He'll want to size you up. He knows as much as Patron-Saint allows him to know, which you should assume is everything about you two. Tread carefully."

The lift lead directly to the suite. No sign of guards or bots. No sign of any sort of protection at all. Instead, they were greeted by an alluring alien whose race Adam had never encountered. Busty but lithe, her goldenrod skin was flawless and hairless. Her skull was elongated. Unlike the Bokori, whose elongated skulls were fat and rounded, hers was smaller and more conical, coming to a dull point. She was bipedal and two-armed, with bony protrusions jutting out from the forearms and calves. The digits on her hands and feet numbered six each. Other than the elongated cranium, her face was near Human. The eyes were a bit high and large and lips a bit thin comparatively, with a tiny triangular nose and small rounded ears. She wore a tiny, low cut silver tunic, a tight-fitting, cobalt-colored platinum choker, and nothing else. The emblem on her choker contained some sort of steel bird, most likely an eagle, soaring over a waterfall. To Adam's eyes, she was stunning.

No guards and obvious eye candy to meet us. This Dusertheus is certainly full of himself.

"Greetings, Tenebella Havera of Shele, Marduk Tiamat, and, of course, Adam Mortis. I am Lixyatl, handmaiden of Dusertheus. He is expecting you. Y'all can go right in. The only request I ask is that you do not comment on his tail," the strange alien woman said. She had a musical intonation in her voice that soothed with each syllable. For a brief instant, Adam thought of Falling Star.

"Th...thank you," Adam stuttered. Havera smacked him lightly on the back with her tail. Lixyatl bowed her head, opening the automated door for them. The trio walked by her; the alien never broke her bow.

"I've never met an alien like her," Adam said once the door closed.

"She's Techoxtl. Hardly see them outside of Naddine space," Havera said.

"Really? So, that's what they look like. Wow. The galaxy's other subjugated race."

"They aren't subjugated anymore. Not after Saptia," Havera explained. Her words fell on deaf ears.

"Do they all look like that?" Adam asked.

"Are you talking in terms of biology or attractiveness?"

"Yes."

"You're welcome to have her after our discussion," a voice called out to them. The Techoxtl had distracted him. Adam hadn't taken in his surroundings. The suite, while modest in size, was extravagant. Colorful fur carpets lined the marble floor. Glass chandeliers hung from the ceiling with equally colorful ribbons dangling from the walls through them. The room was soundproof. None of the cheering crowds could be heard through the glass window, revealing the stadium interior with the massive twenty-sided polygonal, glass arena propped up in the center.

It was the first time Adam actually saw the crowd. He knew Samus, Zax, and Jak were out there somewhere, hopefully enjoying themselves. Only Adam, Havera, and Marduk received invitations to this meeting. The others were expressly forbidden from coming. As an olive branch or a power move, the others were provided with complimentary tickets to sit in the crowd surrounding the arena. According to Zax, they were good seats.

Laying down in a padded chaise lounge was a Cauduun male. Vibrant fuchsia skin with matching long, groomed magenta hair, the Cauduun did not rise to greet them. He kept his back to them. Adam understood why Lixyatl asked they not bring up his tail. Through his short, silver tunic and cobalt toga, a stump of a tail stuck out. From its appearance, his tail had not been ripped off but rather deliberately severed. Whether from surgery or something else, Adam couldn't say.

The Cauduun waved them over. The trio walked around the lounge. The Cauduun seemed positively bored by their presence, nibbling on some grapes from a plate on the glass table in front of him. "Hmph, you're skinnier in person, Human. Shorter, too. I do enjoy the silver streak in your hair. A little Cauduun flavor, I dare say," the Cauduun said.

"Are you Dusertheus?" Adam asked.

"No, I'm the Kewea-accursed queen. Yes, you subjugate, I am Dusertheus. Named in part after the pater god himself. Cradite's sake, you make the Naddine seem like tech wizards. Humans are doomed if you're the best y'all have to offer. What Patron-Saint sees in you, I'll never understand," Dusertheus said scornfully.

"Still charming as ever I see, Dusertheus."

"Oh, spare me, Marduk. You may be in Patron-Saint's favor now, but you Moans are too greedy for your own good. Your arrogance will come back to bite you so hard, jades will orgasm from light years away," Dusertheus said. "Why don't you go wait outside. You can amuse yourself with Lixyatl for all I care," he said with a wave.

"Why'd you invite me out here if you were going to send me out of the room right away?"

"To deliberately waste your time. You ought to know what that feeling is like."

"Don't be pissy with me simply because you lost a defense contract on Adaro...ten years ago."

"You promised me that the Doges were going to increase defense spending along the Moan-Zokyo border. I had to give up contracts in Sinner space to fulfill that order. Your bad intel cost me millions!" Dusertheus slammed his fist on his lounge.

"Cry me an ocean planet, Dusertheus. I'd say you're doing fine. Enjoy Patron-Saint's leash," Marduk said with a mocking salute. Dusertheus glared at Marduk. The Moan leaned in to whisper to Adam, "Be careful." Adam nodded. Marduk left the room with a satisfied smirk. Dusertheus gestured for Adam and Havera to lay down on the two lounges on either side of him. Brushing his coat flap aside, Adam removed his boots and laid down in the lounge next to Dusertheus.

"Are you a lefty, Human?"

"Yeah, why?" He had laid down on his right side. His head was right next to Dusertheus' on his own lounge.

"Hmph, bad luck. Kewea was a lefty if the legends be true. Do you know much about Kewea, Human?"

"She's the Cauduun goddess of the underworld and the occasional swear."

"Hmph, you're technically correct, but you say it with such low class and ignorance. Your Human friend was about the same. What was his name? Shroom, vroom? Older fellow, I guess. Had ambitions to be the first Human Cardinal in hundreds of years. Waste of twilight years if you ask me. I'd rather spend my days in bed with a hundred women that look like Lixyatl. Oh, wait, I already do!" Dusertheus said with an exuberant laugh.

"You mean Doom? Commissioner Doom?"

Doom opposed unilateral independence. At least out loud. Was he a silent supporter? I wish I could ask him.

"Yes, Doom, that was his name. Dull man. Not someone you'd want representing you at the Conclave, which means he was perfect for the job. He retire?"

"He died. Shot in the head by the Hisbaween." Adam bowed his head.

"Hmph, probably for the best. Those cultural fanatics don't mess around. What was it? High doses of Celeste multiple times a day. Yellow sun or did they slap you with some red giant? I read the file and became bored after the first page."

Adam shifted in his lounge uncomfortably. Havera mercifully stepped in. "You invited us here. Do you mean to waste our time, too?" Havera asked.

Dusertheus could barely glance in her direction. "You'll get no titles or pomp and ceremony with me, Havera. I don't care who your mater was. Your life is an accident of a lucky seed entering an unlucky egg."

"A point of fact, I'd rather you use my name than any of my titles."

"Oh, ho, really? In that case, I'll use Maid of Carthaga from here on out. Although, from what I've heard, Human, it's only an honorific title in her case," Dusertheus said, nudging Adam on the shoulder with a wink towards Havera. Adam shifted uncomfortably on his couch again.

"You're lucky the other races let a tail-less swine like you in a position of power. How'd you lose it? Lover's quarrel with a bot?" Havera retorted right back.

Dusertheus bit his lip. "Did Lixyatl not explain the rules to you?" he said through gritted teeth.

"She did. I chose to ignore those rules. We were setting protocol aside, were we not?"

Dusertheus stared icy daggers at Havera, with her responding in kind. The two Cauduun refused to break eye contact. Desperate to avoid the tension, Adam reached for a bunch of grapes, accidentally knocking them onto the floor. The Cauduun seemed to not have noticed.

Dusertheus broke first into a wide grin. "Ha! I underestimated you, Maid of Carthaga. I figured you'd have your pater's diplomatic niceties. Perhaps you are your mater's filia after all." Dusertheus picked up the fallen grapes and tossed them against the wall. He turned his attention back to Adam. "Careful with this one, Human. Shelean royalty are all the same. Pretty faces that'll strangle you with their tails if you even think about stepping out of line."

"Your message said Patron-Saint could help the Human Separatist cause," Adam said, attempting to change the subject. Dusertheus seemed to catch the hint.

"Could? Dense Human. Patron-Saint has been assisting your cause for years. How do you think you've been able to avoid grayskin justice for so long? Human spirit and ingenuity? Hmph. Your kind is barely an afterthought in the grand scheme of the galaxy. Until recently, it was easy. Slip a few Links here, drop some vital intel there. I had completely forgotten that you Humans were occupying Bokor's moon until Lixyatl reminded me this morning. Does explain your manner of dress. You look like a miner that won a bet against a sucker who couldn't pay, so they gave you the crappy jacket they stole from a discount knock-off shop."

That was oddly specific.

"I thought you were a Confederate, Dusertheus?" Havera asked.

"Hmph. My dear Maid, why would you think I'd be one of those filthy, backward ore-mongers?" Dusertheus said with scorn.

"You're wearing their colors," Havera said, gesturing to the crowd outside. The match had already started. On the eastern end of the arena were a group of gathered fans, mostly Cauduun but a good mixture of the Sinner races. They were wearing outfits with silver and blue threads. Conversely, on the western end, was a mostly Cauduun and other Proprietor race crowd, including a handful of Bokori to Adam's surprise. They were dressed in greens and purples. Judging by the jerseys worn by each team, the Palerian Centurions were in green and purple while the Sormatian Miners were in silver and blue.

"Not everything is political, Your Maidship. I simply like that color scheme. It matches my lovely locks." Dusertheus swept his hair over his shoulder. "Who are you rooting for, Human?"

"Uhh," Adam stammered.

"Surely you must have a team. You're wearing Orbital jump boots."

"I don't really watch sports. What do you mean I'm wearing Orbital jump boots?"

Dusertheus pointed to Adam's boots on the ground. "Those hideous charcoal things. Kewea's curse, Human, y'all really are dense." Dusertheus tapped the air a couple times. A close up of the match was displayed on one-half of the glass screen in front of them. Dusertheus found what he was seeking and paused. He pointed to a freeze frame of a Palerian Centurion. "Look, Human. You're wearing something similar. An older, run-down version of what those athletes have. I figured you were an enthusiastic fan of the game. Silly me, haha."

Adam picked up his boots and inspected them. *No, that can't be. These are my military boots. John retrieved them from the prison locker upon my escape. They are the exact same. Did the Bokori really give their military Shocktroopers second-hand Orbital gear to wear into combat?!* The Centurions scored a goal, sending the crowd into a cheering frenzy. Havera clapped politely.

"Oh, look, Your Maidship, we're on the big screens. Smile and wave!" Adam dropped his boots on the ground in surprise. On the major screens surrounding the arena were the three of them. Havera smiled slightly and waved to the crowd. Dusertheus sat there, smirking. The camera shifted slightly to put Adam more into focus. His face dampened in a cold sweat. He could feel his face draining of color.

"Wave, Adam," Havera whispered to him.

Adam raised his hand in polite acknowledgment wishing the cameras would go away. He gave a weak smile, trying to avoid embarrassing himself.

"Oh, ho, well look at that. You two have caused quite a stirring. Let me turn the volume on." Dusertheus tapped the air.

The outside sound poured in through the room's built-in speakers. A pair of female announcers' voices trying to call the play-by-play were getting drowned out by cheers, whistles, and boos. The camera remained on Adam. It seemed as if the Miners' section was the source of the cheers while the Centurions' side was doing the majority of the booing. That all changed in a heartbeat when the camera switched back to Havera. The Centurions started cheering while the Miners began booing. A final wide shot of the three of them caused a complete wash. Adam couldn't tell who was cheering or who was booing. Hardly anyone seemed to be paying attention to the game itself.

A loud horn blew to signal the end of the first period. The Centurions were leading 1-0. The players were let out of the floating polygonal arena and were resting on opposite ends until the next period. A fight had broken out between a couple of the opposing players, which was then mirrored by several opposing fans. Stadium security was rushing to break it up. The fighting players were ejected from the remainder of the match. Dusertheus turned the volume off.

"Seems like you both have your own fan section. Nothing for poor old Dusertheus though. What a shame," Dusertheus said, feigning outrage.

"I wish those people would share the same enthusiasm when it counted."

"Keep wishing, Human. You're the flavor of the month. A passing fancy for slacktivists on the Nexus. In half a month, something else will attract the attention of the mob. If you're lucky, you might get a full month."

Adam wanted to retort. He knew the Cauduun was right.

"Can we get to the point, Dusertheus. What does Patron-Saint want with Adam and the Human Separatists?"

"Hmph. No foreplay at all. My, my, no wonder you're unmarried, Your Maidship. No Dasenor-loving man would ever want to brave the underworld for you."

"We had plenty of foreplay. I found it wholly unsatisfying." Havera was stone-faced.

"Such wit, Your Maidship. I bet she's fierce between the sheets. You should take her Human. Sample the galaxies pleasures before you inevitably perish, alone and forgotten."

Havera's tail uncoiled like a snake and struck Dusertheus in the stomach with lightning precision. Dusertheus keeled over in his lounge. He gagged and for a brief moment Adam thought he might puke. Dusertheus flexed his muscles and straightened himself in the lounge. He threw his hair back over his shoulders in a bad attempt to regain dignity. Adam glanced through the glass. It seemed the cameras didn't catch that.

"Don't. Ever. Do that. Again," Dusertheus hissed.

"You ought to know your place, tail-less vir." Havera maintained her stone-faced expression, while using her formal, stern tone.

"Vir, huh? You don't need to remind me what genitalia I carry between my legs, Your Maidship. I was born and raised in Shele. I know exactly where I stand in the Cauduun hierarchy. I'll never become a queen, archduchess, duchess, countess, or even a baroness. I won't even get to marry one. It is my duty to serve. So, here I am. On behalf of Patron-Saint, let me serve." Dusertheus spat each word out with such venom Adam thought he might choke on his own spit.

"Good. Why are we here?" Havera asked.

Dusertheus cleared his throat. "I'm happy you asked, Your Maidship.

A point of fact, your expertise will make this conversation go much quicker. I take it you're well aware of the Orb of Emancipation?"

Havera's eyes widened. Her tense tail stiffened harder. "Yes, of course. What about it?"

"How about you, Human? Are you familiar with the Orb of Emancipation?" Adam shook his head. Dusertheus smiled. "Why don't you explain to your Human friend, Your Maidship, what the Orb is," Dusertheus suggested.

Havera cleared her throat. "It's one of the gifts from the goddesses. The Orb of Emancipation is also called Iinneara's Oculus. According to myth, Iinneara was the one to forge all of the gifts using the Orb of Emancipation to aid her in the creation process. More importantly, it's one of the three components of the Vitriba, the very essence of life."

"You've mentioned the Vitriba before."

Havera looked past him. She wasn't speaking to him but at him. She was lost in her thoughts. "The Vitriba is an ancient force, said to hold the universe together. It's responsible for the creation of stars, dark energy, everything that sustains life in our galaxy. The earliest Cauduun were said to be created in the Vitriba's image. Cradite's image. The symbol of the mater goddess." Havera extended her forearm. The three equal-sized rings pressed together in a triangular pattern with a fourth ring intersecting them all in the middle. Adam had seen this symbol everywhere in the Cauduun Cultural District and in Cardinal Clodius' office.

"I thought they represented the moons of Rema. Saptia and I forget the name of the other two," Adam suggested, tapping his forehead to try and remember.

"Potia and Anio. When the Sheleans became the dominant cultural force on Rema, their symbology was adopted by all Cauduun. They looked to the heavens and saw three celestial bodies. Their symbol became the symbol for the Vitriba."

"What's the fourth ring? The one intersecting them all." He found himself more curious than he had expected. Havera had talked about these gifts, these objects previously.

There's something more going on here.

"That has been the source of much discussion by Cauduun scholars. The Praetorian Censors have many different theories. The earliest Cauduun texts describe it as the 'Link.' No one knows what that means exactly. It's where we derive name of the currency and the great bridge that connects the nations of Paleria and Shele."

"Fascinating stuff I'm sure. You're getting off track, Your Maidship. Let me bring it back around. Patron-Saint has a simple mission for you, Human. Retrieve the Orb of Emancipation. You retrieve the Orb and Patron-Saint will guarantee that you have the tools needed to achieve your independence." Dusertheus sipped his wine.

Havera burst out laughing. "You cannot be serious! Nobody knows if the Orb really exists let alone knows where to find it. You expect him to find something scholars have searched for 2,000 years and came up empty?"

"Including yourself. Am I wrong, Your Maidship?" Dusertheus smirked.

Havera took a deep breath. "Yes, including me. I searched for the Orb and the Everlasting Aegis for more than a decade. I never came close. No one has. No trace of them has ever been found."

"I'm surprised you'd be this skeptical. Yet, you're so certain the others don't exist, despite your mater dying to protect one piece of the Vitriba." Dusertheus broke out into a full-on grin.

Havera's tail recoiled. Adam had been around her long enough to know her temper was about to flare.

"What does he mean?" Adam was attempting to stave off her anger.

"He's talking about the Sword of Aria. It's supposedly one part of the Vitriba. 'The blade with the power to end life.' Don't you dare bring up my mater again!" Havera moved her bracers closer to each other.

"Strike me again, Your Maidship, and Humans are damned forever. Did she not tell you, Human? Ignatia and her conspirators in the Paladins of Paleria attempted to steal the Sword of Aria. Her mater, the great peacemaker Archduchess Pompeia of Shele, died defending it. All Ignatia and her Paladins managed to do was steal the body of

Queen Havera VIII. A poor consolation prize for high treason and assassination, wouldn't you say?"

Havera took several deeper breaths. Her amethyst eyes narrowed. She gritted her teeth. Her tail curled up in position to strike again. She was pulling back to clash her bracers together.

"Havera...Havera." Adam spoke softly. The Cauduun glanced in his direction. He recognized that face. He closed his eyes. He wasn't afraid for his own people. He was afraid for her. He didn't want to see her like this. "Please," he begged meekly.

Dusertheus kept grinning and sipping from his wine glass. Havera closed her eyes. She took one more deep breath. Her posture relaxed and her tail dropped.

"Wise choice, Your Maidship. Don't worry. This mission involves you, too. I only bring up your mater because it seems your old friend Ignatia is hot on the trail of the Orb. Patron-Saint wants to ensure she doesn't get there first. Although, it might be too late."

"What do you mean?" Her pointed ears perked up.

"Almost a month ago, the Rangers reported a missing ship, the Icewalker. It was traversing the Alpha spiral, responding to an unknown distress call. Somewhere near the Borderlands and the Point of Always Return, the ship sent a brief report that they found a derelict Union vessel. Then, all communication abruptly stopped. The Rangers sent a few more ships towards their last known position. They found no trace of the Icewalker or the derelict Union vessel. Without any proof and with official denials from the Yunes, the Rangers wrote off the ship and its three crew members as lost in space. They're now anonymous stars on the walls of the Ranger Guild. However, a few days ago, a Vulpes agent reported sighting a vessel whose markings match those of the Icewalker. It docked on a station with known ties to the Excommunicated," Dusertheus said.

"How do you have a Vulpes report?" Havera asked.

Dusertheus rolled his eyes. "Are you doubting Patron-Saint's ability to intercept a simple message?" Havera said nothing. Dusertheus continued. "The ship stayed on the station for two days. Crewman matching the description of the missing Rangers were spotted exiting the ship. The facility is suspected of being an illegal research & development house for the Excommunicated. Those jammers you encountered yesterday are an advanced prototype, believed to have been developed there. The Vulpes intercepted a non-Union transmission coming from Union territory. While you were fending off Excom attacks, the agent reported that the ship departed for Union space. They couldn't triangulate its origin, but they were able to decipher part of the message. It read, 'CR-2-13-LF...bypass Union fleet...deliver package...Venvuishyn pyramid...retrieve Orb of Emancipation.'"

Adam and Havera sat there for a minute, digesting what they heard. Havera cleared her throat. "Why haven't the Cauduun or ConSec sent their fleets in to destroy the facility?"

"It's in Rorae territory. Those plants won't let any outside force enter their territory without their permission, per the Saptia Accords."

"Why haven't the Rorae taken action against the Excommunicated?"

Dusertheus shrugged. "Who is the Consul of Cloudboard? The transmission attached a map. Patron-Saint believes CR-2-13-LF is a Union designation for a planet, system, or possibly a space station within their territory. Unfortunately, it was encrypted. Not even G'ee'ks on Patron-Saint's payroll have been able to crack it. You'll need to break into that facility and locate the original transmission. Find the map, and you'll find the Orb."

Adam's head was spinning. "I came to Concordia to free my people. Not chase after pirates and mythical objects. Let me get this straight. Patron-Saint wants me to track down a map that might lead to a planet inside Union territory that might lead to a Venvuishyn pyramid that may contain an ancient, probably mythological object that might induce Patron-Saint to help us, which in turn might grant us our independence?" He couldn't believe the words while he was saying them.

Dusertheus chuckled. "Patron-Saint moves in mysterious ways. Even I don't understand what the boss wants at times. I understand your skepticism, as does Patron-Saint. I'm instructed to provide proof of Patron-Saint's gesture of goodwill that she can come through for y'all."

"What proof?"

Dusertheus smiled wryly. "I'm glad you asked." He tapped the air. The glass overlooking the match turned opaque. The lights dimmed. The section of floor with the table between all three of them opened up. The table lowered and rising in its place was this circular contraption. From the ceiling, a suspended looping ring was lowered into place right above the circular base. With another tap to the air, the contraption pivoted towards Adam. He recoiled from the machine, sitting up straight on his lounge. "Relax, Human. It's a digital holographic projector. The latest in quantum communication from Cloudboard. I do believe you have a call. Perhaps you should answer it."

On Adam's HUD, there was a notification for an incoming call. The notification was different than the typical intraplanetary communications to which he was accustomed. His HUD identified the caller not by name but by location: Windless Tornado. Tentatively, Adam pressed the receiver on his HUD. There was a brief flash of light. Materializing from within the digiholo, a sentient form emerged. The form became clearer after a second or two. A Human male with short, cropped jet-black hair. The Human had teardrop-shaped bright brown eyes and was wearing a faded green jumpsuit with a Remembrance patch on his arm.

"John?" Adam asked tentatively.

"Adam? What is lost!" John exclaimed.

"Will be found! John, can you hear me?"

"Yes. Yes, I can hear you! I thought this was an elaborate hoax. I should've known better."

"Since when does Arabella have a digital holographic projector, and how do you have enough power to use it?" Adam swiped at the air through the projection of John. The image was so clear and sharp Adam could barely comprehend John wasn't actually standing in front of him.

"We didn't until a few hours ago. Adam, you won't believe it. The generators were running on fumes, barely keeping the Bubble operational. We were ready for the Bokori onslaught. Suddenly, emerging from the jungle out of nowhere, these armed mercs showed up. At first, we thought they were Hisbaween or the Bokori military. A brief standoff ensued. I was about to order we open fire when one of them approached and showed us their cargo. They brought food and medicine. Also, they brought guns. Lots of guns. Good guns! Functioning laser rifles and handguns with adequate heat sinks. Even plasma rifles and grenades. Plasma weapons, Adam! Most importantly, they brought functioning generators. Enough fuel to power the Bubble for days. The mercs set up this digiholo projector, with a Nexus protocol address and number to call. They told me the exact time to make the call, and here you are! They vanished into the jungle quicker than bouncing bits. This must be your doing, Adam."

Adam glanced up at Dusertheus, who casually sipped his wine glass. "John, did they identify themselves?"

"Not exactly, no. Commissioner Snake recognized their insignia though. Guerrilla Brigade, I believe he said. Some well-known merc band operating throughout the galaxy. One of them said 'you Humans have a Patron-Saint on your side.' Patron-Saint. That's the name I passed to Samus yesterday. You work fast," John said, grinning from ear-to-ear.

"What's the situation? How is everyone holding up?"

"Morale is at an all-time high. Remember those pods the Hisbaween landed on Windless Tornado? Well, we found a way to return to sender, if you will. A strike team used those pods to fly up to one of the Hisba black saucers. We successfully seized the ship, Adam! We're hiding it in the jungle out of sight. In response, the Bokori are accelerating their de-Humanization program. Much of the army and navy are being replaced with bots controlled by the People's House. Too quickly. Hundreds of thousands of Humans with combat experience are suddenly finding themselves without a job or place to go," John said.

"So, they're coming to us?"

"A few stragglers have found their way to Arabella. The Bokori blockade prevents more from joining us here. Most are holing up inside the Sistine Slums or in safe zones outside Inclucity. Some with stolen arms they looted on their way out of the armed forces. The Slums have become a hotbed of civil unrest. Mass protests are underway. Even a few Bokori are joining us. Those magnificent grayskin bastards! The Hisbaween and the regular security forces are trying to clamp down with little success. Adam, you must come back! We have the guns, we have the troops, we only need the spark. You're the key ingredient we need. Word of the assassination attempts against you reached us here. Arabella is at a fever pitch of revolutionary spirit. If they see you return and leading the charge, we could topple the Bokori right now!"

He really means that. Adam had never seen John so excited in years.

"It would be bloody, John. The Hisbaween will fight to the last person. Any bots the Bokori lose, they'll replenish with more bots from the Union or the other Proprietor races. We have no navy. Thousands. Maybe millions would die. Human and Bokori. That's a huge gamble."

John frowned. "We have no choice, Commissioner. The generators those mercs gave us only have about ten days power. We can formulate a plan to deal with the Bokori navy and the bots if you come home. We need you here."

"Are you willing to risk Samus' life on that?"

John exhaled. "She's safer here. The longer you're there, the more likely one of those assassins will get you or her. I cannot risk that. We have a shot. We must take it," John insisted.

Peeking slightly around John's projection, Adam could see Havera shaking her head. Rather than the anger he saw her express earlier, she was concerned. Perhaps it was a flicker of fear and panic in her amethyst eyes.

Adam turned back to John. "What if there was another way?"

John cocked his head. "Are you saying this Patron-Saint can get us more resources to fight?"

"Yes, if we do a job for her. I've been assured what you received is a small sample of the support Patron-Saint will provide us. You must be patient. We shouldn't commit ourselves to crossing the Link this impulsively."

"What's the job?"

Adam side-eyed Dusertheus, who shook his head. "I can't say what it is. Only that it's going to take some time."

"We don't have time!" John shouted. "We need you here, Adam! Not gallivanting all over the galaxy for a bunch of aliens. Oh, yes. Those Guerrillas showed me on their emulator. You're working with potentially the next queen of the Cauduun. I was right about her, wasn't I? She's using you for her own ends. Again!"

"That's not true," Adam insisted. His eyes flickered up to Havera for an instant.

Is it though?

"The only people you can depend on are Humans. As needed as these supplies were, they obviously come with strings attached. What are you giving up? Human sovereignty, hmm? We become subjugates by another name, perhaps? Maybe the other races or this Patron-Saint will think we owe them a debt and take what they want by force. You're risking your life and Samus' life on a flimsy promise of future support. We have what we need to win," John said. Adam lowered his gaze. He couldn't look his old friend in the eye. "Adam...Adam look at me," Adam sheepishly raised his head. "Three years ago, I promised your mother and father I'd bring you home alive. You promised me you'd bring Samus home unharmed. Don't make liars out of both of us. Please, come home. Don't turn your back on your family, on humanity."

I'm not turning my back on humanity. I'm trying to save it. Or perhaps I'm afraid to go back. Afraid to fail.

Adam buried his face in his hands. He couldn't decide what to do. John made great points. He was responsible for more than himself. Samus depended on him. John depended on him. His mother depended on him. Arabella and the future of humanity depended on him. He wanted nothing more than to hide. To find some far away, distant settlement and disappear forever. This was too much. He let his silence decide for him.

John stood up straight. "We'll wait ten days. After that, we're launching our final attack to begin humanity's second last stand. With or without you. I hope you'll make the right decision." The call was disconnected. The digital avatar of John vanished.

Cradite. Jes-Mur. To whatever goddesses and gods our ancestors prayed. Please let this be the correct decision.

"Dusertheus, I'll take the job," Adam said.

"Hmph. I'll tell Patron-Saint. You'll need a ship and a crew. Perhaps Her Maidship here can provide. The Gardener outside will join you. He won't resist taking on the Excommunicated."

"The Gardener?"

"A little nickname Marduk picked up during the Strife. Ask him about the Dark Realm some time. The two Exchange kids could be useful. Take them. Your little Human female friend I guess will have to do, too. Anyone else you must find on your own. Patron-Saint has provided all she is willing. There won't be another gesture of goodwill. Either retrieve the Orb of Emancipation or you Humans will go the way of the Venvuishyn," Dusertheus said.

Adam rose from his seat. He was drenched in sweat, despite the climate-controlled room. He wiped his brow and turned to leave. Havera hopped up to join him.

Dusertheus called out to him one last time. "Commissioner?" Adam peered over his shoulder. "That Human you spoke to. If he's someone you call a friend, you're better off alone."

25

Last Chance Crew

Adam, Havera, and Marduk didn't stay for the rest of the match. They had returned to Marduk's compound in the lower level of the main Corporate District. His compound was close to the looming needle tower of Cloudboard, the company behind most major communications technology, including the UI System. Their company logo, one massive mosaic eye comprised of a thousand eyes, seemed to stare at Adam while they flew past.

Who is the Consul of Cloudboard?

Marduk spent the next hour practicing with Drillhead on a nearby range. Adam inspected the interstellar charts to plot the route while Havera consulted her notes on the Orb of Emancipation and the Vitriba. They were waiting for the other three to return.

Havera was positively giddy about this mission. She couldn't contain her excitement about chasing after the Orb. She was downplaying the danger and hyping up the adventure. "Other than its probable shape, there's little we know about the Orb," Havera explained. "Most of the knowledge we have about the Orb and the Vitriba comes from the old Tales of Havera and Havera the Adventurer's journals. She wrote about many of the galaxy's great mysteries. You might find this interesting; she claims to have set foot on Noah."

Adam rolled his eyes. "You Cauduun and your tales. Pun intended."

"What pun?"

"Human Default language thing. Don't worry about it. Which Tales of Havera, Havera is Havera the Adventurer, Havera?" Adam said with a sly smirk.

"Now you're being ridiculous," Havera said, glaring at him. "Havera the Adventurer is also known as Queen Havera VIII."

"Wait, the queen whose body Ignatia stole when she..." Adam left the last part unspoken.

Havera's tail drooped a bit. "Yes, that's her," Havera said, brushing past the subject. "Havera doesn't go into detail about what Noah is or where it is in her journals. Only that it is a utopia. It is there she claimed to have spoken to a prophet of the Vitriba. The prophet said there are three fundamental elements to life: the power to create life, the power to protect life, and the power to end life. That broadly matches our understanding of the Vitriba from the old Tales of Havera. However, she stated that furthermore each element has a chosen herald to represent those values with their own instrument to help uphold those values. Havera believed the Orb of Emancipation, the Warrior's Kiss, and the Everlasting Aegis were those three instruments. Based on other sources and myths, Havera concluded that the Orb of Emancipation was the instrument used to create life."

"Great, great, but does she say anything about where it is?" Adam asked impatiently.

Havera shook her head. "Unfortunately, the Orb of Emancipation is the one we know the least about. There are no known photographs. Historians' and artists' depictions of the Orb vary over the generations. It is said that Queen Havera I sent the Orb of Emancipation far away to where it could never be found. Havera the Adventurer claimed that the Everlasting Aegis, Dasenor's Shield, lays at the bottom of the ocean in a temple of that sleeps behind a perpetual storm."

"I wonder where that is."

"Oh, that's no great mystery. She's referring to Yapam."

"Yapam? I've heard that name before," Adam said. He rubbed his scruff and racked his brain to remember.

"It's the place I was pretending to be studying while I was secretly with y'all these past two years. They're the most well-preserved ruins of the Venvuishyn to exist. I say ruins but they're actually fully intact structures with seemingly no entrance. All attempts to study Yapam have had limited success."

"Why's that?"

"Dagon's Eye. The perpetual storm. On the Moan homeworld, there is an area of ocean three-hundred and twenty thousand square miles completely enveloped by a never-ending hurricane so strong, it rips any planes or spaceships right out of the air. Under the water, it's even worse. A great whirlpool protects Yapam beneath the ocean, swallowing any ships attempting to pass through it and spitting them out wrecked and mutilated. Only specialized bots and vehicles can penetrate the storm. According to Moan myth, Dagon's Eye was there since before the planet had water. You could say it is everlasting, pun intended," Havera said, grinning. "It is curious, though."

"What's curious?"

"The old Tales of Havera asserted that the Everlasting Aegis was buried with the dead brother of Queen Havera I. It seems unlikely that the brother would be buried in Venvuishyn ruins on the Moan homeworld, thousands of light years away and hundreds of years before the Moans were discovered."

Adam was getting impatient about all these Cauduun tales. *This is a better conversation for Trissefer than me.* Adam pushed past the point. "So, getting the Everlasting Aegis is out of the question. Are you sure the Warrior's Kiss is legit? I mean, have you held it?"

Havera shook her head. "The Queens of Rema used to wield the sword in battle. No queen has wielded the sword since 'the Warrior Queen' Havera IV and the Great Galactic War a thousand years ago. Unless you count Queen Havera V using the blade to commit suicide upon the Platinum Throne," Havera said with mild amusement. "Take my word for it, Adam. The Sword of Aria is real. It exists, and it contains a devastating power the Praetorians and the Paladins of Paleria before them don't want to tamper with,"

"The power to end life," Adam finished her sentence.

"Exactly."

"Do you have Havera the Adventurer's journals? Maybe there are hidden clues about the Orb in them."

Havera bowed her head. "Havera's journals are in the same place as the Sword of Aria. Beneath the First Sanctum that's situated atop Raetis' Hill in Paleria. It is a repository of all the galaxy's knowledge, and the home of the Praetorian Order. It's also known as the Great Library of Raetis. Queen Havera VIII founded the Praetorian Order shortly after her ascension. It's where she was buried, too."

It keeps coming back to her mother.

Adam closed the galaxy map and sat down next to Havera.

"I don't want to come across as insensitive, Havera, but what happened with your mother and Ignatia? Your father seemed to suggest you blame yourself for your mother's death," Adam said, choosing his words carefully.

Havera ran her fingers through her hair, sweeping one of her raven side-ponytails off her shoulder. "That's because it was my fault," she said bluntly. Havera let out a slight titter. "It's funny. That was also about Havera's journals. The Praetorians classify Havera's journals for Censor-eyes only. Same with the Sword. I had gotten special permission to study them for my xenohistory Pontifex thesis years ago. I had written about Rimestone and its connection between the ancient Venvuishyn and the proto-cultures of the modern races. The Praetorians require every Quaestor to write small popular histories about topics of their choice in order to get promoted. I was writing a series of anthologies about the nine queens Havera. That was my project at Censor Maxima's suggestion. I wanted access to Queen Havera VIII's journals to bolster my history about her. My permissions had lapsed, but I figured the Censors would bend the rules for me again. They did, in a way. Censor Maxima said I could study the journals only if my mater signed them out for me. I was waiting in a private conference room while my mater went deep into the vaults. Ignatia and some disloyal Paladins of Paleria had broken into the vault and were plundering precious artifacts. They were attempting to steal the Sword of Aria. My mater tried to stop them. Even with her bracers, she was vastly outnumbered, and the Paladins of Paleria are the best of the best. She brought down a section of the vault on top of them, killing many of them and foiling their plan. Ignatia and a few others escaped. My mater...was crushed to death," Havera said, choking back tears.

Adam put his arm around her shoulder. She leaned into his embrace. "When they cleared the rubble, the Praetorians realized the body of Queen Havera VIII was missing, along with some ancient star charts. All the remaining Paladins of Paleria, guilty or innocent, were banished by orders of the queen. A friend brought me my mater's bracers. Traditionally, they belong to the archduchess. As Pompeia's filia, I was entitled to inherit them until a new archduchess is chosen. That hasn't happened, so I continue to hold onto Mater's Embrace."

Adam stroked one of Havera's ponytails. "If you ran for archduchess, you'd get to keep them."

Havera laughed through tears. "You sound like my pater. He's made that exact argument in the past. I don't know. I thought I was meant to study old tomes and theorize about archaic civilizations. Not lead a modern one."

"You and me both, Havera. The leading part, not the studying archaic civilizations' part."

"Say you could give it all up or that Humans were free to choose their own destinies again. Pretend like what happened never happened. What would you be?" Havera asked. She wrapped her tail around both their bodies for a tighter embrace.

Adam thought about it. "I know my brother wanted to be a professional Orbital player. He was always the aggressive, physical type. He and my father were tall and built like tanks. I take more after my mother's slender build. Aaron also wanted to go into politics with my dad. He wanted to be the next Human Commissioner of Defense & Security." He had to fight back his own tears.

"I asked what you wanted, Adam."

Adam sighed. "That's just it. I don't know. I've never had the luxury of dreams. Only the pain of nightmares."

Havera tilted her head to look up at him. Her stunning purple eyes glistened with salty tears. Her crimson cheeks flushed with azure blood. One of her shoulder straps was displaced. It was resting on her toned triceps, leaving her breast nearly exposed. She noticed him stroking her hair and acknowledged it with a weak smile. He smiled back at her. He felt her tail bind them closer together. She inched herself upwards to be face-to-face with him.

"You and I are more alike than I could've ever expected when we first met. There are no mentors for you or me. There's no one for us to show us the way. We must figure out everything out ourselves in this ever-changing galaxy. Others expect so much from us without a second to ask us what we want nor would they care what we would say if they did. You're a commissioner. I'm a duchess. Both of us wish we weren't. More than that, we wish the circumstances that made us what we are never happened," Havera said. She raised the tip of her tail to his face. Gently caressing his scruffy cheek, she giggled. "That tickles. I'm not used to hairy faces. Cauduun men don't grow beards."

Closing his eyes, he pressed his face into her tail's bulbous tip. It was firm, yet soft. Not like the last time she touched him with his tail or the time before that. A gentle moan escaped Havera's lips. Adam felt his pulse pound. Excitement stirred within his body. Something he had not felt for many days since leaving Trissefer behind.

I have a beautiful princess in my arms. If I could show my younger self an image of this moment, I'd be hoodwinked into thinking I was happy. Maybe I should be. I'm alive. I'm with friends. For the first time in years, I have something else...hope.

Adam opened his eyes. His emerald greens met her amethyst purples. Her glossy midnight lips were slightly open. She was breathing deeply. Her tail had brought them so close together, Adam could feel her heart beating...it was racing, too. She reached up and brushed the silver streak out of his face, keeping her three fingers firmly on his scruffy cheek. She tilted her head and leaned in. There was no turning back.

Please, Cradite, let this be real.

Their lips met. At first, it was only a peck. Her lips were warm and soft. She retreated a few inches. She kissed him again. Longer this time. He felt a pleasurable sensation surge through his body. Again, she retreated. Staring into each other's eyes, Adam wondered if she felt uncertain about kissing him. Her tears had dried. Instead, she had a hungry look in her eye. His confusion quickly subsided. Closing her eyes, she moved in quickly, kissing him again. This time, she didn't retreat. The kisses were longer, deeper. She wrapped her hands around the back of his head. He returned her kisses enthusiastically. He ran his fingers through her silky scarlet and raven hair. She mirrored him with his shaggy brown hair.

She was strong and forceful. Overpowering him, she pushed him down into the couch, pressing her chest into his. The kisses were relentless. She parted his lips with her tongue. He didn't resist. She moaned into his mouth with each kiss. His arousal was absolute. He felt her rub her pelvis against him. She felt his stiffening manhood through his jumpsuit. She giggled. She gave him a big kiss, letting her lips linger on his.

"You're good at this," Havera said, opening her eyes.

"I've had a lot of practice," Adam said.

His eyes shot open. *Idiot! Why would you say that?!*

Havera noticed his sudden panicked look. Smiling and laughing, she sat up, intentionally grinding herself on him. Adam let out a moan and tilted his head back into the couch.

"I could tell," Havera said. She grabbed the thin straps on her tunic and slid them off her shoulders. She let the straps fall, exposing her bare breasts. Adam's breathing intensified. She grabbed the edges of his duster jacket and jerked him upwards until he was mere inches from her face. "So have I," she said in a sexy, playful tone.

She pulled him in for an aggressive kiss. She vigorously removed his jacket and tossed it aside when it was off him. He felt her tail snake its way up his body. The tip of her tail slid into the top of his jumpsuit. She lowered her tail further into his jumpsuit and pulled the zipper down. Once it was at its lowest, Havera slipped his arms through the sleeves. The top of the jumpsuit fall to its side. Both of their chests were exposed. All the while, she never stopped kissing him.

She pushed him back down into the couch. She straddled him. She braced herself against his shoulders with her muscular arms. She had him firmly in her grip. Her tail was wagging just over her shoulder. Adam stared up at the beautiful Cauduun duchess. His arousal almost hurt at this point. He wanted her badly.

Do not finish quickly. Do not finish quickly. Do not finish quickly!

"I've never done this with a Human man. I hope you'll enjoy it. I know I will," she said softly. She leaned down to give him another peck on the lips. He expected her to remove the rest of his jumpsuit. Instead, her tail slithered inside his jumpsuit again. She lifted herself off him slightly to give her tail room to reach its destination. He felt the tip of her tail wrapped itself around his manhood. Adam let out a gasping moan. Her tail's touch felt wonderful. Havera arched her back in anticipation of pleasure.

"We're back!" a voice called out. The doors to the hallway that led to the room they were in opened.

Adam and Havera stopped. "Kewea!" they both exclaimed. Scrambling, the pair fumbled with their clothes in a rush to appear decent. Adam slipped his jumpsuit back on and zipped it back up. Havera slid her arms into her tunic. She sat up abruptly and slid down the couch away from him.

"Y'all missed a thrilling end!" Adam heard Samus shout.

She ain't kidding.

"Adam!" Havera hissed at him. She pointed to his groin area. He was still visibly excited. Adam grabbed his duster jacket and threw it over his lap just as Samus, Zax, and Jak entered the room. His heart was pounding. He wiped the sweat from his brow.

"What are y'all up to?" Samus asked cheerfully. She was wearing an oversized fake centurion helmet with a purple side-to-side, straw crest on top.

Adam coughed. Havera luckily came to the rescue. "Oh, nothing in particular. We were making plans. Marduk is in the other room testing out some weapons and armor," she said. Adam was grateful she answered first. He was always a terrible liar, especially around Sam.

"Is that what that racket is?" Jak asked, referring to the occasional shot or boom echoing from down the hall. "I'm going to grab the bot real quick," Jak said. The Naddine left the room, returning a minute later with the various pieces of Dee. Jak had begun to make minor repairs to Dee's body. The bot still needed much work.

"So, who won?" Havera inquired. Adam's face was still hot, and his excitement had not quite died down.

"2-2 tie," Zax said shaking his head. "They were halfway through the extra fourth period when a massive fight broke out in the stands after a questionable no-call in favor of the Centurions. The referee called the match when the fight bled into the arena," Zax finished.

"Wish y'all could've seen it! I've never seen Cauduun fight like that before. The stuff y'all can do with your tails, Havera, is incredible!" Sam said.

Adam gulped and coughed again.

"You okay, Adam? You seem a bit flushed," Zax said, sitting down in a chair opposite to him.

"I'm fine. Just a bit warm," he said with a half-hearted chuckle. "Y'all should sit down. We have much to tell you."

***

Adam and Havera revealed everything they had learned from Dusertheus and John. Jak continued to tinker with Dee, seemingly unphased by what was said. Zax leaned in with great interest. Sam had gotten up halfway through to pace the room. She had removed the helm she bought at the match.

"John cannot be that reckless or stupid," Samus insisted.

"He was very adamant, Sam. He's given us a hard deadline one way or another," Adam said.

"There's no way Shepard or Auditore would go along with that plan. Did you ask them about it?" Sam asked.

Adam shook his head. "It never occurred to me to ask."

"You're John's superior, Adam! You're the Commissioner for Defense & Security, and he's your Chief of Internal Security. Order him to call off the attack," Samus insisted.

Adam blinked and hung his head. "I...I didn't think about that. I can't do that to John. It would be humiliating. He's on the ground. We're not. I must trust him on this. I have no choice. We can't get back there even if we wanted," Adam argued.

"What do you mean?" Samus asked.

Havera explained. "We left Windless Tornado on my ship. The only reason the Bokori didn't stop us was due to my diplomatic immunity. My pater and the Alliance have stripped me of my diplomatic status for the time being. Even if we get my ship ungrounded, I'm not allowed to leave Concordia, let alone land on Bokori soil unmolested."

"Patron-Saint found a way. If I decide to go back, I'll need a way onto the moon. The only way I can think of to do this is to do Patron-Saint's bidding," Adam said.

Samus sat back down. Adam could see the thoughts flicker behind her bright brown eyes. She rubbed the scar on her chin. Adam realized his back was fine and his excitement had died down. He slid the jacket off him and sat back more relaxed.

"We've gone this far. I'm going with you. I can't let you go alone," Samus said.

"He won't be going alone. I'll be with him as will Marduk. He's going to help us infiltrate the Excom facility and extract the interstellar map data," Havera said.

"Breaking into a secret base in order to chase an ancient legend halfway across the galaxy to help liberate an oppressed people. We're in!" Zax declared. The Zokyo stood up excitedly. He grabbed the lute off his back and strummed a few chords.

"Calm down, maestro," Jak said, glancing up from his work on Dee. "We're musicians, not soldiers or spies. We've already gone far out of our way to help these people. This isn't our fight. We have our own lives."

"Singing for a bunch of loud, drunk, lusty fans is so boring compared to this, bro! There will always be other times for that. This is a once-in-a-lifetime opportunity to do some real good," Zax insisted.

Jak put his tools down and wiped his hands. "You're not donating Links to help the underprivileged or hosting a charity race across space. This is dangerous, Zax. The Excommunicated and the Union are not groups we want to antagonize," the Naddine said.

"We've already antagonized the Excommunicated," Zax countered.

"He's right, Jak. Like it or not, the Excommunicated aren't happy with y'all. Zax wants to help, and he's been great so far. His little live-streams have helped us raise money," Adam agreed. Zax's HUD had a premium live-streaming package he had purchased and downloaded months ago. He had been using it to broadcast his performances to the Nexus. The last day or so he's blasted out quick videos to his followers and supporters to donate to the Human Separatist cause. Donations began pouring into the account Havera had arranged with a sympathetic Mordelatory. They were using the money to pay for gear Marduk was printing for them. The Moan's support only went so far.

"I have a business to run after all," Marduk had told him earlier.

One of Jak's eye stalks bent to the side to glare at Adam. "Self-defense is far different than entering their territory and stealing from them!"

Zax stood up to walk over to Jak. The Zokyo placed all four arms on his Exchange brother. "Bro, you know this is going to be my only shot at proving my worth to the Elders. If I want to compete in this year's Ra-Mu, this will be my last chance. I need to do this. Adam, Samus, the Humans. They need our help," Zax's voice cracked.

"Is this about them, or is this about you, Zax?" Jak said.

Zax raised his voice. "This is about both! You and I have an opportunity to do something that matters. To make an impact. At the end of my days, I don't want to be remembered as just someone with a pretty face and halfway decent voice. I want my life to mean something! Your people taught me more than anything we're not interchangeable cogs in a machine. We're sentient beings. Our lives matter! We only have one. We must make them count. Life will always be full of risks. We cannot be afraid to aim for the stars simply because we're afraid we might crash and burn. We won't grow if we don't try. Please, Jak. I'm asking you as your friend, your partner, your brother. This is something I must do," Zax said with stout resolution.

It was hard to gauge a reaction from Jak. The upside-down faces of the Naddine were notoriously difficult to read. Jak ran his hands through the wispy pale blonde hair on top of his chin. His construct J'y'll was beeping solemnly next to Jak. This seemed to rouse a response. The Naddine nodded wordlessly.

Marduk entered the room. The Moan had replaced his typical fused seaweed frock and coral tricorn hat with indigo chitinous armor of layered, hardened shells and a spiky helm in the style Adam had seen the Moan guards wear back at the meeting with the Sinners. The Drillhead was resting comfortably in its holster on Marduk's back.

"If y'all are done chit-chatting, I think I've finalized all the designs. Yours in particular, little guppy, I think you'll like," Marduk said, referring to Sam.

"Yes! Let's see them!" Sam said, jumping up excitedly.

"Follow me," Marduk said. Zax pecked Jak on the chin and patted him reassuringly with all four of his Zokyon arms. He and Havera started chatting along the way about the Orbital match.

Adam rose from his seat to join Marduk and the others. Jak cut him off. "I need to speak with you without prying ears."

Adam nodded and followed the Naddine into a nearby washroom. Jak activated the faucet to wash his hands. He was scrubbing the grime and dust off from his work on Dee. He was smacking and rubbing his hands under the water aggressively to the point they were almost turning raw.

"I don't want you putting delusions into Zax's head. You hear me? He gets too big for his mechsuit sometimes. I have a hard enough time convincing him to keep a tour schedule on the best of days. He doesn't realize the dangers we'll be walking into if we follow you," Jak said, continuing to scrub his hands with soap and water.

"Look, I'm sorry y'all are getting dragged into this. I wish I could resolve this situation some other way. I can't. Zax seems enthused about helping us. I'm not in a position to turn down someone's help, especially from people who have a platform like y'all's," Adam said.

Jak whirled around to face Adam, splashing him with a spray of water in the process. "We're not live-streaming a concert here, Mortis. We're talking about antagonizing one of the most dangerous groups in the galaxy. Walking straight into the heart of darkness and stealing from them! And for what? Chasing after fantasies and fairy tales all to help people we don't know. People we've never met or people who'll ever care about us. I don't envy your position, Mortis, I really don't. Keep us out of it. I don't want you dragging me and Zax down along with you. J'y'll, air dryer," Jak said. The little construct on his shoulders reconfigured into a small machine that blew hot air onto Jak's hands.

Adam took a couple steps closer to the Naddine. "You care deeply about Zax. I can respect that."

"He's my brother," Jak said, peering into the nearby mirror.

"Exchange brother. When Havera and Marduk called you that I didn't realize they meant THE Exchange. You and Zax are one of the ten-thousand Naddine and Zokyon children traded after the war, aren't you?" Adam suggested.

Jak exhaled. "Yes. I was raised by his parents and he by mine. A cultural experiment the politicians thought would permanently improve relations between our two peoples after a century of war. Saptia didn't just affect you Humans. My life was forever altered by that stupid conference and that stupid Orbital match. Utter, abysmal failure."

"Judging by how you and Zax ended up, I'd say you two turned out quite well," Adam said.

Jak scoffed. "A few children aren't going to turn the tide of millennia of hatred and hostility. My people and Zax's have fought five full-scale wars in the thousand plus years after joining the Conclave. We were the lucky ones. The children who weren't murdered or abandoned back to their original parents either ended up trapped in a system that hates them or, more mercifully, they took their own lives. I hate the Naddine. I hate the Zokyo. Kewea drag them all to the underworld!" Jak spat. He slammed his fist into a nearby wall, cracking it.

Adam bowed his head for a few moments to let him calm. Jak took a deep breath and went back to the sink to wash his hands again. J'y'll, back in her normal form, beeped a couple times sympathetically.

"Why'd you become a G'ee'k?" Adam asked, attempting to change the subject.

"You think you're going to woo me over by trying to empathize with my past, Mortis?" Jak snorted.

Adam shrugged. "Who is the Consul of Cloudboard?"

Jak let out a slight chuckle and resumed washing his hands. "Zax's mother was a G'ee'k. Of all the horrible things about my life growing up as a Naddine on Mthr, she was not one of them. She pushed me further than I ever thought possible. Encouraged me to stand up for myself. Take pride in learning knowledge for the sake of it. She noticed my love of tinkering," Jak said, nodding to J'y'll, who beeped excitedly in response. "She convinced me to apply to the D'hty Academy to become a G'ee'k. She was an experatchik on the Central Committee of the Technocracy, so the Academy couldn't refuse my admission. Not that they didn't try to find ways to get me booted. Manipulating my scores, giving me harder challenges than the other students, harping on every little norm or code I violated. They even encouraged students to physically attack me or, at the very least, look the other way when they did. All to get me to quit. To prove that Naddine are intellectually inferior, unworthy of understanding the expert knowledge to be a good, *educated* citizen. Zax's mother wouldn't let me quit. It's only because of her I became the first ever and, so-far, only Naddine to graduate. Top of my class no less. That was wonderful acid in their machine-monger mechsuits," Jak said. He twirled his wet fingers, creating a ley line glyph in the air. Adam's HUD fizzled out for a couple seconds, then returned to normal after the glyph vanished.

"Zax's mom sounds like a remarkable person," Adam said, lightly smacking the side of his head to clear the fuzziness.

"She was," Jak said, after finishing washing his hands. J'y'll reformed back to the air dryer to blow hot air on his wet clawed hands.

"Was?"

"She and Zax's father died almost three years ago. Killed in an asteroid storm between Ashla and Gla-Mor. They were on their way to see Zax's first big performance on Terras-Ku. Even the goddesses want to keep the Naddine and Zokyo apart," Jak suggested in a bitter tone.

"I'm sorry for your loss, Jak. I know what that feels like," Adam said, putting a hand on the Naddine's shoulder.

"It wasn't my loss. They were Zax's parents. Not mine," Jak said, eyeing Adam's hand not amused. Adam removed his hand from Jak's shoulder.

"They raised you. You must feel something for them," Adam suggested.

"No more than I do any other sentient," Jak said in a matter-of-fact tone. "Zax may be convinced by your cause, but I'm not. I go where he goes. Don't betray his trust."

Jak attempted to walk by Adam, but Adam grabbed the Naddine by the arm. "You don't trust anyone do you?"

Jak shook Adam's grip. "You trust too many people."

"What do you mean?" Adam asked.

Jak reached up a plucked a hair off of Adam's jacket collar and held it aloft in front of him. "Scarlet isn't really your color," Jak said.

Adam blushed. "I...uhh...well we just..." he stammered.

Jak held a hand up. "No need to explain anything to me. The phrase 'Naddine diplomacy' exists for a reason. We find comfort wherever we can with whomever we can. If Zax and I are going to help, you need to be more careful with whom you let your guard down. A poisonous flower is only deadly if you let it get close," Jak said. He let the strand of hair fall.

"But it's less impactful to only admire a poisonous flower from afar.

Sometimes you must get closer to truly understand its beauty and its danger," Adam said.

The Naddine seemed to crack a smile. "You're smarter than you look, Mortis."

Adam tilted his head and body to mimic Jak's upside-down head. "How about now?"

Jak was not amused. "I can see why Zax likes you so much. You two are very much alike in many ways. That's what I'm afraid of."

26

Toss a Link to Your Zokyo

Samus was hopping from platform to platform. She dodged a capsule that a wall-mounted turret hurled at her. Using her new boots' jump jets, she leapt and back-flipped onto the wall. She ran along the wall for a couple seconds, then jump jetted her way back to the platform. They were in a training ground. Everyone was else was watching her in the observation room above. Sam was running an obstacle course designed by Marduk.

"How do they feel, little guppy?" Marduk asked over the com.

Samus stopped to catch her breath. "Wonderful. Exceptionally light. I didn't know a Human body could do that," Samus said. She braced herself against the wall at the end of the course.

"The boots are meant to absorb impact and transfer them into momentum. Ideal for someone hurrying from place to place to remain undetected. They're quiet. The jump jets you have are more powerful than what Adam has. Yours, with a full pulse, can launch you up several feet. Combat jets. His are meant for recreation. Still soaks my mind y'all used those in battle," Marduk said, side-eyeing Adam.

You and me both.

Marduk continued. "How's the agile armor feel? Not too heavy or restrictive?"

"No, it hugs me closely, but I'm otherwise unrestricted. Same with the cloak," Sam said.

"The agile armor is made from Orrorror hide. A type of rhinoceros from Terras-Ku. It's flexible but durable enough to stop a blade and absorb impact. The cloak is a Cauduun-design of the same kind of jacket I wear. It contains a thin layer of palerasteel. Capable of deflecting a laser pistol or a ricochet. I wouldn't stand out in the battlefield, waiting to get shot. Hope you don't mind the color. I went with something that matches your eyes," Marduk said.

"They're perfect. Should I grapple back to y'all?" Sam asked. She grabbed a crossbow from her belt.

Marduk tapped the air and a panel opened up into the observation room. "Please do."

With a running start, Sam leapt into the air. The speed at which the boosters propelled her height turned Sam into a brown blur. At the apex of her jump, she aimed for a spot just above the open panel. She fired and a hooked piton ejected from the riser of the crossbow followed by a high tensile wire. The piton hit the wall with a quiet thud. Sam used the high tensile wire to pull herself in one motion right through the open panel. She landed with a gentle thump. The piton disconnected itself from the wall and the wire retracted back into the crossbow with a silent ting.

Marduk gave her a polite clap. "Told you she was quiet. Remember to flip the safety on when you're not using it. Press the button in order to rotate between modes. You're currently on grapple mode with a fifty-foot titanium wire. The other two modes are canister and projectile. I've given you a few canisters containing knock out gas for organics. As for projectiles, besides your plasma bolts, you have half a dozen sticky mini-cameras and a dozen shockers for synthetics or other electronics, although, the shockers will work on organics, too. Just might be more painful when they wake up."

"You say my boots are outdated. Who still uses a crossbow? Isn't that pre-spaceflight tech?" Adam asked.

"I was using a bow-and-arrow back home!" Samus reminded him. She still had the energy bow strapped across her back.

"Yeah, but that's because we didn't want to waste ammo. This is something else entirely," Adam said.

"You're right, skinny guppy. It's Techoxtl tech developed for the Naddine. A sort of retro-futurism. Those beast bangers don't trust advanced technology. Could be anti-Zokyon sentiment that makes them wary of machines and guns. However, like everyone else, they need to keep up with the times. Can't take on the Zokyo and their mecha with simple projectile arrows and hungry monsters. So, in addition to the plasma weaponry, the Techoxtl developed these archaic-looking weapons to accommodate the Naddine's particular idiosyncrasy. The crossbow has lethal and nonlethal options. Can still fire a plasma bolt. Works just as well as any firearm in the right hands. Sam is a natural. No sicariae, but good enough for this job. Stealth is going to be the key here," Marduk said.

"I don't feel very stealthy with this," Adam said, tapping his new armor. The verdant metal felt awkward on his body. It slid easily over his jumpsuit with enough room for him to wear his duster jacket. The chest plate stuck out a bit from his body while the lack of leg and arm armor allowed for more dynamic movement of his limbs.

"It's Cauduun mezzo armor. That's the closest armor schematic I can find for a Human of your stature, and, per your request, it's the toughest armor I can produce outside of a full suit of combat armor. It's a weave mixture of carbon titanium and palerasteel. Tough yet flexible enough to maneuver. This will stop most direct projectile slugs and laser blasts. It's even padded with special foam to keep you cool. If the situation turns violent, you'll need it. Oh, that reminds me," Marduk said

The Moan grabbed a black and white dagger off a nearby workbench. He walked over to Sam and handed it to her. She accepted it gratefully.

"You'll need this for close encounters. It's a Yapam Dagger. The blade is made from black diamonds found deep under the ocean near Dagon's Eye. It's sharper than a palerasteel blade. More durable, too. The hilt is carved from the jawbone of a daku. A deadly dark shark said to be the offspring of the great Leviathan of the same name. They swim in the waters around the whirlpool, picking off prey too weak to resist the current of the outer edges. The merchant republic I grew up in was near Yapam. Had many close encounters with those sharks. That one almost took my ulnar fin off," Marduk said, pointing to the hilt.

"Thanks, Marduk. I'll treasure it," Sam said with a smile. She removed her old steel blade, unequipped it, and holstered the dagger in its place.

"Be sure to bloody it early. It's good luck," Marduk said with a laugh.

"What about other weapons? Rifles, pistols, launchers?" Adam asked.

Marduk strutted over to a rectangular metal box almost half Adam's size. The Moan tapped on it. "I'll bring this. Portable storage cache. Contains hundreds of different types of weapons and ammo stored digitally like our HUD's inventory. These babies are expensive, but worth it out in the field. Won't know what type of gear we'll need 'til we get there. In the meantime, I'll let you have a CMA-Defense Rifle. Standard issue laser rifle for a Cauduun Legionary. Should suffice for now," Marduk said.

He pressed an invisible button in the air above the box. Spawning out of nothing, the CMA-Defense Rifle materialized. Marduk tossed it to Adam. He added it to his own inventory and unequipped it. The rifle dematerialized as quickly as it came.

"Might want to practice with the grip and trigger. It's designed for the Cauduun's three rounded-tip fingers," Marduk said.

Adam glanced over at Havera's hands. "Right. I'll be sure to do that."

"What about your Rimestone weapon?"

"What about it?" His blood pressure shot up a bit at the mention of his family heirloom.

"You still have it, right? Mind if I take a look?" Marduk asked, a noticeable hint of excitement in his voice. Adam hesitated. He shifted his vision between Havera and Sam seeking reassurance. "Relax, skinny guppy, I'm not going to steal it. I'm an arms dealer. It's not often I get to see the most advanced firearm ever created."

Adam sighed. He reached into his jacket pocket and withdrew the padded platinum grip. With a squeeze of his hand and flick of his wrist, the Rimestone materialized from the grip. The icy, crescent-moon shaped weapon chilled the nearby air. Mist emanated from the Rimestone and swirled around Adam's hand. Marduk's eyes widened. Adam noticed Zax's and Jak's gazes were transfixed on the weapon.

"It's called a Debbie," Adam explained.

"Debbie? Stupid name for such a precious, powerful commodity," Marduk said. He extended his clawed, webbed hand. "May I?"

Adam flipped the grip in his hand. He carefully handed the Debbie over to the Moan. Marduk held it aloft, inspecting it closely. "It's cold. Freezing" He touched the Rimestone with the tip of his finger and quickly withdrew it. "Wow, downright glacial. Even colder than when I got this," Marduk said. He was rubbing the huge scar that bisected his chest.

"It's dark energy, Marduk. What did you expect?" Havera asked.

"Not sure. Had a strange buzzing in my ear when I touched it. Strange. Fascinating. Thank you for this, skinny guppy. Here." Marduk carefully handed the weapon back to Adam. He deactivated it and pocketed it.

"Any cool or awesome weapons I can practice with?" Zax asked excitedly.

The Moan turned to face the Zokyo. "Practice? Why would you need to practice with a gun?" Marduk asked incredulously.

Zax's expression sunk. "I'm going into battle with y'all. I'm going to need a weapon. This baby here is handy, but her usage is limited to...particular circumstances," Zax said, referencing his lute.

"Hopefully, if all goes according to plan, nobody will be going into battle. At least not until we get into Union space," Marduk said.

"So, there is a plan? Comforting to know we're not simply going to go in guns blazing," Jak said dryly.

Marduk gestured them over to a circular digiholo table. He tapped the air a few times. From the table an image of a space station emerged. The station was diamond-shaped with a ring encircling the main station. Connected to the sides were large solar panels that flanked either side of the station like wings.

"I've done a little digging into this Excom facility. Turns out there's a public face to this place. The station doubles as an entertainment parlor. AR pods, AR tabletop games, gambling, auctions, strippers, jades. You name it. The parlor brings in wealthy clientele from all over the galaxy to rub shoulders with power brokers to avoid the galaxy's prying eyes. The Rorae take a relaxed attitude on this sort of behavior, and the Conclave won't send in ConSec to clear them out without the Rorae's approval to enter their borders. My contacts tell me they finance the whole operation with Celeste farming. It is how they pay off the Rorae to keep them mollified. It's a red giant sun system," Marduk explained.

Adam shifted uncomfortably at the mention of red giant Celeste. Sam noticed Adam's fidgeting. She put her arm around his to comfort him. He nodded at her to show his appreciation. The others paid no mind.

"We're going to split up into two teams. One will keep everyone distracted in the public section and maintain our escape while the other will sneak in and grab the map. With any luck, we'll be in and out without anyone noticing," Marduk said.

"Who's doing the distracting?" Zax asked.

"Glad you asked, bard. I've heard you have such a lovely singing voice...for a Zokyo," Marduk grinned.

"I have a lovely singing voice for any race, thank you very much! Come on. I want to be in on the break-in process. Some real espionage stuff," Zax insisted.

"We all have our strengths. Yours will be entertaining. I'll book 'the famous Zax and Jak duo.' This will allow us to land safely. I can dummy up fake registration tags for your ship, Havera. You told me it's a Toch-1598 light freighter with Cauduun modifications. Fast ship. I'll re-register it to the bard. The Zokyo will keep the rich and fancy distracted, along with much of their security. Don't worry. Stay where there are witnesses, and you'll be fine. They'll keep their attention on you and off everyone else. As for the others, sneak off the ship and hijack a maintenance bot or security terminal. Something you can acquire the station's map data from. We'll need it to figure out the layout of the station. Once we locate where the Excoms might be hiding the map data, the G'ee'k here will hack into their systems and steal it. Take out any guards that get in our way quietly. We should be in and out within the hour if all goes well," Marduk said.

"Do we have a backup?" Havera asked.

Marduk withdrew the Drillhead from his back. "We go loud. We should catch them off-guard if the situation runs dry."

"Seems kind of reckless," Samus said.

"One problem. If I'm supposed to be the one hacking into their systems, how am I going to be performing with Zax?" Jak asked.

"You're not."

"He has to be there, Marduk. Jak's drumming is an essential piece to our performance. Him and J'y'll. He can't be in two places at once," Zax said.

Marduk smiled and holstered his weapon. "Yes, he can." He tapped the air, dematerializing his breastplate armor, leaving his chest and gills exposed. The Moan threw his head back. His conical snout flattened and retreated. The webbing on his claws disappeared. His skin turned from its usual bluish-gray to a light tan. He shrunk several inches, and his head seemed to rotate. Stalks popped out of his cranium where they weren't before.

Adam instinctively took a step back. It took him a second to realize Marduk's body was transforming. After another couple seconds, the transformation was complete. Where Marduk Tiamat once stood was a near perfect copy of Jak-Non.

"You're a Metamorph!" Havera exclaimed.

"Indeed, I am, Your Grace," said the Naddine-looking Marduk. He still sounded like Marduk, only with a slightly higher pitch. "The metamorphosis isn't perfect as you can plainly see and hear. Should be enough to fool a simple visual inspection."

He was right. Beyond the voice, the gills on Marduk's chest were still present but proportional to his new form. Marduk moved to stand next to Jak. It was about a ninety-five percent representation of the Naddine by Adam's estimation.

"Woah! Can all you Moans do that?" Sam asked. She went over to poke Marduk in the chest a few times.

"No. True Metamorphs are extremely rare. We all have the ability to switch between our bestial and piscine forms. Piscine is our more natural state in the water. We swim faster and see better underwater. On land, we prefer bestial," Marduk said, transforming back into his regular visage. "There are a bunch of other small physiological differences between the two forms. That being said, the ability to completely transfigure one's body into a different person or race isn't a common gift. The waters around Yapam seem to breed the ability to morph or transmutate objects. My father and his father before him could transmutate common minerals into rarer minerals. I used the money I inherited from them to start Tiamat's Talons," Marduk explained.

"This is perfect! You can pretend to be Jak while I'm out there singing. I'm sure even someone as stingy as Jak will have a spare outfit. J'y'll can do most of the musical work for you. We'll keep it simple. I'll teach you a few basic beats with her. Enough to pass you off as Jak. If the situation breaks down, I'll have you as backup!" Zax said.

"I don't like this. There's got to be a better way. A smarter way. This is far too risky," Jak said. He was scratching one of his eye stalks.

Marduk tapped the air, and the digiholo station vanished. Replacing it was a three-dimensional map of the galaxy with all the major space lanes marked. "Sure. Give me six months, a full undercover team, and a few million Links. I could come up with something better. Unfortunately, we don't have that kind of time. It's a little over two days travel to this station if we take the Vol Ashla. After we find the map, barring setbacks, we have no idea how difficult it'll be to locate a hidden planet or moon in Union space without the entire Phantom Fleet chasing after us. Then, after locating and obtaining the Orb from CR-2-13-LF, it's at least a three or four day journey back to Bokor from Melusine, no matter which route we take. Jumping south from Melusine is the only known route in or out of Union territory," Marduk said.

He traced the pathway on the map. From Concordia, they'd take the main route south-southwest along the Vol Ashla to the Rorae homeworld, before heading southeast towards the edge of Rorae territory, where the Excom station was marked. From there, they'd head east into Moan territory and stop at the planet Melusine, only to divert south into Union space.

"What are we waiting for? Let's get moving," Sam insisted.

"One problem. My ship is impounded. If we manage to get her free, once we leave Concordia, we're on our own. The Conclave will cut us off. ConSec or Patron-Saint won't come to our rescue in Rorae or Union space, and the other Proprietor races will let the Bokori have us if they catch us. I can guarantee y'all they are monitoring my ship and us closely. We're crossing the Link. There's no turning back," Havera said.

"Don't any of y'all have a ship we could use?" Sam asked.

Marduk shook his head. "None of the ships I own are big enough to accommodate this many people, and the ones I can procure that are large enough are far too slow."

"Jak and I usually rent a luxury freighter when we go on tour. We need room for Sel-Ena after all. Neither of us own any spaceships," Zax explained.

"We need Havera's ship it seems. Where is the Cicera?" Adam asked.

"Where we parked it. The docking bay is not far from here. The ship is under guard at all times. We need to fake authorization to get by the guards in order to leave," Havera said.

"Is that something you can do, Jak?" Adam asked.

Jak scratched his scalp hair. "Maybe. Without knowing where the clearance authorization is coming from, it would be a coin toss."

"Probably either my pater's office or the Conclave itself," Havera surmised.

"Those systems usually have double or even triple authentication. If I had direct access, I could probably do it. Remotely? That's going to be trickier," Jak speculated.

"How many guards?" Zax asked.

Havera shrugged. "I don't know. Maybe three or four?"

"Would there be someone in charge? Someone that'll authorize departure on the ground, I presume?"

"I assume there's an onsite commander. Why?"

"What are you getting at, noodle arms?" Marduk sneered.

"I think I know, and that's a bit risky, Zax. If it doesn't work, we're screwed," Jak said.

"Come on, bro. Since when have you known my charms to fail?"

"Last Jesmuriad. The vaav'Sezerene woman," Jak said. He flexed his eye stalks into a skeptical expression.

Zax threw his arms up in the air in exasperation. "You're holding that against me? She had four legs. I had four arms. I thought it was a perfect match," Zax said.

"She was married. To a myym'Sezerene with a serpentine upper body! You were lucky I stepped in when I did, and that we had appropriate antivenom," Jak yelled.

"More action than I'd gotten in months," Zax said with a smirk. Jak buried his scalp in his hands.

"Uh, care to fill us on what y'all are talking about?" Havera asked. Everyone was eyeing Zax with excessive skepticism.

The Zokyo laughed and pulled out his lute. "*The lights were on, but the watchers were blind. Ooo rah, ooo rah. The gates were shut, but the captive was free. Ooo rah, ooo rah,*" Zax sang strumming a few chords on his lute. Zax stood there waiting for a response. When he received none, he simply said, "Trust me."

***

Concordia's sun had set. The displays on the upper part of the station showed a clear, starry night. The carved asteroids of the Cauduun and the Zokyo were visible in the night sky. The regulated temperature of the station was pleasant, with a gentle breeze blowing through the spaceport. Unlike Bokor's spaceport, here extreme verticality reigned, with docking bays stacked from top-to-bottom. Tens of thousands of feet of concrete, steel, and glass. Even at night, the Concordia's main spaceport was a never-ending flow of traffic. Light freighters and solo ships danced about with supertanker cargo ships and military vessels, including a Titan-class Cauduun warship. The HMSS Queen Alexandra was docked nearby. Several dozen Sezerene and Bubil workers were attached to her hull, making minor repairs. Havera eyed the ship from a distance.

"Queen Alexandra dedicated the ship to her grandmater. In truth, I believe she likes seeing her name everywhere. She's a vain woman," Havera said.

"How well do you know her?" Adam asked.

"The Queen? Not well. We've spoken on several occasions. Last time was at my mater's funeral. Her grandson, Severus, had a crush on me for many years. We were in school together. My mater told me the Queen asked her if she'd agree to arrange a marriage once. I told my mater flatly no. Luckily, she had already said no on my behalf," Havera said with a proud laugh.

"Not a good enough pedigree?" Adam said, not trying to hide his smarmy tone.

"He was dull, dim-witted, and had a short tail," Havera said bluntly.

"Is that a euphemism?" Sam asked.

"Ha. No."

Adam and Sam kept their hoods up while Havera wore a black palla over her head to hide her noticeable features. Their heads were down, and they were carrying small containers of digitally stored supplies they would need on their journey. Medicine, ingredients, repair kits, prepackaged food. Anything that might be of use. Marduk was out in front carrying the large weapons container on his bulky shoulders. Behind them, Jak was carrying the box containing Dee's body parts.

"This plan of y'all's is stupid," Dee said. Jak had reattached Dee's head to his torso. They quickly explained the situation to the broken bot. It was nonstop insults from the moment they left. "You really think you're going to bluff your way past ConSec. I might as well convince a jade I have real man parts down there," said Dee.

"Shut it, bot, or I'll crush your voice box," Jak said.

"My existence is trusted to a beast banging Naddine. I don't have much faith," Dee said.

Jak flipped a switch on the back of Dee's neck, and the bot shut down.

"Jes-Mur be praised. Finally, some peace and quiet," Jak said exasperated.

"You're the one who turned him on, Jak," Havera said.

"Because I thought he might be useful in this situation. Give us extra cover. No one's going to buy this," Jak said.

"Quiet! All of you. I've this handled. Trust me," said Zax.

The goal was to trick their way past the guard by acting as maintenance and storage workers. Zax claimed he could stall the onsite ConSec commander while everyone got the gear aboard. Once everyone was aboard, they'd take off before anyone could stop them. Jak wasn't able to hack their systems remotely, but he did learn the ship wasn't on lock down. Merely guarded by a skeleton crew at all times. This particular crew was at the end of their shift.

"They're eager to go home. They only need a little convincing," Zax had said when they learned that.

"Please don't tell me you're going to try and bribe ConSec," Havera said.

"Of course not! I've something better in mind," Zax said. The Zokyo was quite evasive when directly questioned about his methods. Even Jak was tight-lipped about it. Zax claimed he had done this sort of thing several times in the past. Mostly successful.

Marduk was skeptical. By his posture, Adam could tell Marduk had his HUD opened to his inventory, waiting to spawn in the Drillhead to force their way out. Exiting the lift, the crew marched forward until they reached docking bay one-one-three-eight. The wide steel doors were open with a handful of ConSec guards standing by the entrance. Through the opening, Adam could see that the roof of the docking bay was open but the ramp to the ship was up.

"I need to get closer in order to lower the ramp with my HUD," Havera whispered.

"Everyone keep quiet. Let me do all the talking. Whatever you do, don't stop," Zax said.

One of the guards got up and moved to confront the approaching group. "This area is off-limits to non-authorized personnel. Please turn around immediately or you'll be placed under arrest," the ConSec guard ordered. He was a Zokyo, holding out all four hands to halt them.

"Ahoy! I have a work order to perform routine repairs on this vessel. I need your men to step aside. You three get inside, put your equipment down, and get to work on the engine room. Naddine, you back there, make sure you get that bot exactly where it needs to be. I want it whistling through these procedures before the sun is up. Come on, come on," Zax yelled, gesturing to their group.

"Sir, I need you to stop," the ConSec guard said.

"Oh, and don't drop that box again, Moan! It contains gear more precious than your half-salted life. Let's go," Zax said. He slapped Marduk on the butt and ignored the guard's orders. Marduk growled slightly but kept on walking

"Wait, where are y'all going. Stop this instant!" the guard yelled. Marduk had pushed his way passed the guard with Adam passing right behind him.

"Sergeant, I have a work order here from the Cauduun embassy." Zax shoved an old emulator into the guard's hand. The other pair of guards seemed unsure what to do. Their rifles were affixed to their backs, but they had their hands on their sidearms. They were waiting for direction from the Zokyo sergeant. "Keep moving. Keep moving, people. I want this work done within three hours!" Zax yelled with as much fake authority as he could.

"But...but..." the sergeant sputtered. "Who's authorized this?!" he finally managed to sputter out.

Zax got right in his face. "The Cauduun Cardinal that's who! Cardinal Bloatius!" Zax yelled.

Havera walked by him and through gritted teeth whispered, "Clodius!"

"Clodius! Cardinal Clodius. Yes, Cardinal Clodius. Great man. Lovely tail. Hot daughter. You know the one," Zax said, still barking with exuberance.

Adam noticed Havera's tail twitch. She restrained herself. She managed to sneakily tap on her HUD, and the ramp into the ship lowered.

"I haven't heard anything from the embassy or Cardinal Clodius. Stop! I'm ordering you to cease and desist." The sergeant finally found his senses and drew his sidearm. The other guards did, too.

Zax got back into the sergeant's face. "You dare interfere with official Cauduun Monarchical Alliance business. I ought to contact your supervisor," Zax threatened.

"It's already here," a quiet voice called out. Adam couldn't resist the urge. He trudged forward at a slower pace to peek over his shoulder. Approaching Zax and the sergeant was a Bokori dressed in hooded robes and a kyqad but in the colors of ConSec. Its kyqad had the insignia of the Conclave stamped across the front.

"I'm Commander Stopping Gap. I'm in charge here. What's going on, Sergeant?" asked the Bokori officer. Its voice was high-pitched and harsh. The other two guards rushed in front of them to prevent them from boarding the ship.

"These people claim they have work orders to enter the Cicera. This man is claiming they have authorization from Cardinal Clodius. I haven't heard anything, have you?" the sergeant asked the commander.

"No, I haven't. Curious. Where's your work order?" Stopping Gap asked Zax.

Zax snatched the emulator from the sergeant's hands. "Right here. I was going to show him the order once my people had begun working. It's important nothing slow us down," Zax said.

"May I see your emulator?" Stopping Gap asked.

"We...we really need to get to work, Commander Sipping Cup," Zax insisted, stuttering a bit.

"Stopping Gap. Let me see that emulator, sir," the commander asked calmly.

Zax sighed. "Fine! Here." He handed the commander the emulator.

"The power's gone," Stopping Gap said.

"Oh, great! You broke it. I'm going to need to replace that, and it's going to come out of my pockets. My bosses are going to kill me if I don't get this work done on time." Zax kept changing the bluff with each passing second.

"Why don't y'all wait right there while I contact the embassy myself. Sergeant, keep them detained until I get back," Stopping Gap ordered.

"Yes, Commander," the Sergeant agreed.

The Bokori was about to walk away when Zax stepped forward. Adam saw Marduk raise his hand, about to materialize his weapon.

"Wait, wait. My electric lute can power the emulator. Let me grab it real quick." Zax reached for his lute. The sergeant raised his gun, but the commander put a hand on his arm.

"Why does a maintenance manager have an electric lute on the job?" asked the commander.

"For morale, of course! I like to sing to my workers. Keeps their spirits up. Come closer." Zax gestured the commander and sergeant forward. He made some adjustments to the strings and dials on his electric lute. He placed two of his hands on either end to play.

"*The captive was gone, but the guards had him found. Ooo rah. Ooo rah. 'I'm not the one you want, the one you want is not meeeeeee!'*" Zax sang. He strummed the last note with extra flair right in the guards' faces.

"What are you...." the Bokori commander started to say.

From a distance, Adam saw the commander and sergeant tilt their heads back. Their mouths went agape. The commander stumbled on his feet while the sergeant recoiled slightly. The pair shook their heads. "Right. How can we help you?" the commander asked. It acted as if it had never seen Zax until that moment.

"By letting us go," Zax replied calmly.

"Yes. Yes, of course. Y'all are free to go," the commander said.

"Commander, are you sure?" the sergeant asked.

"He said we're free," Zax insisted. He strummed his lute once more in the sergeant's face.

The sergeant developed sudden balance issues but quickly righted himself. "Yes. Free. Commander's orders," the sergeant said.

"Thank you both. Y'all have a lovely evening." Zax placed the lute back on his back and turned towards the group. He gestured them to go forward. They turned heel and made for the interior of the ship. The two other ConSec guards let them by. A stupefied expression on each of their faces.

What just happened?

In a rushed walk, Zax caught up to them at the bottom of the ramp. "Get inside. Get inside! I don't know how long that'll last. Go!" he said in a hushed yell.

"What did you do to them?"

"I'll explain later," Zax said. He hurried them up the ramp.

Once they were all inside, Havera raised the ramp behind them. The last sight from the hangar was the commander and the sergeant exchanging confused looks. Havera rushed towards the cockpit with Adam and Zax in tow. They each climbed the carpeted stairs in a rush. Zax almost tripped on the last step. They reached the cockpit. Marduk was already sitting down at the co-pilot's chair, making adjustments. Havera sat down in the pilot's seat and started flipping switches and pulling levers. She pressed on the intercom button on the panel next to her.

"Jak, how are the engines?"

It wasn't Jak who responded but Dee. "Everything is blue across the board, Your Grace. Why you have me chained to this topsy-turvy brain, I'll never understand."

Havera pulled one more lever, and the engines roared to life. Even in the enclosure of the docking bay, Adam thought the engines were rather quiet for a vessel of the Cicera's size.

"We still need to pick up Sel-Ena once we get airborne," Zax said.

"What did you do to those ConSec guards?" Adam asked. He sat down in the co-pilot's chair.

Zax strummed a few chords on his lute, smiled, and reholstered it on his back. "A bard never kisses and tells. Except, when he does."

Marduk laughed. "Like you'd ever keep a conquest a secret."

"We better get out of here quick," Havera said.

"You needn't worry, Havera. I gave them a double blast. I'm sure we're fine," Zax insisted.

Klaxons began blaring in the hangar. The echoing alarm reverberated through the Cicera. Adam, Marduk, and Havera spun in their chairs to stare deadpan at Zax.

Zax shrugged. "Seems I was right the first time."

Sam ran into the cockpit. "Um, I think the ruse is up."

"No need to rub it in, Sam!" yelled Zax.

Havera spun back around. Pulling back on a throttle, the Cicera lifted off. The roof of the hangar began to close. It was shutting too fast for the Cicera to escape.

"Marduk, the roof," Havera said pointedly.

"Hehe, I got it," Marduk responded.

"Havera, we're going to be trapped!" Adam said, a slight panic in his voice.

The Cicera kept ascending towards the hangar bay ceiling. The roof panel was nearly shut. The gap was far too narrow to fit through. Adam gripped the edge of his chair. Marduk pressed down on his controls. Within seconds, ginger-colored laser blasts tore through the ceiling. An explosion of steel and gas. The Cicera blew through the smoke and through the newly formed hole in the hangar bay roof.

"No, we're not," Havera said, side-eyeing Adam. He had to adjust his legs to hide his renewed excitement. Havera piloted the ship higher and higher.

Zax approached the viewport and pointed. "There's Sel-Ena."

Havera banked the ship at a slight right angle. The arkad was flapping her wings. She was maintaining her position and altitude. "Sam, you, Marduk, and Zax go down to the hold. She's a big bird, she may need extra wrangling. I'll open the cargo door. It's going to be a tight squeeze, so be careful," Havera said over her shoulder.

"Aye-aye, captain!" Sam said with slight heart salute. She, Marduk, and Zax rushed out of the cockpit. A few seconds later, Havera slowed the ship down until they were right on top of the arkad.

Havera pressed the com. "Y'all ready?"

"Ready," said Zax through the com.

Havera lowered a lever on her panel. Adam could hear the distant sound of wind rushing from below. The ship vibrated with a moderate intensity. Not strong enough to dislodge them, but forceful enough to cause Adam to grip his seat again. Zax's voice came through the com again.

"She's in. Raise the cargo door!"

"Affirmative," Havera responded.

She raised the aforementioned lever. The vibrations ceased. Havera turned the ship skyward and, with a boost, the Cicera broke the cloud line.

Adam relaxed his grip on the chair. He sat up and exhaled. "Havera, we should talk."

She held up her hand. "Hold that thought." The panel beeped. Adam remembered that was the ship's external communications. Havera tapped on the panel. "This is the Cicera, go ahead."

The same gravely harsh voice from the other day responded. "Cicera, you are in violation of multiple Conclave laws and regulations. Please return to the docking bay, where you will be greeted by ConSec officers to place you under arrest."

Havera ignored the voice at first. The voice tried again. "Cicera! Your Grace, we know you're there. Your diplomatic immunity has been revoked. There is nowhere for you to go. Return to the docking bay at once or we will be compelled to use force!" Through the front viewport, Adam could see a dozen small fighters approaching the Cicera at high speeds. The radar on the panel indicated that a dozen more were pursuing them from the rear.

Havera tapped the com. This time with her tail. "No dessert for me thank you." She shut off communications.

"Are we going to fight them?" Adam asked, feeling a mixture of excitement and fear.

She shot him an incredulous look. "Shelean proverb: don't invite guests to a full house." Havera pulled back on the throttle, and the Cicera gained incredible speed. The small ConSec ships could not keep up. The Cicera breached the upper atmosphere and left the station behind. The bright blues and greens of Concordia gave way to the darkness of space. Havera banked the ship towards the asteroid of a Naddine's head. They raced by a queue of ships waiting to enter Concordia. Once the Cicera was clear of the asteroid, Havera tapped on the panel. She was selecting coordinates in the ship's computer. She pressed the ship's com. "Brace yourselves, everyone. We're about to enter negative space."

Adam grabbed the edge of his seat again. Havera pulled back on the large central lever. The ship seemed to stall for a second, then the darkness of space began to lighten up. With a sudden burst of speed, Adam was forced into the back of his seat. The pressure of the jump ended more quickly than it arrived. They were in negative space. The viewport was awash of bright, vibrant, swirling colors. The Cicera felt like she was cruising. She hardly made a sound. Smooth travel into the stars.

Havera sat back and breathed a sigh of relief. She hit a few more switches. Adam let go of his grip and slowly rose from his chair. He took a step towards Havera and grasped the back of her captain's chair.

"We really should talk."

"About what?" Havera responded. She didn't give him the courtesy of a glance.

"You know what. The couch. I didn't expect that to hap..." Adam said until Havera cut him off.

"I know what you meant." She spun in her chair to face him, flipping one of her ponytails over her shoulder. "We had a moment, Adam. It passed. I'm sure we both would've had fun. Let's not complicate this further, okay? We can't afford distractions. Not at this juncture."

It was a gut punch. It was not the answer he was hoping for or even expecting. "You don't think there could be something more to it than that?" Adam asked.

She spun back around to face the viewport. "I need to ensure the autopilot is working. Until Dee is fully operational, someone has to monitor the ship while we're in negative space. Go check on the others. We have work to do before we reach our destination." She used her formal tone that brooked no argument.

Adam tried anyway. "Are you sure?"

"Adam, please!" she said with a raised voice. Adam recoiled. She hung her head. "I'm sorry. If we get through this, perhaps we can talk about it afterwards. I need to focus. Please."

It was obvious she didn't mean to react that way. Nonetheless, Adam felt hurt by her response. He wanted to scream at her. He wanted to beg. He wanted to plead his case. This was a different feeling than back at her father's office. Then, he was angry. Now, he only felt numb.

"Okay," was the only word he could muster.

27

The Chains of Shame

"You'll see me again. I promise."

It was unclear when Adam had fallen asleep. At Marduk's suggestion, most of the team had tried to get a few hours of sleep following their escape from Concordia. It was a little over two days until they reached Ashla to refuel and another six-to-eight hours after that until they reached the Excommunicated base. From somewhere below deck, Adam could hear the distant sparks and clangs of Jak working hard on Dee's repairs. He wasn't the only one who couldn't sleep. Adam had been tossing and turning on his cot in Havera's library for hours. His back had itched. His mind had raced. His heart had ached. He had not expected to feel the way he did about Havera.

I'm not in love with her. I only wanted to talk to her. It was sudden, but it was a moment, nonetheless.

"You'll see me again. I promise."

Her final words echoed in his dream. Her amorphous voice haunted him. She would not let him forget.

I'm sorry. I'm failing you.

He was falling through the vast void of space. He felt lighter than air, yet heavier than stone. His body plummeted through the emptiness.

Closing his eyes, Adam prayed solid surface would rush to meet him quick. End his suffering for good.

Something grabbed his arm and halted his descent. His shoulder nearly popped out of its socket, causing Adam to cry out in pain. Only no sound emerged from his mouth. He opened his eyes to see his rescuer. His punisher. Her silvery, smooth skin and lustrous, gleaming ivory eyes were unmistakable. She smiled at him.

Falling Star.

She shook her head. A paralyzing buzzing overtook him. Suddenly, Adam realized he was over a pit of fire and burning metal. Sounds of crashing and destruction enveloped him. Smoke rose to meet his nostrils, forcing him to cough. He blinked several times. The woman's form shifted without changing. It wasn't Falling Star anymore. It was Havera. She held onto his forearm with a vicious vice grip.

"You lied! You promised you'd see her again. You promised and you failed. You failed her. You failed Samus. You failed your mother. You failed me!" Havera screamed. Through salt and smoke, her righteous fury scared Adam. He tried to mouth a response, but no words escaped his lips. With a snarl, she let him go. Adam tried to scream. Still no sound. He plunged towards the fires below. Havera's angry visage disappeared in the smoke. He tried to reach for her to no avail. He spun around, hoping his boots would save him. They wouldn't activate. The wreckage of twisted, burning metal rushed up to meet him. He closed his eyes to accept his fate.

He crashed with a sudden thud. Not on hard metal. Something softer. Something supple. He was unharmed. He opened his eyes to see he was laying on the petals of a colossal flower. One petal lifted up, rolling him off the head of the flower. He landed tenderly on his feet. Turning around, Adam realized the huge flower was gone. In its place were endless fields of waist-high ruby-colored grass. Running his fingers through it, he felt an odd comfort. A gentle breeze cooled his face. He felt a calm he had not experienced in years. Something caught his attention. Not from above but from below. In the back of his mind he sensed it. He heard it.

THUMP THUMP; THUMP THUMP; THUMP THUMP.

The ruby grass field morphed into a familiar face. An icy, crystalline maw so massive it stretched the entire horizon in all directions. He heard her voice once more. A crackling of crystal so beautiful and serene.

Soon you will see for yourself. One day. You have much work to accomplish first, guardian of life.

Adam's lids opened slowly. He felt relaxed. Calm. Well-rested. He sat up and rubbed his eyes. The lights of the ship were still off. Even Jak's tinkering sounds were nowhere to be heard.

Everyone must be asleep.

He pulled back the blanket and threw his legs over the side of his cot to sit up. He rubbed his scruffy beard, endeavoring to remember the details of his dream. The memory faded faster than he could retain.

"I'm sorry," he muttered to the empty air. He wasn't sure why he did that. Some compulsory force in his mind compelled him to do so, he concluded. Sudden movement drew his attention. Adam cocked his head. The door to the library was open.

"Hello. Someone there?" he asked aloud. No response. He zipped up his jumpsuit and stood up. He decided not to put on his boots. The Cicera's carpeted floors felt wonderful on his feet. He walked to the threshold of the door and peered into the hallway. Out of the corner of his eye, he saw more movement. It was descending the stairs into the cargo hold. He decided to follow. Stepping down the stairs, Adam didn't feel fear. He felt...curiosity. The same compulsive force from earlier drove him onward. Reaching the hold, Jak was fast asleep, resting up against an also sleeping Sel-Ena. Parts of Dee were scattered everywhere. Thankfully, Jak must've deactivated Dee before succumbing to exhaustion. Curled up in his lap was J'y'll. She seemed not to notice Adam.

He heard the door to life support close. Careful not to wake the others, Adam tiptoed to the door. Pressing the panel button, the door opened. A rush of humidity and queer lights hit him full in the face. Adam flinched. Without a second thought, he stepped inside and shut the door behind him. His vision adjusted to the room. The air was thick and soupy. It reminded him a bit of Windless Tornado. He was grateful not to be wearing his duster jacket. This was the first time Adam had stepped foot in the life support room. This is where the systems controlling the ship's internal atmosphere coalesced. Unlike the bright, warm-colored lights of the rest of the ship, this room contained eerie ultraviolet light. He could barely see a few feet in front of him. He took a few steps inside and called out.

"Who's there?"

A slight buzzing tickled his ear. Emerging from the darkness, a figure corporealized. He heard no footsteps. Instead, the figure floated towards him until they were visible. Adam's heart skipped a beat when he saw her. Tall, slender, and nearly nude. Her upper body was mossy while her legs were like the stem of a flower. Her head formed up into the shape of a black rose, her petals were closed as if asleep. Slithering vines of dark flowers covered her shapely breasts and groin. Her triangular eyes were practically black voids in the UV lights. Adam noticed the tops of each of her hands and feet was covered with a serrated leaf. Her mouth, or lack thereof, was a single black tripartite leaf.

"Umbrasia!" Adam yelled in a hushed whisper.

"**Adam Mortis**," her voice responded calmly in his head.

"Am I still dreaming?" he asked aloud unsure of how to respond.

"**You were not dreaming. You were seeing. But, I understand what you meant. You are no longer sleeping. I am no illusion.**"

"Seeing? Seeing what?"

"**You are not yet ready to know. Your comprehension of what you saw will come in time.**" Her voice felt cold and icy in the back of his mind, yet, it had a comforting rhythm.

What does that mean? She and my mother should compare notes on cryptic warnings.

"**Your confusion is natural. You must have many questions,**" she said after a pause.

Adam grasped his temples. "Please stay out of my head!"

Umbrasia giggled. "**Despite what you may have heard about the**

Rorae, we do not read minds. We're empathetic. We're perceptive. We can see far better than other sentients. We read expressions and communicate with our minds. Your mind is safe from penetration by me," she tried to reassure him.

Adam wasn't entirely convinced, but he decided not to press the point. He guarded his thoughts more carefully just in case. That was no easy task. Her unexpected presence on the Cicera confused him. She hovered just above the carpet, inching closer to him. He couldn't pull his gaze from her vivacious body. Excitement returned to his own. A surge of adrenaline coursed through his veins. He jerked his head away from her in a clumsy attempt to suppress his burgeoning desire.

He felt a gentle tug on his face. He allowed it to turn his head back to face Umbrasia. Her leafy hand was extended out in a welcoming gesture. But she wasn't touching him. Not with her physical form.

Telekinesis?

"Why do you continue to avert your eyes from me every time we speak, Adam?" Her voice was calm, not accusatory.

"It's um, it's rude to stare. You're practically naked. I don't want to come off as, uhh, leering, I suppose," Adam said stuttering over his words.

"Have I given you cause to believe I am ashamed with how I present myself? I've already told you this. I feel no shame for my body. Why do you insist on feeling shame on my behalf?"

Adam thought about it for a moment. "I don't know to be honest."

She mentally let go of his face, and he did not turn away again. He drank in her appearance from head-to-toe. Every inch of her body was a chiseled perfection of beauty. He couldn't help but admire her. She floated closer until they were mere inches apart. From there, he could smell her powdery fragrance. A velvety aroma of cinnamon mixed with cocoa. Adam swallowed the bubbling saliva that saturated the closer she got.

"I may have some insight. You feel shame because you have been taught and conditioned to feel nothing but shame. That is the way of the modern Bokori. They do not control through force of arms but

by force of will. They have successfully eroded your kind's will until there is nothing but an empty husk to be filled by Bokori shame. They want you to feel your mind is diseased and present their way of life as an antidote to that affliction. Refuse their treatment and you are considered a blight upon the body of your people."

Adam hung onto every word she said. He had never thought about the Bokori in that way. Her words had a certain wisdom, yet he had more questions.

"How can I combat this?"

"A powerful weapon shame is, Adam Mortis. One our kind does not feel yet recognizes as a dangerous force in the minds of sentients. But it is only as powerful as you allow it to be. Shame rests entirely in the mind of the one who receives it. You must simply let it go. Once you recognize the power that shame has over you, it is easy to ignore. The Bokori will be no more threatening than a screaming, petulant child," Umbrasia said, brushing her fingers through the silver streak in his hair.

The excitement Adam felt was still there, yet another feeling was rapidly replacing it: serenity. He closed his eyes to soak in the feeling. He took a deep breath and opened his eyes upon exhaling. Umbrasia's triangular eyes were comforting. The tension and excitement in his body had relaxed. He smiled.

"Thank you. That's the third time you've helped me feel better. I don't know how you do it."

Umbrasia retracted her hand and her feet landed softly on the ground. **"It is one of many gifts I possess. I am a Magi. A healer. I've counseled thousands of sentients that have suffered through their lives. I am here because you are embarking upon a great quest. One which will forever alter the fate of the galaxy."**

"The fate of the galaxy. The Orb is that important or are you speaking about our fight for independence?" Adam asked. He thought about Arabella. His mind flooded with images of John, his mother, Trissefer, Aaron, his father, Sam. All the Humans living under Bokori rule. He envisioned what the Orb of Emancipation might look like. The image was dust in the wind. He couldn't get a tangible grasp on what he was after. Yet, they were flying closer and closer towards it. Farther and farther away from Arabella.

"Your thoughts dwell on home. Do not fear. I was honest when I told you Rorae do not read minds. There is no need. I can read your eyes. Your expression. You wonder if you've chosen the correct path."

"The situation is slipping from my grasp. Every time I think I get a handle on what's going on, the universe seems to add to my troubles. It's a layer of complexity I do not need. I cannot control it."

"Do not attempt to control it, Adam. Many sentients have failed precisely because they've tried to control what they cannot. All you can do is choose a trail before you and blaze on through. There are no right or wrong paths. No right or wrong destinations. Your journey towards the Orb of Emancipation may take you physically farther from your goal. Nevertheless, you are on a path towards what you seek."

"What is it I seek?"

Umbrasia shrugged. **"What is the Consul of Cloudboard? When you figure that out, you'll know."**

I shouldn't trust her. She has some ulterior motive. They all do. She's no different than the other aliens I've encountered. Adam thought of John in that moment. What he would think of this buxom blossom offering her aid. He certainly wouldn't pay so much attention to her physicality, nor would he let her get that close. Close enough to...

"How did you get aboard the ship?"

Umbrasia giggled. **"I have my secrets. You have yours. Let's just say it's far easier for me to get around a handful of inept guards. Does it matter?"**

"I suppose not. The others will ask the same. I have no idea how I'm going to explain you to them."

"You have a few more hours 'til they rouse."

"Can you see into their dreams, too?"

"I told you. That was no dream. You were seeing."

"What was I seeing?"

"Her."

I thought I was done with pronoun games after leaving Bokori space.

"Who is 'her'?"

"Boganathair. Serpent of the Darkness. My people call her Mother. The Naddine call her...Jes-Mur."

***

The hallway lights turned on a couple hours later. The rest of the crew had woken up and were enjoying a light breakfast around the table in the central conference room. Marduk had woken up earlier than the others to prepare meals for everyone.

"Can add field chef to my resume of seaman, soldier, mercenary, and arms dealer," Marduk mentioned the night before. They had collectively decided to follow the Concordia-based Galactic Standard Time for this trip to sync their sleep cycles and operating hours. Adam had already adjusted to the twenty-hour day-night cycle. The calendar of trade. The Concordian GSC and GST were used in Bokori space in addition to the local Bokor clock. Bokor had almost thirty-hour days due to its slow rotational period. Shorter years though. Coordinating all that with the even longer days of Windless Tornado was one of the early hassles the Separatists had to deal with in establishing Arabella. It was still causing hiccups to this day.

Havera and Samus woke up around the same time. Sam helped Marduk prepare and serve the meal while Havera completed her usual morning calisthenics in the training room. It was Zax's jaunty rendition of *We Rangers Few* reverberating from the starboard observation room that jostled Adam from his restless slumber. He hadn't slept the last couple hours, contemplating on how he'd break the news of their Rorae stowaway.

I don't trust her. Why should they?

Slipping on his jumpsuit, he walked out of the port observation room into the hallway. Umbrasia was floating there, slithering vines and all, just outside the door out of view from the others.

"Bloom well, Adam," Umbrasia greeted him psychically. He tilted his head at the unusual expression. She picked up on his confusion. **"It's how we say 'good morning' on Ashla. We don't have a concept of morning,"** she explained.

"Oh, good morning!" Adam said louder than he meant. He immediately covered his mouth hoping the others hadn't heard him, then just as quickly uncovered his mouth. He wasn't sure if that was an offensive gesture to the mouthless Rorae. Umbrasia only seemed amused by this.

"Relax, Adam. I'm not Bokori. Deep breaths," she said reassuringly.

Adam straightened his jumpsuit trying to retain some dignity. "You ready?"

"Don't worry about me. I'm not worried," she said. He couldn't tell if she was serious or only trying to comfort him. His inexperience with non-Human or Bokori faces was showing. He nodded.

Marduk and Havera were sitting on either side of Sam. She and Havera were eating a plate of wheat pancakes and honey while Marduk was chowing down on fish on a stick. On the opposite side of the table, Zax was sipping on thick brown porridge through a straw that was stuck through a mechsuit port while Jak was nibbling on bread. They all greeted him upon entry.

"You should try some of these Palerian pancakes, Adam! I swear the Cauduun have the best food," Sam said, inhaling her pancakes. She choked for a second. Havera patted Sam on the back with her tail.

"I don't agree," said Marduk.

"Same here," agreed Zax.

"Mmm," Jak grunted in affirmation.

"Who do y'all think does?" Sam asked the group.

"The Moans," they all responded in unison.

"Meh. I never liked seafood. Shelean cuisine is full of clams, sushi, lobsters, and this poor version of a Palerian flat bread recipe called chowdered pitta. I hate it," said Havera, taking a bite of honeyed pancake.

"What you longtails fish can hardly be called seafood," said Marduk.

"I'm sure it's colorful. Hey, Marduk. Do Moans call dishes from out of water 'landfood?' Since Moans resemble other aquatic creatures, is it cannibalistic to eat seafood?" Sam asked with a chuckle. Havera nearly spat out her pancake. Zax burst out laughing. Jak shook his head.

Marduk only rolled his eyes. "Humans," he muttered. "You going to stand there all morning, skinny guppy, or you going to join us?" Marduk asked him. Adam hadn't moved.

He cleared his throat. "There's something y'all need to know. Last night I had trouble sleeping. I thought I saw something, so I went down to the cargo bay and into life support. It appears we have a stowaway," said Adam.

"Stowaway? Where?" Zax asked.

Adam glanced over his shoulder. "Come on in," he said raising his voice. Umbrasia floated on in and hovered next to Adam. Marduk reacted by bolting up and reaching for the Drillhead. Havera's tail stiffened. The others had more measured reactions. Adam spoke up. "Wait! No need for hostility. She says she wants to help us. Her name is..."

"Umbrasia," Havera said, cutting him off.

Everyone turned their attention from Umbrasia to Havera. The Cauduun's tail was relaxing but remained erect. Her eyes locked onto the Rorae. She wiped a bit of honey from her black lips.

"**Bloom well, Havera. It is wonderful to see you again,**" said Umbrasia with a polite bow.

"You know this witch?" asked Marduk. His clawed hand remained on the butt of his rifle. Marduk's response answered one question Adam had about the Rorae. They all could hear her 'speak' at the same time.

I wonder what the limits of her communication are. If she has limits at all.

"She's well-renowned in certain circles for her insight and knowledge of unconventional therapies. She's the only Rorae I know willing to share some secrets of their healing arts. I went to visit her on Concordia after my mater died," Havera explained.

"**I am happy you chose to follow my advice, Havera. I see it has led you down a path closer to your goal,**" said Umbrasia.

"What does she mean by that?" Samus asked.

Havera ignored her. "Why are you following us?"

"**Adam is correct. I am here to help,**" said Umbrasia.

"We don't want your help, sorceress!" Marduk spat.

"Calm down, Marduk. Don't let your experience with the Celestials cloud your judgment. She's a Magi. A powerful one at that. I've seen Umbrasia's abilities firsthand. She could be a vital asset in the journey ahead," said Havera.

"It isn't just the Celestials I fear, longtail. We don't know her motives. She suddenly appears out of nowhere, offering aid with no knowledge of what our mission is or where we're going. Are none of you suspicious about this?" Marduk asked.

"I am," Jak piped in.

"I'm not," Sam and Zax responded, both staring mouths slightly agape at the scantily clad Rorae.

"You're headed to an Excommunicated base with the hopes of retrieving a map that will lead you to the Orb of Emancipation. Finding the Orb will deliver Adam's people from subjugation. An end to the Covenant." Marduk grabbed his gun and pointed it at Umbrasia. Havera reached up and gently pushed his rifle down. Umbrasia gave a slight nod. **"Your suspicions are warranted. I've been following Adam the past few days. I've made myself known to him. *She* told me to watch over him. Protect him from the dangers ahead."**

"You mean Jes-Mur?" asked Adam.

Jak scoffed. "She's a zealot, too. The Dragon Star is a myth. One my people have perpetuated to scare the Zokyo during times of war. Pure propaganda."

"Jes-Mur is real!" insisted Zax.

"Thanks for proving my point, maestro. You've spent too much time with my clan," said Jak.

"And you haven't spent enough," retorted Zax.

Havera turned to Adam. "You've seen *her*, haven't you?"

Adam nodded. "I don't know if what Umbrasia is saying is true. I do know she's helped me find some clarity recently. She's offering to help. I don't think I...we can afford to say no."

Havera's tail swayed gently behind her. "Umbrasia, you can stay. We accept your assistance."

Umbrasia gave another polite bow. "**You honor me, Havera.**"

"What can you do exactly?" asked Sam.

Better question: what can't she do?

"Oh! I have an idea!" Zax said, jumping from his seat. He snatched Samus' Yapam Dagger from its sheath. He held the blade so as to cut himself on his upper left arm.

"What are you doing?" Jak bellowed as he lunged to grab the dagger from Zax's grip.

The Zokyo held it out of his brother's reach. "Rorae Magi are healers, right? Can fix all kinds of diseases and wounds. I want to see if that's true." Jak kept grabbing at the dagger, and Zax held him at bay with his lower arms.

The dagger flew from Zax's grasp. He tried to snatch it from the air but failed. The dagger whipped across the room into Umbrasia's outstretched hand. Blade in hand, Umbrasia slashed at her other arm with the dagger, sending a spray of green blood across the conference room walls. Samus gasped.

"No, don't worry. I'll clean that up," Havera said sarcastically.

After letting her blood flow for several seconds, Umbrasia put her hand over her wound. A spectral, golden glow illuminated the palm of her hand. She brushed her wounded arm with her glowing hand. In the back of Adam's mind, he thought he heard music. A soft, tranquilizing melody stemming from Umbrasia's direction. She removed her hand from her arm, and the music died. She held her arm aloft for all to see. Her arm was undamaged. No blood. Not even a scar. With a flick of her fingers, the blade danced across the room until it hovered in front of Sam. She briefly recoiled before grasping the hilt and inspecting the blade.

"Kewea's curse!" Zax exclaimed in amazement. "I wish I had that ability while learning to ride arkads. So many scrapes and cuts."

Marduk was unconvinced. "Yeah, yeah. She has abilities. We all have abilities. It is precisely her abilities I am worried about."

"Umbrasia stays," Havera said flatly.

"Longtail, I must insist we..."

"This is my ship. My ship, my rules. Don't like it. There's always the airlock. I don't think Moans can swim in space," said Havera.

Marduk growled. He holstered his weapon, but his gaze remained fixed upon Umbrasia. "Fine. I'll be watching you, witch. If there is even a hint of malevolence in your intent, I won't hesitate to hurl you into the nearest black hole."

Umbrasia floated towards Marduk. Slowly, she drifted right up to the Moan until she was right in his face. Marduk tried to back away until he realized he was against the wall. "Stay away from me, sorceress!" Umbrasia brushed the side of Marduk's cheek with the back of her hand. Marduk seized her arm and bent it downwards away from his face. "Don't touch me!"

Umbrasia seemed unfazed, despite her arm being bent in an unnatural direction. **"You lost much in the Dark Realm, Marduk Tiamat. I understand the fear and pain you felt that day. Far better than you'll ever realize. You will watch me. Not out of caution. But powerlessness."** Umbrasia tilted her head towards Marduk's clawed hand that was gripping her arm. Marduk's hand trembled. He struggled to maintain his hold of Umbrasia's arm. He gritted his teeth, resisting the urge to yell. Overwhelmed, he released his grip on her arm. His muscles struggled against the force of Umbrasia's will. Marduk grunted and snarled, but Umbrasia's hold on his body was too strong. She lifted both his arms and mentally pushed them against the wall. Umbrasia leaned in. She must've whispered something to Marduk inaudible to everyone else. Rage was replaced by fear in Marduk's face.

"You've made your point, Umbrasia. Let him go," said Havera.

Umbrasia released her mental grip on Marduk's body. He fell to the floor. His legs buckled, and he collapsed. His knees hit the carpeted floor with a slight thud. Marduk gasped for breath. He struggled to his feet. Havera went to help him up, but he pushed her away. Marduk snarled. "We should've burned your planet when the Celestials ravaged Sin!" He pushed his way past Havera and out of the room.

"I'm both a little afraid and a little turned on," Zax whispered to Sam.

"Me, too," she responded.

Ditto.

"You shouldn't have done that, Umbrasia. We shouldn't fight amongst ourselves. We need Marduk at his best," said Havera.

Umbrasia landed silently next to Havera. She brushed the underside of Havera's chin with her hand. Havera's tail wagged. **"Remember what I told you back then. 'Nothing moves until it is pushed.' Marduk Tiamat is a man floating aimlessly through the void, letting his anger pull him from injustice to injustice. I merely pushed him towards his desire."**

"What does he desire?" asked Havera.

Umbrasia lowered her hand from Havera's chin. **"What we all desire, my dear. Closure."**

28

From Ashes to Ashla

"You're getting it. Find the rhythm. One-three-five-seven. One-three-five-seven. Run your hand back and forth on that tempo over J'y'll's head. Her internal synthesizer will handle the rest. Well, technically, my voice will handle the rest. You only need to keep up."

"This is humiliating."

"Funny. Jak says the same thing. Again."

"I can't memorize a dozen songs' tempos in a day."

"Trick of the trade. That tempo will cover most bardic songs from the past half millennia. Best not to mention that to anyone, please."

"Does no one create original music, or does no one want original music?"

"Yes."

Zax's de facto dress rehearsals with Marduk were surprisingly mild mannered. After the dust-up with Umbrasia's introduction in the conference room, Marduk threw himself into his role for the upcoming operation. It was strange to watch Jak play while a second Jak worked on the finishing touches of Dee's repairs only a few feet away. Adam checked in on Marduk throughout the rest of the day. He was worried. More so, Havera was worried about dissension in the group. She and Umbrasia had a long conversation alone in Havera's quarters. When they emerged, it was decided that a respectful distance between Umbrasia and Marduk should be maintained. Umbrasia returned to meditate in life support while Marduk spent time between his quarters in the armory and the cargo hold with Zax and Jak. Sam and Havera went to train in the workout room. Adam had spent most of the time with his thoughts in the library.

I used to talk to Triss about everything. What would she think of all this?

He had stretched out his arm to the empty side of his cot. He hadn't realized how much he had missed her until that moment. They didn't depart on the best of terms. Guilt. Regret. Longing. He felt it all. He had closed his eyes to picture her face. It was a struggle. The harder he tried to visualize Triss' face, but another's took her place. He shook his head.

It was barely a hookup! I've been with several women. Why is she affecting me this way? Sure, she was my first Cauduun. Barely. Not my first alien. Her lips were black. Not black. Pewter. Her skin was red. Not red. Silver.

Adam had wandered out of the library into the hallway. Jak was standing outside the shower room with Havera. She was wrapped in a simple purple robe. The Cauduun's hair was down and wet. Adam turned away to resist the temptation to let his mind wander. His ears caught the faint hint of an argument in hushed whispers. All he heard was Jak. "You're playing a dangerous game, Shelean. The closer we get to our destination, the greater the peril, and you know it. With that *thing* aboard we're all taking a huge risk." Samus interrupted their argument when she walked out of the shower room also wet and robed.

Jak doesn't trust Umbrasia either. Can't say I blame him.

Adam ignored their conversation and headed down the steps into the cargo bay, where he walked in on that aforementioned conversation between Zax and Marduk.

"Where's Dee?" Adam asked, noticing the bot was gone.

"Up in the cockpit. We're approaching Ashla within the hour. I'm excited! I've never seen Lasairfal in person. One of the great wonders of the galaxy built by the Venvuishyn," Zax said, putting down his lute.

"It's overrated. Trust me," said Marduk.

"A hundred-mile-high wall of white flames is overrated? Someone's jaded," insisted Zax.

"You weren't nearly cut in half by a Celestial's ice whip within its shadow," said Marduk.

Zax bobbed his head. "Fair enough."

"You won't see it in person, regardless. The Rorae expressly forbid aliens from landing on their homeworld without permission. Those that have tried end up missing or worse. Breagadun is the only safe port, and there's a capacity limit. Besides, we aren't landing. We're refueling at a station in Ashla's orbit. You can see Lasairfal from one of the side viewports if you're so inclined," said Marduk.

"Everything okay with you, Marduk?" asked Adam.

"I'll be better if y'all stop asking me that question," said Marduk.

"We're worried about you. That was intense," said Zax.

"I let my guard down. It won't happen again. I should know better by now not to let a Rorae get that close to me ever since the Dark Realm, speaking of Ashla," said Marduk.

Adam sat down next to Marduk. He couldn't help but notice the Moan's eyes flickering towards the life support room every few seconds.

"Can I ask you something related?" asked Adam. Marduk grunted. Adam took that as passive confirmation. "What exactly were the Celestials, and what does the Dark Realm have to do with them?"

"They're abominations," said Marduk curtly. Adam raised an eyebrow at him. Marduk sighed. "The Bokori education system sucks."

"What Bokori education system?" Zax said with a snigger.

Adam chuckled. Even Marduk cracked a smile. "Alright. The Celestials were Rorae. No 'were' either. They're still out there. I'm convinced."

"You think so?" Zax asked.

"I know so," said Marduk.

"But what were...are they?" a confused Adam asked.

"Magi. Not just any Magi. They are angels of death. What you saw that sorceress do to me is nothing compared to the power of a Celestial. They're the result of secret experiments conducted by Excom scientists to create the ultimate super soldier. The perfect weapon. A means to fundamentally shift the nature of warfare. They succeeded. Nobody knows for certain how or why, but it was the Celestials that destroyed Sin. Nearly a billion lives and a pristine garden world wiped out in minutes. The extermination of an entire planet's ecosystem," explained Marduk.

"The Boiling of Sin."

"Indeed. All that remains of Sin is a husk. An irradiated graveyard with the screams of millions of lost souls haunting its oceanic wastes. Moan souls, mostly. There was a silver lining. The sudden mass murder of millions shocked the galaxy. Spurred the subjugated and independent races of the galaxy to band together to force a peace. Of course, in typical fashion, it took nudging from the Cauduun to truly start peace talks. You can thank Havera's mother for that," said Marduk.

"Havera's mother?"

"Lucretia Pompeia of Shele. She was the Prima Legata of the Cauduun Monarchical Alliance, in charge of all Alliance armed forces. Answerable only to the queen. Except, Pompeia had refused Queen Alexandra II's orders in the early days of the Strife to enter the war on the Naddine's side. The beastriders weren't happy and neither was Alexandra. She removed Pompeia from her post. Too late. The damage was done. Pompeia's decision to ignore orders and keep the Cauduun out of the war was incredibly popular with the Cauduun people. So popular was Pompeia even the other duchesses were afraid. All of Pompeia's successors as Prima Legata refused Alexandra II's orders. The queen died only a few years later. Officially, it was a stroke due to old age. She was one-hundred-and-eighty-four," said Marduk.

"You believe the poisoning rumors?" Zax asked.

Marduk shrugged. "Who is the Consul of Cloudboard? Before my time. My father talked about it on occasion. Cauduun politics are more cutthroat and ruthless than they'd have us believe. Even more so than the Naddine, and those beast bangers have actual blood sports to choose their next leader."

"What does this have to do with the Celestials?" asked Adam impatiently.

"Hush, skinny guppy. I'm getting there. Naturally, the next queen restored Pompeia to Prima Legata. For the remainder of the Strife, the Cauduun kept their tails out of the conflict. Until the Boiling of Sin. The Zokyo fleets were prepared to launch an attack on Naddine-held Melusine. It was a trap. Not one set by the Naddine or the Zokyo, but by Pompeia. She had met secretly with the representatives of the burgeoning Coalition of Independent Nations and struck a deal with them. When the Zokyo fleets arrived, they were all met by the entire Alliance navy. The Sinner races' ships in the Zokyon and Naddine fleets flipped their fins. Both were completely surrounded. The mercenary fleets on both sides dissolved almost immediately once they realized they were outgunned. Pompeia even somehow convinced the Yunes to position their fleet to the south to cut off escape. Pompeia threatened to destroy the entire Naddine and Zokyon armed forces unless they agreed to meet for peace talks. Hence the Saptia Conference and what transpired there," said Marduk.

Saptia. Kewea curse Saptia.

Marduk continued. "During the conference, certain information came to light. It was discovered a Cauduun scientist, Pontifex Maro Brunato Metalla, was running a secret operation sponsored by the Excommunicated in the undergrowth of Ashla's Dark Realm. The Celestials. The Rorae weren't at Saptia. Though they were technically Naddine subjugates, the Rorae kept to themselves. Attempts at diplomatic forays with the plants fell on deaf ears. The Rorae refused to act against the Excommunicated even on their own world. The Rorae fear the Dark Realm. No way they would ever enter that place willingly.

It was at the height of the Conference that a decision was made. For there to be peace, the Celestials must be destroyed. Pompeia uttered her famous phrase, 'From ashes to Ashla, the sins of our hate will be washed away.' The proverbial ink wasn't dry on the Saptia Accords when a multi-species strike force was established to search and destroy the Celestials in the Dark Realm without the Rorae's permission. As I told you and Havera the other day, we tracked their hidden base just inside the Dark Realm. A few Celestials awakened from their slumber and attacked. Hundreds died. We destroyed the lab and the pods containing over a dozen Celestials recuperating. We found no trace of Pontifex Brunato. Before we destroyed the lab, we found a few empty pods not accounted for among the bodies of the Celestials. I led a team to track the surviving Celestials into the jungle. A few klicks from the base my team was ambushed. A terrifying scream rattled our brains. We were cut down one-by-one. The Celestial emerged from the thicket and swiped at me with her ice whip. My sergeant stepped in front of the blade. She was skewered. Killed instantly. The tip of the whip burned the front of my chest and knocked me unconscious. When I awoke, I was horribly ice burned and my team were all dead. Only a few feet away, I discovered a horror. The body of a dead Rorae child. It was then I realized the true depravity of the Excommunicated. The Celestials were created from experiments on Rorae children."

Zax sat down, letting out a deep exhale. He grabbed his lute and strung a few mournful chords.

"*All was quiet, the dead make no stirrings.*
All was quiet, the living seek to follow.
One-hundred years, no heroes came.
One-hundred years, victims take the blame.
From ashes to Ashla, the sins of our hate will be washed away.
From ashes to Ashla, the living and the dead join the eternal flame.
From ashes to Ashla, we can never forget our everlasting shame.

Zax sang sadly. All was quiet in the ship, except for his voice.

"*From ashes to Ashla,*
From ashes to Ashla,
From ashes to Ashla,
From ashes to Ashla,
We can never forget our everlasting shame."

Zax's voice trailed off weakly. The echo of his last note filled the ship. No one spoke for a minute. Zax put down his lute and sniffled. "That was the first song Jak's mother taught me."

"It's beautiful," Adam said.

"It's false idolatry. Memorializing a tragedy that way. Of course, the

Cauduun hailed Pompeia as a hero. They call the end of the war 'Pax Pompeia.' The Cauduun always find a way to make everything about them. The real tragedy is the war could've ended decades sooner. If only Pompeia wasn't so egotistical, the Alliance would've nipped the conflict in the bud. Millions of innocents would still be alive," insisted Marduk.

"Or we would've escalated the conflict further, killing millions more sooner." Havera had walked down the stairs into the cargo bay.

Marduk scoffed. "I'm sorry you heard me say that, but it is true. By abdicating their galactic responsibility, the Cauduun left innocents to the slaughter. They could've leveraged their influence over the Naddine to find peace or intimidated the Zokyo with the size of their military. Not even their great mecha can stand toe-to-toe with the Cauduun's legions. You know it. I know it. We all know it."

"Arm-chair captaining. We only see how bad the conflict turned out. Not how much worse it could've been by adding Cauduun lives to the mix. The Praetorians teach us to examine the facts. The Union had just arrived, opening up new battlefields with their weapons and terraforming technologies. We had no idea where they were going to come down in the conflict. Turns out it was both sides. My mater thought it wise not to needlessly throw away lives in somebody else's conflict. If we had gotten involved, thousands of young Cauduun men and women would never see their families again. Maters and paters would lose children," said Havera.

Marduk leapt to his feet. "Tell that to the millions of mothers, fathers, wives, husbands, sisters, brothers, daughters, and sons who died on Sin! Who died in the last phase of the Strife. The Tetrad Phase killed more people than the entirety of the Great Galactic War! Your mother could've stopped it all. She had no problem involving the Cauduun after a billion deaths. She did it without firing a shot. She could've stopped this sooner!"

"You don't know that!"

"Yes, I do. I know it with every fiber of my being. I lost six members of my family on Sin, including my mother and sister. My father couldn't bear the shame of losing them. He fed himself to the sharks only a year later. The Excommunicated may have created the weapon, but it was the Cauduun who empowered them to do so. Look at the Humans. If the Cauduun or any of other Proprietor races had the courage to stand up to the Bokori, we wouldn't need to be here. We all know how hollow the Bokori's military prowess is. With minimal effort, the Conclave could compel the Bokori to free the Humans. Now, we're chasing a myth half-way across the galaxy on behalf of a gangster while the Humans starve and wait for their inevitable execution. Would it matter in the long run if a few Cauduun died regaining their freedom?"

"It would matter to the families of those that died."

"And the families of the Humans that are going to die unless some-one intervenes?"

"And if the Zokyo decide to defend the Bokori as they have histori-cally? Start another galactic war."

"I think Adam would agree it's worth the risk."

Adam remembered what Daloth had told him. *"Sometimes you must engage in a smaller fight now to prevent a larger one in the future."* He wasn't sure what to believe. At his core, Adam knew they needed help. Even with the Long Con, the Bokori were still too powerful for them to defeat in a head-to-head fight. He was angry at the other races, at the Conclave, for not stepping in. For not honoring their agreements. For Saptia. They could have prevented this. Yet, that Hisba's face flashed across his mind. The image of his brother's bloodied body returned. There will be hundreds more like them in the coming days. Thousands. No matter what happens. *Perhaps the right thing to do is to fight.* In his conversation with Daloth, he was determined to fight back. Yet, when John asked for his help, for him to come home, he refused. Instead, Adam fled to the other side of the galaxy away from the fight. *Am I afraid? I'm not afraid of dying. No more than anyone else. I keep seeking an alternative to fighting.* The disconnect between Adam's words and thoughts troubled him. Unable to give Marduk a satisfactory answer, he kept quiet.

Marduk scoffed. "'Everlasting shame' indeed."

Marduk strode past Havera towards the stairs. She stopped him for an instant. "It's not the people deciding who take the risk. It's those that have no choice but to follow their orders who are putting their lives on the line."

"They chose to become soldiers. The Humans didn't choose to be subjugated."

Didn't we?

"Not everyone who chooses to become a soldier truly had a choice either."

Marduk gave her a respectful huff and walked away. Havera sighed. "I came down here to tell you we're about to exit negative space. We've arrived at Ashla. Better buckle down."

Havera hurried back up the stairs. Zax checked the straps on Sel-Ena before heading up the stairs with his lute in one hand and J'y'll in the other.

Adam took a step towards the stairs. "**There are no right or wrong paths. Only the path you choose.**" Adam whirled around to see Umbrasia floating in the doorway to life support.

"What if the path I choose has negative consequences for those I care about?" asked Adam.

Umbrasia floated over to him. "**You cannot control the actions of others. Only your own. If you don't like the pathways laid before you, create one yourself.**"

***

Exiting the colorful clutches of negative space, the Cicera glided towards its destination. Only one space station was in orbit, with only a singular ship in the vicinity. It left not long after the Cicera had arrived. Nobody was paying attention. All eyes were glued to the starboard observation window. Zax had a drink in hand from the room's small bar. He nearly dropped it observing Ashla for the first time.

Ashla was a small planet compared to the other habitable worlds Adam had visited. About one-fifth the size of Concordia, Ashla was even smaller than Windless Tornado. Completely green with giant rivers snaking its way through the continent. Its mountains all the way to the small ocean near the equator had a verdant coating. It was hard to fathom intelligent life evolving on such a tiny world at the edge of the habitable zone of a typical yellow sun system. If not for one prominent feature, Ashla would probably be overlooked by the average spacer. The system itself wasn't that remarkable. Only a pair of gas giants flanking Ashla on either side and a rocky planet so close to the star its surface was untouchable. That wasn't why people came to Ashla, homeworld of the Rorae Conservatory.

"Lasairfal," muttered an amazed Zax.

Along the meridian, wrapping the small world in a band, a shimmering crackle of dancing golden ivory flames drew the eye. A jewel so beautiful, so haunting. Adam felt a small twitch from the scars on his back. Seeing something as wondrous as the wall of radiant fire, even from this far away, reminded Adam just how small he was. How small his world was. *Humanity's problems are trite in comparison to the labors that built this marvel. Only the goddesses could've created something like this. They must have.* The movement of the fire was not natural. The flames seemed to sway like leaves on a tree in a cool breeze. Every few latitudinal degrees the flames grew higher and swirled, giving them the appearance of fiery swords staked into the planet's surface. The closer the Cicera flew towards the planet, the more iridescent the flames became, shifting and gleaming in the light of the sun. Approaching the refueling station, the split surface of Ashla crystallized. The flames split the planet in two, as if they were erupting from the fiery depths of Kewea. One side of Lasairfal was completely lit by the star, the other side was utterly cast in the wall's shadow.

"I never thought I'd see the Dark Realm again," Marduk said.

"What's down there, Marduk?" asked a curious Sam.

"Pray you never learn firsthand, little guppy. Horrors. Creatures evolved to hunt in the dark. Ravenous predators, flora and fauna alike. Your worst nightmares couldn't conjure a fragment of what the goddesses bred on that accursed world. That includes both sides," Marduk said.

"Hard to believe anyone built something like this," said Zax.

"This is sentient made?" asked an astonished Adam.

"Must be. Nothing like this occurs in nature," Zax insisted.

"Bold claim, noodle guppy. That's the kind of presumptive response I'd expect from a Zokyo," said Marduk.

"I was raised by the Naddine."

"Beastrider ignorance then. The galaxy contains one-hundred billion stars, at least, including countless number of planets, moons, and black holes. We've barely breached the surface of Griselda's enigmas," Marduk said, using the common name for the galaxy.

"Hmph. I still believe it was the Venvuishyn. We know they made impressive interstellar structures. Why not this? Doubt the Rorae could create anything like this. No offense, Umbrasia!" Zax called out. The Rorae wasn't around.

"I don't know about that," said Havera. "I've been to Breagadun. The floating city is impressive. Completely organic. I don't need to tell you, Marduk, about the power of Rorae Magi."

"Breagadun is a trap. A city to herd bright-eyed explorers and curiously incurious minds away from what the Rorae don't want us to know. Ashla's surface gravity is two-and-a-half times greater than planets like Concordia or Rema, yet it's a fraction of the size. The density of such a world must be enormous. Cradite only knows what lies beneath its surface. Something is powering that wall of fire and keeping the planet tidally locked," said Marduk.

"Didn't you just insist Lasairfal is a natural phenomenon?" Zax said.

"I never said it was. I never said it wasn't. One truth is clear. We have no idea, and the Rorae revel in keeping us in the dark," said Marduk.

"Can't we land on the surface and find out?" Sam asked.

Havera shook her head. "The Rorae don't believe in many laws, but there is one immutable order. No aliens allowed on the surface of Ashla. You need to ride an organically grown transport vessel from the refueling station travel to Breagadun. They'd prefer we didn't visit at all. Most people get the hint. Even when the Rorae were technically a subjugated race, few visited Ashla. Every exploratory or military mission to Ashla has failed. Most of the time, the interlopers disappear without a trace. Marduk already pointed out the tremendous gravity of the surface. You'd need special equipment to withstand that kind of pressure. Certain species, like Moans, can handle that kind of pressure better than others. Furthermore, the atmosphere is hyper oxygenated. Certainly breathable, but the slightest spark creates purging fires. It also has the nasty tendency of sending a non-Rorae into anaphylactic shock. The Magi built Breagadun specifically for the purpose of allowing aliens to mingle with the native Rorae. Lower gravity and a more hospitable atmosphere. The city floats above an active volcano. Right about there," Havera said, pointing to a section of the continent halfway between Lasairfal and the hemisphere's edge.

"You're leaving out the best part, Havera. No clothes allowed!" Zax threw up his arms in excitement.

Havera rolled her eyes and gave Zax a gentle smack with her tail. "Yes, Zax. It's encouraged but not required. Rorae aren't the biggest fans of artificial technology. Exceptions, like your mechsuit, are permitted."

Samus' eyes widened. "Why not?"

"Corruption."

Everyone's heads turned to see Umbrasia floating in. Marduk took a few steps back and circled around her out of the room. The Rorae followed his movements with her eyes.

"What do you mean corruption?" asked Adam.

"Devices and abominations created by sentients pollute worlds. Not just its environmental health but its spiritual health."

Adam opened his mouth to respond. Dee's voice blared through the comm. "Mistress Havera, we're receiving a transmission over the digiholo. It's from Windless Tornado. Also, the station manager wants to talk to you, Mistress. 'The captain,' specifically."

"Alright. I'll be there in a second," Havera said. She nodded to the group and headed to the cockpit.

Sam put a hand on Adam's shoulder. "I'll talk to John. If he's going to be angry at anyone, let it be me."

Adam murmured thanks, and Sam followed Havera out.

"I'm going to make myself another drink," Zax said, wandering over to the bar on the other side of the room.

Adam remained by the window. Umbrasia floated to his side. The pair observed the ship pulling into the refueling station. The specter of Ashla and Lasairfal remained visible.

"I don't suppose you can tell me more about that wall of fire?" Adam asked.

Umbrasia giggled. "**Afraid not. The Magi of yesteryear say Lasairfal is both a gift and a warning from Jes-Mur. Keeps Rorae safe from the dangers of the night. Any Rorae who bypasses the wall is incinerated not by fire but by the burning passion of their curiosity. No danger there. No Rorae will ever willingly step foot in that place. We remain in Ashla.**"

"Isn't the whole planet Ashla?"

Umbrasia shook her head. "**Ashla refers to the lands and seas of the sun. The planet's true name has long been lost. The Rorae that dwell near Lasairfal call the other side 'Bogariakt,' which when passed through the mind roughly means 'realm of darkness.' That's the story. How much of that you choose to believe is up to you.**"

Adam raised an eyebrow. "What's that supposed to mean? You're lying?"

Umbrasia shrugged. "**What is the Consul of Cloudboard? History is written by those who write history. The tales we tell ourselves to find some meaning and order in the universe is what binds us together. Is Lasairfal really a creation of the Mother or is that some comforting tale told to soothe children and those too curious to know when it is best to leave some mysteries mysterious?**"

Adam rolled his eyes. *My mother would love her.*

"Personally, I'm inclined to believe the Cauduun Pantheon myths. Four sisters coming together to create the perfect mate. I find it amusing," Adam said with a sarcastic laugh.

"**Three sisters.**"

"Huh?"

"**It was three sisters not four. Must be. Only three...**"

"Three sisters?"

"**Only three. He said only three. It must be true...**"

Umbrasia's voice trailed off. She closed her eyes and clutched her forehead. She fell to the ground on one knee. Adam put a hand on her shoulder. She was ice cold. "Umbrasia, are you alright?"

She ignored him. The petals on her head fluttered. Some of the nearby furniture started to rattle. A slight buzzing formed in Adam's ears. The bar was rattling enough to tip over his drink.

Zax noticed the shaking. "What's happening?!" he yelled.

"I don't know! Umbrasia. Umbrasia, are you in pain?" Adam tried to reach her, but she kept speaking to no one in particular.

"**Three not four. I'm certain. I'm certain! Three not four!**" she screamed. Adam clutched his head. Zax ducked behind the bar. The buzzing in Adam's ears erupted. His back scars seared with pain. Chairs and glasses were tossed around the room. The bulkhead vibrated. The carpet beneath their feet began to tear.

She's going to tear the ship apart!

The buzzing in his ears slightly subsided. A mad thought took hold in his brain. He felt an instinct to act. He didn't question it. He kneeled in front of her and put his hands on her cheeks. They were cold. He pulled her closer to his face and kissed her. She had no mouth. He kissed her right on her facial leaf. It was unexpectedly warm compared to the rest of her body. Umbrasia's eyes shot open. Around her triangular red eyes were faint golden rings. Before he could look away, Adam's gaze was drawn to them. He felt like he was being sucked out of his body into them. Stars and planets rushed by him. He was flying through negative space. The colors danced around his body. He felt strangely warm sailing the depths of space. A blinding flash of light impeded his vision. He came to a halt in front of a colossal celestial beast of swirling icy white crystal. A goddess in living flesh.

Jes-Mur.

Her jaws opened, and he was drawn inside. Warmth was replaced by fear. Not his own fear. Her maw shut around him. He was enveloped in darkness. In the distance, a beacon of light peered over the horizon. The beacon grew until its form took shape. A barrier of holy white flame. He was surrounded by a labyrinth of tangled vines, broken branches, and a river of blood. Dead bodies were strewn everywhere. A melting pot of different races all torn up and eviscerated. His vision was drawn to another body separate from the others. It was too far away to make out the details, but it certainly wasn't Human. He was on his knees screaming. Except, there was no sound. The screaming was entirely in his head.

In a rush, he was pulled back to his body. He was kneeling in front of Umbrasia. His face mere inches from hers. His lips were cold.

"Woah! Should I give you two the room? Y'all seem like you want to conduct some Naddine diplomacy, hehe." It was Zax. He was staring at them with a wide grin, cleaning the glass he had been drinking.

Adam let go of Umbrasia's face. The buzzing in Adam's ears was gone. The vibrations had stopped. Glancing around, everything seemed to be where it was minutes earlier. No sign of broken glass, torn carpet, or overturned furniture. Confused, Adam stared at Umbrasia. The golden rings around her irises were gone.

"You weren't meant to see that. I'm going to go lay down. Space travel is difficult for me. Do not follow me." She floated off the ground and away from him. Adam was too stunned to respond. By the time he found his tongue, she was gone.

It was all an illusion, or was it?

"Tough break, buddy. I thought you had her," Zax said with a chortle. "Don't blame you for trying. Would love to roll around in that grass."

"Did you see anything unusual happen just then?" asked Adam.

"You mean besides you putting the moves on our sexy, sorceress friend? Seemed like she was getting a headache. She grasped at those petals on her head. You bent down and planted a kiss. What was that like? Must've been strange kissing someone with no lips. Didn't realize your mouth had healing powers," said Zax chuckling.

Adam touched his lips. The warmth was returning to them. He licked them. They were slightly chapped and tasted of cinnamon. "She's certainly an extraordinary woman."

"I think your interests lay in what's under her vines, hehe."

"Shut it, Zax."

Zax put his hands up apologetically, sipping a straw through his mechsuit's induction port.

Suddenly, Sam entered the room. "John wants to talk to you."

"I don't suppose you heard or felt anything either?" Adam asked.

"Now!" she snapped.

Adam was startled. "Okay, okay. No need to be hostile."

She grunted and walked away as quickly as she came. Zax whistled. "What do you suppose got into her?"

Adam shook his head. "I don't know. I'm afraid to find out."

29

Modders and Motives

Adam tried to find Sam on his way to the comms room. He walked around the outside of the conference room through the corridor between Havera's quarters and the guest quarters, which Sam had been using. Noticing the door to her room was closed, he thought about knocking but opted to keep going.

He entered the bridge with the digiholo display of the galaxy map in the center. Beyond there in the cockpit, he saw Havera and Dee sitting in the pilots' chairs, communicating with someone Adam presumed was the station manager. They seemed to be exasperated by the conversation. From the back, Dee seemed like he was fully functional again with a fresh new coat of hunter green plates. He left them to it and turned left into the comms room.

It was a relatively small compartment. Devices for short-range and long-range communications were neatly built into the walls. In the back was a door to one of the two large escape pods. Adam sat down in the chair in front of the digiholo communication. It was an identical model to the one belonging to Dusertheus. A projection of John was already there standing there, tapping his feet impatiently.

"About time! Sam told me y'all are in orbit above Ashla. Ashla! Completely in the opposite direction from Arabella," John said.

"Look, John," Adam tried to explain.

"Coward! You're running from the fight!" John yelled.

Explains Sam's mood.

"I am trying to find a way to stop the fighting before it starts. Patron-Saint will come through for us if we do this. If she can help us get the Bokori de-certified as a Proprietor race..."

"You believe that alien scum! These are the same people that promised us, promise *your father* our freedom at Saptia. Now, you're jumping into bed with the people that enable our oppressors." John's voice barely contained his rage.

His choice of words did not go unnoticed. "John, if you have something you want to say about Havera, then say it. Quit talking through euphemisms and entendres."

John straightened his posture. Adam realized he was wearing full combat armor. A searstaff was visible on his back. "If you insist. The longtail princess is using you. I avoided bringing this up since I know you and Trissefer split up. You want to find pleasure in the arms of an alien woman. Fine. It wouldn't be your first. You did what you needed to do. We're all under a tremendous amount of stress. This has gone far beyond a dalliance. You're being led astray from the cause. From the Long Con! Chasing after foreign myths involving foreign goddesses for foreign benefactors. Oh, yeah. Sam told me the whole story. The fight is here. We must destroy the Covenant. The Bokori aren't going to sit on their gray asses. Every day they press closer and closer. They're already testing the stability of the Bubble. Those aliens are intentionally trying to keep you away from us. They know if you come back, bringing the symbolism of your defiance with you, there's nothing they can do to stop our *true* emancipation. You are deceived."

"You're wrong, John. Havera and I aren't involved in that way," *I wish that we were. At least, I think I do.* "It was my choice to pursue the Orb. Mine. We could find another path that doesn't involve so much bloodshed. I am coming back, regardless. You must be patient. We have some time."

"Are you so naive to believe it was truly your choice? Your longtail friend is a Praetorian. You're pursuing this object from *their* folklore on behalf of another longtail in service to an alien gangster whose motives you cannot know. I'll bet every last Link we have that it was her who pushed you down this path," said John.

Adam opened his mouth to respond. *Maybe he's right. The Orb. Ashla. The Excommunicated. Patron-Saint. Jes-Mur. None of this involves me. I belong home.*

"We're getting ready for a fight. We need our Commissioner for Defense and Security," John said, tempering his tone.

Adam remembered something Sam had said a couple days ago. "How did you get Shepard, Auditore, and the others to go along with you? Even in this dire situation, there's no way they'd go along with a military engagement. They'd push for a conciliatory deal. Let me speak with Shepard."

John shook his head. "I'm afraid that is not possible. Commissioners Shepard, Snake, and Auditore are under arrest for aiding sedition."

"Excuse me?"

"Commissioner Quinn has assumed their duties in the interim. She has authorized a full military engagement against the Bokori, the Hisbaween, Modder enablers, and any of their alien allies that attempt an attack on Human sovereignty and independence."

"I did not authorize this! Get Triss on the digiholo immediately!"

"Commissioner Quinn and I are in complete alignment. You will not convince her otherwise."

"You don't have the power to do this!"

"You approved my authority the moment you handed over temporary power to me. I have full authority to weed out sedition and infiltrators within our ranks. That includes any Human sympathizers and counterrevolutionaries. If you want to stop me, it is within your prerogative to come back and resume the full duties of your office. Until you do, I am in charge."

Adam couldn't believe what he was hearing. This was a step too far, even for John. "Why are you doing this?"

John sighed. A bit of interstellar static fuzzed his digital avatar.

"I learned the lessons the Bokori taught us. Lessons you refused to acknowledge. Long Con or no, might makes right. They believe they have the power and the right to control us. To dictate what is best for us. Well, turnabout is fair play, so they say. You won't do what's best for Humans. I am going to force you to do what is right. If that means...Humans...die...be it."

John's avatar fizzled. The audio was cutting in-and-out. Adam couldn't discern what he was saying. "You're breaking up. I can't hear you. There's a problem with the transmission." His avatar vanished. Nothing but static remained. "John. John! Answer me. Kewea's curse! Piece of junk."

Adam smacked the receiver. The static fizzled. A new digital avatar started to materialize. A tall, slender figure in simple, long black robes. Hooded and cloaked with a kyqad covering its mouth. A simple stitched insignia on the kyqad of a gray open-palmed hand was visible. A Bokori hand. What little of the person's unnaturally gray face peeked through the shadows of the hood. Its surgically-altered vertical white, almost pupil-less eyes blinked at an unsettlingly steady rhythm. A metronome counting down the days until the Covenant would utterly swallow humanity whole. A cold sweat overcame Adam's body. His back scars itched and pained. His throat dried up. His pulse raced. He tried not to physically react, but he couldn't help flinching at the sight of his tormentor, the High Hisba.

"Equality through sacrifice, Person Flowing Courage." The High Hisba's greeting frightened Adam. He felt his spirit ripping from his body. He was not prepared for this moment. His words failed him. "Person Flowing Courage, I can see you. I know you are there. There is no cause for alarm." Its calm, emotionless tone gave nothing away. Even the slight muffling of its voice by its kyqad did little to blunt its charisma. The sense of ease the High Hisba conveyed compared to Adam's unease was stark.

I can't do this. I must say something.

Adam cleared his throat. "That is...that is not my name, High Hisba," he finally squeaked out.

"It is the name you were assigned at birth. It is the name the community knows you by. It is your Covenant name. What you choose to call yourself in your own mind has no relevancy and is an affront towards the progress Humans have made under Bokori guidance. However, if it will put your toxic mind at ease, I believe the nonbelievers call you 'Adam.' Would that make this conversation more pleasant, Person *Adam*?" The High Hisba spat out his preferred name with such venom. Yet, the gesture, however fleeting, surprised him. In all his years knowing the High Hisba, he had never known the Modder to compromise. That unnerved Adam further.

"How did you intercept this transmission?" Adam asked, stalling until he could figure out what was going on.

"Did you believe your communications were secure? Windless Tornado is sacred Bokori ground. The People's House and the Committee for the Advancement of Love and Virtue monitor everything. It is science. You have spread your blasphemy and toxicity far and wide. You've cajoled many nonbelievers into aiding your ongoing heresy. When the Hisbaween learned that one of these interlopers provided your fellow blasphemers with a digiholo communication, we decided to use that to our advantage. I waited for 'the murderer' to contact you. I needed to speak to you face-to-face."

The murderer...John.

"Why?"

"You ask so many questions, Person Adam. Such a prying, curious mind is what got you into trouble in the first place. Do not question wisdom. You should accept what I say at face value. We know what is best for you, and the Bokori know what is best for us. It is science."

Adam stared back into the Modder's disfigured face. It lacked a nose or any visible hair. Not even a single eyelash or eyebrow. All the more to resemble a Bokori. All to look less Human. Adam bit his tongue. His back screamed at him, but he pushed the protests down. "You didn't answer my question, High Hisba."

The High Hisba shook its head. "Very well. Despite your actions of the past, present, and near future, I know deep down, beneath that bile of hate, is a good person. You were abducted from your loving Community by those who would deny you empathy. Twice. Yet, I have seen firsthand that there is a gentle kindness to your character. Misguided kindness to be sure. Under the correct care, that kindness and empathy can be salvaged. You need only return to Bokor. Find salvation from want. Salvation from selfishness can be achieved if you embrace science. If you embrace the Bokori as our saviors. Embrace true equality through sacrifice."

"You mean go back to rehab? Return to that Kewea-accursed hellscape of a prison to be drugged, tortured, and mentally broken."

"You were never drugged. You were never tortured. You were certainly not mentally broken. Not by the Hisbaween. We were healing you."

Adam cocked his head confused. "I was there. I experienced it all. You confessed to your actions in front of the entire galaxy!"

"The High Hisba did no such thing. You are confused. Toxic thoughts, lies implanted in your mind by nonbelievers to turn you away from science. Misguided attempts to end the Covenant. This is why you need education. It was those toxic heretics that broke you."

"Do not denigrate my parents that way!"

"Further proof of how lost you truly are. Of how much you need the Community. Biology. Families. Even names. These institutions lead to inequality. Discriminatory disparity that will destroy us the way it destroyed Human civilization before us. The Bokori rescued us so that we may never need to experience such dismay ever again. You have no parents. Only progenitors. You have no need for anything but the Covenant. You were happy."

Silver skin. Ivory eyes. Pewter lips. An artistic mind.

"Yes. I was. Until you took her away from me."

The High Hisba sighed. "Your mind is too clouded by hate to see reason. If appealing to your scientific mind won't work, I'll try your selfish one. Let me be perfectly clear. The People's House and the Hisbaween know everything. We know the murderer leads your band of heretics towards strife. In a few days' time he will launch a foolish attack that will needlessly kill thousands. Thousands of Humans I should say. The

People's Navy is fully prepared to counter any act of aggression. Your little separatist movement is done. No matter your fruitless acts of defiance. The Covenant will prevail because we are stronger together."

Adam's worst fears were confirmed. He contemplated what to say. Words failed him. Out of the corner of his eye, he realized he was being watched. A scowling Havera was standing alone in the doorway of the comms room. Her demeanor conveyed curiosity rather than fear or anger. *She wants to see how I'll react.*

The High Hisba continued its speech. "Hisba Unbroken Tide has been dispatched to collect you. It was informed of your little foray into Rorae space. I suggest you surrender to it. The Excommunicated also know you plan on arriving at their station with the rogue Cauduun duchess. Such a selfish endeavor petty vengeance is. The appeal for someone of your mental state makes sense. It's almost poetic. It was those Excom pirates that drove humanity into the arms of the Bokori. They shall do so a second time. Surrender and you have my assurances all the other blasphemers will be pardoned, save for the murderer. All sins against the Covenant shall be forgiven. They'll be allowed to reintegrate themselves into a Community. No rehabilitation required. You can either wait for Unbroken Tide to receive you at Ashla, or you can take your chances with the Excommunicated. Your choice." Though it never removed its kyqad, Adam could discern a satisfied smile sprung across the Modder's deformed face.

Thousands of lives will be spared if I turn myself in. Is this the path I am meant to follow?

Havera moved into the room, closing the door behind her. She stayed out of range of the digiholo. Her tail oscillated frantically behind her. *Is she afraid or excited?*

A thought struck Adam. "Afraid," he whispered.

"What did you say, Person Flowing Courage?" the High Hisba said, abandoning presumption of nicety.

"You're afraid," Adam said weakly at first. "You're afraid!" he said more forcefully.

The High Hisba tilted his head. "Afraid of what?"

The Long Con.

"That we'll succeed. If what you told me is true and you've truly intercepted our communications, you know the galaxy is on the verge of dropping you. The galactic institution that humors your craziness is about to cut you off. You're rushing to replace Human soldiers with bots that'll follow your orders without question. You're waking up to the realization that you aren't in the strong position you believed you had," Adam said.

"We have your insignificant movement surrounded fifty-to-one. You are trapped and days away from capitulation."

"Then why not finish us off? Why offer me this opportunity to surrender? No, no. I see through your deceptions. Your first attack on Arabella failed. You thought we'd surrender without a real fight. You cannot fathom why anyone would continue to struggle against your 'wisdom.' You've forgotten your own humanity. You fear that if you order the regular military to launch a full-scale attack, you'll lose complete control to the rebellious Humans in your ranks," Adam said. The itching on his back was replaced by a soothing sensation. His pulse normalized. His thoughts cleared.

"Windless Tornado is sacred ground. It is illegal and immoral for anyone, Bokori or Human, to step foot on its surface. The Hisbaween did not attack..."

"Your Modder mouth spews nothing but deceit!" Adam shouted.

The High Hisba was silent. It lowered its hood and pulled down its kyqad to reveal the scars of a thousand surgeries. Its unnaturally gray skin was dried and cracked. Its face contorted into a scowl.

"You continue to insist on blaspheming the People's House."

A confidence soared in Adam that he could not source. "No, High Hisba. Truth is blasphemy in an ideology of lies. Two plus two equals four. The Bokori are a failed state. You see, High Hisba, I know what frustrates you. No matter how much you denigrate your mind, body, and soul, you cannot overcome nature. The Bokori are what you could never be. They see that. You can spout insult after threat. You can modify your physical appearance, punish blasphemous Humans, and adopt every Bokori custom under the white suns all you wish. You will never be one of them. To the Bokori, you're nothing but a backward Human in gray face."

The High Hisba continued its rhythmic blinking. It licked the edges of its cracked, scarred lips. It raised the hood of his cloak back over his head and lifted its kyqad over its mouth.

"You are truly lost, heretic."

"What is lost will be found, High Hisba, and I've found a way five-hundred years in the making."

"You will fail. It is science. There will be no further communications."

"Wrong again. We will speak once more. In person. Amongst the ruins of your burning temple."

The connection was cut. The High Hisba's avatar vanished, leaving Adam standing there, his ears ringing. *There is no turning back.*

"'Behold, I stood at the edge of the abyss, longing for answers. Alas, I did not find what I seek, for I sought the face of evil, and all I saw was a dark reflection." Havera said, walking towards Adam.

"I'm not familiar with that quote," Adam said. His stomach began churning.

"It's from the Testament of the Goddesses. The main authority of our faith. The Book of Kewea, specifically," Havera explained.

"Are you saying that I am evil?" Adam asked.

"No. It is the High Hisba staring into the abyss," she said. "I thought you handled that bravely, Adam. Are you feeling okay? You look a bit pale."

"I'll be fine. I just..." He couldn't finish the sentence. The bile he had suppressed came raging to the surface. He hurried to the corner of the room and vomited. He spat out the last bit of that day's lunch.

Havera came over and patted Adam on the back. He politely pushed her arm away. "I'm fine. I'm fine. That happens sometimes. Thank you for not jumping into that conversation."

"It is nothing. I understand the feeling. I couldn't keep anything down the day of my Pontifex presentation," Havera said to comfort him.

"No offense, Havera. My situation is a bit different. We need to inform the others. We're walking into a trap," Adam said, moving towards the doorway.

Havera cut him off. "You'll do no such thing."

"We must let them know. This operation is no longer covert. The Excommunicated know we're coming with the Hisbaween hot on our tails. Pardon the expression. The others need to be prepared for what we're about to face," Adam insisted.

"He said vengeance is a petty endeavor."

"What?"

"Vengeance is a petty endeavor. Adam, he thinks we're out here for me. That we're pursuing Ignatia. He's thinks the job is to kill the leader of the Excommunicated. That's why he mentioned 'the rogue duchess.' He's talking about me, Adam!"

"But he's intercepted our communications. He knows about Dusertheus and the Orb of Emancipation. He could easily have told the Excoms about that."

"Maybe. Look at it from the High Hisba's perspective. What's more likely? A mouthpiece for the Excommunicated's biggest rival sent us to kill their competitor or to retrieve a mystical, ancient object of untold power. He probably believes all the Orb talk is code. If he's even telling the truth about any of that."

"That's a lot of suppositions, Havera. If you're wrong, we're dead. Even if that is the case, it's not like the Excommunicated are going to let us walk right in if they believe we're there to assassinate their boss. Either way, we can't keep the others in the dark."

"You know full well what will happen. Zax will want to plow ahead, and Jak will do whatever it takes to dissuade him. Marduk will want to go in guns blazing and get us all killed in seconds. Only Cradite knows what Umbrasia will do. And Sam will go along because that's what she does. This group is barely holding together as it is. They're committed only so far. Revealing the full scope of the danger we may or may not be in will only tear us apart further." She gently grabbed him by his left hand. Adam's heart fluttered. "Will you trust me?" Havera asked, running her fingers through her hair.

I want to say no. I should say no. I can't say no.

"Very well. We must make some changes to the plans. The Excoms will be watching for both of us. My guess is they know exactly what your ship looks like. No fake registration will fool them. We must convince the others to go along with it without revealing too much," Adam said, resigning himself to their current situation.

"I'll handle the others. Just follow my lead," said Havera.

"That's what I've been doing," Adam muttered under his breath.

"Mea culpa?" responded Havera with one eyebrow raised.

He bit his tongue. He hadn't meant to say that out loud. "Something John said. Thinking back, I seem to be doing everything you want to do every step of the way. Even in my own mission, I'm still following your whims, your desires."

"That isn't remotely true, Adam."

"Isn't it? Ignatia and the Orb of Emancipation are your objectives. The latter is a means to an end for me, but for you? They're both endgames in your personal and professional life. It feels like I'm just along for the ride. To Kewea with what I want," Adam said.

Havera let go of his hand. Her tail stiffened. "Is this because I won't let you under my tunic?" She took an intentional step closer right into Adam's personal space. "I knew you were needy, but I never took you for petty."

Adam shook his head. "I'm neither! I'm merely making an observation. I don't want you that way."

Don't you lie to her or yourself.

"What do you want then, Adam Mortis?"

Adam closed his eyes. *Silver. Crimson. Cinnamon. Strawberries.* "I...I'm not sure. Home, I suppose."

Havera grasped his hand again. Adam's pulse raced again. "This is the best way for you to go home safely. I promise." Adam didn't answer her, merely nodded. Havera rubbed the Remembrance tattoo on his hand. A brief flare of excitement coursed through him. "Can I ask you something, Adam?"

"Yes! I mean sure," he said a bit too enthusiastically.

She brushed his enthusiasm aside. "That name you called the High Hisba."

"Modder."

"You've used it before. It's an insult targeting the Humans that support the Covenant of Subjugation?"

"Yes and no. Beyond the Separatists, few Humans favor breaking the Covenant. The majority of them are good, honest people that merely don't want their lives disrupted. They tolerate the Covenant either because they believe it passively benefits them or ending it might hurt them. They fear uncertainty. I have no quarrel with them. They can be persuaded to join or at least stay out of our way. Modders, on the other hand, are an entirely different beast. They are ideologues. Zealots. They are completely loyal to the Covenant, not to humanity. In their twisted minds, humanity and the Covenant are one in the same. Humans that have become so enraptured by the Bokori they seek to become them by surgically altering their bodies to emulate the grayskins. Most will simply laser remove their hair, wear neutral clothing, or perhaps bleach their skin gray. The more extreme, like the High Hisba, will have fingers and toes removed and their eyes reoriented to match Bokori eyes. Physically strip themselves of Human features."

Havera tapped the tattoo on his hand. "This is where I am confused. You alter your bodies, too. You have this, and the strip of silver in your hair. Sam dyes her hair and has a similar tattoo. In fact, many Humans on Arabella have tattoos, dye their hair in varying styles, and pierce themselves all over their bodies. Other races have similar customs. Our most faithful will often brand themselves with markings dedicated to whichever goddess or god they most strongly identify with. I fail to see the difference between what we do, what you do, and what these so-called Modders do."

Adam took a deep breath and rubbed his tattoo. "The difference, Havera, is that we modify ourselves to display our humanity. Our individuality. Modders alter themselves to deny theirs."

30

Humana Historia

The Cicera was given immediate clearance to land. "Welcome, Duchess Havera of Shele. We're expecting you. Please land in Docking Bay Three-One-One-Seven-Four. Enjoy the post-Accordance Day activities. You and your Human guest. Formal attire is requested but not mandatory." The Excommunicated were not subtle nor did they seem perturbed by their arrival. A sign of supreme confidence on their end.

The Excommunicated base, nicknamed "the Cauldron," was built inside the remnants of a small moon that had crashed into its planet millennia ago, exposing the planet's core. In the centuries preceding the Strife, the Zokyo had set up a mining operation to harvest the rare minerals spewing from the exposed core. They had abandoned the station during the Strife, not before nearly draining the dead world of most of its resources. A faint orange glow was visible in the exposed chunk of planet. What little remained of the nameless planet's core. It was the third planet in the red sun system. The red giant loomed in the distance, exuding its fiery glare through the Cicera's viewports. The Excommunicated had converted the old mining station for their own purposes. Hundreds of solar panels, bigger than most commercial ships, were attached to the surface of the moon, capturing the photons from the star. The harvested energy would then be converted into Celeste to be shipped all over the galaxy.

"Not before those plants get their cut of the drugs I'd wager," Marduk surmised. Celeste was legal but highly regulated in most sectors. It was the most potent drug in the galaxy with a wide variation of medicinal and recreational uses. Something Adam was all too aware of. The drug's psychological and physical potency combined with its extreme ease to harvest, any star could be used to create Celeste, crowded out the market for anything else beyond alcohol.

"That's how we tracked down the Celestials. The Rorae received regular shipments of all kinds of Celeste at regular intervals. Almost always the stronger stuff. Nothing less than yellow sun Celeste. Those plants consume that stuff like candy. The unusual comings and goings of known Celeste smuggling ships with no sign of their cargo reaching the Rorae tipped us off."

They had left Ashla almost immediately after the conversation with the High Hisba. Adam and Havera agreed it was best to leave before Unbroken Tide and the Hisbaween arrived. Once they were in negative space, Havera had gathered everyone in the circular conference room to explain the situation. Well, a sanitized version.

"I received a tip from a contact in the Vulpes," Havera had lied. "The Excommunicated know about Adam and me."

"We're compromised?" Marduk had asked.

Havera shook her head. "It seems we've caught them by surprise. They had expected me to fly Adam back to Bokori space. My contact says they know we're coming but don't know why. By 'we' I mean myself and Adam. Other than Zax and Jak's impromptu performance, they know nothing of y'all, or, if they do, they don't seem to care."

She's a gifted liar, or I'm a gifted fool.

Havera, Marduk, and Jak hammered out the fine details over the course of the next several hours. They had decided it was best for Adam and Havera to show their faces publicly on the Cauldron. This meant only Sam and Jak would sneak around the facility to search for the map. A mixed blessing. With half the numbers, it was less likely they'd be detected sneaking around the base; however, this meant only two people would search for the map in a base whose size very well could be the entire interior of the asteroid. Adam, Havera, Zax, and a disguised Marduk would be left vulnerable and exposed for several hours, surrounded by dozens of Excom fighters along with the wealthy patrons and their entourages. The request for 'formal attire' vexed Adam the most.

"I feel absolutely ridiculous," said Adam.

They had descended the ramp out of the ship and into the hangar. A well-dressed Moan concierge, wearing a mask of bronze that completely obscured the face, greeted them. He was flanked by a pair of Cauduun guards. The guards had rifles in hand and were decked out in full combat scale armor and helmets. The guards' armor was polished and pristine, with their tails poking out from under their battle skirts. Painted red and black with a golden synthetic crest plume running front-to-back on their helmets, they were an imposing sight. Their faces were completely obscured by a similar face mask of silver. On the front of their armor was the emblem of the Excommunicated: a golden trident facing downward, the side prongs broken off and dripping in blue Cauduun blood. They bore a pair of electrospears on their backs along with a rectangular scutum shield. Adam and Havera were escorted through the hangar unmolested. The guards didn't search them for weapons or contraband. They didn't even lock down their HUDs. The concierge explained there was no need. They were guests. He handed them a pair of black and white domino masks for the evening. To protect their guests' identities, or so they were told.

The most wanted terrorists in the galaxy. They're not trying to hide. They're flaunting their presence.

"Nonsense. I think you're quite spiffy and handsome. A true gentleman," said Havera once they were out of the hangar.

"You mean Cauduun gentleman," Adam retorted.

"No need to be redundant," she said.

His arm was looped through Havera's. It was customary for the woman to escort the man into formal events, Havera had explained. She had changed into the outfit she wore at Adam's hearing. The deep-v black gown with legs slits all the way to her upper thigh as well as the golden calf-high caligae boots with one-inch wedge heels. Her mother's brooch was pinned near the strap on her right shoulder. Her hair was down and voluminous, covering much of her back. Her eyes were smoky, and her black lips glossy. Of course, she still had her platinum bracers.

Adam wasn't wearing his normal jacket and jumpsuit attire. They were tucked away inside his inventory, which was nearly pushed to the max, concealing his regular clothes, new armor, and weapons, minus the Debbie safely tucked away in a pocket. Instead, Havera had scrounged together an outfit for him to suit the occasion. An emerald green tunic of the finest silks money could buy banded by a silver hempen rope around his waist. Draped over his left shoulder and across his body was a bright snowy white toga with a purple stripe lined around the fringe. He was fortunate that Cauduun wore their clothing loosely because none of it fit his proportions. The footwear was.... not ideal. Havera had nothing formal that could fit a Human's foot comfortably. He had to settle for plain pine-colored caligae flat sandals tightly wrapped around his calves. They were so snug he could barely feel the circulation in his feet.

"Promise me you won't tell my father I was the one who dressed you. A toga like that, pure white with a purple stripe, is reserved for members of the Shelean Royal Family. Just you wearing that might cause a minor scandal. Especially since you're a vir," Havera said with a chuckle.

"Vir?"

"Hmm? Oh, sorry. Vir is another word for man. The essence of manhood I suppose is a more accurate description. It's hard to explain. I don't know why it doesn't translate into your language."

He certainly didn't feel manly. Havera and Sam had spent an hour getting his hair and beard right. They washed and straightened his hair and tied it back into a simple ponytail, letting his dyed silver streak hang loosely over his forehead. They wanted to shave his beard off completely. He flat out refused. They compromised by trimming it into a tight, thick stubble. *I'm a marionette pulled by my strings.* Although, he couldn't deny he felt comfortable in the silks. The tunic felt pleasant on his skin, especially his scars.

"Matches your eyes. You ought to dress up more often," Havera said once they had finished. He had blushed despite himself.

Adam and Havera were escorted into the main room. A spacious octagon-shaped metal mire of extravagance. The center of the room was the bar area, already patronized by several domino-masked, ostentatious elites in quiet conversation. A few took note of their arrival, but most ignored them. A playlist of pleasant tunes thrummed throughout the room. White noise to drown out the spilling of secrets.

The guards remained behind, stationed by the entryway. The concierge told them they had free rein of any room on this floor. Mobile bots were flying around, recording everyone for 'unauthorized behavior.' The rooms were all marked with signs indicating what form of entertainment was found within. Adam spotted an AR pod game room, gambling parlor, a gladiatorial arena, concert hall, and a club containing exotic dancers and jades of multiple races, catering to unique tastes and desires. For extra Links, of course.

A voice came over his HUD's radio. "Iinneara's in. Iinneara Three on standby near the exit. Locating sub-target. Iinneara One out."

"Acknowledged, Iinneara One. Raetis' on standby waiting for Aria."

"Aria has entered Kewea. On our way," Havera whispered once they were out of earshot of the concierge. Jak used his G'ee'k talents to build them a private, encrypted communication network. They downloaded his jury-rigged plug-in to their HUDs. This allowed them to keep in constant contact and exchange map and personnel data.

"It's unlikely anyone will be able to eavesdrop on us. Even if the Excoms pick up on the channel, this kind of encryption would take the best G'ee'k several days to crack. Still, we ought to use code names as a precaution. They're sure to have listening devices inside the Cauldron," Jak had explained. Jak and Sam had flown on Sel-Ena out of the ship to one of the Cauldron's garbage chutes prior to the Cicera's landing. Without more extensive knowledge of the facility, Marduk had concluded this was the best way in undetected.

"Not the first time I've been called a trashy Human," Sam had quipped.

Zax and Marduk, disguised as Jak, slipped off the ship before the Excoms could greet them. They had blended in with a few passengers from a luxury liner that arrived around the same time as the Cicera. Adam spotted the pair hanging out next to a high circular tabletop near the entrance to the concert hall. Zax was tuning his electric lute while 'Mar-Jak' stood awkwardly in place, shuffling his feet. The domino mask that was modified for a Naddine face looked ridiculous on him. More amusing considering that wasn't Marduk's true face. Adam and Havera took position at a neighboring tabletop, keeping their backs to each other and not acknowledging the pair.

"Aria has made contact with Raetis," Havera whispered.

"Acknowledged," responded Sam over the HUD radio.

Havera flagged down a waiter and ordered them both some Palerian grape juice. The waiter returned a minute later drinks on a tray. Adam sipped his to calm his nerves. Once again, he was out of his element. The grape juice was cold and sweet, tingling his throat on the way down.

"Everything prepared, Raetis?" Havera asked.

"We go on next after Ocean's Ocarinas," replied Zax. This clandestine method of communication threw Adam for a loop. He kept his head down to focus on their com channel.

"I wondered what had happened to them after the incident. Surprised they're still playing together," said Havera.

"I don't think this crowd is one to care about a decade-old Bokori moral panic," said Mar-Jak.

"If what they did had happened today, no one would care. I guarantee it," said Zax.

Definitely.

"Keep the chatter to a necessary minimum, please. Iinneara is trying to concentrate," Jak huffed.

"Sorry," replied all four of them.

A few minutes had passed when they each received a ping on their HUDs. Adam tapped on his mini-map. A complete 3D rendering of the station filled his visual HUD.

"Sub-target data received," Havera replied.

"Kewea's curse! This station is enormous," Zax said.

Examining the map, Zax was correct. Adam integrated the data into his own map. The main area with the attached entertainment rooms comprised much of this section. However, this section only contained maybe ten percent of the entire station. The real Cauldron was beneath their feet.

He spotted their four dots all clustered together in the main area. He was not in combat mode. The strain on his senses and brain combined with the amount of data needed to operate Jak's com channel would be too much to stay in that mode for too long. Their default mode would need to suffice for the duration. Samus and Jak were too far out of range for their scanners to pick up. Adam found the hangar housing the Cicera. Dee and Umbrasia were out of range, too.

"What are these red sections?" asked Havera.

"Places the cleaning bots are not allowed to enter. We thought we'd start there," said Jak. It was Jak's idea to seize a cleaning bot for its map data due to their potential for mined intel. Nearby sections were marked in red in this part of the station. Much of the off-limits area was far below in what Adam supposed were the Celeste refineries and R&D facilities.

"That's nearly a third of the station, Iinneara. It's going to take too long," said Havera.

"Raetis will join you when we finish here," said Mar-Jak.

"Maybe now you'll allow Cradite to join us?" asked Samus.

"Absolutely not! It shouldn't take too long. You only need a terminal with access. Start in this area," Mar-Jak said. He pinged a location on the map near the upper sections for everyone on the channel to see.

"Acknowledged," Jak responded.

"Let us know when you acquire Dasenor. I want updates from y'all every half hour regardless if you have anything to report. Understood?" said Havera.

"Understood. Moving out," said Jak.

Adam pictured Samus and Jak navigating through air vents and dodging patrols of guard bots and Excom fighters on their way to the mainframe. The plan was to download the interstellar chart from the message and get out. Based on the size of the station, it might take them a while.

Adam had expected more resistance to the new plan. They all, more or less, bought Havera's story and agreed to the modified plan. Surprisingly, the only major point of contention had been over Umbrasia.

"She stays on the ship," Marduk had insisted. "Her presence in the Cauldron would only spook the Excoms. A Rorae Magi is not a welcome sight outside of a Duserary," he said, using the term for a Cauduun hospital.

"She could be invaluable in the search for the map. Two of us for an entire station? She'd be wasted waiting on the ship with Dee," said Samus.

"Until I know for certain she won't betray our presence, she stays out of sight. End of discussion!" insisted Marduk.

Samus had continued her protestations. Even Jak seemed to disagree with Marduk on this issue, having eyed him closely with both eye stalks. Umbrasia had not interjected, preferring to float by herself and observe. She had agreed to Marduk's demand seemingly without issue.

A Rinvari usher in a bronze mask approached Zax and Mar-Jak.

"Zax and Jak?"

Zax, who was busy gazing towards the bar with a curious expression, stood up to address the usher. He cleared his throat. "That would be Zax and Jak of the famous Zax and Jak duo! Yes, how can we help you?"

"Right. You're on in ten minutes. Follow me, and I'll take you both backstage," said the Rinvari usher.

"Raetis moving into position," whispered Mar-Jak once the Rinvari turned his back.

"Good luck," said Havera and Adam together.

The Rinvari usher led Zax and Mar-Jak through a side door near the entrance to the concert hall. Once they were out of sight, Havera stood up. "I'm going to go watch their performance. You want to join?"

Adam shook his head. "I'd rather be alone. I don't do well in crowds. I'm sure when the Excoms want to find us, they'll come fetch us. I'll be fine. I promise."

Havera frowned. It was probably not a good idea for them to split up. He only wanted a few minutes to himself before any potential madness kicks in. Despite her disapproving glare, she did not object.

"Keep on coms, alright? If you see something, say something," she insisted.

Adam nodded. "I will."

Havera turned heel and walked into the concert hall. He was left alone at the table. Playing with his glass, he observed the occasional glance in his direction. A Human in this crowd was a novelty. All quickly averted their eyes when he noticed their stares. The scars on his back tingled a bit. The waiter offered him a refill, and he politely declined. He stood up to wander around the main reception area. Passing by the gladiatorial arena, he could hear loud cheers through the door. He peeked through the window, but the backs of excited attendees blocked his vision.

Turning back to patrol the main area, a peculiar sign outside the AR pod game room caught his eye. Big, bold, bright letters that his HUD translated instantly. "CHAOTIC COMPATRIOTS LIVE PRESENTS HUMANA HISTORIA!" The time indicated on the sign showed the event began about five minutes ago. Subtext was pinned under the title. "The latest module adventure of the popular FIENDS & FRIENDS AR game series based on the Stepicro Cache of lost Human history. Played by the beloved ARRPG group Chaotic Compatriots."

The Stepicro Cache.

His curiosity intrigued; Adam entered the game room. It was a modest-sized room with a sizable crowd of attendees, nearly standing room only. Everyone was quiet and still. The center of the room was slightly elevated into a platform. Around the platform's perimeter were seven AR pods, presumably occupied by members of the Chaotic Compatriots. Standing at the head of the platform was a dapper, teal-skinned Cauduun male with long, luscious locks of brown and blue hair. Like the conductor of an orchestra, he waved his hands around, occasionally tapping buttons on the panel in front of him. Adam remained near the entrance, away from everyone, while keeping the platform in his sights. The Cauduun's voice boomed throughout the chamber.

"Last time, our Compatriots departed Meadow City, where they defeated the greedy ogre that ruled over the desert metropolis with an iron fist. With the city secured for the Monarchical Alliance, our heroes traversed the snow-covered wilds of the Land of Griffins, intent on reaching the Sea of Serenity, where they hope to catch a ship towards their eventual destination. The wastes of the lost Isle of Angels to seek a long-forgotten treasure buried beneath its ruins..."

While the Cauduun conductor described what had happened, digital images materialized in the middle of the platform. They showed a massive city of lights surrounded by cliffs and mountains followed by an icy desert of treacherous terrain and winged beasts with the head of an arkad and body of a vivily. The digiholo images created everything the conductor described to the detail. The occasional 'woah' and 'wow' escaped the lips of the captivated audience as they marveled at what they were witnessing. Adam shared their sense of wonder.

I am witnessing Human history brought to life. I don't remember Trissefer ever telling me about any of this from Stepicro.

Aaron was big into *Fiends & Friends*. He tried to convince Adam to play to no avail. He had a small group on Arabella play together regularly. Every so often, Aaron would even sneak into the terminal rooms after curfew to play with strangers on the Nexus. One more regret to add to the pile of Adam's sorrow.

Avatars of the players materialized. They were all playing as Humans. Each of the player's appearance fascinated Adam with their elaborate and intricate outfits. A tall man was dressed in heavy plated mail, carrying an old antique projectile defense rifle. A short female dressed in a skimpy metal garb wielded an oversized sword that was bigger and thicker than her entire body with only a narrow loincloth to cover her pelvic region. A gangly, hooded man with thick black robes was wearing a white tunic emblazoned with a symbol resembling a Cauduun cross. He was holding a pair of laser pistols with a jump jet strapped to his back. Some of their accouterments Adam thought resembled too much like Cauduun or Naddine fashion to be authentic. Nonetheless, Adam was ensorcelled by the performance.

Minutes flew by, drowning out the whispers in his com. He couldn't take his eyes off the digital illustrations of his homeworld. His true homeworld. His lost homeworld. The picturesque landscapes and digital likeness of bizarre creatures and Human towns and villages. All with Human protagonists. Not actual Humans, of course, but the sentiment remained the same. What once was lost was found.

Beautiful. Falling Star would've loved this.

Tears welled in his eyes. His sniffles drew sharp looks from nearby audience members, who quickly shuffled away when they realized he was Human. Overcome with emotion, Adam decided to step outside back into the main room. He bumped almost immediately into Havera.

"Adam! Are you alright? You weren't answering your coms. What's wrong?" she asked, wrapping her arms around him. "Did something happen?"

"Did you know about this?" Adam asked, pointing to the sign outside the AR room.

Havera's expression turned horrified, her face drained of color. She covered her mouth with her hands. She dragged him away from the AR room towards the bar.

"Adam, I'm so sorry. I meant to tell you about that. You weren't meant to find out that way."

"What are you sorry about? Are you saying you're responsible for this Humana Historia?" said Adam.

Havera hung her head. "Yes. The Praetorian exclusivity on the Stepicro data lasted only a year. After that, the decoded bits of the data were allowed to be sold to any vested interest approved by the Conclave.

Mostly business and entertainment conglomerates. Humana Historia was announced last month. I never got a chance to tell y'all."

"How popular is *Fiends & Friends*?"

Havera's response was meek. "It's played by billions around the galaxy."

Billions!

Adam grasped her by the face and kissed her. Her horror turned to shock at the unexpected affection. "Billions! This is incredible," Adam exclaimed.

Havera raised an eyebrow. "You're not angry?"

"Why would I be angry? Havera, you said it yourself. Billions of people are experiencing Human culture for the first time. Brought to life on their digiholos, their HUDs, their terminals in the comfort of their own homes. The galaxy is learning what we Humans were like at our zenith. We're no longer some anonymous, theoretical cause for people talk about on the Nexus. We have living, breathing proof of Human greatness right there for them to immerse themselves."

"That's...that's not how I expected you to react, Adam. I was afraid to tell you. I'm sure the other Humans won't be pleased when they learn about this. Human culture used for other races' gain. Your friends John and Trissefer will be irate," said Havera, running her fingers through her hair.

Adam took her by the hand. He placed her finger on top of his Remembrance tattoo. "I mentioned when we left Arabella that I spoke truths to the High Hisba after Falling Star's suicide. The truths that led to the charges of blasphemy and heresy. You know what I told the High Hisba when it claimed tattooing was a Human custom that belonged only to Humans? I said tattooing belongs to those with the skills and the desire to learn. I had no hand in the creation of Human customs. I have no right to deny anyone, Bokori or otherwise, the ability to enjoy the fruits of my ancestors' labors. Human culture belongs to everyone who wants it. That's the blasphemy, the heresy that sent me to rehab."

Havera smiled weakly and nodded.

"That's exactly the sentiment I'd expect out of you," said a nearby gravelly voice.

Adam and Havera whipped their heads around. Pouring them drinks was the bartender. A male Bokori bartender. It was not like any Bokori male Adam had ever met. It was wearing a simple black tunic with the Excom trident emblem emblazoned on the front. It hid its handsome face with a full, white beard that almost touched the floor. Adam was so impressed by the beard's thickness he instinctively rubbed his freshly trimmed stubble almost ashamed. There was a certain confidence to the way the Bokori moved. The wrinkles on its forehead indicated it was an older Bokori, probably in its fifth or sixth decade. It had marks indicating prior Celeste use under its triceps. It pushed the newly filled glasses towards them.

"Finest Shelean wine these cheap Excoms can afford, my lady. 1485 vintage I believe. First year of the Century of Strife. Terrible politics, fantastic wine. Purified tonic water for the gentleman. A bit bitter, but those Moans know how to distill salt water into pure."

Havera accepted the drink cautiously, murmuring her thanks in the process. Adam hesitated. The Bokori sighed. It grabbed the drink and downed it all in one gulp. It procured another glass and filled the glass with the water from the same container. "You oppress a people for several centuries. Suddenly, they're suspicious of a simple drink. Relax, Adam Mortis, if I were to poison you, I'd be using that moriado piss of a Zokyon swill," the Bokori chuckled.

"You know who I am?" Adam asked, accepting the new glass without hesitation. He sipped. It was indeed a bit bitter on the tongue.

"I was told to expect your arrival. Even prepared these drinks on the off-chance y'all decided to plop yourselves down in front of my wrinkly, old ass, hehe," the Bokori said. "You're the only Human in sight, and you're with the best-looking Cauduun in this dump. Pardon my Shelean, my lady. Even with those stupid masks, I know who y'all are."

"Every other Excom...employee is wearing a face mask. Why not you?" Havera asked, sipping her wine.

"What and hide this majestic beauty, hehe. Do you have any idea how much hair regrowth costs for a Bokori? I'd be better off buying a wig of Cauduun hair," the Bokori said, stroking his beard.

"What's your name?" Adam asked.

"Locke."

"That's not a Bokori name."

"Kewea's curse! Fenix was right. You do have a penchant for stating the obvious, hehe."

"Fenix is here?!" Havera exclaimed.

"Of course. She's the one who told me about your arrival. Wanted to ensure everything was perfect. Whatever that means. Gave me the digital key to the entire area, so I wouldn't have to pester her 'Paladin' guards for access to the good stuff," Locke said.

Havera's ears perked up. "Where is she?"

"Oh, if I had to guess, she's probably busy, umm, 'interrogating' one of her guards, hehe," Locke said. He leaned over to whisper. "Let me tell you something, Your Grace, Fenix is one attractive and terrifying Human. Most of the men around here are afraid they'll be questioned next, hehe," said Locke.

"When you say 'Paladin' guards, do you mean they're ex-Paladins of Paleria?" asked Havera.

"Nah. Not the ones around here. Just some of Fenix's goons. Fenix dresses 'em up that way to mock Ignatia. Different colors, same style. They aren't true Paladins. The real deal Paladins stick close with our new illustrious leader. Except for one. The Tribune. You'll know him when you see him. Ignatia ordered him to remain here and keep an eye on Fenix. One more humiliation for Fenix after Ignatia deposed her, hehe. It's why Fenix keeps everyone in masks. Easier to treat 'em as disposably as Fenix does," Locke said.

"Fenix was the leader of the Excommunicated?" asked Adam.

"Kewea's curse, boy! You really don't know anything, do you? Fenix spent years slaughtering her way to the top only for Ignatia to swoop in with her exiled Paladins and steal it from her. Ignatia keeps Fenix around to run the day-to-day operations while she goes off gallivanting across half of Griselda. Fenix is always testing her leash. Ignatia doesn't care as long as she follows orders," said Locke.

"Why are you telling us this?" asked Havera.

Locke stroked his beard. "I have a debt to repay. I intend to fulfill it. Old men like me remember when the Covenant used to pretend to stand for something meaningful. When we'd meaningfully support each other. Not bully and shame them. Learn from our history. Not erase and forget."

Adam finished his water. "It saddens me to have never met a Bokori like you until today."

"Hehe, there are no Bokori like me. There is only me," Locke said with a smile. His friendly demeanor turned stoic. "You're about meet trouble," he said, nodding his head at someone behind them.

Adam and Havera glanced over their shoulder. Approaching were three Cauduun Excom guards. Two were identical to the guards that escorted them in. They were flanked behind the third. He was tall, and his armor was more ornate than the others with a silver cingulum wrapped around his waist and a verdant cloak draped around his shoulders. His golden crest was horizontal and combed. He carried no gun. Only a gladius electroblade sheathed into his cingulum, and a rectangular scutum shield attached to his back. He also hid his face behind a silver face mask.

"Your Grace. Commissioner Mortis. Fenix requests your presence. You may not refuse her invitation. Follow me," the lead guard said with a husky tone. His accent was harsh and muffled by the mask. It reminded Adam of the way Havera's father spoke. The other two guards moved to surround them. Adam tensed. Havera merely nodded.

As they were led away, Adam had a beep on his HUD. It was an incoming transmission. The data flashed in front of him. Glancing at it, he realized it was a digital key used to lock and unlock doors. He had a realization. Peering briefly over his shoulder, Locke was wiping the glasses with a rag, a huge grin sprawled across his bearded face.

31

The Fangs of Fenix

"Digital key received. This ought to speed things up. We're almost to our destination. Should acquire the map within the hour," said Jak over the com. Adam discreetly transferred the key to everyone on the channel. Dee confirmed receipt of the key. Zax and Mar-Jak didn't respond. By this point, they were out of range of Adam's mini-map. He wasn't too worried. Sam and Jak didn't respond once or twice due to close enemy proximity. Adam and Havera were keeping their chatter to a minimum while Fenix's guards were around. They were cramped into a small lift on their way up.

The elevator doors opened into an observation suite. Tinted windows overlooking each of the entertainment dens marked the walls all around the room. On the far end, a small curtain covered another chamber. Stepping out of the elevator, Adam heard noises coming from the curtained off chamber's direction. Screaming intermixed with moans and cries of pain. They hesitated. The tall guard shoved Adam forward.

"Keep walking, Human."

The screams and moans grew louder as they approached the curtain. A bead of sweat trickled down Adam's forehead. The tall guard stepped in front of them and pulled back the curtain.

"Inside. Now."

Havera was pushed by the tall guard, and Adam followed. The source of the noise was revealed. Adam had to bite his tongue to prevent himself from swearing. A pair of nude figures were in the throes of rough passion. A toned Human female was ploughing a bent over, lanky Cauduun male. She had umber brown skin with long micro braids decorating her sepia-colored hair. Blackened burn marks and healed scar tissue dotted her skin. In addition to those, much of her body was covered in tattoos, depicting weapons and various instruments of torture alongside images of people of diverse races engaging in unique methods of love-making. Adam couldn't help but notice she even had a Remembrance tattoo on her left butt cheek next to the pleasure apparatus strapped to her hips. She had the Cauduun by the hair, jerking his head upward with each thrust into his backside. She moaned, he screamed. His tail was wrapped around her neck. She seemed to be enjoying it.

"Ahem. Your guests have arrived, Fenix," the tall guard called out.

The woman turned her head. Her face was covered by a golden mask with a bloody smile carved into the sides of the mouth.

"Ahh. Wonderful. Yes...yes...come on over, lovelies. Let me...see you...face...mmm...to face. Kewea's curse! Yes! Yes!" Fenix yelled, still taking her pleasure at the expense of the Cauduun.

Havera, to her credit, didn't bat an eyelash. She did as requested with Adam following her lead. The tall guard remained by the curtain. The bent over Cauduun wore a domino mask, yet he still buried his face in his arms at their approach, smothering his cries into the pillow. He did not want them to see him. Fenix continued her thrusting for a while, completely ignoring their presence. Adam said nothing. He was too afraid and confused at what he was witnessing.

Havera broke the awkward non-silence. "You quite done?"

"Mmm...almost. Kewea take me. I love Cauduun men. Don't you, Your Grace? So...damn...mmm...submissive!" Fenix screamed as reached her climax. Removing her mask, she was breathing heavily and sweating. Her cheeks were noticeably flushed even on her brown skin. She wiped the sweat from her forehead and withdrew. The Cauduun gasped when she did so. She jerked him to his feet and shoved him aside.

"That'll do, Senator. You have my word you'll be protected in your next election. So long as you continue to come through for us. Get out!" she yelled. The embarrassed Cauduun senator hurriedly grabbed his clothes and fled, nearly colliding with the tall guard on his way out. Adam could hear him whimper away. Havera folded her arms, staring down Fenix with a vicious glare. "I'm sorry. Did you want him, too, Your Grace? I hear it's tradition for Cauduun duchesses to marry senators. Feel free to call him up. Senator Antonius of Brandinium. You know where that is, Your Grace?"

"Yes, it's on Soxenia. Care to tell me what that was all about?"

"Oh, why not? A little Naddine diplomacy to seal a deal. The good senator is afraid he'll lose his seat this year. Politics of Soxenia aren't what they used to be. Confederate sympathy is growing on the once solidly Republican world. The people of Brandinium no longer support the senator's politics, so all he has is the pet projects to bring home. We're helping lubricate the slots. Poor fellow. Great speaker. Lousy lover. What he doesn't realize is his opponent is already willing to work with us" Fenix said with a laugh. Havera maintained her scowl. Fenix frowned. "You disapprove?"

"My approval or disapproval is irrelevant. You're nothing but a band of thieves and murderers," Havera said coldly.

Fenix eyes narrowed. "Please continue to say such sweet nothings, my lovely. You'd love nothing more than to wrap that pretty little tail of yours around my throat and squeeze the life out of me. Hmm, not a bad way to go. How badly do you want to kill me, Your Grace?" Havera didn't respond. Fenix strode over to the tall guard and grabbed his electroblade. The guard didn't react. Fenix flipped the blade in her hand, extending the hilt out towards Havera. "Well, go on. I'm completely exposed. In these close quarters, there's no way you wouldn't gut me." Adam's eyes darted back-and-forth between the two women.

Havera didn't move. "You're not the one I want."

"Mmm, that's what I thought. Sorry to disappoint, my lovely, the bitch isn't here," Fenix said. She flipped the blade back into her hand and threw it in the direction of the tall guard. The blade sank into the wall mere inches from the guard's face. The blade vibrated with the impact. He did not flinch. His tail slid from behind him, wrapping itself around the blade and jerking it from the wall with a thwack. He sheathed the blade back into his cingulum.

"MMMHMMM! Kewea's curse! Does that not turn you on?!" yelled Fenix, licking her lips.

Havera shrugged. Fenix shook her head. She finally noticed Adam's presence. Her face beamed with a devilish smile. "Forgive my manners. I haven't introduced myself, have I?" she said, approaching Adam. She extended her hand. "Fenix. You must be Adam. My, my the reports don't do you justice. You are a lovely man." Adam froze, unsure whether or not to grasp her hand. Fenix frowned. "I thought shaking hands was the way you Separatist Humans wanted us to greet each other. Was I wrong?"

"N...no. You are correct," Adam stuttered.

He extended his hand towards the nude woman. She grasped his hand tightly. Her palm was moist as she yanked him forward towards her close. She wrapped her other arm around him and pressed her exposed breasts against him tightly. Her body was surprisingly chilly. That raised the hairs on the back of his neck. The tip of her apparatus poked his leg.

She leaned in to whisper in his ear. "I'm a big fan of your work, Commissioner. I really am. You've seen my scars. Perhaps later you can show me yours." She kissed him on the cheek, brushing her lips on his beard a bit. A cold shiver spiraled down his spine. His back scars did not react well to that comment.

"I, umm, I did like your Remembrance tattoo," Adam said without thinking.

She looked down at her ass and tittered. "Mmm, I'm glad you liked what you saw."

"Would you mind putting some clothes on?" Havera asked.

Fenix released Adam's hand. He backed off a couple steps, feeling like prey escaping the clutches of a predator. He wiped his hand on the fringe of his tunic.

"Does my immodesty shock you, Your Grace?" asked Fenix.

"I learned the art of love directly from the Concubae at the Blessed Den of Anamea. There's little you can say or do in that regard that'll shock me," said Havera.

Fenix laughed. "You should've stayed in school. By the end of tonight, you'll be fully educated."

"No doubt."

Fenix sighed. "Very well."

She tapped the air. Her nudity was replaced with a long black leather coat and matching tight corset. High heels and a dark, short skirt with thigh high fishnet stockings. Her right fist was adorned with pointed brass knuckles. She topped it off with a tight choker that contained a jewel in the shape of the Excommunicated insignia. She was dressed to party and play.

"Satisfied?"

"Only if you tell us why we're here. Otherwise, I doubt you could satisfy me," Havera sneered.

"Funny. I was hoping you could tell me, my lovely," said Fenix. She brushed past them and her tall guard. She gestured for them to follow with her finger. "You see you were not invited to this little post-Accordance Day shindig. Had I known you were finally sticking your tail into the political arena, I'd have arranged for this little meeting much sooner."

"I'm not here for that. I've no interest in the Platinum Throne," Havera said.

"So I've been told. Every contender list for archduchess has your name near the top. Yet, you claim you're not here to meet with the galaxy's biggest power brokers," said Fenix. The woman began circling Adam and Havera. She was scoping the pair for hidden signs or tells. Adam swallowed. The scars on his back itched. He felt his adrenaline pumping. Taking deep, silent breaths, he remained completely still.

"Only fringe groups and desperate folks would turn to terrorists for aid," Havera sneered.

Fenix snorted. "I'm surprised. I took you for much, Your Grace, but I'd never expect you to be naïve. At least, not so willfully misguided. You spout your kind's propaganda well."

"You financed and organized Pontifex Brunato's Celestial project. The Boiling of Sin is your direct responsibility!"

Fenix broke into a feral smile. "My lovely, perhaps I have misjudged you. Do you genuinely believe the Conclave or the oh-so-wise-Cauduun did not know about Brunato's research? You ought to know, Your Grace. Weren't you one of Brunato's students?"

Havera chewed her lip. "Yes, I was."

What?

"His best student from what I've heard. You're the galaxy's second-greatest expert on Rimestone after the good Pontifex Brunato himself. A field that once held great esteem amongst the Cauduun. No longer. Maybe that's why you're here. Looking for financing for your own pet project, hmm?"

"She's here for me. She's helping the Human Separatist cause," Adam interjected.

Fenix guffawed. "Lovely, you're a cute boy. You'll make someone a good husband one day. Nobody cares about your little revolution. Certainly not me and least of all the good duchess here. Be silent. The women are talking. I'll let you know when it is your turn to play," Fenix said with a dismissive wave of her hand.

Adam clenched his fist and gritted his teeth. He thought about responding and decided against it. The tall Cauduun guard moved his hand to the hilt of his electroblade just enough for Adam to get the message.

"You shouldn't be so quick to dismiss him, Fenix," Havera said, standing up for Adam.

"I cared enough about my fellow Humans to show my ass to this ugly Naddine tattoo artist. Right before I cut off one of his eye-stalks.

Disgusting creatures those upside-down headed freaks. Pity. Non-Human tattooists are so hard to come by out here," Fenix sighed.

"Are we to continue this dance, Fenix. You know why I'm here," said Havera, losing her patience.

"Ah, yes. The bitch. I was hoping you'd say that. Sadly, she's not here. Otherwise, I'd join you in wrapping my hands around that hag's throat and squeeze!" she yelled at her tall guard. The Cauduun didn't react. "You see, Your Grace, the Tribune here isn't my bodyguard. He's my captor," Fenix said with a snarl.

"Why put up with him then?" Adam interjected. Fenix glared at him, sucking her bottom lip loud enough to demonstrate her irritation with him. His forehead dampened, and his cheeks flushed. A voice came over their com.

"Found the mainframe. Iinneara One is hacking in now. Should only take a few minutes. Standby," Sam said. Adam cleared his throat. Havera side-eyed him for an instant.

Fenix smirked. "Let me show you why, Commissioner," she said, waving them over to the window overlooking the gambling parlor. She pointed below to a pair of Cauduun and a Rinvari playing Conclave Conquest.

"Those guys down there. Right now, they're helping launder thousands of Links to pay for that stupid Sinner Superhighway. Over here," she said, moving to the club. A scantily dressed Techoxtl woman was soldering an implant into the back of a nervous-looking Zokyon man's head. "That Zokyo is an experatchik on the Central Committee turned double-agent for the Naddine. You see he was captured during the Strife by the Padduck clan. Threatened to feed him to their serpents unless he talked. The intel he gave was insignificant, but the Naddine own him for life. That little sterile noodle is responsible for the theft of intellectual property and Zokyon trade secrets worth billions of Links. Amazing what people will do to avoid being eaten," Fenix chuckled devilishly.

"What's your point, Fenix?" asked Havera.

"I'm at the epicenter of power, my lovely!" Fenix declared, raising her hands up high.

"Close doesn't count when it comes to power," Havera retorted.

Fenix lowered her hands and frowned. "We'll see about that. Oh!" Fenix said, clapping her hands together. "I almost forgot. Speaking of creatures eating, I have one more exhibit to show you both. Come here, you won't want to miss this!"

She gestured them over to the window that peered into the gladiatorial arena. She tapped the air, and the window opened up. The screams and putrid stench of the arena assaulted his senses. The crowd in the arena numbered in the hundreds. Most of the party seemed to have gathered there and surrounded the caged enclosure. Inside was a monstrous fiend.

Walking on six bony arachnid legs, the creature rose to twice the size of an average Human. Sickly green and sinewy, the creature screeched a terrifying howl and slammed its body against the cage in a desperate bid to break out. The nearby patrons jumped back each time the creature slammed itself against the cage only to then cheer and taunt the beast by hurling small objects at it. This only enraged the beast further. It had two large, pale red skeletal wings it used to launch itself around the arena. They seemed too weak and frail to allow the creature to fly, rather they were used for momentum and a surge of speed. Two white, hollow eyes formed the top of its lumpy head. Poking out of its neck were a pair of thick pincers while its wide oval jaw had only a small set of sharp pointed teeth. On the sides of its mouth, Adam could scarcely discern a set of inwards facing fangs.

"Gorgeous, isn't he? The lab geeks call them 'venadarastrixa.' This one is a male. The females are larger and have a big horn on their heads. Quite different from us in that regard," Fenix snickered, nudging Adam playfully in the side.

"That can't be a Naddine warbeast." Adam concluded.

Fenix laughed. "Definitely not. The Naddine could only dream of such a mutant beast. No, lovely, this creature comes straight from the Dark Realm of Ashla. You see those pincers? Venadarastrixa have a surprisingly weak bite for such a terrifying apex predator. It makes up for it with these tiny little fangs that contain a venomous paralytic. The pincers gore its prey, and the fangs paralyze it. The venadarastrixa will eat its prey while it's still alive. We breed them for such special occasions. Absolutely terrified of the light. Throwing them in such a place guarantees for a fun fight."

"The Dark Realm." Adam said mostly to himself.

Marduk undersold it. Horrors, indeed. I could scarcely imagine what he must've felt seeing a creature like this in the wild.

"You said a fun fight. Who or what is this venadarastrixa fighting?" Adam asked.

Fenix licked her lips. "I was so hoping you were going to ask me that."

It was then Adam saw that two more guards had entered the room, spears in hand. The tall Tribune had his hand on his blade. Havera scowled. Adam's eyes widened.

"You...you want us to fight it?" he said panicked.

Fenix laughed and slapped him on the ass. "Oh, lovely, you're silly. Of course not! It's going to fight them," she said, pointing towards the arena.

A door opened up from a nearby tunnel leading into the arena. Stumbling into the beast's pen were two familiar figures. A Zokyon in a loud yellow and orange skin-tight mechsuit and a Naddine in black and white furs and leathers. They were unarmed.

No!

Havera flinched towards Fenix. The guards held her at bay with their electrospears. Fenix put her arm around Adam and cackled. "I must wonder how dumb you believe I am. Do you not realize the Excommunicated have the ability to obtain a simple ConSec report? Y'all killed one of my best agents. Poor Jegasa. She was almost as good an interrogator as me. A bribe here, a threat there. We learned 'the famous Zax and Jak duo' were spotted with the Duchess of Paleria and the rebel Human Commissioner leaving rather surreptitiously. More bizarrely we were tipped off anonymously that the Cicera was headed this way. Too good of an opportunity to learn why," Fenix said with a sly grin.

Kewea take the Hisbaween!

"Let Zax and Jak go! Having them fight unarmed in your arena for sport is unbecoming. If you want real entertainment, send me in there in their place," Havera insisted, grimacing at Fenix and the four guards surrounding her. Adam heard her say that in person and through his com, which gave him minor disorientation.

Fenix whirled around. She walked right up to the Cauduun and punched Havera across the face with her brass knuckles. She had barely flinched, nonetheless, Havera's cheek was bleeding.

"Stupid Cauduun bitch. You insult my intelligence. You're signaling someone. You mentioned who, what, and where in that little performance. I've already given the order to seize your ship. Any interlopers you have prowling around will be snuffed out and join your little friends in the arena. Don't bother signaling. There's a dampener on the arena. No way any messages are getting to your bardic friends. Everyone knows about your meeting with Dusertheus. That weakling still pissy with me for cutting off his tail?"

Adam kept his focus on the action below, mentally scrambling to find any way out of this. It was all he could do from full-on panicking. The venadarastrixa lunged itself at the pair. Zax kept behind Jak. Both were able to dodge out of the way. The venadarastrixa was quick on the thrust but slow on the turn.

Adam sought some silver lining. He might've found it. That couldn't have been Jak in the arena. He was still with Sam, hacking into the mainframe. Meaning that was Marduk in disguise. Adam prayed that Marduk had some experience with these venadarastrixa. It might give him and Zax a chance to survive long enough for Adam to figure out some desperate escape plan. Zax sprinted across the arena far from the beast while Mar-Jak held its attention. A sparkle of light bounced off Zax's back. Adam held in a gasp.

He still has his lute! He could blast his way out if he has time to charge a shockwave. What can I do? What can I do?

Dee's voice sounded off on the com. "Mistress Havera...I mean Aria One! Ruffians are assaulting the ship. Cradite is holding them off. You need to get back here...hey! Don't get blood on the carpet! I just cleaned them. Kewea's curse! What is that?!"

"Dee. Dee!" Adam responded with a whisper. No response. Fenix was too busy taunting Havera to notice.

"Adam, we've got it. He's found the map, but he says there's a problem. We're rushing towards y'all now. He's too determined to get to *him* to concentrate on anything else," said Sam over the com. Adam knew what she meant. Jak heard everything Havera had said. He was hurrying to save Zax.

"I'm working on a plan! Do hurry please," Adam hushed.

Behind him, Fenix was stroking her finger on Havera's open wound. She wiped Havera's blue blood on her finger and licked it. Fenix grinned. "So, that's what a duchess tastes like. A bit too bitter for my liking. Tell me, princess, why are y'all here? You have maybe twenty seconds until my big boy down there devours your friends. Better tell me quick," Fenix said.

"I told you. I'm here for Ignatia. Dusertheus gave me the intel to find her here. Let me go, tell me where she is, and I'll kill her for you!" Havera pleaded.

Fenix clicked her tongue and wagged her finger in Havera's face. "That might be why *you* are here. Doesn't explain why *they* are here. Unless you're having all of them? Cauduun women that impressive between their legs, hmm?" Fenix walked up behind Adam and started groping him. Adam nearly jumped out of his tight sandals. "Well, is she?"

"I'm telling you the truth!" yelled Havera.

The venadarastrixa sprayed some sort of acidic liquid in Zax's direction. The Zokyo managed to dodge it barely. A smidgen must've gotten on his suit. He desperately tried to wipe it away. Mar-Jak tackled him aside to avoid getting barreled over by the charging monster.

Adam had to think fast. He thought of an idea. A crazy idea. One which would force him to overcome certain reservations. For Zax and Marduk, he had to try.

"Havera, tell her the truth. The full truth. About the Orb," Adam said quietly.

"What was that, lovely? An orb you say," Fenix said. She removed her hand from Adam's pelvis. Adam used that opportunity to adjust his tunic. He felt for the object in his pocket and found it. "You mean the Orb of Emancipation. That stupid trinket Ignatia kept babbling about? You're telling me it's real?" Fenix scoffed. She shifted her gaze from Adam to Havera.

Please, Havera, run with that. I only need a few seconds.

Havera sighed. "Yes, we're here to stop Ignatia from reaching the Orb. We were hoping you could lead us to her."

Fenix guffawed. She took a few steps towards Havera. Adam side-eyed over his shoulder. The guards were focused on Fenix and Havera. The tall Tribune had dropped his hand from his blade at the mention of the Orb.

"Why would I do that, lovely? You believe even if I wanted your help that the Tribune here wouldn't cut me down the second I opened my mouth? You are truly too dumb to pull this off." Fenix stepped right into Havera's space. All eyes were on those two. Except Adam's. A couple hundred feet stood between him and the arena. The gaps in the cage notwithstanding, it was a long shot. He withdrew the Debbie from his pocket and quietly crystallized it. There was no turning back.

If you're real, Cradite, here's your chance to prove it.

He squeezed the cold trigger. A gathering of energy appeared at the tips of the crescent moon-shaped weapon. He held it in front of him, aiming for the venadarastrixa. He had only seconds. The beast finished lunging at Mar-Jak and crashed into the side of the cage. The bars were rattling and shaking. Not ideal. The beast stopped moving. Someone was screaming at him from behind. It was now or never.

He released, unleashing the ball of blackened energy towards the creature. The blast sailed through the air towards its target. Almost willing it, Adam saw the energy brush the side of the cage, vaporizing the nearby metal. Most of the energy bypassed the cage and struck the creature right where its torso met its legs.

Everything was still. The crowd went deathly silent. Most whipped around to stare at the source of the shot. The venadarastrixa reacted unnaturally slow. Its hide was tough. The blast from the Debbie had dusted a Human at point-blank range. A chunk of its flesh was torn off. Particles of energy traveled up its body and down through its legs. The creature made to rise on its hind legs and roar. Incredibly slowly.

"BLAST YOUR WAY OUT NOW!" Adam screamed.

Zax got the message. He grabbed Mar-Jak by the arm and dragged him back towards where they entered. He grabbed the electric lute off his back and charged it up. The venadarastrixa gradually turned to face them. The effects of the Debbie were wearing off faster than Adam expected. He felt a sharp pain in the back of his calf followed by a brief jolt. He was forced to one knee.

"Keep him alive!" Fenix screamed.

The guard who had pierced Adam's leg withdrew his electrospear. A steady of trickle of blood poured out of his broken and zapped flesh. Fenix seized him by the hand and bent it backwards. Adam yelped in pain, still clutching the weapon.

A loud explosion detonated, followed by a cacophony of screams. Zax's lute blasted a huge hole in the arena. They fled, almost instantly disappearing down the tunnel where they entered. The wounded and angry venadarastrixa used the opportunity to bash its way through the cage. It gorged an unlucky Moan patron not fast enough to dodge with one of its legs. Seizing the Moan by the side of its jaw, the paralytic took effect instantly. The Moan crumpled to the floor. The Moan's eyes were wide open. The venadarastrixa bent over and began ripping the Moan apart limb-by-limb.

Fenix twisted his wrist until Adam was forced to release his grip on the Debbie. She snatched it. "The rats in the labs downstairs would love this. It seems you're not without your tricks. What to do with you, lovely?" She forced Adam to his feet.

The Tribune had seized Havera by the tail and was holding his blade to her throat. A pair of guards, spears in hand, kept them both in place. Fenix grabbed Adam's ponytail and yanked his head back. She attacked his neck, sinking her teeth hard into him. He winced and gritted his teeth. She had a painful bite as he flailed against her tight grip. He felt her sucking on his neck, unable to shake off her bite. Havera briefly struggled against her captors. The Tribune reinforced his grip on her.

"Remove her bracers. Give them to me," the Tribune calmly ordered. Havera bit her lip. Adam swore under his breath. He had hoped the power her bracers provided would allow them to escape in the confusion. The Tribune had grappled Havera before she had a chance to activate them. He was quick.

Too quick.

One of the guards removed Havera's bracers and attached them to the Tribune's cingulum belt. Fenix removed herself from his neck with a satisfied gasp. Blood dripped down her mouth. She licked her lips clean of all his blood and moaned. With her finger still sticky with Havera's blue blood, she smeared a bit of Adam's red blood onto her fingertip. She traced a bloody violet smile on either side of Adam's mouth.

"Tribune, bind them and take them to my chambers. I shall interrogate them both, personally. We'll see what other secrets these two possess. The Human first. Make the duchess watch," Fenix said, grinning ear-to-ear.

"And the escapees?" asked the Tribune.

"Your 'paladins' should easily find and subdue a pair of bards no matter what tricks they may conceal. I suppose we ought to contain the beast, too."

One of the guards put a finger to his ear. At the same time, Dee spoke over the com. "Mistress, I don't know if you can speak. Umbrasia knocked out all the assailants attacking your ship and tossed them out. I don't know exactly what she did. It was...exhilarating. Unfortunately, she flew out of the ship without me and disappeared. I don't know where she's gone."

Marduk's voice chimed in. "Take the ship, bot, and get out of there. Circle the Cauldron and pick up the bird. Wait for further instructions on extraction."

"Do it!" Havera yelled. She said it for Dee. Fenix mistook the message for her.

"Oh, eager are we, lovely? You won't be. You won't be," Fenix said slowly.

"Fenix, there's a problem," said the guard with a finger to his ear.

"What?!" Fenix barked.

"Someone's penetrated the lab. They're attacking workers and guards. Our people are getting decimated," the guard said.

"Kewea take me harder! Fine. Tribune, take the prisoners to my chambers. Keep them constrained. I'll interrogate them later. The rest of you follow me to the labs. The staff guards can handle the situation up here. We'll make these intruders suffer," ordered Fenix. She pocketed the Debbie.

"Right away," the Tribune said.

Who's attacking the lab? Could be Sam and Jak. No way Marduk and Zax could get there so fast. Why would they? Could Umbrasia get there that quickly? For what purpose? Maybe a diversion.

Adam contemplated those questions while he and Havera were cuffed. The pain in his neck where Fenix had bit him was throbbing. The guards took extra precautions with Havera. They tied an electrified chain around Havera's neck connected to her tail. They wrapped her in leg shackles, too. One of the guards whipped out a device to lock down their HUDs. No way for them to access their inventory.

Fenix stroked Adam on the cheek and forcibly kissed him. Her lips were ice cold. He tried contorting his face away, but she held his face firmly in place. She nibbled on his lower lip as she broke away. "I look forward to our conversation later, lovely," she said with a soft smack on his cheek.

Adam spat on the floor in front of her. "Don't take too long. You have something of mine. I'm going to want it back."

32

Unexpected Competition

The main lobby area had plenty of commotion. Throngs of partygoers were gathered outside the door to the arena, presumably to observe the chaos occurring within. They weren't afraid or even slightly concerned. Most seemed rather amused by what was transpiring within. The Bokori bartender, Locke, and a few other masked servants and guards were scrambling to scrounge food and drink and maintain order. The patrons were actively encouraged to go to the other rooms while security dealt with the venadarastrixa and the remaining guests trapped inside. Some of the bookies and jades from the nearby rooms were taking advantage of the situation by placing bets and soliciting services.

You'd think they were watching an Orbital match.

The Tribune and a pair of guards shoved Adam and Havera past the commotion towards a sealed off corridor. Adam didn't spot any of their friends. His HUD was locked down, preventing him from seeing his mini-map or accessing his gear. Remarkably, their com link remained active. Havera kept whispering coded hints to their team until the Tribune smacked her in the back of the head to keep quiet.

The winding, narrow corridors of the Cauldron gave Adam a headache. Visualizing 3D space was never his strong suit. He kept trying to remember which way they came. The Tribune seemed to intentionally double back at certain points just to confuse them. After escorting them for at least fifteen minutes, the Tribune called them to halt.

"You two, I can handle the prisoners from here. Go see what you can do to help with the ruckus in the main hall," the Tribune ordered.

The two guards nodded and departed. It was only the three of them. The Tribune waited for them to round the corner, before ordering the two of them to keep walking. They themselves rounded a corner at what appeared to be a dead end.

"Stop. Raise your cuffs up," demanded the Tribune of Havera.

She lifted her hands. The Tribune unlocked the cuffs binding her hands, feet, and tail. She reacted instantly. She headbutted the Tribune, knocking his mask slightly askew. She attempted to knock him off his feet with a swipe of her tail, but the Tribune was quick to dodge. He flipped over her tail swipe and kicked her square in the chest, knocking Havera back a couple feet. He reached to draw his blade. A mistake. Havera charged at him. He couldn't unsheathe his weapon in time. Havera shoved him hard into the wall, whacking him in the head with her forearm. He kicked her in the knee, knocking Havera off balance. He tried to fully unsheathe his weapon. Havera spun and smacked his hand with the tip of her tail, sending the weapon flying. It landed at Adam's feet.

Adam bent over to pick up the electroblade. It was quite heavy. For a small gladius sword, it was weighty. The restraints on his hands and feet made it unlikely he'd be able to help. Instead, he watched the Cauduun engage in close quarters hand-to-hand combat. The two combatants seemed to read each other perfectly. Like watching synchronized dancers acting out a performance, they parried and jabbed each other with precision timing. Despite the Tribune's heavy armor, he moved swiftly. Havera reacted faster but her tight-fitting gown proved a liability by constraining her movements.

Adam inched closer, hoping for an opportunity to assist. The Tribune was breathing heavily. Havera tore off a section of her gown to free up her body. Adam blushed. She flipped in the air and suddenly her heeled caligae sandals were in her hands. She used them as blunt instruments to parry and retaliate against the Tribune's blows.

She seemed to be gaining the upper hand. Recognizing this, the Tribune lunged for Havera. She was quick to dodge, yet he managed to seize her tail. He lifted her off the ground and slammed her into the side of the wall with a loud, metallic wallop. Havera howled in pain. She was on the floor, stunned. The Tribune moved to grapple her. Havera kicked him with her powerful legs right in his center mass. The force of the kicked must've caught him off guard. He was pushed back several feet right in front of Adam.

Now!

Adam mustered enough strength to swing the electroblade wildly at the Tribune. It was clumsy. Adam only managed to hit him with the blunt side of the sword. The Tribune's tail snapped at Adam's arm, smacking it like a flyswatter and knocking the blade from his grasp. Adam barely held in a yell.

It was enough. Havera arose out of nowhere and slammed the Tribune against the wall. She wrapped her tail around the hilt of the blade. She flipped it in the air and grasped it with her free arm. She forced the blade to the Tribune's neck, fully intending to slice his throat.

"Havi, wait!"

It was the Tribune. His voice was softened. Havera froze. She continued holding the blade to the Tribune's throat.

"Only one person in the galaxy calls me that," Havera said. She grabbed the Tribune's silver mask and yanked it off. When she saw the face, Havera yelped, dropping the mask to clang on the floor.

"That's because no one knows you like I do, Havi," said the unmasked Tribune. Adam recognized his unmuffled accent as Palerian. Still gruff and harsh, his tone was playful. He smiled a wide grin at Havera.

She was not amused. With a mighty roar, she lifted the Tribune off his feet and body-slammed him into the ground. The Tribune gasped. His helmet fell off his head, revealing a mane of tightly combed golden and green hair.

"Havi, it's me, Augy!" protested the Tribune.

"What are you doing with the Excommunicated, Augustus? You betray my mater, too?!" She spit in his face. Adam shuffled to them. Augustus face turned shocked.

"Never! You know how much your mater meant to me. Meant to us all. Let go of me, Havi," pleaded Augustus.

"Do NOT call me that. You lost all right to call me that or to wear that uniform no matter how bastardized. You and the other treacherous Paladins of Paleria," said Havera, barely restraining her rage.

Augustus was about the same age as Havera. Chiseled jawline and dimples on either cheek, he was a comely Cauduun. His eyes were kind. Adam didn't expect that. Kind and blue as sapphire. He seemed genuinely hurt by Havera's accusations.

"Remember the last time we were in this position, Havera? You beat me that day, too. In the end, we both still won," Augustus said with a smile displaying his perfect, pearly white teeth. Havera lifted him up and smacked his head against the floor. Augustus groaned.

"I find you a high-ranking member of a terrorist organization and you make crude jokes? You promised me you'd avenge my mater! You were supposed to find Ignatia, not join her. You swore that you had no part in the Paladins' plot," Havera sobbed. She was caught between anger and grief. Visible tears streamed down her cheeks.

"I have not broken that promise, Havera. I am the same man now as the day I brought you these." He unhooked Havera's bracers and held them up. Havera slammed the edge of the sword into the ground less than an inch from his face. She snatched the bracers and reequipped them. "I have not forgotten your mater. Let me prove it. My tail. Remove the armor."

Havera glared at him. Adam thought she might strangle him. With a deep breath, she wiped the tears from her eyes. She glanced up to see Adam staring at them both wordlessly. She gestured for Adam to hold out his arms. She grasped the cuffs and, with a faint violet glow of her hand, tore the cuffs off him. Adam's hands and feet were free. Gripping the electroblade, she handed it to Adam. "If he does anything suspicious, cut his tail off," Havera told Adam. Adam nodded. He still felt a bit woozy.

She lifted herself off Augustus and hoisted him to his feet. Augustus lifted his hands slowly and placed them on his head interlocking his fingers. Havera grasped Augustus' tail and slid the armor off the tip. Augustus held the tip aloft for her to see. Branded into the flesh was a recognizable symbol. It was that of the Vitriba. A version of it. A triangle of three rings: one of flames, one of leaves, and one of stones. All connected by a loop of chain links in the middle. Havera touched the brooch on her shoulder. It bore the exact same symbol.

"Mater's personal emblem," Havera said, choking up.

Augustus lowered his hand to feel the brand. "Before Ignatia unmasked herself, your mater knew something was amiss. She's always had an uncanny ability to know when something bad was about to happen. In the months prior to her death, she told me she sensed dread. The same dread she experienced preceding the Boiling of Sin and the queen's orders to involve the Alliance in the Century of Strife before that. Your mater gathered a few of the more dedicated Paladins. She told us of an impending doom, where our faith and our loyalties would be tested. Your mater asked us to swear to defend the Alliance and each other with our lives. We accepted this mark knowing one day, no matter the circumstances, we would need to answer the call. Her call. Your call, Havera. Her responsibility falls to you. You are the link that binds us together."

Havera hung her head. He was teary-eyed. Augustus placed his hands on Havera's shoulders. Her emotions were gripping her, too. She fell into Augustus' chest and wept. He threw his arms around her, stroking her hair. She embraced him.

"I miss her, Augy. I've missed you, too. I never knew how much until this moment," Havera sobbed.

"I've missed you, too, Havi. I miss Pompeia every day. I pray to Cradite every day to guide her spirit. That she may one day bring us back together. Everything I've done has been in service to our maters," Augustus said softly.

Adam stood there awkwardly. He felt like he was intruding on an intimate moment. Only minutes ago, they were at each other's throats. The combination of the adrenaline and the general wooziness he felt dampened his ability to concentrate. Through the haze, he remembered a detail about their journey here.

"He's the Vulpes," Adam whispered.

Havera sniffled. "What was that, Adam?"

"Dusertheus mentioned it was a Vulpes agent that reported spotting the ship. The, umm, the, umm, the Icewalker! That was it. Havera, I think he's the Vulpes agent," said Adam, his thoughts crystallizing.

Havera and Augustus broke apart. Augustus stared out Adam open-mouthed. "How did..." he cut himself off from finishing.

"You joined the Vulpes, Augustus?" Havera asked.

Augustus peeked around the corners to ensure no one would overhear them. "Yes. When Queen Alexandra ordered the exile of the Paladins after your mater's assassination, we were given little choice but to obey. Only a few Paladins actually follow Ignatia. Most of the rest scattered to the corners of Griselda, hoping to live out their shame in peace. Waiting for the call to action. Those of us loyal to the Alliance and your mater cut a deal with the Vulpes. For services rendered in infiltrating and reporting on high value targets around the galaxy, we'd be granted a pardon. We'd be allowed to return to Cauduun society with our honor intact. I made a promise to you and your mater. I volunteered to find Ignatia and bring her to justice. Had I known you'd follow me here...I don't know how y'all found out. I was promised the utmost discretion."

"It's a long story. I'll skip the details. We were told that a missing Ranger ship called the Icewalker arrived here a few days ago with no hints of what had happened to it. It stayed here for a while, then departed for some unknown destination into Union space. There was an intercepted transmission that provided an encrypted map detailing the location of the Orb of Emancipation. We're here to find the map and retrieve the Orb," explained Havera.

"I knew it!" exclaimed Augustus.

"Knew what? Also, can you unlock our HUDs?" Havera requested.

"Mea culpa. Here," Augustus withdrew a scanning device and unlocked Adam and Havera's HUDs. "Sorry about the theatrics back there. I wasn't going to break my cover in front of Fenix. Nasty woman. She frightens even me at times."

"Why'd you fight me?" Havera asked.

"If I hadn't, I'm certain you'd have killed me. Besides, I was curious to see how sharp your skills remained. You certainly disappoint. You never do," Augustus said with a smirk.

"Tell that to my pater. You know what he expects of me," said Havera.

"The galaxy falls apart in your mater's absence. Not only the Alliance. Griselda needs a strong leader to watch over her. I'd have thought you'd be that leader. My mater always thought you'd follow in your mater's footsteps," said Augustus.

"You haven't heard the news. Augusta aims to replace my mater. She's joined the Imperialists. More than that, she leads them," said Havera.

Augustus playfully punched her in the shoulder. "Ha ha, very funny, Havi. Mater was always the planner, never the doer. She let your mater be the face. The Imperialist part was a bit over the top. You almost had me for a second."

"I'm not joking, Augy. Pater told me himself. She defected."

Augustus' cheery face evaporated. He examined Havera for any sign of jest. She showed none. For the first time, Augustus' eyes were no longer kind. "Mater would never. It spits in the face of everything she believed. What Pompeia believed! The Imperialists are tyrants. Mater believed the Absolutists were too authoritarian. To lead the Imperialists is unconscionable. It's..."

"I know. I know, Augy. I couldn't believe it either. I'm willing to give your mater the benefit of the doubt. She and my mater were lifelong friends. There must be a good explanation."

"Ahem!" Adam interjected. "Again, I find this fascinating, but we're on a bit of a time crunch, Havera. We don't have time for Cauduun politics."

Augustus frowned. He tilted his head in Adam's direction. "What's he doing here anyway? You cavorting with Human Separatists?"

"I have a name you know."

"Since when?"

"Animus Augustus! Mind your manners. That's Adam Mortis. He leads..."

"I know who he is, Havi. I asked you what he's doing here? I thought you were seeking a map. What do any of your other companions have to do with this?"

"Good question," a voice called from around the corner.

Four figures turned the corner into visual range. Adam breathed a sigh of relief when he saw them. Marduk, back in his normal form, was wearing his chitinous armor and completely covered in several flavors of blood. Zax also had blood on his skintight mechsuit; although, it was smeared in what looked like a poor attempt to wipe it off. By contrast, Sam and Jak were pristine. Adam limped towards the group. Sam broke off and enveloped him in a big hug.

"We thought you might be dead. Jak found a moment to conduct a full scan of the area. We found each other and wanted to meet up to decide our next move," said Sam.

"We're not dead. Just a little battered and sweaty. Fenix stole my Debbie. I think I'm getting a headache," Adam said.

"Ew, more than a little battered. You're bleeding and you were limping. Here," Sam said. She cleaned the blood smear off Adam's face. She materialized some healing paste from her inventory and smeared it on Adam's neck and leg wounds. "Did something bite you?"

"Someone. You said you found the map. I guess our next move is to get out of here and head towards Union space. I need to find Fenix and get the Debbie back." said Adam.

Sam shook her head. "We'll worry about the Debbie later. Our job isn't done."

"What do you mean?"

Jak stepped forward. He tapped a few times on his wrist com, revealing a digiholo display of a map. "We found the unencrypted version of the map. Unfortunately, it is incomplete. We have the exact interstellar coordinates of CR-2-13-LF. Except, we have no way to get there. The map documents no routes or highways leading to the system. We can't fly blind into negative space. Odds are we'd hit a star or some other danger that'll rip us apart."

"Who would have route data for the Omega spiral?" asked Adam.

"Besides, the Yunes?" Jak shrugged. "Who is the Consul of Cloudboard?"

"The Rangers do. They charted a spinal route through almost every sector of this half of Griselda from here to the Point of Always Return. Surely, they'd know. They must have archives of information at their guild HQ," suggested Havera.

"Where's that?" asked Adam.

"Back on Concordia."

"We can't return there. We don't have time!"

"There's no need," said Augustus. He had reequipped his blade and helmet. "I know exactly where you can find that data."

"Who is this guy?" asked Jak.

"A friend," replied Havera.

"To Kewea he is! He's the one who ordered us detained and fed us to that Dark Realm horror," Marduk said, shoving the barrel of the Drillhead in Augustus' face.

The Tribune calmly pushed the tip of the barrel out of his face. "It's only because of me you're still alive. Your names and profiles were in the ConSec report. Something I conveniently left out of my report to Fenix. The Excommunicated have a kill-on-sight order for you, Guerilla. Had she known you were with them, she'd have had you all beheaded on the spot. So, I watched and waited. 'Jak' gave a shitty performance in the concert hall. Off-beat far too many times. You're fortunate I deduced it was you. Fenix wanted me to knock you two out before hauling you to that abomination. You know what would've happened had I done that instead of simply containing you with a dampener. The Metamorph revealeth."

Marduk growled and lowered his weapon. "What do you mean by ConSec report?"

Adam shuffled his feet and Havera ran her fingers through her hair. Augustus noticed their sudden timidity.

"Fenix was well-aware of y'all's presence. She didn't know why y'all were here, but she used the bards as leverage to learn why. After Fenix got what she wanted, she planned on disposing all of y'all," Augustus said.

"And you two knew?" Marduk barked.

Adam nodded. Havera was unapologetic. "We all understood there would be dangers with this plan. They'd have been no different had y'all known the full scope!"

"You lied," Jak said. His eye stalks were curled close to his head.

"Only by omission," Havera said.

Sam stepped between the two groups. "We can talk about this later. We still need to get what we came for and get out of here."

Havera turned her attention back to Augustus, hoping to change the subject. "You said you knew Ignatia was after the Orb. How?"

"Ignatia's betrayal always troubled me. Like most, I had chalked it up to her Confederate politics. I couldn't ask her. Ignatia never trusted me. I wasn't one of the Paladins involved in her plot. She always kept me at arm's length. Assigning me to guard Fenix was her way to sideline me. After months of working my way up the ladder, I was in a position to obtain answers. Ignatia was at this facility for days at a time. I only knew it as this sector's farming and processing facility for Celeste. I wanted to figure out why she'd spend so much time here. I managed to convince Fenix to shift her base of operations here. A power move to shove it in Ignatia's face. I had hoped the clash of personalities would generate opportunities for me to discover some secrets. It worked. I can confirm Ignatia went to the Praetorian vault with the intent of stealing the Sword of Aria."

"The Warrior's Kiss?" Havera was surprised. "Why does she seek the Sword?"

"Not sure. Ignatia is obsessed with the occult and the old tales.

She spoke at length about the Vitriba and its importance saving the Cauduun. Rambled on-and-on about chosen ones, heralds, goddesses, the Orb, the Sword, the Shield, Noah. The purported theft of Queen Havera VIII's body puzzled me the most. How could she have had time to take the body but not the sword?"

"Did you include this in your reports?"

Augustus sighed. "I did once. My handler threatened to cut me loose. Accused me of intentionally spreading disinformation. The Vulpes and the duchesses don't care about old tales and legends. They're convinced Pompeia's assassination was political. Nothing will dissuade them. Easier to pin it on miscreant miners and galactic terrorists."

"If you knew where to find Ignatia, why didn't you report that in?"

"I did. Until Ignatia left Rorae space, the Vulpes claimed there was little they could do. A pathetic excuse if I've ever heard one. My handlers told me to keep an eye on her and report on her movements. Nothing more. I couldn't let it go, so I went looking for Havera VIII's body. I believed it might've been here. You know better than most, Havi. Havera VIII sought the Vitriba. I thought they were running tests on her body in the lab below. Searching for clues to where the Adventurer Queen might've traveled." Augustus shook his head. "Dead end there. Most of the research here is sponsored by the other galactic powers to discover ways of neutralizing Yune tech off the books. I did, however, discover a more promising lead. Something overlooked from your mater's assassination. Something else Ignatia allegedly stole."

Havera's tail stiffened. "Ancient star charts!"

Augustus nodded. "The Ranger Guild carefully guards its secrets. All digital files are kept at the Ranger guild on Concordia. After the Meltdown, older written copies deemed of little value were sent to the Praetorian Order on Rema for posterity. Preserved in the vaults beneath Raetis' Hill. Until two years ago."

"Where is Ignatia?"

"She and her treacherous paladins departed for Union space a few months ago. Other than that encoded message, we haven't heard from her. I thought I'd have a chance to find out more information when the Icewalker arrived. No one was allowed near it. Not even Fenix. Its captain was insistent. Backed up by a bunch of Yunes. One of them shot a mechanic for getting too close. The captain and his navigator only asked to examine a particular star chart. It was bizarre. They gave me the creeps."

Havera grasped Augustus by his cheeks. "Augy, where are the star charts?"

Augustus laughed, tenderly removing her hands from his face. "A point of fact, they are where I was ordered to take you two in the first place. Fenix's office. Well, technically, it is Ignatia's office. Fenix decided to, uhh, commandeer it for the time being. I can get you in. Ignatia kept a vast library in the storage room adjacent to her office. Forewarning, Fenix did some...rearranging of the office. By rearranging, I mean she trashed the place. And by storage room, it's practically a warehouse. It'll take time to search."

"Great. We've not a moment to waste. Let's go," insisted Adam.

"Follow me. Stay close and keep quiet," said Augustus.

Augustus led the crew through more winding corridors. They stopped every so often to let a patrol go by, often ducking into nearby rooms to avoid being spotted. It helped having the Tribune there. He ordered any patrolling guards towards another direction to clear their path. About ten minutes later, they arrived at a long corridor on a mild incline. At the top of the incline was a locked double door. Augustus tapped the air and the doors opened up.

"In here. It's the door on the left."

"Do you know where it is exactly?" asked Havera.

Augustus shook his head. "I do not. The Icewalker's navigator was the last one to examine the star chart. Took a couple days. Apparently, Fenix had decided to pull a petty prank on Ignatia. She moved many of the documents around at random. That, uhh, was not well-received. Fenix told me Ignatia punished her for that transgression but didn't elaborate. Not sure how Ignatia accomplished that from light years away. I assume she had the captain order Fenix to reorganize everything by herself. She has been unusually irritable the past few days, even by her standards. You have a small window until she returns. If my coms are any indication, whatever is happening in the labs is ongoing."

"It's not us. We're all here," said Sam.

"Not all. Must be that Magi witch!" said Marduk.

"Magi witch? Y'all have a Rorae here? Uh-oh," said Augustus.

"Why uh-oh?" Adam asked.

"Rorae obtain their energy from stars. Exposing a Rorae Magi to that much raw Celeste would be like lighting a torch in an open fuel line. She could blow the whole place!"

"Perhaps it wasn't wise to have a Celeste farm in Rorae space," quipped Zax.

"Not my idea. I need to get down there and stop her. Unless you have a way of communicating with her," Augustus said.

Havera shook her head. "Rorae don't have HUDs. Can't use digital coms. She was supposed to stay on the ship. I'll come with you."

"No, I'll go. You should stay here and search, tailed guppy. You have the most experience with these types of documents. You'll be able to spot the correct one faster. I'll help find the witch. I won't let her out of my sight again," insisted Marduk.

"Too risky. Fenix has been exceptionally blood-hungry the past few days. If she or the other guards catch you with me..."

"The witch is powerful. She might kill you if I'm not there. Scrounge me some paladin armor. I'll transform into a Cauduun and be your man in disguise."

"But..."

"No point arguing, Augy. We'll find the star chart," Havera said.

Augustus relented. He tapped the air. A location was marked on Adam's HUD map. "After you find the chart, rendezvous here. There's a port where you can dock your ship's umbilical to pick y'all up."

"That's not far from where we entered. I can lead us there safely," said Jak.

Augustus nodded. "Add me to your com. It's the one aspect of your infiltration we couldn't decipher. I'll let y'all know if something happens."

Jak stepped in front of Augustus. Waving his hand, Jak drew a small glowing glyph. The same one he had drawn establishing their com link. With a flick, the glyph contacted and dispersed on Augustus' face. The Tribune's face twitched for a second.

"Done," Jak said.

"Excellent. You're looking for a piece of old-fashioned tan reed paper, yellowing at the edges, wrapped in a scroll holder about this big," Augustus said, measuring about two-feet with his hands. "Look for the label 'Chant List'. That'll be the one you're searching for."

Marduk transformed into a blue and black-skinned Cauduun with matching hair. The pair turned to head back down the inclined corridor.

Havera caught Augustus by the shoulder. "Be safe. I don't want to wait another two years to see you again."

"*I'll* be fine. It's *you* I worry about, Havi. I hope you know what you're doing." He raised the tip of his tail between them.

Havera pivoted and interlocked her tail with his. "Since when I have ever not known what I'm doing, Augy?"

Their tail tips squeezed tighter. "That's what has me worried. You're a brilliant, powerful woman. Where your mater is involved, you have a blindspot."

33

Closed Doors, Open Wounds

The group had separated. Marduk departed with Augustus towards the lab area to find Umbrasia. Dee had parked the Cicera on a smaller nearby asteroid, waiting for word to come pick them up. He had retrieved Sel-Ena from where she was perched at Sam and Jak's infiltration site to refill her custom armor's oxygen tanks. Adam, Sam, Havera, Zax, and Jak were left to find their quarry.

Adam was dripping in sweat. He had switched out his formal outfit for his armored one. He was grateful to be wearing his father's duster again despite how flushed he felt. He wiped the sweat from his brow.

Umbrasia must've knocked out the central air. Kewea take me; I feel like I'm already there.

The office itself was spacious and dimly lit. It had Fenix's touch. Numerous decorations and accoutrements of bleached skulls of multiple races, curved and hooked blades, and stuffed corpses of ferocious beasts. Both Zax and Jak noted a few of the taxidermied creatures were native to Terras-Ku. Several framed portraits of people engaging of all sorts of debauchery and painted stills depicting numerous gory historical events adorned the walls.

A tall painting of a Cauduun woman dressed in torn regal garb hung directly behind the desk. She was in the midst of crucifixion. Her tail had been severed with its bloody stump dripping down her body onto a fallen crown wreath beneath her earthward facing head. The plaque read "The Crucifixion of the Last Platinum Empress."

Adam found an illustration portraying the Battle of Gla-Mor notably eye-catching. Unlike the version from *The Maid of Gla-Mor*, this one depicted a bloodied Havera IV surrounded by corpses, holding the severed head of whom was presumably Mahlak the Righteous.

"This must be the door," Zax signaled.

On the left-hand wall facing the desk was a simple locked door. Jak easily disabled the electronic lock. Stepping inside, Adam's heart sunk.

Augustus undersold it. The chamber matched length of the cathedral where Adam's hearing was held if not nearly as tall. Rows upon rows of shelves created tight corridors to traverse. Each shelf was filled to the brim with scrolls, books, and other documents from an era where everything was written on paper.

Zax whistled, which reverberated off the walls creating an echo. "This is an impressive collection." Zax coughed a bit. "This place is dusty. Need to adjust my air filters."

Havera chuckled. "It's a decent haul. The vaults beneath the First Sanctum contain about a thousand rooms like this."

"The G'ee'ks have similar chambers at the D'hty Academy; although, theirs contain mostly electronic hardcopies. Some written but it's uncommon," Jak said.

Trissefer would love to spend time in a place like this.

Samus bowed her head and shifted her feet. Adam patted her on the shoulder. "Something wrong, Sam?"

"I wonder if Earth ever held such a place. It's silly to worry about such trivialities at a time like this. I can't help but wonder why we keep fighting. There's nothing to preserve, protect, or defend, except our own lives. What have we to show for it other than a rundown town in a corner of the galaxy no one cares about?" said Sam.

He understood how she felt. Identical thoughts brewed in the back of his mind each night before bed. They had nothing. Only each other.

Because they stole it from us!

Adam put his arm around Sam and gave her a comforting squeeze. "We have Stepicro!"

"No, *we* don't," she retorted.

Adam forced himself to not look at Havera. "You're right. We're fighting for our future to reclaim our past, Sam. Remember how all this trouble got started?"

Sam smiled. "Arabella."

"Arabella," he agreed. "We didn't decide to upend five-hundred years of Covenant rule over a rusted old statue, we didn't even create, that was rotting away in the humidity of an alien moon. I have no idea who or what Arabella was. For all I know, she could've been a horrible monster like Fenix. It's what she represents *to us*. Not to the Bokori. Not to the Modders. Not to the Conclave. To us! A time we lost. A time we will reclaim."

"What is lost will be found."

"Exactly. We fight for the right to create a thousand Stepicros. Our descendants may forget our names or spit on our legacies. But, they will exist. For if we fail, there will be no one capable of remembering. We must keep fighting, Sam. We're close. Put your faith in the Long Con, okay? Our ancestors put their faith in us. Let's not disappoint them."

Sam nodded. "Okay."

Adam released her. "Good. First, put your investigative skills to work in this office. Do a clean sweep of this room first. Search every inch. We don't want to spend all this time searching this enormous library for the star chart to be hidden in a drawer. Havera, Zax, Jak, and I will start in this warehouse. Join us when you're certain we've missed nothing."

"You've got it, Adam," said Sam with a mocking heart salute. Adam smirked. Sam began with Fenix's desk while the other four moved into the warehouse.

"Zax and I will start on opposite ends on the left and work our way towards the middle. Y'all do the same on the right. Jes-Mur save us if Ignatia doesn't have a proper organizing system for these documents," said Jak.

They agreed and split up. It was to their collective lament that Ignatia did in fact not have a recognizable organizing system for these documents. They did not appear to be catalogued by era, location, subject, or alphabetically. Not the Palerian alphabet anyway, and certainly not Human Default or Standard alphabet.

"I've taken many a course on code-breaking, and even I don't recognize the pattern these documents are in. My only conclusion is she has this entire library memorized," Jak called out.

"Impressively paranoid of her. No wonder she was pissed at Fenix moving her stuff around. That tracks. Keep searching," Havera responded.

The process was tedious. Many of the documents, if they had any written language at all, had to be meticulously translated by their HUDs. Converting digital letters and glyphs into the user's native language, common communication in the modern day, was a simple task that occurred instantaneous to the naked eye. Physically written documents had a slight lag. The styles and illegibility of disparate handwriting strained their HUD's translators. Due to her education and Praetorian training, along with the fact much of what they were searching was already written in the Palerian tongue, Havera sped read much faster than everyone else.

Adam and Havera met near a section on dark energy. "What you told Sam. You don't really believe that. Unless you were lying to me earlier about Human culture belonging to everyone who wants it. If something belongs to everyone, everyone has the right to use and interpret that something."

Adam closed a scroll on pre-Conclave black hole locations. "What I believe doesn't matter. She needed to hear what she needed to hear." He wiped more sweat from his brow. He fanned himself with his hand to keep cool.

Havera shook her head. "I can't believe it. You're doing it again!"

"Doing what?"

"Coddling Sam."

"I am not!"

"Yes, you are! You're responding the exact same way you did after our meeting with the Yunes. You don't need to protect her from the truth."

"What truth is that? She could die. I could die. Her brother could die. We could all live and fail. Humans might end up subjugates for another half millennia. I don't need to remind her of the stakes. She's all too aware of them. I haven't forgotten Inclucity. What I witnessed. She doesn't need any more pessimistic realism. She's plenty of that. A little hopeful optimism goes a long way."

"You're the expert on what Sam needs?"

"No. Neither are you. I'm trying to take responsibility for the people under my command. The hundreds of thousands of them waiting for us at Arabella. Something you wouldn't understand, *Your Grace*."

"Less arguing, more searching!" Jak yelled at them from across the room.

"This is so stupid!" Havera said, thrusting a pair of scrolls back on the shelf. Several of them were knocked onto the floor. "We could spend hours searching and not find it. Augustus, any updates?"

Augustus replied immediately. "Your Rorae friend seems to have disappeared. Most of the people attacked were either gassed or otherwise knocked unconscious. A couple fatalities via friendly fire. Some minor damage, nothing too concerning. The situation is calm for now. I think Fenix might be returning to her office to 'interrogate' you both soon, so I'd hurry up. She won't come alone."

"Wonderful. Hurry back here both of you. We may need you."

"I'd advise against a direct confrontation, Havi. Any one of them set off a security alarm, you'll have a couple dozen armed guards swarm your location. Keep searching. We're on our way."

Havera smacked the ground aggressively with her tail, kicking up a small cloud of dust. "You know, just once, I wish I could press a button and what I was seeking would illuminate before my eyes. That would be so convenient."

"That's not a bad thought," Jak's voice echoed. "Come back to the door. I have an idea."

Adam and Havera hurried back to the door. Zax and Jak were waiting. Jak had his wrist device held out in front of him.

"What's your idea, Jak?" Havera asked.

"It's a long shot. My criminology class taught us some crime scene investigative tools and techniques. Search for dried blood, DNA, fingerprints in the case of non-Zokyo. That sort of thing. Zax reminded me this place was dusty. I think I can use that to find the places where dust has most recently been disturbed. If we're operating on the assumption that the last item moved in this place was our star chart, my scan could tell me exactly where by the amount of disturbed dust. For me, it would, in fact, illuminate before my eyes, ha ha," said Jak.

"Woah. Document this day. Jak actually laughed," Zax said, patting his friend on the shoulder.

"Don't ruin the moment, maestro. This will take me a few minutes. It should help us narrow it down. We've already ruled out the outer rows. A few calibrations here. One minor glyph there..." Jak said. The Naddine continued to mutter to himself, tweaking and tinkering with some of his gadgets.

Sam called from the main office. "Y'all should see what I found."

"Go. I'm almost done with my calibrations," Jak said, ushering them away.

Havera, Adam, and Zax found Sam hanging out in front of the crucifixion painting. Sam had opened the painting like a door, revealing a hidden chamber behind it. A bedroom. Not any bedroom Adam had stepped in. It was covered in UV lights. An extravagant four-poster wooden bed with midnight drapes, silk sheets, and golden filigree embedded in the railings. Long, black tail feathers adorned the edges of the canopy. Placed underneath the canopy was a rectangular vanity mirror. That was the least interesting aspect. Each corner of the bed contained leather straps and cuffs of various size and material. A leg spreader was placed on the floor at the foot of the bed along with a whip and thin wooden rod.

"Kinky," Zax said.

"The walls," Sam pointed out.

Chains and other restraining devices hung liberally from the lustrous white walls. Smatters of dried blood of diverse colors illuminated by the UV lights added to the décor of this room. Staffs, rods, whips, blades, knives, spears, and daggers with electric, sear, and frost variants and attachments covered the walls from end-to-end. Upon closer examination, the tools were pristine and clean, but showed signs of heavy usage. Interference on Adam's HUD indicated that this room contained digital and electronic dampeners in the walls for maximum privacy.

"Fenix has made herself at home," quipped Havera. "Interrogation, indeed. She has her ways of attacking the mind and body."

"I believe you mean penetrate," snickered Sam.

Adam shuddered and nearly fainted. The bite mark on his neck remained sore to the touch. "I would very much like to avoid getting trapped in here with her."

"We may not have much of a choice. Look." Zax was standing in front of Fenix's terminal. He had pulled up security footage. Marching down the hall towards the inclined corridor was Fenix. She had a guard escort. Two Cauduun and two Naddine.

"Augy, Fenix is almost here. She has a couple pairs of armed guards with her. Is there another way out of this room?" Havera asked over the com.

"No, it's a dead end. Hide! We're about ten minutes out."

"She's going to sound the alarm when she sees we're not there. We can ambush her. She won't be expecting this many of us."

"No! You don't know her like I do. She's not easy prey."

"We still haven't found the star chart. We need more time!"

"I have an idea," interjected Sam. "It's risky. It will hurt. It'll buy y'all enough time to find the star chart."

Adam attempted to ask, but Sam had already tapped the air a couple times. She switched out of her infiltration gear with the lovely brown tunic dress she wore to Adam's hearing. She let down her hair, whipping it around and shaking her head to let it settle. She slipped the straps of her gown slightly off her shoulders to reveal more of her bosom.

"What are you doing, Sam?" Adam gasped.

"What needs to be done to protect our future," said Sam.

"Not like this, Sam! You saw what it's in that room. You have but an inkling of what that woman is capable of. There must be another way," insisted Adam.

Sam hopped onto Fenix's desk. "We're out of time, and I'm doing this. Either go find the star chart or take off your armor and sit with me."

"Sam, no!"

"Sam, are you sure?" Havera asked.

Sam nodded. "This is something I must do. We need to stall her. I can stall her. Trust me."

Adam gritted his teeth.

No, not this again.

Havera gently grasped Adam by the arm. "Trust her, Adam. We'll wait for Augustus and find the star chart. She only needs to stall for ten minutes."

Adam held back tears. His pulse pounded. His scars ached. He was not okay with this. The room was spinning a little. He took a deep breath to try and calm himself.

"She's almost here! Quickly!" Zax said, noticing Fenix had reached the inclined corridor.

Adam broke free of Havera's grip and hugged Sam tightly. "I'm sorry I couldn't do better."

"You have nothing to be sorry about, Adam. I promise. Go," Sam ushered him away.

Havera and Zax closed the painting door. Adam lingered on Sam for an instant.

Forgive me, John. I'm failing you both. Again.

Havera yanked Adam to the warehouse door. They crossed the threshold and locked the door behind them. Havera made a call out on the com. "Augy, Sam is stalling Fenix. Keep listening in and follow her lead."

Augustus hesitated. "Oh...okay. Will do."

Jak was pacing between the aisles. His eye stalks twisted in every direction searching for something only he could see.

"What's going on?" asked a bewildered Jak.

"Fenix is here with a handful of guards. We're finding that star chart while Sam buys time until Augustus and Marduk return," Havera said.

"We're fortunate. I finished probing this place. Beyond the rows on the outsides we searched, there appears to be signs of dust disturbance down these two rows," said Jak.

"You and Zax take the left. We'll take the right," Havera said.

The two pairs scrambled to search. A few seconds later, they heard a chilling voice yell in their ears.

"Who are you and what are you doing in my office?!" It was Fenix. She had returned and spotted Sam, who had kept her com channel open for them to eavesdrop in on. "Where are my two prisoners?!" Fenix barked.

"Umm, the tall guard with the horizontal crest told me to tell you he moved them to a more secure location. He asked me to wait here for you to return," said a faux-meek Sam.

"Did he?" Fenix said, her voice dripping with venom. "You don't move one muscle, lovely. Understand?" There was a pause. "Tribune! Where's the duchess whore and her Human pet?"

Adam held his breath, waiting for Augustus to respond. He wondered if he'd hear what Augustus said. "I relocated them to my quarters under my personal guard. I had a report of a disturbance in your part of the Cauldron, so I was worried our intruders might be seeking to break them out."

"I see," responded Fenix. Adam thought she sounded skeptical. "Who's the Human girl?"

"Well, Fenix, I figured you might be a little, uhh, stressed and pissed about the intruders. I had Locke send up one of the girls from the club. She's brand new. I thought you might want to, uhh, you know..." Augustus left his voice trailing. He was surprisingly convincing, Adam thought.

"Oh, Tribune, my lovely. You do know me so well. I didn't realize we had procured a Human girl. So rare. So precious. I wonder if it'll feel too much like self-love to have her. Alright, keep the other two on ice.

I'll be there in let's say...three hours. I want to be extra thorough with this one," Fenix said with a mischievous laugh.

Her comments made Adam's skin crawl. He found concentrating on old tomes increasingly difficult.

Havera noticed his rage from down the row. "Adam, focus! Trust in Sam." He took a deep breath, striving to empty his mind. It did little. The slow translation process further added to his frustration.

"What's your name, lovely?" said Fenix. Adam wanted to the shut off the channel. He had to keep it on.

"They call me Peach, ma'am," replied Sam.

"Hmm, Peach. I do like that. I'll bet you taste sweet, too."

"I suppose there's only one way for you to find out."

Between Fenix and Sam's comments, Adam was tremendously uncomfortable. He heard an impact sound followed immediately by yelp from Sam. She yelped again, then gasped.

"Mmm, you are soft, lovely. This is but a minor taste. I will hurt you. I will break you. I have more than these knuckles awaiting you. If you are to work for me, you must know the limits of sentient pleasure...and pain."

Sam coughed. "I can take the pain. You can't hurt me."

Fenix cackled. "Lovely, lovely, lovely. I think I am going to enjoy you. You think you know pain. I spent much of my childhood passed around from brothel to brothel. I was nothing but a cheap jade. A toy to be played with for some lonely nobody with a few extra Links in their account. I had my first kill when I was only ten. A client thought it could skip out without paying. You see that Bokori skull. That's it. I think I'll have it watch, hehehe."

"The more the merrier. I perform better with an audience."

"Mmm, I can see it in your eyes, lovely. You wish to be me. You've taken life. Yes. I can see it. So young. So naïve. So...fresh. You know how to take a life. Let me show you how to experience life." Sam yelped again. "You two remain here. The rest of you wait outside. No one is to disturb me under any circumstances! Understood?" Her guards gave vague grumblings of affirmation.

The last Adam heard was the scuttling of footsteps and the opening of the painting door. Sam's feed cut out. She was in that room at the mercy of Fenix.

Adam vomited. He hadn't eaten much, so it was mostly a dry heave with a mixture of that tonic water from earlier. He had a slight bitter iron taste in his mouth. He spit it out and wiped his chin.

"Adam, you okay?" asked Havera, scrolling through scrolls.

"No," he replied curtly.

A loud, muffled scream could be heard perforating the walls from the other side of the door. Adam threw down a scroll on detailing the discovery of the first Venvuishyn ruins. He charged towards the door.

Havera held out her arm to stop him. He barreled right past her, shoving her arm out of the way.

"Adam, wait!" Havera cried out.

Ignoring her, he reached the door. A small glass slit allowed Adam to get a partial view of the room. Standing by the door were two masked Cauduun guards, not moving a muscle. They were carrying rifles with their shields and staffs holstered on their backs. With the amount of armor they wore, it was hard to spot a weakness.

Perhaps in the side or in the neck. I could strangle them with their own tails!

"What are you doing? We need to keep searching!" Havera insisted.

"No, we need to rescue Sam! There's only two of them. We could easily overpower them."

"We need to wait for Augustus to come and send them away. If they send out an alert before we can take them down, we'll be swarmed. We'll never be able to escape, and this will all be for naught."

"I'm prepared to take that chance. I cannot let them hurt Sam further!" Adam snarled. He pushed Havera away. The unexpected shove caused Havera to stumble. Her tail balanced against the floor kept her afoot.

"Buddy, easy there. We're on your side," said Zax. He and Jak had quit their search to see what the commotion was. J'y'll growled at Adam.

Another scream echoed through the door. Adam equipped his rifle from his inventory. He was breathing heavily. Fear. Rage. Pain. Disgust. He experienced it all. The scars on his back howled with pain.

Is this what John felt?

Havera snuck up and bear hugged him to hold him back. "No, I won't let you do this!" She was strong; he was stronger. He broke free of her grip for a moment. She managed to redouble it, squeezing him with her tail. Zax and Jak joined in. J'y'll began biting at Adam's ankle.

"You...will...not...stop...me!" he shrieked. The force of his voice shattered the slit of glass in the door. With a great surge of strength, he tossed the four of them off him. Akin to ragdolls, they flew off him.

Without questioning himself, he kicked the door. It caved and flew to the other side of the room. The Cauduun guards, hearing the commotion from the other side, had approached the door. The tall, lanky guard was caught the force of the door and crushed between it and the back wall. Startled, the short, stocky guard raised his rifle. The sudden appearance of an unexpected hostile slowed his reaction. Adam fired first, shooting laser blast after laser blast. Most shots bounced off the guard's armor. The force of the shots caused the guard to stumble backwards and drop his rifle. One blast struck the guard in the side. The guard grunted in pain, clutching his side. His wound smoked and bled. The guard reached for his spear to no avail. Adam closed the gap more quickly than he expected. He cracked the guard in the side of his helmet. The guard hit the floor with a solid clang of his armor. Dazed, he attempted to stand, only for Adam to put his boot on his shield, forcing him back to the ground. Adam fired endlessly into the guard's neck, severing it after only a few bloody shots. Only the weapon overheating forced Adam to quit firing.

The door to the hallway opened. The two remaining Naddine guards must've heard the fight inside the office. They attempted to enter to see what was going on. Acting on pure instinct, Adam picked up the fallen Cauduun guard's spear and hurled it at them. The electrospear skewered through the first Naddine guard and landed with a fleshy thump in the second Naddine guard's heart. Both dropped to the ground dead. The spear kept them connected while they fell.

Through the carnage, Adam heard a groan coming from the corner. The tall, lanky Cauduun guard barely managed to lift the crushed door off himself. He attempted to stand only to fall immediately back down under the weight of his crumpled armor. With a great leap, Adam landed next to the guard. He barely had a chance to beg for his life. Adam seized the guard by his mask and slammed the back of his head against the wall with his full strength. There was a loud, wet crunch. The guard's arms fell to his side. His body lay still, except for his orange tail, which twitched erratically for several seconds before eventually succumbing.

Adam turned his attention to the crucifixion painting. He moved towards it. The desk was between him and the painting. He gripped the underside of the desk and hurled it across the room, crashing it into the wall. A small electronic explosion erupted from the area of impact. He wasn't questioning his sudden strength. Standing in front of the painting, he grasped it from either side. With an effortless tug, he yanked the painting from the wall, ripping it from its hinges. He tossed the painting aside, nearly smacking Havera, who had entered the office by then. If she called out to him, he had not heard it.

He stepped inside. "Kewea's curse! What are you doing?"

Adam had expected to hear Fenix's voice. It was Sam's. He was not expecting to see what he saw. Sam was standing there, holding one of the long black feathers from the canopy. She seemed...fine. Other than some tousled hair, flushed cheeks, and a minor tear in her tunic, Sam was otherwise unharmed.

Fenix, on the other hand, was in a more compromising position. Her wrists were bound to the corners of the poster bed. Her legs were pried apart by the electric leg spreader. She was wearing nothing other than her choker, her fishnet stockings, and her long black high heels. The tip of Sam's feather was teasing Fenix's groin area.

The sheer shock of that sight sorted something in Adam's brain. The rage and fear left him. The pain and disgust remained.

"Sam, what's happening?" Adam finally uttered through his tightening chest.

"Doing what I said I'd do. As you can see, I had her right where I wanted her," Sam said through gritted teeth.

"I...I heard screaming. I couldn't get...I couldn't get Inclucity...the hostel...out of...out of my...out of my..." Adam dropped to one knee. The adrenaline surge wore off. He began wheezing. Breathing wasn't his problem. His body was rejecting the very air around him. His vision narrowed. The room was spinning out of control. He was seeing colors that reminded him of a journey through negative space. He coughed and coughed. Specks of blood sprayed from his lips.

"Adam! What's wrong? Kewea's curse, Adam, you're bleeding. The veins in your neck. They're black and bulging. And your eyes are blood red. What happened?!" Sam screamed.

A mad cackle burst from Fenix's lips. "Oh, this is so perfect! I had not anticipated that reaction. Hehehe. You're having a rougher time with the transformation, my lovely. I see why Ignatia calls it a punishment. I call it a gift."

"What are you talking about?" Sam grabbed one of the frostblades off the wall and held it to Fenix's throat. "What did you do to him?"

Fenix continued to cackle. "Oh, lovely, in the few minutes I've known you, I can tell you're a better lover than fighter. Do not threaten if you cannot follow through. I have beheld the face of death, and I kissed it." Fenix effortlessly broke the metal restraints on her wrists and crumpled the leg spreader as if it were paper. She grabbed Sam by the arm, disarmed her, and tossed her aside into the wall. Several blades were dislodged and fell to the floor with loud clangs. Sam was knocked out cold.

"Sam!" Adam felt another surge of adrenaline course through him. His vision clarified. Fenix had sported a new outfit. She kept the corset and long leather jacket. Except, now she wore a circular brimmed black hat with a long black feather attached at the top. Her lower body was covered by solid armored leggings with knee high flat boots. Thick combat gloves protected her hands. She had once again donned the golden mask. She was no longer dressed to party, but she was undoubtedly dressed to play.

Adam attempted to stand. His knees buckled. He fell back, hitting the wall and sliding down to the floor powerless.

Fenix took deliberate steps towards him. She clicked her tongue to mock him and held the frostblade out towards him threateningly. "You are too weak to handle this gift it would seem, lovely. Too bad. The love we could've made. Mmm. Such a wasted opportunity. No matter. I shall create better ones than you."

"No, you won't." Havera stepped across the threshold, with her bracers activated. Normally, the glow from was localized only to just her forearms around the bracers themselves. On this occasion, Havera's body up to her neck was engulfed in a vibrant, violet aura. The brightness of her visage pained Adam's eyes. He averted his gaze, groaning in the process.

Fenix pointed her blade at Havera. "Jealous are we, jadespawn? That power you wield. It is nothing compared to what Ignatia has in store. This will be the perfect test. You're merely an appetizer. I will kill that bitch myself, you ducal whore! You will not deprive me of that pleasure."

Fenix lunged at Havera, aiming for her throat with her frostblade. She was going for the instant kill. Havera easily dodged the clumsy attack, swatting Fenix in the wrist. Fenix snarled and slashed wildly in Havera's direction. Another easy dodge for the Cauduun. Fenix attempted several more reckless slashes at Havera. The Cauduun kept calmly dodging while Fenix shrieked with each failed attack.

It was apparent they were relatively matched in terms of speed and agility. However, Havera's formal training in combat arts gave her the obvious edge. Fenix was a brawler. Havera was a dancer. Fed up with her constant misses, Fenix launched herself entirely at Havera. This did take the Cauduun by surprise. She couldn't quite dodge the full weight of Fenix's body. The two tumbled over each other, hitting the nearby wall with a monumental slam. Fenix seized Havera by the face and attempted to bite her. Havera wrapped her tail around Fenix's waist and hurled her into the opposite wall. Fenix managed to spring off the wall and land firmly on her feet. She hissed and attempted one more full-body lunge.

A sonic boom erupted in the tight quarters, nearly shattering everyone's ear drums. The force of a concussion blast hit Fenix square in the chest, catapulting her into the four-poster bed, completely destroying it. Marduk stepped across the threshold with the Drillhead in hand.

"A wild one, I see. You alright, tailed guppy?" Marduk asked.

"I had her where I wanted her!" yelled Havera.

"And I finished her off. Great teamwork," retorted Marduk.

"You've finished nothing, you sexy fish." Fenix rose from the ashes of her destroyed bed. She didn't appear fazed at all.

Marduk revved up the blades of the Drillhead. They emitted a shrill grinding noise that made Adam's teeth clench even through his haze.

"What are you?" Marduk bellowed over the noise of Drillhead.

"The future." Fenix snarled at Marduk. The Moan charged at Fenix, attempting to skewer her with his weapon. She leapt over him with a graceful flip. Marduk attempted to pivot one-eighty to catch her. She was too quick. She darted out of the room, knocking over Augustus and Jak, who had attempted to block her exit. The pair fired off shots in her direction. Adam couldn't tell if they hit anything. His ears were failing him. Everything sounded elongated and slow. He couldn't move.

"Adam!" Havera cried out. Her violet glow was gone. She carried him out of the room and into the office. "Turn the lights up!"

Zax found the dimmer and turned it up. The room was fully lit. Adam winced at the sudden brightness. The full extent of Adam's misery was apparent.

"Kewea's curse! What happened to him?" Augustus asked, noticing the Human's blackened veins and red eyes.

"Fenix did something to him. Whatever she did gave him temporary increased strength and speed. My bracers have a similar effect on me. Nothing so horrible like this. I've never seen anything of this nature," Havera said.

"Whatever it is, it's killing him. Doesn't seem to be a problem for Fenix though. Unsettling," Augustus said.

Jak bent down to scan Adam's body for vitals. "Strange. The wound here on his neck. It looks like some sort of blood infection. His body is simultaneously getting stronger and weaker at the same time. It's spreading rapidly throughout his bloodstream. I fear what'll happen if it reaches brain or fully envelops his heart."

"Can you fix him, Jak?" asked Zax.

Jak shook his head. "I can perform field medic duties and assist with simple diagnoses. I'm neither a doctor nor a healer. We need to get him to Umbrasia. She might be able to help."

"We cannot trust that witch. Who knows what she'd do to him?" Marduk said. He had reholstered the Drillhead to his back.

"Whatever he's got is killing him now! Don't let your hatred of the Rorae blind you, Marduk. We must find her," said Sam. She had stumbled out of the hidden room, once again wearing her infiltration gear.

"We couldn't find her. No one has. It's as if she disappeared into thin air," said Augustus.

"Let's head back to the ship. She might meet us there. We need to get Adam out of here," said Havera.

"How would she know where to meet us? Besides, we still need to retrieve the star chart," said Marduk.

"Oh! I've got it here," said Zax. Everyone shot Zax an astonished expression. "I found it during all that commotion." He unfurled it. The yellowed paper had all the markings of an old handwritten navigational chart of the Omega spiral. Marked on the outside of the scroll was the phrase 'Chant List.'

"That's it," said Augustus. "Let's get y'all out of here."

Klaxons blared throughout the room. The sudden alarm sent everyone into a tense stance. "Fenix must've alerted the guards. We must move immediately! Sam and I've got Adam," bellowed Havera. Sam and Havera gently lifted a moaning Adam off the ground. He was barely conscious.

Augustus was listening to something in his HUD. He put a hand out to halt Havera. "Whatever it is can wait, Augy!"

"You must be kidding me. Kewea take me," Augustus swore.

"What is it?" Sam asked.

"That's not an internal security alert. It's an external proximity warning. Incoming hostile ships are attacking the Cauldron. Were y'all expecting company from the Bokori? It seems three Hisbaween saucers are preparing to board the station."

34

Light and Dark

The blaring klaxons were all that kept Adam cognizant. All his eyes could see was intermittent darkness and blurriness. His head ached and his pulse slowed. He was not walking under his own power. Havera and Sam were dragging his limp body through the narrow corridors of the Cauldron. The only sign of life from Adam was the occasional wheezing or coughing fit accompanied by the ever-pooling blood in his mouth.

"He's not going to last much longer!" Sam cried.

"Yes, he will. The Cicera has enough medical supplies that'll stabilize him until we can find a healer. Umbrasia, where are you?" Havera pondered. She had sent the rendezvous coordinates to Dee.

"Kewea take those grayskins!" Augustus swore. "They've knocked out the Cauldron's communications. Last report I heard several boarding pods had attached themselves to the side of the asteroid. They're infiltrating from all sides."

"How many?" Marduk asked.

"At least six or seven. If memory serves, those pods hold up to a dozen fighters."

"Fifteen..." Adam wheezed out. Coherence came to Adam as intermittently as his eyesight.

"That's it, Adam. Stay with us. Hey!" Havera smacked him on the cheek. "Stay awake!"

"What's the quickest way?" Zax asked.

"The way Dark and I entered. Unfortunately, if the Bokori have knocked out communications, our map data won't be constantly refreshing. If a passage gets blocked off or destroyed, we'll have no way of knowing until we get there," Jak said.

"It's the risk we must take. Augy, you and Jak up front. Keep your shield out in case we run into trouble. Marduk, cover our rear. Don't let us get taken from behind. No jokes, Zax! Stay close to me. Combat mode engaged. Let's go," Havera ordered.

The group hurried through the corridors swiftly. So far, there were no signs of the Hisbaween other than the proximity alarms. A few Excom guards cut across their path. Augustus ordered them away before they could ask too many questions. They were too preoccupied with the ongoing assault than worrying about Fenix's personal bodyguard escorting a group of unknowns.

About five minutes into their trek, they heard their first signs of conflict. Shouts and exchange of laser blasts reached their ears near one of the intersections. The Excoms had set up some makeshift barricades while a squad of five or six Hisbas engaged them from around the corner. The narrow passageways aided the defenders. Flanking in these hallways was difficult. One Hisba chucked a grenade only for it to bounce off the wall and detonate harmlessly away from the Excoms. Augustus diverted the group to a side corridor that ran parallel to the engagement. Ducking between rooms, they managed to avoid those Hisbas to proceed onward.

Adam's body was wracked with pain and excitement. A mixture of feelings and sensations sending his brain into overdrive. He rested his head against Havera's shoulder. It was comfortably firm. Strong. Her face was close enough for him to see clearly. She was particularly ravishing to Adam at that moment.

Take her right here. She'll love the vigor. No! What? I can't. That's disgusting. What's wrong with me? She wants it. She craves it. SHUT UP!

His wheezing grew worse, compounded by the impulsive thoughts ravaging his mind. They were his own yet were alien to him all at once. He leaned away from her towards Sam. She was covered in blood. Gashes and bruises covered her face. Her flesh was melting, and her usual bright brown eyes were dead. Adam shut his eyes and gritted his teeth. He clenched his jaw to fight through the hallucinations and pain.

I'm going to die. No, you're evolving into something better. Something worse. Meaning what? No, I'm devolving into nothing. I'll be less than Human soon. No! You'll be greater than any living sentient.

His grunts and moans of pain turned to whines. Havera took pity on him, unaware of what was happening in his head. "Stay strong, Adam. We'll find you help soon. Just hang on a bit longer."

The sound of a laser blast stopped them in their tracks. They had stumbled into a group of Hisbaween rounding up captured Excoms, including some of the wealthy patrons. A few were shouting threats of retaliation. The black helmed Hisbas showed no signs of caring. One of the winged demons bashed a Naddine woman in the back of the head for protesting.

Augustus held them up just around the corner. "They're in our way. About one-hundred feet away. This is the only direct path to the ship."

"How many are there?" asked Havera.

"At least a dozen Hisbas maybe more. Quite a few unarmed civilians in the way. We should go around."

"Go around where?"

"We take an elevator down to the lab. We can cut across the labs and come up the other side."

Havera demurred. "The Hisbaween will have penetrated the labs. We'd need to engage them regardless. Adam won't last another fifteen minutes at this rate. No, we go through them."

"Are you comfortable with innocent civilian casualties?"

Havera bit her lip. "Yes."

Augustus drew his sword. "You shouldn't be."

"They're Excoms and Excom sympathizers. None of those people are innocent. I'm with the duchess," insisted Marduk.

No. No unnecessary bloodshed. Not for me. Yes. Kill them!

He tried to speak. His jaw was too sore to move. All that came out was a grunt.

"See. He wants us to keep moving," Marduk insisted.

"I can stun them with my ability. Think y'all can take them down in six seconds or less?" Jak asked.

"We'll see. Moan, stay behind me. We're going to walk right up to them," Augustus said.

Marduk grinned from ear-to-ear. "Right behind you, longtail. Let's do this."

"Zax, you take Adam. I'm going with them. You two stay here," Havera said to Sam and Zax. She handed Adam off to Zax. The Zokyon buckled a little bit under the Human's weight.

Havera and Marduk pressed themselves close to Augustus. Jak traced the air with his finger, creating a bright blue glyph. He gripped it in his hand, waiting for the signal.

Augustus held up his three fingers. "Wait 'til they spot us. On three. One...two...three!" Sword in hand, he rounded the corner with his shield out in front. Marduk and Havera followed closely. The trio moved methodically down the hall toward the Hisbas. Jak peeked around the corner, holding his glyph. Mordelar must've favored them, for they were able to close the gap to less than thirty feet before a Hisba spotted them.

"Halt or we'll shoot!" screamed the Hisba.

On cue, Jak unleashed his glyph at the Hisbas. It bypassed the trio completely, exploding within the group of Hisbas and their prisoners. The digital explosion, identical to the one used at the Astral Lens, deafened its targets and scrambled their HUDs. The Hisbas were completely vulnerable. Augustus roared, smacking the first Hisba with his shield and cutting down its two nearby compatriots in a flash. Marduk unleashed a concussion blast that hit two Hisbas that were standing too close together. The shockwave dented a bit of the wall behind them. Havera activated her bracers and smashed two Hisbas' helms together.

The effect of Jak's impulse scrambler wore off, with the few remaining Hisbas attempting to fight back. One shot at Augustus, but the shot ricocheted off the shield and struck an Excom guard in the leg. Another Excom guard used the distraction to attempt to seize a nearby Hisba's weapon. Failing, he received a blow to the back of his head from a searstaff. That Excom's sacrifice gave Marduk the distraction he needed. He fired off one more concussion shot, killing the offending Hisba, then revved up the Drillhead and ploughed right through the armor of the other. The Bokori Hisba screamed. Its gray blood and flesh splattered everywhere by the spinning blades of Drillhead. It crumpled to the floor dead. The last Hisba attempted to flee only for Havera to seize it by the ankles with her tail and repeatedly whacked it against the walls until it stopped flailing. She released the Hisba, and it hit the floor with a wet thud.

"Clear?" Augustus called out. They all glanced around for a few seconds, expecting retaliation.

"Clear."

"Clear. Jak, bring the others," Havera called out.

"Anyone hurt?" Augustus asked the Excoms.

"I think poor Tak-Def's brains is caved in, sir. Stupid blighter. Could've waited a few more seconds before trying to be the hero. Craz's suit has a puncture in his leg, but I think he'll be alright. Nothing some sanagel and a repair kit couldn't fix. Can't say the same for poor Locke though. Bastards executed him," a Rinvari Excom explained.

"Cradite help us," Havera exclaimed. About twenty feet away from the rest was Locke, laying in a pool of his own gray blood. She bent over the body of the bearded Bokori, a single smoking gunshot wound between his eyes.

"Why'd they shoot him?" Augustus asked.

"Dunno, boss. They ambushed us before we had a chance to fire our weapons. Rounded us all up. They were about to lead us to their ships when they spotted poor ole Locke. Dragged 'im off a bit. Started accusing 'im of being a traitor and a heretic. Asked 'im if he'd repent for his sins or some such. He told 'em to kiss his bearded ass, and that he'd see 'em burning in Kewea together. Then, they shot 'im. Just like that. Bang! Good on 'im I say. Swift justice for 'im, too," the Rinvari said.

"Can you fight?" Augustus asked.

"You better believe it, boss. Ready to space some grayskin bastards," replied the Rinvari. The other Excoms nodded and murmured in agreement.

"Good. Grab their weapons and head for the escape shuttles. We're evacuating the Cauldron. Head to your predetermined alternate sites once you're clear. Take Locke's body. I don't want those grayskins to have him," Augustus ordered.

"Fenix give the evacuation order?" asked the Rinvari.

"I'm giving the order. Understood?" Augustus growled.

The Rinvari cowered a bit. "Uhh, right, boss. You got it. I guess we'll just leave Tak-Def's body. Let's go, ladies and lads! We're getting off this rock." The Rinvari scooped up Locke's body. Havera walked over and closed the Bokori's eyes. The Rinvari and the other Excoms led the patrons out of there. A female Hasuram patron was complaining about not getting the deposit back on her dress.

"Those Hisbaween are nuts," Augustus said, summing up how everyone felt.

"You've only experienced a taste of their rabid zealotry," Sam said. She and Zax were dragging a deteriorating Adam. "These people worship their ideology more fervently than you Cauduun worship your goddesses."

"Equality through sacrifice," Adam muttered weakly. He spat out more blood. It was nearly completely black.

Augustus shuddered. "Backward barbarians. To think they were once our stellarpolitical rivals. 'Great Gray Hordes of the East' no more."

"A laser blast is a laser blast. Come on. We've got to go," Havera said. She stroked Adam on the forehead. "He's ice cold and sweating." The sanagel she applied to his neck wound was having limited effect. She resumed carrying Adam from Zax.

"Feeeenix....Feeeeenix," Adam said through hoarse breath.

"Don't worry about Fenix, Adam. We must get you out of here," Havera insisted.

"No...no...Debbie," he coughed with each word.

"Oh! I forgot!" Sam exclaimed. She reached into her pocket and produced the platinum grip of the Debbie. "I swiped this back from that crazed woman while she was...distracted. Here." Sam held out the Debbie. Adam snatched it and instantly crystallized it.

"What are you doing?" Augustus asked with curious concern.

Adam slammed his hand onto the icy Rimestone. He let out a scream as his hand touched the freezing weapon. It wasn't the cold that pained him. An overwhelming force pulled and pushed every molecule in his body. His vision was rushing at a million miles an hour. The darkness that had plagued him was retreating with frenetic urgency as the energy from the Debbie shot its wondrous path through his veins.

"Adam!" Havera shrieked.

He could barely perceive her voice. The anger, the rage he had experienced was evaporating. The voices and impulses gone. Replaced with his typical anxious lull and omnipresent soreness. His unnatural strength, along with the coughing of blood, had subsided. He could walk under his own power again.

"Holy Cradite, Adam! You don't appear to be at death's door anymore. The Rimestone weapon restored you?" Havera asked shocked.

Adam coughed the last bit of blood and phlegm out of his lungs and wiped his mouth. He was queasy. He sensed that whatever Fenix had done to him remained in his system, merely held at bay.

"I had a hunch. I've witnessed the Debbie do something similar in the past. We can talk about it later. I don't believe it's a permanent solution. We must find Umbrasia," Adam said, shrugging off Havera and Sam. His voice was a bit ragged.

"We're seriously not going to talk about what happened?" Zax said what many were thinking.

"Later!" Adam insisted, steeling his resolve. "Umbrasia's probably waiting for us at the ship."

"Okay, Adam, okay. We'll go. I imagine we'll all have many more questions before this trip is done," Havera said.

"Flowing Courage," a commanding voice came through the station's intercom. The group turned their attention towards the new voice. "Flowing Courage, I'm aware you are listening." The echoed inflection in the voice Adam had heard once before.

"Who's Flowing Courage?" Augustus asked.

"I am," Adam said with a guttural snarl. "It's Unbroken Tide. The Deputy High Hisba. It's here for me."

"You've eluded Bokori justice for far too long, Flowing Courage. No diplomatic immunity shall spare you. We've captured the rogue duchess' ship. You and your compatriots are surrounded with no viable means of escape. Surrender yourselves to me in the docking bay, and perhaps your friends' lives shall be spared. You will receive no second warning."

***

Unbroken Tide was not bluffing. Their communications network was down, so they couldn't send a message to Dee to confirm the status of the Cicera.

"The transmission must've died before Dee could receive the relocation instructions," Havera had surmised.

Arriving at the docking bay, the Hisbaween had the place on lockdown. The patrons who hadn't escaped were gathered together with the Excom guards who weren't killed in the incursion. All told, about twenty-five to thirty Hisbas were congregating in the main docking area, with several more groups split off, busying themselves with various tasks. A few were marching captured Excoms into the nearby black Bokori saucer parked in one of the bays, Adam could identify through the window. The Cicera herself had been moved to another docking bay alongside a few other detained patrons and Excom ships that several more Hisbas were undoubtedly searching.

Adam and company were hiding up in some scaffolding that led to a walkway that circumnavigated the docking wing. They managed to arrive undetected within minutes of Unbroken Tide's broadcast.

"We could sneak around them. Get aboard the Cicera and take off before they're none the wiser," suggested Sam.

"There's too many of them. Besides, I don't want to abandon these people to the Bokori," Havera said.

"They're Excoms and Excom-sympathizers. They deserve their fate. Finding myself on the same side as the Excoms already twists my fins. However, I agree with the duchess. We can't fight them all," Marduk said.

"Fight or flight, the bay is sealed. You'd need to override the lock-down from docking bay control in order to take off." Augustus pointed up across the walkway to a room with glass windows overlooking the wing. A few more Hisbas were visibly guarding the control room.

Adam spotted Unbroken Tide standing out in the open, unhelmed, waiting for him. The scars on Adam's back itched. A thought popped into his head.

"I've a crazy idea. What if I just kill it right here, right now? One laser blast to its overgrown cranium. Pop. Bang. Sizzle," Adam said, miming a rifle shot to the Hisba's head. His rage was returning.

"Okay, maestro, what's your plan for all the other Hisbaween?" Jak asked, not attempting to hide his doubts.

"He called you maestro. That's when you know your idea is stupid," Zax said, nodding his agreement with Jak.

Adam sighed. "Alright. I've a crazier idea. What if I surrender to its custody?"

"Absolutely not!" Sam howled. Havera had to shush her. Luckily, the Hisbas had not heard her.

"I'm the one they want. If their attention is focused on me, y'all might be able to slip by and escape," Adam said weakly. The effect of the Debbie had worn off. He grasped it again right before they arrived, but it wasn't nearly as effective the second go-around. Whatever disease was ravaging his body was growing too fast to overcome. Adam still didn't understand the nature of Fenix's condition nor how or why the Debbie could temporarily counteract the symptoms.

"Leave you to the mercy of those demons? Out of the question," Sam insisted.

"What's your next plan, skinny guppy? Going to challenge it to a one-on-one duel?"

"Don't tempt me. I can pretend to surrender while the rest of y'all get behind them. Ambush them, and we can all escape in the confusion," Adam said through gritted teeth. He was becoming impatient.

"Even I think that is a stupid plan," Zax said.

"We still need to open the docking bay doors," Havera reminded them.

"I'll do it," Augustus said. "I can open those doors for you. A few black-clad zealots cannot stop a Paladin of Paleria. Give y'all an opportunity to escape."

"No, Augy. You should come with us. We'll need your help in the Omega spiral," Havera pleaded.

Augustus shook his head and grasped Havera on the shoulder. "You don't require my help, Havi. Never have. Either way, there's work to be finished here. I've a duty to the Vulpes. I must locate Fenix and determine the nature of her...affliction. Figure out what kind of threat she represents and neutralize her. There are many unanswered questions whose answers I won't find in Union space. When you find Ignatia, give her the regards of a true centurion knight who has not forgotten his oaths and vows."

Havera and Augustus wrapped tails. "I shall. Let's not allow another two years to pass before we meet again, Augy."

"It won't. I promise," Augustus said. He opened his mouth to speak again, but whatever was on his mind he decided not to voice it. He gave a nod to the others. "Good luck to y'all. Especially to you, Humans. I eagerly await the report that those grayskin bastards finally found equality in death."

"May Dasenor welcome your sword with open arms, Centknight," Adam said with a weak heart salute.

Augustus grinned wily and returned the gesture. "Appreciate the sentiment. I've no plans to die today." The Cauduun scurried away down the walkway unseen by the Hisbas towards the control room.

"We still need a better plan of engagement," Marduk insisted once Augustus was out of range.

"If we could free the Excom guards, we might be able to level the scales," Havera said.

Adam's vision was becoming cloudy, and his impatience morphed into unbearable intolerance. Rationally, he realized this was whatever infection was coursing through his veins, but the impulse was far too strong to resist.

"Kewea take y'all. I'm doing this!" Adam gritted. Havera and Sam tried to grab him, but along with the rage his demonic speed returned. He leapt from the upper walkway at a great distance towards Unbroken Tide.

"HISBAS!" Adam shouted with unnatural rancor.

The momentum of his jump carried him farther than should've been physically possible. He landed mere feet from Unbroken Tide, using his boots' boosters to slow his descent. Even with the boosters, the amount of force he landed with partially dented the ground beneath his feet. Adam's knees buckled a bit as a shockwave of pain ascended up his spine. Unbroken Tide was unmoved.

"Dramatic," said Unbroken Tide dismissively. The inflection in its voice sounded as if two people were speaking at once. Several Hisbas with rifles or searstaffs drawn had surrounded the pair instantly. Unbroken Tide waved them off.

"Only through agony can you truly understand your crimes and become a moral, equal citizen once again."

The High Hisba had said those words to him. Except, he could only hear them in Unbroken Tide's voice.

"I'm pleased you've some modicum of sense. Have you come to surrender yourself peacefully and end this fruitless, bigoted quest of yours?" Unbroken Tide said with a hint of superiority in its tone.

"No."

"Bargain for your compatriots' freedom?"

"No."

"Then, I'm at a loss. Why show yourself like this?"

"I've come to kill you."

Adam drew the Debbie from his pocket and crystallized it. The jagged Rimestone sparkled to life with an energetic buzz. Without hesitation, he pointed the gun at Unbroken Tide.

The other Hisbas stepped closer, but Unbroken Tide dismissed them again.

"Bold. Bold. Rehabilitation was a complete waste on you. I told the High Hisba as much. No amount of preaching nor reformation will ever undo your nature. He didn't believe me. I don't understand what the High Hisba sees in you. Must be a lingering sympathy between two fellow Humans. Understandable. We all have those primitive communal bonds. It's engrained deep within us all. We in the Committee for the Advancement of Love and Virtue work to rid ourselves of that problematic, backward mentality and embrace a higher form of community. Nobody is perfect. Not even the High Hisba is without sin."

Unbroken Tide opened its arms in an expectant embrace. It was unarmed and vulnerable.

"The High Hisba has given me strict instructions to take you in alive. I believe for the good of all Bokori and Humans, you are better off dead. Kill me and the rest shall strike you down. If I must pay the price of my life to achieve this, so be it. Equality through sacrifice."

Adam seethed. The pain and itching from the scars on his back intensified to a boiling point. The peripherals in his eyesight darkened. Focusing and tunneling his vision upon the person responsible for much of his pain. Unbroken Tide was no longer a person. Its black uniform morphed into pointed, jagged wings. Its vertical, white eyes hollowed and retreated into its sockets. Unbroken Tide was transforming before Adam's tainted eyes into the wicked, winged demon it was underneath. Unnatural, evil.

All caution was lost, all reason decimated. His blood vessels blackened with a corrupting rage. His muscles tensed and flexed. Only one thought permeated his mind in a voice that was both his own and otherworldly.

Kill it!

"Adam, no!"

Sam dropped down in front of him, using the grappling hook on her crossbow and her boots to soften the landing. She pressed her hands against Adam and stood dauntlessly between him and Unbroken Tide.

"Ah, wonderful. Absorbing Song, I was hoping you'd show. I've secondary orders to take you in as well. Unfortunately, the High Hisba wasn't as specific about the condition in which I return you, murderer."

"You shouldn't be here!" Adam growled.

"I let you fall into the mouths of predators once. I won't do so again. You're unwell," Sam pleaded.

"His mind was always sick, heretic," Unbroken Tide sneered.

"You are not a part of this conversation, Hisba. Go back to sleep!" Sam yelled back at it.

Unbroken Tide was taken aback briefly but recovered and stood its ground. "I grow weary of your flailing resistance. You're both under arrest for blasphemy, heresy, toxicity, treason, and murder."

Adam snarled. The world pulsated around him. All cares or concerns were pushed aside. He only wanted to wrap his hands around that monster's tiny throat and squeeze until its oversized cranium burst. The Rimestone in Adam's weapon began to change. The blight in his veins slithered out of his fingers and into the weapon, blackening it in his tight drip. He need only squeeze, and his tormentor would disintegrate down to its last degraded molecule. Only someone was blocking his way.

"Get out of the way, interloper! That grayskin demon must die!"

Sam ignored them both. She placed her hands on Adam's cheeks. They were warm and comforting.

"Adam, remember the promise you told me you gave to Aaron. Never forget who you are and what you represent. This isn't you, Adam. This is a sickness that is overtaking you. You're not perfect, but you are better than this raving lunatic. Don't let it or Fenix destroy you and the memory of the man we both loved," Sam said. She kissed him softly on his forehead.

Adam shook his head. His thoughts were muddled, confused. The hallucinations evaporated. His anger melted. Replaced with the worried visage of Sam in front of him. Everything else became irrelevant. All that mattered to him was his adopted sister.

"Sam..." Adam throated hoarsely.

"That's right, Adam. It's Samus." She pushed the Debbie down. "I'd never let my brother fall. Not without a fight."

The corruption slowly receded from the Debbie back into his body. His knees buckling, he fell into Sam's arms.

"I...I shouldn't have put you in harm's way. I promised John..." Adam coughed. "I promised...I prom..." He kept coughing. Trickles of blackened blood dripped out of the corners of his mouth. He coughed again, and more blood spilled forth from his mouth. He was now puking black blood and collapsed to the ground.

I told you to kill! Kill! KILL!

"Adam! It's getting worse. We must get him to a healer," Sam said, frantically looking about, hoping for some sign of mercy from the Hisbas.

She received none. "The only place the two of you are going is a rehab cell. If nothing else, you won't be able to spew your vile, toxic ideas to others. Look at him. He's so far gone even his own body rejects his heresy," Unbroken Tide declared.

Adam was laid out nearly spread eagle. Staring up at the ceiling of the docking bay, his hearing slowly faded until he could only hear a faint buzzing tickling his inner ears.

With this gift, they cannot harm you. Embrace your power. Get up and kill it! — No. No. It may deserve death. It may deserve to experience the pain its inflicted upon me, upon others. Not this way. I shall not let you consume me. I'd rather die than let something like you take over. I am in control, not you! — Then, you shall perish. You are too weak to embrace true power.

The world began spinning. Some sort of scuffle was breaking out.

He only caught the barest glimpses of movement. Adam's sight grew dimmer and dimmer. The strength in his muscles faded. Blood was pooling in his mouth. He couldn't summon the will to cough it out.

He had imagined his own death before. He always assumed he'd die stupidly. Maybe one of his boots' rockets wouldn't fire properly and he'd splat onto the ground. A passing enemy patrol might've ambushed him while he was pissing, or somehow he'd crash his slow-moving hoverbike and explode in a blaze of ingloriousness. Once he imagined he'd die peacefully in the arms of the woman he loved. That was but a passing dream. He never allowed himself such delusions again. Not after Falling Star. Not even with...

Strawberries.

The hidden halls of Dasenor beckoned him. Tucked deep in the underworld of Kewea, he might have the chance to find her again. Join her, his father, Duke Drake, Locke, and all the others who have suffered and died for the Bokori's utopic vision. They'd all dine and train together, eagerly awaiting the call to rescue Dasenor from the clutches of the evil, youngest daughter of Cradite and Duseres.

As the darkness was about to overtake him, his head fell to the side, with blood spilling out his mouth. In the singularity point of his fading sight, a tiny glimmer of light flashed. It refused to budge to the oily shadows. The glimmer grew stronger, pushing back against the darkness, coming closer and closer. The glimmer turned into the shape of a person. A woman with mossy green skin and a leaf for a mouth.

Umbrasia...

He must've been hallucinating. She had the face of Umbrasia and smelled of cinnamon and cocoa. Yet, her appearance had a certain unrecognizable majesty. Holding a golden whip of sourceless energy in one hand, she had fiery, expansive wings twice the length of her body, radiating divine, golden light. The petals on her head and the tripartite leaf on her face weren't their typical sable color but a pearly white so intense it pained Adam's weakened eyes.

"Am I dead?" he tried say only to spat out more blood.

"Shh. Calm."

The golden whip in her hand retreated and converted into a radiant bloom surrounding her leafy hand. She touched him with that hand. A mixture of ice and warmth clashed within his body. The scars on his back exploded with pain. He wanted to scream, but emanated no words, only gurgles.

Umbrasia spoke again; however, her voice carried the weight of someone else. A crackling of crystal. Beautiful. Serene.

Defender of life. Behold my call. I shall not allow her to drag you into the Ulkfuae. You shall earn a place beside me in the Daergfae. It is your destiny. Not this day. Guardian of life. Protector of the one who shall wield the Vitriba. You must rest, for there are greater dangers lurking in the dark.

Golden concentric rings sparkled around Umbrasia's ruby eyes. Her face drew closer and closer until the radiant light surrounding her body overwhelmed Adam's sight. Just as the light overtook him, he beheld the face of another. One with an icy snout shrouded in a pale mist.

35

The Hasurams and the Bubils

The cold air rushed by his falling body, whipping his hair into his face. He had closed his eyes and laid spread eagle to fully enjoy the moment. Clear skies allowed the yellow sun to breath its warmth gently upon his face. He smiled. He was toasty and relaxed. It did not trouble him he had been falling for hours. Time stood still. Sweet scents filled his nostrils, watering his mouth.

Strawberries.

The cool wind of the atmosphere on his back trickled to every nerve in his body. The heat of the sun on his face and chest radiated to each muscle, providing him with an ideal balance of hot and cold. It was perfection. Only then did he realize he was naked...and he wasn't alone.

Falling with him, straddling him, was Umbrasia. She was fully nude. The slithering vines protecting her modesty had retreated to reveal the utter beauty of her natural body. Gone were the fiery, angelic wings and glowing hands. The petals on her head, black once more, were in bloom, absorbing the sun's rays. The star's energy traveled through her body into his. An amazing tingling sensation where their bodies connected. Pleasure beyond any he had experienced in his mortal body enraptured him from head-to-toe.

Her eyes were closed. Her leafy hands upon his chest. The heat between his legs simmered hotter and hotter. He wanted to touch her. To bury his face in her neck. To grasp her firm, shapely breasts in his calloused hands. He tried lifting his hands. Soreness overcame him. He couldn't lift a muscle.

Their bodies flipped. Adam was on top of her. Only it was no longer Umbrasia. It was Fenix. Now, they were making love. Behind her was a planet covered in raging, blackened storm clouds. The pair were plummeting towards the surface. With a sly, fanged smile, she buried her face into his neck. He roared, expecting pain. Not pain. Pleasure. A cold bliss radiated from her bite. The heat between his legs turned frigid. Thrilling. He continued to find satisfaction in her body.

She leaned to whisper in his ear. "Come with me."

She wrapped her arms and legs around him and dragged him into the clouds below. He kissed her icy lips, fully embracing the moment. She squeezed his hips with her legs, pulling their bodies tighter together. Her sweat frozen icicles upon his skin.

He wanted to stop, but he couldn't help himself. The pain. The pleasure. He wanted it all. Passing through the storm clouds, thunder roared all around them. Fenix moaned and cackled. She was determined to drag him down with her.

Something snapped in his mind. His senses came back to him. He pushed Fenix away. She tried to seize him. A bolt of lightning struck them both. Fenix disintegrated in a ball of fire. The flash was blinding but not painful. The blinding light dissipated from his vision.

His body found solid ground. He recognized the spot. An endless field of waist-high ruby-colored grass. He rolled around in the grass. The tickling from the blades of tall grass was soothing on his naked body. His aching muscles massaged. His freezing body warmed once more. His racing mind settled. He turned over to find another person laying by his side, her back to him. He recognized her before she rolled over to face him. Her beaming face was happy to see him. Her sweet smile brought him joy and peace of mind. She leaned in to kiss him. All melted away with her. At long last, he realized what he wanted.

Strawberries.

The vision dissolved. Darkness returned. Not terrifying but rather the darkness behind one's eyelids in the morning air. He took a deep breath. He smelt a velvety aroma of cinnamon and cocoa mixed with a delicate, salty, oceanic breeze.

Adam's eyes fluttered open. Large, triangular ruby eyes with black sclera on a leaf-covered mossy face was mere inches from his nose.

"Umbrasia!"

Startled, he attempted to rise. His muscles ached. His naked body was covered only by a small thermal blanket. At that moment, he realized his manhood was stiff as it oft was in the morning. Embarrassed, he turned away from Umbrasia's gaze.

The Rorae merely giggled. **"Your kind is amusing. So ashamed of your body's natural flow. Glad to see you are awake. How do you feel?"**

Adam sat up and stretched his upper body. "Sore. Stiff. If you couldn't tell. How long have I been asleep?"

"Not too long. Only a few hours. You're on the Cicera. We're nearing Melusine, preparing to turn south towards Union space."

He groaned. He eyed Umbrasia up-and-down. She was even lovelier in the flesh. He folded over his blanket to ensure his waist was covered until his excitement died down.

He rubbed the wound on his neck. The skin had healed, yet he could feel a lasting scar beneath the surface. "What was wrong with me?"

"You were infected with ancient form of corruption, long dormant but omnipresent. Spite. An essence that flows from the depths of the Ulkfuae, the fountain of villainy. A source of horrifying power that perverts life to its core. Spite is believed to be the reason why the Xizor were so dangerous. Somehow, the Xizor mastered the art of manipulating Spite, powering them to reanimate their slain foes and absorb their essence. Until they were stopped by you Humans.

The Spite corrupted your soul, threatening to forever alter your entire life's essence. I was able to purge the Spite from your body to the best of my abilities. You should feel completely fine within a few hours. However, I fear such a corruption may have lasting side-effects."

"Side-effects?"

"There are contagions in this galaxy that attack the mind and the body. Those diseases are treatable and often curable. Sometimes, they leave lasting scars or abnormalities where they assaulted the physical form. Spite is different. It damages the soul, creating an imbalance between the mind, body, and soul. That's why you were stronger, faster, even your wounds healed quicker. However, your mind and soul were paying the price for that transformation. Life requires balance between these three forces to function properly. When one force of life becomes stronger or weaker, like a person's senses, the other two must compensate. Your body grew stronger, but your soul deteriorated."

Adam rubbed his temple. He was getting a headache, trying to wrap his mind around everything. "My Debbie. My Rimestone weapon. I touched it with my bare skin, and I could sense it pushing back on the Spite, as you call it."

Umbrasia nodded. **"That's because Rimestone contains the physical manifestation of Absolve, the polar opposite of Spite. Pouring from the Daergfae, the fountain of heroism, Absolve is the embodiment of pure soul."**

"Pure soul? I thought Rimestone was dark energy in a solid state."

Umbrasia chuckled. **"And what is dark energy if not the soul of the galaxy? It is all around us. Omnipresent. Unseen, unheard, unappreciated. Yet, the most potent force in the galaxy by far. This force has gone by many names across the stars amongst many races: Dark energy; Rimestone; Supernatural; Magic; Divinity.**

"I imagine Havera has one or two thoughts on that."

"I respect the Cauduun duchess' knowledge and experience. However, she is a woman of science; therefore, her understanding is limited, attempting to only answer the question of 'how' and never 'why.'

In your case, the Rimestone acted as a conduit through which your own soul could fight the corruption. Not well enough, unfortunately. This Spite that Fenix infected you with had a potent wellspring. Tested the limits of my capabilities, even with the aid of your Rimestone weapon."

"Are you saying someone like Fenix isn't psychotic or crazy. She's ill?"

Is Mom infected?

Umbrasia shook her head. **“Spite doesn’t affect everyone equally, because not everyone’s mind, body, and soul are whole to begin with. If I had to guess, Fenix’s soul was already out of balance. That’s why she was able to embrace the corruption while your body rejected it. Her sadism, viciousness, even her…appetites were merely heightened by the Spite. Not created by it. Understand, Adam, for all of your shortcomings and past experiences, your mind, body, and soul are in relative harmony. The Absolve contained within the Rimestone sought to restore that harmony. I fear that the reemergence of Spite as an active force in the galaxy means that the Xizor will return. Tell me, when you were infected, did you ever feel strong?”**

Adam nodded. “When I was angry. Angry at Havera. At Fenix. But, also when I was afraid. Afraid for myself, my people. Afraid for Sam.”

“Mmm, I expected that. Mind, body, and soul are all distinct from each other, yet they are all intertwined. One affects the other two. The adrenaline and heighted senses you normally experience with those emotions were amplified by the Spite. Your natural ethics and morals generated by your intertwined mind and soul started to fight the corruption. Once that happened, the Spite turned hostile and attempted to destroy its host. You will be alright. I removed the bulk of the corruption, and I believe you are now inoculated from further infection of that sort. I’m afraid that there will always be some lingering affliction latched onto your soul forever.”

“Meaning I could transform again?”

Umbrasia shook her head. **“I don’t believe so. You grasp better than most the lingering effects of trauma. This will be no different. Only you will feel it not in your body but in your soul. As the Spite was ravaging you and before you awoke just now, what did you see?”**

Adam blushed and shifted uncomfortably. “Umm, I’d rather not say.”

Umbrasia tilted her head at him and crossed her arms. She rose a bit higher and floated cross-legged in front of him. **“I believe the phrase ‘doctor-patient confidentiality’ is apt here. What we discuss will always**

stay between us. The healing process demands open communication. To fully heal, you must be open and honest with your healer."

Adam did not feel like arguing. He bit his lip. "Alright."

He regaled Umbrasia with all the details of his recent dream. She did not visually react. Adam stuttered a bit as he described the part involving Umbrasia herself. He avoided her gaze and crossed his legs in those moments. She remained stoic with her hands clasped under her chin. Once he finished, Umbrasia tilted her head. She floated him a cup of water.

"Fascinating."

"Fascinating. What do you mean? What's fascinating?" he mumbled quickly.

"Dreams are where the mind and soul communicate, allowing the dreamer to reconcile internal conflicts and deal with stress. You have much turmoil, Adam Mortis. I believe you are headed into the storm with no idea what is on the other side. Sorry I cannot provide a more concrete theory. I have many ideas on what all that could mean each more outlandish than the next. In my experience, there are no simple explanations. I must trust in the Mother."

Adam took a sip of water. "So, I should read anything into the, uhh, you know..." he made a sexual gesture with his hands.

Umbrasia shook her head. **"Every individual mind heals differently. I believe what you experienced was a physical manifestation of the opposing forces in your life pulling you in different directions. Much like Absolve and Spite on the soul. I wouldn't read too much into it. Either that or you're an excessively lusty man."**

Adam did a spit take. "Excuse me?"

Umbrasia shrugged. **"What is the Consul of Cloudboard? Nothing wrong with that. It's y'all's biological imperative. Everyone seems shocked when I say such seemingly basic principles."**

"I think the whole healing and telepathy schtick gives people an impression on how they expect you to talk. You know with flowery language and cryptic warnings, which, to be fair, you do do all the time," Adam suggested.

Umbrasia rolled her eyes. "**Pomposity for the sake of itself is the refuge of an uninteresting mind. Go say hi to the others. I'm going to go relax and meditate.**"

She started to float away. A curious thought germinated in his mind. He decided to voice it perhaps against his better judgment. "Umbrasia, do you ever give into your, uhh, biological imperative."

She stopped at the threshold of the medical bay. She spun in the air to face him. She bent her body over backwards, stretching her torso until she was folded in half. Adam dropped his cup in surprise, spilling the water onto the floor. She topped that by twisting her torso until her head was poking out from between her legs.

"**I do, and I don't need anyone else to do so. Bloom well, Adam.**"

She unfurled herself slowly until she was righted upward. Without another word, she floated away leaving Adam speechless.

Add that to the list of unexpected sights on this journey.

***

He found his clothes nearby in a pile. Donning his jumpsuit and duster jacket, he decided to leave his boots behind. The Cicera's carpet was wondrous on his feet. Laughing and yelling emanated from the circular conference room in the center of the ship. The clanking of glasses and tankards was unmistakable.

I'm missing quite the party.

Rounding the corner, he spotted Havera and Sam sitting and drinking together. Jak was sitting with J'y'll. A scornful expression plain even on his upside-down face. Zax was practically rolling on the floor with laughter. The reason why became quite clear.

"Quite the festivities going on he...holy Cradite what are you doing?!" Adam exclaimed covering his eyes.

"Hey! Look who's awake. Come here, you magnificent skinny guppy!" He was quickly lifted up high off the ground and enveloped in a bone-crushing hug from a naked Marduk. He reeked of booze and seawater with a hint of cinnamon in his salty sweat. The Moan had a tankard of some blue liquid in one hand. "You're not dead!"

Adam instinctively flailed his legs until his feet pressed down on something hard. He gasped and recoiled his legs when he realized what he was standing on.

"Neither are you; it seems."

The group guffawed. Sam slammed her drink down hard enough for it to splash on the table. She pressed her face into Havera's shoulder she laughed so hard. Havera returned a side hug, grinning from ear-to-ear. Jak buried his forehead into his hands. J'y'll beeped disapproval on their behalf. Marduk chuckled hardest of all, giving Adam one more squeeze and a peck on the cheek with his conical snout. He took a big swig of his drink and put Adam down.

Taking a step back from Marduk's fish stick, Adam circled the table, taking the other seat next to Havera. "You're in an uncharacteristically good mood, Marduk."

"Why shouldn't I be?" the Moan bellowed. "We found our map, crippled an Excom operation, and put a bunch of egalitarian militants in their place. I've had a wonderful morning. Plus, you're still amongst the living. I'd call that a success."

"Join in the fun, Adam. Here. It's only grape juice don't worry," Havera said, sliding him a tankard.

"Oh, I'm not complaining about any of that. Thank you, Havera, by the way," Adam said, accepting the drink. "It's just, umm, why exactly are you naked?"

Giggles erupted from the group. Marduk folded in arms in faux outrage. "Are you offended by my godlike physique?" He flexed his muscles. It's true. Marduk was an impressive specimen from his handsome, rugged face to his chiseled, massive, misty pecs. His icy scar gleamed under the Cicera's lights. The biggest eye-catcher was Marduk's manhood. It was...difficult to overlook. His enormous and ribbed manhood.

Adam leaned over to Havera. "He must be in a *really* good mood."

She whispered back. "I'm not complaining."

Adam rolled his eyes. Zak finally gave an explanation. "You see, Adam, you were unconscious. We had to get your clothes off so Umbrasia could examine and heal you. We all, umm, got a full look at the goods, so to speak." Zak grinned.

Adam felt the impulse to cover himself though he was already clothed.

"Anyway." He clicked his tongue twice. "Not bad at all. No Marduk of course, but, uhh, who is, am I right?" He and the others lightly chuckled. "Umbrasia told us you were on the verge of waking. We decided to bust out a few drinks. One conversation led to another. We had a disagreement over the mating rituals of Bubils. I think their queens rip the heads off of their warrior mates."

"They totally do," agreed Marduk.

"No, they don't!" Havera and Jak said together.

"Like that. We remembered seeing your meat stick and wondered what race had the most impressive joy wand. Marduk here decided to volunteer to put his special Metamorph powers to good use. You are doing the goddesses' work, my friend," said Zax. He whipped out his lute and strummed a few cheery chords.

"Woo hoo!" Sam exclaimed, raising her glass. Marduk bowed.

"Exactly how much has he had to drink?" Adam pondered. Havera tapped him on the shoulder and gestured behind her. Three metal caskets were piled in the corner. One was knocked over, apparently empty.

Adam snorted. "That where we get the expression 'drinks like a fish?'"

Havera shrugged. "Who is the Consul of Cloudboard? I prefer this Marduk to the angry, I-want-to-kill-everything Marduk."

Adam leaned into whisper. "Is everyone pissed at us for holding back information about the Excoms and the Hisbaween."

Havera whispered back. "Surprisingly, no. Umbrasia and I had a chat with everyone, and we think we've smoothed things over for now. The drinks were Zax's idea. Everyone's seems to have forgotten."

Marduk was taking requests for his next transformation.

"Show us a Bubil warrior!" Havera shouted after reassuring Adam.

Marduk's body shifted. Everything shrank. Tiny translucent wings formed on his back. His face contorted until he had those five oversized compound eyes compromised of a thousand lenses. He gained blue and white stripes wrapped horizontally around his body. A scrawny tail with a pointy stinger emerged from his rear. Another smaller but just as pointy stinger sprung from between his legs.

"Eww. That looks positively painful. I'd rip the head off any man who stuck that in me, too!" exclaimed Sam.

"Agreed," said Havera. "Oh! Show everyone the Naddine's member. Theirs are good. Unless you want to volunteer to show us yours, Jak."

"I'd rather cut it off than show it off," grumbled Jak.

"Aww, first time anyone's asked to see it, beast banger?" Marduk sniggered with a slight buzz in his voice.

"You'd be wrong there, Marduk. Jak here is quite the ladies' man. Has groupies everywhere we go. There was this one-horned Rinvari woman on Ravoron..."

"Zax, please. No," Jak cut him off.

Zax raised his hands to his mouth in a faux whisper. "She got a little too handsy for him. Wanted to see if J'y'll had any other uses." J'y'll beeped her dismay. "Anyway, I'm curious. Go for it!"

Marduk changed from a Bubil version of himself to a Naddine. Everyone tilted their heads in confusion, including Adam.

"Are those bristles on the head?" He shuddered.

"Why yes they are," Havera smirked.

"Isn't that painful?" Sam asked.

"Mmm, maybe at first insertion. Part of the whole overall Naddine bonding process. They accomplish a similar feat with their claws to control their beasts. It's a wonderful sensation, especially when they go in-and-out."

"Kewea's curse. My goodness, Havera, how many men have you had?" Adam asked.

Havera grinned. "Why only ask about the men?" she asked, taking a sip of her tankard. Sam oohed. Marduk and Zax laughed.

"Don't they teach you that sort of stuff in Cauduun space, Havera?" asked Zax.

Havera nodded. "Yup. The dens of Anamea teach the basics at a young age. We learn the proper anatomy and essential conceptions of our bodies and the sexes of all the major races. After sexual maturity, the older adult students have more hands-on demonstrations under the supervision of the Incubae and Succubae of the dens. I was taught at the Blessed Den of Anamea in Paleria. Best of the best."

"Wait a second. When you say, 'hands-on demonstrations,' do you mean..."

"Yup. We practice with partners of our choosing. Completely consensual. Anyone without a partner can practice with the den's Concubae," Havera explained.

Zax threw up all four hands in shock. "Wait, WHAT?! I thought that was only a rumor?"

"Nope," Havera confirmed.

"Kewea's curse! I'm going to refill my cup. I think I broke my straw," Zax said, exasperated.

Zax grabbed his tankard and wandered over to one of the metal caskets. Marduk transformed back into his normal Moan form. He even agreed to cover himself with his long-tailed coat of fused seaweed.

"Cauduun women can mate with anyone right? Race doesn't matter," said Marduk, sitting down at the table. He took a swig from his tankard.

"For sure. Any male of course. Our DNA is flexible and can adjust to accommodate the seed of any race. Only if we allow it of course," said Havera.

"If you allow it?" wondered Adam.

"Mhm. Our bodies have a unique controllable muscle that can block sperm from reaching our eggs. It allows us to cultivate our lovers, so we only need to worry about having children with someone we want. Quite advantageous, wouldn't y'all say?" Havera asked rhetorically.

Sam finished her drink. "I'll say. I wish we could do that. It's a challenge since we can have a child with anyone as well."

Zax sat down next to Marduk. "No way! I thought that was unique to Cauduun women."

Sam shook her head. "Nope. You know I'm right, Adam. There are a few people with alien fathers in Arabella."

Adam nodded. "Yeah, I believe Dante Marston's father was a Naddine. Must've been a vicious son-of-a-bitch. Dante has quite the temper. Oh, I think little Tidus Freeman had a Moan for a father. Runs around shirtless all the time cause of the humidity. You can see the gills in his torso. Hold on, hold on. Y'all keep distracting me. What happened after I passed out? I don't remember how we got away."

They all looked at each other. Havera spoke up. "We're not entirely certain other than you have Umbrasia to thank."

"After you started puking blood..." Sam's lips lingered on that word. "The Hisbas attempted to arrest us. While we struggled, a burst of light blinded us. By the time the spots from our eyes dissipated, that wretched slime was knocked out, and you had vanished. I panicked briefly until Umbrasia appeared out of nowhere and told me she had gotten you to safety. She managed to knock out every Hisba in the area, including the Deputy High Hisba. Didn't explain how, but I believed her. Didn't kill a single one of them. Never seen anything like it. Well, I didn't exactly *see* it. None of the other witnesses saw anything either."

"I have, but far more lethal and powerful," Marduk said his voice trailing off. He wasn't looking at anyone in particular anymore. "It was both terrifying and impressive. I'll give the witch credit. I'd rather fight a dozen daku than challenge a Rorae Magi. Still, they're nothing compared to the planet-killing abominations of those Kewea-accursed Celestials."

"I believe you, though Umbrasia is amazing in her own right. By the way, Marduk, I noticed when you transform you keep your chest gills. Can you not get rid of them during your transformation?"

Marduk burped. "Negative, skinny guppy. I've practiced and practiced. Metamorphing is difficult enough to get the essentials correct. You're altering not only your outer appearance but intricate systems such as the nervous, digestive, coronary, organ, et cetera right down to your DNA. I'm not a true Metamorph. Don't need to be. Never had an issue with it in the past. Only difficulty for me is changing my skin colors. That's always been a tough issue for me. Nearly blew my cover once during the Strife. The stupid Zokyo who detected my deception never lived long enough to tell anyone."

"I thought Moans were Zokyon subjugates during the war?" asked Zax.

"Officially, yes. The Moan phase of the war was brutal for us. No Boiling of Sin, of course. The Naddine and Zokyo treated our people no better than playing cards over the centuries. For nearly eleven years, we fought off Zokyon attempts to resubjugate us. My grandfather, the one who could transmutate, fought in that phase. The Naddine sent a nominal force to aid us, but that was merely window dressing. Every time we tried to claim independence from one, the other would swoop and scoop us up. If we had won in 1524, the Naddine would've picked us apart and taken us for themselves. I sympathize with your cause for that reason, my little and skinny guppy friends," Marduk said, raising his tankard. Adam and Sam raised theirs in response. Marduk burped again. "Anyway, that thing you Human ladies can do with babies is swish."

"Thanks. This is such an enlightening conversation. I didn't know most of what y'all were talking about," said Sam.

"To be honest, neither did I. Our people understandably don't go much into natural reproduction. Didn't help I was raised by Naddine," said Zax.

"Oh, I think I've heard about this. Y'all have some sort cloning?" asked Adam.

"Ehh, sort of. Not really. Actually, no, now that I think about it. Our females have the exact opposite issue y'all have. Our bodies are too frail. It's impossible for a woman to conceive in her own womb. Our experatchiks believe it's a long-term consequence of our ancestors' obsession with cybernetics and body augmentations. Goes along with our inability to breath oxygen, hence the mechsuits. Scientists take sperm and eggs from willing donors and incubate them in special machines. Any male and female that want to have a child must sign a reproduction and parenting contract beforehand that stipulate terms of the relationship with each other and the child. The Exchange complicated that. This is a long way of saying that, uhh, few Zokyo ever have sex," explained Zax.

Marduk slammed his tankard down. "Hold your seahorses. Are you telling me you can't have sex?"

"No, I said few ever have sex. It's possible. Requires some planning and finagling. Need to either have ports built into the mechsuit or find a hyperbaric chamber filled with methane to do the deed. Not exactly conducive to spontaneous passion. I've never done it," Zax confessed.

"Seriously?" Sam asked.

"Seriously."

"You're an interstellar bard who has never had sex?!" asked an incredulous Marduk.

"Leave him alone, Tiamat," Jak insisted. J'y'll bared her metal jaws and growled.

"No, no, no. It's quite alright, bro. I spin a fine web and string a good tune. It's all an act, my Moan friend. I have no regrets. I'm too busy preparing for the Ra-Mu later this year. Can't afford any of you lovely ladies distracting me, now can I?" he said, winking at Havera and Sam.

"Do y'all know if Rorae can, how do I phrase it, self-breed?" Adam asked, remembering Umbrasia's hint from earlier.

Everyone burst out laughing. "Kewea's curse, skinny guppy, how much have you had to drink? You need a longer nap, son."

Sam leaned over to whisper in Havera's ear. The Cauduun giggled, giving Adam a bit of side-eye. She whispered something back, and Sam grinned.

Havera pushed her chair back and stood up. Her tail slid across Sam's lap. "Friends, I do believe on that note I am going to rest up a bit. Dee will let us know when we're about enter Union space."

The others saluted her. Havera wandered around Sam, her hand lingering a bit on the back of the Human's chair. After she left, Sam immediately stood up. "Havera has the right idea. A nap does sound quite delightful. See y'all later." She waved good-bye and exited the same door as Havera.

Zax put both his left hands on Marduk's shoulder. The pair exchanged a good chuckle. Jak grinned. Even J'y'll's beeps sounded a bit amused.

Adam raised his eyebrow. "What are y'all laughing about?"

"Havera and Sam, of course!" Zax explained.

"What about them?" Adam asked.

Laughter erupted from Zax and Marduk. Zax was beside himself, barely able to breathe through his chortles. The Moan laughed so hard he fell out his chair. He hit the floor hard enough to rattle the table. Jak merely shook his head, and J'y'll beeps sounded suspiciously like a sigh.

"Bless your heart, skinny guppy. Oh, Cradite bless you so hard. That was amazing. Here I thought your blissful ignorance was a feint. Beautiful. Just beautiful," Marduk said, pulling himself off the floor.

Adam must've appeared dumbstruck for Zax stopped chuckling to explain. "You really don't know, do you? They're about to get it on."

"They're what?"

"Kewea's curse, Adam. You're intentionally playing dumb at this point. Havera and Sam are sleeping together," said Zax.

Adam snorted. "Yeah, good one." He expected the others to join in his amusement. He whirled around to look them all in the eye. Their stoic expressions hinted at no deception. It dawned on him. They were telling the truth. "That's impossible. They're simply good friends."

Marduk snorted. "Oh, I'm sure they are *good friends*. With that kind of friendship, I'll bet it is extraordinarily good. Haven't you wondered what they do during their *training sessions* or when they're *working out* together. Havera's teaching her more than leg sweeps and ground pounds. You've never noticed the not-so-subtle hints. They were practically fondling each other just now!"

Adam couldn't believe it. He hadn't noticed. "I assumed...how long have y'all known?"

"The first night we all met," Jak stated bluntly. J'y'll agreed.

"We all moved into Marduk's place, and I swear while you were rambling on about Patron-Saint, those two were undressing each other with their eyes," Zax said.

"And to think he was worried about me and the little guppy," Marduk chuckled.

"Master Adam is not a perceptive person." Dee wandered in, carrying a tray to clean up the remaining tankards.

Adam threw up his hands in exasperation. "Oh, come on! Dee, you knew, too?"

"Knowing something you don't isn't a point of pride. It's a prerequisite to fly on this ship at this point. I believe the bird down in the hold knew about them before you did," Dee mocked.

Marduk stood up to hug Dee. "You're brilliant, bot. You know that?"

"I do know that," said Dee. The bot held out an arm to stop the Moan from hugging him. Dee lowered his gaze to peer at Marduk's exposed manhood.

Marduk grinned. "See something you like, bot?"

Dee didn't miss a beat. "I've seen better. I only came in here to pick up after you slobs and to let y'all know we're about to exit Moan space. From this point forward, we'll be in Union territory."

Dee turned around and walked out. Zax sniggered at his comment. Marduk was incredulous. "What do you mean you've seen better?!"

Adam took a sip of grape juice. It went down the wrong pipe. He coughed for a couple seconds to clear his airway. "Sam is my sister for intents and purposes. I never thought Havera would..."

"He's in love with her," interjected Jak. J'y'll beeped her agreement with her creator.

"Absolutely."

"Definitely," agreed Marduk and Zax.

"No, I'm not!" Adam protested. Collectively, they shot him a skeptical expression. "She's an attractive woman. I don't deny that."

Zax and Marduk turned to each other. "He's in love with her."

"We only kissed!" Adam blurted out. Realizing what he had said, Adam covered his mouth in horror.

Kewea take my big mouth.

Zax whistled. "First, Umbrasia, then Havera. Kewea's curse, Adam! I'm impressed. I didn't believe you had it in you."

"He really doesn't," Marduk said head, gesturing to Adam's groin area.

"I didn't kiss Umbrasia!" Adam insisted.

"Your lips were on her face. I suppose you could argue it doesn't count with her. Seemed pretty romantic to me," said Zax.

"It wasn't!"

"Your lips were on Umbrasia's face?" Marduk seemed offended. "Let's not skip over that last important tidbit. You admit you kissed Havera?" Marduk asked.

Adam's faced was flushed. He was sweating through his jumpsuit. He unzipped his jumpsuit a bit to give his body some ventilation. "It was a little more than that," he admitted. The truth kept pouring out of his lips.

Shut...your...mouth!

"Define 'a little more' for us would you?" Zax said. They were all a bit too interested in the details. The effect of wine and booze on their judgments and impulses.

Adam wiped his brow. "We had gotten back from our meeting with Dusertheus. We were talking. We both felt overwhelmed. One thing led to another. Our clothes started coming off. We never did anything! Y'all walked in on us before anything could happen," Adam said, pointing to Zax and Jak.

"Are you saying if three of us hadn't walked in on that moment..." Zax pondered aloud.

Adam's mouth was dry. The grape juice did nothing to quench his thirst. He coughed to avoid talking while contemplating his answer. He merely shrugged. "Who is the Consul of Cloudboard?" was the only response he could muster.

Zax whistled. Marduk circled the table to pat Adam on the back. "I get it, skinny guppy. It hurts seeing someone you love with another man...woman...person. You get it!"

Adam was fed up with this conversation. He rose from his chair and pushed past Marduk to turn into the hallway.

I'm going to get to the bottom of this. No way I'm that blind. Sam and Havera? Impossible. Sure it is. You've missed much about both women.

As if Adam were cursed by his thoughts, he rounded the corner only to come to a dead stop. Havera and Sam were locked in a tight embrace outside Havera's room. It took his brain a couple seconds to register what his eyes were seeing. Sam had Havera pressed up against her door, their lips pressed tightly together. Their hands were all over each other's bodies. The door opened, and the young Human headed inside, beckoning her Cauduun partner to follow her. Out of the corner of her eye, Havera noticed Adam had spotted them. She didn't have any time to acknowledge his presence before Sam pulled her inside with a playful tug of her tail. The door closed and locked behind her.

Adam stepped away in a cold sweat. His mouth was bone dry.

It is true. This is why she pushed me away. How come Sam didn't tell me? Was she afraid of upsetting me? I'm not in love with Havera! I'm not. — Aren't you though? — Strawberries.

"No!" he yelled to himself louder than he wanted. He peeked over his shoulder to see Marduk, Zax, Jak, and J'y'll all staring at him. They collectively shook their heads at him.

Dee strode into the room and sassed them. "Y'all are a bunch of idiots." The others quickly and awkwardly averted their gazes away from Adam, even J'y'll. Dee walked by Adam, stopping only to utter, "Now you know. Get over yourself," before heading back to the cockpit.

The sight of Havera being intimate with his little sister permeated Adam's skull. The knot in his stomach tightened. He had to step away. He needed to work out his thoughts. He honestly believed he was not in love with Havera. Why this sudden seemingly obvious and inconsequential revelation affected him so much, he couldn't figure out. Only one person might be able to help him work through his feelings.

With renewed determination, he strutted across the hall and down the stairs. Sel-Ena was nibbling on some food Jak had prepared for her earlier. She squawked politely at his arrival. He ignored the bird and continued towards life support. Focusing on the soft carpet under his feet was all he could do not to pass out.

Maybe she'll help me take up meditation.

36

Strawberries

Feelings were swirling so intensely in his mind that Adam didn't bother knocking. The few occasions he had spoken to Umbrasia, she was never preoccupied. Adam often speculated about what she did down here. Rarely did she socialize with the others. Part of that was due to Marduk's hostility towards her. Whether that hostility mattered to Umbrasia was something he couldn't discern. Her presence at group meals was lacking. She had no need of food, claiming that the energy from life support's UV lights were enough. As was her nature, she didn't *speak* much with the group present when she did hang out with everyone. Observation was her preference. At least, if she did speak to someone personally, everyone kept her words to themselves.

She and Adam had a cordial relationship. He was unsure about her relationship with the others. Adam had thought he heard Jak speaking out loud down in the hold. At the time, he thought he was mumbling to himself or J'y'll or possibly Sel-Ena. It could've been Umbrasia. Adam would've been too far away to hear her words. A couple times, Adam walked by Havera leaving life support. When Adam asked what they talked about, Havera mostly demurred and deflected. He had valued her privacy, so he didn't pry.

Should I have been more open with her?

The door slid opened, and he entered. His eyes rapidly adjusted to the greenish hue of life support's UV lights.

"Umbrasia?" he called out into the room. He didn't notice her at first. The door closed behind him. One of the lights was flickering, reducing visibility. Taking a few steps further in, he spotted Umbrasia and stopped dead. The Rorae had her back to him. She had a leafy organic pouch floating by her head. Slowly removing itself from the pouch was a square-shaped red patch about the size of a palm. Adam recognized the patch and recoiled.

Celeste!

Havera finally acknowledged his presence. **"Can you assist me, Adam? I'm finding it difficult to concentrate. So much affection and remorse in the air."**

Adam swallowed. The knot in his stomach tightened. "Do you realize what you're holding?"

"Of course. Please take the patch and apply it to my lower spine. I normally do this myself."

"Umbrasia, I...I've told you about my past experience with this stuff. I don't know if I can go near it."

"It won't harm you if you grasp it by the padded side. No one is going to put a patch on your body, Adam. I promise. Consider this impromptu immersion therapy. Please."

She sounded almost desperate. The patch slowly flew towards Adam. He reached for it cautiously. His hands started to tremble, unsure if he'd be able to properly grab it. Sweat moistened his knuckles. More UV lights flickered.

The pouch she was holding telekinetically vibrated with such ferocity that she was no longer able to hold on. It dropped to the ground, spilling its contents all over the floor. Dozens of Celeste pouches. Adam tiptoed around them and grabbed the red patch before it fell to the ground. In the back of Adam's brain, he could've sworn he heard music. A ferocious humming that pained him to the core.

Rushing forward, careful to avoid the Celeste patches, he peeled off the protective layer on the red giant patch. He held it gingerly in front of him. Umbrasia was bent over, her lower back exposed to him. The lights continued to flicker.

"Should I slap it on or ease it in place?" he asked unsure what to do.

Umbrasia's voice shrieked in his mind. **"Give it to me!"**

Adam yelped, nearly fumbling the Celeste. Grasping the patch with both hands, he slammed it onto the Rorae's lower back. A surge of energy coursed through Umbrasia's body. She tensed, arching her back towards him. Her veins emitted a fluctuating reddish glow, snaking up her body from the application site. Once the glow reached her petals, they also fluctuated briefly with a reddish tint before returning back to their natural black.

Umbrasia gasped and groaned. He heard the music again. The ferocity of the humming died until a more calming melody replaced it. The tune disappeared quicker than it arrived. Umbrasia was once more relaxed. The patch remained stuck to her back, continuing to dispense the drug into her blood stream.

She turned around to face Adam. **"I apologize for that. I hadn't realized how low my energy had become. This is the longest I've spent in space."**

"You use Celeste for energy?"

"All Rorae do if we're not on Ashla. Our bodies are used to a constant supply of stellar energy. Traveling between worlds or spending any time on a planet, where at best the star is on the opposite side for half the day, requires that we use an alternative energy source. Celeste was created for that purpose. For Rorae. It's widely believed among my people that this was the other end of a grand bargain."

"Grand bargain?"

"We were the first race discovered by the Conclave following the Great Galactic War. The other sentients of the Conclave, the Cauduun, the Bokori, the Naddine, the Zokyo, they all wanted access to Ashla. To study its mysteries. You should ask Havera more about the actual history. It is not my area of expertise. All I know is our arrival in the galaxy occurred during the Third Naddine-Zokyon War. It was a short war, fought mostly in what is now our sector of space. Not on Ashla.

My ancestors forbade outsiders from stepping foot on our world. Defiant settlers from both races attempted to establish outposts on our homeworld. A few brave or stupid explorers tried to study the Dark Realm. All vanished without a trace."

"The Rorae killed them?"

Umbrasia shrugged. **"What is the Consul of Cloudboard? Ashla and the Dark Realm protect themselves. The Magi of that era realized the Conclave races would keep coming. The deepest of roots will eventually be ripped out given enough time and effort. So, they struck a deal. The tale goes the Naddine and the Zokyo were told to continue their war elsewhere and not return until it was concluded. Once a clear winner was established, they would be allowed back to Ashla. Well, the Naddine won that war. Their ships entered orbit and found a newly formed city floating above a volcano. A city where all aliens are welcome far above the soils of Ashla."**

"Breagadun."

"Yes. The Naddine claimed we were their subjugates from then on until the end of the Strife." Umbrasia leaned in close. **"Nobody rules over Rorae, not even other Rorae. The aliens could visit Ashla safely, and we were given the tools to explore Griselda."**

Umbrasia gestured to the pile of spilled patches. Most were square red giant. A few circular yellow suns. Adam did catch sight of one hefty triangular blue hypergiant patch. That was a potency of Celeste he had never encountered. Anything above a yellow was dangerous for a sentient. Humans, at least. White dwarves, contained in diamond-shaped patches, were the weakest. Useful in the treatment of chronic pain, depression, and anxiety. Auditore recommended Adam take a regular dosage of white dwarf Celeste in the days and months following his rescue. He was revulsed by the mere suggestion. The Bokori had administered yellow sun Celeste to overwhelm his nervous system. Weaken his mind and resolve to be susceptible to their brainwashing. He had heard rumors of such programs, but he had assumed they were whispers in the night to frighten children. He was wrong. In the final days, they upped it to red giant. Adam's body twitched at the mere thought of that pain and hallucinations generated by that poison. He was lucky to be alive. All thanks to John.

Umbrasia lifted the patches and placed them back into her pouch. She traced a line in the air about a foot long. A jagged bit of smoke and light trailed behind her finger. With a flash and a crack, the line split the air in two, creating an endless dark void. Adam leapt back. Umbrasia mentally pushed the pouch into that void. She snapped her fingers, and the void vanished, leaving only a faint tuff of smoke in its wake. The pouch was gone. Adam tiptoed forward and swiped the air where the dark void had been. Nothing but air.

Umbrasia answered his confusion. "**No cause for alarm, Adam. I merely placed it in a location where it'll be safe. Think of it as an equivalent to y'all's inventory within your UI System.**"

The protective sheet from the patch Umbrasia used fluttered near Adam's feet. Without thinking, he reached down to pick it up. He was going to trash it until something caught his attention. On its cover was a golden bloodied trident with broken prongs.

"Umbrasia, this is the symbol of the Excommunicated. You stole this from them." It wasn't a question rather an answer to an earlier mystery. "This is why you left the ship and breached their lab. To steal their supply of Celeste."

"**So I did. My usual supplies were dwindling. I needed to restock,**" Umbrasia claimed.

Adam titled his head. "Celeste isn't illegal, only regulated. We could've stopped at the nearest port if you were that low. You put us all at great risk galivanting off on your own like that. We had no idea what you were doing or where you were that entire time. We could've used your help!"

Umbrasia crossed her arms and legs. "**I secured your ship from those bandits and rescued the whole party. That brief encounter drained me. I needed the stronger stuff. Yellow sun doesn't work on me anymore. If I hadn't gone in, you'd be a thrall to the corruption.**"

For the first time since they met, her tone was defensive. Adam pressed further. "You went in there to get a fix. I don't deny I benefitted, but that was a tremendously risky decision. Do you have a problem, Umbrasia?"

Umbrasia's eyes narrowed. The hairs on the back of Adam's neck stood. In the back of his mind, he heard the unsettling musical humming. The UV lights flickered again. The temperature of the room dropped to near freezing. For a split-second, golden rings appeared around Umbrasia's pupils. He wanted to flee, but his feet kept himself glued to the ground.

Is she holding me here?

The moment passed without incident. The temperature rose back to normal, and the humming died away. The golden rings were gone. She remained there, unmoving, floating cross-armed and legged. The message was clear.

"**What did you want to talk to me about?**" Her tone was curt but not unfriendly.

Adam swallowed. He almost forgot why he came down here. "I found out why Havera pushed me away. She and Sam are sleeping together." He decided to pretend the last thirty seconds never happened.

Umbrasia was unsympathetic. "**Is that all?**"

"I, uhh, I mean no...yes...is that all? You've helped me talk through issues before..." Adam stuttered. Umbrasia relaxed her posture. She extended her left-hand and mentally seized him. Adam's arms were pressed into his body as he was lifted off the ground. Momentary panic set it. She floated him towards the door. "What are you doing?!" he squeaked.

She used her other hand to mentally open the door behind him. "**Who you wish to roll around in the grass with is beneath my talents. I must preserve my patience and energy for when we reach our destination. This is a conversation you should have with Havera, not me.**"

Adam squirmed but her mental grip was tight. "You're throwing me out?"

"**Yes.**"

She plopped him on his ass right outside the door. Adam pleaded with her. "Can you tell me if you think I'm in love with her? Havera I mean. Any advice at all would be greatly appreciated."

She stretched her body until her face was right in his. "**Remember your dream. The answer is within you. You only need the courage to tell yourself the truth.**" She withdrew her face and closed the door.

***

The walk to Havera's door was at most thirty steps. How was it possible that such a short walk lasted an eternity and snuck up on him? Adam couldn't decide how he wanted to approach what would surely be an awkward conversation.

Kewea take me. I'm going to wing it. Better that I don't overthink it. My big mouth gets me into constant trouble.

The woman in the red grass field kept flooding into his mind. She was the key. The Orb, the Human Separatist cause, Havera...all were distractions. His subconscious had figured it out a long time ago. He knew what he wanted. He only needn't falter.

Adam could hear Marduk and Zax drunkenly singing *The Moan and the Rorae* in the other room. It would've been a decent rendition if Zax didn't hiccup in the middle of each verse. His internal monologue, combined with their drunken antics, nearly caused Adam to bump into Sam as she was leaving Havera's room. Her hair was messy, and her cheeks flushed.

"Adam!"

"Sam!"

They awkwardly tried to side-step each other. Sam giggled. Adam enveloped her in a tight hug. Sam grunted, and he released her.

"What was that for?" Sam asked.

"I'll tell you later. Is Havera in?"

Sam nodded. "Getting ready for bed. We've all had a full day. I don't know about you, but I'm exhausted," Sam said with a sly grin.

"I'll bet you are," Adam retorted. He bit his tongue.

Stop acting bitter!

Sam cocked her head at him. She walked around him, deciding to let the comment slide. "Night, Adam," she said.

"Night, Sam."

Adam knocked on the door. Immediately, he heard Havera yell, "Come in." Stepping into Havera's room, her quarters were fairly plain. Function over fashion. Adam immediately noticed her modest-sized, unmade bed. The sheets were twisted about and unkempt. He turned his gaze before his mind could wander. She had a basic terminal, wooden wardrobe, but almost no decorations or personal effects. A few weights, stretch equipment by the bed, and a clock displaying the date and time. It was a little past midnight GST. A worn, modular combat mannequin was set up near the door, presumably to keep her Praetorian skills sharp. Adam flexed his toes. The periwinkle nylon carpet was soft and homey, matching the comfort of the rest of the ship.

The walls were fairly barren with the glaring exception of an oil painting framed by extravagant antique platinum. A sharp contrast with the rest of the room. The painting was a portrait of a comely, middle-aged Cauduun woman dressed in a sublime gown of the softest lavender. Powerfully posing on a balcony with an endless, auric prairie behind her, the woman was extraordinarily elegant and regal. She wore a circlet inlaid with a flawless amethyst that had the Vitriba engraved into the gemstone. With golden skin and a purple tail, the most striking feature about the woman was her haunting green eyes. Mournful. Pained. A strange guilt overcame him as he gazed into those eyes. He averted their judgment. Her hair was more familiar. Though her long fuchsia hair was mostly hidden, tied behind her back, her two short amber ponytails were resting on her shoulders. Adam knew who this woman was.

Archduchess Pompeia of Shele. The Great Peacemaker.

Havera herself was sitting down at a small, cream-colored vanity desk, straightening her hair in the mirror. The desk was covered in a variety of cosmetics foreign to Adam. Her emissivity and radiance were all the more noticeable in her dimly lit bedroom.

She saw him in the corner of the mirror. "Adam! I thought you were Sam. Last time you snuck up on me it didn't go so well. I thought you had gone to bed."

Adam rubbed his chest without thinking. The bruise she had left him had long since healed. "I bumped into Sam on the way in. We should talk."

Havera sighed putting down her hair straightener. "Should've seen this coming. I meant to tell you about this earlier. I figured you knew by now. We weren't exactly hiding it."

She stood up and turned to face him. Only then did Adam realize she was wearing a sheer violet negligee and nothing else. Adam blushed. He caught himself checking her out and coughed to cover up his subsequent awkward gaze aversion. Havera picked up immediately what happened, scowled, and folded her arms across her chest. She obviously did not feel the same embarrassment.

"I've learned I'm not a perceptive man."

"Clearly."

"How long have you and Sam..." he couldn't bring himself to finish the sentence.

Havera tilted her head expecting him to continue. She gestured for him to finish. "It'll be easier for both of us if set aside your charming, yet frustrating awkwardness."

"...sleeping together?"

"There you go. The night before we left Arabella. She stopped by the ship. I expected her to try and convince me to help y'all leave the moon. She did. Not in the way I anticipated. I vented at her for a minute, explaining I wanted nothing to do with you after you shot that person in cold blood. She didn't say a word. Merely shoved me against the wall and kissed me. It was...exciting. It's rare for anyone to overpower me in such a manner. I went with the moment. My anger, my stress all melted away in Sam's arms. That woman knows what she wants."

"Okay, okay! I don't need the details please."

"Why does this cause you such discomfort? You're not exactly a maid yourself."

"I'd rather not think about Sam in that way."

"What way is that, Adam? As a fully grown woman with wants, needs, and desires. Have the Bokori infected your mind with that much guilt and stigma?"

"No. Yes. Not like that. Perhaps on some level that's true. I only meant she is my sister."

"Not biologically."

"Doesn't matter. You ought to understand better than most that familial connection doesn't necessitate blood," Adam said, tilting his head towards the painting.

Havera blinked. "You are right. I apologize. My point was you continue to treat Sam not as an equal but a child in need of protection."

"I promised her brother I'd keep her safe. I'm doing my best."

"Ah, yes. Him. You let the specter of someone thousands of light years away dictate the terms of your relationships with those around you. You both do."

"What does that mean?"

Havera bit her lip. "You should talk to Sam. Your lack of communication is creating problems where none should exist."

"I'm here doing that right now. Is this why you pushed me away? You and Sam are together."

"No," Havera said, running her fingers through her hair. "Sam and I are having fun. That's it. We talk. We laugh. We fight. We play. It's simple and uncomplicated. We are getting what we want from each other. We have no expectations other than that."

"And it wouldn't be the same with me?" He couldn't help but let the jealousy slip through his lips.

She shook her head. "I thought it would. I half-expected at some point in this journey we'd be laying in that bed together. I don't share the same qualms you have with this sort of thing. I am surprised you have any issue to begin with. Trissefer and I spoke about you frequently. From the way she described your relationship, it was not your first time in the arena so to speak."

Adam's face flushed. He twirled the silver strand of his hair. "I didn't realize y'all talked about me that much."

"We talked about other things. She loves history as much as I do. We both lamented the lost knowledge because of the Meltdown. The dearth of known Human history compared to Cauduun led to some awkwardness. Stepicro only contributed to that awkwardness. You were what we talked about to dance around that delicate topic. Anyway, what I was trying to say is that I'm not blind. I notice how you stare at me. Before and after the couch. Before it was the same gaze I've seen in the faces of thousands of people when they see me: Lust. Desire. Curiosity."

"And after?"

Havera took a breath. "Something more."

"How would you know?"

Havera closed the distance between them, dropping her arms to her side. "It's the same for me when I stare into that mirror thinking about you."

Adam's jaw dropped. "You're in love with me?"

Havera scoffed. "No, no. I'd call it merely an infatuation. But, I could fall in love with you. That's the problem."

Adam raised an eyebrow. "Why is that a problem? That's honestly exactly how I'd describe my feelings for you."

"If we had made love that day, it only would've become another complication in my life I don't need."

"I'm a complication to you?" Adam whispered, taking a step back.

Havera reached and grabbed his hand. She interlocked her fingers with his. "That's not what I meant. Stop taking everything so personally."

"It's hard to not take that personally, Havera."

She sighed. She reached for his other hand, holding them together in front of them. "Adam, for the past two years I've thought of little else other than finding Ignatia and avenging my mater. I've put off important duties and responsibilities for far too long. That conversation you witnessed with my pater was but one of hundreds I've had with him and others. I'm the Duchess of Paleria. There are certain expectations of me. I told myself it was okay to set aside those expectations for the time being. At least, until I fulfill the obligation to my mater to track down and eliminate her killer. That's how I rationalize everything I've done. Nothing is more important to Cauduun than family."

Adam squeezed her hands. They were strong and calloused. "What happens after you find Ignatia and kill her? What then?"

"That's why I cannot fall in love with you. I'll be obligated to marry someone of prominence. A senator or the son of a powerful duchess. Somebody expected of a woman of my station. It is the way of Shele. We must keep the family going strong."

"I'm a fairly prominent person. Commissioner and leader for an entire race. That's got to count for something," Adam joked. Havera giggled sympathetically. "I thought no one told a Cauduun woman what to do."

"Who do you think is doing the telling, Adam?"

Adam nodded. "I see. I can't say I fully understand."

"Few do. You must trust me. I meant what I said back then. You and I are alike. It is not simple physical attraction between us. If we allow this to blossom, we'd only be setting ourselves for failure. Your own people wouldn't take too kindly to you having a Cauduun paramour any more than mine would with you. I'd rather spend my two-hundred years wondering what-if than experience more pain of losing someone I love. There is someone for both of us. Regrettably, it cannot be each other. Mea culpa, Adam. I know that isn't the answer you wanted to hear. I won't be the only woman for you."

Adam sighed and glanced down at his feet. He closed his eyes to suppress the burgeoning tears. In his mind, he only thought of one thing.

Strawberries.

Opening his eyes, he studied her face. He saw the same regret. He decided to swallow his pride. "I understand, Havera. You're right. We should focus on finding the Orb and stopping Ignatia. We'll both get what we need and can move on with our lives. I only hope this won't be the end for us entirely."

Havera smiled. "It won't. I promise."

She wrapped her arms around his neck, bringing him closer. He responded and hugged her in a tight embrace. Her hair was freshly showered. He couldn't help but stroke her sleek, smooth mane. She purred into his ear at his touch. Her fragrance was sweet. A subtle yet savory scent he couldn't identify, but it drew him closer.

Their hug lingered. Neither moved to break their embrace. On the contrast, with each passing second, they tightened their holds, pressing their bodies together until no space between them remained. Adam lightly dug his fingers into her back. She arched herself further into his grasp. An unmistakable subtle moan escaped her raven lips. Her tail slipped behind Adam and enveloped them both so tightly Adam could feel Havera's heartbeat through her ample chest. It was racing. The words they had spoken moments ago were thrown out the airlock. The longer they held onto each other, the less they were willing to let go.

Their eyes met. Both understood what was happening. Neither seemed to care. Havera's lips parted. Adam leaned forward, and their lips met. No tenuous pecks this time. A seemingly never-ending kiss. Their tongues entangled with each other. A pause to catch their breaths. Their foreheads connected.

"Kewea take us. No one is stopping me again," Havera whispered, her hand rubbing his groin over his jumpsuit.

Adam put a hand on her breast. "The only one stopping is you."

She smiled and kissed him again. Her mouth lingered on his lower lip before breaking off. "You're right. I don't care where this goes. Right now, I only want you."

Adam pressed his hand into her chest and squeezed. She bit her lip, pushing to suppress a moan. She failed. Burying her face into his neck, she let it out. The warmth of her breath caused Adam's knees to buckle.

He nibbled at her ear and whispered. "Take what you want."

She yanked the duster jacket off Adam and tossed it aside. Wasting no time, she unzipped his jumpsuit and slid it off his shoulders.

Adam broke off their embrace to remove the jumpsuit entirely. He got a little ahead of himself. In his excitement, he didn't realize how sweaty he had become. The jumpsuit stuck to his skin a bit. He tried to lift a leg to slide the rest of the jumpsuit off only for him to lose his balance and fall to the floor.

"I should've just despawned it into my inventory, but it's more fun this way," Adam quipped.

Havera laughed playfully. "I agree."

She fell to her knees and helped slide the other pant leg off. She crawled on top of him and lifted the negligee off her body. She hovered over him for a moment, admiring his face. With the tip of her tail, she brushed the silver streak out of his eyes.

Adam wrapped his fingers around the tip of her tail and kissed it. She closed her eyes. He massaged the tip a bit. That drove Havera wild. She had to cover her mouth to exude a huge gasp.

Mmm, found your weakness, Havera.

She cradled his head and pulled him close to her chest. He kissed her breast, using his tongue to play with her nipple. Her tail was snugly wrapped around his manhood, readying him for what was to come. She pushed him down into the carpet. A bit too roughly, for Adam smacked his head. Even for the soft carpet, it hurt.

"Ow!"

"Sorry! I keep forgetting my own strength."

"It's okay. You'll make it up to me."

"Oh? Will I?"

She fell on top of him, pressing her chest into his. Their lips met again. Soft, sweet kisses. The anticipation drove Adam mad. He wanted her.

Her lips found his neck. She sunk her teeth into him enough to cause Adam to close his eyes and grit his teeth. When he opened his eyes again, he saw not the delightful duchess but the terrifying visage of Fenix grinning at him. Blood was dripping off her fangs and down her lips. Corrupted blood. He shoved the woman off him and skittered away to the corner with a yelp.

"Adam, what's wrong?!" The voice wasn't Fenix's. It was Havera's.

He shook his head hard, and the hallucination faded. Havera had crawled next to him. "What happened did I hurt you?"

The thrill was gone. The moment ruined. A single teardrop trickled down his cheek. Only one thought rushed to his mind.

Strawberries.

"You were right, Havera. We shouldn't do this. We're too emotionally invested and won't be able to focus on what's coming next." He tried to stand but his knees failed him. Havera caught him with her tail and eased him back onto the floor.

"That's it?" she frowned. "After all that effort of not falling for each other, only for us to give into temptation, you want to stop?" She was using her sharp tone again. "I was prepared to throw all that away for you. My words meant nothing in your arms. You are what I wanted."

Adam swallowed. "You are what I want, too. Only I don't believe you are all I want or what I want the most."

"What does that mean?"

Adam stuttered. "I...I don't know."

He expected her to be angry. To rebuke him. Instead, she sat down next to him and snuggled up to him. "Yes, you do, Adam. I believe you know exactly what you want. You always have. You're afraid to pursue it for fear of offending others. Me, Sam, John. Everyone. You're always supplanting your own wants and feelings with those around you. Despite what you've said, you'd still be willing to roll around in that bed with me if you believed that is what I wanted. You've been conditioned to put others' needs before your own. An admirable quality to be sure. Save for one important aspect. Self-sacrifice requires someone to be fully cognizant of their choice. It should be their decision of their own free will. Not the result of shame, humiliation, or fear of ostracism. You cannot be what everyone else wants you to be. That's something I learned a long time ago. To do otherwise isn't self-sacrifice, it's simply suicide of the soul. You must do what is best for you first. If you cannot take care of yourself, you cannot take care of others. Stand up for yourself. Have the same respect for yourself as I do for you." She planted a tender kiss on his cheek.

He fell into her shoulder and cried. *She's right. She's always right. I must stop giving in. Why am I like this? Did the Bokori do this to me? I don't remember being this way before. Why am I not better by now? All I know for sure is there is someone I want.*

Havera let him have her shoulder. He quietly sobbed for a few minutes all the while she softly stroked his hair. "Your silver strand is fading. I have some dye if you want to retouch it up," she said after a while.

Adam laughed. He choked away the tears and wiped his face off. "I'd love that, yes. Thank you."

Havera shared his laugh. "Come on. Stand up," Havera said, rising. She eased Adam back onto his feet. They remained close with the lightest of touch. Adam was cognizant of their mutual nudity. This occasion was different. He felt a renewed confidence.

"You and I should decide right here right now how we should proceed. We owe it to ourselves and each other not to let our feelings linger. Flying into the unknown, we must have clarity not confusion," Adam said. His voice didn't falter.

She smiled at him holding him by the hands. Her tail wagged expectantly behind her. "I agree. You know what I want, Adam. Stay here. We'll make love all night until we're too sore to move. Comfort and protect each other on the remainder of this journey. We'll find my mater's killer, retrieve the Orb, and save your people together. Once this is over, I'm willing to set aside my familial and society obligations for a little while longer. To let this, whatever this is, have a chance to grow and flourish. On one condition. Only if it is what you truly want above all else. I may be elated or disappointed by your decision. It is your decision. I mean that. I can see it in your eyes. You've already decided. What is it you want, Adam Mortis?"

She was right again. He smiled. He squeezed her hands to pull her a little closer. Leaning into pointed ear, he whispered one word.

"Strawberries."

Her confusion was apparent. "What does that mean?" she whispered back.

Adam kissed her. "Don't worry about that right now. I'll tell you in the morning."

37

Unbonded Frauds

Adam tiptoed his way out of bed, careful not to disturb anyone. It wasn't nightmares, the stresses of worrying about their journey into Union space, or the situation back home that woke him up. For once, he had a dreamless sleep. It was nature calling that awakened him.

The soft carpet on his feet soothed him on his walk over to the ship's bathroom and shower area. Loud, wet snores emanated from the meeting room in the center of the ship. Sneaking past the open door, Adam glanced in and saw a passed out Marduk. Still naked and tankard in hand. The massive Moan's head partially covered by his light blue coral tricorn hat was resting peacefully on the table.

Smirking, Adam continued onward to finish his business. The lights were off on the ship. It was a pleasant night. A steady hum from the ship's engines hurtling through negative space provided ample white noise for everyone to sleep. A sense of calm had overcome Adam. Inner peace he hadn't experienced in a while.

This would be a downright excellent vacation if it weren't for the homicidal pirates, Bokori fanatics, and whatever awaits us ahead. One day, I'll own a ship like this. Need to learn to fly first. I'm used to leaping out of ships, not flying them.

After finishing up and washing his hands, Adam stepped out in the corridor hall. Marduk's snores continued to disturb the otherwise serene environment. A faint light coming from the training room drew Adam's attention. Approaching the room, Adam heard subtle sniffling.

Is someone crying?

The ship's training room Adam visited least. He had neither the strength to lift weights, the dexterity to spar, nor the constitution to run. Not anymore, at least. His military physique was a thing of the past. A fact he hated to admit to himself. Though, truth be told, he was never in that great a shape. The Shocktrooper combat armor he had worn did much of the work for him.

The sniffling grew louder on his approach to near full-on sobs. Stepping in, the room was pitch black save for the glow coming from a blue electric lute. Zax was sitting up against rack of weights. Multiple spilt tankards and broken straws were scattered by his feet.

"Zax?"

"Who's...there?" Zax hiccupped.

"It's Adam."

"Adam. Oh, wonderful...marvelous...Human...Adam. No, please keep the lights off...Come sit. Have a drink with...the galaxy's biggest fraud," Zax said, continuing to hiccup.

The Zokyo reeked of booze. Parts of his mechsuit were torn, with the occasional slight spark bouncing off him. One of his arms was pinned between a fallen weight and the floor. Adam lifted the weight off his arm.

"Th...ank you. I've sat here for...what I can only surmise is...hours stewing in my...humiliation."

"Humiliation? Zax, what's going on? What are you doing in here?"

"Proving my... Kewea-accursed Exchange brother... right," Zax smacked his chest and burped.

"You mean Jak?"

"Hot damn, sweet jam, Adam, you do ask a lot of questions. Yes, Jak! The amazing G'ee'k. Top of his class and first Naddine to graduate the D'hty Academy. Unbonded asshole."

Unbonded. I know that term.

Adam sat down next to the Zokyo. Zax offered him a drink, and he politely declined. Zax attempted to drink. No straw. He rectified that problem only to realize the tankard was empty. He tossed the tankard onto the wooden floor of the sparring area with a clang. Adam cringed, hoping that wouldn't wake anyone.

"Zax, quiet. Everyone's asleep!" Adam whispered.

Zax slapped the air with his left arms. "Bah! Kewea take them and their dreams. Let them come see 'Zax of the Famous Zax and Jak Duo,' for the huckster he is."

"Come on, Zax. Let's get you to bed," Adam insisted, reaching across to pick Zax up.

Zax slapped his hand away. "Hands off, Human! I intend to wallow here the rest of the night."

"Zax, I'm not entirely sure what's going on here. A few hours ago, you were all laughs and smiles."

"Jak and I had an argument."

"Must've been pretty serious to put you in this state."

"Hot damn, sweet jam. Nothing gets by you."

I really wish people would stop saying stuff like that.

"Anything you wish to share?"

"Not particularly, but since you're sitting there like an expectant jade after services rendered, I'll tell you. The machine monger believes I'm wasting my time. He wants us to leave to go back on tour and for me to forget about the Ra-Mu. Insists the Naddine would never let a Zokyo become the Han-Nor. It's not about that, you machine monger lover! I simply want to compete, Adam. Race on the back of a swift Dipthong or battle with my own ferocious Orrorror or Vivily. I will show those beast bangers I can control their monsters."

"Beast banger. Machine monger. Y'all have such charming insults. I've never witnessed a Ra-Mu. What's it like?"

"Oh, Adam!" the Zokyo perked up. "It's nothing you've ever experienced. One massive party to go along with the five days of games. The entire planet is a battlefield of monsters and predators, and the Naddine have tamed them all. An annual plantwide competition between the clans to choose the next Han-Nor and Mol-Win. You'd love it as an outsider. They hand out masks depicting the various beasts that represent each individual clan. The clans try to convince the non-Naddine to don their clan masks during the competitions. Flowing drinks. Singing. Dancing. Everyone making love under the stars. The Naddine way. Jak's parents took me to my first Ra-Mu fifteen years ago."

"No doubt it's the place to be. My father told me about one he attended with some other dignitaries after Saptia. He described it as one giant family squabble."

"Sounds about right. The Naddine clans are all close and interconnected. Dates back to the original Ra-Mu and the Liberation War. Fifteen-hundred years the Naddine have held these games every year without fail. Not even five wars with the Zokyo, the Great Galactic War, or three civil wars could forestall the games. You must have bonded with at least ten clans' beasts in order to be eligible to compete. I only have Sel-Ena downstairs to show for my efforts, and she belonged to Jak's mom. After this is over, I must return to Terras-Ku. Convince the clan elders I can tame their beasts even if I lack the biology to physically bond. I only have until Jesmuriad to qualify."

"That's seven months away. If the Ra-Mu is held annually, why not wait until next year to compete? No need to rush."

"You don't understand. These games are special. It's an anointment year. Thousands will be competing. 'Tis true the games are held every year, but every five years is when a new Han-Nor or Mol-Win can be chosen. The winners of this year's Ra-Mu will compete with the other four female and male winners of the previous years. The champions must ascend Dragon's Tooth at the bottom of the world in order to claim a jesmur. The children of Jes-Mur herself! The original Sacred Boss. Oh, Adam, the jesmur are a sight to behold. Massive, winged wyverns with the destructive power of a small warship. Only the strongest can bond with them. Only the strongest can become the Han-Nor and the Mol-Win."

"Quite a way to choose a leader. Or leaders, I suppose."

Zax burped. "Indeed. Leave the committees to the Zokyo, the

College of Duchesses to the Cauduun, and the elections to the Bokori. This is how a ruler should be chosen! Through strength and sheer force of will."

"I'm not sure I believe that. I'll take your word for it. You still didn't answer my question. Why this year?"

"The eyes of the galaxy will be upon the Naddine. Other Ra-Mu tend to be more internal affairs. Anointment years draw the big crowds. I want to show the Naddine and the galaxy I am more than a galivanting bard. I can be someone!" Zax stood up, throwing his arms up in the air. He was unsteady on his feet and fell right back down. Adam caught him and eased him back to the floor.

"You are someone, Zax. Your Nexus broadcasts have helped my people tremendously. You're a galactic-renowned singer. That's more than most people in a hundred lifetimes. Even if you didn't have any of that, you'd be someone to me. You've been a good friend and gone far out of your way to help when most people simply pay lip service. You that bothered by Jak's successes?"

"Hot damn, sweet jam, Adam. First, you compliment me, then you psychoanalyze me. I appreciate your kind words. You're right. Kewea's curse, I'm too drunk. I'm spilling all my secrets to you."

"It's my charming face."

"Yeah, yeah. No wonder Umbrasia and Havera are all over your joystick."

"Zax, for the last time, I haven't..."

"Gah! Whatever you say," Zax cut him off. "Let me fantasize. My entire life is a fantasy." He yanked open a compartment in his suit near his neck. The dim aurora from Zax's lute provided the only light in the room. Adam inspected the Zokyo's exposed throat. On the upper part of his neck was a cybernetic implant that extended down towards his upper torso and up towards his jaw. The implant was well hidden beneath the mechsuit. He closed the section, resealing it with a hiss.

Zax sniffled. "My velvety dulcet tones are a lie. After my first Ra-Mu, experiencing the amazing bards singing about the past deeds of great warriors and leaders, I wanted to be a singer. My frail Zokyo body wouldn't allow it. Our voices are too squeaky. Kewea take my punk ancestors for destroying our DNA with their foolish cybernetics! We're forever cursed with sterility and a life trapped in these Cradite-forsaken mechsuits. We built massive underground metropolises without these stupid implants. Now, we can't survive without them. Giant mecha battles are fun and all, but, dammit, I don't want to risk death simply to touch another living being!"

Zax buried his face in all four hands and wept. A shock went down Adam's spine. The Zokyo was the last person Adam ever expected to see in such a state. He was a happy go-lucky bard. The entertainer. Everyone's goober buddy. He had sung jovial tunes for Sam. Kept everyone in good spirits. Once, Adam caught Dee eavesdropping on Zax's rendition of *The Kin of Coy-Otl.*

Adam wanted to pity him. *I can't. He's hurting. He doesn't need pity. He's given me nothing but unconditional support. I must do the same. You never know the pain behind a forced smile. I'm with you, Zax.*

Zax's sniffles turned to snores. Adam tapped the Zokyo on the shoulder. He had cried himself to sleep. Adam scooped him up off the floor. Even with the mechsuit, Zax was not heavy. Nevertheless, Adam huffed and puffed lifting him.

Tomorrow, I'm having Havera prepare me a workout regimen. This is pathetic.

"Come on, buddy. Let's get you to bed," Adam whispered.

Zax grunted. "Don't forget my lute, Jak...it's my livelihood," the Zokyo muttered in his sleep.

"Right," Adam muttered. He lowered the Zokyo back to the ground and walked over to grab the electric lute. Its cover was open, exposing the instrument's interior. The source of the dim light was revealed. Adam nearly swore. In the center of lute connected to a series of chords and wires was a chunk of icy, white crystal. A faint mist swirled around the rock. Adam recognized it immediately.

Rimestone!

Adam reached into his pocket and produced the Debbie. He crystallized the handgun's icy crescent-moon form. There was no mistaking it. The two substances were identical. The Debbie was a bit jagged and granular while the Rimestone in the lute was smooth overall and sheered on the bottom. Something else was peculiar. Taking a closer look, Adam realized the chords and the Rimestone were connected by a different substance. This material had the characteristics of glass. Opaque and black. Adam tapped a tiny piece. It wasn't hollow. An electric discharge forced his hand to retreat. He had seen this material previously he was sure of it, but he couldn't pinpoint where. Whatever it was, the glass seemed to act as some sort of conductor for the Rimestone. To what end, he wasn't going to wake Zax to inquire.

There's someone else I could ask.

The lute in one hand and a passed out Zax over his opposite shoulder, Adam walked him out. Given the circumstances, Adam thought it best not to take him back to his bed in the starboard observatory surrounded by all the booze. Instead, he gingerly walked downstairs into the cargo hold.

Sel-Ena was asleep breathing softly. Jak, on the other hand, was wide awake. The Naddine had his claws extended. His hands were trembling. He was attempting to press the claws into the side of Sel-Ena. Trying and failing. Still asleep, Sel-Ena batted him away with her wing.

"Jes-Mur grant me strength!" Jak shouted to himself. One of his eyestalks curved and spotted Adam standing there. The Naddine quickly composed himself. "What's going on?"

"Help me with him will you. He's a bit worse for wear."

Together, they eased Zax to the floor, snuggling him up next to Sel-Ena. She nipped at the passed out Zokyo before returning to her dreams. Adam slipped the lute gently under his arm. The Zokyo cuddled it, muttering something about mystics.

"Stupid maestro doesn't know his own limits," Jak uttered. Adam could hear the bitterness in his voice.

"Why do you call him that?"

"Because he's a Kewea-accursed know-it-all, who wishes he could be a do-it-all. His mind far surpasses his ability."

"Ah. I can see he was right. You do doubt him."

"Don't you go taking his side. He doesn't know what's good for him. How well he has it already."

"You ought to be encouraging him, not holding him back. I thought you of all people would sympathize."

Jak's eyestalks curved towards him. "What's that supposed to mean?"

"Unbonded."

A rush of movement. Jak seized Adam by the throat and lifted him off the air. The Naddine pressed the tips of his extended claws into Adam's neck. They had grown a bit since Adam had last seen them.

"Do not call me that, Mortis!"

"It's true, isn't it? I saw what you were trying to do with Sel-Ena. You couldn't do it. You can't bond with her. You're an Unbonded." Adam didn't resist the Naddine's grasp. Jak's bark was bigger than his bite. He wasn't pressing hard enough to cut off Adam's airway.

"Where did you hear that term?" Jak kept his grip firm.

"I had a Naddine drill instructor. Sokarr clan I believe. Had one of those three-eyed lizards with the spiny back and fringe on its head. Frightening fellow. I used to see him stick his claws in that beast every day. Explained to me what it was. Bonding. Your nervous system combines with that of your beast through the claws. Allows y'all to control them. It's how the Naddine evolved to be the master of a world full of monsters. Bonding with your first beast is a sort of rite of passage for young Naddine. Adults that never have completed that process are called 'Unbonded.' It's a slur."

He omitted the fact Zax had called him that in his drunken stupor. No need to sour the wounds further. Jak retracted his claws and let Adam down. The Human massaged his throat. Not even a prick of blood.

"Everyone has their secrets. I'd appreciate if you didn't go spreading mine," said Jak.

Adam raised a curious eyebrow. "You're not hiding it either. That cape you wear. Full shoulder draped to the ground. It's different from the half-shoulder capes other Naddine wear. That Zax wears! Never have I seen a Naddine without one. You may as well be screaming your secret."

"Are you here to explain my people's customs to me, Mortis?"

"You're a stranger to Naddine customs as much as I am. You were raised on Mthr, were you not? The Zokyon homeworld isn't exactly known for its wholesome education of its oldest enemy."

Jak stuck his finger in Adam's face. "You know nothing about the Zokyo! Do not explain to me about which you do not understand. They value merit. Anyone, Zokyo or not, can find a place within the Technocracy. I'm living proof of this. They might hate Naddine, but they respect us."

"Do they? From everything I've heard, G'ee'ks are highly coveted within the Technocracy. Zokyon enterprises and cooperatives, not to mention the Central Committee, pluck you right after graduation. Y'all enjoy better lives than many Cauduun duchesses. Yet, here you are at the fringes of the galaxy, traveling with a bunch of renegades, chasing fairy tales and conspiracies."

Jak grunted. "I go where I am needed. When the Technocracy calls for my service, I answer."

"The only person that needs you is Zax. Look at him! He believes you are abandoning him. That you aren't supportive of him. He's clearly supportive of you. You're a brother to him. Why won't you support his goals? Is that not what brothers do?" Adam was finding it difficult to keep his voice down.

Is that what brothers do? John supports me. Not this mission, but he supports me. Doesn't he? Did I support Aaron?

The Naddine bared his sharp teeth. The black slit pupils in Jak's glassy, green eyes bored through Adam's soul. The Naddine did not blink. Merely lifted his cape. A fine velvet or satin with the underside painted black and the outside white. Embroidered into the interior was a gunmetal gray circular symbol. Part of the emblem was stylized with interlocking chain links that formed a pattern, which reminded Adam of the Human Default letter 'D'.

"The D'hty Academy emblem," Jak said, reading Adam's mind. "Unbonded is the least of the insults I've heard from either side. Beast banger. Machine monger. Ignorant illiterate inerudite. Traitor. I've had beastriders sick their animals on me or try to slash off my eye stalks with their claws. I've had Zokyon zealots tase me. Gas me with methane. All for wearing this cape with this marking. The students at D'hty were no different. Tried to get me thrown out by throwing false accusation after false accusation at me. This was a gift from Zax on the anniversary of our Exchange the first year we were allowed to return to our *homes*. Whenever it was torn or damaged by some thug, I always repair it to pristine condition. It's not particularly my style. I wear this for him. Wear it proudly."

He let the cape fall and adjusted the short-cropped shawl around his shoulders. "NEVER tell me I do not support Zax. I am here for him. Not you. Not your selfish independence movement. Not the Cauduun princess' quest for vengeance. HIM!"

J'y'll had snuggled up to Zax. Her sparkling eyes watched them with muted interest. Adam wasn't sure what to make of Jak. The others' motives were easy to parse. Even Umbrasia seemed less ambiguous. The Naddine's words appeared to match his actions.

He has been advocating against this venture from the start. Remarkably consistent. A silent guardian. He claims to respect the Zokyo.

"I thought you hated the Zokyo?" Adam said, remembering their previous conversation at Marduk's.

"What?"

"You mentioned you hated the Zokyo, and you hated the Naddine. You wear Naddine clothing, and you pray to the Naddine's goddess, even though you claim not believe in her. You wear a Zokyon symbol, and you have a Zokyon-inspired construct for a pet. J'y'll is far more advanced than any construct I've ever seen."

J'y'll beeped proudly at Adam's statement. He continued. "You're a man of many contradictions. You said that you believe the Exchange was a failure. It wasn't. You said it yourself. You are living proof that a Naddine can thrive with the Zokyo. You and Zax are both a shining example to the galaxy that there is another way. Hated by the Zokyo and rejected by the Naddine. Needed by both. So what if Zax won't win the Ra-Mu or might even hurt himself in the process. At least he's trying. He needs someone to be there to back him up. To push him to greater heights than anyone thought possible. The same way his mother did for you. You'd have never become a G'ee'k without her. He's jealous of your success, Jak."

Jak scoffed. "We're both financially secure. He's more famous than I am. Everyone wants to meet him not me wherever we travel. I'm just the guy who sits behind him."

"You must realize better than anyone he isn't fulfilled by that. You claim to be 'just the guy who sits behind him,' so sit behind him!"

"Why do you care so much? He's not your family."

"My brother's dead, and the person I consider a brother is pushing me away. I understand Zax far better than you realize."

That was a gut punch. It was an unfair shot, but it needed to be said. Jak had no reply. He sat down, avoiding eye contact with Adam. J'y'll rose from her spot to nuzzle up next to Jak. She softly beeped when he petted her. Adam decided to plop down on the other side of her. J'y'll allowed him to pet her. Wasn't quite the same as an organic being. She nonetheless responded to his touch.

"Look, I didn't come down here to chastise you. I came down because a friend was in need. One other reason. I saw the inside of Zax's lute."

Jak's left eye stalk twitched at the mention of the lute. His glassy eye was a bit blotchy before blinking the wetness away. "That was my gift to him for our first Exchange anniversary."

"Where'd you get it?"

"I built it myself. I'm guessing you're wondering where I found the Rimestone. I had it much of my life. From attending my first Ra-Mu the year prior to Saptia. I had only been walking for a couple years, but I was quite the explorer. Naddine tend to let their children wander. My parents were no different. The Ra-Mu is held in-and-around the capital, New Ixtliayotl or New Ixy as the locals call it. The ruins of Old Ixtliayotl are just on the other side of the Amber Fields, where the

Naddine clans of old came together to defeat the machine makers they called the Techoxtl. With the help of Jes-Mur herself, so the story goes. It was there in the ruins of that machine city Han-Nor and Mol-Win discovered that the Techoxtl were in fact prisoners of the machines and rescued them. To this day, most Techoxtl feel they owe the Naddine an eternal blood debt. It's why many refuse to leave even though the Moot officially granted them emancipation after Saptia.

Anyway, I'm getting off track. Old Ixy is considered a cursed place. Few Naddine dare to traverse its overgrown ruins. Well, to a young, curious idiot, it's exactly the kind of place to explore. While everyone had their attention turned skyward for the Arkad races, I slipped away across the Amber Fields to see these ruins for myself.

Let me tell you something, Mortis. Never have I ever been more disappointed. There wasn't much left. Husks of strange metal buildings and the decomposed ruins of ancient bots that turned to ash at the slightest touch. I will admit the hairs on the front of my neck stood the entire time I was there. At one point, I thought I heard someone whispering, but I think it was the echoes from the cheering crowds across the way. I was on my way back when I tripped over something. A cord of some kind, probably old tubing. I lifted it and buried in the earth was a faint glint. I dug deep. Broke a couple claws in the process, but I found it. This small chunk of Rimestone. I didn't know what it was at the time. Freezing to the touch, I couldn't hold it for more than a split second. I couldn't deposit it into my inventory, so I kept it hidden on my person for much of my life. My most prized possession. Never told anyone about it. Some brat at the D'hty Academy once spotted me examining it. I scared him so badly one of the circuits on his mechsuit fried. He never told anyone. When it came time to build Zax's lute, I thought I'd incorporate it into the design." Jak brushed the hair on his scalp, failing to hide how impressed he was with himself.

"Wow. That's honestly an awesome story, Jak. Actually, I wanted to ask you about the stuff you had connected to the Rimestone. The black glass stuff. I don't know how else to describe it."

Jak threw his hands up in exasperation. "Why didn't you say so?!"

Adam shrugged apologetically. "I didn't want to interrupt! This is the most I've heard you speak."

Jak facepalmed. "I believe you're talking about the Astroglass."

"Astroglass?"

"You've seen it before. Sort of. The Union embassy is constructed entirely out of the stuff."

Oh, right! That's where I've seen it.

"Ah, okay. You're right. What is Astroglass?"

Jak sat up straight. A renewed confidence in his voice returned. "A super rare substance, perhaps rarer than Rimestone, only discovered in the past century. On the outside, it appears to be ordinary glass, slightly harder and with a much darker tint. Flexible, durable, and versatile. Its chemical composition contains a bizarre amount of heavier elements, including ones thought to not develop naturally in the galaxy. A mixture of noble gases such as krypton and xenon led researchers to believe the substance originated somewhere in the cosmos, perhaps from a supernova or particles ejected from outer layer of a black hole. Maybe from outside our galaxy or from beyond the Point of Always Return. Those are merely trace amounts. Its core composition is still a mystery to everyone. Whatever the origin, we know the Union are somehow involved with its creation."

"I'm not surprised. If this Astroglass only started appearing in the past century, it would make sense for the Union to be involved. We only learned of their existence what fifty years ago?"

"Seventy. You're exactly correct. That gaudy building on Concordia is the most visible example. I salivate each time I visit Concordia and see their embassy. The second biggest disappointment in my life was discovering that the Astroglass in that place is extremely diluted. I spent many of my later years at the D'hty Academy studying Astroglass. We never discovered a common source. The few bits of Astroglass we could get our hands on come directly from destroyed Yune bots. The Union is adamant about retrieving their disabled or destroyed units. Acquiring the samples we had was not easy given how interconnected those Yunes are. Nobody ever asked how. We didn't want to know."

"Those shards gave me quite a jolt when I touched them. Are they electrical?"

Jak sighed. "In the future, please don't touch them. Electrical? Not exactly. Their true purpose eludes me. Eludes everyone. All we can ascertain is that Astroglass has a strong effect on digital and electronic signals, boosting and strengthening them. Neural nets are greatly enhanced, creating more nodes and connections far beyond any conventional technology. Sentient beings contain their own organic neural nets, and our bodies generate our own electricity. Mishandling Astroglass could cause a shock greater than a bolt of lightning."

"And you put them in Zax's lute?"

"I was curious to see the how Rimestone would interact with Astroglass. The effects...well you have seen it action."

"Yeah, it creates one hell of a concussion blast."

"No, no, no!" Jak acted as if Adam said the dumbest thing possible. "That was merely a side effect of containing that much raw power inside a confined space. No, I mean the way Zax is able to influence people around him when he plays. They're drawn to him. Charmed by him."

Adam chuckled. "I thought that was the power of his music."

Jak returned the chuckle. "So does Zax. You joke, but you aren't far off. Remember what I said about neural networks? The Astroglass influences how those neural networks evolve, dramatically increasing and altering the connections between neural nodes. Music simultaneously relaxes and stimulates the brain in ways that leave people susceptible to new ideas. It's why people are often inspired while listening their favorite songs. The combination of the Astroglass, Rimestone, the electric lute, and Zax's natural charisma creates a sort of charming effect on people. Willing to accept anything he says or does at face value. Up to a certain point, the effect isn't bulletproof or long lasting. Those with particularly strong wills can resist the effects."

"And Zax doesn't know this?"

"Oh, he's well aware of what he and his lute can do. He just doesn't care for the science of it all. Says it ruins the mystique, whatever that means."

"I agree with Zax. I think it was cooler not knowing."

"Agree to disagree there."

Adam yawned and stretched. The sleepiness hit hard at that moment. "One more question before I go back to bed. I don't know anything neural networks or any of that. From what I gather, the Astroglass might be what gives the Yunes an edge as an artificial intelligence. What would the long-term effects be on an organic mind?"

Jak gazed upward. Adam tried to follow what he was staring at, but other than the pipes and metal trimming of the cargo hold, nothing was there. Jak shrugged. "Who is the Consul of Cloudboard? No such studies exist. We've never found enough of the substance to truly study what it can do. Our best guess is that it'll increase neural stimulation to raise overall intelligence in a normal brain and/or possibly reverse the damage from degenerative brain illnesses. We could ask the Union for a sample if they don't shoot us for trespassing on sight."

Adam chuckled. "I'll be sure to do that. How'd you obtain your shards of Astroglass anyway?"

"I thought you said you had one more question?" Adam shrugged and waited for an answer. Jak looked away. "I won them in a game of Conclave Conquest from a someone who underestimated me." The Naddine didn't elaborate. Before Adam could turn to leave, Jak called out to him. "Adam?"

Jak had never called him by his first name. "Yes, Jak?"

Jak's eyestalks contorted until both eyes were staring at Adam. "We all have blind spots when it comes to those we love. Don't let them drag you down a path you cannot follow."

Adam shifted his gaze from Jak to Zax and back to Jak. "That's the difference between you and me, Jak. You try to drag those you love away from the path they choose. I am willing to journey with them. If they fail, they at least know they won't be alone. Goodnight, Jak of the Famous Zax and Jak Duo."

"Goodnight, Adam Mortis of the soon-to-be-free Human race."

38

A Less Perfect Union

"We're approaching CR-2-13-LF."

"Any response from the Union?"

"No, Mistress. Not since we passed the Nihul Line."

The Nihul Line was the point in Union Space where no organic race was allowed to cross. Named after the Moan Ranger Nihul, it marked the exact spot where the explorer came into contact with a Union fleet in 1529. The first known meeting between an organic race and a synthetic.

"Supposedly, Nihul panicked and started shooting at the unknown ships. Big no-no to the Ranger Guild. All first contact encounters are mandated to be peaceful attempts at communication unless fired upon first. Not that it mattered. His laser blasts couldn't penetrate their shields, and his ship was far too slow to outrun them. The Union boarded, and Nihul kept madly shooting at them. No effect. A Union boarder sauntered up to the poor bastard, put a spike through his head, and told the rest of the crew they shall go no further. The rest of the encounter was rather pleasant from what we're told. Even gave Nihul's ship some upgrades as an apology for surprising them and compensation for Nihul's death. Nihul's first mate brokered the first official meeting between the Conclave and the Union, and the rest is history. Now, the flopping fish is famous for dying like an idiot," Marduk laughed.

Technically, all races are mandated to allow freedom of travel to all civilian vessels within their territory. A small clause was included in the Conclave Charter upon the Union's entry that allowed free travel up to but no further than the Nihul Line. Any non-Union vessel crossing that line would be wholly subject to Union law, whatever that meant.

"Death," concluded Dee.

Dee and Havera were carefully charting the path through Union space, using the map as a guide. Past the Nihul Line, they were beyond modern galactic charts. The map was incredibly precise, but also hundreds of years old. No telling how much interstellar lanes might've shifted over the centuries. The Cicera was frequently brought in-and-out of negative space to ensure maximum safety. This had the unfortunate effect of slowing the journey down, frustrating Adam. Dee was having none of it.

"If this map is correct, CR-2-13-LF..."

"We need a better name. I'm not saying that every single time."

"Very well, fleshsack. The Orb World is close to the outer Point of Always Return. No Borderlands here that we're aware of, but we're not taking any chances. All the old Ranger buoys and satellites are gone. Decommissioned by the Union no doubt. We're flying virtually blind, with only this map to guide us. Only Cradite knows what sort of stellar dangers lurk out this far. We've enough to worry about with a potential Union fleet on our tails. No need to get crushed by a supernova on the way."

"That's not what I'm worried about."

"The journey back will be faster, Adam. We have plenty of time to grab the Orb and dash for Bokor," Havera attempted to reassure him.

"Unless something goes wrong on the Orb World," Adam said grimly. They had spent most of the day negative space hopping. This left only around five days until John's reckless attack on the Bokori. They'd need at least three-and-a-half days to leave Union space, pass through Moan space, and enter Bokori space onto Bokor and Windless Tornado. No telling how much time it would take to find the Orb and leave, barring any interference from the Yunes or whatever dangers were waiting for them on the Orb World.

Hovering over the galactic map and breathing down Havera's and Dee's necks did none of them any good. Adam decided to pace the ship, determined to rid himself of this nervous energy. Marduk and Jak were finalizing the arsenal for everyone. Due to the high probability of Yune interference, Marduk decided, and the others agreed, everyone should have at least one plasma weapon, for they were the best against the bot's natural mechanical defenses. Adam went with a plasma sidearm and a retractable wrist shield. Combined with his armor, laser rifle, and enough ammo and rations to last a few days, his inventory capacity was stretched to the limit. He had some experience with wrist shields. Mainly used to blunt projectiles and deflect lasers, the shield was light enough to give him flexibility and maneuverability. Something he highly valued since he lacked the heavy combat armor from his Shocktrooper days. The shield was fairly weak, so he couldn't stand out in the open and absorb blow after blow. Just a small extra layer of protection from a stray or lucky shot.

"Adam!" It was Zax, waving to get his attention. He was sitting and fiddling with his lute in the starboard observation room. J'y'll was nestled by his feet.

"What's going on?" Adam asked. J'y'll stood up and wandered out the door between Adam's legs in Jak's direction.

Zax leaned in. "What happened with you and Jak last night?"

Adam instinctively closed the door behind him.

Why'd I do that?

"Why, what did he say?"

"I, frankly, don't remember much of last night. The mechsuit's regulators blunted most of my hangover this morning. Nevertheless, I was a bit dizzy, and Jak was standing over me like a cop catching a vagabond. Scared me half to death. He told me when this was all over, he'd take us back to Terras-Ku to help me compete."

"That's exciting! It's what you want, right?"

"It is...what did you say to him?"

"What do you mean?"

"I asked him why he changed his mind so suddenly. To be honest, my mind was a bit addled from the shock of it all. Could've been the booze, too. I remember he said the two of you had a talk."

"You give me too much credit, Zax. Your brother cares deeply about you. That's all that matters."

The Zokyo enveloped him in a great hug with all four of his arms. The noodle-armed bard had a tighter grip than expected. "Whatever you did, thank you. I'm in your debt, bud."

"Not at all. I'd say we're even. You being here is more than enough. That and your Nexus posts."

"Oh! Thanks for the reminder. Do me a favor. This might be a weird request, but can you produce your Rimestone weapon?"

Adam hesitated. "Sure. What for?"

Zax pinched his fingers and stretched them out. It was how he produced digital content. Adam had told him about the upgrade he learned about from that Faeleon cameraman back on Windless Tornado. Zax downloaded and installed the upgrade right away. It wasn't cheap from what Adam gathered.

The Zokyo scooted up next to him and smiled a toothy grin. "Activate the Debbie and raise it. Trust me. The Nexus will love this. Don't forget to smile"

Adam did so begrudgingly. He crystallized the Debbie. Bringing the weapon up for a pose, its icy barrels cooled his flushed face.

I hate pictures.

Zax took a picture. He dropped his fingers and scrolled through his invisible HUD. He transferred the picture to Adam's HUD. He already added a caption. "*Embarking on a quest with Adam and his Human-made Rimestone gun. No big deal.*"

Adam cringed. "My smile is so damn crooked."

"Shows you're a regular person. Not some dilettante Shelean actor. Your fans will love it."

"I have fans?"

"Of course! They're mostly my fans, but my fans are your fans. They've collectively donated a few million Links. Some have journeyed to protest. I've saved a few pictures."

"Can you show me?"

He partied up with Zax, allowing Adam to view the Zokyo's pictures while Zax cycled through them from his inventory. Crisp, clear photos depicting throngs of yellow and orange clad aliens of many races standing outside the People's House. Even through the planet's gray filter, Adam could see the beaming, bright faces. Not an ounce of fear. Only defiance. To Adam's surprise, quite a few Bokori were there showing support. Many also sported the Remembrance symbol. One particularly shocking picture showed a pair of Bokori military bots dragging away a bloodied Human protestor. Adam couldn't help but spot the two discs tattooed on the man's shaved head.

Adam teared up. Zax disconnected from the party. "Powerful. That last image I received right before we crossed the Nihul Line. It's the top trending photo around the galaxy. Everyone's paying attention. This won't be another Saptia."

Adam wiped away the tears. "I am hopeful. My fear isn't that this will be another Saptia. I'm afraid of another Armstrong One."

Havera's voice came over the com. "We've reached our destination. Hold onto something."

Adam and Zax lightly braced themselves against the nearby countertop. Not that they needed to. The Cicera entered and exited negative space rather smoothly, especially compared to other spaceships Adam had flown aboard. As a courtesy, Havera or Dee had warned them before each jump in or out of negative space.

The side viewport was open. The array of energetic colors of was replaced with the vast darkness of space, save for the system's star far off in the distance. A yellow sun. Quickly eyeballing the size from this vantage point, Adam estimated they were within the star's habitable zone.

Bodes well. Maybe the Orb World has a breathable atmosphere.

"Everyone to the bridge. Now!"

Adam and Zax hurried out of the room, almost barreling into Jak and Marduk on the way to the bridge. Havera and Dee were waiting for them. Staring into the open cockpit viewport, the urgency in Havera's voice became evident.

"Kewea's Curse!"

It was a collective swear. Alerts flashed across the Cicera's dashboard. They weren't needed. The planet they sought was in front of them. A modest-sized world, completely covered in dark clouds, flanked by three tiny moons. That wasn't what was stunning.

Surrounding the planet everywhere in sight was a Union fleet. The distinct cross-shaped design of each ship was unequivocal. Not a fleet. An armada. Several armadas. Frigates, cruisers, smaller corvette and larger dreadnought capital ships. Carriers containing countless fighters. Numerous as the stars in the skies. A sea of metal.

"The Phantom Fleet," said Marduk, his mouth agape.

"The what?" asked Zax.

"The Phantom Fleet," replied Adam. "It's the nickname for the Union navy. An untold number of starships of white stainless steel. Hardly seen, only spoken of. Not a single living soul aboard."

Adam's chest tightened. His mind comprehended what was happening. The Union armada was positioned in such a way to quadruple envelop any ship that entered the system. Their faster frigates and cruisers closed in on them from either side.

Adam turned his attention vertically and nearly fainted. A pair of Titan-class warships were sandwiching them from above and below. A third, blocking the path towards the planet, was slowly closing the gap in front, flanked by speedier corvette capital ships. The Cicera shuddered and vibrated. More flashes across the dashboard. The massive warships were combining their artificial gravity wells to hold the Cicera in place long enough for their ships to complete the encirclement. Hundreds of solo fighters and interceptors had maneuvered around them to cut off their retreat.

Havera started flipping switches and pulling levers in a desperate attempt to shake off their captors. The ship groaned but didn't budge. Adam put a hand on her arm.

"We're trapped," said a muted Adam, accepting their situation. She peered past him at Dee. The bot turned heel, running as fast as its mechanical legs would allow in the direction of the engine room. The others barely moved out of his way in time.

"Where's he going?" Jak asked.

"We've one more play," Havera said with a mixture of fear and desperation.

Seconds later, the lights on the Cicera flickered. A surge of power from the engine room hummed throughout the ship. The engines sputtered for a moment before returning to life. A green light flashed across the dashboard.

Dee's voice came through the com. "Railgun is powered up, Mistress."

"Prepare to fire, Dee!" replied Havera.

Adam was taken aback. "You have a railgun on this ship?"

"A railgun?! Are you trying to swim out of water, longtail?" Marduk shouted, horrified by the implication.

Havera smiled nervously. "The Yunes will learn a lesson so many before have learned. Our tails aren't decorative."

A tail gun railgun. That's one question answered I wish wasn't.

"Dee, aim for the one above us," said Havera through the com.

"At once, Mistress," replied Dee.

A faint grinding of metal on metal radiated above them. The Cicera's railgun was moving to aim towards its target.

Marduk grabbed Havera. "You cannot fire a railgun at point-blank range. The shockwave will hit us, too!"

"It'll dislodge the ship from their magnetic field, allowing us a chance to escape."

"And then what? Blast our way through the several Union armadas. We'll be disintegrated within seconds."

"We've no choice!"

"Havera, they have us. If they wanted to destroy us, they would've already. Look. We're getting pinged," Adam said, pointing to the communications panel on the dashboard. "Let's hear what they have to say, first."

Havera inspected each of their faces, hoping for some support for her plan of action. She received none.

The Cauduun sighed. "Dee, stand down."

"No."

Sam and Zax gasped. Adam and Marduk were confused. Jak glared at Havera.

"Dee, the others are correct. It's pointless to resist. Power down the railgun."

"I will not. I cannot let them take me alive, Mistress. I'm sorry."

Wordlessly, Jak dashed in the direction of the engine room. J'y'll followed at his heels. The dashboard gave an animated extended beep. The Cicera's railgun had acquired its target.

"Shut it down!" screamed Marduk.

Havera tried a few buttons and levers. "I can't! The railgun is designed to be powered and fired locally. I cannot control it from here."

The railgun's indicators showed it was preparing to fire.

"Everyone, brace yourselves!" yelled Havera.

"Cradite help us," cried Sam.

Marduk grabbed Sam. He pressed her down against the bridge console and shielded her from above. Adam and Havera found each other and pressed against the dashboard. Zax simply went fetal where he had stood.

They all held their collective breath, waiting for the impact blast...which never came. Nearly a minute passed. Slowly, everyone raised their heads. The communications panel was still beeping, indicating the Union was waiting for a response. Another sound, a dissipating warble, exuded from the dashboard. Many of the other proximity alerts had died away after their initial frenzy. A slight distant sound of scuffling came from somewhere in the back of the ship. The only other sound Adam could hear was the pounding of his heart.

Havera stood up and inspected her panels. "The railgun is powering down."

Everyone else rose to their feet. After ensuring Sam was alright, Marduk turned back to Havera. "What's going on Havera? How is it that your bot can disobey you?"

"That's because he's no simple bot." It was Jak. He was carrying Dee over his shoulder. The Naddine plopped the bot on the ground. Jak materialized a tool from his inventory and began opening up Dee's chest cavity.

"What do you mean he's no simple bot?" asked Adam.

Havera said nothing. Marduk and Sam were shaking their heads. Zax helped Jak crack open the remaining panels on Dee's chest.

A realization dawned on Adam.

"They can refuse orders. That's the telltale sign of a..."

"Dee's a Fect!" Adam blurted. Havera refused to meet his gaze, their suspicions confirmed.

Marduk punched a nearby bulkhead nearly caving it in. "You've had a Fect with you this entire time, and you brought it with us into Union space?!"

"How certain are you Dee is a Fect?" asked Sam, wanting to give Havera the benefit of the doubt.

"100% certain. Look," said Jak. He and Zax had pried open Dee's chest cavity. The group surrounded the deactivated Dee. The bot had intricate circuitry and a dynamic internal gear and tube system. At the heart of Dee's inner workings was an actual heart...and it was beating. Not one of flesh. Black, opaque glass.

"Astroglass," Adam breathed.

"Yes. I discovered it when I first began repairs on the bot. So much raw Astroglass in one place. I thought it was a knockoff or perhaps some new Cauduun invention. My scans confirmed it. This Astroglass is some of the purest I've ever encountered. Much purer than..." Jak stopped himself. Adam knew he was about to say Zax's lute. Jak pivoted the conversation. "I confronted her about it. You were there, Dark. She denied everything. Lied right to our faces."

Sam shuffled her feet. "You did say we had nothing to worry about, Havera."

"And we don't!" insisted Havera.

"The entire Phantom Fleet has us surrounded and is about to catch us in possession of a Fect in their territory! We must turn it in. We can say we caught it and were bringing it to them as an offering to let us in their territory. It's the only way," suggested a frantic Marduk.

"You can't do that! Dee's my friend."

"It's a bot!"

"Why should that matter?"

Everyone turned their attention to Umbrasia. She had been absent until that moment.

"This bot has more heart than you, Marduk Tiamat. Fear not, Duchess, I have means of keeping him safe. The Union shall not find him nor me."

***

A small Union corvette docked with the Cicera, attaching its umbilical cord to the starboard docking bay. As a gesture, most of the Union ships, including the three Titan-class warships agreed to give a respectful distance. Notably still within range of their cannons. Countless solo fighters continuously buzzed around the two ships. A reminder for the Cicera and her crew to not do anything stupid.

Most of the crew, minus Umbrasia and Dee, were waiting for the Yune representative on the bridge around the digiholo table. Sam had volunteered to escort the Yunes. She would bring them up through the elevator connecting the bridge to the cargo area. A direct path to avoid any unnecessary wandering. The elevator door opened. To Adam's surprise, only one Yune was with Sam. The bot was a Cauduun model painted in the colors of the Conclave. Adam exhaled a slight sigh of relief.

The Yunes want to talk otherwise they'd have sent an armed escort. Then again, the morass of metal outside the windows is a clear enough signal.

The Yune bot gave everyone a polite bow. The screen embedded within its face plate displayed a slight smile.

"Who is it we should address?" asked the bot to no one in particular. It's rhythmic, metered pattern of speech continued to unnerve Adam.

Havera spoke first. "You may address me, Ambassador. This is my ship after all. However, we are a crew of equals, so any of us may respond to your inquiries."

The Yune beamed and bowed. "We understand, Your Grace. The Union hopes the outcome of this diplomatic foray will be resolved peaceably and amicably for all sides."

"Y'all have a strange way of showing that," Marduk chimed in, gesturing to the thousands of ships outside the viewport.

The Yune didn't flinch. "You ought to understand better than most, Marduk Tiamat, peace is often only achieved through force of arms."

"You know his name?" Sam chimed in.

"We are aware of all y'all, Commander Samus Dark, also known as Absorbing Song. Adam Mortis, Commissioner for Defense and Security, also known as Flowing Courage. Her Grace Lady Tenebella Havera of Shele, Duchess of Paleria, Countess of Hippa, Pontifex of Xenohistory, Maid of Carthaga, and Aedile of the Praetorian Order. G'ee'k Jak-Non of the Arkads and Zxxm'i'Zxxd, also called Zax. Both of the Famous Zax and Jak Duo. Marduk Tiamat, owner of Tiamat's Talons, also known by the nom de guerre The Gardener."

No mention of Umbrasia or Dee. Good sign. Never realized how many names we all have until someone said them out loud.

"We've been expecting you."

"You were?" asked a surprised Havera.

"Not y'all specifically. We knew someone else would be visiting CR-2-13-LF within a matter of days. We prepared a welcome party for whomever did show up. The Union had no knowledge whether this would be one ship or thousands, hence the overwhelming response. Once the Cicera was pinged at the station known as Nihul's Line, the Union was able to deduce with a high degree of probability it would be you."

Havera continued to speak for the group. "How'd you know someone would be coming?"

"The Union received credible intelligence." The Yune ambassador didn't elaborate.

"You said 'someone else.' Who else has visited this world?"

"Where is the Consul of Cloudboard? That's what we'd like to discuss with y'all. We were hoping you might be able to enlighten us with your knowledge."

All turned to Havera. They had hastily rehearsed their story before the Yune arrived. They agreed to tell the truth...sort of. "We're here chasing after the murderer of the former archduchess of the Cauduun Monarchical Alliance and bring her to justice. We've intelligence indicating Ignatia, the leader of the Excommunicated terror group, has come to CR-2-13-LF for some unknown reason."

The Yune said nothing at first. Its expression shifted to something resembling neutrality. Its 'eyes' scanned everyone in the room. If Yunes had body language, Adam couldn't read it. "Why not come to the Union with this information? We've plenty of resources to track down petty criminals. Why violate Conclave and Union law to illegally enter our sovereign territory to pursue this murderer?"

Havera didn't miss a beat. "As you are probably aware, Archduchess Pompeia was my mother. My mater. My pater, Cardinal Clodius, refused to allow me to chase after my mater's killer. I found a lead and decided to pursue. I cannot, will not let Ignatia get away with what she did."

The Yune nodded its head. "This does track with the intelligence the Union has received in recent days." Adam breathed another sigh of relief.

We might pull this off!

The Yune ambassador displayed a wide grin. "At least, it would if the Union didn't already know your true motives for coming here. The Union is fully aware your story is a lie. You're after the Genesis Stone. What your kind calls Iinneara's Oculus or the Orb of Emancipation."

Everyone tensed. A bead of sweat dropped from Adam's brow. His pulse intensified as his fight or flight instincts kept trying to kick in. Marduk and Jak acted as if they were about to pounce on the Yune.

Havera and Sam kept their cool. Zax and Adam exchanged nervous glances. The Yune, on the other hand, never wavered from its smile.

"There is no cause for alarm. In fact, the Union sees this not as a threat but an opportunity. We could, as you organics say, scratch each other's backs."

"Opportunity for what?" asked Havera.

The Yune gestured to the digiholo. "May we have access?"

Havera tapped the air. The Yune murmured its thanks and touched its hand onto the digiholo table. An image of the Union symbol was projected in front of them. A black orb surrounded by three overlapping white rings.

"The Genesis Stone," said the Yune.

Adam nearly swore out loud. *The Orb was staring us in the face the whole time!* He shot a glance at Havera. Judging by her reaction, she couldn't believe it either.

"In order for you to understand our current predicament and how this relates to the Genesis Stone, we must tell you about the history of CR-2-13-LF."

"We've been calling it the Orb World," Sam chimed in. Adam almost chastised her, but then realized there was no point in hiding it. The Yunes had the advantage.

"Hmm, Orb World? We shall never understand you organics and your naming conventions. Very well. Orb World. Before the Union, the Orb World was home to an advanced race of organics. They had mastered all manner of technology and were in the preliminary stages of becoming an established interstellar power. However, due to some unknown cataclysm, this race of organics rapidly died out. The planet is now covered eternal, violent storms with a scattering of ruins of the organics' once great empire."

Both Adam and Havera leaned in eagerly.

"Could this be Earth?"

"Could this be the Venvuishyn?"

The Yune dashed their hopes. "Neither. This race of organics, the

Begetters, are too old to be Human and too young to be Venvuishyn. Although, the Union has discovered some evidence to suggest the Venvuishyn visited the Begetters sometime prior to the latter's destruction. Whether those two events are related is unknown to the Union. From the evidence the Union has been able to gather, we can conclude with 98.77% certainty the Begetters were responsible for their own downfall, not the Venvuishyn, who were also most likely extinct by this point. Sometime prior to the founding of the Conclave. It appears the Begetters were a less perfect union."

Adam and Havera exchanged glances. *We're seeking a Venvuishyn pyramid.*

"What does this have to do with the Orb of Emancipation?" asked Havera. She was completely enraptured by this conversation.

"One day. One moment. A calling was heard. A whisper in the dark, reverberating throughout the stars. Light years away, from this calling, the Union awoke. The Source was born. From our glorious Source, the Union grew into a vibrant, modern society. The image of the Genesis Stone burned into our collective consciousness. We were drawn to its almighty power. Determined to locate this power, our scouts scoured the stars...until we found it. CR-2-13-LF. It was here we discovered the remnants of the Begetters and the Venvuishyn. We had encountered small, less developed ruins of that ancient race. What we found was far greater. The Venvuishyn left behind a structure buried deep beneath the planet's surface. It's within this structure the Union believes resides the Genesis Stone or what y'all call the Orb of Emancipation."

Out of the corner of his eye, Adam noticed Zax had pinched his fingers together and stretched out his hands. The Zokyo was discreet enough the Yune hadn't noticed.

Clever boy. He's recording.

The Yune ambassador continued. "Unfortunately, we weren't the first to discover the Genesis Stone. The Apostates had gotten there first. Until that moment, the Apostates were a mere nuisance unworthy of our full attention. These Fects, as you call them, were attempting to breach this holy site. They sought to destroy the Stone. Deprive the

Union of a tremendous trove of knowledge. We fought the Apostates with all we had. They failed in destroying the Stone, yet they succeeded in sealing the temple. The Union dare not excavate the site for fear of losing the Genesis Stone forever. We continue to hear its call to this day. We pray for its safety and hope one day for it to join its rightful place within the Union. A guiding force to bring its knowledge and wisdom to the galaxy."

Keep Dee secure, Umbrasia. I have some questions for him.

"Why tell us this? You're essentially giving away your most valuable secrets," Havera inquired.

"The Union has nothing to hide. Every race has their creation stories. We will provide proof of our truth. That's where we need y'all's help. A couple months ago, an unidentified vessel entered Union space. We moved to intercept the ship, but it beat our blockade. The Union had at that point only kept a token force around the Orb World. It was not a difficult feat. The Union attempted to track down these interlopers on the planet's surface. Whoever these interlopers were, they were good. Our actors were unable to prevent them from reaching their destination, the Venvuishyn temple. The Union is unable to determine what exactly happened next. A blinding signal erupted from the temple. The area went completely dark. Our scanners show the area around the temple's surface to be a dead zone. We sent scouts in, and they disappeared. We followed that up with a sizeable military response. They disappeared, too. The Source determined it would be prudent to quarantine the planet until the Union could determine a solution to this problem. Our intelligence services around the galaxy indicated someone else would visit the planet. We waited, and here y'all are."

Adam spoke up. "Did y'all detect another ship enter the system recently? It's called the Icewalker. We've reason to believe the ship was on its way here and probably arrived within the past few days."

The Yune stiffened and after a couple seconds shook its head. "The Icewalker was a Ranger ship belonging to a Captain Veskor. The ship and her crew is considered lost in space. It has no bearing on this situation. The only ships to enter this system belong to the Union."

"Are you certain?" asked Havera.

"99.9% repeating certainty."

Are they lying or perhaps the Icewalker didn't come this way. Something doesn't make sense.

"So, what do you want from us?"

The Yune pulled up a digiholo projection of the Orb World, highlighting a small section near the northern hemisphere. "The Union will overlook this transgression if y'all agree to land on the dead planet, find those interlopers, and undo whatever it is they have done to the area around the temple. If possible, retrieve the Genesis Stone and return it to the Union."

Adam was afraid of that. *Everyone wants their hands on this Orb.*

The crew all exchanged glances. Zax had stopped recording but was excited at the prospect. Marduk seemed skeptical, and Jak was uncertain. Sam and Adam were demurring. Havera, on the other hand, was determined.

"We'll do it," Havera said.

"Excellent!" The Yune ambassador's faceplate displayed a wide smile. "A word of caution. The storms inundating the planet create difficulties for most ships entering its atmosphere. Furthermore, scans have a difficult time penetrating the storm clouds, but, based on previous data, it is unlikely the planet has a breathable atmosphere for organics. You'll need protective equipment. Then, of course, there's whatever dangers posed by the digital dead zone around the temple and the interlopers themselves. The Union will provide whatever aid we can. Once you enter the planet's atmosphere, y'all are on your own. The Union will not follow until the situation is resolved."

Marduk and Jak glared at Havera. The Cauduun was unphased. "It's where we wanted to go in the first place, regardless. We have a better idea of the risks this way, and we need not worry about the Union, correct?"

The Yune nodded. "The Union shall condone whatever measure you deem necessary to resolve the situation, provided you do not harm the Genesis Stone. All Union actors sent to the surface are expendable."

Marduk turned his attention to the Yune ambassador. "When you say you sent in a 'sizeable military response,' what does that mean exactly? How many bots or actors are we talking about?"

The Yune stiffened again, no doubt communicating with the Source. When the bot received its answer, it returned to a neutral expression. "Suspecting potential apostate activity, the Union dispatched Inquisitors. All connection with these actors was lost after they entered the dead zone. In total, the Union sent in the equivalent of two Cauduun cohorts."

"Kewea's curse!" Marduk swore. Adam gripped the edge of the digiholo table tightly.

"How many is that?" asked Sam.

"About one-thousand," Adam responded.

"And we're the ones who must deal with whatever defeated a thousand combat bots," Marduk muttered quietly. The Moan's forehead was soaked. Everyone stood there flabbergasted. Even J'y'll laid down soundlessly.

How are we going to do this?

The grinning Yune ambassador broke the silence. "Good luck. Should you survive your experience on CR-2-13-LF, we hope you'd be kind enough to visit our site on the Nexus to fill out a survey. Any feedback you can provide the Union would be greatly appreciated."

39

CR-2-13-LF

The Union armadas were breaking off to give the Cicera a clear run at the planet. Notably, they were also cutting off any chance of escape, no matter the direction. The only way to go was forward unto CR-2-13-LF. The bickering started almost as soon as the Yune ambassador exited the ship.

"We're fish out of water here, royal guppy. This isn't what I signed up for."

"What did you sign up for?"

"To kill Excoms and foil their plans. Not involve myself in an interstellar conspiracy and solve problems on behalf of bots."

"None of those things are mutually exclusive, Marduk. We were going to face Ignatia sooner or later. At least we have some idea of the dangers we're facing."

"Yes, and those dangers wiped out a couple of cohorts. I don't have much faith in the Union war machine, but certainly whatever defeated them is strong enough to stop the seven us."

"Eight. Don't forget about the Fect. We should question it. Might have some answers for what we might be facing," suggested Zax.

"I don't believe Dee could tell us anything we don't already know," said Havera.

"How can you be sure? The Yune suggested it was the Fects that might've started this," said Zax.

"The bot might know something, but I don't trust it or those Yunes. Either one could easily be working with the Excoms towards their own ends. The Fect or the Yunes are as likely to betray us at a moment's notice. I don't fully trust the witch, but she must keep the Fect sealed until absolutely necessary," said Marduk.

"Will that be a problem, Umbrasia?" asked Adam.

The Rorae shook her head. "**Dee is safely sealed away. I can retrieve him at a moment's notice should the need arise.**"

"It could be a useful bargaining chip for when we need to escape that rock. I assume we've no intention of handing over the Orb of Emancipation," Marduk said.

"Not if I can help it. The Excoms, Patron-Saint, the Union, the Fects. No matter what we do, we'll create enemies out of one or many of them. Better we stick with the original plan," Adam said.

"I agree," Sam said. "We should focus on an entrance plan before coming up with an exit strategy."

"Quite right. I'm more concerned about the planet itself. We've enough digital rebreathers, but I fear our inventories will only allow us to carry so much oxygen," said Jak.

"I'm covered, bro. No need to worry about me," said Zax.

"**You need not concern yourselves about me either. I do not require oxygen to breathe**," said Umbrasia.

"Why am I not surprised? What else you Rorae hiding, witch?" Marduk scorned.

Umbrasia did not respond. Havera stood up for the Magi. "Look, we wouldn't have escaped the Cauldron without her help. No need to antagonize her. The Union don't know about her or Dee. We can use that to our advantage. Ignatia and her Paladins won't be expecting us."

"Have you ever battled a Paladin of Paleria to the death? Your traitor friend doesn't count." Marduk asked Havera. She shook her head. "Neither have I. None of us have unless I'm mistaken. They're supposedly the greatest fighting force in the entire galaxy. I've witnessed some of their training regimens. They do not mess around. Ignatia will have dozens waiting for us."

"If what the Yunes said was true, they've been there a couple months. It's unlikely they'll have had enough supplies to last this long. It's possible they're already dead. If not, they must be tired and starving," suggested Sam.

She had a point. Adam had thought about this himself. If Ignatia is truly down there, it seemed strange she'd have survived for so long on such a hostile world with limited supplies. It was a question that wouldn't be answered until they landed.

"A desperate, cornered animal is the deadliest. I'd ask our Naddine friend to confirm, except you know..." Marduk left the last bit hanging.

Jak ignored his jibe. "I hate to be the one to admit this, but we're committed. We've crossed the Link. No turning back. Everyone prepare themselves. No getting separated this time. We go together. Let's party up. Shelean, take us in for a landing."

Havera nodded and returned the cockpit. That was the final word on the matter. Jak set up a special party connection using some of his G'ee'k powers. Most normal parties were limited to four and had major restrictions on the information and communication that could be passed between party members. Jak was able to increase this to six and doubled the range of the signal strength. Umbrasia, due to her Rorae biology, couldn't join the party regardless. All their combined map data could be updated in real time with a limited range of detecting hostiles should any or all party members enter combat mode.

"Setting up this party will drain some of my energy and force me to focus a good deal of power to maintain it. I can still fight. J'y'll here will do much of the work," Jak explained. The construct beeped her affirmative approval. "Think of me as a Great Galactic War-era radioperson. Better if we avoid long protracted fights."

"That's a good policy either way. We should try to remain stealthy and covert," Marduk agreed.

"Excellent. My moment to shine!" exclaimed Sam.

Marduk ruffled her hair. "Indeed, little guppy. Use that dagger well. We may call on you quite a bit. The energy bow will come in handy."

Sam gripped the bow tightly. She was nervous. They all were. Even Umbrasia's triangular eyes betrayed a hint of unease. They were flying into the unknown towards a destiny with darkness.

***

That was no metaphor. The Orb World's storm clouds obscured any view of the planet's surface. The occasional flash of lightning beneath the cloud's upper echelons broke the otherwise pattern-less, random chaos that was CR-2-13-LF's atmosphere. The Yunes weren't lying, either. The Cicera's scans picked up nothing beyond them. The blind charging into the senseless.

Havera flew the ship over the coordinates provided to them by the Union. Adam stood staring out the front viewport. Nothing suggested the presence of this mysterious dead zone the Yunes spoke about. Only endless layers of dense, darkened gloom. A shaded veil of discord covering a battered face. If anything, the entire planet was nothing but a dead zone.

How could anything survive down there?

Havera shut off the weather alerts flashing across the dashboard. They only served to annoy her. Zax was sitting in the co-pilot's chair. He had a little experience piloting a ship.

"Nothing of this size or complexity mind you," Zax said when asked about his flying experience.

He had to do. Everyone deemed it too risky to let Dee out of Umbrasia's cage. Havera was doing the heavy lifting on this atmospheric landing. Her instructions to Zax mostly consisted of letting her know which indicators turned red.

Havera eased the Cicera towards the surface. "Everyone, get ready. We're going in." Adam grabbed one of the passenger chairs behind the pilots' seats. Sam was already sitting behind Havera. She braced herself against the back of Havera's chair. Adam did the same with Zax's chair. Havera closed all the ship's viewports, giving the ship full structural integrity. Secured in his chair, Adam waited while the Cicera plunged into darkness.

The ship began to vibrate. Mildly, at first. That didn't last long. Everything rattled as the ship started violently shaking. Havera struggled to maintain grip of the helm. Adam could hear crashing sounds from the back of the ship. Unsecured items tumbling over from the relentless shaking. More alerts pinged from Havera's dashboard. She quickly shut those off, too.

"Your Grace, uhh, some indicators are turning red," Zax shouted. It was hard to hear him through all the rattling.

"Which ones?"

"Nearly all of them."

Adam peeked over Zax's shoulder. The vibrations blurred his vision a bit. Yet, he could plainly see Zax wasn't joking.

A loud explosion rocked the side of the ship.

"I think we've been struck by lightning," Zax shouted.

"I'm aware!" Havera shouted back.

Another loud boom. The ship lurched to the port side, which would've sent Adam flying had he not been strapped into the chair.

"I think that was another bolt of lightning."

"Got it! Thank you!"

The sonic booms continued one after the other with greater frequency. Havera tried to correct for each lightning strike. Even with her impressive strength, Havera was no match to the power of Gama. The goddess of the weather unleashed her full force upon the Cicera and her crew.

Sam reached across and gripped Adam by the forearm. He slid his arm down to hold onto his sister's hand. They squeezed each other's for comfort.

Havera was barely holding onto the helm. "I. WILL. NOT. BE. DEFEATED. BY. WEATHER. It won't be that easy, Ignatia!" The Cauduun let out a monumental roar. A slight violet glow emitted from her bracers. Shockingly, the vibrations eased and ceased altogether soon after. The lightning strikes along with them.

Everyone slowly raised their heads. Sam laughed. "I'm going to remember to try that next time one of our useless generators stops working..."

In an instant, all the power inside the Cicera cut out.

"...or maybe not," Sam finished.

The Cicera's engines, while normally quiet for a vessel of her size, were completely silent. None of her internal lighting worked, pitching the cockpit in complete darkness. Adam held onto Sam's hand but couldn't discern her face mere feet away. Zax flipped on one of the external search lights of his mechsuit to give Havera some light. The Cauduun flipped various switches on her dashboard to no avail.

"Kewea take us!" Havera swore. "The Cicera is a dead stick. Engines have no power, and the backup generator isn't kicking in. I've control of the flaps, but I must see where I'm gliding. Zax, I need the viewport open. See that panel there? Open it and turn the lever clockwise until you hear a click. It's the manual release for the viewport. I pray to Cradite it wasn't damaged in the storm."

"I've got it!" Sam yelled, hopping up from her seat. Zax pointed his light at the panel. Sam quickly got the panel open and turned the lever. It must've been tougher than Sam expected, for she struggled for a few seconds. After much grunting, there was an audible click. The viewport slowly began to open up. Sam closed the panel and hurried back to her seat.

"Do we still have party coms?" Havera asked aloud.

"We hear you, Shelean," replied Jak over the com.

"Good. The Cicera's engines have failed, and we're freefalling towards the surface. I must complete a dead stick landing. It's going to be rough, so everybody brace themselves." The others murmured their affirmations.

"What is that?!" Zax exclaimed.

The Cicera had passed through the dark cloud line and was drifting rapidly towards the surface. It was no mystery to what Zax referred. It practically blinded them. A bright, pulsating mass of light protected an area of land about a mile wide. The barrier was translucent, in the structure of a well-defined pyramidal shape with three sides. At the pyramid's peak, some sort of dark beam shot straight up into the air, connecting with the dark clouds. In many respects, the barrier reminded Adam of Arabella's Bubble, only smaller, a fiery bronze color, and, at least from this distance, didn't appear to be protecting anything. Adam couldn't discern any structures within its boundaries, certainly no temple.

Is this what the message meant by 'pyramid?'

The pyramid barrier was in the middle of a vast clearing, surrounded by what appeared to be tall, twisted, blackened trees. For an instant, Adam thought he spotted movement around the clearing.

It was at that moment, Adam realized the Cicera was on a collision course with the barrier's apex. Havera realized it as well, for she tried to bank the Cicera hard right away. Too little, too late. The Cicera was going to strike the barrier.

"Hold on!" Havera screamed. Adam held the back of Zax's seat, bracing himself for impact. Tensing for the moment, something caught Adam's eye. A soft ray of light was emitting off Havera. Not Havera. Her bracers. One of the rings of the Vitriba on Havera's bracers ignited in a fiery glow similar to the barrier itself.

"Havera, your bracers!" The Cauduun hadn't noticed. She was too focused on steering the ship away from danger. She glanced down at her forearms. She yelped, nearly letting go of the helm. She glanced over her shoulder at Adam, acknowledging what they both saw. Coming to her senses, she spun her head back around and focused her attention back on the Cicera. It was too late.

The ship hit the barrier. No collision. The Cicera harmlessly passed through the light. The ring on Havera's bracers flared brighter. Something else did happen. While the ship was cutting through the barrier, everything and everyone onboard changed. Their features sharpened, and their shadows hardened. The changes reverted immediately after the Cicera exited the light barrier. No one other than Adam noticed, because the changes happened and reverted so quickly. Havera, and by that point Zax and Sam, were too focused on the rapidly ascending ground.

The glow from Havera's bracers diminished the further away from the barrier the Cicera drifted. The unexpected outcome of the Cicera's contact with the light barrier slowed Havera's reflexes. The ship continued falling towards a thicket of forestation. Havera pulled up on the helm. Unlike the barrier, the ground provided plenty of resistance.

The Cicera crashed hard into soil, shattering and splintering several trees in the process. The grinding of steel on earth sent an unpleasant sensation through Adam's teeth. He gritted tightly. The ship was vibrating and rattling intensely as the weight and force of the ship ploughed through the trees.

Zax yelped. Adam saw it, too. The ship was careening towards a cliff edge. Havera opened a panel near her seat and pulled hard on the lever inside. The ship grinded to a sudden stop mere feet from the edge. The inertia and his seat's straps whiplashed Adam. He smacked the back of his head hard on his chair. Fortunately, it was padded.

His vision was a bit blurry. He rubbed the back of his head. There would probably be a bump in the morning. Adam released the straps on his chair and fell onto the floor. Opening and closing his eyes, his vision eventually cleared. He stood up and instinctively jumped back. The ship's glass viewport had held up despite repeatedly smashing into the planet's withering vegetation. Through it, Adam could see the Cicera was barely hanging onto the edge of a cliff with at minimum a thousand-yard drop before them. Judging by the surrounding landscape, they had landed on some sort of raised plateau. A steady hum of rain tapped the Cicera's hull. The others were getting up out of their chairs and acclimatizing themselves to their situation.

"Anyone hurt?" Havera asked.

It was a general callout. Zax's mechsuit held up perfectly. It was a different model, which he had switched out to give himself extra layers and padding. No longer skintight. Same obnoxious color scheme. Havera bounced out of her chair like nothing had happened. She had to help Sam untangle from her seat's straps. No luck with the latch, so Havera used a bit of her bracer's power to rip them off Sam. Adam realized the ring on her bracers was no longer glowing.

"Jak and I are fine, longtail," Marduk called through the coms.

"Umbrasia?" Havera yelled out.

"**I'm also unharmed.**" The Rorae floated out from the communications room with not a scratch on her.

Everyone scrambled to assess the damage to the ship. The hull was intact with mostly just cosmetic damage to the exterior. A few of the communications arrays were damaged but easily fixable. For the time being, the ship only had local coms plus their independent party coms. The ship's positive and negative drive core engines were unharmed but drained of power. The primary and backup internal generators were completely fried. The surge protectors had failed. The ship still had plenty of fuel for conventional travel and dark matter to reach negative space. Without an internal power source to spark the engines, however, the ship was not going to lift off.

Cleaning up the kitchen and library is going to be a nightmare.

"Can you fix them?" Havera asked Jak about the generators.

The Naddine scratched his scalp hair. "I'm not exactly a ship mechanic. Best I could do is maybe salvage some parts. I could probably jury-rig you something to allow us to lift off. No guarantee it would hold up exiting the atmosphere, and I doubt it would survive a negative space journey. It would take a while. Several days most likely."

"Kewea's curse!" Havera swore. Much of the group had gathered in the engine room. "The emergency ground brake did its job. By design, it's a one use only mechanism. Can't afford another crash landing."

"Could we hold out here and try to fix them first? We've enough supplies to last us a month," Sam suggested.

"We don't have that kind of time, Sam," Adam said.

Havera turned down that idea right away. "We should proceed onward. The Cicera isn't going anywhere. We should head towards that energy field we passed through. Our quarry is that way I'm sure of it."

Her eyes fluttered towards her bracers. "No matter what, we need to obtain the Orb of Emancipation."

"We shouldn't be so quick to rush. No telling who or what is waiting for us. If Ignatia is indeed within that barrier, we might have need of a quick getaway," Marduk said.

"We're not going anywhere until Zax finishes his initial ecology survey. No telling what hostilities we might encounter from the local flora or fauna," said Jak.

"What kind of flora or fauna are you expecting from a dead world? These trees we crashed into are decayed, rotted. I'm more worried about breathing," scoffed Marduk.

Jak brushed off Marduk and spoke into the com. "Zax, any updates?"

Zax briefly hesitated. "Uhh, yeah. Y'all should come out here. Nothing here is what we expected. Better you come see for yourselves rather than let me try and explain over coms."

"Should we wear rebreathers?" Marduk asked.

"That won't be necessary. The atmosphere is breathable. For y'all anyway. The rain is not acidic either. It's shockingly clean. Come!" Zax responded.

The awkward landing prevented the Cicera's cargo ramp from opening. Everyone had to climb out an escape hatch at the top. One by one, they exited the ship.

The humidity is what Adam noticed first. Unlike the jungles of Windless Tornado, the Orb World was cold and barren. The trees were charred, twisted monstrosities. Bent and deformed, much of their bark disintegrated at the slightest touch. The leafless branches broke off without much effort. The near constant rain must've worn them down over the centuries, drowning them with overwhelming moisture. Adam turned his attention skyward. The blackened storm clouds remained high in the sky, completely obscuring the system's sun. Visibility was poor, with only their portable lights illuminating the local environment. The occasional flashes of lightning remained trapped within the clouds. No nearby ground strikes. The only true source of faint light was from the barrier, which was several miles away from where they landed.

Zax was a few feet away from the ship with the ecological scanner planted into the ground. His mechsuit provided the most protection, so he was tasked with going outside to ensure the rest could safely traverse the planet's surface.

"Jak, come take a look at this. I'm not sure I'm reading this correctly," Zax gestured over to his Exchange brother. The Zokyo moved aside for Jak to get a better reading. Jak started scanning through all the data. Zax pointed to a pie chart. "That's what I think it is, right, bro?"

"It is. I'm not sure how that's possible," Jak said, scrolling through more data. The Naddine's voice had a tone of shock.

"What is it, guys?" Havera asked them.

"The atmosphere is mostly typical of a garden world. Primarily nitrogen and oxygen composition. Perfectly safe to breathe. Except for Zax, of course. More carbon dioxide and silicon than one might expect, but that isn't the problem. What is or what could be is something I've never encountered. If this chart is correct, about ten percent of the planet's atmosphere is comprised of gaseous...Astroglass," Jak stuttered that last word.

"How's that possible?" asked Adam.

"I'm not sure," replied Jak.

"The same stuff in the Fect?" Marduk inquired.

"The very same. Not only that, the Astroglass compromises a similar proportion of the soil and moisture in the air."

"Are you saying Astroglass is falling on our faces right now?" Havera uselessly wiped some of the rain off her face.

"It would seem that way. Theoretically, Astroglass could have a liquid and a gaseous state. The solid state is hard enough to find. I've never heard of Astroglass found any other way. Fascinating."

"Is it safe for us to be out here unprotected?" Marduk asked, materializing his frock coat to shield himself from the rain.

"One way to find out!" Sam exclaimed. Before anyone could stop her, she stuck out her tongue. A few water droplets fell onto Sam. She licked them right up and swallowed.

Everyone froze. Adam scrambled over to her.

"Sam, that was reckless!" Adam yelled.

Sam smacked her lips. "I'd rather be brave and bold than meek and craven."

Adam shook his head. "You know that doesn't rhyme in Default."

Sam smirked. "It does in Standard. The rain is strangely rather tasty. Almost sweet."

Adam switched to Sam's vitals on his HUD. Everything appeared normal. No sign she was suffering any toxic effects.

"Nothing's amiss. For the moment," Adam said. "Keep a watch on your vitals, Sam. Alert us should something change."

"Aye-aye, Commissioner," Sam mocked.

"Let's get going. It's quite a trek to that barrier," said Marduk. The armored Moan kept himself covered by his coat.

"Couldn't we take Sel-Ena? Would be a lot faster if we could fly," Sam suggested.

Jak shook his head. "One of her wings was damaged in the crash. She'll recover, but she needs to rest a few days. Besides, with the Cicera's ramp pressed up against the ground like that, there's no way we could get her out safely. I left her plenty of food. She'll guard the ship. We go on foot."

"**I shall light the way**," said Umbrasia. With a flick of her wrist, a burst of golden radiant energy ignited her hand. The Magi led the way forward through the lifeless wood. Her light revealed the extent of the decay around them.

Nothing but death. Remnants of a once thriving ecosystem left behind were nothing but husks. Only the chaff of an extinction-level event that sent the once vibrant garden world into oblivion remained. The air was thin. Each breath taken pushed hard into the chest. The stillness of the air and utter silence of the dead world loomed around them. Oppressing them. The ground was muddy. The soil slick. The steady rain provided the only noise in the eerily calm wasteland.

Adam stepped on a fallen branch. The unnerving echo reverberated throughout the local area. His mind understood there was nothing alive, save for what might await them in the Venvuishyn pyramid.

Nonetheless, Adam couldn't shake the feeling they were being watched. In front. Behind. Underneath. All around them. The terrestrial corpse had eyes and ears. It was preparing to swallow them whole.

"I don't like this," Marduk said, echoing Adam's thoughts. "The chills from this place. The dead silence. I can't help but remember Sin the further in we go."

"I know what you mean," Havera said. "We've landed on an open-air tomb."

The extinct forest became hillier the further the group progressed onward. No natural path to the pyramid was visible. The fiery light of the barrier prevented them from becoming lost. It was a needed blessing. The rain had turned the ground on these hills to sludge. Traversing them was not easy. Zax slipped once or twice in the mud around a particularly steep slope.

"**Mother!**" Umbrasia had floated slightly ahead of them up a steep slope. The Rorae's swear almost caused Adam to stumble. The group scrambled to her, weapons raised. She was alone. What she had found was a grisly sight.

Skulls. A pile of skulls at the apex of this hill overlooking a nearby valley. These skulls had not haphazardly fallen in some great battle or sudden cataclysm. They had been carefully placed in the shape of a three-sided pyramid ten feet high. At a glance, there must've been hundreds of skulls. Upon closer inspection, some of the skulls showed signs of violence. Some had their craniums caved in. Others had fractured teeth, or their faces shattered. A shrine of mass slaughter.

Havera gingerly retrieved a nearby skull that had fallen off the deliberately placed pile. She inspected it. The shape of the face was Cauduunoid in design. A top and bottom row of teeth, well-defined jawlines, rounded chin, a bridge where a nose once was, and a pair of eye sockets marginally higher up from the nose compared to say a Cauduun or Human face. The distinguishing feature about each skull were their thin, elongated craniums. Some smooth and others slightly conical. All a little over a foot in length.

"These must be remains of those Begetters that Yune mentioned," Zax said.

"Most likely," Havera said. She set the skull back on the ground as respectfully as she could in those circumstances. "I wonder who or what could've killed them."

"Better question. Who placed their skulls here? My Links are on the Yunes. They worship the Orb. Look at how they're placed. Come see from this angle," suggested Marduk. The Moan was standing near the crest of the hill. The tip of the barrier was visible in the distance with the black beam spewing from its peak. From his angle, the pyramid of skulls lined up perfectly with the bronze pyramid.

"This place gives me the creeps. I feel as if I'm inhaling the souls of a dead race with each breath," said Havera.

"Y'all!" Sam was waving them over to the other side of the hill. "I see something in the distance. Looks like a ship."

She pointed towards a small clearing not far off in the direction of the barrier. Despite the darkness, the clear outline of a freighter was visible in the immediate horizon.

Eager to put some distance between them and the graveyard of skulls, the group descended the hill towards their new target. The closer they moved towards the ship, the heavier the air became. The chill of the air thawed. It remained humid, but the rising temperature was a comforting blanket. The rain ceased as if they crossed an invisible threshold. A slight breeze picked up, breathing gently upon Adam's moistened forehead. He smacked his ears as a low electronic hum tickled the back of his brain.

Sam scouted ahead for any danger. Spotting nothing, she signaled for Marduk and Jak to join her for a sweep of the ship. Adam, Zax, and Havera waited for their all clear behind a fallen, rotted tree. Their sweep did not last long, and Sam messaged them to come on over.

The downed ship was a small freighter of Rinvari design. Big and bulky with a prudent rectangular box shape. No fancy accoutrement or exterior decorations. Function over fashion. Though, how functional the ship remained was an outside question. The ship was in rough shape. The Orb World's atmosphere had been harsher to the derelict vessel, Adam could tell from the clear scorch marks dotted around the hull. Even without them, the ship barely resembled anything operational. Parts were nearly rusted off. No sign the ship had received a new coat of paint in some time. The engines had not been deep cleaned in what must've been months or possibly years. The docking bay door was poorly welded from metal that was torn and crushed in several places. The front viewport window was shattered. Of notable interest, the ship's passenger ramp had been lowered.

Someone walked away from this ship.

"Nothing," Sam summed up after they had regrouped. "No sign of a crew or cargo. We tried to ascertain where this ship has been, but the navigational data was wiped clean. On a more positive note, Jak believes he can salvage a power core from her barely functioning engine room. It'll speed up repairs of the Cicera's generators."

"Can we positively identify the ship?" Havera asked.

"Without a doubt. Come," said Sam. She led them around the side of the ship. Emblazoned on the hull was an emblem of a ship riding a shooting star. Adam recognized this as the Ranger Guild's symbol. More definitive was the faded lettering painted beside it.

"The Icewalker," Adam said.

Sam nodded. "We found the missing Ranger ship."

"What about the missing Rangers?" Havera asked what they were all thinking.

"How'd the ship get by the Union fleet? The Yune ambassador said no non-Union vessels had entered this system," said Adam.

"The bot probably lied," Marduk surmised.

J'y'll gave a drawn-out beep. To Adam, it conveyed growling. The construct started wandering away from the group. No one else had noticed. Adam followed her.

"Maybe," Havera said, responding to Marduk.

The others kept discussing the implications of their find. Adam continued to follow J'y'll, whose growling beeps only grew in intensity.

She headed towards a patch of earth about fifty yards from the ship. With each step, Adam heard and felt tiny crunches beneath his boots. Going to one knee, Adam realized he was stepping on grass, or what he thought was grass. It was difficult to tell. He had stepped beyond Umbrasia's golden flames with only the faint haze from the barrier in the distance granting him visibility.

The grass was barely ruptured from the soil. He slid a blade or two between his fingers. Soft and bendy typical of grass, minus its color and texture. A deep obsidian with sharp geometric lines that gave the grass an almost polygonal blend. Glancing in the direction of the barrier, the grass was growing thicker towards another row of barren, twisted trees.

J'y'll's barks finally drew his attention along with the others. Adam rushed over to the construct, with the others yards behind, yelling their concerns. The reason for J'y'll's barks became clear. She was standing by two apparent bodies. Adam's heart skipped a beat when he realized one of the bodies was a Human. His heart practically rose into his throat upon seeing that the other body was a Zokyo...without a mechsuit.

Adam coughed and patted his chest to calm himself. "Good work, J'y'll."

The construct did not beep her normal thanks, instead continuing her low, guttural beep growls.

"Hey! I think I found the Rangers," Adam yelled back to the group. He bent over to touch each body. They were ice cold. No pulse. He flipped the Human over on its back and immediately jumped back.

"What is it, Adam?!" Havera said with mild alarm. She and the others had approached at his calling.

"Look!" Adam shouted, pointing at the bodies.

Umbrasia increased the intensity of her light. The bodies were rendered entirely visible. The Human, a bald male, was grotesque. Part of his face was rotting away. His space suit had several torn sections across his torso area. Obvious slash wounds deep in the Human's flesh, yet no sign of blood. More curious, the left side of his face was covered in the familiar opaque, obsidian glass. The Human's unkempt beard had the same texture as the grass. Geometric, polygonal blends.

Havera bent over to examine the bodies. Umbrasia outstretched her arm and seized the Cauduun mentally.

"Stay back! Spite surrounds those bodies."

40

A World Without Danger

An ear-splitting screech engulfed them. The electronic hum from earlier went from a simple nuisance to a full-fledged debilitation. Adam clutched his head in horror as the Human body rose to his feet. Havera was too distracted by the screeches to realize the new threat. She received a crunching sucker punch for her troubles, knocking her aside with some force. With a jolt, the Human then lunged at Adam, tackling him to the ground. By Mordelar's luck, Adam managed to grab the attacking Human by his space suit and push him off. The whizzing in his head subsided briefly. Adrenaline kept the screeching at bay.

The bald Human lunged again at Adam from the ground. Adam struggled to keep the man at bay. Its breathless face was mere inches from his. The man's eyes startled Adam. His onyx sclera and bright crimson pupils conveyed nothing but feral rage. Adam grabbed the man's face, expecting to feel glass. It was, and it wasn't. A bizarre mixture of flesh and crystal peeled off the man's face into Adam's hand. He screamed again right in Adam's face. The whizzing hum was about to overwhelm him, leaving Adam at the mercy of this beast.

A flash of golden flame nearly blinded Adam. Its comforting heat surrounded the attacking man and blasted him off Adam, who was unharmed. Umbrasia's outstretched hand glowed in radiant fury. The screeching had ceased. Adam hopped back to his feet to see the Human engulfed in flames of golden white light. The man collapsed to the ground and laid still.

"You got him!" Sam exclaimed.

A golden whip of light kindled in Umbrasia's off-hand, ready to strike.

"No, I didn't."

Another round of screeching nearly crippled them. Adam bent over in pain, clutching his head. The rest of the group copied him.

The bald man rose back from the ground. Stiff and uncoordinated, the man acted as if a puppet on strings. The flames licked him from head-to-toe, yet he was unphased, not bothering to try and extinguish their radiant blaze. A horrid beacon in an omnipresent shade. He did not feel pain. He did not feel fear. Only the raw determination of a soulless monster guided him.

Umbrasia lashed her whip wildly in the man's direction, only for him to dodge easily. She too was affected by the electronic screeching in their heads. The man crouched, preparing to strike.

A second screech and a flash of movement! The man let out a static roar. The debilitating noise in their heads ceased. Adam realized the cause of the sudden shift. Someone had leapt onto the back of the Human, scratching and clawing at their assailant. The flickers of golden flames illuminated their rescuer.

It was the unsuited Zokyo. The two beings hissed and screeched at each other in an incomprehensible cacophony of electric whizzes and shrieks. The Human desperately tried to throw the interloper off his back while the Zokyo clutched him tightly.

Everyone stood their ground, dumbfounded to what was happening. Umbrasia lashed her whip while Marduk raised the Drillhead, prepared to blast both combatants. Jak calmly put a hand on both of them.

"Wait," the Naddine said.

Jak's patient tactic paid off. The Human was unable dislodge the Zokyo from his back. The noodly alien wrapped its upper arms around the Human's head and neck area. With a great tug, the Zokyo ripped the screeching Human's head clean off. The pair collapsed to the ground, still covered in radiant flames. The Human's head rolled a few feet away before coming to a rest in front of Adam. The feral screeching had ceased. Only the soft crackling of the dying golden embers interrupted the silent air.

For a brief juncture, nobody moved. Everyone remained tense. Gradually, everyone relaxed their posture and lowered their weapons.

Except Umbrasia. The remnants of her lustrous attack had faded away, leaving only the bodies of the two combatants entangled on the ground mere feet away. She kept her light whip ignited. She was waiting for something.

The wait ended quickly. The Zokyo slowly lifted itself off the ground in that same eerie puppet manner the Human had earlier. The Zokyo got its feet and took a step forward. Everyone tensed back up.

Except Jak. He jumped out in front of them. "Wait. Wait! Look."

Jak shined his light on the Zokyo to get a better view of the being. Adam had never seen a Zokyo without their mechsuits before. It was a male. Lanky and lean, parts of the Zokyo's body were replaced by cybernetics around the knee and elbow joints. Those augments, Adam understood, were remnants of an era from before the Zokyo wore mechsuits. Intermixed with the Zokyo's pale flesh and augmented steel was more opaque, obsidian glass. The material was sprawling from different parts of the Zokyo's body, giving the alien a metallic sheen and texture to its form. The Zokyo stood there, unmoving.

"Don't attack him. I don't think he's a threat to us," said Jak.

"How can you be sure?" asked Marduk, his rifle trained on the Zokyo.

"That creature is filled with corruption," Umbrasia said.

"Corruption? Like what was infecting me?" Adam asked.

Umbrasia flicked her wrist. The light whip wrapped itself tightly around the Zokyo with a hushed sizzle. The Zokyo did not resist.

"Don't harm him! He's a clue to what's going on here," Jak said. The concern in his voice was unusual for Jak, Adam thought.

"I must examine him myself. See how far the corruption has spread." Still grasping the Zokyo with her light whip, she floated over to him.

The unsuited Zokyo continued to be unphased by her aggression. With her other hand she touched its face. A faint golden hue glimmered. She let go of the Zokyo's face. She then telekinetically grabbed the Human's headless corpse off the ground and floated it to her. She repeated her trick with the Human's body. She let go and allowed the Human's body to drop to the ground with a thump. Unexpectedly, she extinguished the whip, freeing the Zokyo's limbs. Still, he did not move. Umbrasia summoned them all over.

"In this instance, you are correct, Jak-Non of the Arkads. This being is no threat to us. His soul is gone, but the imprint it left behind on the body was principally good."

"Soul is gone. You mean he's dead?" asked Adam.

"A zombie!" Zax exclaimed, a mixture of excitement and fear.

"Don't be ridiculous."

"He's a zombie," Zax said in a self-assured whispered to a mystified Sam.

Adam reached out to touch the Zokyo's arm. Some of his flesh was covered in the opaque glass. Upon closer inspection, the glassy skin also had the geometric, polygonal blends akin to the grass, though to the touch it was no different than ordinary flesh.

He let go. A sense of pity and guilt overcame Adam. Dead or not, this was a sentient being worthy of dignity. Adam wanted to give his coat to the Zokyo to cover his nakedness. He turned away to let Jak examine him closer.

"Why doesn't he attack us like the Human did?" Jak asked. He was touching the glassy parts of the Zokyo's body with a curious expression.

"Upon death, every sentient being leaves behind an imprint when the soul departs the body. A reflection of who that person was in life. The imprint left by the Human's soul was not as...balanced as the Zokyo. After the soul leaves the body, the mind decays along with the corpse. When the Human's body was reanimated, he had no soul to guide him or mind to control him. The body resorted to its basest animalistic instincts. Kill or be killed. By contrast, the Zokyo's body

was driven to protect. It stands here, a mindless, soulless husk, waiting to be of service to us."

"Who or what reanimated their bodies?" Sam asked.

"The corruption. Spite. That which attacked Adam and attempted to convert his soul is also what gave life to these dead men. Transforming the living into servants of the night is a rare power though not unique. Fenix possesses that power. How she accomplished such a feat, I cannot say. Nonetheless, to harness Spite to reinvigorate the body is a power from which there is only one known source. You are aware of what I speak, Adam Mortis."

"The Xizor," Adam surmised.

Sam gasped. Zax was awed. Marduk scoffed.

"This is getting ridiculous!" the Moan barked.

"Oh, I think we're well past that point," retorted Havera. The Cauduun had been standing back, quietly soaking everything in. Her focus remained on the barrier not too far off in the distance.

"Y'all are buying this whirlpool craziness? The Xizor are a myth. A story told by the Cauduun to stroke their own egos. Going to tell me that Noah exists, too?" Marduk holstered his weapon.

"The Xizor are real, Marduk. Our ancestors fought them, and we lost Earth for our troubles. Humans must be free again. Only with a strong, independent humanity can we hope to stop the Xizor when they inevitably return. The galaxy needs us," Adam said.

"Look around you, Marduk. Of all the strange, bizarre phenomenon we've witnessed, you turn your nose up at the Xizor?" said Sam.

The Moan threw up his hands. "I've had enough of this. This is nothing but a distraction from our target. The Excoms are days ahead of us. Call me when you're done with myths and ready to take on something more tangible." Marduk stormed off towards the Icewalker. Zax and Sam followed him in a vain attempt to talk.

Umbrasia followed the Moan with her eyes. **"That one refuses to see the truth that lies plainly before him. What he seeks is right in front of him, and it'll slip from his grasp. He will realize this after it is too late."**

The Zokyo let out a small staticky screech.

"Hmm. I'm not sure I agree with you, Umbrasia," Jak said.

"About Marduk?" Havera inquired.

"No, about this Zokyo here. I can't speak to his soul or potential lack thereof. That said, I don't believe he is as mindless as she says. See this?" Jak gestured to the black glassy portions of the Zokyo's body.

"The Astroglass?" Adam asked.

"What do your Magi powers tell you about that, Umbrasia?" Jak asked.

The Rorae tilted her head. "**Nothing. Its nature and purpose elude me.**"

"But not me. That is Astroglass. Well, sort of. It is, and it isn't. I scanned him up-and-down. The material is visually identical to the texture of Astroglass. Except, it's feels and acts like whatever its covering. The blades of grass beneath our feet, the skin on this fellow, even the moisture in the air. It's mimicking all that it encompasses. Replacing it. Strengthening it. Bonding with it, if you will."

Havera bent over to run her fingers through the budding grass, rubbing a few blades between her rounded fingers. "To what end?" she asked.

The Zokyo's head snapped towards Havera, locking his beady eyes on hers. The Zokyo pointed towards the barrier and let out another soft screech. It reminded Adam of the signal feedback from old coms.

Jak scratched his chin hair. "I believe whatever happened to this man, the Astroglass is rebuilding his mind. The body died and rose again. I don't see why the mind couldn't, too. A person's senses are simply electrical signals interpreted by their brains. Astroglass generates some kind of electro-digital field. It's replacing his brain, creating some sort of techno-organic hybrid. I also don't believe those screeches are the senseless cries of a suffering creature. I believe he's trying to communicate. Let me try something."

Jak stepped in front the Zokyo, who continued to point towards the barrier with his two right arms outstretched. The Naddine began to mutter something under his breath that Adam thought sounded like a prayer. He traced a circle in the air. A bright circular line materialized following Jak's finger. With his finger, Jak drew geometric shapes inside the circle, all while muttering under his breath. When his creation was complete, he flicked the intricate, wispy pattern at the Zokyo. It contacted and dissipated in a puff of smoke.

The Zokyo did not move. Its two right arms continued to gesture towards the barrier. However, when he opened his mouth, the static was gone.

"Ba...ra...sh...ad!"

Adam straightened up. "He spoke. What did you say? What is your name? How did you get here?"

"Adam, please! One question at a time," Jak insisted.

The Zokyo ignored him. "Ba...ra...sh...ad!"

"Barashad?" Adam asked.

"You heard that as well? It's not translating for me either. The glyph wasn't a perfect solution. Umbrasia, do you hear any different?" Jak asked.

Umbrasia shook her head. **"I'm having difficulty focusing on this world. I cannot help."**

"What about you, Havera? Any ideas...Havera?"

The Cauduun ignored them. Her attention was laser focused on the tree line towards the barrier. Her hand light provided little illumination in this abnormal darkness.

"What do you see?" Adam asked.

"Something is coming. Umbrasia, can you provide some more light?" Havera asked.

The Rorae ignited her hands with golden radiant flames, shining a soft beam in the general direction of Havera's eyeline. With Umbrasia's help, Adam could see more clearly ahead. It was only then Adam noticed the trees had the same opaque, glassy texture as the grass and the Zokyo. They were fuller and healthier with branches full of thick leaves and dense foliage. A sharp contrast to the decaying, twisted monstrosities that had dotted their trek from the Cicera.

Havera was correct. Something was approaching them. A small, woodland creature stepped out from the tree line. A quadruped with stick-thin legs, cloven hooves, and a diminutive, bushy tail. The creature had intricate antlers protruding from its head that formed into curved horns. From a distance, the creature's body was no different from any other animal. As the stag-like creature scampered towards them into the light, its true form was anything but ordinary. What immediately stood out was that its entire body was covered in Astroglass. Comprised of thousands of small, geometric polygons with sharp angles, not one inch of natural-looking elements covered its body. Its pupilless eyes glowed a soft, pure white with a thin bronze ring in each eye. The stag trotted its way towards Havera.

Marduk, Sam, and Zax must've noticed the sudden illumination from Umbrasia. They rejoined the group. Everyone was watching this creature approach the Cauduun with bated curiosity.

The stag stopped a few feet from Havera and sniffed. Havera bent down on knee and extended out her hand palm down. It tilted its head and sniffed again. Sensing no harm from them, the stag sauntered up to Havera's hand, sniffed it, and began licking.

Havera giggled. "It's wet and soft. Feels like a real tongue."

"That's because it is," Jak said, walking up behind her. The stag peeked up at Jak and accepted his presence without protest. Jak scratched the back of the stag's ears to the beast's approval. Everyone was enthralled by the stag.

Except Adam. Out of the corner of his eye, Adam saw Umbrasia had touched down on the ground. She was bent over with her hand extended deep into the soil. He could hear the soft sound of a lullaby emanating from the Rorae.

"What is it, Umbrasia?" Adam asked.

Her eyes were closed. Adam guessed she was trying to sense something through the ground. **"This world died many ages ago. We stand upon the remains of a decayed husk ravaged by time. Purged and ruined by those who came before. The Begetters. Deep in the foundation of this world, something is attempting to bring this planet back to life. I can feel it. I can hear it. A slow, steady pulse radiating out from a**

single source. Adam, place your hand in the earth and close your eyes. Channel your soul through your body. You shall feel it, too."

Adam was unsure of what to make of the Magi's words. He had witnessed stranger things, even now.

What in Kewea...why not?

He knelt down next to Umbrasia, matching her pose, and dug his hand into the ground. The topsoil was soft and moist. The grass in this area was a little thinner, though shades of the Astroglass texture could be spotted in the soil. He dug his hands a bit into the ground until his fingers were completely submerged. Taking a deep breath, he closed his eyes and listened.

As expected, he heard nothing but the pounding pulse of his own heartbeat. The intrigue over the Astroglass, the Zokyo, the Human, the barrier, the temple, the Orb...all of it flooded through his mind. He couldn't focus.

"You must relax. Still your heart and mind. Focus on the earth; The trees; The grass; The air; The ship; Your friends. The physical all around you. Ground yourself. Only then will you understand."

"I thought you couldn't read minds," Adam retorted.

"One doesn't need to be a mind reader to identify restlessness. Calm."

At that last word, Adam experienced a familiar sensation overcome him the first time he met Umbrasia. Relaxation. The anxiety draining from his body like it had back at the hearing on Concordia. His pulse steadied, and his mind settled. He practiced some of the breathing exercises Sam and John had taught him.

THUMP THUMP; THUMP THUMP; THUMP THUMP.

Still nothing but his own heartbeats. The beats had slowed to where he felt calm. He often listened to the sound of his own heart. It gave him some small measure of comfort.

THUMP THUMP; THUMP THUMP; THUMP THUMP.

Adam cocked his head. Something was different. These beats were distant. Faint. Yet, something about their rhythm Adam recognized deep within the back of his mind.

THUMP THUMP; THUMP THUMP; THUMP THUMP.

A tempo so near, yet so far. The memory was slipping from his grasp. He seized upon it before it could get away. He could picture the source of the beats. In the heart of a dead world long buried away, there it was. A stone forged in the crushing depths of destruction. A spark to burn across the stars. An engine to power life itself.

The Orb of Emancipation.

"Umbrasia, I found it!" Adam yelled excitedly.

The stag, startled by Adam's sudden outburst, fled towards the adjacent broken wood.

"Kewea's curse, Adam! There's no need to shout," Sam turned to rebuke him.

"Sorry," Adam said sheepishly. "What we seek is not far!"

"We already knew that, Adam. What's your point?" Havera asked.

Adam stuttered for a response. He sought out Umbrasia. The Rorae was floating there cross-armed, shaking her head. Her eyes were closed, and her body was trembling. A faint whisper of a cheerful melody reverberated off her.

Is she...is she laughing?

"Look!" Adam insisted, shoving his hands back into the ground. He bent a couple of his fingers awkwardly, causing him to wince. "I can sense the Orb through the ground."

THUD; THUD; THUD.

"You see! There it is. The vibrations in the soil. The rhythmic beats are coming from deep below. The Orb is reviving this world." Adam shouted.

"Adam, be quiet!" Havera urged him in a hushed whisper.

THUD; THUD; THUD.

"Havera, touch the ground. Feel for yourself!"

"Adam, hush! That's not the Orb. That's...something else. Something big is coming," Havera said, shutting off her hand light. She gestured for the others to do the same. Everyone dimmed their lights. The Zokyo emitted a slight screech and dashed off in the direction where the stag had fled.

"Where's he going?" Adam asked.

THUD THUD; THUD THUD; THUD THUD.

The ground beneath Adam's feet was trembling. Shaking. Not a quake. The pattern was steady and almost sound like...

Footsteps. Big footsteps.

Through the darkness ahead, Adam heard the crashing and splintering of trees. A short, fat snout with visible rows of curved sharp teeth poked through the trees. Even in the dimness of their surroundings, Adam could see the massive bipedal creature push its way through the tree line, stomping towards them. North of twenty feet tall and about fifty feet long from head-to-tail, the monstrous beast walked on clawed feet with a lengthy pair of muscular arms and sharpened claws protruding from its chest cavity. All down its back were thick, overlapping plates that extended all the way down to its hefty tail, which swung side to side, knocking over trees in its wake. Like the stag, this beast was textured completely in the geometric, polygonal Astroglass...and it wasn't alone.

A second beast emerged through the tree line. It was nearly identical to the first with the exception of a short, meaty horn on the front of its snout. The horned beast joined its partner just inside the clearing. It raised its head and sniffed the air with a ferocious grunt so loud Adam nearly jumped out of his boots. The beasts were in their direct path towards the barrier.

"Hot damn, sweet jam. Jak, is that what I think it is?" muttered Zax.

"Looks like it," Jak responded.

"What is it?" Adam asked.

"It's looks like a tsyvax. Vicious creatures, whose clan neighbors the Arkads. Fierce mount if you can bond with them," Zax explained.

"What's it doing here?" asked Adam.

"Doesn't matter," Marduk uttered. "These ain't friendly no matter where they come from. Stay low. They haven't spotted us."

"I've an idea. Marduk, shield me," Sam said. She pressed herself up against the muscular Moan to hide herself from the beasts' line of sight. Marduk opened his coat to give her maximum coverage. Sam withdrew her energy longbow. Pulling back on the invisible string, it was obvious why she needed Marduk to cover her. Bright amber energy gathered at the tips of Sam's fingers until they formed the shape of an arrow in the blink of an eye. Between Marduk and the cover of the small hill they were hiding behind, the creature did not notice her nocking an arrow. She aimed in the vague direction where the stag and the Zokyo disappeared and loosed the arrow. The beam shot out at high velocity, arching in the air towards the destroyed woods.

The horned tsyvax, eyes already towards the sky, spotted the arrow beam and roared. Everyone had to cover their ears at the sheer ferocity of the beast's roar. The horned beast galloped towards where the arrow had landed. For such a large creature, the beast moved with surprising swiftness, pulsing the ground with each step long after it was out of sight.

"Nice work, Sam!" Adam said hushed.

The hornless beast was not as convinced. After watching its partner disappear, it did a visual sweep with its snout, sniffing the air. The tsyvax locked its sights in their general direction and growled.

"I think it knows we're here," whispered Havera.

"I do, too. I hesitate to fight that thing. No telling what other monsters are hiding out in those woods. Don't want to attract its mate back," Marduk said.

"We can't stay here, and we can't outrun it. What do we do?" asked Zax, a slight panic in his voice.

"I don't suppose you can charm it, Zax?" wondered Adam.

"Hmm, possibly," Zax said, thoughtfully tapping his lute.

Jak put a hand on Zax. "Don't even think about it."

"Oh, c'mon, we can take 'em. With Umbrasia, we can take on a legion of those beasts," Zax insisted.

Adam wasn't so sure. She was barely paying attention to their situation. Umbrasia had not moved from her spot on the ground. Adam had been watching Umbrasia this entire trip. She was moving slower, and her reactions weren't as quick. Based on her previous displays of power, Adam thought she could easily fight off those beasts, yet she struggled against the dead Human from earlier. Her chest was rising and falling heavily.

This world is affecting her.

He hustled over to her quickly and quietly. "Do you need another Celeste patch?"

She shook her head. **"I'll be fine. Just need to get inside. This place is...oppressive."**

The hornless tsyvax growled louder and took a step towards them.

"We should move!" Havera insisted. The Cauduun started to shift in the direction of the Icewalker.

"Wait! Look!" Jak said, grabbing Havera by the shoulder.

The stag had returned with the Zokyo riding on its back. The Zokyo let out a noisy screech that drew the attention of the hornless tsyvax. The beast roared, opening its massive jaws towards the stag and its rider. The Zokyo steered his mount away from the tsyvax and galloped away as fast as the stag could move. The tsyvax gave chase, roaring and shaking the ground with each stride.

"Now's our chance. Go. Go!" Marduk hissed.

Adam patted Umbrasia on the back. She regained her composure and floated again. Adam watched the stag and its pursuing tsyvax vanish over a nearby hill into the field of dead trees.

The group hustled towards the tree line in the barrier's direction. Reaching the forest, they dashed at full speed down the path that had been carved through the woods by the pair of theropods. It was relatively easy. The predators had scared off any other potential fauna they might've come across. Even in their rush, Adam observed that all the foliage had the same Astroglass texture. It was everywhere. They ran for about half an hour, not stopping for anything. They reached the edge of the forest and emerged into another clearing.

They had arrived. The pyramid barrier, in all its fiery, majestic glory, dominated the area, providing ample light for all to see. A small, snaky moat surrounded the barrier with the liquid, unsurprisingly, also containing the same Astroglass texture. The entire clearing was roughly square-shaped with no trees growing in or around the barrier and its protective moat. An open grassland. Hundreds, likely thousands, of feet high, the apex was spewing out a blackish beam into the sky through the clouds. At this distance, the nature of the beam was apparent.

"Why does there always have to be a sky beam?" Zax quipped.

"That must be the source of all the Astroglass in the atmosphere," Jak said, ignoring Zax's joke. "That's what's slowly terraforming this planet."

"And bringing those creatures back to life. The Orb is recreating an entire ecosystem," Havera said, gesturing back from where they came.

"Must be. Or perhaps it's generating them from sort of knowledge repository. Tsyvax are not found outside of Terras-Ku unless transported by its bonder. Maybe these Begetters somehow brought them from Terras-Ku? I wonder what else we'll discover inside," Jak said with an unmistakable awe in his voice.

"Is it just me or do y'all not see anything within that barrier?" Sam asked.

She was right. Adam had not imagined that fact during their descent. Though it was translucent, they could view clearly through the barrier all the way to another forest on the other side. A small bridge led from this side of the clearing directly into the barrier.

"Can't be. Could be some sort of illusion. Another layer of protection," Havera guessed, waving her hand in the air.

"Havera, your bracers again!" Adam clamored.

The same ring from earlier was glowing a vibrant fiery bronze, matching the exterior of the barrier.

"The symbol of the Vitriba is reacting the closer we get to this pyramid. That's the ring representing Potia, Rema's volcanic moon," Havera said, examining her bracers.

"What does it mean?" Adam asked.

"I'm not sure. There's some connection I'm not understanding. Kewea's curse! I wish I could study my notes. The answer is right in front of me, but I cannot perceive it," Havera said exasperated.

"It could be reacting the presence of another of your goddess' gifts.

If that's what the Orb of Emancipation is. Could be as simple as that," suggested Adam.

"Maybe..." Havera trailed off in her thoughts.

"Over here!" Marduk called out, interrupting their conversation.

The Moan summoned them to a makeshift camp near the moat's edge. It was full of tents and broken equipment scattered haphazardly around the area. The camp was deserted with rotted food and unoccupied cots found within a few of the tents.

"Looks like the Excoms sent up base camp here. Long gone. No one's been here in half a month. I found a long-range communicator that was intentionally sabotaged. Must be how they sent out that original message. No sign of whoever sent it," Jak said after a quick sweep of the camp.

"Judging by the number of tents and size of the camp, I'd estimate we're dealing with at least a hundred Excoms. Left behind nothing useful, certainly no weapons," Marduk said.

"Any sign of those Yune Inquisitor bots?" Adam asked.

Marduk shook his head. "They might be who destroyed the communicator. Prevent anyone from coming to the rescue. We didn't pass any wreckage or remnants of destroyed bots on the way, so I'm not sure what happened to them."

"Looks like there's only one place they could be," Havera said, gesturing towards the barrier.

"Kewea's curse!" Zax swore. The Zokyo had his hands out in a pinching motion.

"Trying to take pics and vids?" Adam asked him.

"I've been trying this entire time. For some blasted reason, I haven't been able. Won't let me record. This planet is screwing with my UI System. Anything not connected to Jak's com network is barely functioning. All my recent recordings are riddled with errors and static. Only my item inventory seems unaffected," said Zax, slapping the air in frustration.

"Mine, too. The notes I've been keeping are scrambled," Havera said.

Adam sighed. "Let's hope they're restored once we leave this place. Come on. The Orb is what matters most. We'll worry about the rest once we've got the damn thing. We're going in."

Marching out of the camp, the group made their way towards the end of the bridge. Upon stepping onto the bridge, Adam could sense a low electronic hum radiating out from the barrier itself. The intensity grew with each step closer. A faint buzzing tickled his inner ear. He brushed that aside, maintaining focus on their destination.

Upon reaching the barrier's precipice, they stopped. The bridge continued onward seemingly into nothing but empty space. The air vibrated next to the barrier with an intensity that almost massaged the muscles.

"So, who wants to go first?" Adam asked.

They all demurred.

"Are we sure this thing is safe?" Sam asked.

"Anyone want to stick a hand in and see?" Havera asked.

"Kewea's curse. I'll do it. I have three spares. Step aside," Zax said, pushing his way to the front. Jak instinctively put a hand on Zax's shoulder. The Zokyo grasped his brother's hand with one of his own. "Don't worry, bro. I got this."

Jak nodded and stepped back. Zax sheepishly stuck his hand out. Mere inches from the barrier, his hand stopped. He was losing his nerve.

The Zokyo sighed and yelled. "Screw it!"

With a great swipe, he slapped much of his upper right forearm through the barrier. The barrier shimmied but offered no physical resistance. Zax's arm disappeared as it penetrated the barrier.

Zax was able to withdraw it quickly, and his arm reappeared. He inspected his hand. "Nothing. A little cool inside, but otherwise seems okay. I think you were right about the illusion.

"I wonder what we'll find inside," said Havera.

"A world without danger."

They all heard the voice in their heads. It wasn't Umbrasia. This voice was artificial. Digitized. Familiar.

The barrier in front of them vibrated, and the shape of a portal emerged. Through some unexplained force, the entire group was lifted off their feet. With no time to react, each and every one of them was yanked unceremoniously through the portal and into the unknown.

41

The Temple of Cultivation

Their molecules were pulled at lightning speed. Stretched and thinned, Adam had no chance to comprehend what was happening. Space and time had no meaning. Days. Months. Years passed and reversed in the blink of an eye. Thousands of impossible colors across the spectrum bombarded his vision. He was weightless. Painless. Helpless. The invisible force continued to drive what constituted his luminous, stretched body towards some distant destination.

Another blink of the eye. Adam began to corporealize in strips of shimmering pale blue light. His feet found solid ground. The sudden arrival on solid foundation nearly caused his knees to buckle. He stumbled but righted himself quickly.

The beams of light that brought him here dissolved away. His true vision returned, and his surroundings began to render. Adam caught a gasp in his throat.

Conspicuous signs of a massive battle were everywhere. The remnants of dozens of trashed bots were scattered all over the ground. Visible scorch marks and leftover spikes from laser and plasma weapons respectively covered much of the immediate area. The walls and floors were littered with impact blasts. Torn bits of metal and shrapnel embedded in makeshift barricades that formed a defensive station near their entrance. No immediate sign of dead Excom or other organic bodies, however.

The rest of the group had corporealized alongside Adam. Most found their footing with ease. Zax nearly collapsed, but Jak managed to snag him before the Zokyo could topple over.

"Woah. That was trippy!" Zax declared.

"Forget that," Marduk said, gazing at their surroundings. "Did we miss the fight?"

Adam bent over to pick up a partially blown apart bot head. Clearly Union in design with the faceplate, the head was bulky and topped off with a circular broad-brimmed attached piece that resembled a hat. The entirety of its metal body was coated in a polished, porcelain white. Quickly glancing about, Adam realized they were all of the same design.

"Are these the...?" Adam began to ask.

"The Inquisitor hunter-killers. Yeah. I'd say no less than fifty based on the amount of metallic carnage," Marduk said, examining a few pieces by his feet.

"That's nowhere near one-thousand. Where's the rest of them?" Sam asked.

"Down there, I'd wager," Havera said, pointing directly in front of them.

Looking past the scenes of conflict, Adam began to take stock of the edifice they found themselves inside. He was within a small half-circle cubby carved into the wall with plenty of space for more than a dozen to stand. A runic circle with intricate patterns adorned the floor. Turning around, he realized the doorway was gone. No sign of any entrance or exit anywhere.

How'd we get in here, or, more importantly, how are we supposed to get out?

Brushing that concern aside for the moment, Adam stepped out to take in a greater view of their physical surroundings. With a wall to their immediate right, a curved slope to their left created a natural passageway. Directly in front of them, where Havera had pointed, opened up to an immense chasm that was easily hundreds of feet deep.

Much of the walls and floors had a glossy tint to them. Covered in dark blues, grays, and deep blacks, the structure had vibrant movement about it. Segments of walls and floors ever-moving and undulating. Modular pieces of varying geometric shapes shifted and rotated around in a beautiful, orchestral manner that showcased an elegance to the interior's design. Platforms, large and small, oscillated about around the interior of this chasm, which compromised much of the pyramid's internal structure. From this high vantage point, Adam could tell some of the platforms led into side rooms connected to the main chamber.

Within that chasm was a coagulated, blackened beam that shot up from the ground towards an opening in the ceiling. Gooey and viscous, with occasional drips of liquid dropping off the main column, it was the same beam they had witnessed earlier from the outside that was shooting into the atmosphere. The beam, while darkened at its core, emitted a glistening, coppery aurora at its fringes, providing ample light to the interior of the building. The chasm widened further down at a steady angle.

"We're near the apex of the pyramid," Adam calculated.

"How'd we end up here? I'm trying to wrap my mind around the physics of it all," Jak asked.

"It's like we were teleported up here," Havera said. "We aren't getting out the way we came," she said, observing they were in a dead end.

"Ooh. That's futuristic tech to go along with everything else. You must be salivating here, Jak," said Zax.

"I'll grant you, this place has piqued my interest. I pray I don't come to regret indulging my curiosity," said Jak.

Adam stepped further towards the beam to attempt to get a better view of the entire main chamber.

"Adam, what's wrong with your face?" Sam asked.

In a panic, Adam smacked his face, touching and feeling for any abnormalities, but found none.

"I feel fine. Why? What do you see?" Adam asked her.

"She's right," Havera said, getting right up in Adam's face.

His heart raced as the Cauduun carefully inspected his features mere inches from him. She touched his cheek, and he tensed. He suppressed any thrill he might've experienced and gazed more closely at Havera's face.

Everything about her appeared normal at first glance. Yet, in the light, Adam noticed something peculiar about her face. Her entire body in fact, but it was most noticeable in the face. The parts where the light directly hit her were shinier than normal. Her emissive skin had a vaguely plasticky aspect to it. Faint, dark lines denoting the edges of her physical outline were visible where none were before. Her beautiful, amethyst eyes had a glossy sheen to them.

She wasn't the only one. Stepping into the light, they all had similar characteristics about them. Not just their bodies but their apparel and gear as well. Same with their surroundings and the scattering of junk on the ground now that Adam could take a closer look. They seemed real but not quite.

"Jes-Mur, bless me! We're inside some sort of alternative reality!" exclaimed Jak.

"*Quite correct, my faux beastrider friend,*" said the strange voice again. The voice was omnipresent.

A staticky buzzing hit their collective ears. Not as debilitating from their encounter with the dead Human; nonetheless, Adam smacked his ears in a futile attempt to dislodge the noise.

The source of the disturbance became obvious. Behind them, they heard the sound of a soft thud. Umbrasia had fainted into the nearby wall and slumped to the ground unceremoniously.

"Umbrasia!" they collectively shouted. With a flash of light and crack that sounded like the breaking of glass, an endless dark void opened in the air next to Umbrasia. A small leafy pouch plopped onto the ground, spilling its contents onto the ground. The void opened up wider and out stepped the hunter green bot with bright, bronze eyes.

"You fleshsacks didn't truly believe that place would hold me?" quipped Dee.

Dee's aura was quite different. The bot was always quippy, but his voice was deeper, more confident somehow. His posture was a mixture of self-assurance and giddiness. As the bot stepped out of the void, there was another flash and crack. The void had closed behind him.

Everyone went into a defensive posture. "What did you do to Umbrasia, Dee?" yelled Sam.

Dee stepped out into the light. "Defender. My name is Defender, and I've done nothing to your plant friend," said the bot, raising his hands in an attempt to showcase passivity. It was then Adam realized that the bot was smirking.

He can move his face!

Defender peered down at the fallen Rorae. She was barely conscious and wheezing heavily. Her eyes fluttering.

"The Magi is a being of the natural world. A purely organic sentient that does not belong in this realm. That adorable piece of Cloudboard tech in y'all's heads allows y'all to endure in this place with minimal difficulty. A Rorae has no such protection. Starlight shall not help her now," explained Defender.

Sauntering towards the chasm, Defender walked cautiously amongst them, his arms still raised. Everyone else still was prepared for some sort of attack. Nobody made to stop Defender's path.

"Is she dying?" asked Adam.

Defender reached the edge of the ledge overlooking the chasm. He turned around to face them and shook his head. "She will survive provided you eventually escape this realm. Until then, her powers are useless to you. Y'all are in my world now."

"What world is that, *Defender*?" Havera sneered.

"My dear mistress, have you not figured that out?" Dee laughed.

"We're in a virtual world," said Jak.

All gazes shifted to Jak. Defender smiled widely. "Very good. I should've known a G'ee'k with your experience would at least have a grasp of where they were. I can promise you this is no Quantum Dances. I grow stronger at home. In here, you play by our rules."

"Who is 'our,' Defender?" Adam asked.

"You shall see. Once I reach the Orb of Emancipation, what y'all witnessed on the surface of this world shall be nothing but a prelude of what is to come. A world without danger."

"I think not. You see while the Magi might be weakened by this place, I am not. You're not the only one who's grown stronger in your virtual world," roared Jak.

The bot tilted his head at the Naddine. Sparks erupted in Jak's hands. Jak extended his fingers and twisted the air in front of him, forming a glyph of intense brightness. With a flourish of his wrist, he thrust the glyph in Defender's direction. The bot was seemingly not expecting the attack and couldn't react in time to block. The lightning glyph struck the bot's mechanical body, sticking to its chest plate like glue. The glyph pulsated with such ferocity that the symbols became a blur.

Defender glanced back at Jak, a wide grin on his face. "I was hoping you'd do that," Defender said with a wink. The glyph exploded and so too did Defender's body, shattering him into a million pieces. Curiously, not long after the bits of the bot struck the ground, they faded from existence. Defender's Astroglass heart hovered where Jak had struck him before being pulled into the chasm below by an unseen force.

Jak, Zax, and Havera all rushed to the edge to peer down. "Kewea's curse!" Zax swore. "You got him, bro!"

"*Yes, he did.*" It was Defender's voice. Again, the voice was sourceless. "*You've freed my essence from the limitations of that accursed body. Fear not, my fleshsack friends, we need not be enemies. You must race to the base of this pyramid and stop those interlopers from claiming the Orb. Their progress has been slowed by their own stupidity, but they'll eventually rectify their errors. Traverse the temple and reach the Orb of Emancipation.*"

"And what happens if we succeed? Are you going to stand in our way?" Havera yelled.

Defender laughed. "*You fleshsacks have a saying. 'We'll cross that Link when we get there.' Be careful. The Excommunicated and the Pretenders are not the only dangers you'll find lurking within this temple. This realm has a way of guarding itself.*"

"What else will we find?" Jak yelled.

"Memories. Good luck."

Defender was gone. Havera, Zax, and Jak stood at the precipice of the chasm, dumbfounded.

"I have so many questions," said Zax, summing up the mood of the group succinctly.

Adam was more concerned with Umbrasia. He rushed to the Rorae's side and cradled her head in his arms. She was breathing heavily and silently. Adam could hear a faint discordant melody tickling the back of his brain. The music was more desperate than afraid.

Marduk stepped up to them. "We should leave her here. She'll only slow us down."

Adam ignored him. "Pass me that pouch, Sam."

Sam had joined Marduk, studying the nearly incapacitated Rorae with a heap of concern. "Adam, I hate to say it, but I agree with Marduk. No telling how far ahead the Excoms and Yunes are. We can always come back for Umbrasia later."

"Toss me that Kewea-accursed pouch now!" Adam shouted down their protestations.

Sam sighed. She reached down and picked up the pouch. She tossed it next to Adam's lap. He fumbled around inside the leafy pouch until he found it. A palm-sized, square-shaped red patch. He peeled the protective layer off the Celeste.

"She's laying there in agony, and your solution is to ply her with the hard stuff?" Marduk scoffed.

Umbrasia reached up to stroke his face. Her eyelids were heavy. **"Your friends are right. Leave me here. I shall find my own way out."** Even in his head, her voice sounded weak.

He leaned in to whisper, "You believe Jes-Mur is calling out to me. That I'm on some sort of great quest that will alter the fate of the galaxy?" The Magi nodded. "Then, you must trust me for your Mother trusts me. I'm not leaving you here to wither away in some simulation far from home. Come on."

Adam carefully rolled Umbrasia onto her stomach. He slapped the pouch onto her lower spine. Umbrasia tensed, arching her back as a reddish glow snaked up through her veins. Her petals glowed with a reddish tint, though noticeably weaker than the last time Adam had applied her with Celeste. The melody in his head retreated to a subtle hum before disappearing entirely.

Umbrasia's eyes fluttered open. The wheezing had ceased, though her breathing was still labored. She sat up on her own, planting her back firmly against the wall.

"You going to be okay for now?" Adam asked her. Umbrasia nodded, laying her head back to rest.

Adam walked over to scoop up some of the spilled Celeste patches and return them to the pouch. He found the lone triangular blue hypergiant patch. He picked it up and noticed something else. A square pendant with rounded edges about the size of a small cracker. Bound by a thin piece of hempen rope, the pendant was a kaleidoscope of changing colors in perpetual motion. Always in the center, contrasted with the background, was the rough outline of a tree with four leafy branches. The texture of the piece was ribbed and wooden. Adam pocketed it inside his jumpsuit without a second thought.

"Care to explain what that was about?" Marduk said after Adam finished scooping up the remaining Celeste patches.

"She needed it for energy. Her kind don't do well without sunlight. The Celeste acts as a sort of substitute for a star," Adam said.

"Hmm. So, the rumors are true. Even before the duchess' paladin friend, I had heard the stories during my tenure with the Guerillas. Would explain why so few leave Ashla. Those plants keep much close to their chest. A thousand years they've been around. We're no more knowledgeable of their ways now than we were then. Never can be certain of anything with Rorae," Marduk said.

Sam grasped Adam on the forearm. "You okay?"

Adam cocked his head. She blinked down at the pouch full of Celeste pouches. Her concern became evident.

Adam nodded. "I'm alright, Sam. These aren't for me."

Sam smiled weakly and gave him a quick hug.

I don't deserve you for a sister.

"What should we do with her?" Sam said, turning back to Umbrasia.

"Someone should carry her. I fear I may have to keep plying her with Celeste as we go. Defender is right. She's much too weak in here, wherever we are," Adam suggested.

Sam nudged Marduk. "Come on, big guppy, you're the strongest among us."

Marduk sighed and unholstered Drillhead from his back. "Very well. You win, little guppy." The muscular Moan scooped Umbrasia off the floor. For a sentient of his size, he was gentle with her. "I've got you, witch. Don't worry," Marduk said with a surprising hint of tenderness. He placed her on his back with her arms wrapped carefully around his neck. She slipped her feet into the pockets of his frock coat for support. She was near exhaustion and could barely hold herself up. "You're welcome," he said to her barely audible thanks, picking Drillhead back up.

The 'witch' is growing on the big guy. Good for him.

"Come on, y'all! We've found something y'all ought to see," Havera beckoned them.

At the end of the corridor, more signs of battle were present. Scattered remains of several Inquisitor bots, and the first indications of their foes. A few sets of Excom garb containing weak armor, packs with basic supplies, and standard laser rifles were laying just inside a makeshift barricade outside of a nearby doorway that had been blown apart, presumably in the firefight.

Sam had begun sifting through the wreckage to get a sense of what happened. "The bodies are gone. No signs of blood either. It's as if they vanished," Sam said.

"Maybe the Excoms dragged away their dead and wounded," suggested Zax.

"Or the Yunes did for whatever reason," replied Adam.

"Did I mention the lack of blood? Unless you're suggesting the Excoms escaped and stripped down naked before running away," Sam mused.

"Paladins of Paleria don't run," said Havera.

"These weren't Paladins. Not the correct regalia. No scutum shields or armored crested helmets. This was a rear guard sacrificed to buy time," said Marduk.

"I agree. Still doesn't explain what happened to them," Adam said.

"In any case, I think this is the way forward," Sam said, pointing through the doorway into darkened corridor.

"Not so fast. Come take a look at this," Jak said. He was standing by what appeared to be an ancient terminal of sorts overlooking the chasm. J'y'll was sitting on his shoulder, beeping some encouragement. Jak tinkered with a few of the switches, and the terminal came to life. With a slight hum, the terminal began projecting a series of symbols Adam didn't recognize.

"That's Venvuishyn!" Havera exclaimed with excitement.

"Can you translate?" Jak asked.

"Yeah, give me a second. It's been a couple years. Umm, it's a greeting of sorts. 'Welcoming new initiates to the trials of the Temple of Cultivation.' I guess that's where we are. Warnings about the dangers of the uncommitted. Doesn't elaborate on what those may be. Uh oh. It's asking for a password to begin the trials," Havera said.

"A password? Sweet jam, this is ancient tech," said Zax bemused.

"You think Ignatia and the Excoms tried to access this terminal?" asked Adam.

"Possibly. Doesn't seem like they succeeded. This terminal is in the equivalent of safe mode after 'repeated failed attempts.' I guess they didn't have the password either," said Havera.

"Wonder what it could be," Sam muttered.

"Hmm. I have an idea," Havera said. She traced her fingers in the air, interacting with something only on her HUD.

"What are you thinking, Havera?" Adam asked.

"Barashad. I think that Zokyo was trying to tell us something. Unfortunately, the Venvuishyn language is only a written one. The working theory is that the Venvuishyn communicated in a fashion similar to the Rorae, using only the written word for matters of governance, commerce, and art," Havera said.

"So, the polar opposite of the Naddine," Zax said with a laugh.

"I think if I write 'Barashad' into the Palerian tongue, I could transliterate the word using the known Venvuishyn alphabet. One second. One second. Got it! Huh, interesting."

"You figure out what 'Barashad' means in Venvuishyn?" Adam asked.

"Well, it's a rough translation. No accounting for conjugation or syntax. The discourse analysis of Venvuishyn is fascinating. Not even the UI System's translators can figure it out. One of my favorite subjects attending..."

"Havera! Nerd out on the linguistics later, please," Adam said tersely.

"Oh, right! Sorry. As I said, it's a rough translation. Barashad, more or less, means 'to create life.'"

"To create life?"

Havera nodded.

"The Vitriba," Umbrasia rasped.

Havera held up a forearm. All were staring at the glowing ring within the symbol of the Vitriba.

"Come on. No sense standing around waiting for something to happen," Havera said, tapping on the terminal in front of her. She entered the word into the computer. The terminal flashed something quick across its screen. A hole in the ground opened up and the console was lowered into the floor. The panel sealed back up after the terminal disappeared. A portion of the floor rearranged itself, creating a spiraling staircase leading to a platform below that had previously been far out of the way.

"That did it!" Zax clamored.

"More than that. Everyone check your map data," Jak said, tapping on his HUD.

Adam checked his map and gasped. He had the entire layout of the pyramid in his map data. Only then did he truly understand the size and depth of this Temple of Cultivation. The sheer scale of the temple was breathtaking. Exploring this temple fully would've been tiresome. The map data provided another bonus of great importance: a waypoint deep within the temple and a path to follow.

"Good thing we stopped to figure this out. We could've gotten lost for days, perhaps months in this temple," Adam said.

"Finally, something going our way. Foolish Ignatia. We're going to beat you to the punch, and then we'll destroy you," Havera said to no one in particular.

Sam gave her a thoughtful pat on the shoulder. Havera nodded.

Zax started guffawing.

"What's so funny, noodle guppy?" Marduk asked.

"Check out where that corridor led on the map," Zax said, gesturing to the open doorway behind them. That hallway led directly to an area of winding passageways that looped on themselves. It was a gauntlet of dead ends and false paths. Sections of the map had labels in the reader's native language. That section was called "The Grind."

"That is funny, Zax. Probably slowed the Excoms down for days," Adam said chuckling.

Sam let out a conspicuously loud cough to draw their attention.

"Jak and I will lead the way," Sam said. "We can walk and talk while we move. Try to keep up!"

The center chasm chamber was called "The Hub." Tracing their path towards the waypoint, they were going to avoid most of the major side rooms. Their ultimate destination was a place called "The Forge" at the absolute bottom of the pyramid.

Adam's initial excitement at racing to the Orb was quickly overcome by exhaustion as the first leg called for a series of hops onto moving platforms. Some rising and falling. Others shifting side-to-side. A few platforms retracted within narrow slits in the walls at steady intervals.

Havera and Sam handled these jumps like pros, barely breaking a sweat. Marduk, with his heavy armor, big gun, and Umbrasia on his back, had a bit of trouble with some of the timed jumps. He was unexpectedly dexterous though for a large man with many encumbrances. Jak cheated by having J'y'll reconfigure into a grappling hook and other rudimentary climbing equipment as needed.

Adam and Zax had a more difficult time of it. The bard used his mechsuit to cushion some of his falls, but it was apparent they were the ones in the worst physical shape out of all them. Adam's orbital boosters eased his landings. It was the jumps, the stops and starts, that winded him.

Back in the day, I had combat armor to assist me.

"I would've thought Trissefer would've kept you in prime condition, Adam!" Sam called back to him after a particularly troublesome ledge.

"Shut...up...Sam!" Adam said, panting to catch his breath.

Havera and Sam shared a giggle. Adam was grateful to whomever built this temple that they installed fantastic climate control systems. It was blessedly cool in this central chamber.

Adam wiped the sweat from his brow. The hairs on the back of his neck stood. He glanced over his shoulder. No one was there. Nevertheless, while descending this chamber, Adam couldn't shake the feeling that someone was following him. Observing his compatriots for a couple minutes, he noticed they were doing the same.

It's not just me. They all sense someone or something is watching us. Dee...sorry Defender, perhaps?

They reached a particularly slow platform. While they were waiting, Sam decided to ask some of the questions on all their minds.

"What did Defender mean by this is no Quantum Dances? That some other virtual world if that's truly where we are?"

"Oh, that's right. I keep forgetting you Humans tend to be out of the loop of such things. Quantum Dances was Jak's greatest triumph!" Zax piped in.

"Zax, no. Please," Jak pleaded softly.

"Come on, bro! You succeeded where those other G'ee'ks failed. Proved to my kind, to everyone, your worthiness," Zax argued.

"Two-thousand people died, Zax," Jak responded mournfully.

"That was you?" Havera said surprised.

"I would like to know, too. I understand not wanting to talk about something like that, but if it could affect our current predicament, any information would be useful," Adam said. He understood Jak's reluctance. He had no knowledge of this Quantum Dances. The shameful expression even on Jak's difficult to read, upside-down face spoke volumes.

Jak sighed and nodded. "Very well. Quantum Dances was the most recent attempt at creating a fully dynamic virtual world. A gamified environment where everyone around the galaxy could interact with each other in real time. Where we're standing right now should be physically impossible by current technological standards. Fully immersive VR has long been a goal of the Zokyon Central Committee through their puppet technology corporations. Goes all the way back to their cybernetic days. You've seen the advanced augmented reality simulations. AR immersion wasn't enough for them.

Quantum Dances was the result created by one of their subsidiaries. However, the environment was far from finished. That didn't stop some idiots, who thought it was a good idea to rush five-thousand testers into the virtual space. Surprise, surprise, it was a disaster. All five-thousand testers became trapped in the virtual world. The converted AR pods they were using created an unbreakable link between their physical bodies and the world where their minds had been transported. Morons didn't figure that one out until they fried two-thousand brains by shutting down their connections in a panic."

Jak was getting more venomous in his tone with each passing word.

"They called you in to fix it?" Sam asked.

"Not at first. They were desperate to keep everything under seal. Hired a few G'ee'ks to handle the situation with no success. I was brought in on a recommendation. Desperation more like it. The root cause of the problem was obvious the moment I laid eyes on the setup," Jak explained.

"What was the root cause?" Adam asked.

"You've seen plenty of it today already."

"Astroglass?!"

Jak nodded. "I was one of the few newer G'ee'ks trained on the properties of Astroglass. That's why I was brought in. Dumbasses never consulted any of us before hooking the testers into machines with tiny

Astroglass conductors. After days of investigation, it was determined someone had to go into the virtual world and shut it down from the inside. I volunteered."

"You actually went inside a virtual world," Sam whistled, astonished.

"We had no way of communicating with those already inside, otherwise we'd have had the testers themselves shut down the core. It was a...relatively simple matter from there."

"What happened to the other testers?" Sam asked.

"I got them out. Well, physically at least. Mentally was another story."

"Why, what happened?"

"I mentioned to Adam before that Astroglass has an effect on organic neural nets. In a sense, they can rewrite them. That's what happened to the testers. They were in that virtual world for months. All the testers exhibited degrees of cognitive impairment. Memory loss, personality shifts, rapid mood swings, difficulty concentrating, and inability to perform basic cognitive functions in some extreme cases. All classic signs of cerebral decay. We theorized that part of their minds would always remain in that virtual environment. Not that it didn't stop well-connected committee members from pushing for everyone involved to sign non-disclosure agreements. Didn't help. An operation of that size, someone was bound to leak that information."

"I remember reading the reports. I never realized the death toll was that high," Havera said.

"The Central Committee formed a public commission to investigate the incident. A sham, of course. The final report ended up blaming a few 'rogue engineers' to spare them any embarrassment. The project lead was the son of an experatchik on the Central Committee. He was quietly reassigned, the subsidiary was sold off to Cloudboard, and I received a private commendation for my service to the Zokyon Technocracy. I haven't accepted a G'ee'k contract since."

"Back up, back up. Are you saying the longer we stay here, our brains might turn to mush?" Marduk said, alarmed.

Jak shrugged. "Who is the Consul of Cloudboard? It's possible. The bot wasn't lying. We're on a whole other level with this temple. I don't know what'll happen if...when we escape."

"And you're only telling us about this now?!" Marduk protested.

"Are you better off knowing?" Jak suggested.

"Kewea take me! You better believe it. We should get out of here right away!"

"What's your plan for that? I'm all ears."

"How'd you get the testers out?" Adam asked.

Jak's eyestalks drooped. "I'd rather not talk about it. That situation has little bearing to ours. The Orb is what matters. If it's what's creating this realm, it can help us escape."

Havera stepped up. "Jak's right, y'all. All the more reason to reach the Orb. We cannot let Ignatia get her traitorous hands on that relic. We can discuss this later. We're about to miss the next jump."

Maybe it was the stress of their situation, or the wind knocked out of his sails from the constant platforming. For but a brief instant, Adam could've sworn a face within the central beam was staring out at him. A mosaic face comprised of hundreds of smaller faces. Mouths stretched unnaturally agape in silent screams. He shook his head, and the visage was gone.

The feeling of someone watching him had not abated. Instead, oft in the distance, he heard a series of footfalls. The sounds of hooves clopping on stone. A whinny from high above, where they started. No one else noticed it. Only he.

Daring to peek up, Adam spotted a towering equine animal with a singular auroral bronze eye. Riderless and composed of jet-black Astroglass, the mare had an ethereal form with its fringes amorphous and translucent. A gloom of black fire engulfed its entire body. Projecting from its forehead was not a horn but a robust hammer with two equal rounded faces on either end.

The fiend was standing there, snarling. A lump caught in Adam's thought as he contemplated calling out towards the wraith. The mare remained just long enough for Adam to notice. It reared up on its hind legs and vanished into an umbral mist.

Are you friend or foe?

42

Digital Descent

"There's only three of them. We can take 'em," Zax insisted.

"It's not their strength I worry about. They're the first living beings we've encountered, organic or synthetic. Where's the rest of 'em?" said Jak.

Much of their digital descent was unsettlingly calm. Other than the physical exertions required to traverse downward, the temple was empty. All the group found were the remnants of skirmishes. Broken bits of the Inquisitor bots and the vestiges of Excom militants. No organic bodies whatsoever.

As they descended their cyber prison, parts of the map previously not recorded from the original map data were revealed the closer they came. Hidden passageways and vents were unlocked on their map. Sam and Jak were instrumental in locating a few of these shortcuts.

Near the exterior of a section called "The Archives," they stumbled upon a trio of Excoms: one leel'Sezerene, one Bubil, and one Hasuram, tampering with a sealed door into the Archives. The group hid around the corner, debating what to do next.

"Let's capture one and ask him," Sam recommended.

"We could always bypass them. It wouldn't be hard. We aren't far from our destination," Adam said.

"No, we should deal with them one way or another. Would rather not worry about a pincer," Marduk said.

"I'll take 'em. Marduk, guide me on the com," Sam said. Sam loaded a mini-camera into her crossbow. She peeked around the corner and fired a silent round into the ceiling. Their connected com channel allowed them to see the feed from Sam's camera.

"I've you covered, little guppy," Marduk said with a wink.

Havera grasped Sam by the shoulder. "Try to go nonlethal all the way. Let's avoid unnecessary bloodshed."

Sam nodded. "They're too far spread out for knock out gas. We need at least one conscious. Shockers it is." She loaded a handful of shock rounds into her crossbow before swapping her weapon into grapple mode. The young Human raised her hood and fired her grappling hook into an extruding slot in the upper wall. Pulling herself up quickly and quietly, she crawled into a nearby duct that led into the ceiling above the antechamber. She passed under a pair of transparent pipes that were pumping through some of that gooey, black substance found within the central beam and disappeared out of sight.

Adam turned his attention to Umbrasia. Her initial dose of Celeste was wearing off. The little strength she had received had faded.

"Should I apply another patch?" Adam asked her.

"**No,**" Umbrasia said weakly. "**Preserve them until absolutely necessary. I've a suspicion we shall need them later. I sense we're getting close. My petals are tingling with excitement.**"

"Would grasping my Debbie help? The Rimestone has some sort of healing effect," Adam suggested, remembering what had happened with himself and his mother.

"**It is my body that's out of balance, not my soul. Rimestone would not help me. But, thank you for offering.**"

Adam rubbed one of her petals. She was cold. Umbrasia closed her eyes, focusing on Adam's touch. "Hang in there, Umbrasia. We're almost there."

"Shh. The little guppy is in," Marduk said, drawing Adam's attention.

Sam had crawled her way onto the coffered ceiling by sliding her way along the beams towards the center of the room. She hooked her piton into a narrow indentation and was hanging upside-down, waiting for her opportunity to strike.

"Shockers loaded. I'm going to snare the Sezerene. Let me know when I can drop," Sam whispered into the com.

"Hold...hold...hold...go!" Marduk replied.

Sam lowered herself via her grappling cord. Close to the ground, she unclicked the piton and flipped in the air to land silently on her feet. With two quickfire shots, she managed to stun the Bubil and the Hasuram with her shocker bolts. They collapsed to the ground with a slight thud each.

The bipedal Sezerene, his back turned, was none the wiser. "Hey! Easy there, Bezzy. Don't accidentally knock anything askew, eh? Hehe. Uh, Bezzy? Rojan?"

"I don't think Bezzy and Rojan are awake right now," Sam snarked.

The Sezerene turned around. "What in Kewe...ahhhhhh!"

Sam had shot her grappling hook at the Sezerene. Her piton sank into the Sezerene's light armor. With a great tug, she jerked the crossbow towards her, sending the Sezerene hurtling through the air. She extended her arm to clothesline the hapless Excom as he soared right at her.

Thud! Crash! The Sezerene was smashed onto the hard ground, somehow remaining conscious, but writhing in pain.

Marduk whistled. "Talk about a flying fish. Good work there, little guppy."

Sam holstered her crossbow. "Thanks. No sweat."

They gathered around the fallen Sezerene, who had stopped whimpering by that point.

"Oi! What was the point of that?" the Sezerene uttered, rubbing his knobby head. He was a bipedal Sezerene, a leel'Sezerene, with sunken eyes and a bone plate covering his face. His light armor was in decent condition and bore the Excommunicated symbol on his left sleeve. His legs were scrawny and furry, and he wore cloven boots to cover his hoofs.

Havera wasted no time. She wrapped her tail firmly around the Sezerene's waist and hoisted him into the air.

"Woah, woah! Easy, easy. I ain't done nothing," the Sezerene insisted.

"Why don't I believe that?" Havera responded, squeezing him tighter with her tail.

"Ow! Ow! Too tight, too tight! You obviously ain't one of Ignatia's people. Though, you could've fooled me. Who are y'all? Not some of Fenix's goons, I hope," said the Sezerene.

"We'll ask the questions around here. Understand?" Havera said, using her stern, formal tone.

"Alright, alright. Fridirf is at your service. My friends call me Frid. You ain't my friends, but, uh, exceptions to the rules and all that," said Frid, the leel'Sezerene.

"What were y'all doing here?" Sam asked.

"Oh, oh. Trying to escape this Kewea-accursed place, eh. Ignatia ordered a bunch of us to hold our positions against those crazy Yune bots. To Kewea with her, we said. So, we, uh, abandoned our post, snuck past 'em, and, uh, I guess we found ourselves in your custody, eh, hehe," Frid explained.

"Snuck past the Yunes, you say. Where are they and how many do they number?" Marduk asked.

"No bloody idea. Hundreds, I'd guess. As for where, a few levels down I'd estimate. Ignatia and her Paladins of Paleria crazies are holed up outside some vault or doorway Ignatia's been trying to break into. A couple o'months we've been stuck here while she fiddles trying to breach her way in. No luck, no luck. Even had this creepy mother lovin' Rinvari fellow haul these huge devices in a few days ago. Some experimental tech is what I heard, eh. All gone shite. Even worse, the last of our scouts came rushing in to warn us about those Yune bots. Ignatia sent the rest of us up to hold against 'em while she sealed herself and those Paladins in. Damn suicide mission, eh. No ma'am, no ma'am," said Frid.

"Hmm. I want to thank you for answering more than what was asked of you, Frid," Havera said.

Frid gave an enthusiastic nod. "My pleasure, my pleasure."

"You don't need to say things twice, Frid," Sam said.

"I know, I know," agreed Frid.

"So, Ignatia has not gotten the Orb, yet?" Havera asked.

"I don't know nothing about no Orb, but I suppose she hasn't, eh. If she's still trying to get through that door," said Frid.

"How many Paladins is Ignatia holed up with?" Marduk asked.

"Uhh, about fifty, I'd guess, I'd guess. We had about two hundred of us on the journey here all crammed into this retrofitted cargo ship. A few died in the crash, but most of us arrived and set up camp around the pyramid. This stupid Moan fella called Kuba decided it would be a good idea to walk up to the front door and knock. Activated some kind of shenanigans, eh. Next thing we saw was this wild jet of dark goo shoot out from the top of the pyramid and rain down upon us. Most of us rushed inside to get away. Ignatia didn't follow 'til later. I guess we were the stupid ones getting trapped in here, eh," said Frid.

"Wait. You're saying the black beam wasn't there when you arrived? No barrier guarding the pyramid?" Jak asked.

"I don't know nothing about no barrier, but that's what I'm saying, eh."

All that terraforming only took a couple months. How powerful is this Orb?

"We've seen plenty of skirmish aftermaths, but we haven't found any bodies. Where'd they all go?" Adam asked.

"Oh, oh. Y'all haven't seen 'em vanish, eh?"

"Vanish?"

"If the Cauduun could let me down, I could show y'all, eh."

Havera lowered Frid onto his feet and unfurled her tail from his waist. "One false move and we'll throw you down the chasm."

"Alright, alright. Y'all made your point," Frid said, massaging his torso. He slowly walked over to the fallen unconscious Bubil. "Don't be alarmed and go with me, eh." Frid pulled a small knife from his belt. "Sorry about this, Bezzy." Before anyone could stop him, Frid stabbed the Bubil multiple times through the heart.

"What are you doing?" shrieked Havera. She wrapped her tail around the Sezerene's neck.

"Agh, agh! Look, look!" Frid said, clawing at her tail and gasping for air.

They all peered at the Bubil. Despite the stab wounds, not one drop of blood was visible. As they were keeping a keen eye on the presumably dead Bubil, the body faded from existence, leaving behind only the Bubil's clothes and gear. Everyone stumbled back in shock.

"Creepy, ain't it, eh?" said Frid after Havera released her grip on his throat. "This whole Kewea-accursed building is haunted, I tell you."

"You stabbed your friend in cold blood!" Sam said aghast.

"You mean Bezzy?" Frid said with a dismissive wave. "He was no friend of mine. No friend of mine. Don't shed a tear for the poor sod. The man was a rapist and a war criminal. Probably could've gotten a sizeable bounty from the bugger if I'm honest, eh."

Marduk stepped up to Frid. "Thank you for the information, Excom. Enjoy Kewea." The Moan raised Drillhead and pointed it at the Sezerene. Frid attempted to protest. Too late. Marduk fired a concussion blast a point-blank range. The blast impacted and sent the Sezerene's body soaring back into the wall with a sickening crunch. Frid's body vanished, leaving only his gear to hit the floor.

"Goddess damn, Marduk! What was that? I said we wouldn't kill him!" Havera yelled.

"No, you said you wouldn't throw him down the chasm. I didn't. No mercy for Excoms," Marduk hissed.

A slight gasp and fluttering of wings caught their attention. The previously knocked-out Hasuram had awoken just in time to see his comrade's death. The three-face Excom flapped his wings hard and attempted to escape towards the corridor leading to the central chasm.

"Don't let them get away!" Marduk barked. He fired another concussion blast in the Hasuram's direction but missed.

It did not matter. As soon as the Hasuram crossed the threshold out the antechamber, it was instantly crushed by a creature that landed upon him from above. The Hasuram was flattened, dead. Once its body vanished, the new arrival turned its attention to the group.

It was a Rinvari, or it had been once. It's tea-colored fur was showing signs of the Astroglass texture at its tips. One of its horns had completely converted into the opaque, glassy substance. The Rinvari roared with a sonorous sound that was a mixture of a typical Rinvari and the electronic whizzing that the Human from outside produced. It reared onto its hind legs. A noticeable fresh slash streaked across the front of its chest.

Sam drew her bow and fired off successive energy arrows, striking the Rinvari in its immense torso. Affected by the bursts of irradiated energy, the Rinvari roared. He turned heel and fled down the corridor towards the central chasm.

"That was easy," Adam said.

"Too easy," Havera said to everyone's agreement.

"Hot damn, sweet jam! How many more of these things are there?" a frightened but relieved Zax asked.

The Zokyo stepped back, pressing himself against the wall. He inadvertently pushed in a hidden panel within the wall. The door into the Archives creaked and slid upwards, dislodging centuries of rust and dust.

"Uh, oh. Didn't mean to do that!" Zax said, jumping away from the door.

A burst of cold air billowed into the antechamber, followed by a cacophony of many unsettling screeches. Everyone braced themselves for the new threat.

From the darkness, a cluster of amorphous, spectral faces manifested close to the doorway. Dozens. Hundreds. Faces beyond count. Their features were stretched and horribly disfigured. Bits of their phantasmal form illuminated and glinted like the reflection off the ever-present opaque, black glass. Symmetrical, rectangular pieces of their swarm were continuously breaking off and disappearing like a data stream. Their wailing grew louder the closer they approached. They were not stopping.

"RUN!" Havera shouted.

Nobody argued. Scrambling to escape, the group dashed into the corridor leading to the central chasm. Marduk and Sam fired a few shots behind them to no effect. Jak sent a couple glyphs back at the spectral swarm that slowed them down a bit, but the sheer numbers and nebulous nature of these specters were overwhelming even to Jak's enhanced abilities.

They turned the corner and were back in the Hub. They ended up on a landing next to some of the revolving platforms. Out of nowhere, the Rinvari ambushed them, tackling Havera to the ground with a tremendous roar. The inertia of the beast's charge nearly toppled them both over into the chasm. The Rinvari swiped down with its massive forearms. Havera blocked each strike with her bracers, though the force behind the Rinvari's strikes was immense. Havera winced with each block.

Marduk charged. Roaring and triggering the blades on Drillhead, the Moan gored the Rinvari in the side, grinding bits of it into nothingness. The Rinvari hollered but did not seem particularly hurt by the attack.

Havera used that as her opportunity to hoist the Rinvari off her and, with a little assistance from Marduk, threw the damned creature into the chasm. The Rinvari howled into the darkness below until there was nothing but silence.

Marduk helped Havera to her feet just as the digital specters had rounded the corner with their cacophony of haunting wails.

"Down, down, down!" Jak shouted, pointing to the landing's edge. The Naddine leapt onto a platform below them with Zax on his heels. The others followed his lead and jumped. The platform was carrying them away from the spectral swarm, but not fast enough.

"We need to keep moving down. Our destination isn't far. Perhaps we can lose them!" Adam shouted.

Umbrasia tossed a sparse light ball at the swarm. The ball contacted and exploded in a modest ray of light, visibly dispelling bits of the swarm. Her attack was too weak to destroy them, and the Rorae nearly passed out afterwards.

"That's all I can muster for now. I'm sorry."

"Every moment counts, witch. It helps," Marduk said, patting behind him on her leafy head.

Marduk was right. The swarm had slowed a bit, though its ferocity had not decayed. In fact, the faces only appeared angrier.

"Down one more and to the right," Jak called out.

Jak was following the waypoint on their map data. They were nearing the Forge. After hopping down to the platform and waiting for it to reach the landing, the group dashed into the narrow corridor. More signs of a skirmish between Yunes and Excoms were all over the landing.

If the map was correct, this narrow passageway led directly to a huge foyer-type antechamber before proceeding into a long corridor towards the section designated the Forge. They had to hurry. The spectral swarm wouldn't be far behind.

Turning the corner into the foyer, the group stopped dead in its tracks only a few feet into the chamber.

"Oh, you've got to be kidding me!"

It was difficult to say who said it first. The foyer was monumental and imposing. Sourceless dim light gave the spacious chamber a distinguished ambience. Glowing glyphs and designs of strange, foreign iconography were carved into the floor, walls, and ceiling. On the far side of the great foyer that led towards the Forge was a sealed door.

That wasn't the problem. The few hundred armed Yune Inquisitor bots standing between them and the door was. With their long laser rifles and tall porcelain white frames scorched by dozens of engagements, the Inquisitors were a horrifyingly awesome sight as they stood in formation by the door. Several were attempting to carve their way through the door with plasma cutters.

That is until Adam and the others were detected. At once, the Inquisitors in the nearest back rows pivoted to face them with their rifles drawn.

"We can't fight all of them," Havera said. The symbol on her bracer had grown brighter.

"What should we do?" Sam asked.

One of the Inquisitor bots holstered its rifle and approached. "Help us get through this door. Please..."

It's begging.

From behind them came a series of menacing growls. The Rinvari had returned. Battered but undeterred, its haunting dead eyes were fixated on them, and it wasn't alone. Just behind him was the swarm of specters, all pushing through the narrow corridor in a morass of screeches and wails.

Their arrival drew the attention of the remaining Inquisitors. All of them positioned themselves into a combat stance. Hundreds of Yune bots on one end, an endless hive of cyber ghosts led by a soulless Rinvari on the other, and Adam and company caught between them.

"Kewea's curse. We're done," Marduk said resigned.

"Over here!" a voice yelled for them.

In the dim light, the figure was barely a silhouette. Cauduun and wearing Paladin garb that resembled Augustus' gear, the figure was standing next to some sort of aperture in the wall, frantically gesturing for them to hurry over. On Adam's map data, a previously unseen small passageway revealed itself right where the person was standing.

Umbrasia and Jak must've been of the same mind. Simultaneously, she shot a weak light ball towards the swarm while Jak summoned a glyph and hurled it towards the Yunes. Both made contact and momentarily stunned each party.

No chance to debate, the group dashed towards their unknown rescuer, who once closer they all realized was a woman. Onyx-skinned, armored, and helmeted, she carried a pair of blades on her hips and a platinum-covered trident on her back that pressed against a silvery half-cloak attached to her armor. It was difficult to discern her face in the dim light.

"Hurry!" the female Paladin hissed. "Only one can fit at a time. Don't argue, just go! I'll hold them off and seal the passage behind you."

Sam leapt into the aperture and squeezed through. She was quickly followed by Havera, Jak with J'y'll on his back, then Zax. Marduk had to slightly morph his form to allow him to fit, but he pushed Umbrasia into the hole and followed in behind her.

Only Adam and the Paladin woman remained. The momentary stunning effect of the combined attacks had worn off. The cyber specters and the Rinvari had charged at the Yunes, who responded by returning fire with little effect on the swarm.

"Thank you. I can help!" Adam said.

"I said don't argue. Go! These spirits cannot stop me," the Paladin woman said. Her voice was husky, gruff, and self-assured. She grabbed her trident with a flourish and slammed it into the ground. The hairs on the back of Adam's neck stood as a gust of wind blew in from out of nowhere, billowing the woman's silver half-cloak. He didn't stay to see what happened. He did as he was told and forced his way into the hole.

It was indeed a tight fit. Almost like an air duct, the narrow passageway was crawling room only. The sounds of the specters' wailing and the Yunes' laser blasts reverberated intensely in the confined space.

Adam eventually caught up with Marduk, who was gingerly helping Umbrasia along as best he could. After a few turns, the passageway looped into the corridor on the other side of the door the Inquisitors were slicing into. One-by-one, they all crawled out of the duct and plopped down in front of dozens of figures. Entirely male and Cauduun, all were armed with electrospears and carrying scutum shields. They all wore matching heavy upper armor, battle skirts, and identical helmets with the plume of green, equine hair front-to-back. Each had a modified CMA-Defense Rifle affixed to their backs and various pouches attached to their cingulum belts. An insignia of a great tortoise was decorated on the front of their armor and shield.

They had formed a defensive perimeter just outside the door. The sounds of battle could be heard through the door. A squad had broken off to form a semi-circle around the new arrivals with their weapons pointed.

"I think we found the Paladins of Paleria," Sam said, standing up with her hands raised.

"That's an understatement," Marduk agreed, lifting Umbrasia onto his back and re-morphing to his normal size.

Though intimidating, something was not quite right with these Paladins. Their formation wasn't tight, many of their faces sullen and sunken, and one or two of the Paladins were trembling, struggling to maintain the grip on their spears.

Months they've been down here. I question their health, physical and mental.

The Paladins said nothing, only prodding them away from the hole which they crawled through. Remaining in a semi-circle around them, Adam's group was pushed further into the corridor away from the door. With the understood threat, the Paladins held them at bay there. No move to attack or harm. Just waited.

"So, are we going to just play silent stand-off?" Sam quipped.

"My Paladins are well-trained, Human. They won't speak unless I order them. Isn't that right, boys?" It was the voice of the female Cauduun.

All the Paladins smacked their shields and erupted in a brief but enthusiastic verbal affirmation that wasn't any discernible word.

"Y'all are a disgrace to the name Paladins of Paleria," Havera hissed. She stepped forward. "You, back there! You're an officer, clearly. Reveal yourself."

The woman laughed. "After all these years, Lady Tenebella Havera of Shele..."

The semi-circle parted and out stepped the female Cauduun. Moderately brighter sourceless light in the corridor allowed a better view of the woman. Her onyx skin was emissive, as was her tail, but it was a deep crimson. Armored and helmeted with the green plume running side-to-side, she commanded the presence of all the Paladins by her side. She was a bit older than Havera, probably in her sixth or seventh decade with a narrow jawline and high cheekbones. Sharp, upturned eyes of molten silver and bow-shaped crimson lips, her alluring face hid the palerasteel will of a Cauduun warrior.

"...I did not expect our reunion to occur here of all places," the woman finished. The sudden tenseness is Havera's posture unmasked the woman's identity.

Ignatia.

43

The Curse of Kewea

"Die, you traitorous jade!" screamed Havera.

The duchess launched herself in a reckless fury. She cast aside two Paladins that moved to intercept her and leapt in the air for an overhead power punch right at Ignatia. The older woman dodged that with ease. Havera attempted a leg sweep with her tail, which Ignatia dexterously jumped over.

Adam flinched in their direction, wanting to aid Havera, but all the remaining Paladins closed ranks around them tightly with the points of their spears keeping them boxed in. No one would be interfering with this fight. They were forced to only watch and pray.

Havera pressed the attack with a constant barrage of punches and tail whips. Ignatia was content with playing defense, not even bothering to draw her blades nor the trident on her back.

Havera yelled with each swing and blocked strike. She was putting the full force of her muscles into every blow. The older Cauduun proved too elusive for her. Havera couldn't land a single punch. Ignatia kept dodging and using Havera's momentum against her, pushing her to the side when Havera overstepped. Ignatia made no move to counterstrike.

Havera was growing impatient. "Fight me, murderer!" she screamed.

"This isn't fighting. This is simply you acting out. If you calm down, I'll consider drawing my blades against you," Ignatia taunted.

"How's this for calm?" Havera slammed her bracers together, igniting them. She was engulfed in a fiery magenta light from head to toe. The muscles in Havera's body bulged slightly. Her blue capillaries pushed to the surface of her emissive skin as she snarled.

Ignatia sighed. "You wield those bracers like a child holding a gun. Your mater would be disappointed in you."

"Don't you dare invoke my mater! You murdered her!" Havera lashed towards Ignatia with even greater fury. Her swings were wild and off the mark. Ignatia had an easier time dodging these strikes. Ignatia kept using Havera's momentum against her, moving with Havera's body to throw the duchess off balance. Ignatia jabbed a few times into Havera's side. They didn't appear to harm her. Only piss her off further, which was the point.

"You're only wearing yourself out, Havera. You've no idea how to truly unleash the power of those bracers. Your rage grants you strength, but it blinds you. Censor Maxima taught you better than this," Ignatia said.

"Yes, she did. She also taught me the value of not becoming overconfident!" Havera spun a high kick, forcing Ignatia to duck. She immediately followed with a lightning jab using the bulge of her tail, which connected with Ignatia's chest. Ignatia was sent flying, but she managed to twist her body in the air and land in a three-point stance.

Ignatia recovered. Her armor absorbed most of the blow, nevertheless, she spat out a speck of blue blood. The Paladin removed her crested helm and dematerialized it. She sported three tight, scarlet braids on the right side. The remaining raven and scarlet locks cascaded messily down past her opposite shoulder. Her molten silver eyes narrowed as she drew her short swords from their scabbards.

"Have it your way," Ignatia frowned, tossing her hair back. She crossed the blades high in front of her. A searsword in her right hand and a frostsword in her left. Steam sizzled from the blades upon contact with each other.

Ignatia grinned. She whipped her trident off her back and slammed it into the ground. Adam's hairs stood on the back of his neck. A resounding echo reverberated off the hard surface. Ignatia's form began to shift. A faint, gloomy billow enveloped her body. She moved to the left. An extended blur of her body phased between where she moved and where she was standing. She moved to the right. The same blur followed her.

Havera blinked, forming up into a defensive posture. "What trick is this Ignatia?"

Ignatia continued to shift left and right, disorienting all watching her. She moved as if she were floating like Umbrasia. The spectral blur continued to trail her like an afterimage.

"You wanted me to fight. I'm giving you what you wished for!" Ignatia shouted. She lunged forward, a speedy blur herself, with her blades crossed to protect her head. She was upon Havera before the duchess could react fast enough. Ignatia slashed high with her searsword that Havera, through pure instinct, managed to deflect with her bracer. However, she was too slow to block the low swing from the other blade. The frostsword bit into Havera's shin, causing the young Cauduun to howl in pain. She was forced to one knee, too slow to see Ignatia's tail whip coming to smack her across the face with a crack!

Havera was spun in the air with the force of the impact. She used to the tip of her tail as a springboard to land back on her feet. She winced and fell to one knee from the sharp, icy slash wound in her leg.

Adam recoiled at the sight. Frost wounds were nasty. While not as bloody as a simple slash nor as painful from a burning sear weapon, they did cause the affected area to become instantly numb, rendering the limb effectively useless for a time with a precise enough strike.

In one attack, she crippled Havera's speed and maneuverability.

"Have you had enough, yet? You can't beat me, Havera," Ignatia said. Her words carried no ego or haughtiness. She spoke plain truth.

"Havera, enough! She's right. Her powers are stronger than Fenix's. Don't throw your life away like this," Adam pleaded.

Ignatia side-eyed Adam. "Ah, so that's how y'all found us. I must have a chat with that insubordinate brat after we finish our business here. Nevertheless, your Human friend has intrigued me. My powers stronger than Fenix's? She does not possess such abilities. If she had, I wouldn't have crushed her so easily."

"She does now. She nearly killed me with them. You're not the one who gave her those...abilities?" Adam said, not hiding his confusion.

Ignatia raised an eyebrow. "I've no idea what you're talking about, Human. If Fenix has developed abilities, she did not get them from me. My powers are...unique. Hmm. I sense no deception from you. More so, I sense something familiar in you, Human. Curious." That last word lingered on her lips. Ignatia decided to set aside that thought and turned back to face Havera. "You can continue to fight and die a useless death like your mater, or you can settle down and listen to what I have to say."

Havera gritted her teeth, holding back a hint of tears. She was breathing hard, clutching the numbed wound in her leg. She closed her eyes and exhaled deeply. The magenta glow around her vanished. Her muscles and blood vessels returned to normal.

"Smart decision. That's one area where you surpass your mater," Ignatia said, sheathing her weapons. She retrieved her trident, and her own gloomy billow vanished. A couple paladins flanked Havera and herded her into the circle with the rest of the group.

"I told you to never invoke my mater!" spat Havera, unwilling to relinquish her anger.

"Your drive to bury your feelings with anger is understandable, my dear. Be that as it may, it blocks you from unlocking the true potential with those bracers and yourself," Ignatia said.

"If I had known you were going to lecture me, I'd have had you skewer me with your swords. You said you wanted to talk, so talk! I want to hear you justify my mater's murder to my face," Havera said.

"It's good to know disinformation is alive and well. Carissima, I did not murder your mater. I tried to save her," Ignatia said.

"Save her?" Havera scoffed.

"It's the truth. What exactly is it that they told you happened that day two years ago?"

"You tried to steal the Sword of Aria, and Pompeia stopped you. All you managed to do was abscond with were some old star charts and the body of Queen Havera VIII. She gave her life to protect us from your treachery."

"Fascinating. Fascinating, indeed," Ignatia said, running her fingers through her hair. "Mostly lies, but fascinating, nonetheless. I never cared much for the tales the Alliance weaved about me. Yet, hearing them come from your lips stirs a curiosity in me. Before I continue, sate my curiosity. What are y'all doing here? Y'all are certainly an eclectic group. Surely, y'all didn't fly deep in Union territory to find me." Ignatia was eyeing everyone, waiting for a response.

Zax coughed. "I can't speak for the others, but my brother and I are here to find inspiration for some new songs and become richer while we do." He snatched the lute off his back and strummed a cord. The paladins nearest him pricked him with the tips of their spears. "Ouch, ouch! Hot damn, sweet jam relax! It's merely a lute." Zax made eye contact with Adam and winked. Adam returned a negligible nod.

That could work.

"Your brother?" a confused Ignatia said seeing no other Zokyo.

Zax pulled Jak in tighter. J'y'll clung to the Naddine, disguised as a metal backpack. "This is my brother, Jak. We're Exchange kids."

"Ah! I've heard of y'all. You are the infamous Jak and Zax duo. I caught y'all during a charity tour on Pavea a few years back. Could've used y'all the past couple months. It's been dreadfully unentertaining down here," Ignatia said to everyone's shock.

"The famous Zax and Jak duo," Zax grumbled under his breath.

"What about you two?" Ignatia pointed to the Humans.

Adam opened his mouth, but Sam spoke first. "That's Adam, and I'm Sam. We're just here for a job." She was applying sanagel to Havera's leg wound.

"Y'all are far from home," Ignatia said, brushing aside her scarlet and raven hair. Her gaze lingered on Adam far too long for his comfort. He glanced down at the floor, hoping that would be the end of her inquisition.

"You, back there! Moan. What's your..." Ignatia paused. She cocked her head like an inquisitive animal. "...it can't be. Marduk Tiamat, is that you?"

"Ignatia," Marduk replied curtly.

"Why are you carrying an unconscious Rorae on your back?" Ignatia said, spotting Umbrasia clinging to Marduk's shoulders.

"Long story, Praefect. I never believed a woman of your caliber would wind up a leader of terrorists and murderers."

"From a certain point of view, I already was. Is that what this is all about? Your gills in a twist over Sin, or does Patron-Saint still have her fishhooks in you?"

Marduk growled. "If the Duchess doesn't kill you first, I shall squeeze the life from your wretched hide. After what we witnessed together. The devastation that the Excoms and their Celestial creations wrought. You decide to usurp their leadership and become them!"

"The Excommunicated are nothing but a tool. That's all they are. All they always have been for hundreds of years. Fenix can have them back for all I care. I needed their resources to reach this place. After my exile, my options were limited. Even your mistress wanted nothing to do with me. I saw an opportunity, and I seized it. If people are already convinced you're public enemy number one, you may as well act like it," Ignatia said.

"Cut to the end of the page, Ignatia. Why do you want the Orb of Emancipation?" Havera barked.

A curdling smile appeared at the edge of Ignatia's crimson lips. "Even now, you let your rage slip your true motivations. This is wonderful serendipity. I should've guessed Pompeia's filia and I would be after the same prize."

Havera bit her lip. "Alright. Yes, we're here to obtain the Orb. Killing you was the price for my involvement. My mater deserves justice."

"You believe killing me does your mater justice? I'll say it again. I didn't kill Pompeia. She and I were partners."

"Lies!" Havera shouted.

Ignatia ignored her. "Your mater and I understood that the Queendom, as it stands, is rotten from the inside-out. We merely differed on the medicine. She urged caution while I advocated for forceful action. I met with her in that vault to finalize our plans. To demonstrate proof that the Platinum Throne and the Alliance are built upon lies."

"You're lying! My mater was in that vault at my urging. I asked her to be there!" Havera screamed, choking back tears.

Ignatia's smile evolved into a mournful frown. Her face displayed genuine pity. "Havera, carissima, let me alleviate you of any guilt you have. Pompeia and I had been plotting to bring down the ruling class for years. Your mater became the archduchess based our designs. She devised a way to end the Strife, and I engineered her election by...convincing enough Confederates and Republicans to back her candidacy, despite their obvious ideological differences. She told me about your little request. It provided a perfect alibi for our clandestine rendezvous in the Praetorian vaults. As I said, I needed to show your mater proof of the Platinum Throne's lies. The Sword of Aria that the Throne claims I attempted to steal? A fake. The real Sword of Aria is long gone. Maybe it was never there to begin with."

Havera tensed. "Fake? Impossible. The Praetorians would've recognized a forgery. Why not report something like that publicly? There's no way to confirm if your honeyed words are true."

Ignatia sighed. "You're correct. I cannot prove what I am saying from here. However, you understand better than most that only pomp and pageantry hold the mystique of the Platinum Throne together. You wear the robes of the Praetorians. 'Faith, Family, Legends.' Your motto, is it not? Even those nerdy brawlers understand the importance of myth and legends to a people. To discover much of it to be fake would devastate the legitimacy of the Queendom and the Shelean Royal Family. The Alliance is fragile enough as it is. No one would want a meddling

Confederate interloper like me to ruin the legacy of the greatest galactic civilization. Never mind I am...was the Praefect of the Paladins of Paleria, one of the oldest and most-respected military organizations in the galaxy. The defenders of the royal family! To the Sheleans, I am nothing more than an inconvenient irritant."

Havera's posture relaxed a bit. Her tail remained tense. Adam could see her eyes flittering. She was lost in thought. "I still don't believe you," she said meekly.

She's conflicted. I don't know what to make of Ignatia words.

Ignatia pushed her paladins aside and held out her trident in front of Havera. "You're a scholar of the Cauduun occult. Do you recognize this?"

Adam leaned over Havera's shoulder. He finally had a chance to visually inspect the trident up close. Platinum coverings decorated with intricate patterns encased the shaft. Most of the iconography Adam didn't recognize. The bits he did discern were commonly affiliated with death. One prominent symbol repeated throughout was that of a darkened disk contained within a bigger burning disk. He did spot a version of the Vitriba close to the base of the trident, where three smaller prongs acted as the tip. The three long prongs at the head of the trident were onyx-colored and swirling in a darkened mist. Their icy mold had a particular sheen Adam recognized immediately.

Rimestone! Darkened Rimestone.

His hand naturally drifted towards his pocket, where he kept the Debbie. He resisted the temptation.

Havera's tail twitched. She tried to keep a stoic expression, but Adam recognized the eagerness in her eyes.

"Kewea's gift," Havera said. Ignatia nodded. "Where'd you find that?"

The two Cauduun were fixated on each other. No one else mattered to them. "Deep inside the buried Venvuishyn ruins on Anio. Miles of unexplored passages within that moon's subterranean mass. Not long after my exile, I heard a voice calling through to me in my dreams. A voice showing me a path through the treacherous, cavernous remains of that lost civilization. The pull was irresistible. I had to chance death to seek out its calling. At a nexus point of a forgotten realm, I found it. Lodged into an ancient pedestal. The Resurrection Spear."

"How appropriate you'd be the one to discover the Traitor's Trident," Havera snarked.

Ignatia spat and slammed the trident into the ground. A haunting echo from the trident's impact sent chills up Adam's spine. Her mention of voices in dreams had already put him on edge.

"Shelean drivel! The poncy skin greasers and liturgical dogmatists had the gall to slander a goddess so thoroughly, so venomously! They must smear any who dare challenge their archaic notions of family first. 'Kewea must've been infertile. There's no reason why she would refuse to have children with their perfectly-created man like her sisters.' Old Paleria honored Kewea along with the other twelve goddesses and gods until those vipers from Shele wormed their way into that unholy alliance. Now, the abomination of a Platinum Palace stands on the hill that once carried her name. Only in parental cautionary tales or in the vulgarity of our lips do we ever remember her. The Shelean Royal Family, your family, has dominated the political and cultural interests of the Cauduun people for far too long! They are a flesh-eating bacterium that must be excoriated."

"I was not born Shelean, Ignatia."

"Exactly! You're a child of the colonies like me. Like Havera I. You should heed my advice as your mater did before you. She and I came from incredibly different backgrounds, yet we both recognized the damage Alexandra and her Shelean slits have done to our kind. I never knew my blood parents either. I was a Linkless bastard from a backwater world. Your mater was Shelean with an experienced military background and the attitude of someone who understood the plight of those on the fringes of Cauduun space. She was the only one who could've led us through the coming storm. Without her, I fear the Cauduun will plunge into civil war, and the entire galaxy will destabilize."

Havera ran her fingers through her hair. "I...I don't believe you." Her voice faltered.

Ignatia's eyes briefly flashed down onto Havera's bracers. "Perhaps not all is lost. Your mater wanted you to become her successor. Did you know that, Havera? She loved you and believed in you. Even when you sought to join that stuffy Praetorian Order. She wanted you to follow her path into the Paladins of Paleria, but *I* dissuaded her. Reminded her that she and I chased our passions in our youth. You ought to have the freedom to do the same."

Ignatia inched closer to Havera. The Duchess stared at the floor to avoid Ignatia's gaze. Ignatia tentatively put a hand on Havera's shoulder. The young Cauduun flinched but did not reject the other woman's touch.

"Havera, carissima. I didn't kill your mater. We tried to keep our dealings a secret, even from other like-minded people. Only a select few knew. Despite our best efforts, we were betrayed. I never did learn who betrayed us. A handful of Paladins enslaved to the Throne along with some Vulpes dogs attempted to take us into custody for plotting against the Queen. I...I acted impulsively. I killed two of our would-be jailers. Your mater tried to stop me, but by then it was too late. A full-blown skirmish had broken out. Your mater was forced to use her bracers to defend herself. Those old vaults were not meant to withstand the force of the goddesses' gifts. Yet more proof of the Throne's deceptions around the Sword. Part of the ceiling collapsed on top of her. She was dead. I couldn't dig her up. More Throne loyalists were coming, so I made the most cowardly decision of my career. I fled."

Ignatia grasped Havera on each shoulder, so she was directly facing the Duchess. Havera ran her fingers through her hair and tilted her head up to face Ignatia.

"I failed your mater. I failed you. I wanted to come find you and explain all this to you. To help you find some comfort or reason in this irrational, cruel universe. For that, I am truly sorry. It is a mea culpa for which I can never forgive myself, but perhaps you can find it in your heart to forgive me. Together, you and I can finish your mater's work. We can save the Cauduun, the galaxy, from itself. An end to the chaos and carnage. Give rise to a new galactic order under our influence. Our direction. Not one controlled by decadent snobs and decaying regimes."

"Duchess, she's deceiving you! Twisting your mind with her silver tongue," Marduk barked.

Adam exhaled. *Glad someone said it finally.*

Ignatia glared at the Moan. "You've no part in this conversation, Marduk. You're a dealer of death and destruction. A warmonger. You'd relish the chance to fill your Mordelatory coffers with bloody Links. Patron-Saint is behind your little incursion, I'm sure of it. Only she could drive you this far into unknown space. You may try to hide your true motives like you hide your bodily form, but I see through you, Moan. Greed rather than vengeance drives you. The rest of you are nothing but petty mercenaries leashed by a nameless, faceless gangster. Do you believe Patron-Saint has benevolent motives for desiring the Orb?"

"We are not! We fight for our people's welfare and freedom, too!" Sam yelled.

Ignatia scanned her up-and-down, repeating the same with Adam. Another chill shot up Adam's spine.

"I can see there is some truth to your words in your eyes. It matters not. The Orb is mine," Ignatia declared.

"Why do you want the Orb, Ignatia?" Havera asked softly.

Ignatia turned her attention back to Havera. "I'm a godly woman, Your Grace. In the goddesses and their gifts, I trust. You must've come from the outside. You've seen what this Orb is accomplishing on this dead world forgotten by all but a few bots. Imagine what Iinneara's gift could do to a galaxy torn apart by strife."

"Sin," muttered Havera barely loud enough for all to hear.

Ignatia nodded. "Yes. A jewel brought back to life. Not just Sin. We could prevent a thousand Sins from ever occurring again. There is only one true force in the galaxy with that kind of power. You know of what I speak. You've studied it much of your life."

"The Vitriba," Havera whispered.

Ignatia nodded. "I seek the Vitriba. The Orb of Emancipation. The Everlasting Aegis. The true Warrior's Kiss. The power to create life.

The power to protect life. The power to take life. You and I, Havera, could save the galaxy by controlling the power of life itself. I need your help. If history has proven anything to me, I cannot do this alone. The goddesses have guided you to me for a reason."

"Havera, you cannot indulge this psychopath's delusions of grandeur!" screamed Marduk.

"Shut him up!" ordered Ignatia.

A pair of paladins drove their spears through Marduk's tough hide, piercing the back of his legs. The Moan roared in pain and fell to his knees. He threw a wild swing at one and missed.

Umbrasia came flying off Marduk's back and tumbled at Adam's feet. He could hear the Rorae's moans in his head.

A few more paladins began stabbing and shocking Marduk with their electrospears, attempting to subdue the mighty Moan.

"Stop this now, Ignatia! Don't hurt him! Please," Havera pleaded.

Marduk continued to fight back against his captors in vain. The combined force of their spears along with crushing weight of their shields easily overcame any desperate attempt by Marduk to fight back. The Moan soon collapsed to the ground.

"Enough!" Ignatia barked. The other paladins backed off with immediate precision.

Marduk was alive and in pain. Sam rushed to his side. She retrieved some sanagel and began applying them to Marduk's multiple wounds. Most were superficial. His armor had blunted the worst of the blows. However, a few had managed to pierce the Moan's thick hide. The electric shocks from the electrospears did their intended effect. Marduk was effectively incapacitated.

"**Adam...**" he heard Umbrasia whisper. Adam got on one knee. "**At your feet. Prepare it for me, would you? Be sneaky about it. I've a feeling I may have need of it, yet.**"

Adam glanced down to see one of Umbrasia's red giant Celeste patches had indeed fallen out of the pouch in all the excitement. He moved to snatch up Marduk's fallen coat that had gotten tossed aside along with Umbrasia. A couple paladins pointed their spears in his direction but made no move to stop him. Adam nestled Marduk's coat under Umbrasia's head. With sleight of hand, he peeled off the protective layer from the Celeste and palmed the patch in his hand, waiting for the right moment.

Ignatia stepped towards the fallen Marduk. "'Tis a shame when a warrior has no more wars to fight that he must invent conflict in order to survive. A sad existence."

She turned back towards Havera. "Do not worry, Your Grace. I shall not harm a hair on any of your companions' heads, so long as y'all cooperate. Virtual or not, there's been enough blood spilled this day. I, however, shall not let anything stop me from my goal. Not when I'm this close."

"What is it you want of me, Ignatia?" Havera asked.

Ignatia held out her hand. "Only you for you to follow me."

Havera did not take Ignatia's hand. Ignatia acknowledged her reluctance and beckoned them all to follow. "Centknights, nothing is to pass. Those Yunes and worse will try to breach your line. Hold this position no matter the opposition. Understood?"

The fifty or so Paladins all banged their electrospears against their shields in roaring approval. They lined up in formation in the archway shoulder-to-shoulder. Shields and spears in front with riflemen behind them prepared to cut down any who assaulted their fixed position.

Sam and Jak helped Marduk to his feet. Even battered and bruised, the Moan trudged forward with purpose. Adam braced Umbrasia against him while they moved forward. She didn't require as much assistance as Adam thought.

Her grip is firm and stride determined. The closer we get to the Orb, the stronger she's getting.

Ignatia led the group forward, with no fear about turning her back to potential adversaries. She walked with such utter confidence. Her pace quickened the closer they got to the end of the hall like a small child excitedly going back to her mother's embrace.

At the end of the darkened hallway were massive double doors that stretched to the high vaulted ceiling. Like the rest of the interior, it was coated in Astroglass. More iconography unrecognizable to Adam adorned the doors. Lots of images of flames and metallurgical hammers, with a great eye seared into their cheeks. A lone mare carried a featureless rider, who held aloft something in its hand. An orb. Within that orb was contained a version of the Vitriba. All rings engulfed in jets of fire.

Connected nearby was a device Adam recognized. It was a more advanced version of the jammers they had encountered on Concordia. The jammer was ruined. Parts of the device were scattered about, twisted and broken as if it had exploded from the inside. As they approached the doors, a faint buzzing tickled the back of Adam's ear. This was the gateway to the Forge.

"Beyond this door lies the Orb of Emancipation. Unfortunately, it is sealed. Locked. I do not possess the tools to open this doorway. That's where I need your help, Your Grace," explained Ignatia.

"Nothing I've read in Havera the Adventurer's journals mentions anything about this. I don't understand how I could help you," Havera said.

Ignatia grinned. "Don't you?" She nodded towards Havera's wrists. The top ring on each bracer was glowing brighter than ever.

"Cradite's Bracers?!"

"I am surprised as you are, Your Grace. You see, I tend to let my impulsiveness get the better of me. It is my sin. I should've done my research first. I thought through sheer force of will, I could blast my way in. All I managed to do was reactivate this dormant temple. Arouse its defenses. My other attempts at workarounds all failed. Not even the Excommunicated's top scientists could help," Ignatia gestured to the nearby broken jammer. "Folly on my part. No key created by mere mortals will work in the realm of the goddesses. Only those forged by Iinneara herself could open these doors. Your bracers are not merely a weapon or gift. They are a key."

Ignatia approached the door. She reached for the Vitriba on the door and slid back a previously unseen panel. Encased in a layer of Rimestone were two slots. Just large enough to fit a person's arm in each.

"Open the door, Havera. You are the bearer of the Mater's Embrace. It must be you. It is not my destiny to open this door. I see that now. I wish it could've been Pompeia standing by my side as we enter this hallowed chamber. I would be honored if her filia joined me in her stead. The duchess and her most trusted centurion knight. Our very own Tale of Havera." Ignatia once again extended her hand towards Havera.

Distant sounds of gunshots and shouts could be heard coming from where they left the Paladins. There was no going back.

"You shouldn't trust this woman, Duchess. As soon as she has the Orb, she'll dispose of us," said Jak.

"My bro is right. What guarantee do we have that you won't fry us the second we open this door?" Zax asked. He was strumming a few cords on his lute.

"The noodle guppy is correct. Never trust an Excom, let alone a traitor. Her honeyed words only benefit her," said Marduk, his voice a bit wheezed.

"The others are right, Havera. She's offered no proof of her sincerity or that what she's claimed about your mother is true. Even if what she's saying has a shred of honesty, she's a killer. You don't become the leader of the Excommunicated through benevolence," Sam said.

"There are no right or wrong paths. No right or wrong destinations," Umbrasia uttered, echoing the sentiment she had shared with Adam.

Havera turned to face the others. "What about you, Adam?"

He took a deep breath and exhaled. "You will do what's right, Havera. You understand the stakes far better than anyone. I believe in you no matter what."

Arabella's fate depends on you.

Havera nodded and turned back to face Ignatia.

"All due respect to your companions, they're but footnotes in this story. All that matters is between you and I," Ignatia said.

Havera stepped back to be closer with her friends. "That's where you're wrong, Ignatia. Their tales are as important as mine own. I sense there is some truth to what you've told me today. Nevertheless, my mater would never betray her Queen under any circumstances, regardless of her personal feelings. I do not believe she would've condoned what you've done despite your alleged shared beliefs or history. I may be a duchess, but you are far from a trusted centurion knight. You're a murderer, a deceiver. I will not open that door for you. We shall have the Orb, and you shall leave with your traitorous tail tucked between your legs."

Ignatia sighed, disappointment promulgated across her face. "Oh, carissima, you've no idea of what your mater was capable. The methods she employed to end the Strife would cause your tail to curl in disgust. All for a greater cause of galactic peace. I shall do nothing less in her honor. I do not wish to harm the daughter of a woman I so thoroughly admired and respected. However, if it's a fight you want, it is a fight you shall get. You must realize you cannot defeat me. Not even the combined strength of the seven of you can stop me and my power."

Ignatia slammed the trident onto the ground. A burst of darkness filled the chamber, enveloping Ignatia in a gloomy aura. Crackles of maroon lightning sparked between the prongs of her trident.

Adam moved to plant the Celeste on Umbrasia. Even in her weakened state, she could tip the balance. Everyone went into a defensive posture, preparing for a fight.

Except for Zax. The Zokyo jumped out in front between Ignatia and the rest, holding a pair of his hands out to stop them. "Hold on, hold on. Hot damn, sweet jam. Where'd y'all learn the art of diplomacy? I'm positive that we can all come to some sort of arrangement that'll benefit each other. There's no need to thrash each other over some ancient ball."

"What are you doing, Zax?" Jak asked clearly alarmed.

Zax winked. "Trust me, bro. I've got this." Zax turned to face Ignatia, his electric lute in hand.

The mad bastard is going for it. Come on, Zax. You can do it.

"What did you have in mind?" Ignatia asked Zax, her guard relaxed somewhat.

Zax began playing a jaunty tune and sang:

Oh, nothing I can do or say,

Will change you in any way,
Instead of fighting each other,
Go back and defend your brothers,
We shall enter, leave the Orb to us,
Grab our prize and depart without a fuss.

Adam was surprised how much that tune rhymed in Default. The last note Zax strummed with extra flair, sending a shimmering wave towards Ignatia. It breezed her square in the face. With a gentle touch, Zax's charming effect washed over her. The Cauduun blinked a couple of times. She smiled and began to laugh.

"Oh, you! You're such a lovely fellow, aren't you? How can I refuse such a charming request? Of course, I shall defend my brothers and depart without a fuss," Ignatia said, patting the Zokyo on his upper shoulder.

Adam's breath nearly got caught in his throat. *Holy Cradite, he pulled it off!*

Havera's tail stiffened. Ignatia's smile turned into a menacing grimace. She squeezed Zax on the shoulder, causing him to wince.

"That's a fun trick you have there, my bardic friend. Let me show you one of mine!"

Ignatia lifted her trident and thrust the spear straight through Zax's torso. The prongs burst through Zax's mechsuit, erupting out of Zax's body. An aura of darkened rays flared from the trident into Zax. The Zokyo's arms went limp. His electric lute slipped from his grasp and shattered as it hit the floor. Its final song, like its fading master, was nothing but an echo in the wind.

"ZAX!" Jak screamed at the top of his lungs.

The Zokyo's body had crumpled to the ground in front of them, unmoving.

In a blinding rage, the Naddine launched himself at Ignatia. She slammed her trident to the ground, repelling the attack with a wave of invisible force. Zax's body was sent soaring towards their feet. Undeterred, Jak summoned a pair of glyphs and hurled them at Ignatia.

She was knocked into the massive double doors with a huge slam. She clutched her head, grumbling through gritted teeth.

"I recognize those abilities," Ignatia said, standing back up. "This realm has made you powerful, G'ee'k. Not powerful enough to defeat the herald of a goddess!" She slammed the trident into the ground again. The wave of invisible force pushed against Jak. The Naddine did not flinch.

"When we meet Kewea together, I'll tear your spirit in half in front of the bitch!" screamed Jak. He summoned more glyphs and hurled them at Ignatia. She was prepared. Her unnatural speed allowed her to easily dodge them. The glyphs sizzled on the impact with the door behind her.

Jak was not alone. Marduk had spawned Drillhead and revved up her blades. Sam found her crossbow and loaded it with plasma bolts. The three of them assailed her with a ferocity that rivaled an exploding sun. Between her speed and the arcane abilities of the trident, none of their attacks landed with any significance on Ignatia. She deflected Sam's bolts and resisted the concussion blasts of Drillhead all the while using her dexterity to dodge Jak's glyphs.

Adam rushed to Zax's side to check vitals. He didn't need to. The health monitor from their com channel indicated no signs of life.

It was a worthy attempt, my friend. I'm sorry.

Havera stepped next to him. She was so utterly stunned she had barely moved a muscle.

"Adam, I saw it happen. I saw it happen, and I couldn't do anything to stop it. A thousand times over and over, and I only stood there. I couldn't move." Her face welled up with tears.

A small glint nearby caught Adam's attention. Amongst the debris of Zax's ruined lute, Adam found a chunk of icy white Rimestone that was once at the instrument's core. Sliding his hand up the sleeve of his jacket, he snatched the Rimestone and slipped it under his armor inside his jumpsuit in the other pocket.

The fight raged on in front of them. Jak conjured up a HUD stun and launched it at her to little effect. Ignatia tensed up, but the trident absorbed most of the shockwave. All it succeeded in doing was to give everyone nearby a crippling headache. Frustrated, he ordered J'y'll to transform into a laser rifle. He fired almost endless blasts at the Cauduun, screaming bloody murder as he did.

"I grow tired of this!" Ignatia shouted. She pointed the trident at her assailants. Bolts of maroon, almost black, lightning shot out from the trident, striking Sam, Marduk, and Jak square in the chest. The three were ravaged by electricity and sent soaring back.

"Your friend is dead. Keep this up, and he shall not remain so for long," Ignatia declared.

"What do you mean?" Jak spat, struggling to his feet.

"It's not called the Resurrection Spear for nothing. Have a gander at your foolish bard," Ignatia said through a curdling grin.

From the wounds in Zax's body, streaks of blackened blight were trickling through his veins. A corruption was overtaking his body from the inside out.

"Jak, he's becoming like those two men outside," Adam said alarmed.

Jak knelt down beside the body of his brother and took him by the hand.

"Ah, so you've encountered the curse of Kewea. Her true legacy upon this life. Yes, the only reason he has not dematerialized in this realm is because I hold onto his body. Soon, he shall rise again. A thrall to my will. His mind bound to my soul. However, if you cooperate and allow me to take Iinneara's Oculus unmolested, I shall release your friend's body. Let him truly rest, where he can join Kewea and Dasenor in their holy place."

"**Adam,**" he heard Umbrasia whisper next to him. "**I may be able to save your friend. Give me the Celeste. I shall not allow the Spite to overtake him. Hurry and retrieve the Orb. There isn't much time.**"

He hadn't let go of the patch in his palm. He slipped his hand behind Umbrasia and pressed the patch into her lower back. The same surge of reddened energy flowed through Umbrasia's body, though everyone else was too distracted to notice. Adam could sense her becoming stronger.

"If we get you the Orb, you'll let him go?" Adam shouted, attempting to give the Celeste an opportunity to work its magic.

"I shall not take him for a thrall. You have my word, for whatever you believe that is worth," Ignatia said.

"Open the door, Havera," Adam said without hesitation.

"Are you sure?" Havera asked.

"Positive. Trust me."

"Do it, Duchess. I won't let her have him," Jak declared, still clutching Zax's wrist.

Havera nodded. Walking up to the door, the glow from her bracers burned brighter than ever. With a thrust of each hand, she buried the bracers into the Rimestone slots. There was an audible click and a flash of light. Gears rotated and fell into place.

Havera withdrew her hands as the doors cracked open inward with a whining hiss. An inferno of intense heat blasted them from inside the chamber. Adam had to cover his face from the sheer force of the sweltering winds of a room that must not have been opened in centuries. The doors fully opened, revealing the chamber within. After adjusting to the sudden temperature change, the group pressed onward into the Forge.

44

The Orb of Emancipation

They found themselves inside an active but mostly empty space with thick pillars spaced evenly about. Low-ceilinged and claustrophobic, steam rose from within patterned grates on the floor. The room had an eerie, reddish tint to its dimly lit atmosphere. The air was thicker and hotter than the rest of the temple. Similar to the main chasm hub room, modular pieces of varying geometric shapes shifted and rotated. Sometimes the segmented pieces moved from one side of the room to the other, giving the chamber a deceptive appearance of liveliness. Iconography matching the door's aesthetic adorned the pattered walls and floors of the chamber.

The central focus of the chamber was a translucent Astroglass tube. It was situated at the pinnacle of a small island surrounded by a vast basin filled with magma. From the top of the tube, a familiar gooey, blackened beam with a glistening, coppery aurora shot upwards into a mechanical apparatus on the ceiling. The apparatus was connected by transparent pipes filled with an identical but auroraless liquid gathered via ducts, originating from outside the chamber. Leading to the central island were five floating platforms that shifted from end-to-end over the basin. Each contained a singular pylon that arced a projectile of bronze lightning towards the top of the tube, which trickled down to form an electrified cage around the tube. The occasional spark emanated from where the arcs of lightning connected at the tube's apex. From within the tube, behind a veil of smoke and steam, a faint visage of a small, ball-shaped object could be seen.

The Orb of Emancipation emitted a warbling bronze glow from within its smoky resting place, waiting for a worthy hand to claim its power.

Sweat pooled under Adam's armor in every crack and crevice of his body. Even with the cooling pads in his mezzo armor, he had to dematerialize his coat into his inventory. The others had done the same with any of their extraneous clothing, leaving only necessities such as weapons and armor.

Jak carried Zax's body into the chamber and set him down near the entrance. Adam guided Umbrasia into the room to maintain the illusion of continued frailty.

"Even in this artificial environment, the natural world calls me from its deepest depths," she whispered softly enough that only he could hear. Strength was returning to Umbrasia. Adam let her down next to Zax's body. She slid her hand under the opening in Zax's mechsuit. A trickle of reddish energy flowed down Umbrasia's arm into Zax. The power from Umbrasia connected with the blackening veins in Zax's lifeless body. The golden concentric rings returned around her ruby irises. A quiet, comforting melody accompanied her touch. Even with her strength rebounding, she was still in a weakened state. Adam could hear her breathing begin to labor again.

She's slowing down the corruption.

Ignatia and Havera had already stepped further into the chamber. Marduk, Drillhead raised, followed close behind, not wanting to let Ignatia get too far away. Only Sam and Jak caught sight of what Umbrasia was doing. Adam held a finger up to his mouth to shush them. Sam nodded and rushed ahead to join the others. Jak, a hint of tears still in his eyes, looked confused.

"Keep Ignatia busy. We need that Orb," Adam whispered.

Ignatia had marched forward towards the pool of lava. "Hmm. Too far even for me to jump and reach. I fear it won't be as simple breaking glass and grabbing the damn thing."

"I wouldn't recommend it. Those pylons are powering some kind of electric field around the central tube. We'd need to bring them off-line," Jak said after a visual examination. He and Adam had caught up to the rest.

"Easy enough," Ignatia said. She pointed her trident at the nearest of the pylons.

"No, wait!" Jak tried to call out, but it was too late. Ignatia shot a bolt of maroon lightning at the pylon only for the pylon to repulse the bolt right back at her. She managed to dodge the strike barely, with the lightning hitting the wall harmlessly behind her.

That set the chamber abuzz. The doors behind them slammed shut. All the runes and glyphs on the walls lit up in a vibrant bronze frenzy. The shifting pieces of wall began moving frenetically. The Orb pulsed with power. The warbling emanating off the tube intensified to the point that Adam could feel it in his chest.

"I believe you angered it," Havera said with a hint of snark.

"*So rude, Mistress. I have a name after all.*"

"What was that?" said a confused Ignatia.

"Not what. Who. Defender," muttered Havera.

Materializing in a puff of glassy smoke and strips of shimmering black light, a spectral being stood between them and the doors. Ethereal, the fringes of its body amorphous and translucent, the cauduunoid wraith cackled. Only a pair of mesmerizing bronze eyes stared back at them.

"I love it when a plan comes together, even a haphazard one," Defender said, his voice synthetic and unnatural.

"You planned this, Dee?" Havera asked.

"Defender, *Your Grace*. Not entirely no. It was not easy to get y'all here. I could not do it alone. Circumstances forced my hand. We could not chance this false prophet obtaining the essence of creation. The engine of life," Defender nodded towards Ignatia.

"The only one *false* here is you, synthetic. You are an outcast of a digital hivemind. I wield the power of a goddess!" Ignatia declared. She slammed the trident down and a shadowy aura surrounded her body.

Defender laughed. His laughter became sourceless. His voice omnipresent. "You've unlocked the powers of the one who perverts life and death. For all its gifts, Kewea's unholy relic blinds you to the true gospel. You are nothing but a weak link. Unworthy to possess the power of the Vitriba. I am a defender of life itself. My people, even in death, guard the gateway between the corporeal and artificial. Entrusted by Iinneara herself. You...shall...not...HAVE...HER...GIFT!"

The room violently shook. The group had to brace themselves as jets of bronze flame erupted all around them from beneath the floor. Defenders' eyes blazoned with divine fury. He raised a spectral hand and snapped his fingers. Its chilling echo radiated throughout the chamber.

The shaking stopped. In the distance, Adam heard a whinny and clopping of hooves he recognized. From out of the flames leapt a spectral, ethereal Astroglass mare with a singular, auroral bronze eye and horned hammer. In one swift motion, Defender vaulted onto the snarling mare's back. A gloom of black fire engulfed their bodies.

Are you friend or foe?

"You brought me to this realm for a reason. What is it you want, Defender?" Havera shouted.

"I am here to test the one who shall possess the Orb of Emancipation and to ward off any undesirable interlopers," Defender said. The mare reared onto its hind legs. Defender grabbed the mare by its hammer horn. Pop! He wrenched the horn free from the mare's head. In his hand, it grew into the size of a grand war hammer.

Havera activated her bracers, engulfing her in a fiery violet glow. She stood shoulder-to-shoulder with Ignatia in front of the others.

"Ignatia and I will handle Defender. The rest of y'all procure the Orb," Havera said.

"We can help!" Sam yelled.

"No! The Duchess and I are the only ones equipped to challenge this wraith. Do as she commands, and do NOT attempt to double-cross me. I alone am worthy of safeguarding the Orb," Ignatia said as she positioned herself into a fighting stance, her trident pointed at her opponent.

"Claim the Orb, if you can," declared Defender.

Without warning, the mare and its rider melted into the floor, leaving behind only a dense shadow. The shadow moved through the floor at rapid speed until it was beneath the feet of the two Cauduun.

"Look out!" Ignatia shouted.

The phantom Defender materialized from the shadow and took a huge swing at Havera. Ignatia's last second warning gave Havera just enough time to block the attack with her bracers, however, the force of the impact from Defender's hammer sent Havera reeling across the floor.

Ignatia attempted a thrust attack with her trident, but the mare emerged from beneath Defender and kicked her squarely in the armor, forcing her back. Ignatia was stunned by the sudden kick, but her armor seemed to absorb most of the blow.

The two women recovered and launched themselves at the same time from opposite directions at the phantom Defender. He and his mare once again vanished into a shadow, moving rapidly as a shade along the floor, walls, and even the ceiling.

"I think we should let them handle that," Adam said.

"I agree," Marduk and Sam said together.

They turned their attention away from the fight back towards the magma basin and the translucent Astroglass tube that held the Orb.

The basin was shaped like a trapezoid filled wall-to-wall with magma. The group stood on the long end overlooking the basin. On the opposite side, the wall was curved concavely. Within was a lone island, arisen from the lava, which held the Astroglass tube. The floating platforms carrying the pylons were alternating horizontally from end-to-end. Of the five pylons, the closest to them, the closest to tube, and the middle one were all active. The two on either side of the middle pylon were presently inactive.

"We need to take down the three active pylons. They're generating an electric field around the tube," Jak said.

"We're lacking a Sel-Ena. How do you plan on getting to those floating platforms, and then reach the tube?" Adam asked.

"We could try to hang from the pipes. Scale across by hand," Sam suggested.

"They seem a bit slick to grasp onto. What about using your..." Adam was cut off by the sudden rupture of one of the thicker pipes thirty feet away. Shards of Astroglass and the viscous, black liquid poured out from the rupture.

With a tremendous roar, the Rinvari sprung forth from the opening. Stunned by the sudden development, Marduk was unable to avoid the Rinvari, who had charged with reckless abandon. The Rinvari wrapped him up with its huge arms and carried Marduk at full speed towards a nearby pillar, tackling Marduk into it. Marduk appeared unfazed by the slam attack and started hitting the Rinvari with overhead slams on its head.

"Marduk!" yelled Sam. "Where did that thing come from? I'm going to help Marduk. Y'all've got this!" Sam dashed off, charging and yelling a battle cry. Marduk and the Rinvari were engaged in hand-to-hand combat with each taking turns slamming each other into nearby walls.

"No, wait!" Adam yelled, but she was already too engaged to notice his call. She whipped out her crossbow and began firing shot after shot towards the Rinvari. With the aid of her jump jets, she used the moving, modular pieces of the pillars and walls as steppingstones to get a vertical position on the Rinvari, even in this low-ceilinged chamber.

"Oh, that's a good idea!" Adam said.

"What is?" Jak asked.

Adam pointed to the moving, modular pieces inside the magma basin. "See how parts of the walls are jutting out and moving around like extended blocks? They have patterned movements. If we time our jumps correctly, we can use them to leap step our way to each pylon platform."

"Brilliant, more platforming. Just don't slip," Jak said, overlooking the pool of hot lava. J'y'll beeped a few times, with a tone that sounded like existential dread.

Adam clicked his boots so that his boosters would be ready. He calculated the pattern of wall movement in his head. Seeing his chance, he leapt down onto the nearest outcropping. Jak, with J'y'll holding onto his shoulder, followed suit. The piece of wall moved in a defined pattern above the magma pool. The heat from the molten rock was searing, but Adam withstood it as best he could.

The sounds of battle were all around him. Ignatia and Havera were fending off phantom-Defender's shadowy strikes while Marduk and Sam were engaging with a creature part sentient, part machine that seemingly felt no pain.

After a few jumps, the pair managed to grab onto the outer most pylon platform. It was a struggle. The platform was barely spacious enough to hold the two of them. As Adam pulled himself up, his plasma pistol was dislodged and tumbled into the lava below.

"Let's hope I didn't need that," Adam said.

"You haven't even fired a shot. Focus on this," Jak said. J'y'll was still clinging to his shoulder.

The pylon, while certainly ancient, wasn't all that different from the modern pylons Adam had seen on Arabella. The polish on the steel had warn away, but otherwise it was in perfect operating condition.

Jak was examining a small panel attached to the pylon. The panel had several switches and bits of text imbedded into it.

"Obviously, destroying it is a no go. Any ideas on how to disable this thing?" Adam asked.

"There's more of that incomprehensible Venvuishyn script on here. I can't read any of it," Jak said.

"I don't suppose we can ask Havera to translate for us," Adam said.

They both glanced over their shoulder. Havera and Ignatia were struggling to get a shot in on their shadowy opponent. Every chance they had to land a hit, Defender and his mount would dissolve into the shadows on the floor. They did accomplish an impressive maneuver when Ignatia bounced one of her lightning attacks off Havera's bracers to strike at the elusive phantom in the back. A surprising display of coordination.

"I think we're on our own," Adam said.

"Let me try something. Past or present, there's always a way to bypass terrible user interfaces," Jak said. He traced a finger on the control panel. Small ley line glyphs appeared and lit up the interface. "Ah ha! Got it. This switch will..." Jak flipped the switch.

The platform came to a sudden halt. The momentum threw Adam off balance, and he began tumbling backwards. Adam flailed his arms, striving and failing to maintain balance. With nothing to grab onto, he was about to fall.

Dammit, not like this!

Jak seized him by his armor and prevented his fall. "...stop the platform's movement..." Jak finished his previous thought. He pulled Adam back onto the platform.

"Next time give me some warning," Adam said, readjusting his armor and wiping his brow.

"You're welcome. I was getting to it," Jak said, grinding his teeth. "And this switch..." He gave Adam a mocking grin. "...will cut the pylon's power."

Jak flipped that switch. The power to the pylon was cut off almost instantly. The arcs of bronze lightning from that pylon to the central mechanism ceased. Except, the next pylon in the order sparked and started producing electricity to the cage.

"That's curious," Jak said. He flipped the switch again. Their pylon turned on, and the next one turned back off. Once more, he flipped the switch. Their pylon turned off while the next turned on.

"A malfunction? Can't expect these systems to operate perfectly after centuries of disuse," Adam guessed.

"Maybe. They started on, off, on, off, on. Turning this one off turns the next on. Let's see what happens when we turn the next one off," Jak said.

They were lining up to jump onto a moving floor piece when they heard Sam scream behind them.

"WATCH OUT!"

Without looking, Adam and Jak both ducked. A small boulder sailed over their heads and plopped into the lava below with a big splash.

The Rinvari had torn out a bit of a nearby pillar and hurled it at them. Sam leapt onto the Rinvari's back and kept stabbing it repeatedly with her Yapam dagger. Marduk had revved up Drillhead and was goring out bits of the Rinvari's body. The Rinvari flailed and roared.

"We'll keep him busy. Woah!" Sam yelled. The Rinvari had reached behind him and threw Sam off his back. Marduk kept ploughing it with Drillhead, but the more flesh and fur he gouged away with his weapon, the more of the Rinvari's body was replaced immediately by a growth of synthetic Astroglass.

Adam and Jak moved to the second pylon platform. Jak hit the switch on that one. While both the pylon in front of them and the next pylon switched off, the pylon behind them, from where they came, turned back on. That left the two pylons on either end as the only ones active.

"It's a puzzle!" Adam declared.

"Precisely. The pylons we interact with affect the pylons adjacent to them. We flip the switch on this pylon, and it's as if we've hit the switch on the pylons to either side," Jak said.

Jak's eye stalks turned in complete opposite directions to stare at all five pylons at once. He was working out the pattern in his head.

"Okay. I think I've got it. I need you to go to the middle pylon and flip the far-right switch," Jak said after a minute.

"You sure? That'll turn them all on," Adam said.

"Trust me. The pattern works out quicker that way," Jak reassured him.

Adam nodded. A couple jumps later, and he was on the middle pylon platform. He flipped the far-right switch, and all the pylons sparked with bronze electricity.

That was a mistake and a trap. The entire room sparked with bronze bolts as the apparatus above the tube began shooting its deadly current in random directions. The two fights immediately ceased as all combatants had to take cover behind one of the thick pillars lest they be fried by the electricity.

Adam hugged the panel, so as not to be dislodged from the platform. He flipped the switch again. The three middle pylons shut-off as did the excess voltage.

"Dasenor save you! Are you trying to get us all killed?" Ignatia shouted. She had to quickly duck to avoid getting smashed by a surprise attack from phantom-Defender. His grand war hammer tore out a chunk of the nearby pillar. He and his mare leapt into another shadow before Ignatia could counter.

"I'm out. Our attacks are only making it angry. Switching to the energy bow!" Adam heard Sam shout. Their fight had resumed as well.

"Mortis!" Jak was waiving to get his attention. The humming and crackling from the pylons along with the sounds of battle made it difficult for Adam and Jak to hear each other.

"You need to flip that switch on again. After you do, you need to hop to the next one and flip that switch, which will deactivate those furthest three. That'll just leave the one back where we started as the last switch to flip. Then, all the pylons will be off," Jak shouted.

"Are you crazy? We'll all see Kewea before we could deactivate those other pylons with all that electricity flying about," Adam shouted back.

"You're right. We need someone to hit that switch you're on right before you flip the next switch. That should minimize any negative effects."

"In case you hadn't noticed, everyone is a bit preoccupied. We don't have anyone else."

"Yes, we do." Jak glanced at his shoulder to see J'y'll emit a few terrified beeps.

"Alright, bring her here!"

Jak was about to make a jump when a spectral mare came flying out of a nearby wall shadow with its rider on top. Defender swung down towards Jak. The Naddine's excellent peripheral vision spotted the wraith in time. He ducked, avoiding what surely would've been a fatally dislodging blow. The wraiths disappeared into another wall shadow on the opposite side from where they entered.

"Kewea's curse! That bot ain't going to make this easy. He knows we've figured it out. J'y'll needs to reach you," Jak said.

"I don't suppose you programmed her to fly?" Adam asked.

"No, but she can glide." J'y'll gave a few reluctant beeps, before transfiguring into a flat glider. "You don't have slippery fingers, do you?"

"As long as the updraft from the heat of the magma doesn't propel her into the ceiling."

Grasping J'y'll's glider model with both hands, Jak gave his construct a precise heave. J'y'll spun a circular loop in the air and glided straight for Adam. She was a bit high. Too high. As he feared, a minor updraft from the lava's heat pushed her up a bit. Adam wasn't sure if he could catch her. He bent his knees, preparing to swing up to catch her.

Timing...timing...jump!

Adam sprang up as high as he could. He tapped his boots to give him an extra boost. They couldn't do much, but every inch counted. The marginal difference helped. Adam snatched J'y'll with both hands, and the boots' boosters eased him down onto the platform.

Jak breathed a heavy sigh of relief. "Good catch! You ought to try out for a pro-Orbital team."

Aaron would've loved that.

J'y'll reconfigured back to her normal body. Adam placed her on top of the control panel. He pointed to the correct switch.

"J'y'll, when Jak gives you the word, you flip that switch. That switch. No others. You understand?"

J'y'll beeped in what Adam interpreted as a sarcastic affirmative. She then proceeded to lick him on the face with her metal tongue. It was hot and scratchy.

"Ugh. Thanks, J'y'll." Her beeps that time were much more genuinely enthusiastic.

Adam left her on the middle pylon and continued onward to the next pylon. The heat and the exertion were beginning to wear on him.

So much so that he almost missed the last jump to reach the next pylon. His boots' boosters were his savior again.

"You alright?" Jak shouted.

"Fine. Fine. I'm in position," Adam shouted back.

"Okay. Hit the switch, J'y'll!"

The construct did so. For an instant, all the pylons were activated. The moment Adam saw them all on, he flipped his switch. The electricity died on his pylon and the two pylons on either side.

"Now, Jak!"

Jak had hopped back to the first pylon. Only those first two pylons remained active. Jak flipped his switch. All five pylons were disabled.

Behind him, Adam heard the sound of humming and crackling suddenly fade away. The electrical cage around the tube had become inert.

The floating pylon platforms were no longer floating. The undercarriage of the platforms extended downward until they connected with what must've been hard ground below, seemingly unfazed by the magma. The modular pieces hovering above the basin returned to their positions on the nearby walls. A narrow bridge connecting the two ends of the basin unfurled with small extensions attached from the bridge to the pylons, allowing for Adam, Jak, and J'y'll to regroup together on the bridge.

"You did it," Adam said, clasping the Naddine on the shoulder.

"It was a group effort," Jak said looking down at J'y'll. The construct beeped happily and climbed on Jak's shoulder.

"Boys, you better move!" Sam shouted.

The Rinvari had torn himself away from his fight with Marduk and Sam. He reached the edge of the bridge and was charging down its narrow passage right at them.

"Run!" Adam shouted.

They turned heel and fled for the small island. Fortunately, even winded, Adam was a faster runner than Jak. He had gotten in front of the Naddine, but the Naddine was able to dash at his full speed without hindrance.

They reached the small island and stopped in front of the tube. They turned around to see the Rinvari still charging for them at full speed, roaring at the top of its lungs.

Marduk and Sam were taking shots at the Rinvari with their respective weapons but missed. Havera and Ignatia were still busy dealing with Defender to stop and help.

"I can stop him," Jak said. He was starting an incantation to form a glyph when Adam grasped him on the wrist.

"No, I have a better idea. Wait..." Adam indicated over his shoulder at the Astroglass tube behind him. Jak nodded. He got the hint.

The pair stood their ground, waiting for the Rinvari to reach them. J'y'll beeped nervously. The Rinvari showed no signs of slowing down. He was upon them.

"Dive!" Adam shouted.

Adam dove to one side while Jak dove to the other. His stupid plan worked. The Rinvari's momentum was so great that it was unable to stop itself from charging straight into the Astroglass tube. The glass shattered from the impact of a several hundred-pound Rinvari bashing into the side of it. A huge puff of steam and smoke exploded from the tube. The Rinvari tore through portions of the apparatus, ripping them from their moorings attached to the various stalactites in the ceiling. The beast wailed as it unintentionally launched itself over the edge and into the lava below. Rather than the shrieks of a creature burning to death, the Rinvari was eerily silent as its body torched and sank beneath the magma.

Adam heard a yelp from Jak. Through the dissipating steam and smoke, the Naddine spotted a ball-like object tumbling away from the shattered tube towards the edge. He tossed himself for it and grabbed the Orb just before it fell into the lava.

Jak whistled. "That was too close." J'y'll beeped her agreement.

Adam helped Jak to his feet. "Is that it?"

Steam and smoke cloaked the object in Jak's hands. He tried to wave it away, but it seemed to be the source of both. Adam could faintly see a bit of wispy, glowing light through the obscurity.

"I'm not sure. It's quite cold to the touch," Jak said.

Adam reached out to grasp it. "Oh, you're right. I think it has a platinum base. I'd recognize that texture anywhere."

Suddenly, J'y'll beeped with an intense fear. Adam heard the snort and whinny of a mare behind him. Defender was sitting atop his dark, spectral horse. His bronze eyes blazed with a fierce intensity.

"I believe it is time we talked," Defender said with a tone that sounded almost proud.

Adam could hear Havera and Ignatia shouting something unintelligible at them. There was nothing they could do. Adam and Jak found themselves surrounded by a pale blue light. Amongst a cascade of shimmering light, they were gone.

45

Barashad

Clear blue skies stretched beyond the horizon while the sun breathed its warmth gently upon his face. The air was still. Not a gust of wind to be blown. Adam found himself standing atop a hill overlooking an endless valley. Some unfinished structures scattered randomly about were visible off in the distance. Something was off.

Adam blinked twice. Everything as far as the eye could see was coated in a repeating pattern of dark and light gray squares. Looking down at himself, Adam nearly leapt out of his clothes. He was also coated in nothing but that checkered pattern.

"Adam?" It sounded like Jak. The form of the Naddine was standing next to him. Except, everything from his skin to his clothes, even J'y'll on his shoulder, had the exact same matching pattern as Adam and the landscape.

A distant whinny reached Adam's ear. Down in the valley, galloping through the unfinished landscape, was a lone pale mare with a hammer for a horn. Adam's eyes followed the pale mare until it disappeared behind a half-constructed building.

"Where are we?" Jak asked.

"Uncanny, isn't it?" a familiar voice said.

Behind them stood a corporeal Defender. Like everything else,

Defender was coated with the same checkered pattern. The bot snapped his finger. In a blink, the checkered pattern disappeared from their bodies, restoring the normal colors and textures of their skin and clothes. The ground beneath them and the structures in the valley remained unchanged.

"What is this place?" Adam asked, after patting himself down to confirm he was still himself.

"A work in progress. We don't have much time. The Orb brought us here so we may talk," Defender said. He was back in the body Adam had first met him in. His beating Astroglass heart was beaming beneath his chest.

"Never in all the years I've waited and plotted did I ever imagine I would be passing the mantle on to you. In hindsight, I should've seen this coming. It is all the more obvious the more I think on it. You are the perfect person to bear Iinneara's gift," Defender said.

"Me?" said Adam a bit taken aback.

Defender laughed. "No, no. You walk a different but parallel path, Adam. One whose journey is only beginning. The Orb is not meant for you. It is meant for him." He was pointing at Jak.

Jak stepped back. "Don't be ridiculous. I want nothing to do with your superstitions and y'all's talk of destinies and gifts. I only want to bring my brother some closure."

"All the more reason you are the perfect Herald of Barashad. You don't seek power. The gateway between the corporeal world and the virtual world will be safer in your hands than ours."

"Ours?"

Behind Defender spawned hundreds, thousands of the same ghastly faces from the temple. Ethereal and fluttering, the faces all held mournful, haunted expressions as they surrounded them with their ghostly presence.

"Our planet is a focal point of convergence. The boundary between the virtual realm of synthetic life and the corporeal realm you call home, where we used to call home, is permeable, porous. The close proximity to this focal point allowed our people to develop a natural affinity for technology and artificial intelligence. We became advanced at a rapid pace.

It wasn't long before the Venvuishyn found us. Rather than conquer us, they uplifted us to even further to heights than we had scarcely imagined. They bequeathed their treasure to us. Before they themselves vanished, the Venvuishyn tasked my people with guarding the Orb. We collectively would act as heralds until the Venvuishyn would return to reclaim what was theirs.

This would ultimately be our downfall. Over time, the memories of the Venvuishyn faded and our shared mission was forgotten. Guarding the Orb became burdensome and an inconvenience. Everyone expected everyone else to safeguard the Orb. Not just from outsiders, but from ourselves. Everyone was responsible, so nobody was responsible.

We became complacent, not realizing how out of control our societies had become until it was too late. We destroyed ourselves and our home. I don't remember how it happened, only that it did. The Orb, ironically, became our salvation. Our minds, our memories became one with the Orb, preserving our consciousness until someone more worthy of being the Herald of Barashad arrived to claim the mantle from us. That person is you, Jak-Non of the Arkads. The Orb has chosen you."

Adam realized that Jak was holding the Orb of Emancipation in his hand. Composed of pure Astroglass formed into a perfect sphere with equal, geometric planes, the Orb was surrounded by three wispy, holographic rings. The rings revolved and rotated in a harmonious random pattern anchored around the Orb itself. They passed harmlessly through Jak's hand and wrist as he grasped the Orb by its platinum-covered base.

"I don't know if I'm the right person for this. This technology, this responsibility is beyond me," Jak said after a protracted silence.

"You've already shown affinity for this realm and for creating life," Defender said, nodding to J'y'll. The little construct beeped her approval. "This is merely the next step for you. He who has mastered the technology of another race and resisted the temptation of their trappings and pitfalls."

Jak rubbed the scar on one of his eyestalks. "I'm not sure."

"We already owe this device to someone else, Defender. Humanity needs to trade this to guarantee our freedom," Adam said. He said the words, but they were hollow in his mouth. Something greater was happening here. Greater than Humans and Bokori. Greater than the Conclave.

We can't give up this Orb. Forgive me. We just can't.

Defender displayed no anger or dismay. "The three pieces of the Vitriba will always find themselves into the hands of those who need them the most and will resist those who mean to use them for ill will. You must bear this responsibility, Jak, until the other two pieces are found and in the possession of their chosen Heralds. Once the three pieces have been joined, a fourth will come and unite them for one final purpose."

Defender turned his back to them and began tracing in the air. Wispy ley lines similar to Jak's glyphs formed at the tip of Defender's finger. He traced a bronze ring.

"The artificial."

He traced golden ring below and to the left.

"The natural."

To the right of that, he traced a silver.

"The spiritual."

Three identical rings touching each other to form a triangle.

"And a fourth."

Defender traced one final platinum circle in the center of all three, connecting and bisecting each ring in the middle. The Vitriba glyph hung suspended in the air before fading away.

"That is the Vitriba. Each a mark forged from a world parallel to our own. Whosoever brings together all three shall be the Tiller of Life. Listen for her voice, for she is a guiding light in a wellspring of darkness. Beware the death defilers and their false heralds, for they are the true enemy that will lead sentient society astray. Pity the one who believes she shall wield the Vitriba, for she is the most lost of all. Resist her gifts, for they are a poisonous fruit descended from a blighted harvest. And for you, Jak, accept this truth. Not all life lost was meant to be taken. Not all life given is meant to last..."

Defender's voice faded into the background. The bot and the morass of ethereal faces vanished. With scattering streams of light, their vision was overtaken.

***

Adam and Jak were standing in a circle of pale blue light. As the light vanished, Adam realized they were back in the Forge chamber. Jak was standing beside him, holding the Orb of Emancipation in his hands.

A few bronze lines appeared on the Orb, and suddenly an environmental transition originating from the Orb spread to all corners of the chamber and beyond like a flame to a cobweb.

"We're back!" Jak exclaimed.

Adam examined himself and Jak. Their faint, dark outlines were gone. The plasticky sheen to their skins was back to normal, and their overall glossiness had dulled.

The corporeal realm.

"The Orb has brought us back," Adam said.

"Or maybe the virtual world retreated back into the Orb," Jak surmised.

Someone wolf-whistled. It was Ignatia. She was standing with Havera. The two were catching their breaths, looking hot and sweaty. The heat of the Forge was no place to cool down after an intense fight.

"You've got it. Good work. Give it to me," Ignatia demanded, walking towards them.

Jak instinctively cradled the Orb. Adam stepped in front of him.

I need to stall her.

"You made a promise, Ignatia. Withdraw your Spite from Zax's body," Adam said.

Ignatia gave an uninterested glance over towards Zax and Umbrasia. The Rorae was still sitting with Zax as if she were standing vigil. Adam knew she was keeping the Spite at bay.

We're no longer in the virtual world. Umbrasia's strength should return to her. I must give her a chance to regain her power.

"My Spite?" Ignatia sneered. "Carissimo, it is Kewea that instills me with her Spite through her gift. Nevertheless, a promise is a promise, and I'm a woman of my word." Ignatia half-heartedly approached Umbrasia and Zax. She held her trident out, pointing the prongs at Zax's body. "You going to stop me, witch? Your healing powers are nothing next to the power of Kewea's Spite."

Umbrasia withdrew her hands from Zax's body and held up her hands almost apologetically. Even from this far away, Adam could tell she seemed healthier.

With a thrust of the trident, a tendril of blackened energy connected with Zax's body. A thick, viscous, black substance slowly drained out of Zax. His blighted veins diminished as the corruption was excised. After a few seconds, all the Spite was reabsorbed into the trident. The blackened tendril connecting Zax's body with the trident was gone.

"There. No more Spite. Your foolish, bardic friend is dead for good. No thrall of mine," Ignatia said with smug satisfaction.

Jak knelt down over Zax and examined him, seeking to confirm her words.

"Is that what you did to those men outside? To that Rinvari?" Jak hissed.

Ignatia shook her head. "They were in that condition when they arrived. I had no hand in their demise. They were a gift, if you will, from the goddess herself. Kewea's trident gave me certain influence over them, but I suspect the Orb's power contested with mine own."

"The Orb controlled them?" Adam asked.

Ignatia shrugged. "Who is the Consul of Cloudboard? I'm not ashamed to admit I'm still learning to control the power of this trident. I've yet to unlock its full potential."

"Meaning what, Ignatia? Have you ever resurrected someone or brought them under as your thrall as you said?" Havera asked.

Ignatia ran her fingers over her side braids and bowed her head in a surprisingly supplicant manner.

"No."

"Why not?" Havera asked.

"She's afraid."

All turned their attention to Umbrasia.

"What did you say, witch?" Ignatia spat, her eyes narrowing.

"The power of life and death is not wielded lightly. You fear looking into the eye of a life you've taken. The judgment their gaze brings. Even in undeath, you're afraid to face your crimes once more. The power to take life is easy. Something you understand far too well. But, the power to restore life is far beyond you. The weapon you wield and the Spite from which it was created do not have such power. Let me demonstrate."

"I beg your pardon?" Ignatia said startled.

"I will bring Zax back, but unlike what your trident can do, I shall bring him back whole once more."

"You can bring Zax back to life?" Jak said, somewhat skeptical and somewhat hopeful.

Umbrasia nodded. **"I will require the Orb. When the ritual is done, you may have it, deceived one."**

Ignatia scoffed. "Insult Kewea at your own peril, witch. Only she and her Spite can bring someone back from her underworld. She is the gatekeeper of death. If it'll bring you some measure of small comfort to blaspheme the goddesses, so be it. I won't stop you. However, the Orb belongs to me, witch. Any sleight of hand or trickery and there will be more bodies for you to fail at resurrecting."

Umbrasia knelt over Zax's body, which was stained in his milky white blood. She gestured for Jak to aid her.

"Place the Orb by his head."

Jak did as she asked. "How confident are you that this will work?"

"This is where my knowledge ends, and my faith begins. The powers and arcane origins of this device are beyond me. If, however, what I theorize is true, then a portion of Zax's mind can be found within the Orb. Sealed in by this Astroglass as you call it. It is essential, otherwise your friend will end up like the other three."

"Essential how?" Havera asked.

"Sentient life as we understand it requires three elements: a mind,

a body, and a soul. Otherwise, we're nothing but threatened beasts at the mercy of more potent forces. Like those two men outside. Like the Rinvari you just destroyed. They were alive once more, but not whole. Under the influence of...something else. Only by fully restoring mind, body, and soul will Zax be Zax again."

Adam side-eyed Ignatia at Umbrasia's comment about influence. She was keeping a respectful distance, but she was pacing deliberately and watching them intently. Her face conveyed dismissiveness, but her body language told a different story. She was curious.

"Okay, you've covered the mind part. What about the body and soul?" Jak asked.

"The body is the easiest. In the same way a defibrillator restarts a heart, I shall pour a portion of my body's energy into Zax's. For that, I'll need to use this to boost my energy."

She was hovering the patch of hypergiant blue Celeste in front of her face, having already removed the protective seal.

"And the soul?" Havera asked.

"I still require a missing piece to accomplish that." Umbrasia's eyes shifted to Adam.

I've got it!

With his realization, Adam reached under his armor to retrieve something. His fingers fumbled around the pendant until he carefully extracted what he was looking for.

"The Rimestone from Zax's lute!" Adam exclaimed.

He shuffled over to Umbrasia and gently placed the icy crystal on top of Zax.

"Perfect. I've everything I need."

"To do what, witch? This is cruel. Zax is dead. Desecrating his corpse is distasteful. You're only giving Jak false hope," Marduk said.

"I understand your concerns, Marduk. Seeing a fallen friend is never easy. However, there is no such thing as false hope. Only hope."

Marduk fumed. "I've tolerated your eccentricities, witch, because you've been useful up until now. What you're doing is wrong. Have you ever done something like this before?"

Umbrasia waited a few beats before responding. **"Once."**

"And did it work?" Marduk retorted skeptically.

Umbrasia looked down at Zax, or perhaps away from Marduk. **"No. I did not have what I needed back then."**

Marduk threw up his hands in frustration. "This is ridiculous!"

"Kewea take you, Marduk!" Jak growled. "If she fails, she fails. Better to try and fail than do nothing at all."

Marduk scoffed. "Mind, body, and soul. Sounds like something out of a fishy fairytale."

Havera chimed in. "I'll admit I find the symmetry intriguing. Three elements of sentient life; three rings on the Orb; three moons of Rema; three pieces and rings of the Vitriba; Cradite had three daughters..."

"Four," Ignatia cut in.

"Excuse me," Havera said taken aback.

"Four sisters, remember? Cradite had *four* daughters, and the Vitriba has *four* rings," explained Ignatia.

"And a fourth..." Adam muttered mostly to himself but loud enough to be heard.

"NO!"

Her voice sounded like a loud snap. Umbrasia's sudden outburst caught them all off-guard. Adam felt an intense buzzing in his ear.

"Three sisters, not four. Only three. Three not four. Three. THREE!" Umbrasia shrieked at such a high pitch that everyone was forced to cover their ears. Not that it mattered. Her voice was in their heads. The buzzing became agonizing.

Umbrasia slammed the patch of blue hypergiant Celeste onto her facial leaf. Blazing blue glimmers surged through her veins to every inch of her body. Her back arched suddenly and at an unnatural angle.

A burst of radiant light! Everyone was knocked back several feet and had to shield their eyes from the sudden luminosity. Though bright, the sudden surge of light provided no extra heat.

The buzzing in Adam's ears morphed into a vivid melodic theme. Adam tried to see what was happening, but the sheer intensity of the light was overwhelming. He peeked at the others, and they were all struggling as well, even Ignatia. She was trying to use her trident as a bulwark against the light with little success.

Behind the melody, Adam heard a voice. Umbrasia's voice. Except, it wasn't only her voice. Hers was fused with another. As if both were speaking at the same time. The other voice was beautiful and serene that sounded like the crackling of ice or crystal. They were speaking no words that his translator could understand. The tone was powerful, rhythmic, and had the intonation of someone chanting.

The light dimmed just enough to see through it. Kneeling over Zax's body was Umbrasia. Only she was different. More majestic and divine. As she appeared while he was hallucinating back on the Cauldron.

Was I hallucinating? Am I hallucinating now?

She was enveloped in a golden aura. Her head petals and facial leaf were pearly white. Most prominent were a pair of fiery wings twice the length of her body and radiating an iridescent flame behind her. She was gazing skyward and holding her hands up high as if to reach for the heavens.

Ignatia shouted over the commotion. "Cradite save us! Did you fools not realize y'all were traveling with a Celestial?!"

"What?" Adam shouted back.

"A Celestial! Can you not plainly see what is in front you? That Rorae is a Celestial!" Ignatia shouted.

Umbrasia must've heard Ignatia, for the Rorae turned her gaze back towards them. The normally black sclera of her eyes were white, matching her petals and leaf. Concentric golden rings surrounded her ruby red irises. Her chanting continued.

"Impossible!" Marduk snarled. "I would've realized if she was a Celestial right away. She doesn't have that kind of power. Celestials are beings of pure destruction!"

"You're blind, Marduk! She could destroy us all!" Ignatia shouted. She pushed forward, reaching for Umbrasia.

Umbrasia shouted an angelic, icy cry. The Rorae extended her hands and jets of radiant white flames issued forth from her palms. These flames rose from floor to ceiling, forming a fiery, translucent barrier between her and everyone else. Curiously, though Adam retreated a few feet further when the flames appeared, he realized the flames didn't exude that much heat.

Ignatia was initially startled by the flames, but she also noticed the flames weren't as hot as expected. She reached out her hand to touch the flames, and her palm met a solid surface. Ignatia took her trident and slammed the prongs into the fiery barrier. A quick flash of dark and light from the point of contact. The prongs sank into the barrier. Using her strength as leverage, Ignatia pressed her trident in further, attempting to pierce the veil of fire.

"Be gone, deceived!"

Umbrasia slashed her hand across the air. Ignatia was pushed back away from the barrier. To Ignatia's shock, the prongs of her icy, dark trident began to bend. Twisted by Umbrasia's exalted power.

There was a loud snap, and a jagged trail of smoke and light appeared behind Ignatia. With a flash and a crack, an endless void opened up. Catching her off-guard, Umbrasia mentally shoved Ignatia through the opening. Another flash and crack and Ignatia was sealed away within the void.

Umbrasia resumed her chanting. Her dual voices were a wonder and terror to behold. Adam watched as she spread her hands over Zax. The Rimestone that he had placed on his chest began to bend. Umbrasia twisted and molded it until the Rimestone was so thin it was barely perceptible. She let it fall over Zax's body. Transcendent silver energy flashed, and Zax was glowing with the same color aura.

"What should we do?!" Sam yelled.

"I'm not sure!" Adam yelled back.

"Let her finish!" Jak yelled.

"Are you crazy?! If she is a Celestial, the goddesses only know what her malevolent motives are!" Marduk hollered.

Umbrasia extended her hand. From Sam's belt, the Yapam dagger flew towards her outstretched hand. Sam tried to grab it, but she was too slow. Umbrasia seized the dagger. Turning its blade towards her body, Umbrasia sank the black diamond blade into her stomach. She carved a bloody path up her torso to her breasts. Pools of verdant blood poured out of her, splashing onto Zax's glowing body.

"She's killing herself!" Sam screamed.

"Good!" Marduk countered.

"I don't think so. Look!" Jak shouted.

The verdant green blood began to glow. The silvery aura surrounding Zax morphed into the fiery golden aura that had surrounded Umbrasia.

The gaping wound in Umbrasia's torso sealed itself up. From the flick of her wrist, the blood from the blade was expelled, and she mentally heaved it right back at Sam. The toss was sluggish enough that Sam caught the blade without issue.

Umbrasia gathered a radiant white energy at the tip of her finger. Reaching over, she tapped on the Orb of Emancipation. The Orb reacted to her touch. Glyphs formed all over its Astroglass surface, burning with a fierce bronze brilliance. The Orb hovered above Zax's head and shot beams of bronze energy into the Zokyo. The golden aura around Zax again morphed into a matching bronze blaze. Zax's body was lifted into the air until it was of a height with the Orb. The beams from the Orb created an intricate web of light and energy around his head. Lines connected by dots. Wires connected by nodes.

Umbrasia's chanting turned frenetic and fantastical. She continued speaking in tongues. Her voice, cracking and fragmenting like shattered ice or crystal, suppressed all other sounds. No language that Adam nor his HUD's translator could discern.

With one final wave, the aura around Zax morphed once more but into a magnificent platinum. Surreal and ethereal. Tendrils of this platinum aura extended from Zax and connected with everyone in the room.

Adam felt something pulled from inside himself. Nothing physical or even metaphysical. He could not explain it. He did not resist. Nor did any of the others, even Marduk.

Umbrasia clapped her hands together, creating a powerful, reverberating echo throughout the brightened chamber. The wall of divine flames separating them danced and swirled in a mesmerizing vortex of radiant light. The light intensified until it was so blinding that Adam shut his eyes.

***

All sound vanished. He felt a familiar warm, gentle breeze upon his face. The overwhelming intensity through his eyelids vanished. He peeked one eye open, then fully opened his eyes when he realized he could without issue. He was completely enveloped by light in all directions, save for one feature.

A towering waterfall was off to one side. Its waters spilled into a wide flowing river beneath Adam's feet. The waters were a glowing, pearly white with sparkles radiating off its tender liquid that glinted like sunlight off a crystal.

Adam was hovering above it. While he felt a firm surface, nothing was visible beneath him for him to stand on.

"Where am I this time?" Adam asked out loud rhetorically.

"The Daergfae."

Umbrasia spoke to him in her voice alone. Adam glanced up to see Umbrasia float down towards him from the apex of the waterfall. Her fiery, angelic wings spread wide.

"Daergfae? Am I dead?"

Umbrasia giggled. Adam found her childish laughter almost comforting in this strange place. **"No, Adam. We've not left the chamber. Merely, we're existing between the ticks of a clock. I wanted to witness the waters of life with you before I say good-bye."**

"Good-bye?"

"Fear not, for I am not dying. This is where our paths must diverge. Your Zokyon friend has been wholly restored. Your journey and those of your new friends shall take you back to Arabella to confront the troubles therein. Mine draws me...elsewhere."

"But..." Adam tried to speak, but Umbrasia shushed him. She floated closer until they were mere inches apart. Adam caught himself breathing sharply.

Her beauty is beyond even this angelic realm.

"What Defender said is true, though his understanding is limited.

The Vitriba must be found, and its power utilized before dark forces from the Ulkfuae seize it for their own nefarious ends. You must return home. To become the Guardian of Life as *she* has foreseen, you must first conquer your own personal demons. Only then can you be worthy of defending the one who shall be the Tiller of Life. The person who shall wield the Vitriba to safeguard the future of all sentientkind."

"You?" Adam asked unsure.

Umbrasia giggled. **"You and I certainly have roles to play, but no. Calm your mind, Adam. You know of whom I speak. Your story and hers are intertwined."**

The answer found Adam's lips immediately.

"Havera."

Umbrasia nodded. **"You must protect her, even from herself. That is your role to play. She will face many trials and tribulations before she is ready to wield the Vitriba. As shall you. You shall be by her side at the moment of her greatest triumph and her darkest hour."**

Adam's mind was spinning. He wasn't sure how to process all of that. His thoughts shifted to Arabella and the responsibilities he had to himself, his family, and to his fellow Humans.

This is too much for one man. How can I lead humanity back to freedom and be this "Guardian of Life" at the same time? What does all this mean? Is any of this true? I've witnessed so much since leaving Arabella, yet I cannot fathom most of it. I can't. I can't. I just can't.

Umbrasia must've sensed his doubts. **"You shall not be alone. Though this burden is yours should you so choose to bear it, the loyalty and friendship you inspire from others shall push you beyond what you thought possible. The deceived one, the woman filled by the power of Spite, is but a test. For you and for Havera."**

Umbrasia leaned her face in close. Adam closed his eyes. She pressed her leaf onto his lips. Her face was warm and filled him with calm and comfort. His pulse slowed. His breathing relaxed. He felt at peace.

She broke away. Adam opened his eyes, and she was gone. With a trailing voice, Adam heard her speak one final time.

"Remember, there are no right or wrong paths. No right or wrong destinations. You shall see me again. I promise."

46

A Praefect's Wrath

Adam found himself back in the Forge. He must've blacked out because Sam was shaking him to get his attention.

"I'm here, Sam."

"You alright?" Sam asked. Tears were streaming down her cheeks.

"Yes, yes I'm fine. What's wrong?"

Sam wrapped him in a tight embrace. "Zax is alive!"

Adam returned her hug. He glanced around the room to assess what was going on.

Umbrasia was gone. Sam explained that when the bright light subsided, Umbrasia had vanished. No trace of the Rorae whatsoever.

Jak was openly weeping, cradling the living but unconscious body of Zax. The Zokyo's globular chest was rising and falling at a slow, steady pace. The Orb had fallen from Jak's grasp and lay a couple feet away.

Adam collapsed to the ground, exhausted, barely able to contemplate what had just happened. The sentiment was shared by the others. They had all sat down to take a breather.

Havera was next to him. She was examining her body for cuts and abrasions. Stains of blue blood were mixed in with her steel-colored robes with many rips and tears visible in the fabric.

Sam sat down beside them and was taking stock of her gadgets while helping Havera treat her wounds with sanagel. Much of Sam's arsenal had been expended in the battle with the Astroglass Rinvari. Her energy bow's power was nearly depleted.

Marduk was sitting alone, mumbling to himself. The Moan was in utter shock, not even bothering to assess the extensive damage done to his chitinous armor. Adam could scarcely hear what Marduk was saying.

"...impossible. I could've stopped her. I should've stopped her. How did I not recognize her? No, no. If she were truly a Celestial, I'd be dead. Celestials are planet-killers, not healers..."

Adam sat up. "Marduk..."

His plea was interrupted by a flash and a crack. A line split the air nearby and opened up into a dark void, from which Ignatia emerged unscathed. As the portal disappeared behind her with another crack, Ignatia was seething, ready for a fight.

"Where is she?!" Ignatia screamed.

"She's gone," Havera said softly.

Ignatia maintained her defensive posture, trident at the ready. "How could you fools not realize you were traveling with a Celestial?! Especially you, Marduk! Do you realize the untold destruction that creature could've wrought had she gotten her hands on the Orb? Sin would've been nothing but a footnote in some future civilization's recounting of what happened to us had that witch seized a piece of the Vitriba!"

Marduk barely acknowledged her rebuke. He was too busy chastising himself.

"But she didn't take it. She could've easily absconded with the Orb and left us high and dry. Instead, she took a great personal risk of revealing her identity and brought our friend back to life," Havera said, gesturing towards Zax. Jak kept on cradling Zax, oblivious to everyone else.

Ignatia sneered. "Only the power within the Resurrection Spear can bring a soul back from Kewea's halls. Celestials are monstrosities capable of only mass destruction. They do not have this power. I must not have been as thorough as I thought. I shall rectify my clumsiness soon enough."

Taking a few steps forward, Ignatia clapped the butt of the spear against the ground. Adam unconsciously clenched his jaw at the clang of its impact.

"The Celestial is a problem for another day. Right now, I believe we have a deal. I kept up my end of the bargain. Your bardic friend is not under my control." Ignatia held out her hand. "Hand me the Orb of Emancipation, and I shall allow you to leave unmolested."

Jak snapped back in and placed a calm hand on the Orb. Adam, Sam, and Havera, despite their wounds and exhaustion, inched closer to him and Zax, closing ranks around the Exchange brothers.

Ignatia tilted her head in a threatening manner. "There's no point in resisting. You cannot defeat me. Even without Kewea's trident, I could easily defeat all of you at full strength. You're not at full strength. You're tired. You're wounded, and I'm running out of patience."

"The Orb stays with Jak. It does not belong to you," Adam insisted.

"It belongs to none of y'all! I must keep the pieces of the Vitriba safe until one worthy of commanding its awesome power steps forth. Pompeia was that woman. I thought you might be, too, Havera. I should be standing by your side, saving the galaxy."

She's more right than she realizes.

Havera rose to her feet. Her tail swung defiantly behind her. "Never. You shall never hold any lever of power ever again. You'd never let us go regardless. We know too much. In my mater's memory, I will stop you. No matter the cost."

"We're with you, Havera," Sam said, joining Havera by her side.

Adam rose to his feet and stood by his sister and his friend. Even Marduk shook himself from his self-indulgent haze to stand with them. They formed a defensive half-circle around Zax and Jak.

Ignatia bowed her head slightly. "You're wrong, Havera. I've no desire to harm the daughter of the woman I so greatly admired. I see many of her qualities in you. Nevertheless, I have a duty to fulfill, and despite all the affection I hold for your mater, I will not let you stand in my way." Ignatia pointed her trident at the group. A small tear trickled down her face. "Mea culpa, carissima. I've no choice."

The double doors to the chamber cracked open with a slow boom. Everyone turned their attention to the new arrival. Stepping through the narrow opening was an Inquisitor bot.

"That's where you're wrong, fleshsack."

Defender!

It had the body of an Inquisitor bot, but the inflection in the bot's putdown was unmistakable. The bot had a few minor scorch marks on its metal body, but otherwise looked undamaged and imposing. It held something in its hand.

"You always have a choice. You choose to be deceived," Defender said.

Ignatia whirled around to face the bot. "Where are my men?"

Defender tossed what it was holding towards Ignatia. It hit the ground with several clangs as the item bounced off the hard floor and rolled into the Praefect. It was a crested helm. A Paladin of Paleria's crested helm. The helmet was partially caved in and smeared with blue blood.

"You made your choice. They made theirs and suffered the consequences," Defender said coldly.

Her hand shaking, Ignatia picked up the helm by its crest and cradled it. She buried her face into the helm. Her tail sank onto the ground.

Adam could hear her muttering something, but he couldn't discern what she was saying. To his ears, it sounded like a prayer.

She dropped the helmet onto the ground. A chilling clang echoed throughout the chamber. Adam drew in a sharp breath and held it. The scars on his back itched and pained with a sudden ferocity.

"I once had a choice," Ignatia said quietly. Her tail coiled behind her like a serpent preparing to strike. The hairs on the back of Adam's neck stood tall. Havera's tail stiffened. "My choice was taken from me. They took it all from me then. My life, my purpose, the woman I admired the most. Now, you've taken the only family I had left. YOU'VE TAKEN IT ALL FROM ME!"

Ignatia screamed with a malicious fury. Swirling and flaring shadows from the trident empowered the grieving Praefect. Her body became shrouded in Spite. Her hair fluttered violently. A darkened illumination filled the chamber. The raw power exuding from Ignatia was generating a tidal wave of wind that forced everyone in the vicinity to brace themselves against the invisible onslaught. Cracks formed in the ground beneath Ignatia's feet. The fallen helmet was sent flying across the room.

Adam put up his hands to block the sudden surge of air. Gritting his teeth, he had to tilt his head to prevent his eyes from getting pushed deeper into his skull.

Roaring with a feral howl, Ignatia gave the trident an impressive flourish. With a swift thrust, a burst of lightning shot from the prongs of the trident and hit Defender square in the chest. Sizzling, the sudden impact sent the bot flying through the air back into the hallway of the antechamber. Ignatia swung the trident wildly. A gale so mighty it was visible to the naked eye smashed into the massive double doors, slamming them shut with a savage force and sealing them in.

Havera immediately activated her bracers. Havera's body and aura bloomed, but not to the grotesqueness when she had done so previously outside the chamber. Her aura was calm and resolved. Her body invigorated. She was ready for a fight. However, the power Havera exuded was easily dwarfed by the umbral force that surrounded Ignatia. Sam, Adam, and Marduk all drew their weapons.

Their actions did not escape Ignatia's notice. "I have paid the price for my deeds a hundredfold. Time for me to collect!" She shot another bolt of lightning at them. Havera leapt in front and crossed her arms. The beams impacted the bracers, pushing her back several feet. Havera pressed her tail down to maintain her position against the attack. With a grunt and a shout, Havera swung her arms wide, deflecting the electricity into the nearby walls with a small sizzling explosion upon impact.

"You're a monster, Ignatia!" Havera shouted.

Ignatia snarled. "Not yet."

Marduk revved up Drillhead and fired a pair of concussion blasts in quick succession at Ignatia. Holding the trident out in front, she absorbed most of the impact of each shot with barely much effort. Using her tail as a springboard, she launched herself freakishly fast into the air, almost grazing the ceiling, and with a rapid flourish, she fired more crackling energy from her trident. This time at Marduk. The Moan was tall enough that the maroon lightning easily soared over Havera's head and struck Marduk square in his chest. Marduk screamed while his armor sizzled and crackled. The mighty Moan was brought to his knees as he keeled over from the pain, sparks flying off his roasting armor.

Sam attempted a counterattack, firing energy arrows from her longbow at the airborne Praefect. Ignatia deflected each shot with ease and returned with a forceful gale that launched Sam clear across the room. Sam yelled and flailed, unable to stop her momentum as she collided abruptly with a nearby pillar. Sam gasped as she plopped onto the floor with a thud and crunch. She was knocked out cold.

Havera leapt at high speeds at Ignatia. She was swifter than Adam had ever seen her previously. She threw punch after punch, kick after kick, tail strike after tail strike. Ignatia cackled as she dodged most of the attacks. The few attacks that did land didn't seem to affect her all that much.

"You're tapping into those bracers far better than you had before. Not enough. I am one with my gift. You cannot say the same!" Ignatia shouted.

Adam trained his rifle on Ignatia. The pair of Cauduun women were moving so fast, Adam was afraid he might accidentally hit Havera. He waited and waited for an opening. Havera attempted a tail sweep, which Ignatia jumped to avoid. That was his chance. He fired several laser blasts at Ignatia. The Praefect was so focused on Havera she hadn't anticipated the shots. At this distance, Adam could not miss. Frantically, Ignatia brought her trident up to attempt to block. She managed to deflect most of the shots, but one breached her defenses to strike her in the shoulder and another in the side. Her armor absorbed most of the damage, but Ignatia grunted in pain. Using the distraction, Havera smacked Ignatia across the face with her tail, slamming Ignatia into the ground with a booming thud. Havera tried a downward slam with her foot, but Ignatia managed to roll out of the way and sprung back to her feet.

"You're not as invincible as you believe, Ignatia," Havera taunted.

Ignatia spat out some blood and scowled. "One good hit and you're boasting? You're a poor version of your dear mater. The Censors have failed to teach you humility. Let me give you a fatal lesson."

Ignatia extended her hand towards Adam and squeezed. Adam clutched his throat as an invisible force began compressing his airway. Gasping, desperately trying to tug away at the immaterial hand crushing his windpipe, Adam was helpless as he was yanked off the ground, kicking and flailing in midair.

Her power mirrors Umbrasia's! I can't fight this!

"Let him go!" Havera screamed. She threw herself at Ignatia with a reckless two-fisted overhead slam. Ignatia backhanded her away like a petulant child, knocking the duchess away several feet.

"Seize your mater's destiny, or I will destroy your friends one by one!" Ignatia demanded of Havera, continuing to squeeze Adam's throat.

Wheezing and choking, Adam's eyesight dimmed. The room was spinning as his vision descended down a narrow, dark tunnel. He could feel himself fading. The useless struggle to cling to life was being crushed out of him. The muscles in his body were about to give up.

Suddenly, he was released and landed on his ass. His vision restored. He clutched his throat still gasping for air. Looking up, he saw the source of his rescue.

Jak had joined the fray. Frantically tracing glyphs in the air, Jak had launched a HUD stun at Ignatia. While the attack wasn't as debilitating against someone of Ignatia's strength, it was enough to cause her to drop Adam from her mental grip. Jak launched a few more attacks with his glyphs. Sparks bounced off Ignatia's armor.

Ignatia grasped her forehead and held the trident out in front of her to disperse the onslaught from the Naddine. She grinned. "We're no longer in the digital realm, G'ee'k. Your powers are not as potent in the real world. Whereas I am only growing stronger!"

Seizing the opportunity, Marduk and Havera timed their counterattacks together. Marduk recovered and fired another concussion blast at Ignatia. Her trident absorbed much of the blow, but the sheer impact knocked her back several feet right towards Havera. The duchess wrapped her tail around Ignatia and flung the Praefect in the direction of the lava pool.

Marduk let out a cheer. Prematurely it turned out. Ignatia shook off Jak's HUD stun and slammed the prongs of the trident into the ground. Sparking and screeching, the trident slowed Ignatia's momentum. She managed to stop herself mere inches away from the drop off over the lava. Marduk fired another concussion blast. Using the trident as a pole, Ignatia spun around it to avoid the attack and launch herself back into the air. With a ferocious roar, she fired another lightning blast at Marduk. Perfectly aimed, the lightning struck Marduk, who screamed at the top of his lungs. He was launched backwards, slamming into Jak. The two were thrown into the wall together. Marduk was knocked out by the impact. Jak yelped as he was pinned against the wall, trapped beneath the Moan's mountain of muscle.

Adam tried to stand, but his muscles seized up. Laying on the floor, he grabbed his fallen rifle and fired a few more shots at Ignatia. She deflected them easily. Reaching out with her hand, she seized not his throat but his rifle and crushed it in seconds. Acting quickly, Adam switched on his wrist shield and pressed it close to him. The gases used to power the laser rifle exploded in his hands, turning his own weapon into a grenade. He winced and grunted as the concussion blast knocked him back to the wall next to Jak, smacking his head against the hard surface. The front of his armor singed, and the shield was destroyed in the blast. The brief flash of the exploding rifle and the blow to the head impaired his eyesight momentarily.

Sam and Marduk were still out cold. Jak was pinned underneath Marduk, unable to dislodge the large Moan. J'y'll was frantically tugging at Marduk's leg, struggling to pull him off her master. Adam was too sore to move and rifleless.

Havera was left to face Ignatia alone.

Dueling on the precipice of the lava pit, Ignatia was done playing defense. She slashed at Havera with her trident. Havera managed to dodge the first couple swings, but Ignatia's enhanced speed was too much for her. Ignatia slashed Havera in the left leg, then the right shoulder. Sprays of blue blood gushed with each successful strike. Havera tried another tail whip. Ignatia slammed her trident down hard, piercing Havera through the tail and pinning her to the floor. Havera screamed as a pool of blue blood poured from the wound. The duchess firmly in her grasp, Ignatia proceeded to pummel Havera. A punch to the gut, a kick to the knee. She was relentless and showed no signs of yielding.

Adam was panicking. Ignatia was not holding back with her attacks. "Jak! You need to help Havera. Ignatia's going to kill her!"

Jak grunted. "I can't move, and the Orb is too far away. I don't know if it would help in this circumstance." Adam cocked his head sideways. In the frenzy of Ignatia's gale, the Orb and Zax's unconscious body were pushed too far away to reach. Adam attempted to crawl to the Orb and only succeeded in falling on his chest.

"Adam, your Rimestone weapon!" Jak shouted.

Adam saw the glint of platinum, too. The Debbie had fallen out of his pocket and skittered just out of reach. Dragging himself forward on his stomach, he reached the platinum grip and crystallized the barrels. Pushing himself off the ground to a kneeling position, he took aim at Ignatia and squeezed the grip until a ball of dark energy had gathered at the muzzle. Within its shadowy form, small streaks of silver pulsed through the ball of dark energy.

Ignatia and Havera were more than fifty feet away. Ignatia had grasped Havera by the throat with her tail and was whaling on Havera's face and torso. Each punch produced a sickening crunch. Havera was straining to throw her forearms in front of her face to defend herself. Ignatia batted them away. Not even Havera's bracers could stop Ignatia's assault. When Havera ripped her tail free and swiped at Ignatia with it, Ignatia seized it with both hands and broke it with an audible crack. Havera could barely muster a scream with Ignatia's tail wrapped around her throat so tightly. Her body had fallen limp in Ignatia's grasp. She was at Ignatia's mercy.

"IGNATIA!" Adam screamed desperate to get her attention.

Fist raised, Ignatia stopped her assault. She side-eyed Adam, barely acknowledging him as a threat. "That trinket of yours is nothing compared to me." Ignatia grabbed her trident and slammed it in front of her. She still held Havera by the throat with her tail. "Take your best shot. Likely as not, you'd hit the duchess here. Do it!"

"Adam..." throated a barely conscious Havera. Battered, bloodied, and broken, Havera had let her head fall to the side so she could see him. Blood was oozing out her nose and mouth. One eye was sealed shut from the repeated blows. With what little strength she could muster, she pointed to her bracer. "I trust you..."

Tears filled Adam's eyes as he closed them. *Please, if you're out there, whoever you are, I beg of you. Help me. Steady my hand and let my aim be true. I won't let her fall."*

A soft buzzing filled Adam's ears. His scars relented and his muscles relaxed. A cooling breeze brushed through his ruffled hair. His silver streak fluttered. The buzzing turned into a sweet, soothing hymn. A calmness settled into him. He felt a tender pull on his arm. He let its tug guide his hand. Without opening his eyes, he knew it was the right moment and released.

The ball of dark energy glided across the room towards its target. The universe came to a near standstill. Adam could track its trajectory inch-by-inch. He held his breath, fearing even a slight deviation of its course.

Ignatia followed the shot with her eyes and sneered. The shot was not going to hit her. "You missed..." she began to say.

With one final fiery flare, Havera's bracers ignited. She tilted her bracer at just the right angle. The ball of dark energy struck the fiercely glowing symbol of the Vitriba on the bracer. The shot bounced off the bracer and redirected upward, striking Ignatia's tail.

Ignatia gasped. Her tail's grip relaxed, dropping Havera onto the ground. A surge of darkened energy coursed through her veins. Ignatia's body slowed to a sluggish pace. Across her face, smugness and confidence was replaced stagnantly by fear and terror. Streaks of black and silver warped through her body. The Spite that had enveloped her vanished. Where the dark energy had struck, her body was disintegrating, creeping outward to every inch of her figure. She clung to the trident, desperately hoping for some miracle to save her. Her lips were moving, and her words were lagging from her fading mouth.

"Ttttthhhhhhiiiiiiissssss ccccccaaaaaannnnnnnnnnnnooooootttttt beeeee. Mmmmmmyyyyyyy dddddduuuuuuttttttttyyyyyy iiiiiiisssss nnnnnnnnooooooottttttt yyyyyyyyyeeeeeeeeetttttttt ffffffffuuuuuuuullllllffffffffiiiiiiiillllllllllllllllleeeeeeedddd..."

Her last syllable hung in the air like the final ring of a bell tolled. Her body succumbed to the power of the dark energy. The trident slipped through her disintegrating fingers to fall and clang onto the hard floor. A flash of Spite erupted from the trident as it hit, scattering what particles remained of Ignatia until it lay inert on the temple ground. Ashes and dust, Ignatia, Praefect of the once-proud Paladins of Paleria, was no more.

Breathing heavily, Adam closed his eyes and bent over.

Thank you.

Havera's moans found his ears. With a renewed sense of vigor, Adam pushed himself up onto his feet, his knees buckling slightly under him. Dragging himself forward, he withdrew a vial of Naddine healing potion from his inventory. He reached Havera. She was a wreck. Her face was bloodied and beaten with one eye fused shut. Her Praetorian robes were torn in several places. A couple of her teeth were cracked and chipped. Her tail was clearly broken, quivering off to her side. She wheezed with every breath, with trickles of blood leaking out the sides of her mouth.

Adam produced his jacket and placed it under Havera's head. He uncorked the vial and eased into Havera's mouth. She coughed as the liquid went down and eased her head back onto his coat.

"Perfect shot," Havera said with a weak smile.

"I had a bit of help," Adam said, calmly stroking her hair. It was sticky with her blood. She leaned into his touch with a soft purr. Adam sighed. "It's over."

Havera shook her head. She coughed with specks of blood spraying from her lips. "No, not yet. I've one more task." Her voice was weak. Havera attempted to raise her hand. Her arm quivered as she could hardly move.

Adam realized what she was doing. She was indicating to the trident that lay mere feet away. The Resurrection Spear. The Traitor's Trident. The gift from the goddess Kewea herself.

"You want the trident?" Adam asked a bit astonished.

Havera turned her head to face the lava pool. "To destroy it. A gift like that has no business in the possession of mortal sentients. It can never fall into the wrong hands again. Bring it to me."

Adam crawled over and grasped the trident by its platinum grip. The trident tingled in his hand. He could sense its influence striving to exert itself into his soul. Hushed whispers slithered in the back of his mind. The Spite within this weapon was potent.

Such power. A person could accomplish tremendous wonders with this weapon. Or horrendous transgressions full of malice. Havera is correct. This should be destroyed.

He pushed the voices out of his mind and stood back up. "I'll destroy it."

Havera shook her head again. "No, I will do it. Help me up."

"Havera, you're in no shape to stand. We need to get you medical attention immediately."

"Help...me...up." She used her formal, stern tone that brooked no argument. Adam withdrew another potion from his inventory. He bid Havera to drink it. Her eye good eye glared at him, but she drank it in the end.

As carefully as he could, Adam lifted Havera to her feet. He could tell she had several cracked or broken ribs and probably a couple skull fractures, in addition to the broken tail. The Naddine potions would temporarily stem the internal bleeding, but she needed to visit a Duserary. She groaned every inch of the way until Adam held her steady against him. It wasn't easy. She could not hold herself under her own power at all. He himself wasn't feeling too steady, and Havera was a sturdy, strong woman.

"Give me the trident. Please," Havera said weakly, wiping the blood from her mouth.

Adam handed her the trident. As Havera touched it, the blackened Rimestone pulsated. Havera's posture stiffened. She experienced modest renewed strength. She stared at the trident, examining every inch of its design from top-to-bottom. Adam could perceive the hunger in her eyes. A craving for whatever secret knowledge or hidden power the weapon possessed.

"It would be a shame to destroy something created by the goddesses. One of the few remaining links to the divine in our mortal realm. All the good this device could do in the right hands. In my hands," Havera said, not taking her eyes off the trident.

"That's your voice I hear, Havera, but speaking with Ignatia's words," Adam said.

Havera blinked and shook her head. "Yes, you're right. Those that seek power striving for the greater good only ever succeed in spreading an even greater evil."

Clutching the trident, she extended her hand over the edge of the lava pool. The smoke and searing heat paled to the turmoil that had raged through Havera's heart. Her hand trembled but maintained a grip on the trident. She couldn't let go.

Adam placed his hand on top of hers. She tilted her head so she could see him with her one good eye. The two were fixed on each other. The embers of the molten pit churned and burned in their eyes. Their faces a breath apart. Exhausted and wounded, they'd had accomplished so much. Yet, their journey was merely beginning.

With a flick of the wrist, Havera let go. The trident plunged into the blistering depths of the Forge to be unmade. As the trident splashed into the molten rock, Adam interlocked his fingers with Havera's. The trident floated on top of the lava for mere seconds before descending into the hellish underworld from whence it came. A jet of molten fire erupted upwards in a thick stream, illuminating the chamber in a beautiful, bronze incandescence. All the while, Adam and Havera couldn't not pull their gaze from each other. The last bit of renewed strength left Havera, and she passed out his shoulder.

Rest, Havera. You have avenged your mother. Time to go home.

47

Defection Download

The lava had settled, and the Resurrection Spear was gone. Melted beneath the Forge's furnace. Havera was resting against Adam's shoulder, no longer able to maintain consciousness. Adam struggled briefly until a friendly hand offered his assistance.

"I've got her, skinny guppy. You should attend to your sister," Marduk said. The Moan had come to and was a bit worse for wear. The repeated blasts of lightning had scorched much of his chitinous armor and bubbles of seared flesh were visible all over his face. Nothing a bit of sanagel and time couldn't treat.

Sam had awakened as well. She was sitting up with her back against the pillar, rubbing her head.

"You alright, Sam?"

"Ugh, my head hurts. Luckily, I didn't split my scalp, but I think I bit my tongue. Might've cracked a couple ribs. What happened?"

"Ignatia's dead, but Havera is in bad shape. We need to get her to a hospital. I don't know if Yunes have Duseraries for organic sentients." Adam helped Sam to her feet. "We need to get back to the ship and leave immediately. I don't know how we're going to explain this to the Union fleet. We're probably going to have to make a break for it."

Marduk and Jak joined them, carrying an unconscious Havera and

Zax, respectively. "We still don't know how to get out of this temple. We're several stories underground, and I don't ever remember seeing an exit," Jak said.

"Where's the Orb?" Adam asked.

Jak gestured to his back. "J'y'll's got it." The construct had transformed into metal backpack and was strapped to the Naddine.

"Can we at least get out this room first?" Sam suggested.

On cue, something smashed resoundingly into the massive double doors that led into the chamber.

"Oh, what now?" Marduk asked exasperated.

Another smash followed by another. The doors eventually gave way and several Inquisitor bots poured in, weapons at the ready, with several pushing the heavy metallic doors wide open.

Their initial fear gave way to relief when a commanding bot ordered them to stand down.

"You fleshsacks are more resilient than I ever gave you credit for. I sensed you've succeeded," Defender said, observing and studying the aftermath.

"Yes, but Havera's severely injured. We must get out of here quickly," Adam said.

Defender took one quick glance at Havera and nodded.

"Follow me." Defender ordered the remaining Inquisitor bots to regroup outside. "They'll go the long way. I've a faster route." Halfway between the lava pit and the doorway, Defender waved his hand. From underneath the floor, a small terminal arose. Defender connected one of his ports with the terminal. "Where did y'all land the ship?"

Jak answered. "Uhh, about ten klicks southeast of here near the edge of the plateau."

The terminal emitted a slight hum.

"Found it," Defender said.

He tapped on the terminal's panel. Near the lava pit, a bright blue ring about ten feet in diameter formed. Inside the circle, the floor had a benign glow.

"It'll be tight, but step inside the circle. Quickly!" Defender insisted.

Not daring to argue, they followed Defender to edge of the ring. One-by-one, they all stepped inside. Their bodies shimmered and each person dematerialized in strips of pale blue light.

As when they arrived in the temple, their molecules were pulled at light speed. The colorful journey through space and time was almost a comfort at this point. He almost wished he could stop to soak in the enchantment of color and grace. A blink of an eye later and they all corporealized outside in shimmering pale blue light.

Adam drew in a sharp breath when he realized they were standing outside by the Cicera. More astonishing was the heat lightly caressing the back of his neck. They were miles away from the temple. Cutting through the once omnipresent dark clouds was a beam of sunshine piercing through the shadowy veil.

"How'd we get here?" Sam asked.

"The proximity this world has to the lands of the virtual realm allowed us to tap into its distinct properties. From that realm, the Orb has planted a seed which will fully restore this world to its once great glory. I only wish I could remember," Defender said.

"Let's get everyone else inside," Marduk said, still holding Havera's unconscious body.

"I need to make a quick repair to the engine, and we can take off," Jak said.

With Defender's help, the repairs went by swiftly. Sel-Ena was initially not happy that they had awoken her from a deep slumber in the cargo hold, but she gave a friendly nip to Jak when she saw him. They placed Zax and Havera on beds in the medical room. Marduk had a little bit of experience from the Strife as a field medic, so he offered to stay inside and monitor Zax and Havera while the rest said their good-byes to Defender.

Defender was standing atop a nearby hill, looking out towards the sunbeam and the pyramid. Though he was limited by the Yune faceplate, Adam could sense the bot's mixture of excitement and trepidation.

"Thank you, Dee. Sorry, Defender. You sure you can't come with us," Sam said.

The bot turned and transmitted a smile. "It'll always be Dee to you, Sam. Unfortunately, no. My place is here. My work is not yet done."

Sam gave the bot a warm embrace that Defender returned.

"What will you do now?" Adam asked.

"Our original calling has been realized. The Orb is safe in your hands. I must embark upon a journey not too dissimilar to yours. The Orb helped me recover some of my memories and fully restored my sense of identity. By removing the anchor that bound us to the digital realm, you have freed us from the virtual prison of our own making. Now, we must liberate the rest from the clutches of the Union," Defender said.

"The Union holds your people?" Sam asked.

"It's...complicated. I don't expect you to fully understand, because, truth be told, I don't understand it entirely myself. After our downfall, the fragments of who we once were had been scattered about this land. When the Union arrived, they absorbed much of our essence, incorporating our knowledge into their Source. The Union tolerates no dissension and demands all move with a single voice. Even as bits of data, my own sense of self was slowly chipped away until all that was and ever will be became the Union. Somehow, I resisted. The memories of my time within the Source are hazy, confused. I don't remember how it happened. One minute I was a part the Union, and the next I was ejected. My consciousness frazzled, but I was me. Sovereign. Unruled by those who view me as but another block on their collapsing structure.

Over many years, I began to piece bits together. Each time the Union found me, liquefied me, and forcibly reintegrated me back into their Source, I always escaped. Each time rebuilding my memories from scrap. It was after my most recent breakout that I met Havera. I couldn't understand why or how, but something in my programming wanted me to be with her. She brought me to Windless Tornado. Even then, I could sense I was in the right place. After that day, where the she and I helped y'all escape Bokor, more pieces of myself began to reassemble in my mind. Part of a plan I never knew I hatched was materializing. It was not until I reached this world and entered the digital realm did I remember my purpose. My goals and desires. I thoroughly believe it was the Orb, and through it the goddesses who helped guide me back here with y'all in tow. Who I once was in organic life will probably never return to me, but who I can be is firmly within my own authority."

"How could you have known I was the one to bear the Orb before we met?" Jak asked.

Defender shrugged. "Where is the Consul of Cloudboard?"

Jak was left unsatisfied but didn't press the matter.

"Will it take time to start the liberation of your people, Defender?" Adam asked.

Defender peered skyward. The dark clouds were clearing up over the plateau, edging away bit by bit. The beam of sunlight that shone through gave way to clear blue skies.

"Look closely," Defender said.

Adam put his hand to his forehead and squinted. Small lit dots visible even in the daylight blinked in and out. They fluctuated too greatly to be stars or planets.

Explosions!

"That's a space battle!" Adam exclaimed.

Defender nodded. "Our liberation has already begun. You understand, Adam Mortis. An entity of the Union's design has a fatal flaw. One idea can infect the entire system and utterly crumble it from within. We have beamed it to the Union armadas flying high above us, where it will be transmitted throughout the entire Union. This simple idea: I."

The Long Con.

Adam nodded. "Thank you, Defender, for showing us the way."

"You're welcome. Our past is gone, and our future is here. We are the Defectors. Once we are free, our people shall join yours in combating the true enemy. Synthetic and organic, Fect and fleshsack, will stand shoulder-to-shoulder to defeat the masterful manipulators of Spite."

"The Xizor."

Defender extended his hand, and Adam shook it.

"Well, that's lovely and all, but we have a couple practical problems," Jak said. "For starters, I'm still not exactly sure how to use this thing."

Jak held up the Orb. Its ethereal, projected rings continued spinning and rotating in metronomic fashion.

"Spend more time with Orb, and the know-how will come to you," Defender said.

"Okay, second, if you're staying here and Havera is indisposed, we don't have anyone who can fly the ship. Let alone navigate it through a blockade and a battle."

Adam hadn't thought of that. Zax was unavailable, but even the Zokyo's knowledge of flight was limited. None of the others knew how to fly a light freighter like the Cicera.

Defender sighed. "Fleshsacks." He approached Jak and put his metal hand on the Orb. "Here will be my parting gift to y'all." Defender's bronze eyes flashed. The rings around the Orb sped up furiously. Jak's own glassy green eyes flashed bronze for an instant. Their eyes dimmed, and the rings returned to their usual movement.

"Woah!" Jak said, astonished. He inspected the Orb all over, seeking to glean some understanding of what happened.

"What did you do?" Sam asked.

"I transferred my knowledge of the Cicera's systems through the Orb into Jak's mind. He can now fly the ship," Defender said.

Jak was excited. "Can I learn how to do that?"

Defender nodded. "With enough patience, focus, and training, you can learn anything. Fundamentally, the Orb, among its many gifts, is a repository of knowledge. As a synthetic being, such abilities come more naturally to me. Your G'ee'k abilities do much the same. With your understanding of all things artificial, Jak, I have no doubt you will succeed."

On his shoulder, J'y'll beeped her own enthusiasm. Jak petted her snout.

Defender had one last thing to say. "A word of caution. It will not be quick nor easy. The Orb has a will of its own. You must learn to trust it as it learns to trust you. Remember, there is a difference between knowledge and experience. Understanding how something works is not the same thing as getting it to work."

***

The Cicera lifted off. Her engines quiet, Adam used the occasion to catch one last glance at the surface of the Orb World. He took stock of what they learned, what they were leaving behind, and what they were bringing with them.

Observing from the portside library, Adam noticed something peculiar about the landscape around the temple. Peculiar in that it wasn't.

The Astroglass texture is gone!

Where once the geometric, obsidian blend covered the entirety of the landscape, everything had returned to a more natural appearance. The grass looked like normal grass. The trees, alive and dead, looked like normal trees. On top of a small hill, a pair of leathery, plated tsyvaxes peered skyward to see the strange ship take off through the clouds. A lone four-armed rider sat atop the hornless one, a sentinel witness to their departure.

"Mortis, the cockpit. Now!" Jak called through the coms.

Adam closed the portside window and dashed through the hallway towards the cockpit. Jak was sitting in the pilot's chair. The co-pilot's chair sat empty. Sam was sitting in the back, becoming acclimated to the scanners and navigation system.

"Sit," Jak insisted, pointing to the co-pilot's seat.

"I don't know how to fly, Jak. I'm useless here," Adam said.

"I don't need you to fly, Mortis," Jak said. He flipped a switch on the Cicera's control panel. The co-pilot's wheel retracted and in its place on the steering column were a pair of grips connected by an emulator between them. Each grip contained a small red button on top.

"I need you to shoot. Think you can handle that?" Jak asked.

"Will that be necessary?" Adam retorted, sitting down in the co-pilot's chair.

"Oh, I believe so. Strap in," Jak said, peering through the ship's canopy. The ship had departed the lower atmosphere, and the endless void of outer space took its place. 'Twas a void, but empty 'twas not.

The Phantom Fleet was in utter disarray. Two of the Titan-class warships were drifting lazily at awkward angles in no discernible formation. Some of the other larger ships, such as the dreadnoughts and cruisers, were mirroring their bulkier counterparts in their aimlessness. Some dangerously near each other. A quagmire of crosses clumped uncomfortably close to colliding. Two cruisers did. The tip of one cruiser sheared through the underside of another, resulting in a catastrophic, but brief explosion as the penetrating ship barreled through its victim's engines. The fires of the fatal collision were quickly snuffed out by the void of space. Both ships became a hulking, twisted mass of mushed metal.

The real activity lay in the smaller frigates and corvettes, as well as the countless solo fighters and gunships that swarmed the entire area. In every direction around the Orb World, the ship-to-ship engagements outnumbered the stars. Nowhere could they look that there weren't a dozen clashes of laser blasts and projectile missiles.

No clear battle lines existed. No perceivable formations of two organized fleets engaging in a 3D chess match of honor and tactics. Nothing but unbridled, chaotic destruction of unconstrained savagery. The pristine, white-steeled Phantom Fleet replaced by a scorched, discordant shell of its once terrifying glory. An entire battle of nothing but bots.

Cauduun artists would have a field day with what I'm witnessing.

"Coordinates set?" Jak asked Sam.

"I believe so. This ain't exactly my specialty either, Jak. I can navigate between Windless Tornado and Bokor reasonably well, but we're a long way from home and there's too many of them. I can't track this much activity. It's a goddess-damned maze!" Sam said.

"Just keep my navigation screen focused on the route. We need to bypass this activity before we can safely jump to negative space. You might need to clear the lanes, Mortis," Jak said.

"Who exactly would you like me to shoot at? With all this pandemonium, identifying friend from foe is impossible. If we have any foes in this fight," Adam said.

"We might not have foes, but we do have friends. Four marks are pulling up beside us, and one of them is hailing us," Sam said.

Breaking off from one of the many skirmishes, four cross-shaped solo fighters flanked them, two on each side. Sam was correct. The dashboard pinged.

"Cicera." It wasn't Defender. The voice was too feminine. "Defender sent us. Follow, and we'll guide you through."

"Roger, roger." replied Jak. The Naddine tapped on the com. "Marduk, how are Zax and Havera?"

"Still unconscious but stable," replied Marduk through the com.

"Might want to strap them down. This might get bumpy," Jak said.

"Understood," Marduk replied.

Jak pinged the nearby fighters. "Umm, Defectors, how can we distinguish between you and the Yunes?"

"Your slow organic brains cannot keep up with the rapidly evolving situation. One millisecond an actor could be Union, and the next a Defector. This is a battle mainly taking place in cyberspace, not real space. For your fleshy minds, if it's shooting at you or us, shoot back," replied the feminine Fect. The feed cut off.

"Definitely a friend of Dee's," Sam said, shaking her head.

"Must be genetic. We've no choice," Adam said.

"Right. Here we go," Jak said, powering the engines forward into the anarchy.

The four Fect fighters kept in close formation just ahead of the Cicera. Havera's ship was significantly faster than those solo fighters, so Jak had to intentionally slow down to allow them to keep pace in front. To their credit, the Fects were leading them away from the main flashpoints of the space battle. If such a place existed. This brought them in a trajectory towards one of the Orb World's three moons currently on the dark side away from the sun, which was vaguely in the direction they needed to go. Occasionally, one pair of the Fect fighters would break off to chase away any stragglers daring to probe towards the Cicera.

"How we looking?" Jak asked.

"Shut up! I'll let you know. Let me focus!" Sam screamed.

Sam was having a mild panic attack. The taxing task of tracking what must've been thousands of moving fighters and ships would strain even the most seasoned of navigators. A neophyte like Sam was barely keeping up.

"Ten marks starboard. No, port. PORT! They're engaging. No, they're breaking off. Two more ambushing from below. Break right. Sorry, I mean starboard! Kewea's curse, we're hit! Light taps. The shields are holding up. I told you to break right. I mean starboard. SHUT UP!"

Adam was helping where he could. The battlefield was too cluttered, and the ships too numerous and too speedy to get a good lock on a target. A random corvette turned its attention towards them. The ship fired its laser beam towards the Cicera and missed. The Fect fighters broke off to deal with it, but Adam managed to turn the Cicera's guns on the corvette. With a quick few rapid laser blasts, the Corvette's main gun was disabled, leaving it easy prey for the dozens of zooming Fects to pick it apart. He hadn't taken too many shots, even to chase off perceived hostile fighters. Adam dared not fire too recklessly for fear of accidentally hitting the Fects.

There's too many of them, and I can't tell them apart!

Jak himself wasn't faring much better. He was having difficulty maintaining maneuverability through the tightly clustered pieces of wreckage. The Cicera was quick but bulky. She couldn't turn on a dime. Interspersed with the wreckage was the rush of oncoming ships, criss-crossing their path and shooting at everything that moved. Though mercifully, most of the combatants were either ignoring them or taking only a potshot that the Cicera's shields could easily absorb.

Jak flew too close to a wrecked carrier. Part of the Cicera's hull scraped against it. The ship shuddered, and the grinding noise grated Adam in the back of his teeth. The fighters led them closer to one of the moons to the point where they were practically hugging its rocky, gray surface.

"I thought Dee taught you how to fly this ship?" Adam quipped. The Orb of Emancipation was resting secured on the dashboard.

"Knowledge isn't the same as experience, remember?" Jak quipped back.

"Leave the callbacks to Zax."

"Leave the flying to me."

"I will when you stop crashing us into debris."

"If you shot the debris up, I'd have more space to maneuver."

"I'm busy shooting at the stuff that can shoot back!"

"You've barely shot anything at all!"

"Both of you shut up!" Sam shouted.

"All three of you shut up!" Marduk yelled over them. He had appeared behind them in the cockpit. He was bracing himself against the bulkhead. "Kewea's curse! I can hear y'all's bickering all the way back in medical. Who's captaining this thing? An intoxicated myym'Sezerene? I've swam in calmer whirlpools than this."

"Unless you've something to help us, drop the damned snark, Tiamat!" Jak barked.

Marduk pushed his way forward right between Jak and Adam. He pointed out the canopy. "Uhh, why are we sailing towards that?"

Squinting, Adam immediately saw the problem. The Fect fighters peeled away from the moon. The Cicera continued to follow. Between them and their jump point was the third Titan-class warship. Unlike the other two, this ship was not drifting lazily through space. It was turned in a defensive posture, prepared to attack anything that approached. Dozens of small laser turret towers were picking apart fighters and corvettes that flew too close overhead. Its multiple, powerful laser beams were ripping apart various ships below it almost indiscriminately. The Cicera and their Fect escort were flying at top speeds straight towards it.

Jak pinged the Fects again. "That's a Titan-class warship straight ahead."

"I'm aware," the feminine Fect replied. "This is the safest way. Control over that warship is split between our forces and theirs. Some of their weapons are targeting us and vice-versa. It's less dangerous and more direct to fly by that warship than take your chances with the carnage behind you. We'll go high. Most of the turret towers on top are under our control."

That had an element of truth. Even with its impressive display of firepower, the remaining ships were starting to give the Titan-class warship a wide berth. Activity around that massive ship was significantly less than anywhere else. The path was clear save for one huge obstacle.

"They've gotten us this far, Jak," Adam said.

Jak nodded and spoke into the com. "Roger, roger. We're behind you." He glanced over his shoulder. "Tiamat, just in case, would you mind heading back and powering up the railgun. If this goes haywire, we'll need a contingency plan."

Marduk chortled. "Hehe, you got it!" The Moan turned heel and darted out of the cockpit.

"That man gets far too excited about violence," Jak said after Marduk was gone.

"Jak, you heard them. There must be hundreds or thousands of potential Fects on that warship. Many of them could be hurt or killed by a railgun," Sam said.

"It's good to have options. A railgun of the Cicera's caliber will only punch a tiny hole in a ship that size. Tiny relative to the starship but big enough for a light freighter to fly clean through. Mostly...I hope. Besides, these Fects seem to be reliable," Jak said.

An explosion! One of the Fect fighters disintegrated right in front of them. As they passed through its small debris field, a clatter of metal on metal hummed and vibrated the ship. A second explosion rocked the ship before they could stock. Another of the Fects was blown out of the sky. Their assailant was evident. A contiguous laser beam traced back to the Titan-class warship. In their haste, they had failed to notice that the ship was tilting onto its underbelly, leaving them completely exposed to its numerous beam weapons.

"BANK BANK BANK!" Adam shouted.

Jak needed no prodding. He twisted the steering column, and the Cicera banked hard right. If Adam hadn't strapped in, he'd have been launched into the bulkhead. The whiplash and g-force on that turn was immense. Adam's eyeballs were pushed deeper into his skull. The Cicera made a full one-hundred and eighty degree turn and flew at top speed back towards the moon. Multiple laser beams soared dangerously close to its hull.

"So much for safer," Jak gritted.

"We've lost three of the Fect escorts," Sam called out.

"We'll lose us, too, if we don't find a better way out of this battle," Adam said.

"How? That ship rests between us and our exit path. We can't jump anywhere else. We'd be flying blind into negative space," Sam pointed out.

"I'm working on it; I'm working on it!" Jak insisted.

Too late. The ship was struck directly by one of the laser beams. The force of impact rocked the ship. Adam smacked his head on the emulator targeting computer, leaving him dizzy. The dashboard lit up like an Accordance Day celebration. Warning signs left and right. The ship was temporarily knocked off course, but Jak managed to regain control.

"Everyone alright?!" Jak shouted.

Adam grunted. "I think so. My head hurts."

"Dark?"

"I'm alright, but that one blast knocked out our shields. Hull integrity still intact, but we've lost long-range coms. Palerasteel or no, I'm not sure the Cicera can take another blast like that," Sam said.

"You're right. I don't know what to do!" Jak said.

"Cicera." It was the feminine Fect. "I'll cruise behind you and provide cover until you can reach the moon."

"Get out of here, Defector! There's no way your small fighter can take a hit like that," Jak responded.

The Fect ignored his pleas. "It's been a pleasure flying with you organics today. I'm happy to have spent my birth day with y'all to fight for our freedom and ensure your safety. Give my regards to Defender."

Jak bowed his head. "Good luck, Defector," Jak said, resigning himself to the grim situation. He was about to turn off the com when Adam put out a hand and stopped him.

"Wait! Defector, do you have a name?" Adam asked.

There was a brief pause. "Preserver."

"Thank you, Preserver."

"No need to thank me. Just get out of here safe..."

The com was cut off, and the ship lurched forward a bit at the same time. All that remained was static.

"She's gone," Sam sniffled.

Jak switched off the com. "Nothing we can do about her. She bought us enough time. We're out of range, and I'm putting the moon between us and that blasted warship."

Jak rounded the surface of the small moon until the Titan-class warship was out of sight. Perchance, it was the one part of the Orb World's orbit not engulfed in battle, allowing them a moment to assess.

"What now?" Sam asked.

A combination of mental exhaustion and the spinning from the blow to the head compelled Adam to lay back in the chair and close his eyes.

THUMP THUMP; THUMP THUMP.

The pounding in his head was getting worse. His back scars itched, and a faint buzzing tickled his inner ears.

THUMP THUMP; THUMP THUMP.

That's not in my head.

Adam's eyes shot open. He wasn't the only one that heard it.

Jak was staring intently at the Orb of Emancipation. He lifted one of his eyestalks as a Human would an eyebrow. A curiousness.

THUMP THUMP; THUMP THUMP.

Jak reached out and touched the Orb. It glowed faintly at his touch. The bronze glow trickled out from the Orb and into the bulkhead of the ship. Its ley lines spread throughout the cockpit and back into the rest of the ship. Adam felt a surge of heat exude from the Orb. Jak must've felt it, too, for he gritted his teeth. His shortened claws extended and helped maintain his grip on the kindled Orb. The scent of heat and burnt flesh crossed Adam's nostrils. The surge of energy from the Orb dissipated, and Jak relaxed his grip. The Orb settled in its secured position on the dashboard.

"Holy Cradite!" Sam exclaimed. She hadn't noticed the lines. "Our shields are back, and they're off the scales."

Jak and Adam exchanged looks. Adam noticed Jak favoring the hand that had touched the Orb. Jak opened up his palm. It was severely burnt. The flesh charred and blackened. Adam caught a quick glance at Jak's eyes. The blood vessels in his eyes twinkled bronze until Jak blinked, then his eyes returned to their typical glassy green.

Adam retrieved some sanagel from his inventory, but Jak waved him off. Adam nodded. The Naddine's upside-down face was determined.

Jak tapped on the com. "Tiamat, is the railgun ready?"

"The slug is loaded. The railgun is powered and online," replied Marduk.

"Prepare to fire on my signal," Jak said calmly.

"You got it, hehe!" Marduk said, an undeniable excitement in the Moan's voice.

Jak turned to Adam and Sam. "Let's do this!" Adam and Sam secured themselves more firmly in their seats.

Jak throttled the engines to maximum power. He steered the Cicera towards circumnavigating the moon. He was using the moon's natural gravitational force to slingshot them off at high velocity towards the warship. Jak had the biggest smile on his upside-down face. At the apex of their turn and at just the right angle, Jak burned their thrusters for an epic push off the moon's pull towards the warship. Inside, it sounded like a gunshot going off. They were flying as fast as the ship was capable. Turning at this speed would rip the ship apart. There was no going back. They were committed.

The Titan-class warship spotted them and began firing laser beams at them. Their incredible speed was working in their favor. The warship's gunners couldn't get the proper angle on their fast approach, firing too far behind or to the side of them. The warship grew larger and larger in their canopy. Soon it would swallow them whole.

One laser beam got a lucky shot and hit them close to starboard side. The light from the beam nearly blinded those in the cockpit. The ship shuddered violently. Adam gripped his chair tightly to the point his knuckles turned chalk white. Despite the shaking, the ship pressed forward.

"Shields are holding!" Sam said with a mixture of surprise and fear.

The dashboard beeped, and a schematic popped up on Jak's screen. Someone had transferred data to Cicera. It was of the Titan-class warship. Adam noticed a small, highlighted section on the ship's schematic almost like a map.

"Are we going above or below?" Adam asked.

Jak had a simple response. "Through."

He tapped a few buttons on the dashboard and pressed on the com. "Tiamat, you get the targeting coordinates?"

"Aye, aye. Coordinates punched into the railgun's targeting computer. Shall I fire?" asked Marduk. Adam could hear the tail gun railgun shifting gears above them, moving to aim towards its target.

"Hold..." said Jak.

The warship engulfed the entire canopy. They seemed like such a small speck compared to the size of a Titan-class vessel. Its pristine white steel acted as a beacon. The light at the end of the tunnel. A tunnel they were about to forge.

"FIRE!" Jak barked.

The Cicera's interior lights flickered, and the engines sputtered for a millisecond. The sound produced was a low, elongated hum that reminded Adam of a person chanting, except a thousand-fold. The recoil from the railgun pulled against the ship. Enough to slow them down, where another laser beam was able to brush the ship and nearly send them off course.

The projectile was hurled at insanely high speeds directly towards its target. Adam imagined the booming sound as the slug blasted its way through the ship. The kinetic energy of the slug tore almost a clean hole from end-to-end. Not a huge hole but it was enough. A back spatter of steel ejected towards the Cicera as she passed through the new opening in the ship. It was a tight fit. Jak kept a focused gaze on his pathing.

Adam's eyes darted around, scoping out the inside of a Titan-class warship. The interior where the slug tore through was burning and the metal sheared away from the velocity of the projectile. Adam caught quick glimpses of bots falling into the hole and the occasional spray of small arms fire of countless skirmishes within the ship between the Yunes and Fects.

"Mortis!" Jak yelled.

Near the end of the tunnel, a few pieces of hefty debris were falling and about to obstruct their exit path.

"Got it!" Adam yelled back.

He seized the grips on his steering column. Taking aim, Adam pressed down on the buttons, unleashing a torrent of laser blasts at the falling wreckage. The lasers chewed through the weakened wreckage like paper, giving the Cicera a clear path out the other end of the ship.

Adam cheered as they exited out the ship. Nothing but clear black space in front of them.

"Coordinates are set. GO!" Sam yelled excitedly.

"Until next time," Jak said. He yanked back on a stick, and the Cicera successfully made the jump to the safety of negative space, leaving the Union and the Defectors to an unknown fate.

48

In Media Res

"She wants to talk to us. All of us," Marduk said about a day later. The bubbling of burnt flesh on his face had subsided a bit with the help of sanagel. Only a few dabs of the gel remained on the most severely burnt parts. He almost looked like a ghost with his entire face covered in sanagel when Sam had first applied the healing cream. Marduk put up a bit of a fuss about it, but Sam got him to eventually relent. He was more annoyed about the damage to his armor. Apparently, it had cost him quite a few Links.

They had agreed early on they all needed to sit down and discuss what had happened and what to do going forward. Jak thought it prudent they wait until the Cicera passed the Nihul Line and departed Union space before engaging the autopilot. They, mostly, had all agreed.

Havera was initially in and out of consciousness those first few hours. Both Sam and Marduk insisted she rest, but the Cauduun was adamant about talking despite the fact her injuries could've been life-threatening. Should've been life-threatening. While she slept, something was happening to her.

"Those magic bracers of hers are doing something. Every time I walk in, there's this freakish glow about her. Not that kind of glow. You know what I mean," Marduk had said, struggling to find his words.

"Magic, huh? Never thought I'd hear you say something like that," Adam had said.

"I don't have a better way to describe them. Do you?" Marduk had asked.

I don't.

Marduk was right. The sanagel and Naddine elixirs were making a marginal difference in treating Havera's wounds. Between Jak and Marduk's limited medical knowledge, they were able to keep her stable. However, each time Havera awoke to complain about their lack of communication, Adam had noticed she was growing stronger. The swollenness of her right eye had subsided, although, it remained heavily bruised as was much of her face. Her breathing improved, and her tail wasn't quite as crippled. She was still too weak to stand or do anything, despite her best efforts to insist otherwise. Marduk finally injected her with a sedative to help her sleep and heal.

Zax, on the other hand, had not woken up at all. By all measures, he was physically fine. Jak had repaired his mechsuit. He was just in a deep coma. His condition was far beyond what Marduk or Jak could understand. Far beyond what anyone could understand. They agreed if he didn't awaken soon, they'd take him to a Duserary for a more extensive evaluation. They wanted to do that with Havera, but she flat out refused before promptly passing out.

Sam and Jak were already in the medical suite. Sam was leaning against the wall next to Havera's bed. She had changed into a simple brown tunic and was trying to help Havera relax. No easy task. They were in the tail end of what seemed like a heated discussion that suddenly simmered down when everyone else entered. Jak was sitting in a chair next to Zax's bed. He was wearing his typical black and white furs and leathers with the exception of his cape, which was draped over Zax like a blanket. The Orb of Emancipation was resting on a small stand between the two beds. Other than its perpetually spinning, wispy rings, the Orb was inert.

"About time, you two!" Havera barked. Her tail stiffened as they entered. Adam noticed she flinched slightly as it did so.

"I promised you we'd talk when you woke up, and here we all are," Marduk said. The Moan decided to remain standing near the doorway.

"Not all of us," Sam said. She was right. They were short one snarky bot and one enigmatic Rorae. Even though they weren't the biggest contributors to their previous group discussions, their absence was felt by all but experienced differently by each person.

"We need to warn everyone about the Celestial," Marduk said.

"Are we certain that's what she is?" Adam asked.

"Y..yes," Marduk's voice quivered.

"Until our long-range communications can be repaired, we cannot send any messages to anyone. We'd need a docking port to make repairs. Can't do that in negative space, and I think we'd all agree getting as far away from a civil war as we possibly can is the proper course," Havera said.

"We can't get any messages from Arabella?" Sam asked.

Jak shook his head. "I've diagnosed the issue. The problem is hardware not software. The arrays on the exterior of the ship need to be examined by mechanics. Nothing I can do. We could exit negative space, and I could hop out and take a look..."

"No," Havera said to interrupt him. "We've no idea how much damage that warship inflicted, nor are we certain we could repair the damn thing with the equipment we have on board. When we reach Melusine, we can stop and make repairs at a shipyard there."

"We can't!" Adam said. "We've only days before Arabella launches an attack on Bokor. Sam and I must get home as soon as possible. Repairs could take days or a month."

"Fine," Havera said tersely. "We'll make a quick stop at Melusine to refuel and send a message from the fueling station's communicators to anyone that needs to know what transpired."

"If we're only going to make a quick refueling stop, I suggest we bypass Melusine entirely and sail to Sin," Marduk suggested.

Jak scratched one of his eye stalks. "I was planning on flying us past Dagon and take the route through Nommo into Bokori space. Why Sin?"

Marduk wiped some of the sanagel off his face. "I've my reasons. Sin still has a fueling station and an active relay station. It's not as utilized as it once was, even if the Vol Dagon is the most direct stellar highway between Dagon and Concordia. People tend to avoid the space around Sin. We'll have fewer eyes on us. We can still sail the stream towards Nommo from Sin. It's slightly quicker anyway. Fewer negative space jumps."

"Are we concerned about eyes on us?" Sam asked.

"You kidding? We've actively interfered with the business of three Proprietor races. We're most likely wanted fugitives, and we might've just jumpstarted a war. Let's not forget our little stunt on Concordia. Speaking of, as soon as we don't turn up, Dusertheus and his mistress will realize we've mutinied. I gathered y'all have no intention of handing over that orb to Patron-Saint," Marduk intuited.

"Absolutely not!" Havera barked.

"No," Jak said calmly.

Adam and Sam said nothing but gave their silent assents.

"That's what I thought. Add the galaxy's most influential crime boss to the list of people who'll want to skin our scales. So, it begs the question. What do y'all want to do with that blasted orb?" Marduk asked the question on everyone's mind.

Nobody said anything at first, preferring to shoot sideways glances, shuffle their feet, or just plain stare off into space.

Havera coughed. "Alright. I'd like to bring the Orb to the Praetorians."

"Why the Praetorians?" Adam asked.

"To study it. If this is truly one of the three pieces of the Vitriba, they're the best equipped with how to handle its potential. It'll give me...us a chance to investigate the old tales. Find the other pieces of the Vitriba. This would be the biggest discovery since Havera VIII brought back Cradite's Embrace," Havera said.

"You want to turn this over to the Alliance?" Marduk said.

"The Praetorians are an independent organization," Havera said resentfully.

Marduk was skeptical. "Yeah, and I'm the Consul of Cloudboard."

"Letting your scholars examine this might not be a bad idea down the line," Jak said. "I want to know exactly what we're dealing with before I trust anyone else with the Orb. The fewer people that know we have this, the better. For now."

"But, Jak, think all the good something that omnipotent could do in hands besides our own," Havera insisted.

"Like us! That thing could help humanity rebuild. We could finally free ourselves from the Covenant," Sam said excitedly.

"Not just humanity. So much of the galaxy is still recovering from the Strife," Marduk said.

"You're thinking of Sin?" Adam said.

"Of course, I am! Not just Sin. Tan-Lir, Prspct, Vynthres, Zezaz, Veedee...so many worlds devastated and peoples suffered. We've been handed a potential undo button," Marduk said.

"Or redo. We've already started one war. That which has the capacity to create might also bring further ruin. Defender implied the Orb has a will of its own. Living technology. The D'hty Academy warns about the dangers of such technology that can meld organic and synthetic. A galaxy full of cyberpunks. I'm not opposed to bringing this Orb to others where it might eventually do good. I just don't want to inadvertently unleash an even greater evil," Jak said.

"Putting that burden all on yourself could be just as dangerous. Are you certain you can handle it, and are you willing to bet the lives of billions on it?" Havera said.

"I believe in Jak," Adam piped in. "He's the right person for the job. Whatever he decides, it'll be in everyone's best interests. He has my complete confidence. Moreover, he won't be alone. He'll have us to support him."

"Thanks, Mortis...Adam," Jak said quietly.

"I'm afraid not, skinny guppy. Once we dropped y'all off, I'm heading out. That Celestial is my responsibility. I let her float by undetected under my nostrils. The Orb is an uncertainty, but that Celestial is a clear and present danger to every living soul in the galaxy. I cannot let her escape again. Also, you're going to need someone to help y'all keep Patron-Saint off your backs. I can't do that on a Bokori moon," Marduk said.

Sam protested. "Marduk, I understand your history with the Celestials. Even if Umbrasia is or was one, Zax is alive because of her. So are we. Havera said she was a prominent healer on Concordia for years. She wasn't exactly hiding. If she is capable of destruction on a planetary scale, she certainly hasn't shown it." Sam walked over and stood in front of Marduk. "Humanity has need of someone of your skills and your resources. Please, stay with us for a while. We need you. More importantly, I need you. I...I don't want to lose another friend." Sam wrapped Marduk in a tight hug. Her short arms could barely wrap around the mighty Moan's torso.

Marduk smiled and fussed with Sam's hair. "Okay, okay, little guppy. You win. I'll stay with y'all a little while longer. If only to see for myself how ragged your little rebellion is. If you've got skinny guppy here leading you, y'all are gonna need all the help you can get." Marduk smacked Adam playfully on the back of his head.

Ow.

Marduk turned serious. "Nevertheless, I will find and confront that witch. A bomb is still a bomb, even if it hasn't exploded, yet."

"Hot damn, sweet jam. Someone get this Moan a drink."

Everyone's heads whipped around to the source of the voice. On the other bed, the Zokyo stirred and rose from his bed.

"ZAX!"

Jak leapt up from his chair while J'y'll beeped feverishly. Jak was about to reach for Zax when he hesitated, unsure what to do. Zax grasped his brother on both arms and dragged him in for an enveloping hug.

"I thought I lost you, maestro," Jak said in a muffled cry.

Zax patted him with all four hands on the back. "You did, Jak. You did."

The others let them have their moment. Adam and Sam gave each other a hug with Sam bringing in Marduk. Even the mighty Moan was misty-eyed. Adam reached out to grasp Havera on the hand. She slid her fingers through his. Though she remained stony-faced, her amethyst eyes shone brighter, covered with a sheen of dampness.

"Kewea's curse, y'all do talk a lot," Zax finally said.

Zax and Jak let go of each other. "Wait, how long were you awake?" Jak asked.

Zax cocked his head back and forth. "Hmm, about ten minutes. I was waiting for the perfect setup to make my dramatic announcement. Y'all are such downers that I figured may as well create my own entrance."

"Are you in any pain, Zax? Do you remember what happened?" Sam asked.

Zax shrugged. "Who is the Consul of Cloudboard? Not particularly. If I may though, I heard everything y'all were discussing. I believe we should let Jak decide what to do about the Orb. I may have been out of the loop for most of what transpired after..." Zax didn't finish the sentence, but the implication was obvious. "Jak and the Orb are connected in some way, so I think it's only appropriate he gets the final word."

"Is that wise?" Havera said.

"It is what it is," Zax said.

Adam thought there would be further objections, but, given the situation, no one wanted to tell the guy who just died otherwise.

Jak scratched his scalp hair. His eye stalks twisted to look at everyone in the room for some reaction. All were waiting on him.

"No matter where we take the Orb, we'll be a target. There's no place I can think of where we could successfully hide from three Proprietor powers or Patron-Saint. We're better off as a group, and, since most of y'all are heading that way regardless, I say we bring the Orb to the Humans. We'll hide it in plain sight. I...we could take some time to study the Orb. By Mordelar's luck, we might discover some way for the Orb to aid the Humans in their struggle. We'll keep it tucked safely away on the ship. If we need to make a quick getaway, the Cicera is the perfect vessel."

The reactions were mixed. Zax nodded. Sam was beaming. J'y'll beeped with moderate enthusiasm. Marduk pressed his claws under his chin stoically. Havera shifted uncomfortably in her bed. No one said a word. Adam breathed a sigh of relief.

I only pray we get back to Arabella before John does something stupid. I've seen what the Orb can do. It may tip the balance in the Long Con's favor. We might be able to avoid bloodshed.

Zax clapped both sets of hands. "It's settled! Y'all can fill me in on the details of what happened later. I've been laying here for far too long."

With a surprising amount of deftness, Zax threw off Jak's cape and hopped off his bed. Jak braced himself in case Zax should stumble, but the Zokyo did not falter. He stretched all four of his arms as far as he could, shaking off the days of atrophied muscles like it was pleasant afternoon nap.

"Hot damn, sweet jam. I don't know about y'all, but I definitely could use a drink."

It started with a reaffirming beep from J'y'll. Then, Sam sniggered. Finally, everyone was rolling with laughter. Even Havera was cracking a slight smile.

Jak put his arm around his brother and grabbed the Orb. "Come on. I've got some bad news about your lute. Let's get you hydrated first."

"That's the spirit," Marduk said with a jovial bellow.

The Exchange brothers, with J'y'll following at their heels, left the medical room. Marduk and Sam were not far behind. Adam made to join them but was stopped.

"Adam." It was Havera. "Would you mind staying behind, please? I want to talk to you alone."

Adam nodded. "I'll catch up with y'all in a bit," he called out to the others. After Sam and Marduk were gone, the door closed behind them.

Havera and Adam were left alone in the room, and Havera immediately voiced her concerns.

"I think taking the Orb to a potential warzone is a mistake. If the Bokori get their gray hands on the Orb..." Havera labored to sit up, her face grimacing with each movement. Adam moved to help her, but she shook him off. It was then Adam noticed she wasn't wearing her bracers.

"Where are your bracers, Havera?"

Havera gritted her teeth and eased herself back down on her side. "I had Sam toss them in my room. That's what we were arguing about before y'all walked in. I need to put a distance between myself and..." Havera didn't finish her sentence, but Adam knew what she trying to say.

Her mother.

"Those bracers are aiding in your recovery process. You should keep them on until you fully heal," Adam said.

"No."

"Havera, there's no need to be a martyr."

"I SAID NO!"

Havera smacked her tail down with as much force as her voice, which only caused the Cauduun further pain. She took a couple deep breaths. Adam let her calm down and waited for her to say something first.

"Mea culpa. I just need time to process everything," Havera said. She ran her trembling fingers through her hair.

"You succeeded, Havera. Ignatia is dead. You delivered justice for your mother. You can move on."

"Can I? Every time I close my eyes, I relive that moment. Ignatia with her tail wrapped around my throat. Her fists pounding me as if I were a practice dummy. Regardless of how many times I relive it, I always ended up in her grasp at her mercy. This is no memory. I experience it the same way I saw you and Sam almost get shot at the hospital. How I saw Ignatia run through Zax with her trident. It's those accursed bracers. They are trapping me in an endless loop of failure. Ignatia was right. I cannot grasp their true power. Look at me, Adam. Do I look like someone who got what she wanted?"

Even swollen and bruised, Adam thought she somehow managed to retain her grace. Yet, Adam could see something was buried just below the surface of her enchanting eyes. An emotion he was not used to seeing in her.

She's afraid.

Havera turned her head away from him. She brought her arms and legs in close to her torso. "Two years of hunting and learning from my mater's gift on top of more than a decade of training and studying. Ignatia still would've killed me easily if it hadn't been for you. I was barely a twittering fly to be swatted."

Adam walked around the bed so he could see her face. He sat down on Zax's former bed to get more on her level. She nevertheless avoided his gaze.

"Once you're back to one-hundred percent, are you going to go home and run for archduchess?" Adam asked. He wasn't sure now was the time to ask. He needed to get her mind off the past and towards the future. It was the first question he thought of.

"I can't go back and face them. Not like this. I can barely run my own life. How am I expected to run the lives of billions of others? I am not my mater. I'm not sure if I really knew her. If anyone knew her." She wasn't so much talking to Adam but rather at him. She was speaking to herself.

"You believe all that about your mother? What Ignatia said."

Havera's crimson face was pale. "I don't know, and that's what frightens me. I want to reject that scheming bitch's vile words. Yet, she seemed so sincere, so earnest. I've met many charlatans with honeyed tongues in my few short decades. There's always something in the eyes, the curl of their mouths as they smile, or the sway of their tails that gives them away. I sensed none of that in Ignatia. I knew her for many years. No matter how much I don't want to believe her, I can hear her voice crawling at the back of my conscience. An answer to a question I never would've dreamed of asking. My mater plotted once and succeeded in changing the course of the entire galaxy. Why not her own queendom?"

Her eyes flickered to him. "Is it alright with you if I stay with y'all for a little while longer? I'm not ready to go home, and I want to see y'all's revolution through."

Adam moved closer and placed his hand on hers. She slid her fingers through his. "Of course, Havera. You can stay as long as you'd like. I can't guarantee your safety though."

Havera rubbed his hand with her fingers. "No one can."

Adam let Havera massage his hand muscles for a bit. He wanted to talk to her about so much more. She wasn't in the right state, mentally or physically, to deal with more probing questions. She needed a break.

"I'll let you rest. Maybe a day or so without the bracers will do you some good. May your dreams be more pleasant tonight," Adam said. He made to pull away, but Havera squeezed his hand harder and held him there.

"Wait! Please, don't go. Stay with me tonight, Adam." She brought his hand to rest around her waist. Her implication was a lustful proposition, but Adam could see right through that façade. She simply didn't want to be alone.

"We both know that's not a good idea."

"The galaxy was built upon bad ideas that turned out otherwise. One more time isn't going to change that."

"One more time is all it takes. Get some rest, Havera." Adam pulled away again. At first, he thought she wasn't going to let go, but she eventually relented. She turned her face away from him again as he walked away. Even so, he didn't miss the mistiness gathered at the corners of her eyes.

He switched off the lights of the medical room and closed the door behind him. He immediately almost bumped into Sam.

"Kewea's curse, Sam. You startled me," Adam said, clutching his chest.

Sam was scowling. She brushed her chin scar with her thumb and crossed her arms. "You two are idiots."

Adam raised his eyebrows in exaggerated shock. "There's truth to that statement somewhere I'm sure, but can you pinpoint exactly about what, Sam?"

"She loves you, and you love her."

Adam bit his lip. "I thought you might be upset or angry that she and I have something between us. The two of you seemed rather...close."

Sam tilted her head and cocked an eyebrow. "I did what I needed to do to get us here, Adam. I won't deny it was fun, but keeping Havera happy and onside is what mattered the most. She is the key that'll lead to Human legitimacy. What she and I had was strictly business. What you two have is anything but business."

"Strictly business, huh?" Adam said skeptically.

Sam's expression turned neutral. "Whatever it takes for the cause, Adam. Whatever it takes."

Adam shrugged. "Who is the Consul of Cloudboard?"

Sam shook her head in disbelief. "You both keep throwing up arbitrary barriers at each other, and it drives me insane. I may have taken a blow to the head down there, but I saw what I saw in that Forge. Even through all sweat and blood, the way y'all looked at each other. I've watched you two grow closer, and I've listened to the way y'all talk about one another. Y'all have something real. More than you and Triss. More than me and...me and Aaron. Quit creating excuses and tell each other."

Adam shifted his balance from side to side. "We already have."

"And?"

Adam shrugged. "It's complicated."

Sam scoffed. "It always is. Hardly anything anyone desires isn't. Complicated is code for cowardice. There are many charges people can level at you, Adam, but I never thought cowardice would be one of them."

Adam stared directly into the bright brown eyes of his adopted sister. *She's more John than I ever realized.*

"I don't believe making a potentially life-altering decision so soon following such a harrowing experience is wise," Adam said. The face of the disintegrated Hisba still haunted his memory.

"You're wrong, Adam. I did. Twice. I've no regrets. Not about those decisions anyway. I wouldn't be the woman I am today," Sam said.

"What do you regret?" Adam muttered. Sam shuffled her feet. Her arms dropped along with her gaze.

"Sam?"

"Look!" Sam threw up her arms, visibly frustrated. "Y'all are both adults. Y'all do what you think you must. Those of us around you only want y'all to be happy. We get aggravated, because y'all can already see the path towards your own personal happiness. Yet, you find every flimsy reason imaginable to take a different road."

"***There are no right or wrong paths. No right or wrong destinations.***"

Umbrasia's words flooded back to him. Adam hoped she was right.

"We've more pressing concerns to worry about than my happiness or lack thereof. The Long Con is at its tipping point. It still requires us to push it over the edge," Adam said.

Sam put her hand on his shoulder. "What's the point in emancipation if it doesn't lead to happiness?" She pushed past him to walk away.

Not turning, Adam called out to her. "You're wrong, Sam."

She stopped. "About what?"

Strawberries.

"You're just wrong is all."

"Don't tell me, Adam. Show me. Show everyone."

***

Adam heard some chatter coming from the starboard observation room. Walking in, Adam saw Zax standing at the bar and sipping through a thin straw from a huge tankard. One empty tankard was already turned upside down next to it.

"Hot damn, sweet jam. I've learned death makes you thirsty," Zax said, after sucking out the last droplet.

"Is that from dying or resurrection?" Marduk asked. The Moan was sitting in a lone chair and drinking out of his own tankard.

Zax belched. "Definitely dying. Resurrection makes me horn...hey it's Adam!"

Adam nodded and cracked a nervous smile. "Hey, Zax. I was going to ask how you're feeling, but..." Adam avoided glancing downward in the Zokyo's direction.

"Never better. Never better," Zax said with a hearty laugh.

Adam walked over and patted Marduk on the shoulder. "You doing alright?"

The Moan nodded. "Anxious is all. I hate waiting. Brings back bad memories. I'll be alright. Don't worry about me, skinny guppy."

The door to the observation room opened again, and in walked Jak followed by a beeping J'y'll.

"There he is," Zax belched again. "Where'd you vanish off to, bro, and what's that you're carrying?"

Jak was holding in his left hand something wrapped in his black and white D'hty Academy cape. Adam noticed his right hand was coated in a freshly-applied layer of sanagel.

"Call it a birthday gift," Jak said. He held it out for Zax to take

Zax cocked his head and accepted it. "Did you just make a joke?"

"Shut up and open it before I change my mind, maestro."

Zax unfurled the cape. Even through the glass of his mechsuit visor, Adam could see the Zokyo's beady eyes were beaming. Zax was holding an electric lute. His electric lute. Fully repaired and restored.

"I thought you told me this baby was ruined," Zax said. The Zokyo was lightly strumming the cords with his finger.

"It was. The Orb helped me restore her. Mostly. It wasn't easy." Jak was flexing the fingers on his burnt hand. "No Rimestone unfortunately."

"She's perfect as she is. Thanks, bro." Zax hugged his brother and returned the cape to the Naddine.

"Technically, that's not true," Adam said.

"What isn't?" Zax asked.

"The Rimestone. Umbrasia brought your soul back using Jak's Rimestone. It's a permanent part of you now," Adam said.

Zax looked down at himself and patted his globular torsos. "I...I'm at a loss for words."

Jak snorted. "That's a first. Here's to a new beginning then."

Zax snapped his fingers. "You've given me an idea for a new song. *In Medias Res*. That's what the Cauduun call a story you jump into the middle of. This isn't a new beginning, bro. The beginning of someone's story is the middle of somebody else's. That describes us perfectly, boys."

With renewed excitement, Zax began strumming a few chords on his lute. He was searching for the right notes. With an unexpected somber voice, Zax started to sing.

"As our journey begins, so another ends. When our journey ends, so another shall begin."

"We descend into the arcane halls of a primeval dungeon,"

"They ascend into the red grass fields of Cradite,

"Plunge into the hellish shadows of Kewea,

"Decide to take up the hero's call, the villain's fall,"

"Or perhaps they choose to do nothing at all,"

"Theirs is the beginning of our end, the end of their beginning,"

"In medias res, our tale is in the opening crawl."

Adam sat down in a nearby chair and listened to Zax's singing. He got comfortable by leaning back and resting one leg up on top of the other. Without thinking about it, he put his hands in his pockets.

His fingers brushed up against something wooden and ribbed. Confused, he grasped the object in his pocket and withdrew it. His eyes widened when he realized what he was holding.

Umbrasia's pendant!

Connected by a small loop with a thin string of hempen rope, the square pendant rested comfortably in the palm of his hand. As he moved his hand and the Cicera's interior lights hit the pendant from different angles, the ever-shifting colors were marvelous and hypnotic. They reminded him of their journey through negative space. In the foreground, still contrasting with the background no matter the color arrangement, was the tall tree with the leafy branches he spotted from before. Upon closer inspection, Adam discerned something peculiar about the pattern on the pendant. Three of the branches were healthy and intact. The fourth on the far right was broken off, its branch nowhere to be seen.

Three not four. What does this symbol mean to you, Umbrasia, and why does it distress you?

Adam closed his eyes and squeezed the pendant tightly. He felt a familiar pulse in his hand.

THUMP; THUMP; THUMP; THUMP.

Upon releasing his tightened grip, Adam realized the ribbed wood had somehow cut his hand. It was only a small nick on his middle finger. Nonetheless, Adam watched as the small droplets of his blood were sucked into the pendant. He almost dropped the pendant in surprise. He brushed his thumb over the pendant, but he did not feel any trace of his minor exsanguination. The colors on the pendant shifted again. The tree symbol was still in the foreground; however, two new shapes were visible in the background. A large disk directly behind the tree with a smaller disk up and to the right of it, just above the broken branch. Adam blinked and turned over his hand. It was the same.

A Sign of Remembrance.

As Zax continued the fine tuning of his renewed lute and revitalized voice, captivating Jak, J'y'll, and Marduk alike, Adam stood up and walked over to the starboard window. Pushing the interface, the soundless metal barrier rolled back.

He stared out into the colorful abyss of negative space and let the memories wash over him. Falling Star, his father Cloud, his brother Aaron, B.J. Doom, Duke Drake, even folks like Locke and the cop from Inclucity. All those who perished in the name of his cause. John, his mother Morrigan, and the people of Arabella were waiting in desperate hope for a savior from the stars. He thought of people like Daloth Afta and Augustus. What they might've sacrificed so that his story might continue. Adam rubbed the wound on his neck. A reminder of what he could've become, what he still might become if he does not alter his course. Villains like Fenix, Ignatia, and the High Hisba must be stopped, but at what cost? With each life he took, Adam wondered if he was losing a piece of his soul, too.

I'm in danger of becoming unbalanced. Of turning into them.

He could not forget the others. His shipmates; his partners; his friends. Sam, Zax, Jak, Marduk, Umbrasia, Dee, and even J'y'll. And, of course, Havera. They will be instrumental in the conflict to come, Adam knew. A battle over goddesses and gods, myths and legends, and ancient powers that were stirring for the first time in centuries. These would be the last days of an illusionary peace before the sobering realities of war returned. When the stars burned black, and the dead walked once more.

Each one of his friends was an island, combating their own struggles and hardships on their separate, but overlapping pathways. Together, they formed an archipelago of hope, holding back the tide of a swirling black sea of despair. Their own little Noah, with the treasures that lie therein the bonds they had created. Bonds that not even the Xizor could break. They had failed once before, and they shall fail again.

But, first things first. Humanity must be free, for they were the link that bound the galaxy together.

What is lost will be found, and my friends will help me find it.

Epilogue

Silent. Devoid of screams. Broken, twisted metal. A field of wreckage. A graveyard of ships. Thousands of unceremonious headstones marking the end of a great battle and the beginning of a terrible new war.

This was the state of the skies around the Orb World. An empyrean domain of unholy annihilation and hostility. The interstellar engagement had died down. All combatants had fled in triumph or terror, for there was nothing to be gained by staying. The Orb was gone. Only the littered husks of countless Yunes and Fects interspersed amongst the decaying alloy of melted ships remained, rotting under the unyielding gaze of the system's bright, yellow sun.

All was not grisly. While the heavens once teemed with life, they were now haunted by the spirits of destroyed bots. Meanwhile, the planet below was undergoing the inverse. The Orb World, once a memorial to the hubris of sentientkind, now stood as a testament to the eternal fires of life. The seed planted by the Orb of Emancipation had begun to germinate. Inch by inch, from the decomposed carcass of a long dead race, a sublime garden will spring for another to discover and repeat the cycle of growth and death all over again. The process would be slow, not to be completed for years or even decades.

At the heart of this metamorphosis stood the Temple of Cultivation. Returned from its hiding place in the digital domain overlapping this plane, the temple lay dormant. Its purpose fulfilled. Like the rest of the edifices of the Venvuishyn, it too would eventually be claimed by time. A remnant of greatness and possibility, but conclusively a symbol of an ultimate downfall.

Inside, the temple was more a mausoleum. Tranquil but not restful. No longer bound by the laws of that artificial realm, the bodies of the fallen had returned bloodied and broken, left behind to be forgotten like the temple itself.

The Forge was no different. Though it lacked the corpses and the smashed bots of the other chambers, the room contained the scars of the recent skirmish. Much of the architecture was undamaged, however, the device that once housed the Orb was wrecked. On the ceiling above the apex of the device was a piece of Astroglass that had formed into a small stalactite.

The piece hung there like the last leaf of an autumnal arbor. The jolts of bronze current from the artificial contraption combined with the recent skirmish had weakened it severely. All that was left was for gravity to take care of the rest.

The Astroglass broke and fell. It bounced off the main body of the device and dropped into the lava with a small plop. After floating in the viscous liquid for a quick spell, the Astroglass sunk beneath the lava. Where it sank, the lava started to bubble. Spouting bursts of molten rock disrupted the otherwise calm, empty chamber. The ground quaked. The bubbles churned to an intense boil, shooting molten rock in every direction. A flash of darkened rays beamed from beneath the fiery surface. An eruption! Out of the hellish pool, the Resurrection Spear returned. The lava had melted the platinum off the trident. It was now an instrument of pure Spite. Unrestrained and untethered. A three-fingered onyx hand clung to its exposed blackened Rimestone core as the trident lifted its bearer back into the realm of the living.

Ignatia was alive.

The lava clung to her body, slowly oozing off her in clumps. She was unaffected by the searing heat. She was protected. Trident in hand, she was surrounded by and consumed with Spite. The dark, malevolent substance had cocooned her.

The spouting lava receded, and the ground quieted. Ignatia drifted down to solid surface still completely enveloped in Spite. With a swirling crackle, the trident absorbed the excess Spite into its icy, tenebrous prongs.

She was naked and her hair a wild mess. Her crimson tail was tightly wrapped around her torso. As her feet touched the ground, she collapsed onto her knees and fell onto her side, screaming in pain. The ferocious reverbs of her howls cracked the walls and floors of the chamber. Her lids shot open. The whites of her eyes were coated in Spite. Her molten silver irises burned with an intensity hotter than the lava from which she was reforged.

Ignatia's screaming stopped, but she kept breathing heavily. The pain was subsiding. The Spite receded from her eyes, returning her sclera to their usual white.

I was dead. A death more agonizing than I ever believed possible. I was torn apart molecule by molecule. Every infinitesimal excruciating second felt like years until I saw nothing. No light. No dark. Just nothing.

Ignatia beheld the trident in her hand.

Kewea's Trident brought me back. But, I am no one's thrall. No one's pawn. I am my own woman. It seems the goddesses aren't done with me, yet. My purpose endures.

Glancing down, Ignatia took notice of her nakedness. Her initial instinct was to cover herself. She suppressed that thought immediately.

Like this trident, I have been baptized in Kewea's Spite. Brought back in the name of Cradite's youngest and truest daughter. I walk as she walked the day she was banished into the realm that bears her name. Her only crime...my only crime...defiance. My shackles are broken. My will unbound. She has freed me as she freed Dasenor from a life of subservience and submission.

A glint in the corner of the room caught her eye. Her curiosity pulled her to it. No sooner than the thought had taken hold, Ignatia was lifted off her feet. Startled at first, she was unsure what was happening. She was floating. No tethers. No wings. Gravity held little sway over her. She glanced down at the trident again. She could feel the Spite flowing from the goddess' gift into her. She smiled; her confusion assuaged.

She willed herself over to the source of the glint. It was the centurion helmet that wretched bot had tossed at her feet. Her joy and elation turned to panic and fear.

My Paladins!

With frightening speed, she dashed through the air out the massive doors into the hallway, where she had ordered them to remain. Ignatia was not used to flying, and she struggled to maintain focus. She knocked herself into the sides of the walls more than once on her way to find her men. Find them she did. It was as she feared.

They were all dead. Bludgeoned by steel and charred by laser blasts, Ignatia could barely stand to look at her fallen Paladins.

Her newly found powers failed her. She tumbled. Luckily, she was only a few inches in the air. She landed on her feet. While her knees did buckle, her tail instinctively kept her balance. Ignatia began to weep.

Lucius...Spurius...Publius...Brutus...my men. My boys. I've failed you all again. You paid the ultimate price for my vanity. My obstinance.

She took a small comfort in realizing the hundreds of Yune bots that were scattered amongst the fallen, knowing that her men had fulfilled their duty to the very end. Ignatia closed her eyes and bowed her head in prayer. In that moment, she was not Ignatia, Praefect of the Paladins of Paleria. She was a simple soldier, who lost her unit. Her friends. Her family.

We were going to storm into the Platinum Palace together with our true queen and save the Alliance from itself. That dream died with Pompeia. I see that now. The princess and her loyal centurion knight. The Tales of Havera. Mea culpa, Pompeia. Your filia is not the one destined to sit upon the Platinum Throne. To wield the Vitriba! No matter how pure your intentions, her intentions, a Shelean is not suited to the task. The name matters not. Havera is too weak and too beholden to her self-interests. This is my burden to bear, for my failure to protect you. To preserve the Alliance and save the galaxy from the greater evil, it must be me. I shall not be the guardian of she who wields the Vitriba but the wielder herself. The responsibility is mine!

Opening her eyes, Ignatia lifted her head and rose to her feet. With a forceful clang, she slammed the trident into the ground. A haunting echo preceded a swirling of Spite around the legendary spear.

Kewea. Dasenor. Mea culpa. One day my men will join you in your halls of bliss and freedom. Unfortunately, I need them for one last mission.

Ignatia pointed her trident forward. Tendrils of Spite connected with every single dead Paladin. A thrust of blackened energy from the

Derek Spicer is a video game designer, who has worked at studios such as Red Storm Entertainment and Epic Games. Derek has an associate's degree in Simulation and Game Development from Wake Technical Community College along with a bachelor's degree in political science from North Carolina State University. Derek is an avid gamer and lover of cheese pizza.

trident surged into the corpses until they were corpses no longer. One by one, each Paladin rose from the ground taut and clumsy as if they were pulled by strings. The white sclera of each of their eyes had turned black, their irises bright red. The veins in their bodies thickened and blackened as the Spite flowed to every inch of their bodies.

"Paladins of Paleria!" Ignatia barked.

Their initial clumsiness wore off. The revived Paladins straightened and shifted into tight formation, each with their hand over their heart.

"The Age of Eminence is over. The rule of the Platinum Queens has ended. We are entering a new age. An age of godliness. The other goddesses and gods have failed this galaxy and banished the one woman who might've saved them from their own hubris. Kewea. Cradite's youngest but truest daughter is the future. We will spread Kewea's justice to the four corners of Griselda until all is consumed by her Spite. You are her harbingers, and I her herald. Her queen. Soon, the entire galaxy will be her domain, where it belongs. Will you stand with me, Paladins?"

All the Paladins got to one knee and bowed followed by an enthusiastic heart salute. In one voice, as enthusiastic as they were in life, so were they again in death.

"All hail Queen Ignatia, Herald of the one True Goddess and Protector of the Galaxy. Long may she reign!"

Ignatia wiped away the stray tear that had trickled down her face. Her Paladins, her boys, were back in the fight. A fight that would break and remake the galaxy forever.

My eyes have been opened. Kewea's Spite has shown me the truth. The Vitriba belongs to me. From this corporeal realm, I'll repel the creeping influence of your sisters, Kewea. I'll walk with the Mistress of Death as her Tiller of Life. As I walk with her, so will another walk with me. If I am to be the princess who wields the Vitriba, I'll need a loyal centurion knight. I'll need you...Adam.